Domini Taylor is the pseudonym of a well-known English author. She is married and lives in Hampshire.

DOMINI TAYLOR

The Tiffany Lamp

WARNER BOOKS

by Little, Brown and Company

This edition published by Warner Books in 1995

Copyright © Domini Taylor 1994

The moral right of the author has been asserted.

*All characters in this publication are fictitious
and any resemblance to real persons, living or dead,
is purely coincidental.*

A CIP catalogue record for this book
is available from the British Library.

ISBN 0 7515 1245 1

Printed in England by Clays Ltd, St Ives plc

Warner Books
A Division of
Little, Brown and Company (UK)
Brettenham House
Lancaster Place
London WC2E 7EN

THE
TIFFANY
LAMP

CHAPTER ONE

THE LAMP SPOKE to Elinor across a hundred yards of darkness. The lamp said: Right, this is right, this is the moment, kill now.

The lamplight came from a circlet, a kind of wreath, of six flat-mounted electric bulbs. This strange antique arrangement had been devised by its maker for his rich clients, to cause the lamp to glow with extraordinary brilliance. In the days before there was such a thing as a thousand-watt bulb, a great light, in a domestic setting, could be produced only by many bulbs: so they arranged them in a halo, head to tail. The light came through curved and shaped panels of glass which were honey-coloured and sea-green and crimson and daffodil, the glass divided by strips of lead in voluptuous curves to form a giant tropical flower, the blossom of an exotic and erotic dream, luxurious, redolent of Edwardian cocktails and discreet affairs, of Fifth Avenue apartments and large hats and cars with French chauffeurs.

The light came from the upstairs oriel window of the Guardhouse, the smaller subsidiary house where such disgusting things had been going on. The light travelled along the cliff-face to the terrace of the château called la Moquerie, travelled along the path which had been carved out of the cliff. No vagrant gleam of the light dived to the foot of the cliff, to be reflected in the smooth implacable river which raced almost inaudibly between its towering banks. It was a big river, a fast and very dangerous river, but a stranger would scarcely have known it was there, standing with Elinor in the darkness of her terrace.

Elinor knew it was there, all right, fifty-six feet below the parapet by which she stood. She was vividly aware of it. She was about to use it. It was her murder weapon.

She looked at the lamp and she read its message and she knew that it was right. The gradual, elaborate preparations were complete. Everything was in place. Everything was done that had to be done, everything that could be done in advance. It had taken an intolerable time. Elinor had remained outwardly calm (most of the time), smooth of brow and gentle of speech, but the effort had been terrific. She had seen or imagined obscenities which had made her physically ill, made her gag with disgust and hatred, so that to wait and to be patient and to be bland had many times, over the weeks, seemed more than she could manage. That phase was finished. The lamp said: Now, tonight, do it.

These emotions were new to Elinor. Betrayal was new because love was new. Nothing had prepared her for pain so intense, rage so acrid, for the feeling of screwdrivers in the gut. She had always supposed that the poets and novelists had exaggerated, for artistic or commercial effect. She had not believed in obsession which was like illness, loss which was like amputation, love which was like torture.

No doubt it was all more intense because she had come late to it. She was thirty-three. Physically she had bloomed in the last few years to an almost incredible extent. Everybody said so, and it was true. She had been a dim little dumpling in the English countryside, and now she was a raving international beauty. Everybody said that, and she knew it was true. But behind that miraculous mask she had been ignorant and vulnerable. Young love would have acted like a kind of inoculation. Her heart should have been gently, prettily broken when she was about twenty-one; it would have healed quite quickly, and given her defences against this. In her early twenties she was not quite physically virginal but she was spiritually deaf and dumb. She was hurt and disgusted and repelled by the one serious man in her life, but her soul had not been touched, and she had developed no immunities against this new agony.

Tonight would lance the boil. The lamp said so. The steel rope in Elinor's hand said so, and the barely audible hiss of the big black river.

She would get her beloved back.

La Moquerie loomed behind her, the gaunt towers badged with the golden rectangles of lit windows. The night was warm, windless, cloudy. There was no moon. The sky was completely black. The masonry of the château, by day the colour of butterscotch, was invisible against the sky. A few insects ticked and rustled. There was no voice nor any music. The month was August, but there were no holiday-makers here, no caravans or campings, no cafés or night-clubs or heavy trucks.

The river was the Tarn, rising in the south-western bastions of the Massif Central and sliding rapidly through bare, sparsely populated hill country until it descended to the ancient promenades of Albi and the fat vineyards of Gaillac. The hills were grey and yellow in the morning, violet in the evening. Much of the country had been deserted. Dry grass feathered the flanks of the hills like the down on a plucked bird. Castles had crumbled from uselessness here, and farms from the poverty of the land. There were kites in the sky and lizards on the ruined walls.

The nearest road – only a little road – ran parallel to the river two kilometres to the north, on an east–west ridge of higher ground with enormous wayside views of almost nothing. A tortuous pot-holed drive, running north-westerly from the house, joined la Moquerie to the road; another, shorter but not short, running north-easterly, joined the Guardhouse to the road. Rocks and ravines so placed themselves between the two drives that even where they were closest, above the river, no vehicle could go directly from one to the other. God had made a ridiculous arrangement. A carload of groceries, or an infirm person, had to go five miles round to travel the hundred yards from the big house to the small one. Since the small house was the annexe of the big one, traffic was continuous between them.

This was the reason for the path on the cliff-face.

Elinor knew every yard of the path, naturally, but she still treated it with respect. There was – had been – a good stout rail of cast iron set in concrete uprights. The rail made the path quite safe, although it would not have done to let a drunk along it, or a young child unaccompanied. It was needful that the rail and its posts be inspected regularly, tested, mended or replaced if they showed the least sign of weakness.

The rail was being mended now, a ten-yard section of it to be replaced in new uprights. It was a time just now to be very careful on that path. Elinor told everybody to be extra careful. She was very careful herself on the path, because of the big dangerous river fifty-six feet directly below.

A very little amber light seemed to leak out of the windows of the château on to the terrace that overhung the river. In it could just be seen the flagstones of the terrace, and the stone balustrade, and the stone arch which marked the end of the cliff-face path. Nothing could be seen beyond

4

the balustrade except the lamp in the window of the Guardhouse, which illuminated only itself. A person could have seen that Elinor was there, a person on the terrace with her (but she would not have allowed anybody to be with her, since she was committing a murder). But that person would not have been able to see whether Elinor was beautiful.

She knew she was beautiful that night. She was more than usually beautiful because she was excited, because she saw the end of misery, the recovery of happiness and love. She had paused by the full-length mirror in the hall of the château, the great cloudy gilt-framed mirror by the foot of the stairs, put there by Bruno in a good military tradition.

'You enter and leave a barrack through a guardroom,' said Bruno, 'which stops intruders coming in and deserters going out. By the door onto the outside world they have a looking-glass, a full-length looking-glass.'

'Every barracks has that?' said Elinor, amused and incredulous, although she was herself the daughter of a general.

'Every good unit,' said Bruno. 'Every regiment with pretensions to smartness. The point is that soldiers can check their turn-out at the moment they step out on the town. Cap straight, belt horizontal, buttons done up. This is pride and discipline. It is an extremely good idea, eminently imitable.'

'Eminently imitable,' repeated Elinor. 'Imminently emitable. What rubbish you do talk.'

'Without a little vanity we are hobbledehoys and scruffs, we are dowdy and down at heel, there are dribbles of soup on our cardigans and our ties are frayed at the knot. You would not be so beautiful if you were not vain, and nor would I.'

This was evidently quite true. Elinor's beauty was not

accidental. She fell into the habit, as soon as the mirror was hung, of checking her appearance in it each time she passed it (often a hundred times in a morning) and she did so with increasing satisfaction as she became more beautiful.

More and more beautiful. Stunning, dazzling. A lot of people said so, and she was photographed for glossy international magazines.

Bruno was proud of her, and she was proud of herself.

That day she had glimpsed herself in the big mirror two or three score times, perhaps; an awful lot of times. In the morning she had crossed and recrossed the hall, between the salon and the flower-room, between the dining-room and the garden, between the terrace and the bedrooms, because she was doing the flowers. It was a difficult time of year for cut flowers, in that place and on that thin soil, but, as serious young men said in the magazine articles about her, she insisted on there being fresh flowers in every room, at every season. It took ingenuity, originality, a particular eye. There were silvery grasses and tobacco-brown leaves and the black berries of spiny, desiccated shrubs, and effect could be conjured of a subtle and surprising beauty.

There were roses in the garden also, masses of roses, cosseted and mulched and sprayed, on the steep banked beds behind the house: but Elinor did not pick roses for the vases of the château. It was an English thing to do. She would have picked roses in England – had done so, naturally, in her father's garden in Dorset – but a bowl of roses here would have struck a note like that of a cricket bat, an Old Marlburian blazer, a tobacco-jar with the arms of an Oxford college, a Victorian water-colour of Salisbury Cathedral. None of these things was bad, but at la Moquerie any would have looked uneasy and unconvincing. Elinor had been quoted to this effect, on very stiff and shiny paper, in a narrow rivulet of type between sumptuous photographs of her château and her pictures and herself. It was a fancy way to talk, but that did not stop it being right. Bruno had laughed at her when he read the article, but really he agreed with what they said she said.

Bruno had probably put the whole idea into her head, of a bowl of roses being too impossibly English for la Moquerie.

She remembered the episode that morning, as she prowled in and out with armfuls of metallic herbage. She remembered it as she glanced at herself in the big mirror. She smiled at the memory, so that her reflection smiled at her.

She was *en beauté* because she was preparing to be happy again.

She was tall and slender, with the height and presence of one of those million-dollar models. She had glossy black hair and wide grey eyes. Her skin was touched with a pink-gold tan, and her cheeks had a high healthy colour, a happy colour. Her broad brow and high cheek-bones gave her in certain lights, in certain moods and colours, a Slav look, but her narrow, high-bridged nose was purely Western European, as aristocratic as a coronet.

She was dressed that morning exactly for what she was doing, in yellow cotton trousers and a green checked shirt with flapping tails, with old faded espadrilles on her narrow feet, and a spotted handkerchief tied piratically round her head.

While quite demure, quite modest, the thin clothes revealed the magnificence of her body, the high breasts, broad shoulders, small waist, long legs. She was a marvellous clothes-horse even in these casual and sloppy garments. Very many men – most men, perhaps – would have speculated involuntarily about how she would look without them. Anybody who was by could have seen, when she had a quick swim at one-fifteen in the pool behind the château: but there was nobody by. The others were away or busy in the Guardhouse; there was no servant on the premises that day; no callers were expected. Elinor swam in nothing but a bathing-cap. She went indoors in a towelling wrap. She noted the colour of the wrap, as she saluted her reflection in the mirror in the hall: a charming faded terracotta. Bruno had acquired the wrap many, many years before, at the Mamounia Hotel in Marrakesh; it was almost threadbare, but still useful and a delightful colour. Dozens of people had worn that wrap after swimming in the pool at la Moquerie; an exhibition could be mounted of photographs of people in the terracotta wrap. It had probably been washed more often, and ironed less often, than any other item in the château.

Elinor put on a little blue cotton dress, for her solitary lunch. She glanced at herself in the hall. She thought how well that particular blue would go with the terracotta towelling. It was a familiar combination, much used by professional interior designers, but it was still soothing and suitable for this climate and a good background for people.

She had lunch on the terrace, in the shade of the awning. She had salad and cheese and fruit and a young white wine from Cahors. She looked at a *New Yorker* left behind by a visitor.

She could not concentrate on the articles in the *New Yorker*. She stared uncomprehendingly at the cartoons. She was too preoccupied to take in the jokes. Her mind buzzed round and round the project for the night, the blazing and brilliant act of ten hours later, the midnight miracle.

It was punishment and deliverance, justice and release. It

was death so that Elinor might have life.

It had taken weeks of preparation to bring things to this point, to the imminent midnight moment. When the time came it would be just that, a moment, the wink of an eye, pouf, a snap of the fingers: and for Elinor a different world, paradise regained.

It was impossible not to be frightened and excited: to be a little aghast, and at the same time joyful at the prospect of the future. It was impossible not to be tense, tight-strung as a banjo-wire, fingers trembling and eyelids twitching with the suspense.

Elinor struggled to be calm, to be cool and rational and in total control. What she had to do was simple. She just had to do it exactly right.

It was no good saying that nothing could go wrong, because a million things could go wrong. A sudden thunderstorm, keeping everybody indoors. A car-load of festive, unexpected visitors – some of Bruno's friends from Paris or Milan. She herself suddenly incapacitated by a burst appendix or a brainstorm.

Elinor had wanted a siesta. An hour's nap in a long chair on the terrace would have been a good idea. But it was unthinkable. Even to sit still was difficult: to sleep would have been impossible. She filled the morning with flowers, forcing herself to think only about flowers, allowing herself, besides flowers, to glimpse the future, to put a toe in the blessed waters of her future happiness. But now as the hands of the clock swivelled with infinite slowness it was impossible to think about anything except—

Just pulling sharply on a wire rope. That was all that was involved. No weapon or mess. Nothing that could be heard. No trace that could be left, no wisp of evidence, not even any questions that could be asked.

Elinor was neither a nail-biter nor a smoker. She did not have those recourses of the tense. She forbade herself any more to drink. She felt alternately very large and powerful, because she was about to play God, and very small and frightened. Happiness leaned over her shoulder and touched her cheek with its cheek.

She could say it was punishment, what she was about to do. She could say it was the unlocking of the door. Actually it was murder. It was those other fine things, but also it was murder.

Well, all right, yes, it was murder. Round and round went Elinor's brain, churning, spinning: yes, murder, but retribution and liberation and restoration, good things, morally excellent, handsome and holy things.

Nothing would go wrong. Everything could go wrong.

It was natural that Elinor should inspect yet again the repairs to the cliff-face path, the integrity of the temporary railing that made it usable. It was her responsibility. It would have been negligent of her not to keep an eye on the situation. The safety of others was involved – her own safety, too.

It did not matter that she was openly scrutinising the path and the rail and the rope, in the glaring mid-afternoon. It did not matter who saw her. Lots and lots of people could see her, because it was all right for her to be doing what she was doing. She would be able to describe, afterwards, exactly how things had been.

She looked cautiously down from the path, fifty-six feet to the surface of the river. It was smooth, in spite of the awesome power of the current. The water was absolutely clear, the gin-clear trout-haunted water of sporting tradition. The bottom of the river was so clearly to be seen in the sunshine that it was as though there was no water at all. The bottom was made of grey rocks, with hints of dark green and red. There was no weed in this part of the river, no underwater vegetation at all, because the current scoured the bottom clean. It was like a painting Elinor had seen in a friend's house, a Rowell Tyson of the rocks and pebbles of a river-bed seen in bright sunshine through clear fast water. Elinor had liked that picture, so Bruno had tried to buy it from the owner. That was perhaps a little uncouth, but the thought was kind.

On the path, five of the concrete uprights had been judged unsafe. Elinor said they had been inspected and found dubious. Elinor had been alone in the house when the man from the ministry came. Nobody else saw him. But nobody doubted that he came when she said he came, that he said what she reported him as saying; nobody would suffer that inconvenience and expense unless it was all truly necessary. Elinor caused builders to come out from a town to demolish the condemned uprights. She ordered cast-iron posts to replace them, which would be indestructible if they were regularly painted. The new posts had to be machined, cut to precise lengths, drilled for the cast-iron rods which formed the rail. These things were happening but they had not yet happened. In a few days, the builder said on the telephone, the truck would come to la Moquerie with the iron posts and the concrete mixer, and then the job would be very expensively completed.

Meanwhile a steel hawser was stretched at a height of four feet along the outside edge of the path, where the concrete posts and their rails had been removed. It was pretty satisfactory as, literally, a stopgap. It was so safe that it could, at a pinch, have been made a permanent arrangement. This was never an option that Elinor seriously considered. The steel hawser was temporary. For this reason it was not anchored at both ends as it would have been if a fixture. At each end it overlapped by a yard the existing cast-iron rail, and the overlap was wired to the rail by a few feet of galvanised steel wire. This also was perfectly safe and satisfactory for a few weeks in the summer.

Elinor took a pair of pliers when she went in the afternoon to inspect the rail. She fussily involved herself in adding twists to the end of the wire lashing, at the château end of the gap in the rail. She could have been seen to inspect the other end also, but seemed satisfied that the wire there was sufficiently twisted.

Almost certainly nobody was looking, because the people in the Guardhouse were busy or away, but in case anybody was looking, what she did was innocent and responsible.

A person seen from a distance to be twisting wires together with a pair of pliers may just as easily be untwisting them. The physical movements of hands and wrists are the same. An observer would have to know whether the wires had been twisted clockwise or anticlockwise. The wires holding the hawser to the rail were twisted clockwise. The French builder was right-handed, and it was natural that he turned his pliers from left to right. Elinor busied herself with her pliers, improving the builder's handiwork. Not one person in a thousand would have noticed, from a distance, particularly, that she was twisting the pliers anticlockwise, even had there been anybody at a window to notice. Elinor untwisted the wire lashing except for one single final turn. This one turn kept the lashing in place, which kept the steel hawser in place on the rail. But the single final twist could be undone by hand, in the dark. Then the wire lashing could be unwound in a few seconds. Then the end of the hawser would be free. It would fall to the round. There would not be any rail on the outside edge of the cliff-face path.

To anybody who came and seriously inspected the wire lashing, who came to that spot with the specific intention of inspecting it, what Elinor had done would be obvious. It was so unlikely that anybody would do such a thing that the possibility could be dismissed. A thousand people could walk along the path, and see the wire lashing, and not notice that the twists that secured the end of it were reduced to a single turn. It was highly unlikely that, in what remained of the day, any single person would use the path. One of the people in the Guardhouse would use it after dark. By that time there would be no lashing, and no steel hawser, nothing between the person on the path and the fifty-six-foot drop into the river.

The steel hawser could easily be put back afterwards, so that the path became perfectly safe again. The hawser was not very heavy. Elinor was strong. She could manage it. It would be covered in her fingerprints, of course. Since she lived there, since she used the path constantly, it would have been a peculiar, suspicious circumstance if the hawser had not been covered in her fingerprints. She could put the wire lashing back, with a sufficient twist at the end to keep it in place for the moment. She could do that quickly and in the dark and without tools. She had very thoroughly rehearsed the whole operation, in the dark. The business of the wire and the hawser was quite simple, and after the event there would be plenty of time. Before and after there was more than enough time, the hours of darkness before the path was to be used by the one person who would use it, and all the hours until dawn after it had been used. Elinor would lose some sleep. But when she did sleep, it would be in tranquil happiness.

Elinor had a thin coil of nylon rope, bought as clothes-line. She kept it quite publicly hanging on a hook in the flower-room of the château, the small stone-flagged room with a big sink and shelves of bowls and vases. This cord would be knotted to the free end of the steel hawser. It would have been nice to have had that knot tied in daylight, but it would have looked distinctly strange, a nylon rope knotted to the steel hawser. Nobody using the path by daylight could have failed to see it. Almost certainly nobody would use the path in daylight, that day, but it was an avoidable risk. Elinor had practised knotting the nylon cord to the end of the hawser, in the dark, relying on touch only. A series of half-hitches made a sufficient knot, to join the nylon to the hawser. The more the cord was pulled, the more the knot would tighten. But when the pressure was taken off, the knot would almost undo itself. The nylon was very light. Elinor's forty-metre length weighed only a few pounds. She could carry the coil on her forearm, leaving her hands free for other things.

Her hands had to be free for the searchlight.

This was the one piece of equipment which had been difficult to get, difficult to find a credible, innocent reason for getting. Why would anybody want an immensely powerful electric light who was not mounting a *son et lumière*, floodlighting an ancient monument, or advertising a nightclub?

Security.

Security against what?

Thieves, intruders.

In that place? There were none. There was nobody at all within miles, except the people in the big house or the little house, or servants who occasionally spent the night, or friends who were staying.

Ah, but people did come. They were heard. They left their vehicle on the road, and crept up the drive on foot in the small hours. They stole a small eighteenth-century bronze from the formal garden, a putto carrying a bird-bath on his head. They tried to steal a marble also, but that was massively cemented to its plinth. The light was to be mounted on a bar over the back door of the château, automatically to come on if anyone approached, to blaze out over the yard and gardens. It was a familiar security device, as anti-social as a screaming burglar alarm if there were near neighbours, but harmless in this context and doubtless an effective deterrent.

The two clamps which secured the searchlight were widely adjustable, so that it could be installed wherever the householder required. They could grip almost anything up to five inches across. Elinor assured herself, before she bought the searchlight, that she could clamp it to the cast-iron railing of the cliff-face path. She tried the clamps on various bits of metal pipe in the house. The clamps worked fine, and were easily tightened and loosened by hand. What the clamps did do, if firmly hand-tightened, was to scratch the surface of whatever they gripped. It was practically certain that nobody would take a microscope to the railing of the path, see tiny scratches identifiable as new, relate the scratches to the clamps of the searchlight, guess correctly why the searchlight had been put in such a peculiar place. Not Mycroft Holmes himself would deduce that method of murder from those scratches. But the deduction was theoretically possible: it was another avoidable risk. Elinor bought a chamois-leather duster from a garage outside Albi, where she stopped for gas. She cut it in half. She tried the searchlight clamps on the waste-pipe below the sink in the flower-room of the château. Lined with the pieces of leather the clamps did not mark even the soft lead of the waste-pipe.

Had there been intruders? *Had* the bronze putto disappeared?

Elinor herself had heard the intruders, had seen the gleam of a small flashlight, without at the time realising what she had seen. She said so in the morning. The putto had gone away in the back of a car, no doubt to be sold to a dealer who asked no questions. It had gone away in the back of Elinor's car, wrapped in an old raincoat. She had disposed of it, quite legally and openly, to a man a long way away who had never seen her or heard of her. She had never much liked it. Debased Italian rococo garden ornaments were not to her taste. Bruno liked it, but Bruno was almost too eclectic.

The disappearance of the putto, and a few cold-chisel marks in the cement at the base of the marble, made all too credible Elinor's report of the intruders and their flashlight. It all made sense of the purchase of the searchlight.

The new searchlight came with a moderately long flex which could conveniently be plugged into a socket in the back passage, when the light was in service as an anti-burglar device. When it was being a murder weapon it had a very long extension lead which was coiled on a plastic drum.

Why on earth would Elinor want a fifty-yard electric flex with male and female plugs, an extension lead of such extravagant length?

She needed it for an electric garden tool, an edger for the geometrical patches of the knot-garden. This was something Bruno, eclectic again, with an oddly unscholarly approach to style, had created on one of the terraced areas behind the château. It could be described as cute. It needed to be kept impeccably tidy. It was certainly labour intensive. It was not certain that, in the event, the electric edging-tool was much of a trouble-saver, what with stretching all that flex up steps and round corners, and cleaning the machine after using it, and rolling up the flex again . . .

In its security role, the light was switched on by a photo-electric cell. This automatic switch could be overridden by a manual switch, turning the light on and off. The manual switch could be operated by a cord of any length, because it was foreseen that the searchlight might require to be mounted in places difficult to reach, such as the top of a porch or the roof of an outbuilding. Elinor had a spool of heavy nylon monofilament fishing-line. She could switch the searchlight on or off from any distance. Buying the fishing-line involved only going to a sporting-goods shop in any town, and talking of a present to a friend. There were great numbers of fishermen, locals and visitors, in the valleys of the Aveyron, the Lot and the Tarn. Miles of monofilament were bought daily. Elinor's spool of the stuff, like a fisherman's, fitted into a pocket.

All of this took time and thought, and practice and rehearsal and experiment. Nothing Elinor did during those weeks was to be seen as strange or surprising. Nothing was to set anybody thinking, or to be remembered as odd.

Somebody said that genius was an infinite capacity for taking pains. Elinor's knowledge of art history made her aware that this was nonsense: but what she was doing certainly required a capacity for taking pains.

The shadows lengthened on the terrace, and the racing waters fifty-six feet below turned strange colours of serpents and unknown metals: and the stained-glass art nouveau lamp from Tiffany suddenly bloomed through the twilight, from the upstairs oriel window of the Guard-house.

Elinor prowled. She was hopelessly restless. She could

not sit still for two seconds, although the hands of the clocks were sitting still. She prowled out onto the terrace and in, out at the back and up the garden, and a short way up the drive towards the road, with her shadow bouncing eastwards over the rocks and the dry grass.

She did not go to the cliff-face path, or anywhere near that end of the terrace. She was pulled in that direction by fascination, by magic forces, but she resisted. She gave an appearance of being busy in almost every other part of the house and garden. But she was not busy at all: she had nothing whatever to do. Everything was done that could be done before dark. She wished there was much to do, anything whatever to do, any task to occupy her mind, to kill a few minutes.

She passed and repassed the big mirror in the hall. She saw with self-derision that she was clutching her hands in front of her like a tragedy queen in a melodrama. She forced herself to drop her hands to her sides, to relax her shoulders, to turn her head, to smile at her reflection over her shoulder. Then she looked down at her hands, and found that they were clutched together, the knuckles white, the fingernails of her right hand gouging into the back of her left.

Her light and healthy lunch had formed itself into a lump of iron behind her breastbone. She could not face the idea of having any more to eat. She was sure it would be a bad idea to have anything to drink.

Any physical fumbling, any clouding of the judgement, would be a bad idea.

She reminded herself that what she had to do was not difficult, that she had rehearsed many times every one of the few simple actions required, so that she could do them in the pitch dark, so that she could have done them in her sleep.

She thought she would be the better for one glass of wine.

She went through the kitchen to the larder where the everyday wine was racked. She took down a bottle, and stared stupidly at the label, and put it back again.

In this condition of extreme tension, half a glass might set her roaring and staggering. Or perhaps a bottle would have no effect at all. She had no experience to guide her about the effect of wine in such circumstances. There had never been anything like this in her life.

Dear God, the time moved slow. She sun hung interminably on the edge of the sky. The river below the terrace was streaked with black and purple.

There were little livid marks on the back of Elinor's left hand, where she had dug it with the nails of her right hand. She despised herself for this neurotic weakness.

She tried to listen to a Mozart CD, but the music was simply irritating.

She wondered if anybody would notice the little pits dug into the skin of the back of her left hand by the fingernails of her right. Would anybody guess how they got there, interpret the little marks, read in them the acute tension Elinor had been undergoing, link that tension to a sudden death?

Probably Ailie was the only person observant enough to remark those tiny wounds. Ailie was sensitive enough, intuitive enough, to read them as the marks of tension. But Ailie was away. Ailie would not be back until all this was finished.

Neither Ailie nor anybody else would know what had happened. There would be nothing to show what had happened. They might think it was an accident, or another suicide. It would not, in fact, very much matter what anybody thought, because nobody would actually know anything.

Eventually the body would be recovered. It might be washed ashore quite quickly, in a kilometre or so, but Elinor thought it would go on downstream as far as the big weir across the river at Albi. It would hang up on that. It might not be all at once identified. It was going to be interesting to see how all that worked out, how long it would take and what guesses would be made. Elinor faced that aspect of the future with lively curiosity.

Darkness fell by infinitesimal degrees, more slowly, less dramatically because the sky had become cloudy. The air was warm and dry. There was no threat of rain, thunder, hurricane. Stars would have been nice, perhaps, but they were not important to Elinor's plans.

Restless, Elinor passed and repassed her reflection in the big mirror in the hall. She saw herself lit, now, by the old-gold light of the bulbs in the alcoves of the hall, indirect light bouncing politely off the porcelain and bronzes in the alcoves. She had changed her clothes again, with the going down of the sun. She wore a long silk skirt which was one of the colours of the sunset, a cool mysterious crimson. She wore with it a silk shirt, completely simple, the colour of clotted cream. Her feet were bare, as often in the house and on the terrace. She wore no jewellery nor any make-up. She wondered about her lips and eyes, about rings and earrings. In one sense, what she was doing was so important, so momentous, that she felt she should dress up for it, even though she would be quite alone and in pitch darkness. But to make herself beautiful in order to kill somebody? It made her think of Clytemnestra, Messalina, Lucrezia Borgia, who were vulgar women without taste or self-discipline. Elinor thought she would feel easiest if she were barefooted and barefaced.

Her reflection in the hall told her that she looked beautiful enough. She was hardly yet used to what it told her. She was not yet used to being so lovely and so loved.

By ten o'clock it was full dark, inky dark, starless and moonless, as dark as it ever would be. Out on the terrace there was a very little honey-coloured light from the windows, reaching no further than the balustrade, than the arch on to the cliff-face path. A warm, motionless curtain of absolute blackness hung all round the terrace, pierced only by the unearthly art nouveau colours of the Tiffany lamp, a hundred yards away in the upstairs window of the Guardhouse.

In the hall, Elinor assembled her *matériel*. There was not much of it.

Barefooted, noiseless as the shadow of a candle, she went out on to the terrace. She went to the arch at the end of the terrace, and very carefully along the cliff-face path. She would be unhurried, because there was no hurry and everything must be exactly right.

She slid her hand along the cast-iron rail, until her fingers met the overlapping end of the steel hawser.

She was almost halfway along the path now, halfway to the Guardhouse, halfway to the surreal beacon of the Tiffany lamp.

Her fingers found the twisted ends of the wire which lashed the hawser to the rail. She untwisted the wire. She unwound the lashing, twenty or thirty turns which took only a few seconds to unwind. Released from the lashing, the hawser fell to the floor of the path. She led it along the inside gutter of the path, tucked close in under the cliff. She could do this confidently in the dark. But she moved slowly and carefully, because there was now nothing between her and the fifty-six-foot drop to the river.

She took the free end of her coil of nylon cord, that she

had bought as clothes-line, and hung innocently in the flower-room of the château. She tied the cord to the steel hawser with half a dozen half-hitches. She went very carefully back to the terrace, uncoiling the nylon cord as she went. She put the rest of the cord on the ground, on the flagstones at the base of the arch.

She did not know that anyone had ever killed anyone by exactly this method, ever before, but she was quite sure it would work.

She picked up the searchlight and the pieces of chammy leather. She carried the searchlight along the path to the end of the proper rail, to the beginning of the gap in the rail. She lifted the searchlight so that it rested on the rail. She fitted the pieces of leather inside the clamps, and clamped the searchlight to the rail. She swivelled the light so that it pointed up the path, away from the château, towards the Guardhouse. She tilted it a little upwards, so that it would shine into the face of anybody who came along the path from the Guardhouse. She slotted the plug of the searchlight into the plug on the end of the extension flex. She went back along the path to the terrace, uncoiling the flex as she went from its plastic drum. She kept the flex well into the gutter beside the path. She led the flex across the terrace and into the château. She plugged it into a floor-plug in the hall, near the foot of the stairs.

She went back along the path to the searchlight, with her spool of monofilament fishing-line. She attached the end of the monofilament to the switch at the back of the searchlight, her fingers confident in the dark because she had practised this so thoroughly.

She went back to the terrace, uncoiling the fishing-line as she went. There was no need for her to touch the nylon, and she did not do so. Afterwards she would wind the nylon

22

back on to the spool, and nobody would have any way of knowing that it had even been unwound. She put the spool on the ground beside the arch, with the coil of cord.

It was terribly tempting to pull on the fishing-line, to switch the searchlight on for just a second. Elinor resisted the temptation. It would have been a foolish thing to do. She knew that the searchlight worked and that the switch worked.

She thought that it must be almost midnight, that she must have been labouring for two hours. But the whole thing had taken twenty minutes. It was not ten-thirty when she was completely ready.

She had an hour and a half to wait. Midnight was the time. It was absurd that she had to wait so long. It was infuriating. But she herself had named midnight as the time. It gave her a comfortable margin of error, in case anything went wrong with her preparations. Since nothing had gone wrong, she had another interminable gulf of time to kill.

When she went indoors, something drove her out on to the terrace. When she was out, she wanted to sit down or read or at least to be able to see, so she went indoors again.

She went in and out, in and out. The weird stained-glass lamp glowed unceasing from the upstairs window at the far end of the path.

She passed and repassed her reflection, in the mirror in the hall. She might have expected herself to look haggard with the tension that she felt. But she looked beautiful even by her standards, barefooted and without make-up or jewels, adrenalin giving her a focus and glitter that even the most passionate sex had never brought about. She wondered if she had to kill somebody, in order to look her very best. She tried to laugh at this grotesque proposition, but she was too tense for laughter. Later she would laugh. Later she would laugh and dance, in freedom and pure joy.

Five minutes to midnight. She went upstairs, and turned on the bedroom light which was the signal. It meant that all telephoning was finished, all risk of interruption was gone.

She went downstairs and out. She crossed the terrace quickly, on narrow bare feet, silent, almost invisible. She picked up the nylon cord, and held it in her right hand. She picked up the spool of fishing-line, and held it in her left hand. She waited.

She thought it was a funny irony that, when she was more beautiful than she had ever been, she was all alone in pitch darkness.

She heard a sound that was too quiet to hear, a click from the far end of the path. A dim rectangle of brownish light appeared, at ground level, as a door was opened. The light disappeared, as the door was closed. Footsteps could now be imagined, possibly heard, crossing the narrow terrace of the Guardhouse and starting along the path.

There was a wavering firefly, at waist height, approaching along the path: the beam of a small flashlight. It approached at moderate speed: somebody who knew the path, who was not frightened of the dark, who was not silly or impetuous.

The flashlight told Elinor exactly how far the oncoming person had come. The person was ten yards short of the gap in the rail: five yards short.

The person was level with the gap in the rail, with the place where there was no rail. Elinor pulled sharply on the monofilament fishing-line with her left hand. The light blazed, glaring full into the face of the person on the path at a range of five or six feet. At the same time, Elinor heaved on the cord which was tied to the hawser. She dropped the spool of fishing-line, to use both hands on the cord. Very quickly and with all her strength, Elinor pulled on the cord so that she pulled the hawser off the ground and up across the path. The hawser caught the person just above the knee. The person was already dazzled and unbalanced by the sudden, overpowering glare of the searchlight. The hawser pitched the person off the path. The person gave one short strangled scream, and clawed at the air for a moment, and was tipped off the path, over the edge into nothingness, fifty-six feet down the cliff into the lethal river.

At the moment of the victim's fall, at the irremediable moment when balance was lost, Elinor had seen the victim's face full in the glare of the searchlight.

Elinor began to scream. She screamed and screamed, in madness and misery and horror.

CHAPTER TWO

ELINOR'S JOURNEY to la Moquerie started on a curious and obscure branch line in her life. She found herself at a station from which you would have thought that no useful journey could begin. She was attending a function quite unlike any she had ever seen before: unlike anything she had ever wanted to see.

She was among people who filled her with frightened boredom, whose conversation was incomprehensible, who wore clothes with the evident intention of looking as horrible as possible. These people were dangerous and dirty, but at the same time they were dull.

The place was an art school, the occasion its annual summer exhibition of students' work. It was Milchester College of Art and Design, on the outskirts of that ancient Wessex cathedral city, its campus neighboured by a small industrial estate and a large Baptist chapel. The college awarded degrees in Fine Arts, Textile Design, Photography, Ceramics, Interior Design, Animation, Print and Packaging. Its students worked hard at looking like art students, and so did many of its teaching staff.

Looking round at the crowd at the exhibition, Elinor thought the girls were all too fat and the boys were all too thin. The hall they were in was too small for the crowd, but the pictures were too big for the walls. Elinor thought they were pictures pretending to be important by dint of size, while the older people present, with beards and pewter brooches, were pretending to be important by dint of the loudness of their comments. Elinor did not at the time admit that she knew nothing about modern painting. She did not admit that she knew nothing about people.

Elinor was at that period extremely intolerant. She had been bullied into intolerance throughout her childhood, but also it came naturally to her.

Intolerance was in the air breathed by the people of Milchester. It was the provincial capital of the quietest and richest region of southern England, full of beechwoods and river valleys, birdsong and cathedral bells, and retired generals with disgruntled wives who no longer had house-maids. Elinor had grown up among these things, and they had formed her.

Elinor's father's house was in a village six miles from Milchester, a village of which it was said that if you threw a stone you were certain to hit a retired general with a Georgian house or a Lloyd's broker with a weekend cottage. All the young girls had ponies, and their fathers read the lessons in church.

When Elinor was a little girl, she was just like all the other little girls in that pampered area, except that her mother was even more snobbish than the mothers of the rest.

Going between Milchester and their village of Conyng-ham Smedley, Elinor had passed the College of Art and Design some thousands of times. It was just off their road. In the 1960s it was rebuilt. In the 1970s it was partly hidden from the road by the demure, hangar-like factories of the industrial estate. In the early 1980s, at a time of optimistic public spending, it was further hidden behind a belt of ornamental trees: but these were so vandalised, and their replacements vandalised, that the Council lost heart, and thereafter the college could be seen between the factories. There was a big sign on the road, pointing to the college, the design of which did everybody credit, but Elinor had never noticed the sign, nor glimpsed the range of low yellow buildings. She had heard of the Milchester College of Art and Design, because a cousin of her mother's was a member of the Board of Governors; but she had not seen it, nor had any idea where it was, nor cared.

As a building, or group of joined buildings, it rambled over a large acreage. Elinor already found, in that one evening, that it was a place it was easy to get lost in. It was said that people were quite often hopelessly lost, and never seen again, their bones being found by later generations of students or contract cleaners. This confusion was not the result of change or historical accident, but simply of incompetence on the part of the administration. Elinor's mother's cousin often said so. She said she came away from meetings of committees crippled with nervous indigestion, brought on by helpless rage at the idiotic decisions taken, the money wasted. Elinor had been hearing this for years. It had never interested her.

Almost the whole of the college was given over to the exhibition, which included the degree shows of all the students who were graduating, and which comprised all the different disciplines. Elinor wandered among pots and prints and textiles, which was when she got lost. She steered back towards the centre of things by aiming at the loudest noise, and by following signs to the Browning Gallery.

All the passages were hung with exhibits, paintings, drawings, monoprints and etchings, fabrics, reliefs, objects of unguessable function behind glass. People thronged the passages, students in tattered black jeans and provocative

T-shirts, the earnest, baffled families of students who had failed to keep their families away, local dignitaries looking for the girl with the tray of plastic cups of wine.

All roads led at last to the Browning Gallery. The paintings thought to be the best were hung there, because it was the best part of the college. It was new. It was the handsome, well-lit, effectively ventilated, capacious, adaptable exhibition space the college had needed and could not afford. They found a benefactor, the Browning of the gallery's name, a local art-loving tycoon. Elinor knew all this from her mother's cousin. She heard that Mr Browning was a charming man with, for a businessman, an astonishing knowledge of art.

'He strikes them all dumb,' said Cousin Octavia Crossley. 'Not just the pompous old burghers of Milchester, but the professors too. He knows more than they do. He's seen far more. His travels are truly admirable and truly enviable. He seems to have seen every picture in every gallery in the world. And a million pictures in people's houses, too, private houses the public isn't allowed into, he knows everybody who's got good pictures. Everybody! Greeks and Americans and Italians and I believe even Australians.'

'Japanese?' asked Elinor.

'I don't know if Mr Browning knows any Japanese. There might not be so very much point. They buy pictures for millions in order to lock them up in their cellars.'

'Why do they do that?' asked Elinor, not interested but because she was trained to politeness.

But Cousin Octavia was not interested in the conversation, either, and her mind went off on to something else.

It was Cousin Octavia, of course, who brought Elinor to the exhibition, which was a piece of hopeful tactics. Elinor needed a new sense of direction. Her function had disappeared, because her father had died. Now that she had no one to look after, she had nothing to do.

Lieutenant General Sir Bernard Leigh had not reached a great age, as measured by other people's calendars. He was born in 1916, so that he was six years short of his eightieth birthday when he died in the early spring of 1990. A stranger, meeting him, would have said he was six years short of his century. He had seized all the privileges of extreme age. He required all his opinions to be listened to. He had the tyrannical pettishness of the very old; he had their double standard, which allows them to indulge any whim, while it obliges everybody else to adhere to exact routine.

The trouble with Bernard Leigh was that he was spoiled rotten all his life.

He was born two months after his father's death on the Somme, youngest of five children of whom all the rest were girls. He was a living memorial to his heroic father. He was a godling, surrounded by a shining aureole. From his infancy, adoring women competed to win his smiles, with food, games, gifts, stories, piggybacks, funny faces, with laughter at his jokes, applause for his exploits, instant forgiveness when he broke things, spilled, tore or stole things, pulled his sisters' hair, or screamed with frustrated wilfulness. Since he was a big, strong boy, he was not disciplined by his contemporaries at school. His form-mates could not wallop him for his puppyish arrogance. He was also a hero among other little boys, for being success-fully cheeky to the masters, and for being good at football.

His father having died gallantly on the Somme at the head of the Pink Hussars, he was commissioned without fuss or delay into that resplendent regiment, in 1936. His mother and all his sisters did his packing and polishing when he was posted to India.

He was popular in the army in India. He liked it very much. From the angle at which he viewed it, life had not changed for a century. He liked being a privileged member of a master race. He had a comfortable private income, on top of his pay. He left his sisters' letters unanswered and often unread. He played a good game of polo, and he was an adequate shot. He was a big, strapping, handsome man, with very thick glossy black hair and a black cavalry moustache, grey eyes in a tanned face, broad shoulders, and a proud, soldierly bearing. He expected to be obeyed by men and adored by women.

He had a creditable war, in which he was neither captured nor wounded. He finished it with a DSO and the acting rank of Lieutenant Colonel. He came back to England in 1946, to a job at the War Office. He was bigger and glossier than ever, though no longer tanned. He belonged to the Cavalry Club and the Hurlingham Club and the Four Hundred Club. When he was not in uniform, he wore a stiff collar and a curly bowler. He hunted with the Heythrop in the winter, and fished for salmon in the summer. He was not one of those who polished his own tack or tied his own flies.

In 1948 he met, in 1949 married, Daphne, second daughter of the Earl of Crondall. It entirely fitted his picture of himself to have a wife called Lady Daphne. The Earl was important at village level. He was a great man for five miles round. His stately home was a school and his fortune had gone with the wind: he was pleased to have a glamorous son-in-law who smelled of professional success.

Daphne was a clever girl. She had inherited brains and artistic talent, perhaps from her mother's family. She knew that these should not be allowed to show, being irrelevant or even disgusting to the kind of man she wanted.

As to that, she had always been quite clear. The man was exactly defined, in romantic novels and adventure stories. He was tall, with thick dark hair and grey eyes. He was a cavalry officer. He was brave, with medals. He hunted and played polo. Men obeyed him and women adored him. This man eluded Daphne's search until the summer of 1948, when she saw him crossing a neighbour's lawn, in the early evening, in white flannels after tennis. The sun was behind him, and he had at once for Daphne the aureole he had had for his mother and sisters.

She lost her heart, but only provisionally. Daphne asked necessary questions, even before she and Bernard were introduced over the tray of Pimm's. It was all right. He was a colonel in a famous regiment, and he came from a good military family. Daphne could allow herself to fall in love, which she therefore did.

She was not a person who ever admitted she was wrong, so she never admitted she was wrong.

They had various postings abroad. Sons were born in 1952 and 1955, and a daughter in 1961. Elinor was an unsought, unwelcome afterthought, born when her father was forty-five.

In these years, Daphne lived much in officers' messes, and other enclosed, far-flung societies. The temptation was to conform, to be one of the bunch, to lower standards: to entertain people in your quarters whom you would never have allowed through the door at home: to drift into tolerance of the uncouth and intimacy with the common. Daphne was alert to these dangers, especially on behalf of her children. Neither she nor anyone else forgot that she was the daughter of an earl.

They lived in army quarters and rented houses for nearly twenty years, but they wanted a base, a family home in which their children could put down roots. Daphne wanted to be queen of a village as well as an army base. In 1965 they found the Old Rectory in Conyngham Smedley, a substantial Georgian house with barns and stables and fifteen acres. Elinor was four when they moved there; she did not think she remembered any other home.

Daphne did not relax, returning to English rural life. It was more than ever necessary to maintain standards. Terrible things were happening in the world – socialists on the rampage everywhere, hysterical mobs of adolescent girls screaming at something called the Beatles – and fingers must be jammed in dykes against the threatening flood of egalitarianism. The future, of course, lay with the children. It was hardly too much to say that the future of civilisation lay with the manner in which a few people like Daphne brought up their children. It was an awesome responsibility, a gigantic challenge.

Elinor and her brothers, in other words, were given extremely expensive educations.

Bernard was knighted with his promotion to Lieutenant General in 1971. He retired from the army two years later. He was at once involved with the county Red Cross, the regimental museum, the Committee of Milchester Races and so forth. But he was far more often at home. Elinor was twelve at the time of this change, and during the school holidays she felt the smack of firm government.

At this point Elinor, being twelve years old, graduated to a new school. It was a small establishment with indifferent examination results. It was the most expensive girls' boarding school in England. It had a high incidence of titled parents, and divorced parents, and of titled and divorced Old Girls.

'Why on earth are you sending the child there?' asked

Daphne's cousin Octavia Crossley.

'She will submit herself to the judgement of her peers,' said Daphne.

Octavia laughed incredulously.

'Octavia has her priorities seriously wrong,' said Daphne later to Bernard. 'She was talking about A-levels and university entry and understanding computers.'

'Oh yes,' said Bernard, who did not think the education of women was of any importance at all, and who had objected in vain to the enormous school fees.

'The point is that we rely on her generation to keep the flag flying. Otherwise we relapse into chaos.'

'Oh yes,' said Bernard.

'Judgement of her peers,' quoted Octavia derisively, to her friend who was manager of the principal Milchester bookshop.

'Whatever does it mean?'

'It means that a bunch of toffee-nosed little snobs will tell the child what's U and what's non-U. They'll tell her what sort of bra it's admissible to wear, and what to call elevenses, and where to hunt.'

'Are you serious?' asked the bookseller.

'I'm not, but Daphne bloody well is.'

So Elinor soldiered on through her teens, subjected to the judgement of her peers and of her parents. (Her brothers were by this time figures of distant glamour. She had never known them well, and now she did not know them at all.) As she later – much later – said to Bruno, 'The requirements they made on me were paradoxical. In a fundamental sense, they wanted me to have high heels and flat heels, to wear both all the time, to be two kinds of people all the time.'

'I don't understand,' said Bruno, uncharacteristically.

'Nor did they.'

Elinor approached her eighteenth birthday; she approached leaving school, embarking on life. What now? Nobody had any idea.

Some of her schoolmates were embarking on parties, art-history courses in foreign cities, higher education in the areas of cookery and flower-arrangement, or, in the cases of the dimmest, secretarial training.

Elinor?

Friends of the family suggested Winkfield, Florence, something in South Kensington. Elinor's parents reacted apathetically to these ideas. Nothing was decided. There was plenty of time.

Elinor was now a big dark girl, too big and dark and beefy for the taste of the time. She was too shy and silent for the taste of any time, too clumsy, too apt to break things.

Elinor when small had been almost an only child, her brothers being so much older, and thus subject to a most unwelcome spotlight. People looked at her because there was no other child to look at. It was unfortunate and unfair. She had been rather an inconvenience, an uninvited and unwelcome extra; her parents were incapable of the crudity of saying so, but they were also incapable of the artifice of concealing that this was how they felt. Elinor was made aware that she was a limiting factor, a brake on freedom of movement and of expenditure.

'But for Elinor we could spend six months in Australia.'

'But for Elinor we could buy another ten acres and a thoroughbred broodmare.'

If you are a big girl, and you hear this kind of thing, then you bump into occasional tables and break pieces of china.

She made up for this, as best as she could, by winning rosettes at gymkhanas. She was better in the saddle than on foot, more graceful and confident. There were days when her father could be proud of her, and even say so. This instructed Elinor in the sort of person she was supposed to be – more the flat heel than the stiletto spike, more the boot than the shoe.

In the summers, during her teens, Elinor often stood in for her mother, being her father's gillie on the banks of rivers, carrying his gaff and his flask and his sandwiches. In the winter she was his gun-bearer and dog-handler. She was taught that these things were fun.

She hardly ever went to London. When she did she was lost and exhausted. She never went abroad at all.

She sometimes stayed with schoolfriends in the holidays, when she was fourteen and fifteen and sixteen. The friends had brothers. These boys tried to squeeze Elinor's breasts, already prominent, through her sweater, or even to push their hands up under her sweater. Some of her friends said that these things were fun, too, but Elinor did not find them so.

Of sex, Elinor's mother said, 'Ladies have to do it sometimes, of course, but they don't discuss it.'

Elinor's friends said they couldn't wait, and some of them said they hadn't waited. Elinor looked at the boys that her friends said were gorgeous, and she saw the spots on the backs of their necks.

So Elinor approached her eighteenth birthday, approached leaving school and embarking on adult life, knowing no more than she had at thirteen, knowing no more than her King Charles spaniel did.

And at that point her mother was killed, running into the back of a tanker on a motorway slip-road. She wrote off her car and herself, messily and needlessly; it was most uncharacteristic.

Elinor's brothers, Timothy and Simon, said she should stay at home, at least for a time, to look after their father. They had agreed between themselves that this arrangement would be a great deal cheaper than the alternative, which was to hire a housekeeper, whose wages over a period would make a hole in the estate.

Elinor's brothers' wives, Caroline and Tricia, said that she must stay to look after her father. They were both appalled at the prospect of looking after him themselves, giving up a spare bedroom, having him at every meal, rearranging their lives round his needs.

Bernard himself said that Elinor must give up the idea of going to London, or any other idea she might have had. He said she must stay at home. He said he had spent his life looking after her, and now it was her turn. She owed him no less. He said he needed her, and almost at once she realised that it was true. He had never in his life done anything for himself. He had never cleaned his shoes, made his bed, bought a packet of biscuits, made a pot of tea, sent a Christmas card, put the cufflinks in a shirt.

Elinor accompanied her father to church, to race-meetings, and to cocktail parties given by the elderly for one another. He required that she did him credit, as her mother had done, so she assembled a wardrobe of tweeds and a rack of brogues, and for Christmas her sisters-in-law gave her scarves from Hermès.

She was a tall girl, a big strong girl, and the tweeds she wore made her look bigger than she was. When she was dressed up for the races or the covert-side, it would have taken a brave young man to make a pass at her. She also dressed up for hunt balls, to which she went in large and noisy parties; the clothes she then wore were not much less stiff, not much more revealing. She wore silk as though it were tweed, and carried herself like a guardsman. It still took a brave young man to make a pass at her, but there were often young men at those dances made brave by drink. Their faces were flushed when they danced with her, their white ties askew, and they took her out onto balconies. There they inexpertly kissed her, their hands sweatily busy over her bosom. She hoped there was more to life than this.

It was no better when she was twenty-five than it had been when she was fifteen.

Her father liked what he called 'proper food'. He meant sausages and potatoes and puddings, treacle pudding and jam roll and spotted Dick, suet puddings and dumplings, macaroni, baked beans. He did not care for thin slices of anything. He was fretful and ill-tempered if he was hungry. Meals were to be punctual to the minute. Obviously Elinor shared her father's diet, since the great majority of their meals were eaten by the two of them together. Although, therefore, she took plenty of exercise, her shadow did not grow less. She became not so much fat as solid.

Her hair was done once a month, by a girl in Milchester.

She suffered from solitude. An unmarried girl of her age and background, living at home in the mid-1980s? She was a freak, a dodo, member of a vanished species. English villages of the well-barbered sort had been full of young spinsters in 1910 and 1920, at the earlier time because the young men were in India, at the later because the young men were dead: but in 1980 the daughters of generals had jobs in London. They spent a few weekends a year with their parents in the country, the number varying with the power of emotional blackmail, but they lived within the sound of wine-bars. Elinor's situation, once common, had become unheard-of. Midweek tennis parties had become impossible, and amateur theatricals with *ingénue* parts.

When Elinor went to the village shop, she saw nobody of her class of less than twice her age.

She did not grieve that she had never seen a Giacometti or a Warhol, read Borges or Updike, heard Messiaen or even Cat Stevens, because she had never heard of these people. Her days were filled with weeding and walking dogs. Television having made a belated but overwhelming entry into her father's life, the screen dominated every evening. Horizons narrowed by the month. Mister Right (Captain or Major Right) was a distant schoolgirl dream.

Then Boots Cookson won the Grand Military, causing an explosion which bade fair to blast Elinor's life into orbit.

The Cooksons were another army family, though Derek Cookson had only been in the county regiment, and only risen to command of a company in that. Derek named his son Robert, but called him Boots from birth. He caused everybody else to call him Boots, too, so Boots was Boots in the nursery and at school and in the army. Derek's reasoning was that Boots would grow into his nickname, and be a dasher and an amateur steeplechase jockey and a hard man to hounds and a breaker of hearts and a successful general. By the time Boots was twenty-five, this strange, simple-minded strategy was more or less working. This success was due less to Boots's nickname than to his mother, a lady known locally as Mrs Beige, so anxious not to disgrace her dashing menfolk that she never said anything to anybody. But she had plenty of money, her father having been a successful builder. Boots consequently went to a smarter school than his father's and into a smarter regiment, and was thus able in some ways to live up to his nickname.

Why was Boots a dashing nickname? It just was. Everybody saw it as such, and many people said it suited him. It derived, perhaps, from a minor character in *The Memoirs of a Fox-Hunting Man*.

Mrs Beige's three-quarters of a million bought an eight-year-old thoroughbred gelding for Boots, as a prize for being promoted to the rank of captain. It registered Boots's racing colours and paid the training bills and entered the horse in various hunter-chases, and Boots won three small races and believed everything his father said about him.

Boots was tall and thin, with shiny light hair and close-set eyes. He had square, stubby hands inherited from his maternal grandfather, but in other ways he looked like a gentleman. Sometimes, owing to a small, pouting mouth and a pointed chin, he looked a good deal like a lady.

Stupid girls thought Boots was wonderful. He did not meet any clever girls.

Boots's life and career had nothing whatever to do with Thatcherite meritocracy, or John Major's vision of a classless Britain. His type was more enduring.

Boots won the Grand Military Gold Cup, at Sandown Park in March, on his own horse Vicar of Bray, the two horses in front of him having fallen at the notorious pond fence. He finished twenty lengths clear of the second, to loud applause, because regular cavalry officers riding their own horses were rare creatures, even in army races.

Elinor Leigh was there with her father. It was a meeting they never missed.

'That's a good boy, that one,' said Bernard. 'I like that boy.'

Bernard was wearing a dark brown tweed suit with a blue overcheck, his regimental tie, and a hairy bowler with a curly brim. His white moustache was brushed upwards and outwards, and his white hair grew glossy and thick over his ears. His bearing was still so soldierly that he appeared to have been starched, or to have a broomstick for a backbone. Elinor was also in tweeds, hers oatmeal. She wore brown brogues and thick stockings and her mother's diamond regimental brooch, and on her head a large beret of shaggy buff-coloured wool.

The Cooksons lived only six miles from the Leighs' house in Conyngham Smedley, but the families hardly knew one another. Lady Daphne Leigh had snubbed Mrs Beige whenever the Red Cross or the Friends of Milchester Cathedral brought them together. Bernard snubbed Derek Cookson, too, but this was not obvious, since Bernard's manner was always so stiff that extra stiffness was not remarked.

Boots Cookson was pleased to be congratulated by General Sir Bernard Leigh, who exactly personified Derek Cookson's ambitions for his son. A great many people congratulated Boots that afternoon, including royal persons, but Sir Bernard's words were specially to be valued.

Bernard's daughter's, also. Boots had known Elinor by sight for most of his life, but they both considered her to be above him. Elinor knew that her mother ignored and deplored Mrs Cookson. Boots knew that his father would have loved to be a crony of the general's. It was altogether sweet, therefore, to see admiration in Elinor's eyes and to hear congratulations in her clear alto voice.

Boots was now well and truly Boots, sure enough, unmistakable.

Boots could clearly now do what had previously been unthinkable. He could make a pass at Elinor Leigh. He could probably screw Elinor Leigh. Doing so would prove whatever else needed to be proved.

Boots could actually screw anybody he wanted. He was

the most glamorous and dashing young cavalry officer in the British Army. All the girls thought so. He thought so himself.

He said to Elinor, on the way to the car park after the last race, 'Are you ever in London?'

'No,' she said, 'because of my papa.'

'Well, you can get to Milchester?'

'Yes, of course.'

'Would you meet me for a drink sometime? I mean dinner?'

'Me? Really? Well,' said Elinor, knowing that thousands of upper-class girls would murder to have those words said to them by that man on that day. 'Well, yes, I suppose . . . I mean, I could, you mean in the evening? Yes, I suppose I might.'

Elinor rejoined her father, who had paused at a Gents' on the way. She did not say anything to him about Boots Cookson's invitation. This was because she thought it was an invitation to a good deal more than dinner.

Boot's eyes had flickered from her legs to her breasts and back again. On his face was an expression Elinor recognised, although the other ones had been drunk. Boots was drunk, but with victory. That was fair enough. Boots was not subtle. He was too honest and brave to hide his feelings. Elinor felt proud and excited. She felt herself coming alive, and not before time.

The winner of the Grand Military! On his own horse! Mummy had been silly about his mother being the daughter of a jerry-builder.

On a Tuesday, after five covert telephone calls, Elinor said. 'Daddy, I'm going out tomorrow night, if you don't mind.'

'Out?' said Bernard. 'Out? Out? Out? Out? Out?'

'I have been asked out to dinner. I have been asked to a party,' Elinor lied.

'Out? Out? Out?'

'To a dinner party.'

'Dinner.'

'Dinner,' said Elinor, rolling the word around her mouth, certain that more than dinner was involved. She had read enough romantic novels to know how to feel.

It was touch and go for twenty-four hours.

Having said 'dinner party', Elinor had to invent hostess and place and occasion, pitching these outside her father's acquaintance but inside his notion of the permissible. She had to stop him ringing up an imaginary household on the other side of Milchester, a call he would have attempted not so much out of jealousy or suspicion as to give himself something to do.

He wanted to come to the dinner party, too. Elinor struggled to persuade him that he would not enjoy it, that the conversation would be arty, that there might even be foreigners present.

It all invested the assignation with a great weight of labour, a burden of exhausting falsehood, a quite excessive importance. The date loomed too large. Nothing could have lived up to this atmosphere of epiphany and thunderstorm.

It all might have gone all right, in spite of this handicap, if Boots had not had three double whiskies before they met.

He felt he needed them. He had taken himself out of strict training, and he had some ground to make up. If he stopped to think about it, he was still a bit frightened of Elinor, of Elinor's certainty. At the other end of the swing of his mental pendulum, he saw himself as a man who could get away with anything. Want a drink? Have a drink. Have two, have three. The girl won't like it? Yes, she will. You're doing her a favour. Drink up.

Elinor smelled his breath in the foyer of the Eastgate Hotel. Whisky on breath was ominous; horrible hunt balls had made her familiar with it. It was manly, though, and anything could be forgiven to the winner of the Grand Military. It was something she might have expected, but it was not terribly pleasant.

Boots was wearing a dark suit, and a striped institutional tie. He looked quite old-fashioned.

Elinor was wearing a dress of crimson wool. She looked old-fashioned. Nobody had given Elinor advice about her clothes since her mother's death, and her mother, when alive, had given her bad advice. Her father did not notice what she was wearing, as long as it was not surprising. The crimson wool dress was not surprising, except that it was intended for a lady of fifty.

'Elinor!' said Boots, with jovial urgency. 'Great that you made it!'

Elinor felt herself smiling nervously. 'Hello,' seemed a grossly inadequate reply to his greeting, but it was all she could think of.

'Shall we have a cocktail here, or go straight in?'

'Whichever you like.'

'No, whichever *you* like.'

Elinor did not know which she liked. She had no opinion in the matter.

'We might go straight in,' she said doubtfully.

'Or we might have a bit of a gargle here first.'

'Well, yes, if you like.'

'No, if *you* like.'

Elinor's elation, her guilty joy, had problems surviving undiminished this indecision about drinks before dinner.

She was too nervous to make conversation, though conversation seemed necessary. Meanwhile there was no obvious reason why they should ever make a choice in this matter of drinks.

Boots was standing close to her, as though a crowd was pressing him from behind. The whisky was obtrusive on his breath, as he continued to defer to her preference.

The place had been redecorated in the style of its multinational owners, who had also decreed the anonymous piped music and the striped waistcoat of the waiter. This absence of character was reassuring, since it gave one the feeling that nothing that happened here really happened.

They did have a drink, Boots a large whisky and Elinor a medium sherry. There was a glitter in Boots's eye as he stared at the neckline of her dress.

Conversation over dinner, dreaded in anticipation, was easy in the event. Boots talked about himself, four large whiskies and half a bottle of wine making him fluent and rather loud. Elinor only had to say, 'God, how super,' a few times.

Between courses, he put his hand on her knee under the tablecloth. When they reached their coffee he could keep it there, and move it a little up her thigh. He was beginning to look a little pale and sweaty, and to repeat his stories about himself.

Elinor was a bit aghast at the situation she found herself in. She wondered what her mother would have said. But this was the winner of the Grand Military. Thousands of girls would give their eye-teeth to have Boots's hands on their thighs.

When they brought him the bill, Boots had a good deal of trouble calculating the tip. He had to borrow a ballpoint from the waiter, and take his hand from Elinor's leg, in order to do sums. He tried to continue lordly during this phase, but it is impossible to be lordly while counting on the fingers. He was a bit too drunk to do arithmetic. Elinor was powerless to help. It would have been presumptuous; also she had never in her life tipped a waiter in a restaurant. She told herself not be embarrassed, because he was the big race winner.

He said he knew a place. He said it was all fixed. He said he had paid a deposit, which they had the bloody cheek to demand. He was confident now. He had paid a lot of money for dinner, far too much for that dinner. He had drowned any atavistic nervousness. He was entitled to assume that she would come with him.

This was, as it were, part of the contract. Fair play was demanded. All those thousands of girls would give their eye-teeth.

They went in his car, leaving hers in the car-park of the Eastgate. He insisted on driving, in order to be masterful. He drove very slowly, with exaggerated care. His breath reeked, in the confined space of the small car. They went to the Hartleap Motor Inn, on the Milchester bypass. They went straight from the car to cabana number seventeen, of which Boots already had the key, having made these grown-up arrangements in advance.

'Let's get going,' said Boots thickly, 'let's get going.'

They sat on the bed in the pink plastic motel room, and he began kissing her wetly. He tried to push his hand down the front of her dress, but it was too tight. Elinor was worried that he was going to tear the dress. He tried to undo the hook and eye at the top of the zip at the back of the dress. This was too difficult for him, on account of the whisky he had drunk before dinner. Elinor reached up to the back of her own neck, and unhooked the fastener. This act had symbolic significance. It meant that she was going along with all this, that she was making it easy for him, that she was even making the running.

He pulled her clothes off and his, and stroked and prodded. She was sure he laddered her tights, but it was not a moment to be worrying about that. He climbed on top of her, and what followed was painful and unpleasant, devoid of the magic promised by fiction, heavily flavoured with whisky and the smell of sweat, mercifully extremely brief.

He slid out of her and away. He said, 'Oh Christ,' and vomited over the side of the bed. The little clean room was full of the acrid smell of his vomit.

The thought came clear and hard and sharp to Elinor, lying on her back and still pinned down by his weight, hurt and ashamed and embarrassed and disgusted, that this was by far the most horrible experience of her life. Nothing had prepared her for anything so squalid and beastly.

Boots was asleep, or had passed out. She heaved herself out from under him. She felt close to being sick herself. She washed and dressed, finding that she had to run one of her shoes under the tap. Boots was out like a light, his breath bubbling loudly in his throat. His head overhung the indescribable mess he had made.

Elinor's first idea was to find his car-keys and take his car. But then he might surface in the small hours, find her and the car missing, and ring her up at home, still drunk. Everything would be discovered and the recriminations would be ghastly.

Her next idea was to telephone for a taxi. But she did not know the number of any Milchester taxi, and there was no telephone book in the room. She could go to the reception desk. They would have the numbers of taxi companies. But she was ashamed to do this, to admit the kind of disaster that would make such a thing necessary.

All she could think of was to walk back into the middle of Milchester, to where her car was parked by the Eastgate. It took her just over an hour, and when she got to her car she was almost too tired to drive it.

'And may I respectfully enquire,' said her father, halfway up the stairs, in his pyjamas and dressing gown, at two-thirty in the morning, 'in whose house a week-day dinner party ends at this hour?'

Elinor had been raped by a drunk, and she had walked four miles in high-heeled shoes. She had had more than she could take.

'Shut up and mind your own business, you boring old bully,' she said.

Bernard's legs buckled, halfway up the stairs. He rolled ten steps to the foot of the stairs, and lay in a rag-doll heap, one of his slippers having fallen off.

'Well, not to put too fine a point on it, it's what we call a stroke,' said the doctor. 'He may last for hours or days or weeks.'

'Which?' asked Elinor, by now so tired that she was hardly less helpless than her father.

'Which what?' said the doctor, who was also very tired.

But Elinor had forgotten what question she had asked.

Bernard lived for three months, not speaking again or apparently aware of his surroundings or knowing Elinor. The nurses made a larger hole in the patrimony than any housekeeper would have done.

Elinor felt racked by guilt every time she saw the emaciated yellow face on the pillow. She had done this. Boots had done it. Sex had.

Elinor's brothers and their wives came with hushed voices and a keen eye for economies. They wanted a good lunch, and they went away immediately after it.

Bernard died in his sleep at five in the morning at the end of June. Elinor, deeply asleep and utterly exhausted, knew nothing about it until the morning. The night nurse was asleep, too, although she never admitted it.

'Not with him?' said Elinor's brothers. 'Why not?'

They came to supervise the funeral and the memorial service. Their wives came to manage the catering at these events. They all came to load up their Volvos with furniture, pictures and silver before the contents of the house were valued for probate.

The family put the house on the market. Elinor was to stay there until it was sold. She was the one to show people round, as she was there all the time anyway, as she had nothing else to do.

It was at this point that Elinor's mother's cousin Octavia Crossley rang up, full of busy practical charity, to invite Elinor to the annual exhibition of the Milchester College of Art and Design.

'She needs knew interests,' said Octavia Crossley to her friends. 'She needs a new beginning, a new direction.'

Thus it was that Elinor came to meet Mr Bruno Browning, and quickly become a completely different person.

CHAPTER THREE

BRUNO BROWNING'S LIFE had equipped him to deal with almost everything, except a girl like Elinor Leigh.

Ironically, his tough, simple, cunning father would have had no trouble with her at all. He would have tugged off his cap and called her 'Miss' or 'Madam'. Bruno called nobody 'Miss' and only royalty 'Ma'am'. His very brilliance placed him, at a moment like this, in a social quandary. He saw at once that communication between Elinor Leigh and himself would be impossible.

His father was Albert Browning, who with his younger brother Edwin had run the Old Forge Garage in Milchester. They mended cars and sold petrol, starting in 1935. They were moderately successful from the beginning, since they were involved in something that was growing fast. Bert's hobby was racing motor bikes. In 1937 he had a spectacular smash, breaking his leg in six places. He walked thereafter with a limp, and concentrated his efforts on building up the business. Edwin – Ted – was no businessman, but a wizard with machinery. Under his hands dead engines sprang to life, groaning and screaming engines purred with contented efficiency, extravagant engines became economical. The brothers complemented each other perfectly. They respected each other's ability. Each, indeed, was awed by the other's particular genius, Bert standing amazed when Ted tinkered with a motor, Ted dumbstruck with admiration when Bert acquired a new agency, stole a competitor's client, and drew up the balance sheet.

At the beginning of the war Ted joined up, an immediately valuable craftsman in an army rapidly mechanising. Bert had one leg four inches longer than the other, and they told him to keep the wheels turning on the home front.

At this point the evacuees arrived. Populations were being moved from cities where bombs were expected to villages where they were not. Wherever there was room, in the quiet places of England, families from the back streets were billeted.

There was no room in the Browning family's little house on the edge of Milchester – both sons still lived at home – but next door there was a childless elderly couple called Stanley and Ruby Leaf, and into their two extra bedrooms moved Rosa Greenbaum and her younger brother and sister. They were the orphans of a gas-main explosion of the previous year. Rosa was nineteen, and would have been sent to a factory making armaments, but she was evacuated with the children because she was a mother to them. Rosa was thin and dark, with delicate features and large eyes. When she was tired, her eyes sank back into her skull, into dark mysterious pools of shadow. She was often tired, because the kids were a right handful, and old Ruby Leaf treated her as a grateful slave.

Bert and Ted's father called them 'the Ikeys over the fence'. Their mother suspected them of eating animals slaughtered in funny ways.

To Bert, the Ikeys over the fence were first an irritant and then a threat and then an obsession. The irritant was Bernie and Miriam, skinny little things, active as spiders, noisy, always climbing over the lean-to sheds behind the houses, peeping and fiddling, inquisitive as monkeys, chattering and calling and mocking and forever asking what Bert was doing.

Why where they a threat? They just were.

It was Rosa who became the obsession.

If Bernie and Miriam were inquisitive about him, he became, by degrees, that first bitter winter of the war, passionately inquisitive about Rosa. He peeped at her when she was hanging out the washing in the Leafs' back garden, peeped from an upstairs window, or from behind the net curtains downstairs. He regretted the cold weather, because it caused Rosa to be encased in layers of stiff wool. He created occasions to talk to her, his ingenuity honed by successful years in business; and then he was too shy to say anything. She never spoke to him at all, but she was aware of him. He did not know how he knew this, but he knew that she watched him, too. He was a good-looking young man, in spite of his limp or even because of it; the girls in shops said so. Rosa asked Bernie and Miriam what he had been doing in the shed behind the house, and she asked the neighbours about the Browning family.

Bert found out about the Greenbaums, ever so casually asking Stanley Leaf in the pub. Their grandfather had come from Hamburg. He became a tailor's assistant in Catford. His wife was also German, but she had come with her family from Poland. They lived in a tenement with other Jewish families. They had five children, but they never had any money at all.

The youngest son also became a tailor, but he was called up in 1915 and spent three years in the trenches. He was a sergeant at the end of the war, in an intelligence section of a brigade headquarters. He was lucky to have a business to go back to in 1919. He was married by then, and Rosa was born in 1920. The others followed several years later.

The gas main blew up when they were demolishing a building in Poplar. Six people were killed, who were all waiting for a bus.

Rosa, who had just left school, got a job as an office junior, and learned typing and shorthand at night-school. Neighbours helped with the children. Rosa told the Leafs all about it, and Stanley Leaf told Bert.

Rosa became, for Bert, heroic as well as fascinating. She had struggled and she had managed, although with her bird bones, her tiny wrists and ankles, she looked too fragile to withstand a strong wind.

Stanley told Bert that Rosa went to Milchester Cathedral to listen to the music. She got books on art out of the public library. Her parents, seemingly, had started her on that sort of thing.

'Jewish, you know,' said Stanley, as though everything could be explained.

Stanley was proud of Rosa, though Ruby Leaf still exploited her. The younger children were top of their class at school.

Rosa got a good secretarial job with a feed-merchant. Bert made excuses to go to the feed-merchant's offices, although he had no animals and no conceivable use for any of the firm's products.

Bert's obsession with Rosa was noticed. Of course it was noticed. It became a local joke. Ted came home on leave and heard about it within minutes. Ted teased Bert about it, and they had a fight, in the yard behind the garage. Ted was astonished when Bert attacked him.

Bert could talk fluently enough to customers and sales-men and suppliers, and the snoopy little bureaucrats who controlled petrol, and to his mates in the pub and friends of his family, and to retired judges and generals whose cars Ted fixed before the war; but he could not say a word to Rosa. There were no words in his head to express what he felt. He could not have told himself or Ted or any friend what he felt: it was beyond any word he had ever used or heard.

They knew about it at home, but they did not talk about it. They thought it was something that would go away.

The weather got better and the news worse.

France fell, and everybody thought Britain would be invaded.

Bert, peeping, saw Rosa in a cotton dress hanging out the washing in the Leafs' back garden. A gusty summer wind whipped her skirt round her legs, slim little legs, not skinny or sticklike, fragile but nicely shaped. The wind pressed the front of Rosa's dress against her chest when she turned to face it, when she reached up with the clothes-pegs to the line. She had small, sharp-pointed breasts, like the hills in a child's drawing. Bert felt ill with desire. He felt a great tenderness for this tragic and heroic waif. He felt throttled by words he wanted to pour out, which he did not know, which he would not have dared to use even if he had known them.

Little Miriam said to Bert, 'Why don't you ever talk to our Rosa?'

'She doesn't want to talk to me,' said Bert.

'Yes, she does. She said, "Why doesn't Bert Browning ever talk to me, when he goes on like a gas-rattle to everybody else."'

'She never said that.'

'She did. Cross my heart. "I wouldn't half mind passing the time of day with that Bert Browning sometimes." That's what our Rosa said.'

'Crikey. I wish I could believe you.'

Miriam giggled, and disappeared over the roof of the Leafs' garden shed.

Then when it happened it was ridiculous.

Bert came face to face with Rosa in the yard behind the feed-merchant. They both stopped dead, a metre apart, their faces solemn.

They both spoke at once, using identical words.

'Miriam says you want to talk to me,' they both said, at exactly the same moment.

'Sorry,' said Bert. 'Carry on.'

'No. I'm sorry,' said Rosa. 'You carry on.'

'Miriam says . . .'

'Miriam says,' said Rosa. 'What did she say to you?'

'That you wanted to talk to me.'

'I never said that.'

'You don't want to talk to me.'

'Yes, I do, but I never said so to Miriam.'

'Gum,' said Bert. 'She made it up, then, saying you said you wanted . . .'

'And she made up that you said . . .'

'She must have. She got it right, mind, but not because of anything I told her.'

'She always was a monkey,' said Rosa. 'But now we're talking to each other. I was beginning to think we never would.'

'I was scared.'

'How could you be?'

'I was.' Bert groped for words to say things he had never said before. 'It was too important. You was too important.'

'Me important? I'm not important.'

'You are to me.'

'Honest?'

'The most important thing in the world.'

'Am I, Bert?'

'I believe you know that.'

'I believe I do. But I thought you'd never say it. I won't half belt that Miriam when I get home.'

'Don't do that,' said Bert. 'I do love you, Rosa.'

'I love you, Bert.'

'I don't understand. How can you? How can you possibly? Me, walking with a ruddy limp like a paralysed ostrich.'

'What difference does that make, that you've got a limp? It's you I love, not four inches missing off your leg.'

'How do you know it's four inches?'

'I know everything about you. Every last little thing. You don't have no secrets from me. I asked and asked and learned and learned.'

'Blimey, why?'

'Can't you guess, you dear old fathead?'

'Oh Rosa. How would it be if I kissed you?'

'Just what I was going to suggest.'

They had one of those Spartan little wartime weddings. Ted got a seventy-two-hour pass, and made a speech. They had a three-day honeymoon in Torquay, and came back full of secret smiles.

Their son was born in October 1941. It was a difficult birth, owing to Rosa's narrow hips and the blackout and an exhausting pregnancy, and Rosa was ill for a few weeks and weak for some time after. She recovered all right, and the baby bloomed, crooned over by Bert's mother and Ruby Leaf and Miriam.

Rosa could not have any more children.

They called the boy Brian. Rosa said she had always wanted a son called Brian. The sun rose and set round

Brian Browning's birdlike shoulders.

He resembled his mother, as firstborn sons are apt to do. Even when he was very small, his face had a hawklike, exotic quality.

Probably if she had had other children Rosa would not have loved her son with such intensity of devotion.

Rosa wanted Brian to have everything. Consequently it was necessary for herself and Bert to acquire everything. It was easy and cheap to acquire property during the war, as a basis for future dealings. You needed faith in the future – faith that there was a future, that the war would be won, and normal capitalistic life resumed. Rosa had faith because she had Brian.

Rosa had a business brain at least as good as Bert's. She could handle or oversee any secretarial work. She was good at mathematics, and she had longer sight and a broader vision than Bert's. The two of them made a formidable team. When Ted came back with his mechanical skills, the world was their oyster. It was Brian's oyster, and the pearls would be Brian's pearls.

Books, music, art: Rosa was feeding them to Brian when most little boys were still with Flash Gordon and Percy F. Westerman.

Education. Bert had a good brain, and Rosa had inherited a first-class one. As soon as he went to school, it was evident that Brian had inherited the best of both. His teachers talked about a scholarship to the Milchester Royal Grammar School. Bert's family had never raised their eyes one-tenth so high, but to Rosa it was all obvious.

Brian got the scholarship in 1953, coronation year. That summer saw the conquest of Everest by Hillary and Tenzing, and the conquest of the scholarship examination by Brian Browning.

He inherited his mother's appearance of fragility, and his father's reality of toughness.

Brian moved up through the Grammar School, collecting prizes. He played the piano and the oboe, but he was not going to be a professional musician. He painted, very well taught at the school, but he was warned against any hopes of being a professional artist.

'Music and art will be lifelong joys,' said his teachers, 'even if they are not how you make your living.'

This was not so very disappointing, because it was already clear how Brian would make his living.

It would be a pretty good living.

Ted had come back after the war, as a Staff Sergeant in the REME. He married a local girl called Margie Winch-field. They called their son Frederick. Margie always wanted to call him Freddie, but in the event he was always called Fred. Fred was eight years younger than Brian. Margie wanted Fred to be like Brian, but this was not going to happen, since Ted was unlike Bert and she herself was unlike Rosa.

The business picked up, but the brothers were not content to go back to where they had been before the war. They looked about for areas of diversification – they discussed a chain of filling-stations, a car-hire business, a factory. In 1955 Rosa said, 'People all the time want a bulldozer for a day. They want to dig one ditch. Or they want to cut up half a dozen trees. They don't want to buy the machinery, just for that one job, just for a few days a year. They want—'

'To hire,' said Bert. 'I wonder.'

'People don't want to have to bother with maintenance, servicing – all that,' said Rosa. 'They want it all done for them. If machinery's on hire, it's used all the time, instead of once every six months. That means the cost is amortised double-quick.'

Plant hire. Everything from nine-inch electric mowers to bulldozers that could pile Pelion on Ossa. It was a new industry of rapid growth. Rosa had exactly defined its point.

Bert looked after the business and Ted looked after the machines, as before, and they grew and grew, and the red and black logo of Browning Machinery was seen over a wide area.

This was when Brian, one of two heirs apparent of the business, came under the brilliant influence of Oliver Outhwaite.

Oliver Outhwaite was a Yorkshireman drawn south by civilisation, as he saw it, as Goths had been drawn to Rome and Americans to Paris. Among the soft and tolerant southerners, far from his Calvinistic roots, he could be himself. He was an aesthete. He was interested in women only as wearers of clothes or models for artists. He was much travelled, an accomplished linguist. He had no creative talent: he was the supreme type of those who cannot do and therefore teach. He genuinely loved teaching and was very good at it, with the serious qualification that he played favourites. His energies were devoted to those few who would benefit. He did not exhaust himself trying to breathe the divine afflatus into clods. The headmaster of the Grammar School knew this and tended to deplore it (although an elitist himself) but Oliver Outhwaite was safe in his job because he coached his favourite pupils to scholarships at Oxbridge.

Oliver Outhwaite made a sincere and sustained effort not to fall in love with his pupils, but he could not resist Brian Browning. He appreciated the toughness beneath the fragility, the quick, accurate brain, the nascent seriousness of taste, the infinite teachability. He saw the fine bones of the face, the shadowed, deep-set eyes, the narrow and strangely aristocratic skull, the touch of exotic fascination; he saw also the impeccably kept fingernails, the invariable snowy-whiteness of collar and cuffs, the marks of pride, care, self-respect, fastidiousness. All this was unusual in boys of this age, and not altogether to be ascribed to a loving and protective mother. The cleanliness and delicacy was intensely attractive to Oliver Outhwaite. It also soothed moral doubts. The boy was thereabouts already. There could be seduction without what the world called perversion.

Brian was flattered by the special attention which the teacher paid him. He was dazzled by the man's knowledge and accomplishments, his languages, the people and places he knew. He was intoxicated by the promises Oliver Outhwaite made regarding his own future, the worlds to be charmed and conquered.

The first physical episode was delicately done, so that it almost became part of a tutorial. Brian was not shocked, because he had been gently, sedulously indoctrinated with classical and renaissance precedent, with Alcibiades and Leonardo. He was made to feel adult and beautiful. He was made to feel part of a great aesthetic tradition, one of the elect, an Athenian, a Medici.

Oliver Outhwaite was determined that Brian should win a scholarship to Cambridge, and in 1959 he did so. His subject was modern languages, French and Italian because in these Oliver Outhwaite was most fluent and learned, and in both of these Brian was already quite well read. The dons who examined him were impressed, though one remarked that he was so accomplished that he had probably already peaked.

Bert Browning was dumbfounded by his son's success. He had not really taken in what sort of son he had, even though he had been married to Rosa for all those years. Because Brian was like him in some ways, he had not realised how unlike him Brian was in other ways.

Of course Brian had changed since he was a little boy, changed a lot in the last couple of years at school. He had changed more than Bert noticed, because Bert was so busy making Brian's fortune.

Rosa was passionately proud of Brian's success, of course she was, but she wasn't in the least surprised by it, of course she wasn't.

Brian's Uncle Ted was dubious about all this art and literature. He wasn't exactly against these things, for teachers and suchlike, but he did not see the relevance to people of their sort. Brian was to take over the business one day, with his own boy Fred, and what good were all those poems and pictures for that?

Ted's wife Margie took the opposite view exactly. She did not confront her husband with her opinion, but she dinned it into her son. Brian was the sort of person to be. He was superior. You could tell by just looking at him. He had risen above his background, as all great men did. It was marvellous to hear Brian using French words, and talking to his mother about Michelangelo and such. That was what Margie wanted for her Freddie.

Fred was nine years old when Brian got his scholarship to Cambridge, and Margie reckoned that gave her time enough to turn Freddie into Brian. If she didn't manage that, it wouldn't be for lack of trying. She knew her duty as a mother.

But Fred already showed clear signs of preferring machine oil to linseed oil or midnight oil. Fred took after

Ted in more than name. Fred trotted about after his father among the mowers and diggers and dump-trucks, the axles and gearboxes and lathes and grease-guns. When Margie gave him a book of German engravings, he used the pages to make a gasket for a carburettor.

The funny thing was that Brian and Fred really liked one another. They would never be in competition because they were so different. Brian knew that Fred could already do things that Brian couldn't do, and though he, Brian, didn't even want to do them, they were still good and useful things to be able to do. Brian knew that his own future, the future of Browning Machinery, depended on people like Fred as much as on people like himself. There was still plenty of his father in Brian, as well as so much of his mother.

Cambridge then was a hive of creativity, and what people were busiest creating was themselves. Wherever you looked, there was a talented young man reinventing himself – a medical student becoming a star revue performer, that sort of thing. Bliss was it in that dawn to be alive, for somebody like Brian Browning, and to be young was very heaven.

Brian had a quick ear. As a musician and a linguist he was an accurate mimic. He imitated the voices of the Old Etonians, and those of certain rather precious lecturers, so that soon their way of talking became his way. Although he could assume the burr of his native wood-notes, well enough to fool even his family when he was at home, this comfortable Wessex was the performance, and that other was his real voice.

'Bruno' came to him when he was looking at an Italian primitive in the Fitzwilliam. He told people it was what everybody called him, so that soon it was what everybody called him. It was a really good idea, that. It was a legitimate nickname punning from his surname; it suited his colouring, his black and tragic Semitic eyes, his thick black hair; it suited his exoticism, and his areas of study and of taste. It expressed the sort of person he had decided that he was. 'Brian', though his mother's choice, expressed to him exactly the person he was not.

Bruno began his serious travels in the vacations. He inserted himself charmingly into cultured households in Rome and Milan and the Veneto. Everywhere he studied pictures and buildings, and learned their history; he went to concerts and operas, and met everybody he could. People handed him on to one another, and with each group he became known to other groups, in France as well as Italy, and then in Spain and Greece. He had an excellent memory. He also had a filing system, kept in a drawer in his rooms in Cambridge, dealing with art, people and wine; it was modelled on the system devised by his mother for the head office of Browning Machinery.

He did not ask his new friends home to Milchester, but he did entertain with delicate luxury in Cambridge.

His tutors said he was spreading himself too thin to do himself justice academically. He knew this was true, but he had his own clear sense of priorities.

He became a tremendous snob. If he was derided for anything, it was that. He was a name-dropper and a lover of princes.

He was a lover of princesses, too. He liked the company of women, and there was for him powerful sex appeal in social rank. He was bedded by a few bored Italian wives, smitten by his apparent fragility and his studied weariness, and he was neither disgusted nor discredited. Indeed his lack of predatory brutality was itself successful with these women who had to live with machismo. He was not passionately involved in these adventures. They were a means of returning and ensuring hospitality.

The Browning business meanwhile continued to grow, and Bert increased Bruno's allowance. Bruno was able to begin collecting. He began with unfashionable things that he liked – historical and allegorical paintings of the Italian eighteenth century, early Victorian neo-classical sculpture, and a few very young moderns. He bought some metal sculptures made out of welded bits of machinery from a student at the St Martin's, and paintings from the Young Contemporaries exhibitions at the ICA. It was difficult to find room for these things. Rosa struggled to appreciate the modern pieces, but her taste was rooted in Vermeer and Velazquez. Bert less and less understood how he could have been responsible for his son.

In Paris in 1961 Bruno was asked to join a party in a box at the Opera. The party included a stranger, an American, a silent grey man, very tall and elegant, treated with awe by Bruno's friends. His name was Wentworth Pollock. He said he was no relation of the painter. They called him Wenty, though Bruno did not at first venture to do so. Wenty lived in Paris, recreating the *déraciné* life not of Gertrude Stein and Hemingway but of Henry James and Whistler. Wenty was rich.

Bruno had to go back to England the next day. The Cambridge term was beginning. He had an appointment with his tutor. He had to be there. He was cutting it fine, by staying in Paris this final night.

Bruno sat at the back of the box, behind the girls and the others. Wenty was with him there. Bruno felt electricity. He felt a communication from the dark figure beside him, a message of sadness and gentleness. He felt not so much excited as affectionate. It was very strange.

Already in the back of the box, in public, in the middle

of *La clemenza di Tito*, sitting beside a person to whom he had hardly yet spoken, Bruno felt an emotion new to him outside his own immediate family, an emotion remote from the physical itch, the vivid sensation of his affairs: he thought he felt love.

How could this be?

The music formed a silken spaceship, in which his emotion flew away from the known world.

Their fingers touched in the darkness. Wenty gripped Bruno's hand. Bruno felt that Wenty's hand was trembling.

'You can't go.'

'I must go.'

'If you leave me now, I shall die.'

'That's simply not true. I'm sorry to go. You know that. I'm broken-hearted. I think you know that.'

'If your heart were touched at all,' said Wenty, 'you would stay.'

Bruno repeated that he could not. Wenty, educated, would understand that Bruno's education was supremely important to him.

Wenty at last gave up his passionate attempt to keep Bruno in Paris. He shrugged, and tried to smile: and Bruno's heart was wrenched to see that unhappy little false smile.

'Take this with you then,' said Wenty.

So Bruno carried Wenty's gift with him, on his journey home. It was a large and awkward package, heavy, fragile, precious: brilliant stained glass, leaded like a medieval window, as kitsch as could be but of its kind superb, supremely self-confident in its garishness and its sweeping voluptuous lines.

'It expresses what I feel about you,' said Wenty. 'It is

feminine, sexy, strong, pretentious, a little vulgar, beautiful and adorable.'

Bruno did not know, all at once, what to do with the lamp when he unpacked it in his rooms at Cambridge.

Three days later he had a letter from Paris, from one of the friends who had taken him to the opera. Wentworth Pollock was dead. He had committed suicide. He had taken an overdose. He left a note saying that he was too unhappy to be bothered with living any longer.

'*C'était une âme triste*,' said Bruno's friend's letter.

Thereafter and for ever the Tiffany lamp was Bruno's most treasured possession.

Bruno came down from Cambridge with a 2.2 (not what was expected of a scholar of his college) and joined his father and uncle in the business.

He was diligent and efficient. A lot of people were surprised.

He moved out of his parents' house into a flat in a big converted house behind the cathedral close. There he installed most of his still-growing collection. There, in the middle of the principal room, the Tiffany lamp presided like a tutelary god, like a symbol of another and a better world.

Bruno was Bruno in the light of the lamp. He was Brian round the corner in his parents' home, and in the offices and workshops of the firm.

Boys came and went in the lamplight, art students from the college, young clerks and apprentices and messengers from various businesses in the city. Nobody ever came who worked for the family firm or had any connection with it. Nice girls came to tea or Sunday supper in Bert and Rosa's house.

Cousin Fred joined the firm, straight from school, in 1968.

His mother Margie had had a mad dream of Fred following his cousin to Cambridge, but there was never the least possibility of that. Instead he went off on courses with various manufacturers, becoming a certified expert in the repair and maintenance of their machines; he went also part time to the Milchester Poly, acquiring impressive qualifications in mechanical engineering. In 1972 he married, too young, a nurse at the Milchester hospital who was too young. They rented a cottage, the merit of which to Fred was a huge garage and workshop. The marriage was under early strain from Fred's oily fingerprints on the curtains and chair-covers.

The pleasant smell of lubricating oil entered every room with Fred. It did not leave the room when Fred left, but remained.

Bruno and Fred – Brian and Fred – continued to like and respect one another, as their fathers had done, and still did, though they were a good deal more different than their fathers had been. To Fred's mother Margie, the friendship was one of the redeeming features of a situation otherwise deplorable.

The other redeeming feature was that her men – her Ted, her Fred – were in their oily-handed ways making plenty of money.

They made a great deal more in 1983, when the firm went public.

Bert was over seventy, and Rosa wanted him to retire completely. Neither he nor she would really retire while they were still on the spot, in Milchester, in walking distance of the office and workshops. The only thing was to go right away, to Cornwall or the Scillies, and take to growing hydrangeas and playing Scrabble.

'It's not fair on the new lot, us still sitting on their heads,' said Rosa.

'New lot,' said Bert, laughing through his chronic bronchitis. 'Brian's about forty-five.'

'He's forty-three.'

'That's about forty-five.'

The family retained a substantial holding. They continued to run the company, though now with outside directors from the institutional shareholders who were the new joint owners. Bruno became Chairman and Joint Managing Director. Fred was the other joint Managing Director.

Fred's wife let herself be bought out. She went off to Wales with her money, to start a nursing home. She said she had to go as far as that, to get away from the smell of lubricating oil.

Bert and Rosa kept a sentimental stake in the company, enough to come to meetings and vote. But Bert was now almost entirely immobile, gone in the hips and knees and back, because he had limped all his life. Rosa was still alert and elegant, and frightening to the young. She was more than ever exotic, and very beautiful.

Bruno could take more time off, as his cousin Fred become more involved with management. Now that they had gone public, the management team was stronger and more varied; the company was in good professional hands. Bruno could with a clear conscience spend more time in Florence and Venice, Cleveland and Malibu, Dresden and Prague. He could go to auctions all over the world, though he could not, to be sure, bid against the Japanese industrialists or the Australian brewers. He could with greater leisure cultivate duchesses and curators, and negotiate invitations to wonderful little parties in wonderful little palaces.

He was able to help young artists, certain brilliantly

talented lads, with patronage and hospitality, with money and encouragement and constructive criticism, and little trips abroad which dramatically demonstrated the inter-action of art and life and love.

Bruno was often, in this company, made the victim of treachery and ingratitude. But he remained optimistic and sunny-tempered, like his father, and committed to the cause of the arts, like his mother.

Bert died in Torquay in 1985, of bronchitis and bore-dom.

Bruno and Rosa had a long, vehement argument about Bert's money. It was all left to Bruno, Rosa to enjoy a life interest. Bruno said Rosa was to have all that income, as Bert had intended. Rosa said she wanted about a fifth of the income, and Bruno had better enjoy the rest while he was young enough to do so.

'You want more pictures and more trips abroad and more champagne,' said Rosa.

'No I don't.'

'Of course you do.'

'I want you to have them.'

'I will have them, dear.'

'Not enough.'

'More than enough.'

Rosa won the argument. She always won arguments. Bruno was immediately much richer.

Rosa moved to St Ives, and went to painting classes. They tried to turn her into a modern, but she was not having any of that.

Bruno did buy more pictures, and more Concorde tickets, and more champagne. He made a massive gift to the Milchester College of Art and Design, as a memorial to his father; after many acrimonious meetings, the gift was earmarked largely for a new multi-purpose exhibition space. There was a proportion also for annual prizes for student work. These were in the form of travelling and other scholarships. Aware of miserable precedents – such as Shaw's bequest to the British Library – Bruno insisted on very precise and permanent rules, breach of which was to render the endowment forfeit. Extraordinary bitterness was secretly felt and covertly expressed about this tying of the College's hands. Rosa had warned Bruno that this would happen. He did not know how she knew.

The other substantial new outlay Bruno made could not in any way be thought of as a memorial to his father. He found and fell in love with a decrepit château on a bluff over the river Tarn, north-east of Albi. When he saw it, in the spring, the lush patches of meadow beside the river were blue with orchids, and the ground just behind, higher and drier, powdered with millions of golden cowslips; and the caramel-coloured stone of the château glowed in the afternoon sun like something made for an enchanted giant's birthday dinner.

Rosa came out to the Tarn, to look at la Moquerie. Bruno could get it – the big house, the little house, three hundred metres of river frontage, seventy hectares of land – for less than £100,000.

'Ooh, there's a lot of work here,' said Rosa.

'Yes, but what fun to do it.'

'It's a long way to come, dearie, for a couple of hours in the evening putting up shelves.'

'It's an easy journey. An hour from Toulouse.'

'But the time!'

'I've got the time.'

'How many days a month? How many weeks a year?'

'Lots. I'm shifting into a part-time mode.'

'Handing the day-to-day to Fred?'

'It's what he wants. He's old enough. We might lose him if he isn't given more clout. I'll still be there wearing my buttonhole in public.'

'Don't give it up, love. Your dad invented it.'

'I won't give it up, darling. I'm still part of Milchester and part of the firm.'

This was true, to a qualified extent.

Bruno bought a long lease of a house in the Close, a heavy-featured four-storey seventeenth-century building two doors from the Deanery and four from the Diocesan Library. He spent about a third of his time there; he was regarded as a resident by the residents, as a neighbour by his neighbours. He bought tickets for all charitable and artistic events. He remained a presence at the Milchester College of Art and Design, keeping a tactful but resented eye on the progress of the Browning Gallery, meeting the students who won the prizes he had given.

In his new house he installed the parts of his collection which belonged there, paintings by Richard Wilson, Alexander Cozens, Francis Towne, the Gainsborough drawings, the two Nollekens busts. He did not overfill the house with furniture. Rosa had in her later years – her taste educated and her bank balance copious – assembled a small but excellent collection of English furniture, which included some flamboyant pieces in the Empire style. Rosa particularly liked this brief and happy imitation of the French taste at its most hubristic.

'I like it too,' said Bruno. 'But, you know, it's vulgar. It's opulent and brash. It's the style of someone self-made and self-educated, like Napoleon himself.'

'Like me,' said Rosa. 'I think we like it because we're Jewish.'

'Like Edwardian financiers with astrakhan coats and diamond tie-pins?'

'I'm surprised you haven't got a diamond tie-pin.'

'As a matter of fact,' said Bruno, 'I have.'

Bruno left the house in the Close quite sparsely furnished, since in due time those pieces of his mother's would take their places there. Meanwhile she had to be restrained from giving him everything she had.

He entertained occasionally, always quietly.

In the midst of the big drawing-room, on a table behind the sofa facing the fireplace, stood the Tiffany lamp. When it was switched on early, before the shutters were closed or the curtains drawn, on dusky winter evenings when the sky was dark before teatime, the magical barbaric colours of the lamp could be seen from windows two hundred yards away on the other side of the Close, colours out of dreams, unmatched in nature or in the great windows of the cathedral.

In regard to the firm, Bruno's idea was to be useful to it, powerful in it, without stepping on the managerial toes of his cousin Fred.

Fred said, 'You don't have to be so bloody tactful with me, Brian. You're older than me and cleverer, and you're Chairman, and anyway I rely on your judgement. I want your opinion wherever you've got one. For God's sake don't ration your input out of concern for my feelings.'

'Ration my input?' said Bruno. 'That sounds completely extraordinary. Why, ration my input! It could mean going on a diet. A politically correct description of trying to lose weight.'

'Jesus, you do talk,' said Fred.

But Bruno continued to be tender of Fred's feelings, partly because he was deeply fond of him, partly because he believed the firm was best served by Fred having the confidence of executive control.

Which allowed him to spend eight months of the year abroad.

La Moquerie took much of his time, in those last three years of the eighties.

He early decided that he did not want to do anything twice – that whatever he did he must do right first time. He decided he was never going to undertake anything like this again. He decided that the result of his labours should approach perfection of craftsmanship and taste.

'I aspire to set a standard,' he said, 'by which all future yuppifications will be judged.'

His listeners knew that he spoke only partly in self-mockery.

It took a lot of money, and a lot of time.

It was obvious that spending the time reduced the useless spending of money: that only by spending much more money could you get away with spending less time. He had, and spent, plenty of both.

It was done in overlapping stages, the plumbing and wiring interlocking with the rebuilding. Some decisions had to be taken before he was ready to take them, such as the placing of wall lights and power points. The stone floors at ground level were repaired and restored, nowhere replaced. The terrace was extensively and expensively repaired, to make it safe, and the 120-step zigzag stairway from the terrace to the jetty in the river.

As the château took shape, it consisted of two massive stone towers, east and west, one of seven and one of six floors, topped with steep roofs of stone cut into fish-scale semicircles: the towers joined by a central block, much restored, on three wide and airy floors. There was a spiral stone staircase in the east tower, a zigzag wooden staircase, replacing ladders, in the west tower, and a broad marble staircase, taken from a demolished Edwardian hotel, in the middle.

Archaeologists had been consulted, historical plans drawn up, but the past had not really dictated the arrangements of the present. Throne-room, guardroom, dungeons, were not kept to their original shapes or functions. Crumbling walls were rebuilt to include great south-facing windows over the terrace and the chasm of the river.

Bruno was not coy about his efforts. He did not repel photographers. The glossies charted the progress of la Moquerie from picturesque ruin to gracious home, and few satirical voices were raised to comment.

Bruno liked showing people round, discussing his plans for the garden, his disposition of paintings and sculpture.

He began giving parties, indoors and out, long before the work was finished. He gave parties to baptise the pool, the rose-garden, the fountains, the main marble staircase, the new kitchen; he considered but rejected a whimsical idea of a party to baptise the bathrooms.

After three years the main house and garden were just about finished, though it was true that neither house nor garden would ever be definitely finished. There remained untouched the little house, the annexe, the subsidiary building a hundred yards away identified by the experts as the guardhouse. There the small garrison of the château had stood alert, or lay in drunken slumber; there a whole new project lay ready, a marvellously situated compact house, picturesque as a cocked hat, romantic, potentially very practical, a canvas waiting for another painting. But Bruno was tired. He felt exhausted at the prospect of starting all over again, charting the course of pipes and wires, choosing window-frames, siting fireplaces, enduring noise and dust. Somebody else could have the Guardhouse as a hobby.

Pending that restoration, the cliff-face pathway between château and Guardhouse was smoothed and fenced and made quite safe.

Rosa saw some of this; she saw all the magazine articles and photographs. She knew that some of the large spaces of wall would be hung with pictures she did not understand; but in general she was deeply happy. From the moment she had known she was pregnant, months after that chilly little wedding, this was what she had hoped and worked for.

She refused to come and live with Bruno, in the château or in the Guardhouse. She was seventy, too old to up sticks. She had a kind of awareness, unvoiced even to herself, of aspects of Bruno's life she did not care for. She was not shocked or sickened, as she might have been without her knowledge of art history: but she did not want to live in the same house as episodes she was careful not to imagine.

Fred also came, for the brief holidays he allowed himself. He liked the château and its position, though he hated the contents. He tinkered with the electric pump which drew water up from the river for the fountain, for the runnels which tumbled over the terraces and sustained the gardens. He improved the efficiency of the pump. He was as happy as a lark while he was twirling his screwdrivers.

Bruno offered Fred the Guardhouse, on a lease as long as he liked. Fred was tempted.

'When I retire,' he said.

'Go part-time. Give it three months a year.'

'I haven't got three months a year. But when I have I'll take you up on it, if the offer's still open.'

Bruno bought an eighteenth-century putto with a

bird-bath on its head, for the middle of the rose-garden. He bought a marble nymph by John Gibson, in the manner of Canova, a pensive and drooping girl with dimpled knees, slightly more than life size; he put her at the top of some stone steps, and surrounded her with foaming lavender. This was more Rosa's style. She was glad when a man came to photograph the Gibson for a glossy magazine.

He was a very young man. He was the sort of photographer who took pictures of garden statuary, not of murders or Bosnians. He was the sort who had really wanted to be a painter. Rosa thought him gentle and witty and too thin.

Bruno thought him gentle and witty and just the right shape.

The boy was called Mario Robinson, not because he was half Italian, or for reasons like Bruno's, but because his mother had seen *The Great Caruso* at an important crossroads in her life.

Bruno asked him to come and stay as soon as Rosa had gone home, but not before.

'Are you ashamed of me?' said Mario.

'Yes,' said Bruno.

Mario laughed very much. He was still laughing when Bruno kissed him.

Mario was a freelance. He took pictures when he was asked to, or when he needed the money. Staying at la Moquerie did very well instead of taking photographs. Bruno got him painting again, and encouraged and inspired him.

Rosa died very quickly in the spring. Fred had sent for Bruno, and Bruno was there just in time.

Her affairs were simple, and in perfect order. There was very little property of her own – she had been enjoying a life interest in a small part of what Bert had left. She left a couple of brooches to her sister-in-law Margie. Her death increased Bruno's furniture and fortune. Bruno was, in a curious way, heartbroken without being upset. He had adored his mother and been close to her; he would mourn and miss her greatly. But he knew she would have hated helplessness, walking-frames and wheelchairs, the maddening dependency, all the frustration she had seen Bert undergo. Even more she would have hated the sense of losing her marbles. She would have been mad with rage at the thought of being mad with a stroke.

Bruno went home to Milchester, to see the lawyers who were also the executors. He arranged for the furniture and so forth to be brought up from Cornwall. He had long ago decided where everything would go. The Empire pieces looked very fine in the light from the Tiffany lamp.

Fred was grumpily comforting. He was a comfort, too.

Bruno put in some time at the office, and some at the Art College. He went to half a dozen exhibitions in London; he went to a concert at the Barbican and a play at the National. He went to a couple of parties where he saw the art critics of the serious papers.

At the end of May, he went back to la Moquerie, where there was much to be done and where Mario was waiting for him.

Mario was there, but not waiting for him. Mario was as high as a kite on something or other, with an insolent young German who had broken into the wine cellar. Bruno had to wait until the servants came, before he could throw them both out. He was sick with disgust, with the messiness in himself which made him the victim, the captive and the dupe, of a guttersnipe like Mario. It was depraved and humiliating and horribly expensive, to indulge his itch for the Marios of the world.

77

He was sick with disgust, and with heartbreak. He missed the gentle and funny Mario of their golden moments with a sharpness of pain that made him bite his pillow at four in the morning.

He swore: never again the humiliation and squalor of such an affair. He swore: never again the misery at the end of such an affair.

In this mood he went back to Milchester at the end of June, for the annual exhibition of student work at the College of Art and Design; and in this mood he met the strange and unspeakable Elinor Leigh.

CHAPTER FOUR

S HE WAS A HORSE, perhaps a cow. She was a Sherman tank, a bulldozer, a rhinoceros in an unbecoming cotton frock, with the wrong shoes and the wrong hairdo and the wrong lipstick, and absolutely the wrong expression on her face.

She was much too young for all these wrongnesses, which were of a kind familiar to Bruno in older women, the wives of his senior employees in the business, librarians, shopkeepers, women in French post offices.

She could have been handsome. She might still, perhaps, if she remade herself inside and out. She carried herself well, with an arrogance Bruno admired. He liked that posture. He had attempted it himself, but his spine persisted in its ingratiating curve.

The dinosaur was staring at a small painting which had done nothing to arouse the hatred that she showed. Perhaps it was her response to any painting. Perhaps it was her response to the whole of life.

Bruno identified the painting as *Landscape VII*, by Ailie Huxtable, Fine Arts, Year One. Ailie Huxtable had evidently been awarded one of the Browning Prizes for this picture, by the committee which made the selection. Bruno wondered why the committee had chosen this muddy little semi-abstract, with its debt to painters whom only the oldest Academicians would nowadays consider adventurous. This picture was obscure and opaque without even being modern. Its palette was turgid and its intention baffling. What was it for? Why had Ailie Huxtable painted it?

Was Ailie a boy's name or a girl's?

Bruno looked again at the picture because the Sherman tank was looking at it. He was inclined to be prejudiced in its favour, because the tank hated it so much. Perhaps for this bad reason he began to see more in it. There was a subtler, more original deployment of those pessimistic colours than he had at first realised, a precocious assurance and lyricism in the brushwork.

The selection committee had been right. It was clever of them, because this was not a picture to reach out and grab you by the lapel – not at all one of the brash, callow screams for attention which covered so many yards of wall so very uselessly. This one murmured, wove a gentler spell, stayed in the mind after the eye moved elsewhere. This was pretty good stuff. It did the College credit.

The artist? The artist was generally to be found near a prize-winning piece, answering questions about it, enjoying a moment of notice which, in most careers, would never come again. Was the artist here? Was this the artist? This cringing urchin, this anorexic waif, this grubby little number?

'Are you by any chance the artist?'

'Yes.'

It seemed this was a girl, though it might have been a very skinny and small-boned boy, the flapping, formless clothes hiding any evidence of a figure, if this undernourished creature had a figure.

'You're Ailie Huxtable?'

'Yes.'

'Ailie. That's a curious name.'

'Yes.'

'Is it short for something?'

'Yes.'

Bruno waited for her to say what Ailie was short for, since a little harmless small-talk might put the child, now laconic with terror, more at her ease. Bruno was sufficiently impressed with the painting, now that he looked at it properly, to want to communicate with the painter. He had sympathy with the tongue-tied young, with anybody frightened. He was on the side of anybody who was trying to express things, to make beauty. Of course he would try to communicate. But it was going to be hard work.

'Is this an actual scene?' he said, 'a landscape taken from nature?'

'Yes.'

Bruno waited for more, but no more came. The girl had a little sharp face, the eyes too large for the rest of it. She had long, straight, pale hair, pretty clean. She must have been eighteen or nineteen at least, to have finished a year at the College, but to look at she might have been twelve, hardly on the threshold of puberty.

The painting, said Bruno to himself, had perhaps the sexless purity of extreme youth. But the organisation of the elements into a composition, the gentle restricted palette, the eloquence of the brushwork, were really mature. There were none of the awkward, perfunctory passages which almost always betrayed student work, even the most accomplished.

'I think you have been very well taught,' said Bruno.

'Yes,' said the child.

'Mr Bruno Browning,' said a busy and pasty administrator, 'Miss Elinor Leigh.'

Bruno had forgotten for a moment the diesel truck standing in the same part of the gallery. How she did tower over the painter! It was the world's most awkward threesome, none of whom was able in any way to get through to either of the others. They stood gawping at one another. Bruno had not in twenty years felt such social despair, such a sense of gaucherie.

But, having been introduced, Bruno and Elinor Leigh were supposed to say something to one another. They were supposed to include Ailie Huxtable in their conversation. How could this be done?

Training told, as with a guardsman. Elinor Leigh inclined towards Ailie Huxtable. She said, 'Your painting?'

'Yes.'

'Ah. Super. Really.'

'Thank you,' said Ailie Huxtable, in a tiny, frightened, bored voice.

'Explain it to me.'

'What?'

'Can you explain the picture to me?' said Elinor, more loudly, as though talking to a foreigner. 'I don't understand it.'

'It's a landscape.'

'Yes?'

But Ailie Huxtable had said all she was going to say. She did not want to talk to a big, ignorant woman from a county background. She did not want to explain her painting.

It came to Bruno that Ailie Huxtable could not explain her own painting. This was sometimes the case. It was a refreshing change from the usual modern situation, in which artists were all too ready to explain their work at inordinate length, and to write impossibly pretentious accounts of themselves in exhibition catalogues.

'Although the painting is taken from nature,' said Bruno to Elinor Leigh, 'I take it that it is not an exact account of what our young friend saw. If she had wanted a photograph she would have used a camera. Right?'

'I haven't got a camera,' said Ailie Huxtable. 'I can't afford a camera.'

'She could have drawn what she saw, which is what anybody else would have seen, which there is therefore no point in doing.'

Bruno saw that both girls were listening intently. That was nice.

'You see,' he said, 'no painting of serious merit could have been done by anybody else, except in freak cases such as Picasso and Braque. A painting expresses the artist as much as the subject. It expresses the impact of that subject on that artist. If a lot of people see things in exactly the same way, paint them in exactly the same way, there is no point in any of them bothering.'

Ailie Huxtable nodded briefly, dismissively. She knew all this stuff. It was what they were taught.

Elinor Leigh frowned at the painting. She did not have anything to say. Bruno thought he was wasting his time, lecturing a bulldozer on aesthetics.

He excused himself, and moved away. Glancing back, he saw that Elinor Leigh was looking after him. Her expression was inscrutable. She had one of those trained, upper-class faces, disciplined from an early age to hide contempt, pity, enthusiasm. Probably Elinor Leigh had never felt pity or enthusiasm. She was an awful sight. That was a pity, because she might have been a striking female.

Ailie Huxtable was not looking after Bruno. She was staring at her feet, which were shod in heavy black boots. Apart from these aggressive boots, she had the cringing look of someone very shy and very bored.

'I saw you were talking to my young cousin,' said Miss Octavia Crossley, known to Bruno as a governor of the College and a fan of himself.

'Oh? Which one?'

'The larger. The darker. The older. Elinor Leigh.'

'That creature is your cousin, Miss Crossley?'

'Daughter of Daphne Leigh, who died a few years ago. Also of Bernard Leigh, who died a few weeks ago.'

'The General?'

'That's the one.'

'His wife was Lady Daphne.'

'Not half,' said Octavia vulgarly.

Bruno at last had Elinor placed. He ought to have done so at once, usually alert to these matters, but he had been distracted by the noise and by the girl's shoes. Elinor had not seemed at first to fit into any significant scheme of things, but now she did.

All was explained.

No wonder she looked like that, so good, so dreadful.

Her mother had been practically the only authentic aristocrat in a very wide radius from the middle of Milchester. Somehow all the resident lords, and the squires of ancient family, had died out or sold out, or gone to live in the Bahamas or the Isle of Man. The blood of belted earls was hardly to be found in that landscape. The territorial magnates were now insurance companies, and the stately homes were schools. There were judges and generals by the score, giving an illusion of aristocracy, but no real blue-bloods, except Lady Daphne.

Lady Daphne had been well known to Bruno, by name and reputation. He would, when young, have been frightened to meet her. He heard that she looked down on nearly everybody. She cut the bishop, because he had been to a grammar school. That was what they said at the time. In 1980! There might be something crass about that, but there was something magnificent too.

And here was her daughter, granddaughter of an earl. This was the authentic article, beside whom Italian *principesse* would curl up like pieces of plastic. No wonder the girl carried herself so arrogantly. And of course she thought she could wear any shoes she liked.

Bruno remarked to himself, in a secret part of himself, that the Brownings had come a long way in a single generation: from back-street garage owners to the party companions of the granddaughters of earls.

He rejoined Elinor Leigh. She was still moored by Ailie Huxtable's painting, as though she had been told to wait there until she was collected by a grown-up. Bruno found himself resuming his lecture. Elinor Leigh listened intently, her interest flattering, her mind, presumably, being broadened by the minute.

On the subject of Ailie Huxtable's painting, Bruno got rather carried away. He heard himself using art-critical jargon which he normally avoided. He glowed with an enthusiasm which he also normally avoided. He wanted to get a response out of Elinor Leigh.

He also wanted to cheer up Ailie Huxtable. She looked as though she could do with all the cheering up anybody could give her. The prize he had sponsored might cheer her up a bit, and lyrical praise of her painting ought to be good for her, too. He had now convinced himself, after a second and third inspection, that her work really did show exceptional talent, an individual vision. She was the sort of person he wanted to help. For the moment, talking was the only way he could do this, so he talked.

She did glance up at him, once or twice. She glanced at his face when he was saying how sensitively she had addressed the problem of recession in a semi-abstract context. She looked as though she was surprised to hear that she had done anything of the sort. Bruno realised that he was interpreting her own picture to her. He felt a bit silly. He felt he was being a pretentious old booby. He did not mind this so very much, if in the end Ailie Huxtable felt better about herself, and Elinor Leigh woke up out of her long sleep.

Round them, the party was beginning to die. The supplies of warm white wine had dried up, or been diverted to cubby-holes where students were playing at wickedness. Backs were aching, feet becoming painful in party shoes on a warm evening. Milchester parties ended early.

The strip lighting was cool and merciless on all those big, garish, self-important student paintings, with their modish irreverence, their urchin obscenities.

Across the room, through the thinning crowd, Bruno saw his cousin Fred. Fred was talking to an elderly couple in sober clothes. They were people Fred knew. Bruno did not know them, but he knew that Fred knew them, because Fred would never have been talking to people he did not know. The idea of starting up a conversation with a stranger at a party would have appalled Fred. The idea of small-talk appalled him. It played no part in his life. He was incapable of it.

Of course Fred preferred looking at a couple of people that he knew to looking at these pictures. He would not do that if he could help it. He would not have come to this exhibition, if he could have helped it. But he was Managing Director of Browning Machinery, and this was the Browning Gallery, paid for, as everybody knew, by the profits of

Browning Machinery, and he was a Browning, one of only two Brownings left in the company; it was an inescapable requirement of Public Relations that he make an appearance at the exhibition.

Fred admitted this. He promised to come. 'Just keep me away from blokes with beards,' he said the day before.

'The women are worse,' said Bruno.

'Worse beards?'

'I was thinking, worse voices.'

'I know. The quacking sort. Hens out of hell. God preserve us. I hope there'll be some whisky there.'

'Certainly not. You're supposed to be intoxicated by the art.'

'Bugger that for a lark,' said Fred.

But of course he would come, and here he was, and Bruno felt a surge of affection for this grumpy, unimaginative cousin of his: an affection he knew was returned, which had lasted all their lives and would last all their lives. It was not to be explained by consanguinity, or propinquity, or by anything except itself. They were devoted to one another because they were.

They were as comically different in appearance as in everything else. Fred was a muscular, compact man, a little under six foot. His hair was curly and gingery, his skin very fair, his eyes pale blue. He went pink and then purple in the sun, like his mother Margie. He had a squashy, turned-up nose and a broad mouth. He was very Anglo-Saxon, very rural. He looked innocent and decent and practical. He looked a man you would lend money to, trust the repair of your car to. He looked a man who might laugh at your joke, but would not tell you a joke back.

Fred had been photographed for the *Milchester Herald*, with the Principal of the College, in front of a prize-winning sculpture. The sculpture was made of welded metal rods. Fred quite liked it, though he was not impressed with the quality of the workmanship. He would not have offered the sculptor a job in his workshops. But he put on a cheerful face for the camera, the public face of Browning Machinery.

He kept the cheerful face, more or less, by dint of looking at people he knew rather than at the exhibits; he kept it by avoiding blokes with beards and women with quacking voices.

He saw his cousin Brian in the distance. He kept clear, not because of Brian but because of the people Brian was with.

Certainly not because of Brian, who was a pretty good old thing. He was a snob and a poseur, but his kindness was infinite and his enthusiasm was genuine. He seemed phoney to a lot of people, but at bottom he was quite real. He did care about people. He was hipped on all this barmy art, and he did know a hell of a lot about it. Fred would have crossed the room to foregather with Brian, except for what Brian was talking to.

There were two of it, two females. They were the sort of females life was too short for. Fred did not know either of them, and he was determined to go on not knowing them.

One was a tall, forbidding woman, ten or a dozen years younger than Fred himself, a big strong Girl Guide kind of woman, a natural leader, a District Commissioner of the Pony Club, a bossy, humourless, glamourless, sergeant-major kind of woman. The countryside round Milchester was lousy with women like this, running fêtes, raising money for the British Field Sports Society, walking labradors. This one struck Fred as an extreme example. She was one of the ones who terrorised shopkeepers and objected to developments and bullied old men at the Red Cross Centre: the ones who should have been destroyed by the march of progress, left behind by history, buried like the dodo, but they were too tough, they were still all over the place. Each one was far more trouble as a customer for a firm like Brownings' than a dozen factories.

Fred had an eye for a pretty girl, when he looked up from his machines, and this was not one. He had an eye for a pretty frock, a dash of style and sex-appeal and fashion; this female had none of those things. She had a dress like a chair-cover and shoes like suitcases. She did not look in the smallest degree arty. It was a wonder that she was talking to Brian.

The other girl was arty, all right. She was far too arty. She was arty all over, through and through. She was skinny and shabby and untidy, with no make-up, dressed out of somebody's dustbin, her boots stolen from an old soldier. She looked the way a lot of the art students looked, only more so.

Both these creatures looked the way they did on purpose. This was how they saw themselves.

Fred was not dressed as he saw himself. He was wearing a dark business suit and a dapper striped shirt and the tie of a vintage car club. He looked like a farmer dressed up as an accountant. He saw himself, he thought, exactly as others saw him, in greasy overalls. But he knew enough to wear disguise at parties.

Elinor Leigh, for her part, hardly noticed Fred Browning. She saw him, at most, out of the corner of her eye, a local worthy in a dark suit. He would not, to her, even be worth looking at. He was evidently a local business or professional man, a shopkeeper or builder. He belonged in business hours, behind his desk or counter.

After the first few minutes, Elinor had also ceased to notice Ailie Huxtable. She had painted the picture, but she did not seem to understand what she had done. She could not or would not talk about it. This was just as well, because Mr Bruno Browning talked about it, and about a million other things.

Mr Bruno Browning mentioned, as he spoke, some of the people that he knew. He mentioned the places he had been to, the things he had seen. Elinor was obliged to pretend to have heard of some of them. He made them sound the only things that mattered.

Elinor had the sense not only of doors opening which had been locked, but of the existence of doors in what had been a blank wall. The blank wall was between her and the rest of her life. Here were doors into an astonishing future, perhaps, into a world she had not even guessed at.

There might be other ways of living, than any she had seen.

Really her parents' life had been pretty dull, ever since she could remember. Perhaps India had been fun, but Conyngham Smedley was no fun at all. The people were all too old. They were dull. Everything they did was dull, and their gardens and conversations and even their dogs.

What else was there?

The lives of her brothers and their wives? Lloyd's, the Stock Exchange. A house in Battersea, a flat in South Kensington. Weeks in Scotland, fortnights in Spain or the Caribbean. English spoken. Photographs taken, shown proudly, stuck in albums. Children's sports-days. Dinner parties, charity committees, Ascot, Goodwood.

Elinor might have married into all that, without a bloodsucking father to be fed and soothed, especially if she had been two inches shorter. She had regretted missing that chance – at least, people spoke as though she had sure enough missed it. But maybe she should not be regretting that at all. The lives of her sisters-in-law? Fun? Exciting? Satisfying? Fulfilling?

Compared to the life Mr Bruno Browning was allowing her to glimpse?

'Are those any good?' asked Elinor abruptly to Mr Bruno Browning, pointing at the big garish canvases on the opposite wall. 'I think I'm beginning to understand about this one, but what about those?'

'What do you think about them yourself?'

'I don't know what to think. I don't know enough to think anything about them.'

'What do you feel about them? Let yourself feel something about them. Try to experience them, as though they were a place, or a dream, or an adventure.'

'Is that the right way to look at paintings?'

'It's one way. A supremely right way, a necessary way. It's one of the necessary ways.'

'What are the other ways?'

'Context. Personality. History. Some people wouldn't agree about some of that. Deconstructionists wouldn't.'

'Who are they?'

'We'll talk about them another time. What did I say a moment ago? Context. You must look at a picture with awareness of the context in which it was made. What was going on in the world? War? Famine? Earthquake? What was going on in his world? Divorce? The illness of a child?'

'Context. Yes, I see. That's obvious.'

'I'm sorry,' said Mr Bruno Browning drily.

'It's obvious, but I never thought about it. Yes. If everybody was starving when he painted the picture, you ought to know that if you're trying to understand it.'

'You have taken my point. What else did I say? Did I say personality? I probably did. I am a very strong believer in the importance and integrity of the individual personality. If that does not express itself in a picture, then the picture is inhuman and artistically meaningless.'

'So I ought to know if the artist was happy or sad.'

'Or drunk, or a sadomasochist, or deeply religious.'

'And you said history.'

'Art history. The large sweep. We'll come to that another time, too. You asked about those canvases opposite. I invited you to react emotionally. Do that – react emotionally.'

'They're too big,' she said. 'The colours clash. They're ugly. I don't think they mean anything at all.'

He said, 'You're right that they're too big. The colours are meant to clash, like discords in Schoenburg or deliberate bathos in the *Four Quartets*. So that—'

'Stop. Explain about them.'

'Another time, I think.'

'Another time?'

'This had better be continued in our next. At this moment I will say merely that those large, immature, ill-organised paintings are better and more interesting than you think they are. Now I must immediately pick up my feet and go hoppity-hop away, like a rabbit. I must go with my cousin Fred, visible yonder, who is giving me a lift, but I think we have by no means exhausted this subject, nor dried the well of this conversation.'

He was smiling. He was distinctly beautiful, in a fragile and rather effeminate way. He looked very foreign. He spoke like a gentleman.

It came to Elinor, as a strong and clear and important message, that Mr Bruno Browning would not drunkenly

92

rape her in a motel, nor be sick over her shoes beside the bed.

(She knew she had not really been raped, but she used the word to herself as an excuse for her behaviour.)

It came to Elinor that she was safe with Mr Bruno Browning, and that he would guide her into a new country that would be more interesting than the one where she had been living.

He was well dressed without being overdressed. Her father would not have disapproved of his clothes, although there was perhaps something a tiny bit fancy about the height of his shirt-collar and the size of the knot of his tie. He was taller than herself, but he swayed and undulated as he talked, so that his head sometimes swooped lower than hers. He had a sweet smile, but his eyes were sunken and tragic.

She said, in her gruff shy alto voice, 'Do you live here?'

Bruno was used to people knowing who he was and where he lived. He thought everybody in Milchester knew his house, certainly everybody at this party. He was amused that the single aristocrat did not. He saw that this was salutary. He made a note of this, as a story to tell against himself.

He told her that he was sometimes in his house in the Close, but more often abroad.

She said, 'I've got some pictures. I inherited some. I don't know if they're any good. I don't know if they're worth anything.'

'Would you like an opinion? My opinion? For what it's worth. It is worth, I should interject, rather a lot, although I shall not charge you more than the cost of a drink.'

Elinor laughed.

Ailie Huxtable smiled. She had been listening to all this.

Elinor had forgotten her existence.

Mr Bruno Browning was also reminded of Ailie Huxtable. He said, 'Is your picture for sale? May I buy it? For £200?'

'Buy it?' said Ailie Huxtable, in a tiny astonished voice.

To Elinor, Mr Bruno Browning said, 'I must look at the diary on my desk, before I suggest a time when I am to come and sponge a drink off you. You're in the book? Shall I telephone? Tomorrow morning shall we employ the instrument? I have enjoyed myself.' He turned to Ailie Huxtable, and said, 'Renewed congratulations. You will let me know if my offer is acceptable. A note left for me in the office here will worm its way to me eventually. If you're bent on haggling, I could go a little higher, but not much, because I disapprove of overrewarding the young. It gives them false ideas of their future viability. Good night, my dears. I am desolated to leave you, but I can see that my cousin is pawing the ground.'

They both stared after him, Elinor Leigh and Ailie Huxtable, the one towering over the other. They did not look at one another, or exchange any further words.

Bruno Browning wondered what he thought he was playing at.

Was it just because she was the granddaughter of an earl?

She had been insulated from anything important, anything exciting. He had already drilled a hole in that armourplating, that fibreglass or asbestos which divided her from life. Did he not have a duty to make the hole bigger, big enough to drive a coach and four through? Should he not set himself to dissolve the wall altogether? Mightn't it be rather amusing?

An awful lot of hard work. He had enough on his plate,

with the company and la Moquerie and his friends all over Europe. He would ring up and say he could not come to inspect her pictures.

He foresaw the pictures. Imitation Sartorius, and Lionel Edwards prints. Possibly some water-colours by a great-aunt, and a Victorian pastel of a cocker spaniel.

Going to look at the pictures would not only be going to look at the pictures. It would signal a commitment. Too much. Over the top. Exhausting. Odds against success. Life too short. A labour of Hercules. Pish to it all.

There were bones in her face that might have a sort of marmoreal magnificence, framed with the right hair, painted with the right paints. Was he to be Michelangelo, liberating the statue from the marble in which it already existed?

Was he trying to be Pygmalion? If so, Galateas were coming heavy-weight this season.

Bruno Browning went to bed certain that he had been carried away by a mixture of snobbery, idealism and philanthropy: certain that he should on no account commit himself.

Bruno was awake at three in the morning, a pulse in his left temple remembering the warm supermarket white of the exhibition.

He found himself thinking about Mario, and about the oily army of Mario's predecessors. He was fed to the teeth with those treacherous little oiks, those nasty youths.

He, Bruno, was profoundly indebted to a teacher who had wished him well. He had been trying to repay a debt to God, ever since, by helping as he had been helped. Look where that had got him. Betrayed, robbed, humiliated. Again and again.

Wasn't it time for a change?

A shining morning, hangover erased by further sleep. The euphoria of toothpaste, the cleansing ritual of shaving. Orange juice, coffee, toast, Bruno in the sunshine amidst the working surfaces of his kitchen, amongst the soft whirring of his electric machines. It all put quite a different complexion on things.

Hope, benevolence.

He rang up Elinor Leigh, and they made a date for him to look at her pictures.

Elinor had an idea that she ought to dress up.

She had been weeding the border, in corduroys and a flannel shirt. She came in to change.

How do you dress up for the visit of an internationally celebrated connoisseur of the arts, a man of limitless knowledge, fashion, worldly-wisdom and sophistication, for a drink before lunch on a weekday in the country?

Tweeds? Jeans? A silk cocktail dress?

The clothes she pulled out of the wardrobe were just clothes, the clothes she had, more or less correct for the things she did, passing muster, arousing comment neither admiring nor derisive. They were dull. They were like everything else about her life. She saw them suddenly, glimpsed them for a second as they lay piled on her bed, with the eyes of Mr Bruno Browning: as she had perhaps seen through his eyes that little dun-coloured picture by that little dun-coloured girl. He gave her new eyes. She had seen the picture through the new eyes, and understood that it was good. She saw all her clothes through the new eyes, and saw that they were awful. It was a depressing experience.

Her father had thought her clothes were all right. At least, he had not said that they were wrong. Nobody else had ever said anything about them at all.

She had got too big for pretty clothes. She had got too old.

She was old and massive without ever having had any fun.

Elinor burst into tears at the sight of herself, a big strapping healthy boring woman in bra and girdle, in the full-length mirror in her bedroom. She wept at the thought of herself, at what somebody like Mr Bruno Browning would think of her.

'You live all alone here?'

'Yes, since my father died.'

'Shall you continue to do so?'

'Oh no. We'll sell it, if we can. There are three of us. It's left to the three of us.'

'Ah, it has to be snipped, trisected, yes, sometimes a shame. Not, I think, a shame for you?'

'In a way it is. It's what I'm used to. I've lived here nearly all my life. I don't know where I'd go. Except for boarding-school I've never lived anywhere else.'

'Then, if I may say so, it's high time you did.'

'Yes,' said Elinor. 'Yes.'

The day being fine, but with a cool and gusty north-west wind, she had settled on a worsted skirt with a cotton shirt and a cardigan. The colours were brown and green, both tending to khaki. She wore brownish tights and brown brogues and an amber necklace left to her mother in 1938.

'These are by somebody called Henry Alken. I expect you knew that.'

'Hum,' said Mr Bruno Browning.

He either did not know they were Henry Alkens, or he

knew they were not Henry Alkens.

'A very prolific artist, prolifically imitated,' he said. 'I always think his trees resemble vegetables cooked *al dente*.'

Elinor smiled and nodded, as though she knew what *al dente* meant.

He was wearing a Prince of Wales suit of pale grey checks, with a blue shirt and a silk tie with a muted Paisley pattern. His hair was thick and dark and glossy; it was like her father's hair when her father was in his prime, in photographs taken in India with polo sticks and mahseer and the corpses of tigers. From his hair came a faint, pleasing fragrance which, to her astonishment, Elinor recognised. It was the same stuff her father had used. Every morning, ever since she could remember, her father had smelled like that. It was extraordinary that her father and Mr Bruno Browning used the same stuff on their hair.

'Is that Trumper's *Coronis*?' she suddenly and childishly asked.

'Yes,' he said, evidently much surprised.

'Yes. I thought so. My father's dressing-room always smelled of it.'

'I shall always evoke for you your father's dressing-room. I am not sure whether to be proud or apologetic.'

'I just think it's extraordinary.'

'Your father was a man of nice discrimination.'

'I suppose in some ways.'

He said, after looking at some reproductions of engravings after Pollard, 'Has there been much interest in the house? Are purchasers beating a path to your door?'

'They say it's too expensive. The agent says so, too. My brothers fixed the price. I've been showing people round.'

'How ghastly.'

'Sometimes they're quite rude about some things.'

'Naturally. They denigrate in order to bring the price down. They must appear to despise the property, to be doing you a favour by taking it off your hands.'

'I understand that, but it's horrid when it's your home.'

'Each time like undressing in public.'

'Yes, exactly. You've done it, too.'

'Never, *grazie a dio*.'

'Then how do you know it's like taking off your clothes in public?'

'I imagine that is how it must feel.'

He not only used the same hair-stuff as her father, he also correctly imagined the feeling of humiliating exhibitionism, when one opened the door of the pantry or the guest bathroom or one's own wardrobe.

He was not dressed quite as her father would have been. He was dressed better than her father would have been. There was deep sadness in his deep-set eyes.

He said, 'I know a man who's looking for a decent period house, with a bit of grazing, in a quiet village.'

'Might he like this?'

'I think he might. Has the agent got one of those brochures, with photographs?'

'I had some. I've run out. I gave the last one to a foul couple who kept talking about the "lounge".'

'More can be got. Who's the agent? Oh yes. I take it people come by appointment only?'

'They're supposed to have appointments, but they just turn up.'

'And you have to show them round, in case they're the ones.'

'I have to. It's a bore. It's thoughtless of them.'

'I will ensure that my friend behaves.'

'I expect all your friends behave.'

'Oh no.' He laughed. 'If they behaved all the time they would not be my friends.'

She laughed also, intrigued. She wondered in what ways his friends misbehaved. If they had orgies, they must be very cultured orgies. That might be nice, if one could overcome embarrassment. The great thing was for people not to be sick over one's shoes. Elinor did not think Mr Bruno Browning's friends would do that.

They strolled round the garden. At twelve-thirty she offered him a drink. There were bottles in a sideboard in the dining-room. She suggested sherry or gin and tonic. These were the drinks she knew about.

He said, 'Is there such a thing as a glass of white wine?'

'Oh,' said Elinor. 'I don't know what wine there is. My brothers took most of the wine. I hardly ever drink it.'

'That is another change I think you should make.'

'I should like to change just about everything.'

'Oh? Explain.'

'I can't. I don't know.'

'Not everything,' said Mr Bruno Browning. 'Some things you should not change. For example, I am sure you should leave your eyebrows alone.'

Elinor laughed. She felt herself blushing. She still blushed easily. It was proof to herself how far she was from having grown up, though already old.

She found half a case of Muscadet which her brothers had missed.

'Will this do?'

'To admiration.'

They sat in the sun on the terrace outside the French windows of the drawing-room. It was out of the wind. Elinor took off her cardigan.

'As to the pictures which are the excuse for these indulgences,' said Mr Bruno Browning. 'I am slightly at a loss to know what to say.'

'I should think that has never happened before,' said Elinor.

He laughed.

She blushed again. 'That was rather pert.'

'The fact that you are self-conscious about making such a remark,' he said, 'shows how seldom you make them. It is another thing you should do.'

'Drink wine and make rude remarks?'

'Not rude. Perceptive and epigrammatic. You are tall and striking. You should make use of those attributes.'

'If I was small I couldn't be rude?'

'Very small persons should be rude all the time, like Truman Capote.'

'I think you think the Alkens are imitations.'

'Yes, but the best imitator of Alken, and the most sedulous, was Alken. This is the case with many commercially successful artists. Some of the Dutch genre painters were shameless. Witness also Canova, Renoir and all those damned milkmaids, Utrillo and the streets of Paris, Dufy at Le Touquet, Bernard Buffet, Warhol and his silk-screen prints, Roy Lichtenstein and his dots and comic-strips ... I'm sorry. I'm showing off.'

'Why are you?'

'Nervousness.'

'Rot.'

'I assure you. This wine is making me drunk, or something is.'

'It can't be the wine.'

'I read the other day that a glass of wine, on an empty stomach, taken as it might be in the late morning, can have quite a terrible effect even on a hardened fellow. If one were to be drinking neat gin – or let us say Polish vodka – then the system would ring alarm-bells, and shut doors to seal off the stomach from the bloodstream. But wine, gentle and insinuating, arouses no such furious panic in the system, and this wine is even now racing madly through our veins. What follies do you suppose we shall commit?'

'I only committed one proper folly in my life,' said Elinor. 'It was ghastly.'

'It is high time you committed more follies.'

'Because I shall soon be p-p-past it . . . ?'

Elinor burst into tears, tears of Muscadet, of knowing that she was too big and too old and that even her Henry Alkens were no good.

He put his arm round her. He soothed her and stroked her head, as though she were a child with hurt feelings, or a frightened dog.

She said into his shoulder, 'What shall I do? Tell me what to do.'

'Leave here and start living.'

'Yes. Where? How? I don't know anything.'

She sniffed into his shoulder. He gave her a handkerchief. She blew her nose.

He took her face between his hands, and pushed back her hair from her temples. He put his thumbs on her cheeks, and gently pushed the flesh back over the bones. Under his hands he revealed the structure and strength of the bones of her face. He stared at her. She stared back, tears still rolling, puzzled.

He said, 'Stand up.'

Obediently she stood.

'Stand on tiptoe.'

She rose.

'Raise your arms above your head. Push them back. Stand as tall as you can. Oh yes. Amazonian. A victory, unwinged.'

'This is uncomfortable. I shall fall over.'

'Sit and drink. Sit and get drunk. Tell me, why do you wear clothes the colour of compost?'

'Compost.'

'You should wear the most brilliant and overpowering colours, wild clashing purples and scarlets, vermilion and orange, greens of acid and arsenic, colours cold and hot, the colours of the skins of serpents. You could be a sensation.'

'I'm too big. I'm too fat.'

'Stand again. Take off that dreadful shirt.'

'What?'

'Trust me. And that awful skirt.'

'But we've only just . . . Why are you telling me . . .'

She found that she had stood, that with trembling but obedient fingers she had unbuttoned her shirt and unhooked her skirt, and she stood now in bra and girdle, as she had stood two hours before in front of the mirror in her bedroom.

'It is a question of how badly you want it all,' he said.

'Want what? Can I put my clothes on?'

'The world at your feet. It will take more than diet. You will have to work at it. No, those clothes are awful. They are the colour of manure, the colour of shit. You look much better without them. When you have lost twenty pounds you will look better still. You will look like a goddess. Then we shall begin to dress you, although in a way it will be a pity to do so.'

'Am I to be a clothes-horse?'

'You are to be a phenomenon.'

'A pheno . . . I think I am drunk.'

'Don't cry any more.'

'I'm crying now because I don't believe any of this. Why did I take my clothes off?'

'There must have been a reason. You must not be embarrassed. That is the first lesson, never cringe. You must be arrogantly shameless. You must cash in on your advantages. From where I sit, you have several. But you're right that they are too large. You will look very nice, when you have lost twenty pounds.'

'How do I do that?'

'Come with me to London.'

'All right.'

Elinor liked the thought of being thin, and of all the colours she was going to wear. She thought it would be nice to be a phenomenon. It would be nice to drink a lot of wine, and be aggressively shameless, and wittily rude, and live somewhere amusing, and know about all those people Mr Bruno Browning had mentioned.

'Bruno,' said Elinor. 'Bruno. It's a good name. It suits you.'

'Elinor. Don't let anybody call you Elly. Except in France. Yes, you could be called Elly in France, except they might think you were a man.'

'Nobody will think I'm a man,' said Elinor, suddenly laughing, so that her tummy jumped in and out above the waistband of her girdle.

'As people have said a wearisome number of times,' said Bruno, 'this is the first day of the rest of your life. We've almost finished the bottle. Let's finish it.'

'Yes.'

CHAPTER FIVE

E LINOR COULD NOT AFTERWARDS believe that episode. She thought she must have been drunk. She
thought Bruno must have been right, that wine hit
quicker than gin.

But if she remembered him saying that, how could she
have been drunk?

But if she was not drunk, why in God's name did she pull
her clothes off?

Was she in love with Bruno?

She rang up both her brothers to say that the house was
unsaleable at the price they had named. They must take the
agent's advice. She was fed up with hanging about, with
showing people round who were never going to spend that
amount of money.

'I won't take any more trouble about it, unless you get
realistic,' she said.

Her brothers were astonished at this cheek from the baby
of the family.

Inside Elinor, something was already happening.

Bruno could not afterwards believe the episode in Elinor's
garden. He thought that both Elinor and himself must have
been drunk. The general's daughter, the earl's granddaughter, standing in the sunshine out of doors in her

underclothes, displaying her spare tyre to a virtual stranger . . .

Where was this leading?

What were his plans? What did he want? Was this a good game? Was that big girl going to become important to him? Why? Did he want to carry such a large extra burden? Could he afford all this?

What would people think? The Italians? The Americans?

Meanwhile he paid for the little landscape, and two days later collected it from the office of the Head of the Department of Fine Arts at the College. He tried it here and there in his house in the Close. It was not obviously at home in any of the rooms. Though an English scene by an English painter, it did not harmonise with his English pictures or his mother's English furniture. He decided to take it to la Moquerie. A corner could be found for it there. Probably the picture was a waste of money.

Even while trying the picture in this room and that, Bruno's mind was going round and round his other problem.

He had an idea. He thought it was a good idea, perhaps cruel.

He rang up a woman he knew called Salamis Torquemada (who did not pretend, as Bruno sometimes did, that that was her real name) who had a dress shop, not called a boutique, in the Fulham Road. Salamis had clothes with very fancy designer labels, at greatly less than the original price. You would hardly know they had ever been worn.

To Salamis, Bruno said, 'I want a silk cocktail dress. I think what I want is still called a cocktail dress, although I don't think anybody drinks cocktails, do they?'

'Do you call a Bloody Mary a cocktail? If not why not?'

'I am speaking of a dress of high sophistication, for a lady of about thirty. The measurements should be exactly those of Linda Evangelista. My friend has a pale skin, dark hair, grey eyes. The colours should be powerful. Pastel me no pastels. Blood red, electric blue, I want ferocious colours.'

'I have exactly what you need. A thing of Gianni's.'

'Who is Gianni?'

'Versace.'

'Oh. Is it vulgar?'

'Yes, of course, but it can be carried off.'

'Revealing?'

'Quite.'

'Slit?'

'No.'

'Colour?'

'A green I think you would call veridian. And a crimson you would have to call alizarin.'

'Is this a good dress, Sally? Shall I like this dress?'

'It will take a bit of wearing. It's not a dress for a mouse.'

'I've got Bodicea to wear it.'

'That might do.'

'One more thing. How does it do up?'

'A zip at the side.'

'Perfect.'

'Don't you want to know what it costs?'

'For God's sake don't tell me,' said Bruno, 'or I shall change my mind about the whole thing.'

Elinor stood once again in bra and girdle. She felt the silk sliding over her bare shoulders and delicately brushing her diaphragm. The girl tried to zip it up.

'Oh,' said Elinor. 'Oh.'

'Do you like it?' said the girl. 'Because if so I've got news for you.'

'Oh. I've never seen such colours. I can't wear this bra with it. Can I wear any bra with it?'

'It's yours when you can zip it up,' said Bruno.

She said over her lunch (over her salad and Perrier), 'Why are you doing this?'

'If you go into a room,' said Bruno, 'in which one picture is hanging crooked, what is your instinct?'

'Is it my room? Am I allowed to touch?'

'It is not your room, but you are allowed to touch.'

'Then I straighten the picture, I suppose.'

'You could not bear not to do so. At least, I think I could not. Straightening the picture is something that screams to be done.'

'Are you answering my question? Am I just a picture hanging crooked?'

He did not answer this silly question, but said, 'You must go away for a week, ten days, almost at once.'

'The house. I can't go away. Not yet. Somebody has to be there to show people round the house.'

'Tell your brothers it's their turn. You've done enough.'

'I couldn't possibly do that.'

'Yes, you could.'

'Why do you want me to go away? Where to?'

'You might quite like it. Some people do. There is a smell of vegetable soup. You have massage and so on. The problem is boredom. Do you speak French?'

'I learned it at school.'

'Do you speak French?'

'No. I suppose not. I've never actually tried.'

'There's a way you learn now with a video. That will keep you busy. Also books. I'll give you books. I'll come and see you, too, if you like. Your life will be a round of pleasure, hardly time to fit everything in. But you must promise not to cheat. If you do, you'll never wear that dress.'

'Whatever are you talking about? Where am I going?'

'To a health farm, of course.'

'Forest Mere or something? I can't afford that.'

'I can.'

'Bruno. I can't let you spend all this money on me. I can't give you anything in return.'

'Yes, you can.'

She blushed. She said, 'I am not for sale. It's my house that's for sale, not me. You're mixing me up with my house. I admit we're about the same size.'

'I'm not buying you, Elinor. Nobody's rich enough to do that. I'm simply straightening a picture that's hanging crooked. Speaking of crooks, the friend I mentioned does want to see the house.'

'Is he a crook?'

'Oh yes. One of your brothers can show him round.'

'I'd better not tell them he's a crook.'

'No, don't tell them that. But I'll tell you something. You're already more amusing than you were a week ago.'

'Good God,' said Elinor. 'What a bloody patronising remark.'

Elinor's brothers spoke to one another on the telephone. They were surprised and annoyed that she was going away.

'What's the girl thinking of?'

'Herself. Spoilt. Typical.'

'Is there a man?'

'After her money.'

'If she doesn't sell the house, she won't have any money.'

'*I* can't get down there.'

'*I* can't get down there.'

'The agent will have to do it.'

'It's not at all satisfactory. It's damned thoughtless of Elinor. What a time to choose.'

'Why am I learning French?' said Elinor to Bruno.

'Have you ever heard of Edouard de Pomiane? He wrote a cookbook, very witty and practical. He says that when you get home, the first thing you do is put on a saucepan of water. Even before you take off your hat, you start heating up a saucepan of water. Do you know why?'

'No. Why?'

'Because you might need it. Simply that. My cousin Fred always carries a screwdriver, in case he might need it. You should carry the ability to speak and understand French. You'll probably need it.'

'If I go to France, I suppose.'

'You'll probably go to France.'

'Anyway, it'll be something to do while I'm living on fruit juice.'

Elinor did not exactly enjoy the health farm, but she became absorbed in the challenge. She weighed herself twice a day, on the big machine outside the steam-room.

It was satisfactory. Her weight went down and down, within days. Her diet hadn't really been very wrong, her father's schoolroom diet. She looked different. She began to contemplate herself, nude, in the full-length glass in her little bedroom, with something approaching satisfaction. She greeted her ribs, so long invisible, and the inward curve of her legs above and below the knee.

She had good legs. She really had very good, long, strong, beautiful legs.

She was passionately hungry, quite often, and the video

tapes that were teaching her French were not a sufficient distraction.

She was massaged, manipulated, thumped, squeezed, soaked and dried, her skin emptied of oil and filled up with oil. She was made to feel pampered and important. A couple of the girls who worked there loudly envied her figure, the figure she was already getting.

Bruno came, as he promised.

She was wearing only a dressing-gown, when they told her he was waiting in the foyer. She felt silky and beautiful, after the luxurious rigours of the morning.

People were walking about in their dressing-gowns. It was a place of dressing-gowns, and all kinds of ridiculous slippers. Elinor was glad she had thought to bring her father's crimson silk dressing-gown, stained about the collar but still with an imperial magnificence.

'Those, I think,' said Bruno, 'are your very best clothes.'

'That is true, but rude.'

'It hints at what is below. The less that is more. Have you been going through the agonies of the damned?'

'Yes. A bit. But it's nice having ribs.'

'May I see your ribs?'

Still she felt unthreatened. She felt proud of herself. She felt entitled to show off what she had done to herself, by deprivation and flagellation and life in a wilderness of khaki soup.

'You can come and see my cell,' she said, leading him towards the soothing pastel box where she slept and studied the language videos.

'There is hardly room for two of us,' she said. 'Why am I doing this? Why should I?'

'Because you are proud.'

'Oh yes. I am beginning to be.'

'Stand tall. Be proud. Let's see those ribs.'

Her instinct was to cringe and cover herself, but she overcame it, and stood proud and tall.

He reached out and touched her delicately, as though she had been carved or woven. She slightly jumped. Fear and embarrassment blinked on and off in her face. He touched the upper slope of her breast, and then her ribs below and behind the breast. His palm moved down to her waist and to her hip, and down her thigh.

'You will be a goddess,' he said. 'You will be the object of adoration and of the most bitter envy.'

He touched her cheek and her hair.

He said, 'I think you should stay another week. And then we must go very carefully into the question of your hair.'

'I will decide about my own hair.'

'No, darling.'

Elinor found that Bruno had excellent and wide-ranging contacts. Her father's contacts, military and sporting and marginally aristocratic, had always seemed limitless, but they were sketchy and specialised compared to the network of a man who was a successful business operator as well as an internationally celebrated connoisseur of many of the arts, including the art of being entertained.

Bruno was just the man to sell the Leighs' house for them.

He sold it rapidly and not badly, considering the calamitous state of the market. He sold it not to the friend he said was a crook, but to another who was only a bit of a crook, a Harley Street consultant, semi-retired, a dry-fly fisherman and gardener. The purchaser was a man designed to appreciate life in that village, among admirals.

Bruno's role in the sale was known to Elinor and to the

agents, but not to Elinor's brothers.

They came to the house again, to make decisions about the remaining furniture and pictures. Elinor was not there.

'Where has the damned girl got to now?'

'Miss Leigh rang to say she is detained,' said the man from the house-agent's.

'Where? How? What could be detaining her?'

The house-agent's man did not know.

Elinor had left the health farm, but she was not yet ready to relaunch herself. She wanted her family to have difficulty recognising her. She had an appointment with a hairdresser in London, Bruno's choice made after consultation with beautiful women that he knew; she had an appointment also with a woman who was to teach her how to do her face.

'I was taught all that when I was sixteen,' said Elinor.

'No, you weren't,' said Bruno.

She was not yet ready to buy a lot of clothes. She had not yet received her share of money from the sale of the house; and she had not yet lost twenty pounds. She bought a few unserious clothes, clothes for the summer and for travelling. It was now the end of July, not a time for serious shopping.

Her hair was done. It became sleek, like a metal helmet. Her face had meanwhile become thinner, the bones more prominent. The skin had become smoother and softer.

After she had been taught how to do her face, she used less make-up than she had when she dressed up for parties in the old days: when she made herself up to go out to dinner with Boots Cookson. It was lucky that she used only a little of the various sorts of goo that they gave her, because the stuff was hideously expensive.

She had to let Bruno pay for some of it.

'All right,' said Elinor. 'All very splendid so far, all very fine and large, but where am I actually going to live?'

'I said you'd be needing French,' said Bruno. 'You'll be needing French.'

Elinor made one further and final visit to her father's house.

She had expected to feel a sorrowful nostalgia, a sense almost of amputation. It was the only home she had ever known, and she knew every knot in the floorboards, every hairline crack in the ceilings, every twig and pebble in the garden and paddocks. She found that she was simply thankful to have got rid of the whole lot. It had been her life only because she had had no other. 'Prison' was too strong a word, but only just too strong.

She sold one of her horses to a riding school, and gave the other, almost a pensioner, to a family who could be trusted to look after it.

There were two labradors and a spaniel, all clean, biddable and characterless. The labradors were good gun dogs, and the spaniel was good at cleaning up scraps of food under the kitchen table. All three were well known locally, and Elinor found homes for them.

Disposing of the animals was not as much of a wrench as she expected. They were part of the albatross that had been hanging round her neck. They were bars in the not-quite-prison. It made her feel almost weightless, to have shed that responsibility.

With her share of the price of the house, and of what remained of her father's capital, Elinor could have bought a small house, with stables and grazing, and lived more or less the life she had always lived. She would have expected herself to do that. Everybody certainly expected that. She might have married into the life she had been leading, or become a hearty sporting spinster, probably breeding Jack Russell terriers. But now, suddenly, all that was no longer an option. A corner was turned. It was a new road she was on, leading in completely new directions. The road signs were in other languages, and the sky was an unfamiliar colour.

She wanted to see her brothers and their wives, before she went. More exactly, she wanted her brothers and their wives to see her.

Her brothers said she looked well. They said she looked different. They did not know what they were seeing. They were cross with her for being idle about selling the house, for making them bring the price down; but they were not really interested. For them, her usefulness was at an end. They no longer had a job for her. They did not much care where she went or what she looked like.

But in the eyes of their wives Elinor saw what Bruno had promised she would see.

She was ashamed of enjoying it. It was morally reprehensible. It was like something forbidden by her diet, too delicious to resist.

Where she had for years seen patronising pity, impatience, disdain, she now saw envy.

Bruno had to spend another three weeks in Milchester, on and off, with shareholders' meetings, annual reports and such. Elinor did not want to go back to Milchester, at least not yet. There was nowhere particular for her to go. She could not stay with Bruno, well known as they both were. She could have asked herself for a few days to any of a score of households; the prospect of staying in any of those places filled her with apathy.

Bruno had the use of a small house in Fulham, whose owners were in Brazil. He installed Elinor there. They did not use the word 'install' which had negative and misleading vibes.

London in August was said to be empty and dead. Elinor did not find it so. It made no difference that everybody was away, since she knew nobody in London anyhow. If there were more foreign and provincial tourists, there were fewer Londoners, so she imagined the discomforts evened out. Museums and galleries were open, shops and restaurants and wine-bars and libraries were open. It was the first time in her life that Elinor had ever spent more than two days in any city.

She enrolled at a health club, where she bounced and sweated three mornings a week. She was not only improving her fitness and figure, but also learning exercises for use in perpetuity.

They said that she might grow idle about doing those exercises, as she might get weak-willed about diet. But she thought she never would. She would only have to remember the glare of helpless envy in the eyes of her sisters-in-law.

The weight came off more slowly now, but still she lost four more pounds in her first London week, and three in the second.

She flattened her nose against Bond Street windows. She tried on dresses in the big stores. She could now get into anything she wanted to wear. She bought an exiguous one-piece swimsuit.

She saw herself with amazement in shop windows, a tall slender sleek brunette, arrogantly strolling or prowling, followed by the avid inscrutable eyes of the Japanese tourists and by the lovely whistles of men on building sites.

She bought one wonderful crazy red and white broad-brimmed American hat. She laughed out loud at the reflection of herself which she glimpsed by chance in a window in Knightsbridge. The whole street laughed, in admiration and glee.

A woman rang up the Fulham house, asking for her, speaking French.

'*Je suis amie de Bruno. Il m'a invitée de vous donner un coup de téléphone.*'

Haltingly, but without much difficulty or embarrassment, Elinor replied in French. She asked Josette Maréchal round for a drink. Josette came, a little brown woman of forty, speaking only French. She knew about painting and about Bruno. She knew Bruno's house in the Tarn. She was a chatterbox. Her enthusiasm was infectious. She got Elinor talking about herself, her life with her father, her plans. She briskly and kindly corrected Elinor's French, getting her pronunciation just so, telling her which word exactly was the most colloquial, or most socially acceptable, increasing her vocabulary. Elinor remembered which words to use: she remembered the new words Josette taught her.

Elinor realised after she had left that Josette had given her a priceless French lesson.

Josette had left a telephone number. Elinor rang in the morning. They arranged further meetings, visits to galleries, an expedition by boat to Greenwich. Josette was wickedly malicious about everybody. She made Elinor laugh very much. She refused to speak one word of English.

She sold Elinor hard on French painting of all types and times. She introduced her to French lyric poetry, to Villon and Ronsard, de Vigny, Alfred de Musset. She said the moderns were for later, if ever. Elinor found to her astonishment that she understood and enjoyed the poems, and that she memorised them almost without meaning to.

By this time she had realised that Josette was being paid by Bruno to teach her French. She no longer minded. She did not feel patronised or manipulated. Her life was careering in these new and delightful directions, and the cost of the ticket was unimportant.

What was Bruno's motive? What was in it for him?

'Who cares?' said Elinor to herself, to her reflection in a shop window, where she could see also the people who were admiring her admiring herself.

Bruno went to an organ recital in Milchester Cathedral. On his way out he met Miss Octavia Crossley, which came as no surprise.

She said, 'What's this I hear about my little cousin?'

'Which little cousin would that be, Miss Crossley?'

'You know very well which cousin, Mr Browning.'

'What do you hear about her?'

'That she has been transformed by a monstrous magic.'

'No no.'

'And by you.'

'I simply gave advice when asked for it. As to a hair-dresser, for example.'

'The hair is one of the things I am told of.'

'Yes. She has been, it seems to me, in a measure, by the recent tragedy, liberated.'

'Indeed yes. The abolition of slavery arrived in her life. I would say, arrived at a stroke, if that were not in the circumstances rather a sick joke.'

'I shall probably not quote it. But what I had not realised, what nobody told me, what I had no means of knowing, is what a clever girl that is.'

'She would be, you know. Her mother was a clever woman, though she was careful to hide the fact.'

'Why?'

'Women did, Mr Browning. Some women. Very snobbish

women. A blue-stocking was a terrible thing to be. I know, I was one. How has Elinor given evidence of her brain?'

'Apparently she has become quite a bore on the subject of French poetry. She recites it interminably.'

'Good gracious,' said Miss Octavia Crossley. 'Lord love a duck.'

Elinor did after all have to go to Milchester, to talk to the lawyer who was her father's executor.

How do you dress, in mid-morning in mid-August, for a meeting with an elderly solicitor in a cathedral city?

The funny thing was that only a few weeks previously Elinor would have known. There would have been no problem. She would hardly have thought about it. She would have put on a cotton frock and a cardigan and medium heels. She would have worn clothes which she then wore constantly and which now she would never, ever wear again.

She had still not done any serious shopping. She had not yet got any serious money. She knew that she needed guidance. Bruno would know who to ask.

She dressed demurely, for the train journey, for the streets of Milchester, for the lawyer's office, for lunch afterwards with Bruno. You would not have known that demure was what she was, from her reception at the lawyer's. The old gentleman treated her as though she was radioactive. She was not on this occasion aiming to knock anybody's eye out.

She learned that her money would be slower coming than she had expected, and that there would be less of it.

She went on to Bruno's office, an arrangement made because she had not known how long she would be. Bruno was in his shirt-sleeves, wearing apricot-coloured braces.

With him was a stocky, blunt-faced man, very fair, in age between Bruno and herself, whom she had seen but not met.

'Do you remember my cousin Fred?' said Bruno. 'Elinor Leigh. You met, or perhaps didn't, at the exhibition at the college.'

Fred nodded to Elinor, and said something she did not hear which was not obviously rude, but not polite either.

Elinor had come through a showroom and some outer offices, to arrive at this functional little sanctum at the back. This gave her an idea of the sort of company it was, a firm which was about machinery and which was housed in concrete, a firm with bare girders in the roof and a pervasive smell of lubricating oil. She saw that it was not that Fred was a funny cousin for Bruno to have, but that Bruno was a funny cousin for Fred to have: Bruno was a funny person to be associated with any of this.

But they said he was very good at it. In the company he was known as 'Mr Brian.'

'We're redecorating the staff canteen,' said Bruno. 'Here's a drawing of it. It's amazing how quickly it gets grubby. It's because they all like fried food. The industrial psychologists say we should have clear, soothing colours. They recommend this one. They call it "peach". It is ergonomically correct. Do you like it? Is it soothing?'

'Too soothing,' said Elinor. Remembering an episode of her past, she said, 'It is like the foyer of a motel. It would be all right if you jazz it up with peacock blue and purple and pillarbox red.'

'La,' said Bruno. 'How fancy, how very designer. Which glossy mag have you been studying?'

'How often does it actually need doing?'

'How often, Fred?' said Bruno.

'Every other year,' said Fred.

'Then it doesn't matter terribly if you go over the top,' said Elinor. 'It's only there for two years.'

'A curious view,' said Bruno. 'Extravagant and anarchic. I suppose you think like that because you're so rich. Are you rich, after your meeting?'

'No.'

'I was afraid you might not be. Wills never turn out as you expect. I don't know why I bother. We'll go to the Eastgate. Are you coming, Fred? Will you join us?'

'No,' said Fred. 'I've got a company to run.'

Elinor thought this graceless. Perhaps he was shy. Perhaps he was preoccupied, genuinely too busy to come. If so it was a relief. It was impossible not to be glad that such a spiky character was not lunching with them.

'We are lunching together, *à deux*, in the middle of Milchester,' said Elinor. 'People will talk.'

'Fred won't,' said Bruno. 'Fred never talks, except about gaskets and camshafts.'

'Gasket,' said Elinor. 'It sounds like an Elizabethan word for a loose woman.'

'Ho, snivelling gasket,' said Bruno. 'And a camshaft is something she is wearing, a yellowish undergarment.'

The manager of a travel agency saw them having lunch, and laughing very much about something.

'Your cousin,' he said to Fred, 'was buckling on the feedbag with a very startling female.'

'She's changed, that one,' said Fred. 'Before she changed, I used to think she was the most horrible kind of woman in the world. Now I realise I was wrong. She was only the second most awful kind of woman in the world.'

121

'What's the most awful?'

'The kind she's changed into. What she is now.'

'Well, I thought she looked pretty good. What's wrong with her? I thought she looked pretty sensational. Why is she so awful?'

'She's overdressed, pretentious, bossy, arty, fancy and arrogant.'

'Christ,' said the travel agent, who had not realised that Fred knew so many words.

It was time to go. They went. They flew to Toulouse, arriving in time for lunch. Bruno had arranged for a car to be waiting for them, the key in the Air France office.

'It's a hundred and fifty miles,' said Bruno. 'We could get there in time for tea, but we won't.'

'Why not? You know I'm dying to see it.'

'You must see St Sernin first.'

So Elinor saw one of the greatest Romanesque buildings in the world, and they had a drink in a bar which had an air of being full of students at other times of the year, and then it was time for a nap before dinner, in a hotel which did not care who they were, but was too polite to say so.

They had never slept under the same roof before. This thought came as a surprise to Elinor, although there was no reason it should have surprised her. Their relationship had jumped to intimacy without any intimacy.

'We have adjoining rooms,' said Bruno. 'In case you get nightmares.'

'It will be a comfort,' said Elinor.

This was true. She knew it, and she dimly understood the reasons. It was to do with her childhood. Even she knew enough about Freud to understand that. In her childhood she had been treated sometimes as a dog, to be shouted at and whipped for disobedience and fed at stated times: and sometimes as a mechanical toy, to be wound up and shown off on a table top: but never as a person.

And Boots Cookson had treated her simply as a rubber appliance.

She had a shower, and then lay with a Pierre Loti novel on one of the beds in her room, in a dressing-gown. This was not her father's resplendent silk robe, worn for display at the health farm, but a skimpy cotton affair of faded blue, a threadbare relic of her schooldays, something to be rolled up and pushed into a corner of a suitcase.

Bruno knocked at the door which connected the rooms. He came in carrying a tray, on which were an open bottle of champagne and one of cassis and two glasses. He had also been showering, and he was dressed as she was, though his dressing-gown had a pattern of red telephones.

She dropped her book and sat up. He poured. They smiled at one another by way of toast, and drank. She lay back on her pillows.

He loosed the belt of her robe and folded it back, opening it away from her body like the flaps of a package. She lay naked on the pillows except for her arms, which were still in the sleeves of the dressing-gown. She looked up at him doubtfully.

He felt with his fingertips the corrugations of her ribs, and then her nipples. He stroked her legs and the cushion of her pubic hair.

She groped under the front of his robe, and ran her palm over his bare chest. He kissed her forehead and breasts and lips.

They remained thus, half lying, half sitting, half kissing, half caressing, not more than half making love, not less than half doing so, comfortable, excited but at ease, smiling, not trembling, neither approaching climax, not within a mile of self-forgetfulness.

Elinor, smiling, extricated herself sufficiently to drink her drink. There was neither rejection nor escape in her movement, but only desire for the drink. Bruno smiled and refilled her glass.

'It is a great thing,' said Bruno over dinner, 'to know what one needs in life, and more particularly what one does not need.'

'What one does not need, and what one is better without,' said Elinor. 'I suppose like smoking.'

'That image is unnerving,' said Bruno. 'The phallus and the fireball, flare, heat and smoke, then deadness and ashes . . .'

'And mess and stink,' said Elinor, remembering spilling ashtrays in her brother's house, remembering the vomit on her shoes.

'Thrills,' said Bruno, 'are to be got from the arches in the crypt of St Sernin, which we saw today, and from the Toulouse-Lautrecs which we shall see in Albi tomorrow.'

'And guilty, sinful thrills,' said Elinor, 'are to be got from this *pâté de lièvre.*'

It would have been pretentious and teachy for Bruno to have spoken French to Elinor when they were alone. He did not do so, except in so far as his conversation was apt to be peppered with French and Italian phrases. But when they were with the French – with waiters, shopkeepers, chance-met people on roadsides or in cafés – Bruno nudged Elinor into French conversations.

She soaked it up like a sponge.

Bruno thought she was quicker than he had been.

She soaked up the magnificence of the cathedral in Toulouse, the paintings in the Bishop's Palace at Albi, the castles and landscapes that they saw.

There was by lucky chance a concert in the cathedral of Albi the night that they were there, renaissance music sung by a small and disciplined choir. Elinor soaked up this pure and complex music. She afterwards tucked away the little printed programme, so that she had a record of the names of the composers. Bruno had done the same, thirty years earlier, when he was reinventing himself.

He had been ten years younger then than she was now, but she had all the eagerness of youth, the malleability, the quickness of reaction, so that experience printed in immediately and deeply. She was thirty years old and she was a teenager, because her youth had been stolen.

'The risk with you is cultural bulimia,' said Bruno. 'The risk is that you gobble up so much that you make yourself sick.'

'*Pas moi*,' said Elinor. '*Pas de mal.*'

So they came to la Moquerie in the evening.

There was a small sign in the verge of the road. Bruno turned into a smaller and rougher private road, which snaked through an unthreatening wilderness of golden-grey rocks and ash-blond grass. They topped a rise and came on the château waist-deep in the countryside, so that they could not see it all until they were much closer. They saw the river, and the high and empty far bank; they saw the rays of the setting sun slanting up the gorge of the river, so that the rocks had pink faces and purple shadows.

Bruno stopped the car when they reached the last steep slope at the top of the garden.

They got out.

'How can you ever bear to leave?' said Elinor.

'I don't want first-growth claret every day of the year.'

'I do.'

They came down into the courtyard at the back of the château. A man and a woman came out of the house, servants. There were reunions and introductions. The folk were well used to Monsieur Bruno's glamorous friends.

The things were unloaded from the car and carried into the house. Among them was a picture, the little drab landscape by the little drab girl in Milchester.

CHAPTER SIX

ELINOR THAT EVENING put on the Versace dress, the first time she had worn it since trying it on in Salamis Torquemada's useful establishment. It was a hot evening. She wore the dress without underclothes. No straps peeped, no ridges punctuated the smooth contour of buttock and thigh. It was the right way to wear the dress if the wearer's figure was good enough. Elinor's was.

Years of riding and hunting, gardening, walking dogs, carrying things along river banks and up and down stairs for her father, had in fact – in deeply ironic fact – been much better for Elinor than she had ever guessed. The muscles had been overlaid with stodgy nursery food, but they were muscles and they were there. Massage and exercise only fine-tuned them, while starvation melted away the ambient flab.

Almost unknown to herself, she had been an athlete. That was why the magic worked so quickly.

It had all come together, bone and muscle, slenderness, arrogant grace of carriage, and now a daring and spectacular dress. Elinor stared at her reflection with incredulity.

The servants had an air of applauding, when she came into the salon at eight o'clock.

'I don't think I ought to be proud about any of this,' said

Elinor, 'and I don't think you ought to waste time being considerate and tactful. Tell me what to read and see and listen to. Tell me what to hear and say. Tell me what to think.'

'I can tell you what I think,' said Bruno. 'But it's necessary that you start disagreeing with me.'

'I won't do that.'

'Oh yes,' said Bruno sadly. 'Oh yes, you will.'

There was a retired schoolteacher in a cottage in the village, engaged on a critical edition of an eighteenth-century pastoral poet of whom nobody had ever heard. Since it was clear that this work would never be finished, his attention wandered from it, and he had time on his hands. The teacher was a fierce old man, socialist and atheist, looking back with intense nostalgia to the remembered intellectual ferment of his student days, despising the ambitious conformists of the nineties.

He despised also Bruno's aestheticism, deplored his wealth, poured furious scorn on his politics and morals. The two of them wrangled over five-course lunches, after which the old teacher was taken home and poured into bed.

He was called François Delalain, and he became Elinor's scourge and bully and teacher of French. He said that by Christmas she would pass anywhere as a native Frenchwoman of superior education. But she suspected that the French he taught her was on the pedantic side (like the kind of English Bruno had taught himself at Cambridge) and she corrected the balance by learning from other sources – the bars and markets of the towns, the garages and épiceries. She developed, partly deliberately, a mixture all her own of the elegantly scholarly and the racily vulgar. She found that this mixture startled Bruno's French friends – a fancy and fastidious bunch – into shocked admiration, astonished laughter.

She took to being outrageous in English, too.

People began to come to la Moquerie in September, on their way back to the cities from the yachts and islands and mountain-tops where they had been summering. In the early autumn of that year, Elinor began to meet people in numbers, the inhabitants of the new world of which she had been given an entry visa.

They discussed her, chattering softly on the terrace over the river. Of course they did. When they got to Paris and other places, they continued to discuss her.

When Bruno took her to Paris at the end of October, she found that people had heard of her. Heard what? They were curious to meet her. Heads swivelled when she came into rooms, because people were wondering what she looked like; silences fell, because people wondered what she would say. They expected her to give them delicious shocks. Some were prepared to be resentful and contemptuous. Elinor tried not to disappoint any of them.

Bruno's most fashionable female friends took her shopping. The prices were frightening. She was now dressing to her new personality; consequently she looked audacious and arrogant and all the time laughing at herself.

They spent three weeks in a borrowed apartment in the Avenue Victor Hugo. Elinor went again and again to the Louvre and the Musée d'Orsay. She went to concerts and operas, and to films and plays about which, afterwards, she was ordered to write detailed accounts in French for François Delalain.

She met Americans and Italians of terrible sophistication, or else a lot of money, and no English persons at all.

She began to learn Italian from a girl whose husband

refused to allow her to have a job, and who had nothing to do except teach Elinor Italian. She came from Tuscany. Bruno said that Elinor must not learn Italian from a Roman, Piemontese, Venetian, Lombard or Neapolitan, owing to the accent she might pick up.

'If you think I'm a snob, wait until you get to know them,' he said.

'I like their clothes,' said Elinor.

'Yes. You want to wear Italian clothes in Paris and New York, though you want to wear English clothes in Italy. We'll make a raid on Milan.'

'Tomorrow?'

'First I must go to Milchester. Fred says my signature is required on six million documents. Will you come?'

'To Milchester?'

'You don't have to.'

'I won't unless you need me. I'll come if you want me.'

'I think you're too overpowering for Milchester. I think you'd frighten them.'

'Yes. I'll go home.'

'Home? Where is home?'

'La Moquerie,' said Elinor. 'That's my home.'

'Has it occurred to you,' said a music critic to a fashion journalist, 'that our dear Bruno is repeating his achievement in a new medium? He is restoring, recreating, not so much rescuing as reinventing. Of course it is the nearest the poor boy can come to creativity, as with so many of us. Having remade his house, he is now remaking his girl.'

'He's doing a good job,' said the fashion writer.

'Yes indeed, but one trembles to think what he may start on next. The Eiffel Tower?'

*

Elinor saw Bruno off at Charles de Gaulle, and took the train to Millau. They met her with a car. Her heart lifted when she saw the silver fishtail stones of la Moquerie's roofs, and the toffee-coloured stones of its walls; it lifted again when she passed her reflection in the big mirror in the hall.

She resumed her lessons with François Delalain. She read French novels and poetry. She gave an hour a day to Italian instructional videos, trying to keep the two Romance languages apart in her head, finding that in fact knowledge of one often helped her find a word or construction in the other. She revisited the buildings and pictures of Albi, and inspected many lesser marvels mentioned in the guidebooks.

Berthe came four days a week, sometimes bringing two old cousins to scrub the stone floors. She left Elinor's dinner in the oven, or left ready the materials for dinner for Elinor to cook when it suited her. Berthe arrived in a little pick-up truck with Pierre, who was butler and gardener and odd-job-man. These two were devoted to Bruno. They said so, and Elinor was sure it was true. They cheated him only moderately, food and some wine and things out of the garden, possibly a little linen, probably no silver. Elinor wondered what they made of herself, her status, her relationship to Bruno.

She sometimes wondered what she herself made of her status.

She wrote postcards to people in England, with photographs of cathedrals and remarks about the weather. She sent cards to her brothers and her cousin Octavia Crossley, and the judges and admirals of Conyngham Smedley. She wondered what they made of her, too, and if any of them had heard reports from Paris.

She missed Bruno, but not achingly. She thought some of the pictures might have been better hung.

She came to be particularly fond, mysteriously, of the little dun-coloured landscape by the little student in Milchester. She hung it in her bedroom, wondering if Bruno would approve of this arrangement. It was not only that she now saw in it all the qualities that Bruno had explained to her: it was also that this picture had been her magic carpet, key, open sesame, passport, catalyst – something like that, one of those things – which had turned her round and wound her up and started her off.

On a day at the beginning of December, a day of blustery wind and fitful sunshine, a day belonging to Normandy in March rather than the Tarn in midwinter, Elinor took it into her head to look at the Guardhouse.

That was what Bruno said it was.

It was made of the same materials as the château, and was in the same style, if you could use that word of either of those lumpy medieval buildings. It was a miniature version, a single tower on four floors, with a narrow terrace over the river. It had little square windows placed haphazardly, and a single pepperpot turret which Bruno said was a privy. It had long ago been looted of anything of the least value which could be prised out and carried away.

It had somehow never been the right moment for Elinor to go along the cliff-face path to the Guardhouse. There had always been other things to do, more interesting, more useful, a chapter to read, leaves to rake in the garden, a new CD to listen to. One forgot about the Guardhouse, one ignored it. It was like an abandoned shed at the bottom of a garden, nothing to look at except the corpses of spiders.

But on this blowy Boudin day, Elinor remembered something Bruno had said, soon after they arrived: 'We won't inspect it now. It won't go away. One day somebody might do it up. That would be an amusing challenge, for which personally I am too tired. Then, when it is all done, when it is comfortable and elegant, it can be let to discriminating tenants, from whom we shall require the highest references. They can come for a fortnight at a time, at huge profit to me. This is a growth industry, you know – expats letting their converted barns to rich folk from the Home Counties. We could pay some of the bills with that. Never mind about it now. It's all something for later.'

Now it was later.

Elinor picked up a sweater, and went out on to the terrace.

At one end was the arch which gave on to the interminable stone stairway to the river-bank, to the jetty and the little dank boathouse. The river was now cold, steely, inhospitable. It looked very big. It was very big. It was dangerous at this season; it was dangerous at every season. It was beautiful. It was always beautiful. This was not a day for going down all those steps to the rim of the river.

It was a day for the other end of the terrace, for the squat stone arch at the mouth of the cliff-face path.

The path made use of some kind of natural jut in the face of the cliff, as though the cliff had been sliced laterally by a titanic knife, and the top half pushed back a yard. Of course the natural ledge was not as tidy as that. The path had been gouged above and filled in below, masonry set God knew how to create a horizontal walkway a hundred metres long. They had once had wooden posts, it seemed, slotted into holes in the masonry or in the living rock, the posts joined by rails which were probably also wooden. That would have been a hazardous arrangement, unless they were awfully careful about keeping it in repair. It was easy to imagine men-at-arms, awkward in steel plate and burdened by weapons, stumbling on the path and crashing through the flimsy wooden barrier and dropping like gleaming boulders into the river . . .

Over the centuries, it was credibly said, the rail had been strengthened as the path itself had been improved; and somebody just before the war, in 1938 or thereabouts, had planted concrete posts carrying tubular steel rails. There must have been a notion, at that moment, of rehabilitating the château. The war killed the notion: probably the owner also. Bruno had found the concrete posts, sole evidence that anybody in living memory had taken any interest in la Moquerie. Bruno had the concrete posts inspected, and where necessary replaced. He improved some yards of the path. Most of it was pretty good, holding up well in that kindly climate. Nowadays the path was hardly used, because nobody went from the château to the Guardhouse. There was nothing to go there for.

Not yet.

Elinor had only a very few times walked along the cliff-face path, in all the weeks she had been there. She had only walked along it to see it; having seen it, she had seen it. That mission was accomplished. It was not an important experience. There was no need to repeat it.

But today was different. She went along the path not as an idle sightseer but as a potential restorer of ancient Guardhouses. She thought she might take up Bruno's challenge.

She inspected the path as she went. It would become important, if she went ahead with this project. The path would be used constantly, by themselves and their friends and the servants, and by people who were paying rent, if they followed up that idea.

The face of the cliff here and there beetled above the path, as in the Gorges du Tarn the banks beetled over the river; here the path had been carved into the rock with an infinity of ancient chisel-blows. At other points the face scooped away from the path, as the cliff folded into chimneys and recesses. The floor of the path was here and there masonry, here and there recent concrete, with some stretches of living rock tool-smoothed and bootsole-smoothed, and stretches of firm-trodden gravelly dirt. The path was all right, quite comfortable walking. Stiletto heels in the dark might have been a risk, and tender bare feet unhappy on the gravelled sections: but Elinor thought that nobody sensibly shod would have any trouble with the going. That was one problem already solved.

The rail, the balustrade? This would have to be safe, before anything else was contemplated.

Elinor thought that an engineer, an expert, had better test the integrity of the concrete uprights, but meanwhile they seemed perfectly sound. They were ugly, square and yellowish, but reassuring.

The path would just about take the width of a small wheelbarrow or a narrow wheelchair, but not anything that you could call a truck or tractor, cart, vehicle, trailer. Therefore everything sizeable – masonry, cement, plumbing, drains – would have to come to the Guardhouse by road, by its own drive from the highway.

Elinor had never explored that back drive. She had had no occasion to use it. Within her memory, as far as that went, Bruno had never used it. Nobody had. What sort of state was it in? How much would need to be spent on it, to prevent the builders' trucks getting broken axles?

This thing was liable to open out into an ocean of expense. How far would Bruno go?

Elinor's head for heights was pretty good, but she was not made of iron. It was unnerving to lean over the rail and look straight down at the river, even though the metal rail and the concrete posts were evidently safe. The water was so smooth and fast, so very far down, so metallic and implacable. It was creepy that such rapid and powerful water was so silent. The thunder of falls or the rustle of shingle would have humanised the river, normalised it. The power and silence of the water was one aspect of la Moquerie that Elinor still found foreign and alarming.

She turned away from that water which was not like water. She went on to the narrow terrace of the Guardhouse, which was paved with golden stones. It was hardly wider than a path, on the south and west sides of the building. Was there room for furniture, like the lovely wrought-iron on the terrace of the château? If not, it would be a terrible waste of this marvellous position. What would it cost, to widen the terrace, to build it out over the river?

The massive oak door should have been locked, but the lock had been broken time out of mind. The door did not even shut properly, owing to the frame having warped away from the stone. Elinor pushed open the distorted door, into the dank blackness of the ground floor. The door opened with difficulty, the hinges being caked in honey-coloured rust. The oak of the door had the feeling of iron. The air inside the building had the feeling of stone, old damp stone long buried. There was a feeling of insects and of slimy things.

The darkness inside had an indescribable smell, of mildew and ancient drains. It was not in fact completely dark. When Elinor's eyes had adjusted, she saw that there were two incompletely shuttered windows, high in the walls, one of which faced south over the river.

She thought: where there are two windows there can be ten; where there is a small window there can be a large one.

The ceiling was high, and virtually invisible. It was impossible to see from below if it was about to fall down. There was no staircase, but a crude ladder, with rungs missing, bolted to the east wall. It was obviously folly to risk the surviving rungs of the ladder. Elinor hesitated, then committed the folly. She went very carefully up the ladder, testing the rungs and the sides of the ladder before she put her weight on them. The dust in the air was thicker as she rose, and cobwebs festooned themselves over her hair and shoulders. She could not see her hands in the dark, but she knew they must be filthy. She should have worn something on her head; she should have worn gloves and old overalls. She should not be climbing this dangerous ancient ladder with nobody within earshot. If she had any sense she would go down immediately. She went on up.

If she looked upwards, things fell into her eyes. She climbed slowly, expecting to hit her head on a trap-door. But her head went through the ceiling and into the chamber above. The ladder passed through an opening about a metre square, in which there must once have been a trap-door, in which there was now a wooden frame of gigantic oak to which the centuries had given nothing except greater strength.

More cobwebs festooned themselves on Elinor's hair and brow, as she rose like a deep-sea creature into the new level. It was lighter. Because it was lighter, and more could be seen, it was more destroyed, shabby, dirty. It was more dangerous, with slabs of wood with ancient square nails rustily protruding, and gap-toothed floorboards over joists and beams, instead of stone over stone.

There were windows in the east and west walls, looking

along the bank of the river upstream and down. Elinor supposed a window could be put in the south wall, overlooking the river. When that had been done, this room could be ... She tried to imagine what it could be. It was difficult. She was completely new to anything like this. The chamber was big enough to be made into two rooms, three, but that might be a pity. There was an awful lot of thinking and planning to be done.

The dusty twilight of the place was hung with tendrils of cobweb, thick, greasy to the touch. Birds and bats and small animals with teeth lived here, or had long ago died here.

Seeing more clearly, Elinor saw that another section of ladder went up to another floor, through another empty square where a trapdoor might have been. It looked a very dubious ladder, though it was made of large pieces of wood. There was a great chimney-breast in the north wall, and below it a great fireplace. This was where the soldiers had cooked and eaten their rations, and drunk the wine sent to them along the cliff-face path from the château.

All of that could happen again.

Elinor rose into the room, and reached a yard across the wall to the foot of the next ladder. She put her weight on the ladder cautiously, gradually. She tried not to inhale cobwebs. She heard or sensed the skittering of a million tiny claws on the floor and ceiling and walls.

The opening at the top of the new ladder was a pale square. There was more light above, much more. Part of the wall had collapsed, or there were more and bigger windows.

She thought she was dirtier than she had ever been, larded and hung about with greasy ropes of dirt, ancient grime on her hands and cheeks and lips and eyelids. This place was a coalmine in the middle of the sky, a reversal of the natural order, something mad. It was inconceivable that it could be turned into a residence where a person could have a drink and a conversation with other persons.

Elinor was frightened of the next ladder. She was going to be a long way up off the ground. It was a grotty old ladder, with missing rungs. But there was brightness above. She dared herself to go on up.

She climbed slowly towards the square of brightness, which was bright because of the gloom below. She was more suspicious of the rungs of this ladder because some of them were missing.

Her head rose above the level of the next floor, and she saw the oriel.

It was a big, beautiful window which immediately, all by itself, if there had been nothing else here, made restoring this place worth while. It was obviously later than the rest of the building, a happy afterthought, perhaps of the early sixteenth century. In style it was very late gothic, with long-gone glass held in a flattened arch and contained in the remains of elaborate stonework. Somebody had wanted to make the place nicer. Elinor imagined a guard commander who was a cadet of the noble family of the château, or the renaissance quirk of an effeminate, even a female, commander of the guard, or the use of the Guardhouse, in some period of peace, as a dower-house or guest house or presbytery. It all suggested the time of François I. Perhaps he was somehow personally involved. Elinor immediately decided that her favourite French king was directly or indirectly responsible for the oriel window.

In which case Leonardo da Vinci had doubtless sketched from it.

Thinking on these lines was distinctly unscholarly, a bit girlish. But it was an idea Bruno might have had. Was

Bruno girlish? Could you use that word of him, without gratuitous cruelty?

Elinor began the perilous journey across the corrupt floor to the oriel window, to see exactly what view it commanded, what Leonardo had drawn.

The window looked up the bank of the river, towards the château. Obviously it was visible from the château, in full view of the west-facing upper windows of the west tower. Why had Elinor never seen it? Why had nobody remarked on it? Why had Bruno not pointed it out to people, as a charming and unusual feature of his property?

Elinor supposed that she had never really looked at the Guardhouse, the forgotten half-ruin which nobody bothered with. She did not deserve her luck, her glorious oriel.

This would be the Oriel Room. It would be famous.

Elinor inched across the floor towards the window, treading where she could see there were joists under the floorboards, where, sometimes, there were no boards hiding the joists.

She saw that there had been shutters. There were still the splintered remnants of shutters. She wondered whether she should restore them. It was a question for later.

She found herself looking down on the eastern end of the Guardhouse's narrow terrace, where it might be very nice to have breakfast in the early sunshine; beyond was the cliff-face path, and a hundred yards on the big terrace of the château. Behind rose the toffee-coloured bulk of the château itself. About sixty feet below the path and the terrace (they said it was just short of sixty feet) shone the silver-green polished surface of the river, into which malefactors had long ago been dropped.

(François Delalain said they dropped their servants in the river, when they caught them stealing or fornicating; he said that sort of seigneurial justice was a major cause of the French Revolution. Elinor agreed with him that such arbitrary ferocity was very shocking. This was a phrase which translated well into the pedantic French which François Delalain was teaching her.)

There was a small west window which could presumably be enlarged. A window could be made to the south, on to the river. They would not have any windows in the north wall, by the great chimney-breast and the fireplace which duplicated the one below.

Whatever they did with the rest of the house, this floor would remain one big room, as it was now. It was far too early to make decisions, but Elinor made this one.

It would be the Leonardo Room, and people would come from all over the world to photograph it. Elinor caught herself in this pretentious daydream. She laughed at herself. She had acquired from Bruno the habit of self mockery. She thought how different the lives of both her parents would have been, if they could have caught the habit too. They would have been quite different, and much better.

The Leonardo Room. The da Vinci Chamber.

What about the walls? What colour? She would be guided by Bruno's practical experience, of course, but ought she to be guided by his taste? She was aware that hers was already moving a little away from his, into greater simplicity and stronger colours.

Curtains inside the shutters? Curtains instead of shutters?

Elinor was looking round the half-lit room, ideas elbowing one another in her head and raising urgent hands for attention, so that she was not quite so carefully looking where she was going. There was a sudden crunching and crackling noise, and the floor gave way under her right foot.

She screamed. She grabbed at the floor. There was a great choking new cloud of old dust, and a curtain of greasy cobwebs came from nowhere to drape her face. Her foot was stuck in the hole in the floor. It was not a big hole. She was not in any danger. She had hurt herself, she was scratched and bleeding, but she thought she had not broken any bones. She extricated her foot from the splintered floorboards, and crawled to the top of the ladder.

She was trembling with the shock, the sudden terror, the moment familiar from nightmares when the earth opened underfoot. She waited for calmness, for the sense that she had a grip of herself. She needed to be fully in control in order to cope with the ladders.

She went down very slowly and carefully, motionless for long moments.

Berthe screamed when she saw Elinor crossing the hall of the château.

'Madame Elly!'

Elinor tried to reassure her: but Elinor had not at that moment yet seen herself in a mirror. When she did so she understood why Berthe screamed. She looked as though she had been having a fight to the death with a wildcat in a coal-cellar. Her clothes were torn and filthy and there was blood on her leg.

Elinor said there was nothing wrong with her that would not be put right by soap and water, sticking-plaster, and a clean shirt.

'Madame Elly! Madame Elly!'

This was what they called her. Elinor was not sure how they spelled it, if they ever had reason to spell it – Elli? Eli? Ely? – nor how they had arrived at 'Madame'.

Elinor thought the servants had been told by Bruno what to call her. That was all right. She was happy with it. She did not mind what they called her, as long as they liked her, and they seemed to do that.

Madame Elly in the Leonardo Room.

Berthe followed Elinor upstairs, with a scattergun of anxious concern. A bandit? An avalanche? A helicopter falling out of the sky?

'*C'était le corps-de-garde,*' said Elinor. '*Le plafond.*'

'*Le plafond,*' shrieked Berthe, imagining of course that the ceiling had fallen in.

'*Je veux dire le plancher, au deuxième.*'

'*Le corps-de-garde, le corps-de-garde!*'

Elinor thought: why *corps-de-garde*? Why not *maison-de-garde*? She made a mental note to ask François Delalain about this illogical usage, which he would doubtless hotly defend on patriotic grounds. Meanwhile the important thing was to get clean and to pacify Berthe, two things which it was difficult to do at the same time.

'I wondered when you'd get round to it,' said Bruno. 'Do you want an architect, or just a builder?'

'Just a builder,' said Elinor. 'And somebody to tell me if I'm breaking any laws.'

'I'll help, but only from a distance. I'm not climbing any ladders.'

Elinor did the programme of exercises with which she ended the active part of the day, having begun the day with a slightly different programme. Then she had her bath. Bruno was having his bath, in his separate bathroom. After his bath and hers, Bruno came to her room, carrying a bottle of champagne and two glasses. It was their reunion. They kissed and caressed with affectionate friendship, happy to be together, not avid or trembling or self-forgetting.

Elinor dressed up with particular and bizarre magnificence for dinner, as a way of saying 'Welcome home.'

Elinor had new ladders put in the Guardhouse, and new planks laid temporarily over the floorboards.

She called in the builder Bruno had recommended, one of three who had worked at la Moquerie. The builder and Bruno between them recommended plumbing and electrical contractors. These people poked about in the Guardhouse and its environs, and conferred with Elinor and with one another. Elinor began to make drawings. She set on foot a tactful search for cast-iron spiral staircases.

It was odd that the oriel window should be so little noticeable from the outside, from the upstairs windows of the château – it seemed the odder to anyone who had seen it from the inside, seen how striking it was, what an important feature of the building.

It would look different when the stone had been scrubbed and the whole big window had been glazed and there was a light inside the chamber.

'Then,' said Bruno, 'it will be a magic casement opening on the foam of, well, a perilous river.'

'What are you quoting, if that's a quotation?'

'Oh God, I am once again forgetting how illiterate you are. So smart and fancy you've become, I forget that you're completely uneducated.'

'François Delalain doesn't think so. He thinks he's educated me.'

'I must say, your French is quite good. Let's go and try your Italian on the Italians.'

So they came to Milan and Florence and Rome, and Elinor tried her Italian, and tried on Italian clothes, which were to be worn, according to Bruno, anywhere except in Italy.

Bruno had prepared the way for them, with telephone calls to friends. Rumour and hearsay also preceded them. As in Paris, Elinor was greeted with intense curiosity, much goodwill, some suspicion, considerable envy.

Among Bruno's Italian friends, much more than among his French ones, it was relevant to reactions to Elinor that her grandfather was an earl. It was an aspect of herself about which, in the previous few months, she had quite forgotten. But in some of the Italian houses the spirit of Elinor's mother was an almost palpable presence.

There was a curious misunderstanding among several of the Italians. Elinor's sobriquet at la Moquerie became Italianised and joined up: she became Signora Madamelli, or Donna Eleanora Madamelli, or even, in the shops, la Contessa Madamelli.

It was partly for this reason that she was so often photographed. Her face appeared in all the magazines which her new friends pretended not to read.

Because she was involved with the Guardhouse, she was alert to any ideas which were to be got about building and decoration, fixtures and fittings, furniture, colours and textures and fabrics and papers. She made notes and a great number of sketches.

She saw the first mural paintings she had ever seen, first some by a pupil of Veronese, then some by Tiepolo. She had known that there were murals in cathedrals, and great paintings on the ceilings of palaces, but she was startled and delighted to find allegories and nymphs and landscapes covering the walls of rooms in private houses. This was surely an idea to consider. She made a note of it.

There were certain people who met her when she first

arrived in Italy, and met her again when she was about to leave; these people were astonished at the difference in the way she spoke Italian – the confidence, fluency and accuracy she commanded after so short a time. But it was not really surprising. She had simply been given the chance to practise what she had already diligently learned. Much of what she said was very Tuscan and correct. But she had an appetite and a memory for racy, demotic Italian as well as the literary language of Bruno and his friends. As in France, she was able to startle and amuse people.

'Another country at your feet,' said Bruno. 'Where will it all end?'

Elinor was in no more hurry with the Guardhouse than Bruno had been with the château. She kept it no more of a secret, either. She was a marginal celebrity, compared to girls who took off their clothes while singing pop songs, but still her photograph was in magazines, so her recreation of the Guardhouse was in magazines.

Of course she had it far easier than Bruno, for many reasons. He could give her the benefit of recent, hard, practical experience, in every technical area, in every phase and factor of what she was doing, where he had had to find it all out for himself. Then, her project was on a far smaller scale, more manageable, artistically more graspable as a whole, less calamitously expensive if errors were made. Then again, and most significantly, her project was an annexe, a folly, a toy, where his had been a major principal residence, a stately home. This did not influence the standard of the building work, or the plastering or plumbing or wiring, but it did influence the size and number of the bedrooms and other rooms, their windows and arrangements for heating and lighting, and, profoundly, their decorating and furniture.

Elinor was in the lovely position of being able to go over the top without going over the top.

Bruno, nearly all the time, hid his dismay.

Bruno was an old square.

Elinor had discovered in herself an utterly unforeseen potential for social and sartorial audacity; now she indulged it in bricks and mortar, in plaster and paint.

It was going to work, as a place to use and live in, but it was going to take a bit of getting used to.

'Some people will never get used to it,' said Bruno. 'I shall never be quite used to those spiral staircases.'

'I shall change it before anybody's used to it,' said Elinor. 'The trouble with the world is people being used to things.'

'Um,' said Bruno, not really grudging the expense.

Pictures of Elinor Leigh, pictures of the *corps-de-garde*, appeared in magazines which appeared on the coffee-tables of Milchester.

There were some dreadfully jealous people.

There were those who claimed to have known Elinor intimately well, and to be very surprised, or not at all surprised, at her metamorphosis. There were many accounts of the realities of her relationship to Bruno. There was much incompleteness of knowledge here, some concealed, some boasted. The people who knew Bruno well did not know Elinor at all. These included the staff of Browning Machinery, staff and students of the Milchester College of Art and Design, and residents of the Close. The people who knew Elinor well – her mother's relations, her father's sporting friends, elderly neighbours in Conyngham Smedley – had never heard of Bruno, although some of them had hired his hedge-clippers.

Miss Octavia Crossley knew both Elinor and Bruno. She was much amused at the imaginable reaction of her late cousin Lady Daphne to Elinor's notorious liaison with a garage-owner.

Fred Browning knew them both. He thought he understood them both. He thought Bruno was a social climber and Elinor was a gold-digger.

Little Ailie Huxtable had met them both. But she never saw the kind of magazines which carried pictures of Elinor and la Moquerie, and she never met the kind of people whose gossip might have touched on these topics.

CHAPTER SEVEN

BRUNO WAS VERY PROUD of Elinor. He felt for her a great tenderness; he was constantly surprised that she continued to surprise him. His emotion was in part parental, in part the proprietory love of an artist for his creation, in part the gratitude of a battered pilgrim for the benison of a comfortable haven.

Bruno was safe with Elinor, from treachery and extortion, from blackmail and heartbreak, from all the wounds inflicted by simple excess of emotion.

Bruno applauded with silent rapture when Elinor startled parties with her clothes, with her own special multilingual mixture of pedantry and raciness, with her idiosyncratic, her often outrageous, her never ill-considered views on practically everything.

Bruno watched with delight, without envy, when Elinor effortlessly took centre stage, as he had never had the zing or charisma to do.

Bruno did not allow himself to feel much like a puppeteer or a parent; he did not feel much like a lover, or an author, or a brother.

When Bruno was asked, as he sometimes was, how things stood between himself and Elinor, he said that they were friends.

They were friends in spite of the piles of Bruno's money

spent by Elinor on the Guardhouse. Partly they were friends because of this money. Everybody loves the person they give money to, who thus represents an investment. Elinor was Bruno's investment, as well as his invention.

It was not so great an outlay as it easily might have been – as Elinor urged that it should be. The saving was in the matter of the terrace. Elinor had called for it to be made broader, to reach dramatically out over the river, as a Frank Lloyd Wright house hangs over a waterfall in Pennsylvania. Elinor admired that effect, studied in a photograph. She imagined a kind of shelf, on gigantic brackets, on which she and her friends would drink chilled wine.

'What you suggest would introduce a note of intrusive modernity, of high-tech steel and concrete. It is something an Arab would do.'

'You only say that because you're half Jewish.'

'As a matter of fact, it is something a Jew might do. It is an architectural excess imaginable in Tel Aviv or Miami.'

'Then where am I going to have breakfast?'

'With me, on the proper terrace, at la Moquerie.'

Elinor was mutinous. Independently, she got another opinion from a consulting engineer from Toulouse. He gave her an idea of the figures involved. She better understood Bruno's position, which he had pretended was aesthetic. She continued to simmer for a time, but she never boiled over, and she accepted in the end, with a fair grace, that the existing narrow strip of terrace better suited the proportions of the building.

Inside the building, the most striking and memorable feature, the most often photographed throughout the period of the works, was as Elinor had immediately predicted. It was the second floor (the third floor, to Bruno's American friends): it was the Oriel Room.

It was the Oriel Room because Bruno had teased Elinor out of her more fanciful and pretentious ideas. He could not, however, stop her from telling everybody that Leonardo da Vinci had sketched from the oriel. Why not? He might have done. The date was right. He was in France for all those last years of his life.

But the room was the Oriel Room, and it took up the whole of its floor, with the spiral staircase in the north-east corner coming up from the floor below, and going on up to the floor above. The other three floors, two below and one above, were divided up, probably not at all as they originally had been, to make bedrooms and bathrooms and a big kitchen-dining-room and a small study: but the Oriel Room stretched from wall to wall, and it was to have large pieces of furniture with large spaces between.

The Oriel Room had its glorious oriel window in its east wall, a new long window (completely out of period) over the river in the south wall, the great fireplace in the north wall, and a single small oblong window on the west wall, which for compelling technical reasons could not be cloned or enlarged. There were to be pictures above bookshelves each side of the fireplace, pictures each side of the windows in the east and south walls. What about the west wall, a wide and inviting space, with only a single small window at one end?

Elinor had an idea about that west wall, but she needed to think about it for a long time before she even discussed it, even with Bruno.

Three-quarters of that year included the anniversaries of Elinor's deflowerment by Boots Cookson, her father's death, her meeting with Bruno, her rebirth as a modern goddess, her installation at la Moquerie.

Quite a year.

Elinor spent most of the three-quarters of the year after Christmas on the conversion of the Guardhouse; she found, as Bruno had said she would find, that being on the spot saved incalculable time and money (her time, his money). Bruno spent some part of those months in Milchester, to which Elinor was not interested in going. Bruno continued to make a lot of money, paying himself a large salary for his part-time contribution to the company, receiving large dividends from his shares.

(The recession was kind to people who hired things out, since their customers were reluctant to buy things.)

Much of that time, Bruno and Elinor were apart. Much of it, they were together. They were sad but not distraught when they were apart. They were happy but not delirious to be together.

Writers and photographers of the glossiest kind came often to the Guardhouse, pointing their cameras at the oriel window and at Elinor, describing the spiral staircases and Elinor, commenting on history and on Elinor. Bruno was there or he was not there. He bowed Elinor into the centre-stage position where she so fabulously blazed.

Bruno laughed a bit; Elinor was the only person with whom he shared his laughter.

Bruno continued to make money in those months; he maintained his benevolent and cultural activities in Milchester; he popped in and out of congenial houses in London and other cities.

He did not embark on any passionate adventures. He did not want any more horrible young men in his life.

He was also busy, on a small scale, at la Moquerie. The house being pretty well perfect, he was putting more time and thought into the garden. He made a knot-garden, from ancient drawings discovered in an ancient house.

Elinor was preoccupied, naturally. She was deep in large labours and decisions. She did not have an eye to spare for Bruno's knot-garden.

It was a very little garden, half the size of a tennis court, planted with herbs credited in the old books with scarcely credible powers of healing and divination, their beds contained within miniature box hedges and grass paths inches wide. It was elegantly and delicately geometrical, in a plan that might have been drawn up by Piero della Francesca. Bruno was awfully pleased with it. Elinor ought to have spared it more than a glance. But she scarcely did. It was not her cup of tea. She went for the big, bold gesture, the strong colour and the sense of drama. Bruno's knot-garden was, perhaps, all too quintessentially Bruno's, delicate and fancy and precise, clipped and disciplined and understated. It was psychologically obsessive rather than hysteroid; it was aesthetically middle class, rather than casually aristocratic or untidily plebeian.

Elinor was simply too busy to bother with the knot-garden.

She was too busy to be bothered with Bruno's new present to himself, the little bronze putto bird-bath he found for the middle of the knot-garden. It belonged in an Italian town garden, perhaps, or among the demure parterres of a neo-classical villa in Twickenham or Kew. Elinor thought it looked completely out of place on the bold terraces of la Moquerie. She did not say so, but she did not make huge efforts to hide that this was what she thought.

In October they downed tools, and Bruno took Elinor to America. They saw people and pictures, both of widely

153

varying merit. New York was exciting and exhausting. Bruno shrivelled a little, among the overwhelming American art-lovers and socialites. He was in that company more than ever European, over-refined, gimcrack. Elinor was relieved, on his account, when they escaped back to an environment where he was not dwarfed.

On her own account she was disappointed when they left. Nothing she had met dwarfed her. She liked huge buildings, huge avenues, huge personalities. She understood what Sylvia Plath had meant, about wanting people and things powerful enough to stand up to her.

The Oriel Room was painted at last, in a crimson which nearly gave Bruno palpitations. He thought he remembered a similar colour on a ceiling in Venice, but all four walls of a very large room . . .

He came away, and returned, and came away, and returned, and stared, and Elinor watched his face with an anxious smile.

Furniture and pictures began to colonise the room. Elinor mixed the ultra-modern and the neo-classical and the gothic, metal and glass and wood; she had an eye for juxtaposing opposites which the glossy magazines said was trend-setting.

Bruno came away, and returned, and his eyebrows went up and down like the leaves of an indoor tree beside an electric fan.

The room was famous before it was finished, Elinor Leigh's Oriel Room in the *Corps-de-garde du Château de la Moquerie*.

Cousin Octavia Crossley was one of hundreds who climbed the spiral staircases to see it. Octavia sat down on a chair which had been made of glass in the Bauhaus in

1930. She said, 'I am too old for this.'

A memory disturbed Bruno, pleasurably, but maddeningly, because its face eluded him. Something about Elinor's crimson walls rang a bell in his brain, in his guts. He was not used to having bells ringing in his guts; he thought the fugitive memory must relate to powerful emotion. That being so, he hoped that whatever it was would remain forgotten. He had done with powerful emotion. He had given it up, as a heavy smoker puts away his cigarettes for ever.

Not only a Venetian ceiling, that particular singing, crying, lambent electric crimson, but something else too, a magical object with a shocking electric charge.

Somebody's nail-polish?

A detail in a Titian, a nipple or scarf or blossom?

The petal of a subtropical flower in his mother's garden?

Some dreadful drink, some awful cocktail?

A yard inside the oriel window, Elinor had placed a table. It was massive, as the position demanded: an imaginative near-replica of one dug up at Pompeii, an item of luxurious solidity.

What should she put on the table?

One thing? A clutter of things?

Vases, flowers? Large illustrated books? Stacks of glossy magazines? Pot-pourri, alabaster, small bronze statues, cigarette boxes, books, bottles, a tantalus?

A lamp? What lamp?

Not in the middle of the night, not in his bath, but in the salon of la Moquerie in the early evening, looking at a recent copy of the Sotheby's *Preview*: that was when and how

Bruno traced the original of that crimson.

It was part of his life, of his innermost essential person.

In physical actuality, Elinor had never seen that example of that crimson. Yet she had chosen it for the Oriel Room.

How? Magic? Love?

Magic.

That blazing bloody crimson was a few little slivers of glass in the Tiffany lamp, darts and daggers between the black curving lines of lead, details in the opulent tropical blossom which the lampshade was. Those touches of the hot-cold crimson were vital to the success of the design, otherwise all greenish-blueish, cool, even insipid.

This was amazing.

Elinor had never seen the lamp, Bruno thought, unless by chance when she walked across the Milchester Cathedral Close on a winter afternoon, after the lamps were lit but before the curtains were drawn.

She had not got that colour from any such memory, oh no, the idea was preposterous. It was a colour she had chosen – no, invented, caused to be mixed for her special purposes.

The consequence was inescapable.

Pierre carried the package, ever so carefully, up the first corkscrew of cast-iron stairs and up the second. The package was heavy and of awkward shape. Pierre grunted with effort, and contorted his leathery face. He was always one to dramatise, to groan with martyrdom.

Elinor followed Pierre up the stairs. Bruno waited at the top.

Pierre, groaning, lowered his awkward burden to the floor by the oriel window. There was space for it, for all of them, between the table and the window. Pierre took out his clasp-knife and began to cut away the elaborate wrappings.

'*Doucement*,' said Bruno.

Pierre was gentle. He freed the object from its wrappings as though liberating a precious mummy from its cerements.

Berthe had laboured up the spiral stairs, and now joined the group in the window. She knew that something important was being revealed. She lent as always an air of drama and solemnity to the occasion.

Pierre unwrapped the Tiffany lamp, and placed it, under Bruno's direction, on the table which faced the oriel window.

'Oh,' said Elinor. 'Oh. This is genius. This is perfect. I never would have thought of it. Even if I'd thought of it, I never would have found it. The colour. Those splinters of colour. That red.'

'It matches remarkably,' said Bruno, his voice unsteady.

'Is that why you're doing this?'

'Partly. The coincidence is extraordinary. I don't believe in coincidence. It is inartistic. I am sickened by novels which depend on coincidence. This is no coincidence, that you chose a colour that pre-existed in my lamp.'

'I sort of agree. I prefer to think it not a coincidence that I chose this colour.'

'You made this colour. You conjured it. It existed in my lamp, but not in the manufacturer's catalogue.'

'I made the colour. No, it wasn't a coincidence. But I don't know what it was.'

'It was magic, of course. That is why I brought the lamp here, to demonstrate a miracle. That is one reason. Another reason is that it goes well here, don't you think? It looks fine. It looks supremely at home. It is too grand and declamatory for most contexts, for any normal niminy-piminy domestic environment, but here it is in its element.'

'It is histrionic.'

'Goodness, what a long and learned word. Yes, that is a good word for it. This lamp is an actor, it pretends, it is make-believe, it is a great show-off.'

'Like so many of us.'

'And there is another reason why I brought the lamp here, which I do not really want to talk about.'

Elinor nodded. She thought she understood the reason, and she also did not want to talk about it.

There was really nothing to say about it.

It was not exactly love, but it was difficult to know what else to call it. Bruno's word 'friendship' was an evasion.

Elinor said, 'I am passionately in love with that lamp.'

In the weeks that followed, there was an article in one of the glossies about the refurbishment of ancient French buildings, one about new directions in interior design, and one about Tiffany's. All these pieces carried photographs of Elinor's Tiffany lamp, in her Oriel Room in the *corps-de-garde*, two of them with Elinor alone, one with Elinor and Bruno.

One might have supposed that the world would have grown tired of Elinor and her room in her funny old house, but the magazines did not think so.

It was all right with Elinor. She had a sneaking, unworthy hope that her brothers' wives saw the magazines.

The Guardhouse now had hot water, loos that flushed, a cooker that cooked. It was beginning to be habitable. Elinor spent nights in it, first with a sense of adventure, then with a sense of settling into a nest. Bruno spent nights in it, as Elinor's guest. For once they shared a bathroom.

*

Bruno came away from the Guardhouse one evening, going carefully and safely by the cliff-face path. He left Elinor busy about something. He entered his own house, and on a sudden impulse went upstairs not to his room but to Elinor's. Elinor's room faced west, downstream, towards the Guardhouse. Bruno went to Elinor's window, and looked out.

The Tiffany lamp showed like a demented star, a luminous epigram, across a hundred yards of dark chasm.

It was the Olympic torch. He had been handed it, and he had handed it on. Now it was Elinor's lamp, because she was what she was.

What it expressed could not be put into words.

That was not quite right. What the lamp expressed could only be put into words too embarrassing to say or write or frame or name, words too near the knuckle, altogether too sick-making and mawkish.

Like all good symbols, the lamp did instead of words. Wenty Pollock had known that, and Elinor knew it.

Bruno had always been a ready weeper, often to his acute embarrassment. He had tears on his cheeks now, when he turned away from the window, from the little blaze of barbaric colour in the distant oriel.

And the memory he had tried to bury, the memory of course was of Wenty Pollock. Wenty had been evoked by the crimson walls, because they remembered their splintery pre-echoes in the lamp.

Bruno killed Wenty Pollock, who had given him the lamp. Elinor would not kill Bruno. If she did not exactly love him, in the ordinary sense of the word, what else would you call it?

★

Elinor, left behind in the Guardhouse, was not visibly busy with anything. She was invisibly busy. She was thinking. She was staring at the west wall of the Oriel Room, the big blank wall that she had so far done nothing with.

Bruno had said, and other people had said, 'Why not pictures?'

Elinor had smiled and waved her hands (long beautiful hands), as though she had many excellent secret reasons for leaving the wall blank. There was actually only one reason, which was that she was waiting for an idea. When it came, it would be astonishing and triumphant. That was all she yet knew about it.

Elinor was by now apt to see her life in theatrical terms. This was inevitable, because she was on a stage and in a spotlight: people were all the time taking her photograph and asking her opinion and reporting her actions. Since she was giving a performance, about which she was not at all unselfconscious, she wanted clear cues, dramatic pauses before her entries, pulverising one-liners, great curtains, and plenty of dizzying emotional switches of the kind Pirandello contrived. In her life as in her conversation, she wanted to add surprise to surprise. So here: she wanted to match the Tiffany lamp at the east end of the room with something equally extraordinary.

She wanted something with particular qualities which she found hard to visualise or verbalise. Something very strong, remarkable in form or colour or both. It should not occupy much space; Elinor had seen some very large Alexander Calder mobiles which would have been most happy there, but they would have taken up too much room. If it was to be a painting, it was not quite any painting she had ever seen; nothing was quite right that she had ever seen or imagined. She kept thinking negatively – Hockney was too brash, Lichtenstein too predictable. Chagal too fey, Bacon too ugly, Freud too vulgar, Matisse . . .

Of course she wanted a Matisse, one of the St Petersburg ones.

Since she could not have a big Matisse, the last thing she wanted was an imitation Matisse.

Whatever it was, it had to be classy. This word revolted Elinor, but in its revolting way it was exactly right. Something classy was exactly what she meant.

It had to be at the same time classy and lurid. It had to be like Goya. On a large scale, and in two dimensions, it had to have the qualities of the Tiffany lamp.

Bruno said, 'If you want somebody to do something astonishing, then get them to do something they've never done before, never thought of doing, never been allowed to do, never dared to do. You, for example – you did something astonishing which was completely outside anything you had imagined for yourself.'

'What did I do so amazing? I've never done anything amazing.'

'You turned yourself from what you were into what you are.'

'You did that. You turned me. Anyway, I want somebody to do something astonishing now.'

'I know you do. That is why I mention the matter. You want somebody to paint a mural on the west wall of the Oriel Room.'

'How do you know?'

'That wall screams for it.'

'It screams for Matisse.'

'Yes. Those dancers in a circle, stolen from Poussin. What I think you don't want to do is get hold of somebody who's done something vaguely, nearly, approximately right. You'd get a replay, because that's what you'd be asking for. It would still be nearly right, no more nearly right than what he's done before, not exactly right, and also not fresh, something rehearsed, something already explored. You want somebody whose qualities you admire, but who has never dared or been allowed or had the chance to attempt anything like a mural, a mural in that place, in that context, with that competition.'

'You've been thinking about this.'

'Of course I have. It's the kind of thing I spend most of my life thinking about, thanks to my cousin Fred. This is a time to take a chance.'

'I suppose, if it doesn't work, we can scrub it out,' said Elinor. 'But that would be awful. What would you say to the artist? Or would you not tell him? Then he might come to see it, to show it to his new girlfriend. He'd say, "Look what I did – er – er –" I suppose it could be removable, painted on pieces of hardboard, or strips of canvas on a row of stretchers, made to fit exactly. Isn't there a Titian like that in the Academia? But I wouldn't want that, really. I don't know why. I want an actual mural on the actual wall, painted on the fabric of the building.'

'I would want that, too. I also don't know why.'

A little greeny-brown painting, a landscape, semi-abstract, influenced perhaps by Graham Sutherland. Nothing very much here, but –

Achieving, in an understated way, an almost tentative or tactful way, a sharp individuality of character, of mood and vision –

Achieving a sense of illimitable distances, even on this small scale, even without a horizon, without evident perspective –

Bruno had not said anything much about Elinor's appropriation of the little picture, which he had bought for a small sum out of the exhibition at the art school.

'Oh, you've hung it in here,' he said. He was not much interested in the picture, although he had explained it so brilliantly.

He had not kept in touch with the artist. He did not know what had happened to her. He had not thought her interesting as a personality. Indeed she had been heavy work to talk to, responding to every overture with bleak, shy monosyllables.

Elinor remembered that she had at first seen nothing in the painting. Bruno had said that there was something in it. He showed her what was in it. Did he show her more than there was in it, altogether overstate the matter, perhaps out of kindness to the little girl who had done it? Was Elinor now more attracted to it than it deserved? Had it become a habit with her? Was it undeservedly iconic, because of the moment at which it entered her life, the role it unwittingly played in her transformation?

What was all the fuss about?

So Elinor thought, circling the little picture, in the evening, in her bedroom, as though she could learn more about it by looking at it from different angles, as though she were stalking it with a view to pouncing and catching it.

Bruno's sermon was: Look inside yourself for an authentic, personal emotional reaction to a work. If there is none, it may be your failure or the artist's failure, but the point is that there is no communication, the art experience has not happened.

It was easy to imagine or invent an emotional reaction, to think oneself into being moved by Michelangelo or shattered by Guernica. It was also dangerously easy to react to the easy, the flashy, the fraudulent, the second-rate, to be suckered by the histrionics of Caravaggio, the false exoticism of Delacroix, the adolescent vapourings of Edvard Munch, the vulgar posturings of Augustus John, the pretentious feyness of Georgia O'Keeffe.

Was Elinor falling into these traps, pretending to a reaction she should have, or having a reaction she should not have?

Elinor was uncertain when she went to bed. She was still uncertain when she awoke to a morning shining after midnight rain.

She took the little picture off the wall. She turned it over. On the stretcher was written, in felt pen, 'A Huxtable Yr 1'.

A? Anne? Augusta? Alexandra? Elinor thought she had heard the name, but she had certainly quite forgotten it. Probably it was no matter – it was not terribly likely there were two A. Huxtables at the College.

Elinor wrote:

Dear Miss Huxtable.

You may possibly remember that we met 18 months ago at the Milchester Art College, with Mr Bruno Browning, we discussed your prize-wining landscape painting, which Mr Browning afterwards bought.

The picture is now here. I am looking at it as I write. I am writing partly to tell you how much pleasure it continues to give me.

We are at present engaged in restoring and redecorating a smaller building attached to this château, in which there is a large second-floor room with a big window and a fine view. There is a blank wall at one end of this room, for which we are considering a mural. We have not yet come to any decision as to artist, medium or subject.

Whoever undertakes this commission will of course live here as our guest for as long as is necessary. (If they wish to do so.) We would have the wall prepared as required (eg plastered and painted) though fresco would present difficulties owing to availability of craftsmen of sufficient experience. We would provide tools and materials as required.

The total dimensions of the wall are approximately 30 foot × 13', but there is one small window at the right hand (southern) end, about 4'6" × 2'.

I would not wish to impose any preconceived ideas on any artist who undertakes this job, but would say that a strong and colourful design is probably required given this particular situation.

We would pay a reasonable fee. I imagine we would have no difficulty in arriving at an agreed figure.

If you think you might be interested in this project, please write to me here. It would of course be helpful if you could enclose photographs of recent work (prints or transparencies). I imagine you will wish to postpone any creative decisions (eg subject matter) until you have seen the site.

We will be awaiting your reply with interest.

Yours sincerely,

Elinor Leigh.

Elinor addressed the envelope to Ms A. Huxtable, c/o the Milchester College of Art and Design.

She did not tell Bruno anything about any of this. It would have been too painful, watching him stopping himself from interfering.

There was no knowing if the letter would find the girl. A. Huxtable might have left the college, flunked out, emigrated, died, moved house, anything. Or an uncaring, overworked secretary might lose or bin the letter, or . . .

Or the letter might arrive without result. A. Huxtable might remember Elinor with dislike or contempt; or she might not remember her, in which case she might regard the letter as impertinent or frightening, or she might have devoted herself entirely to miniatures or to print-making or sculpture, or she might be a trendy red and consider doing murals only in a works canteen or an underground station, or . . .

It did not terribly matter. Writing to A. Huxtable was a bow at a venture, a long-shot, a whimsical freak. They might decide against a mural. There were thousands of competent established muralists. There was no hurry about any of it.

Then Bruno said that they should go to California, and Elinor was distracted by the problems of what to pack and what to read on the flight.

Elinor was not a celebrity in San Francisco or LA. There had been no jungle drums, no warning orders, as in Paris and Milan. Nobody had heard of her. She was not asked on morning TV chat-shows. She met a handful of people interested in the arts, and who enjoyed conversation and wine and looking at pictures. Some of these people were gay, some straight, some Jewish, some Wasp, as elsewhere.

In San Francisco they had been lent a suite in a residential hotel, where they had adjoining, communicating bedrooms. The comfortable ritual was observed: Bruno knocked; he entered Elinor's room, soon after her bath and his own, when they were relaxed and soap-scented and pinkly clean, and wearing only robes of cotton or terry; he carried a tray with glasses and a bottle of champagne. They drank together, and caressed in loving friendship.

After two weeks, Elinor was homesick for la Moquerie.

She never once thought about A. Huxtable, all the time she was in America.

Ailie Huxtable thought of Elinor, though, and of Mr Bruno Browning, thought furiously about them from the moment the letter arrived in her hands.

Her life was at a low point – low even by the standards of a life which was all the time intolerably low.

She reckoned she had never had a chance. The cradle into which Providence had placed her at birth was the most hopeless of imaginable starting points. It was a ramshackle, dirty, ugly, wet, worm-eaten cradle. Nothing good, beautiful or happy could grow from such a place. This was not due to natural disaster, evil fortune, or anybody's malice. It was due wholly to mismanagement: to stupidity, crassness, inefficiency, arrogance.

No, not stupidity, not exactly. Not exactly stupidity at all. That was the irony, the sick and bitter joke. Not stupidity but silliness. Obstinacy, wrong-headedness.

The result was the same.

Ailie had to escape, but she couldn't, but now perhaps suddenly she could.

If her desertion killed her parents, that was what it did. There was no way of escaping them except physically escaping them, going away. They would not be killed by grief, but only by resentment, by a sense of betrayal and ingratitude.

Ingratitude! Ailie owed several debts to several people, neighbours and teachers and a few friends, but she owed her parents nothing at all, nothing except rage.

It was all very much worse for a very peculiar reason. Ailie was a lady. Incongruously, calamitously, irremediably. She spoke like a lady, and she was clean and fastidious and delicate in her manner of eating. It was how she was. People could take it or leave it. She scorned to pretend to be working-class, dirty and uncouth, which some people did for self-protection: they adopted camouflage when they became students, so that they could pass unchallenged, unmocked, unbullied. Ailie could not pretend to be common. She would not. She spoke the way she spoke and ate the way she ate. She would not swear as the others swore, or wear dirty socks.

Her parents were useless and selfish and impossible, but as it happened they were well born and well educated. Ailie was brought up in a gutter, in a midden, but the people there spoke Oxford English and read the music reviews in the *Guardian*.

Probably it was not really Sarah's fault. She was maddening, sure, she was ceaselessly plucky and stoical and loyal, when she should have screamed and struck out, but she was probably as much a victim as Ailie was. But Adrian, Adrian the wispy-bearded, the pig-headed, the complacent knowall, the whinnying whingeing genius who couldn't work a tin-opener, who had never had a job because he always despised potential employers, the fatuously arrogant failure at absolutely everything –

Ailie loved them both, with despair, helpless to help them, exploding with impatience and frustration, wondering how in God's name their genes had produced herself.

Which they sure enough had. There was no doubt about her parentage.

It was why Adrian and Sarah got married, necessary if Sarah was to keep her tiny remittance, on which they lived. As an unmarried mother she would have been given the chop by the family trustees.

Adrian couldn't even manage a condom.

The catalogue of his incompetencies included every avenue of human activity in which he had ever engaged, including copulation, at which he was no good, or all too good.

It was all a mistake, like everything else in both their lives.

Francis Huxtable had a decent house and a small agricultural estate near Leamington, sustained by a family manufacturing business in Coventry. The business had been started in 1880 and the estate acquired in 1910. Francis inherited control of both in 1937, having also inherited (or assimilated in infancy and childhood) a hard-working, high-minded, humourless personality which pretty well suited the role he had been called upon to play. He had a couple of admirals in his ancestry, which licensed him to say that he ran his business and his estate like ships – like happy ships, he said, which meant not a sloppy tolerance but healthy discipline, a brisk, alert, eye-on-the-ball jump-to-it way of doing things.

Not everybody liked it. Not everybody liked him.

Francis Huxtable believed in practical Christianity and the Tory Party and the Empire and the importance of tidiness. He was a man who always put trees in his shoes.

Francis did not go to the war, because as a manufacturer of machine-tools he was doing work of national importance. He married and had children instead. He had three sons and two daughters. His second son was born in 1942. Bombs were dropping on the Midlands in Adrian's infancy, and the Socialists began ruining the country in his early childhood.

Francis regarded himself as a Christian gentleman. He asked of his sons that they follow him into the family firm and that they be Christian gentlemen, too. He sent them to

Rugby, which was convenient, where they learned about the classics and football and God. He permitted them to go in for culture, if they wished (some gentlemen did, though not Francis) but they were not to be arty. They were not to talk about it, or have arty friends. Their friends, when they grew up, were to shoot partridges and play golf. The Huxtables were to have creases in their trousers and to be loyal to their background.

It was odd that only one of the three was a rebel. Some people who knew the family thought that all five children should have been rebels, but in the event only one son and one daughter were.

The daughter rebelled by running away to live on a Greek island with a fisherman. She ran back again, but she could not be reclaimed. It was too late. She had tasted freedom, and she would not rejoin a world of family dinners, tennis courts, and the *Daily Telegraph*. She got a job with the BBC and nobody heard of her again. She was quite a successful rebel.

But Adrian was a failure even as a rebel. He ran away from Rugby when he was sixteen. He ran away to London, but only as far as an aunt who gave him a bed in the basement. He lived on the wretched aunt, and on surreptitious handouts from his mother. He was offered jobs such as scrubbing floors, the only jobs for which he was qualified, but he would not take them because he had his pride. He had been brought up to be a gentlemen, and he remained one. You could tell by the way he talked, though not by the way he looked.

He wanted to drift to India and Kashmir, but he did not have the energy or the courage to drift any further than Milchester.

He went to Milchester because Sarah Moon went there. Sarah was beautiful, fey, artistic. Many people thought she had a screw loose. She came from a family much like the Huxtables, so that she spoke as though she might be walking down Sloane Street in green Hunter boots. But she gently, almost imperceptibly, walked out of that world. Her family hardly noticed her departure. Her father was busy having lunch at the Travellers', and her mother was meeting friends at Fortnum's, so that they had plenty to occupy their minds. Sarah had been given an expensive education. What more did she want?

She wanted to have her cake and eat it, in a very peculiar regard. She wanted no part of her family's boring, constricted, conventional life, which was governed by rules she found absurd. Therefore she became yet another of those rebels, of whom there were such a number at that time. But in rejecting her parents' habits and habitat, she was not rejecting herself. She was what she was. It did not occur to her to pretend that she came from a back street in Brixton. This made it difficult for her to make friends in the world of squats, since the people there were, or pretended to be, gritty and bitter-minded proles. Then she met Adrian, who had his pride. They recognized one another with relief.

Sarah had a tiny private income from a family trust. She could just about live on it. She did not want a job, because she was an artist. She did not go to any art school, because she was too muddled and disorganised to get a portfolio together, to attend on the right day, or to fill in a form of application. She drew and painted with any materials that came to hand, on any available surface. In style and subject she was completely traditional, because nobody had taught her about being modern.

Somebody told her about the Milchester College of Art and Design, and she went there with the idea of beginning her serious education. But she attended on the wrong day, empty-handed, and she resigned herself with her usual gentle fatalism to never being an art student.

Adrian followed her to Milchester because his aunt and his mother had run out of goodwill. He was too arrogant to take advice, and too prickly to show gratitude. He still wore clean socks and spoke like a schoolmaster, but he began to grow a beard and to wear strange night-shirts brought back by someone from Afghanistan.

Adrian and Sarah found some sheds – a chicken-house, a toolshed and a corrugated-iron garage – at the bottom of an orchard below a farmhouse which had been swallowed up by the new Milchester bypass. They paid a token rent to a distant landlord. By now they had drifted into living together, as a result of which, and of absent-mindedness, a child was conceived in the summer of 1972.

In order to continue to receive her remittance, Sarah had to have a periodic interview with, and report from, a member of the establishment, as if she were applying for a passport. She went to a JP, a builder who was a leading figure in the local Methodist community. She dressed herself up to look respectable, which her background equipped her to do to a surprising extent; but she could not disguise the seven months of her pregnancy. She had to say that she was married. She then had to get married, or her bluff would have been called. Nobody made speeches at that wedding, or drank champagne. Ailie was born in wedlock, though only just.

Adrian's father wrote to Sarah's father; he said he washed his hands of his son, who had been entrapped by a hippy, and was thenceforth the responsibility of the wife's family. Sarah's father replied, on Travellers' Club writing paper, saying that, on the contrary, his innocent little daughter had been seduced by a layabout, and the latter's family must assume the small burden of providing for the couple.

The other members of both families said, 'Well, what is the Welfare State supposed to be for?'

Fatherhood made Adrian very serious and keen. He became energetic about growing food and being self-sufficient. But digging was dreadfully hard work; he got blisters and backache; and the soil was poor and poisoned; and he had his pride.

They stuffed rags between the boards of their dwelling. They acquired a broken, dangerous, but not useless wood-burning stove. Sarah scrounged all manner of odd pieces of fabric, as well as food and old clothes and discarded furniture and chipped plates and saucepans.

Adrian collected the serious newspapers of each previous day, and on Mondays all the serious Sunday supplements. He spent much of each day keeping in close touch with all cultural developments. He was formidably well informed. There was nobody he ever met worthy to talk to him about these matters, which were the only things worth talking about.

They brought their daughter up to know all about everything, and to speak and behave like a lady.

Ailie went to a local school, where she was completely isolated. Nobody had ever met before this combination of extreme poverty and a lah-di-dah accent. Teachers, pupils and parents all found it grotesque. Ailie was bullied rather a lot, for not having a bicycle or the right shoes, for talking posh and being clever.

She had a wretched childhood.

She developed the quick-witted realism of the urchin, of the desperate: so that she was still very young when she understood that her parents' folly was the whole reason for her misery.

At the same time they were kind to her. They cared about her. According to their lights, they did well by her. They were not evil. Ailie did not wish to kill or torture them, but only to get away from them.

She got as far as the College of Art and Design, three miles away, more organized than her mother had been, better advised. She had a grant (like almost all her fellow-students) which paid all her tuition. It paid for some of her materials, and a bit towards her maintenance. As a student she was below the poverty line, but she was richer than she had ever dreamed of being.

As a student, at that time in that place, she was just as isolated as she had been among the beef-fed peasants of the village school. She was bullied. Her accent was imitated and her locker vandalised.

Physically she was a late developer, perhaps because of her diet in childhood; in her first year at the college, when she had her nineteenth birthday, she was still a skinny little thing, flat-hipped, small-breasted. She was nevertheless honoured by the beery attentions of some of the male students, in the dark corridors by the cafeteria. They did not believe her when she said no; they jeered when she dodged and escaped.

She ran home, to find Adrian plucking at his stringy beard and railing at the ignorance of the book reviewers in the *Guardian*: and Sarah trying pluckily to conjure a stew out of odds and ends and left-overs and handouts.

Meanwhile she was well taught that first year, with weekly life classes in which she got covered in charcoal, and then painting classes with the teacher who became her tutor, and who much encouraged her.

The other students bought big, elaborate plastic bait-boxes for their paints and palette-knives, easels, pads of expensive water-colour paper, canvases ready stretched, fistfuls of brushes and buckets of tubes of paint. Even at subsidised prices in the College shop, Ailie could only afford the barest essentials. Her tutor slipped her some materials of his own – half-squeezed tubes of oil paint and acrylic, hairy old brushes, linseed oil and white spirit. He understood how things were, though Ailie never mentioned to him her problems with family or money. He was very good to her. She thought he was a man of great kindness, and a wonderful teacher. She did not much admire his own paintings – chilly landscapes in the manner of Paul Nash – but he exhibited and sold in London, and other people liked them, and he was anyway kind and clever.

In the middle of her first summer term, she painted a small landscape which was derived from nature but did not imitate it; the picture was more influenced by her teacher than other things she had done. Perhaps for that reason he was very nice about it. It was selected to be hung in the main gallery, where the best student paintings were, in the end-of-term exhibition.

That was the beginning of the worst year of Ailie's life.

CHAPTER EIGHT

IT WAS ANNOYING ENOUGH for Ailie's fellow-students – the thirty-seven First Year Fine Arts intake – that her little landscape should be selected for hanging in the Browning Gallery.

There was talk then of her sucking up to Kenneth Yorke, the Head of Painting. He was her tutor. Not many of them had him as tutor. They had tutorials, the two of them, in his office. What went on there, eh? There was talk of her getting round the old sod with her spindly legs and her lah-di-dah voice.

The boys who talked like that were jealous yobs, said some of the girls.

There was talk in the queues in the cafeteria, in the dark tortuous corridors of the college, in the Print-Making Room and the echoing squalor of the Sculpture Area.

The envious girls were mingy bitches, said some of the boys.

She sucked up to Kenneth Yorke by imitating his style of painting, as well as in lots of other ways, nudge nudge, wink wink, boom boom. His style of painting was brain-dead anyway.

They sniggered and whinged behind her back, and there were graffiti in the loos.

★

Out of the pieces chosen for display in the Browning Gallery, a committee selected the annual prize-winners. These received much honour, the possibility of photographs in the *Milchester Argus*, and vouchers for moderate sums, redeemable at the college shop for art materials, subsidised by Browning Machinery.

Who was on the committee? Why, the tutors, the teaching staff, the very people who had short-listed the pieces for display in the gallery. They were the same people, subject to the same pressures, the same flattery, bribery, blackmail or whatever.

It was a racket.

It was like the Best Seller List and Top of the Pops and the Booker and the Turner – all rackets, Buggins' turn, your girl this year and my boy next year, open your legs and win a medal.

Diabolical, really.

How in God's name could anybody seriously think that little Hux did a better painting than mine? Honestly, now? I mean, really? For God's sake?

Little tart. Little slag. Those airs, and they live in a pigsty, you know that? That voice. Okay, those legs and cheekbones I grant you, but what's that got to do with talent?

Kevin fancied her, you know that? He made it with Sue, but it was Hux he really fancied before that, you know that? She wouldn't look at him, her bleeding highness wouldn't, had bigger fish to fry, had prizes to win, didn't she?

Get screwed by the professor, win the prize, easy ennit?

But there was an end-of-term, end-of-year feeling, and most of them had got through, for another year of postponing maturity by way of grants, and the bullying of Ailie was half-hearted, absent-minded. There was two more whole years for that.

Mr Kenneth Yorke, the Head of Painting, was end-of-termish, too. He was apt to be end-of-termish even in the middle of a term. He had a couple of gins in the Faculty Canteen, and then saw Ailie Huxtable, his protégée, in the corridor outside the Animation Studio. The weather was sultry, and she was scantily clad in the manner of art students – a skimpy T-shirt, and tattered trousers of a papery, debased artificial fabric. She was a skinny little thing. She looked fragile. In a delicate, epicene way she was really elegant. She was touching. She had long legs and very slim wrists and ankles. Under the curtains of pale nondescript hair she had a sweet wide mouth, wide eyes, wide cheekbones. If Kenneth Yorke had been feeling better, he might suddenly have wanted to paint her. As it was, he wanted to eat her. He saw in her, for the first time, a high-bred beauty which was unique in that large and low-bred institution. She was mighty desirable, to a randy, half-drunk, middle-aged minor artist who had had a couple of lunchtime cordials.

'We'll have one more tutorial, before we put the shutters up,' he said, a little thickly.

'All right,' said Ailie, startled. 'Thank you.'

Tutorials with Kenneth Yorke were rare events, red letter days. He was one of the very few tutors who sold work, who was known outside the walls of the college. He was hard to pin down. He cancelled most of the appointments made for him by the Office of the Director of Fine Arts; he failed to turn up for many of those that he left on the timetable, being busy with drinks in the Faculty Canteen, or dickering with a gallery in London, or chasing a girl from a supermarket checkout.

Ailie was therefore astonished and flattered.

Dotted about the college were scores of small rooms of awkward shape, bitterly cold in the winter and suffocating, as on that occasion, in midsummer. Their proportions and position were due to the incompetent design of the buildings: they had no windows or huge windows; to enter one of them was to be downhearted. They were called 'Seminar Rooms', and indeed small groups sometimes miserably squatted in them, on folding chairs, to discuss one another's paintings under the chairmanship of a member of the staff.

Also the rooms were used for tutorials.

Into one of the rooms, Kenneth Yorke led Ailie Huxtable. She followed, innocently, proudly. She was carrying a home-made portfolio (hardboard and strips of canvas) with recent drawings. Kenneth Yorke shut the door behind them, and to Ailie's surprise put a chair against it.

Nobody had told her about him. Nobody had told her what they said about herself. She was not plugged into the whispering and sniggering of the queue in the cafeteria. She had no idea what was going on.

She had no idea about anything. Her parents had told her nothing. They did not know anything. Her friends had told her nothing. She did not have any friends.

She was utterly unprepared for the sudden embrace, the slobbery gin-flavoured attempts at kisses. She gave a little scream, and struggled like a trout, and twisted clear. He had a handful of her T-shirt. She ducked round to the far side of the plastic table, the narrow grey metal-edged institutional table on which students sometimes spread their work: she put a yard of solid table between herself and his blubbery face, but still he had a handful of her T-shirt.

He crowed, and pulled at her T-shirt.

He said, 'Don't be a silly little bitch, sweet little girlie, why do you think you got a prize for your painting?'

Ailie was unable with her slim little fingers to free her shirt from his hand, a big blue sweating hand with black hairs across the backs of the fingers.

He yanked at the shirt, intending to pull her towards him across the table-top. But his tugging had the effect of pulling her shirt off. He nearly pulled it over her head. She saw that the only way to get out of this situation was to get out of her shirt. She wriggled out of her T-shirt, leaving it in his grasp, and pulled the chair away from the door, and slipped out of the room in her little teenager's bra, which she scarcely needed.

She had never let go of her portfolio. She held the portfolio in front of her, hiding behind it, as she scampered away along the corridors.

Of course she was seen, scudding along behind the portfolio, as though she were a skiff and it a sail: it was seen that she was practically naked to the waist, and that she came out of a room where Mr Kenneth Yorke was sitting on the floor, having fallen over a chair, clutching a dishrag or some such.

So what's new?

It was impossible thereafter to believe – for even the most charitable to believe – that Ailie's painting had won its prize on merit.

So she was fair game for all those irresistible guys in Ceramics and Package Design.

It was lucky it was the end of term.

It was the eve of the big annual do, the public open day, the party at which the College tried to impress its neighbours and justify itself to its patrons: the end-of-year exhibition of student work, with the very best displayed in the Browning Gallery.

Ailie had to go, of course. It occurred to her that she ought to dress up. But she had nothing to dress up in. She was to be available to answer questions about her work, about her theories and aspirations, her motives and hopes and dreams. That was what they said she must be available for. She thought they must be mad. She had no theories, and her dream was having enough to eat and some nice clothes and going to Paris.

She crept into the College on the evening that the exhibition opened, the evening of the party. She crept into the Browning Gallery, and to the area where her picture was hung, one of only three by students of her year.

Kenneth Yorke more or less said that she won the prize because he fancied her, because he wanted to kiss her and so forth.

Some of those boys had wanted to kiss her, and do those other things they said they did, the things they did right on the TV screen in the documentary about Van Gogh, which Ailie saw at the College (there was no TV at home). It had not happened between any of those boys and Ailie. That was because the boys were too clumsy and smelly, and also too cocksure and brash and macho.

Of course they thought, and loudly said, that it was prudery, unawakened virginal ignorance. It was true that Ailie was unawakened, but not out of prudery. She had no view about the moral aspect. She had been brought up a rebel, agnostic and amoral. What she took a view about was those particular boys. They were smelly yobs. She was fastidious. She was choosy, and she did not choose her fellow-students, or Mr Kenneth Yorke.

She was painfully shy. She was ill-dressed. She was scrubbed clean. She had never owned any make-up, or ever used any. She was undernourished. She had been proud that her painting won the prize, but now she wondered if she had any right to be proud.

She thought it was a good painting. It had surprised her, developing and improving under her hands. She did not quite know what she had done, but she was sure it was the best thing she had done. The other tutors must have seen it, too, seen it and judged it, not just Mr Kenneth Yorke. He was only one member of a committee of half a dozen. Anyway, what he said when he was drunk might not have been true. He was just trying to make her feel grateful. It could be like that. Nobody else would believe it, but perhaps her painting had been given the prize on merit.

At any rate, she had to pretend that she thought so. They all had to pretend they thought so.

They had to pretend to one another, and to the guests and civic bigwigs and benefactors. They had to pretend to this incredibly smooth man with incredibly smooth hair, a face she had sometimes seen in the corridors, Mr Bruno Browning.

When he came up and spoke to her, she wished with passionate violence that she had something proper to wear. Probably Mr Bruno Browning never spoke to anybody dressed as miserably as she was. Certainly she never spoke to anybody who was dressed as glossily as he was. She was so overwhelmed by the contrast between his style of clothes and her style of clothes that she scarcely heard what he was saying.

He seemed to be kind.

He had an educated, cultivated voice, like her parents, like herself, unlike almost anybody else in the college.

There was somebody else looking at Ailie's painting, a big young woman, not so very young, but certainly very big. She was not so much dressed as upholstered, like a big sofa. She was handsome in a way that was too strong, too bossy and masculine. Her hair and lipstick and ear-rings were all quite wrong. Her appearance was pretty awful, and she looked as though her personality was pretty awful. She looked like the Head Prefect of the kind of school which Ailie had only read about, in stories from the library.

She talked to Ailie, as well. She did not seem to enjoy doing so, as Mr Bruno Browning pretended he did. He had really good manners. The woman thought she was doing her duty. She was like a guardsman, and she was doing her duty like a guardsman. Ailie hated being talked at by this terrible female.

The woman wanted Ailie to put her ideas about the painting into words. She did not know how to do that. She did not want to try. She thought a painting ought to speak for itself, without any need for explanation in words.

To Ailie's astonishment, the glossy Mr Bruno Browning began explaining to the female guardsman. He said that it was derived from nature, from a particular scene, but was not an imitation of that scene. It was a painting made out of what she saw and felt about that scene, not an attempt to be a photograph. He said all that, and it was exactly true. He said that a really good painting could be painted by no one else except the person who painted it, and probably at no other time than that when he or she did it. That was exactly right. Ailie's painting was good for exactly that reason, that it was not quite what anybody else would have done, not quite what she herself would have done the day before or the day after, when she was feeling different and the sunlight was a bit different.

Some of the other things that Mr Bruno Browning went on to say about the painting were pretty good rubbish, Ailie thought. She had been exposed to a lot of pretentious art talk, for example from her father, and this was some of it. A lot of what he said she did not understand, although she nodded her head as though she did.

The female dragoon was listening intently, taking it all in, but it was impossible for Ailie to guess if she understood it, either.

Mr Browning and Miss Lee (maybe she spelled it like that; perhaps not) began talking about some pictures she had. It seemed to Ailie that she was asking for a free valuation from an expert: it was like somebody meeting a doctor at a party and wanting a free consultation.

She was going to pay for his expert opinion with a drink. How much would be that, in money? Ailie had never bought a drink, or seen one bought anywhere except in the college beer-bar, and that only at a distance.

Ailie suddenly giggled. Miss Lee (or whatever) was surprised. What amused Ailie was the idea of herself being part of a three-way conversation with these two creatures from another planet.

From two quite different planets, both illimitably outside the range of the telescopes on her own world.

The way they were all dressed! They must be a bloody funny sight together, like a painting of a brothel by Botero.

Mr Browning saw her giggling as well, so he wiped the smile off her face by offering to buy her painting.

For £200.

Ailie was thunderstruck. She was what they called gobsmacked. She made some kind of small rabbity noise, which was not what she would have wished. She was incredulous. This could not be happening.

She did not want to sell the painting. She would do so. She had to. It would be madness not to.

He told her to leave a note in the college office. He said

he might even pay a bit more than £200.

He said he had to leave, to go away with his cousin. Ailie identified the cousin. He was a strange cousin for Mr Browning to have – a solid, stolid, peasant sort of man, a farmer or a builder in his best clothes, not interesting in any way.

Miss Lee was interesting in one way, which was that she had sort of got off with Mr Bruno Browning. He was going to have a drink with her, at her house, and look at the pictures she had inherited. He was more interested in her than he was in her pictures. That was a triumph, really. Ailie wondered how she had done it, what made her interesting enough for Mr Browning to bother.

Ailie was sort of jealous of Miss Lee, in an odd way.

She pictured Mr Browning coming to her own home, her parents' half-converted chicken-house. The idea was so ludicrous that she giggled again, secretly, into the colourless curtain of her hair.

Ailie wondered whether to open a bank account with the money. It was not a thing which she knew how to do. She walked past a bank in Milchester, and peeped in at the hushed efficiency, the brisk girls in spectacles, the men with brief-cases. It was a foreign and frightening world, of which she had no experience at all. She was afraid to dive into it, to make a fool of herself, to be cheated and derided. They would sneer, and then give her a bill that used up all her money.

Her parents would eat up all her money. If she let them so much as sniff it, guess its existence, it would simply melt. There would be nothing to show for it. There would be no new garment or gala meal, saucepan, rug, bicycle, anything. It would blow away, like the ash of a burning newspaper on a windy day.

She said the prize-winning painting was hanging in the college office, or would be one day, when framed.

She did not ask her parents' advice about her money, or about anything else, because she knew that their advice would be worse than no advice.

That summer vacation, she got a drab little part-time job in the café of a garden centre. There was immediately a row about her shoes. They said she must wear proper shoes. She had no proper shoes, and she could not afford them until she got her first pay-packet, and then they would have to be very cheap shoes.

She would not nibble into her £200 for things like shoes.

She weathered the row, but the manageress was after her from that time on, because she had been pert and rebellious. It was a beastly job, boring and exhausting and humiliating. The lads in the kitchen were bullies, and so were the sour middle-aged waitresses. She had to wear a grotty green overall and a striped cap. It was the only job she could get. She was lucky to have it. It paid very badly. They kept back her tax, as though she worked full time and all the year round. She foresaw an awful hassle, getting a repayment out of the taxman. She never saw her share of the tips.

She spent some of her wages on food, and gave the rest to her mother. Sarah lost it or caused it to melt, to blow away like the ashes of a burning newspaper.

In the time that she had, she painted. It was more difficult to do it at home than at college, because there she did have a space, although it was a very little space, and she was surrounded by Them. She could not use her prize money to buy materials, because it took the form of vouchers on the college shop, and the shop was shut in the vacation. She had to buy some paints, some linseed oil and white spirit and some fine brushes. She could scrounge surfaces to paint on, hardboard and cardboard and pieces of wood, but not materials to paint with. They were expensive.

To buy the things she needed, she withdrew £30 from her Post Office savings.

Adrian never noticed anything, since he was not interested in other people, but he could smell the spending of money. He detected that Ailie had come by more tubes of oil paint, and a new big jar of oil and a plastic flask of white spirit.

She said the money had come out of her wages at the garden centre. She did not much like lying to her father, but it had always been impossible to live without doing so.

'That money ought to go to your mother,' said Adrian. 'You ought to give her more of what they give you. You ought to contribute more than you do.'

'I already contribute more than you ever have in your life,' said Ailie, stung, exhausted by her day's work, speaking as she seldom spoke.

Adrian went into a sulk, because he was unable to contemplate the possibility that he was inadequate in any way. The victim of his sulk was not Ailie but Sarah her mother, victim of everything about Adrian, though really just as hopeless herself. Ailie felt guilty, because her flash of useless truth-telling had the effect – the solitary effect – of discomfort for Sarah.

But after a few days, Ailie became the victim too, when Adrian started nagging her about the money she was or was not giving Sarah.

When Adrian got hold of an idea, or an idea got hold of Adrian, he went on and on about it until everything around him wilted from boredom and exhaustion. The idea that obsessed him, that July and August, was that Ailie was selfishly, irresponsibly, spending her earnings on luxurious and needless paints, when she ought to have been helping her mother with the housekeeping expenses.

No logic could touch this obsession. No argument shook it. That Adrian had never contributed – that Ailie's earnings were tiny – that an art student had to have paints . . .

Sarah sometimes looked at Ailie with a mute and anguished appeal. She never said anything that could be construed as disloyalty to Adrian. She did not herself nag Ailie. She just wanted the noise to stop.

Ailie burst out, one evening of interminable whining, 'If you must know, I sold a painting.'

'Impossible,' said Adrian.

'It's true.'

'To whom?'

A sudden instinct of self-preservation, much needed in her life, made Ailie say, 'One of the governors of the college. I don't know his name.'

'How could you not know his name?'

'I did. I've forgotten it.'

The same careful instinct made her say, 'He paid me £50, on condition I spent the money on painting materials.'

'What a grotesque condition,' said Adrian. 'What an offensive liberty, to attach strings in such a fashion, what a pompous and patronising way to go about things.'

'It's his money,' said Ailie. 'At least, it was.'

'He bought one of your paintings. Have we been allowed to see this painting? Are we deemed worthy to cast an eye over it?'

One source of grudge had been removed, that of the division of Ailie's pay-packet, but at awful cost. Hydra-

188

headed, the grudge spawned a forest of new grudges. There was Ailie's secretiveness. Then there was her stupidity, in forgetting the name of her patron. Then there was the intolerable arrogance of the purchaser, making conditions as to how the money should be spent. Then there was the suspicion that anybody who made money in any way was somehow certain to be cheating.

Ailie lost her job at the garden centre, owing to losing her temper with the manageress of the café. Adrian was bitter about that. He talked about it at great length.

The rest of the vacation, the whole of September, passed in a miserable atmosphere. It was a relief when the term began at the beginning of October; at least, it would have been a relief, but the boys renewed their slobbery gropings, and the girls were sniffy and envious and bitchy, and Mr Kenneth Yorke was coldly indifferent because she had sort of humiliated him; and Ailie found it very difficult to keep up any self-confidence, to do any work that really expressed herself, so she sunk further into the shadows at the college, in the life class and the seminar rooms and the cafeteria, and nothing she did was much looked at, and nothing she said was listened to.

During the terms that followed, Ailie occasionally saw Mr Bruno Browning, glossy and cosmopolitan among the scruffy professors, his cultured, precise, slightly affected voice drifting like incense down a corridor as he paused, in the company of the Principal or some other recipient of his patronage, to give a metropolitan comment on some piece of provincial work. He was awfully exotic.

To the students, Bruno Browning was a bit of a joke. He was a posturing pansy, overdressed, pretentious and too rich and talking about painting because he couldn't do it.

Ailie boiled silently – silently because she did not dare to stick her neck out: boiled because those students were ignorant and ill-judging – they were largely wrong although, annoyingly enough, they were a little bit right.

Because, well, yes, he was pretentious and affected, Ailie could see that. Anybody who knew her father Adrian knew all about pretentiousness. But Bruno Browning was kind, truly benevolent; and he did actually care about art. There was no way the students could know this, but Ailie knew it.

Ailie knew that she knew what she knew, unlike her fellow-students, who knew nothing at all about what they thought they knew. Ailie knew she was not a fool, although her ignorance and shyness and lack of worldly experience might make her seem stupid. She was not a fool and she was not insensitive. She could see and feel other people, and understand them. All her life she had had to do so, in order to stay sane. She had to understand her maddening and impossible parents. She did understand them, and kind of loved them, but they remained maddening and impossible. Because she was clear-sighted about her own family, she was clear-sighted about other people. She was dispassionate and a bit merciless, about her family and her fellow-students and Mr Kenneth Yorke, about anybody she had had a chance to get to know at all.

She had had a chance to get to know Mr Bruno Browning. She thought that he was on the side of the angels.

She wished she could have made a better impression. She thought she must have struck him as a moron, a ninny, a very stupid little girl. She had acted like that, rude and silent and gauche. She did not know how else to act.

Well, what the bloody hell did anybody expect, the life she had led?

She blamed everybody but herself for the way she was, until she came to the conclusion that she had nobody but herself to blame. She had allowed herself to be trodden and compressed into the miniperson that she was. She must simply expand into a different sort of person. Other people had done it. Artists, writers, actresses, politicians. Many of them had had to change themselves fundamentally – change their way of talking, for instance, like Maggie Thatcher. Ailie did not have to do that. She started with advantages.

She what?

Until she got away, right away, she was screwed into this little bottle she occupied. She was screwed into genteel poverty, into being the scrubby little art student on the fringe whom nobody would ever pay any attention to.

(Although she won the prize. Why did she win the prize? They all thought they knew why she won the prize. Instead of being respected, she was despised for winning the prize.)

Sometimes in the middle of the day Ailie despised herself for being so sorry for herself. But always in the middle of the night she was just sorry for herself.

Her second year should have been better than her first year, because she won the prize. It was worse, partly because she won the prize. Her third year should have been better still, but it was worse still, because she clearly faced, that spring, the prospect of failing to get a degree. Lack of confidence, lack of guidance, lack of materials, lack of anywhere to work at home undisturbed, lack of friends and of peer-group encouragement . . .

On the credit side?

She had thought she had some talent, but twenty months of discouragement made her doubt if she had any.

The boys made passes at her. Did that mean she had sex appeal? Was it a good thing to have? Did she want it? She thought the passes meant that the boys were yobs who took her 'Yes' for granted, spoiled macho bullies who thought all doors and legs were open. Did having sex appeal mean you were for ever exposed to that kind of mindless exploitation?

Had she actually got any of this thing the magazine talked about?

She examined herself dubiously, in the nearest her parents had to a full-length looking-glass.

She was not much like Elizabeth Taylor, or Jerry Hall, or Raquel Welch. She had seen pictures of somebody called Twiggy, apparently a star in the sixties. She was a bit like Twiggy, perhaps.

Whatever she had, it made those oafish boys think they owned her. To them, she had the quality not of a person but a slave-girl. That was intolerable. It was one of the worst things about her life, being a waif that everybody thought would be grateful for a smile. The thing to be was the opposite sort of girl, a big powerful girl – somebody like Miss Lee (was that how she spelt it?). Nobody would think they owned her. That would be a comfortable way to be, though not very pretty.

The way Ailie was was the worst way to be, and it got even worse still when Sarah came to her weeping and asking for money.

It was terrible to be wept at by your mother asking for money. It was shattering. Ailie was filled with guilt at not having given Sarah all the money from the sale of the painting. She was filled with rage that Sarah was so footling, so improvident and hopeless.

Ailie gave her mother £75, to pay the electricity bill. After the money she had spent on paint and such, over eighteen months, that left just £30 of her £200.

She was just as bad as they were. That noble, gigantic sum had flaked away in featherweight ashes, like a burning newspaper in a high wind.

What in God's name could she do, with £30?

What in God's name could she do with the rest of her life?

'A. Huxtable? That's you, isn't it?'

'Yes.'

'Letter for you. Been here for a bit. You have to come and collect your mail, you know. You can't expect us to run around after you like page-boys.'

'I'm sorry.'

'French, eh?' said the secretary, looking at the envelope. 'Got a boyfriend in France, have you? Good luck to you. Can't stand the place myself.'

The crowd in the cafeteria pricked up its ears. Little Hux had a letter from France, ooh la la, nudge nudge.

Ailie looked at the envelope incredulously.

Ms A. Huxtable, c/o Milchester College of Art and Design.

A French stamp sure enough; the postmark illegible.

The paper of the envelope was far heavier and more expensive than that of any letter Ailie had ever received. She had received very few letters in her life.

A gangling, lank-haired boy in sawn-off jeans twitched the envelope out of Ailie's hands as she was about to slit it open with a tin cafeteria knife.

'Give that back,' screamed Ailie.

'Give thaaat baaack,' said the boy, in crude imitation of her accent.

There was a general jeer of unthinking laughter.

Ailie tried to grab the letter out of the boy's hands. He

held it above his head, far out of her reach. He laughed. This was fun. The others laughed, a ring of boys and girls baying with heedless laughter.

Ailie lost her temper. She hit and scratched at the tall boy. He laughed louder, effortlessly pushing her away with one hand while holding up the letter with the other. The rest laughed. It was funny, to see little toffee-nose losing her cool.

The tall boy passed the letter to another. Ailie attacked the new holder of the letter, with fists and fingernails. She was beside herself. She was screaming. They all laughed. The boy passed the letter on. They passed it from hand to hand, baiting her, laughing as she sobbed with rage and frustration, in the dingy concrete cafeteria, among the plastic tables.

One of the boys dropped the letter. It fell among the cigarette butts on the concrete floor. Ailie dived to get it. The boy put his foot on it. He put a great black military boot on the letter on the dirty floor. She screamed at him.

'Say please,' he crowed, as she crouched on the floor by her letter.

She bit him suddenly, as hard as she could, in the fleshy part of the thigh above the knee. He yelped and recoiled. She picked up the letter.

She said to them all, 'You bloody swine.'

They fell back a little, silent.

There and then she slit open the envelope and read the letter.

Elinor Leigh. Not Lee. Big lady.

We want a mural. Who's we? La Moquerie. Where's that?

Mural. Good God.

Live free, in a French château. Be paid on top of that.

Strong and colourful, otherwise no limitations. Thirty foot by thirteen.

Photographs? Colour prints? transparencies? She had never been able to afford any of those. She had never thought her work important enough to photograph.

Her degree? Probably she was not going to get a degree anyway.

Write, enclosing photographs she didn't have, and then wait maybe months for a reply that might never come, that the stupid office here would probably lose . . .

Ailie looked round the dreadfully familiar peeling posters for amateur rock concerts and Animal Liberation rallies, and at the gritty concrete walls and at the faces of her fellow-students. She suddenly knew what she would do, and what her £30 was for.

You could read the letter upwards, downwards, sideways, backwards – study it from every angle, read between the lines or between the words. It still did not add up to an actual invitation to the place. Such a thing might come later, but it had not come yet.

'Send transparencies, write letter.'

Instead of doing those things, Ailie went to the main Post Office in Milchester, and drew out all the poor rest of her savings. She also bought a temporary passport. Apparently you no longer needed one to go to France, but she felt safer and more adult with a passport, and she might find herself going to other places.

Miss Elinor Leigh was a remembered dragon, but she said she liked Ailie's painting. Mr Bruno Browning bought that. It was his money Ailie was taking out of the Post Office. Was it his house, the château Elinor Leigh was writing from?

Ailie asked in the college office. They were surprised by

her curiosity, her cheek. They said yes, Mr Browning did
have an address for urgent mail in France, he was there part
of the time, never mind who he was there with, he was a
busy and important man and he was not to be bothered by
students.

It was his house. It was Bruno Browning who was really
asking her to France. He was kind and he cared about art
and he had bought her painting, and he had even explained
her painting to herself.

'I'm going away for a bit.'

'Impossible,' said Adrian, to whom all things were
impossible.

'You ran away from school. You're always boasting about
it.'

'Hush,' said Sarah.

'I've been offered a job,' said Ailie.

'Impossible,' said Adrian.

'I thought I'd better tell you, in case you wondered where
I was.'

The extraordinary thing was, that they simply refused to
believe her. The more exactly she told the truth (the truth
as she had rewritten it) the more they thought she was
raving. They did not believe that she would strike out on her
own to a far country, since neither of them had struck out
any further than Milchester. They did not believe that
anybody was interested in her, since nobody had ever been
interested in them. They refused to be shocked, impressed,
or sad. Ailie regretted mentioning the matter. It would have
been better just to go, but she was not ruthless enough to do
that.

She bought a sweater and an anorak at the Oxfam shop.
She bought a rucksack for a pound from a girl at the college,

who had bought a new backpack for many, many pounds. She knew roughly what clothes she would want, and she had none of them, so she would have to make do with what she had, which were shabby and childish. She packed a sketchpad and pencils, socks, pants, toothbrush. She put on her boots, and hitched in a cattle-truck to Portsmouth.

The ferry used up most of the rest of her money. She was seasick, which was to be expected, and homesick, which was not.

When she stepped ashore on French soil, she was committed, because she had no money for a return ticket.

CHAPTER NINE

D AY FOLLOWED DAY that lovely spring in the valley of the Tarn, and no word came from A. Huxtable at the art college.

It was probably just as well.

There was no point in following it up.

If one letter failed to arrive, another letter would fail to arrive. If one arrived and got no answer, so would another.

Bruno would be in Milchester, off and on, in the coming months, but Elinor was not going to burden the poor dear with hunting out a furtive or unwilling student, even though she had done one nice painting.

To Bruno, Elinor said, 'I did have an idea about that mural, but nothing came of it.'

'Have another idea.'

'Yes, and you have one.'

'Oh no. You're not dragging me into this.'

Other things claimed their attention: the garden, and a stream of visitors, who came to the Tarn in the spring like songbirds to England.

'I must confer with my cousin Fred,' said Bruno two days later.

'Confer on the telephone. That's what it's for.'

'We must put our little heads together, over some pieces

of paper. We must scrutinise diagrams. Plans. Architect's drawings. I would leave it all to him, but he refuses to be left. He requires my opinion. It's flattering, really.'

'You can't go to Milchester now. You've got the people coming about the terracing, and the people coming about the drains . . .'

'I know, it's the worst possible moment. So I've asked Fred here. He hasn't been here for two years. He rather loves it, I think. Not that you can tell, with Fred. He doesn't wear his heart on his sleeve. As a matter of fact, he doesn't often wear a sleeve.'

'He's coming here?'

'Will you be nice to him?'

'Yes, of course, but he won't be nice to me.'

'There does seem to be a failure of sympathy between you. I can't think why. I love you both. Why can't you be tidy-minded about it, and love one another, as commanded in the book?'

'Your cousin Fred thinks I'm ghastly. He's wrong, as we all know, but he's absolutely entitled to his opinion. I suppose I have to allow that he's entitled to his stupid opinion. I think I'll go away for a bit. When is Fred coming?'

'The second week of April.'

'Just the time I should like to be in Venice.'

'All by yourself?'

'Probably not. I'll recruit a girlfriend. Ortensia or Louise or Marie-Claire. One of my mates who'll come and look at the pictures with me.'

'I don't want you to feel I'm throwing you out.'

'It's time I went to Venice again. I've only been once. I want to have lunch on Torcello.'

'Yes, that's a good thing to do.'

Ailie spoke a little schoolgirl French, learned not at school but from Adrian and Sarah. She was immediately obliged to use it. She had to speak French, as best she could, because the level where she found herself the people did not know other languages.

She rapidly picked up the phrases needed for hitching lifts in lorries, for admitting that she was hungry, for saying that she was not a tart.

She got very dirty, which she hated. She crept into a motel outside Bayeux, and found a bathroom, but a maid found her before she got into the bath, and she was thrown out. Her feet began to feel too big for her shoes, her T-shirt too big for her shoulders.

She had to jump out of a van, in Alençon, at traffic lights, because the driver was too busy with his free hand, expecting to be paid for the lift.

She got scraps from the back doors of restaurants, late at night, competing with cats.

It was nothing like as bad for her as it would have been for most girls, because she had been scavenging and begging and surviving on other people's crumbs all her life.

She lost weight, although it might have been supposed that she had none to lose. She thought that her feet and face and hair would never be clean again.

She zigzagged southwards, trying to hurry but unable to do so, living from minute to minute and from mile to mile. Sometimes there were road-maps at a bus-station, or outside a *Syndicat d'initiative*. She could not afford to take a bus, but she could look at the maps, and see how far she had to go, and in what direction.

She slept on roadsides and in railway stations, ignoring the usual differences between night and day.

She sometimes wondered what the hell she thought she was doing, begging and stealing and creeping her way across a large, indifferent foreign country.

It seemed to grow larger and larger, but it was daily less foreign.

Sharp necessity accelerated her learning of the language. Some of the French she picked up was not elegant, but it produced sausages and wedges of cheese, and sometimes cups of coffee and glasses of beer; it got her lifts which took her east and west and gradually south.

In Blois she did a drawing of old men fishing from the bridge over the Loire. She sold it to a middle-aged Belgian couple, who had parked their car and were strolling. She had not meant to go as far east as Blois, but a busy little salesman's busy little Renault took her there, and she was very happy that it did. She sold the drawing for two hundred francs, which bought her the best dinner she had ever had in her life.

Getting the message, she did another drawing, more careful and elaborate, from the same bridge in Blois. She sketched in her mind the bath and the night between sheets that it would buy. She left her pad on the parapet of the bridge, to stretch her cramped legs for a minute. The picture, water-colour over pencil, was almost finished. She knew that it was good, in a traditional and saleable way. She was almost ashamed of doing so conventional, so old-fashioned an English water-colour, but she was being a professional, doing it for her bread. She was a few yards away from it when a young schoolboy darted up and took the pad, with the picture, and ran twinkling away like a rat into the lunchtime crowd in the Place de la Résistance.

That was when she cried. It was the only time.

She was hungry again, in spite of the dinner she had

eaten, because of the work she had put into the picture.

She crossed the river, and tried to get a lift towards Amboise.

Fred came a day before they expected him. It was a misunderstanding, the fault of a secretary in the office in Milchester.

It made Bruno anxious, because his two favourite people were really best kept apart. It saddened him, but it was so. They simply did not see the point of one another, and obviously never would.

Bruno's life had always been lived in two watertight compartments, even as a schoolboy at the Milchester Grammar. What Elinor and Fred did was to personify the compartments, to dramatise them, and remind him how watertight they were.

In these two worlds, different languages were spoken, with different accents and vocabularies, treating of different subjects. Bruno himself had both voices, both accents, both vocabularies, and he spoke of both sets of topics, one in each language. He was cut in half, as Berlin had been.

Dinner at la Moquerie was fraught, that Thursday night. It was sadly evident to Bruno that each of the others wished the other was not there. Elinor thought Fred a rude mechanical, Fred thought Elinor a pretentious hag. They were both wrong, but there was a tiny fragment of truth in both opinions.

'Why did Elinor never marry?' Fred asked Bruno, over nightcaps, after Elinor had gone to bed.

'She was kept at home as a slave until it was too late, or she thought it was.'

'Ah. Pity, I suppose. Bit of a waste.'

'Don't you go taking her away from me.'

'Christ Almighty, I'd rather take a diesel locomotive, a thirty-ton truck, a bloody dragon.'

'Why did Fred never marry?' Elinor asked Bruno in the dawn, when she was getting ready to drive to the airport for an early flight.

'He did. She was a nurse. They were too young. She pushed off.'

'Why?'

'She said it was the smell of oil.'

'You mean hair oil? Like your Trumper's?'

'Lubricating oil.'

'You've got no heirs between you. It's a shame there's no one to inherit the business, after all you've done, all both your fathers did.'

'I expect between us we'll find people to hand it on to,' said Bruno. 'I expect when we make our wills, we'll think of some names of people we care about.'

Bruno did not give these words any unusual weight, nor look with unusual meaning at Elinor when he spoke. But she understood, and she knew that he intended her to understand.

'You said you were going to give it to me to play with,' said Fred to Bruno in the Oriel Room of the Guardhouse. 'I was rather looking forward to that.'

'You missed the bus,' said Bruno. 'I couldn't wait for ever. It probably would have been twenty years before you got round to it.'

'I wouldn't have done it as well as you have,' said Fred. 'It's just as well I was too busy. I think this is really good.'

'I agree, but it's no thanks to me.'

'Balls.'

'No no. I did none of this.'

'Who did?'

'Elinor.'

'I don't believe you.'

'I assure you. She took every decision here, with such professional advice as she chose to call on. This fantastic colour, for example. That window. These chairs. I blenched when I saw them. I am innocent of any hand in any of it.'

'That lamp is yours,' said Fred. 'I recognise that lamp.'

'It was mine,' said Bruno. 'I've given it to Elinor, to go in this room, to be the jewel in its crown, in her crown.'

'Looks well here.'

'Doesn't it, indeed. Looks well, looks happy, if that isn't intolerably whimsical.'

Fred thought it a shame that Bruno had given away his beloved lamp; but it crossed his mind, looking round the Guardhouse, that Elinor had earned it.

Elinor expected Fred to be gone, when she got back from Venice. But he had stayed on an extra two days, owing to a fresh sheaf of plans having been faxed to la Moquerie for discussion by Bruno and himself.

It was slightly inconvenient, because the château and the Guardhouse were both going to be full, for a festive long weekend coinciding with Elinor's return. With some shuffling, room could be made for Fred among the glittering arrivals: and it would have been madness for him to have gone away, all the way back to Milchester, only to return a day or two later for the discussions they had to have.

'Oh yes,' said Elinor. 'I see the logic. Of course he had to stay. But I don't think he'll enjoy the party, will he?'

'He can sit in a corner with a drink,' said Bruno. 'Or take himself off to bed.'

As Bruno predicted, Fred sat in a corner, nursing a long weak whisky for several hours. He was neither amused nor amusing. But he did not go to bed. Elinor had the sense that he was watching her, maybe with suspicion, maybe with venom, maybe not with these things. She was made uneasy.

They played after dinner the game in which you perform an action 'in the manner of the word', a game the correct name of which no one could remember. The adverbs which people acted were in English and French and Italian. It was a very knowing party, everybody being clever in three or more languages. Fred could scarcely have been enjoying it. But he sat there, and Elinor saw that it was true that he was looking at her – she was not making this up. But she was laughing and enjoying herself, and showing off and flirting, and looking stunning and aware that she was doing so, so that she was able to forget Fred and his fixed pale-blue stare.

The yellow headlight of the little three-wheeled vegetable cart skewered the sign on the roadside: la Moquerie.

Ailie could hardly believe it. It was a mirage. It was a different place of the same name. It was a cruel joke played by a cruel God.

She was exhausted and dirty, short of sleep and of food, completely out of money, her boots shredded and her clothes unspeakable. She did not dare to sniff any part of herself that she could approach with her nose.

It had taken her three and a half weeks to zigzag to this wild, empty, midnight place. Those days in retrospect had the quality of film or dream, illogical, episodes not caused by other episodes but jumping up out of the roadside, things happening to someone else, flickering, not in any order, events not defined by time or place, not fixed in geography or the calendar or the clock, dreamlike feasts of incongruous ingredients at the back doors of cafés in the small hours, bumping interminable lifts in the backs of lorries never going in quite the right direction, rain, hair and clothes gradually drying in the sun after rain, uneasy sleep among the feet of travellers on railway platforms, and always the astonished inner voice saying, 'This can't be happening to me.'

The driver of the fruit cart looked like Yasser Arafat, thick-lipped and stubble-chinned. He had a half-smoked but unlit cigarette in his mouth, which he seemed to have forgotten about. He was absolutely silent for the thirty-five minutes Ailie sat beside him.

He said he knew where la Moquerie was, but he did not know who lived there, or if anybody did, or if anybody was there now. He had never seen the house, but only the sign by the road. That he was sure of, because he had once had a puncture there. He was going that way. Mademoiselle could come. No problem. That was all he said. Thereafter he was completely silent. Ailie was sorry, because she had got in the way of talking to the people she met. She practised her French. She was learning all the time, and also it was more fun. She became more confident and outgoing when she spoke French. She was a different sort of person. This was most odd, but she noticed it about herself. She had always had strong views – too strong – but for the first time she was expressing them, more and more so as she learned more words.

She had need of very few words this time. She climbed down from the machine. Its engine, ticking over, sounded like an old motor mower. Ailie pulled her bundle of clothes from the back of the cart. She had almost no surviving clothes. They had not been sturdy when she started – none of them had been bought new – and now most of them were rags in litterbins in various departments of France. Her rucksack had perished, and also her Oxfam anorak.

She shook hands with her chauffeur. She thanked him, in clear accurate French. He nodded; his cigarette twitched. He let in his clutch, and banged away into the night behind his single yellow headlight.

It was now completely dark. It was darker than dark, because she had been seeing by the light of the headlamp. But Ailie had become used to dark roadsides. Even on moonless and starless nights they were not quite dark. Only inside four walls were you totally unsighted. Presently she would get a sort of idea of what was around her, where the road went that led to the château.

Her vision was a long time coming, and when it came there was very little of it.

She began to pick her way along a road that was not much of a road, between banks that were hardly banks. She had a sense of boulders beyond, but she did not know why she thought they were there, as she could not see them. She was not certain that what she was on was a road, not certain that she had not left it, even if it was a road, not certain at all if it led anywhere, if the sign saying 'la Moquerie' meant that this was a road to la Moquerie.

It was too early in the year for the noise of insects, too late in the night for the sound of birds. Ailie's ruined boots scuffled over the broken surface of the drive, and some-times her breath whistled loudly out of her nose; the noise of her boots and the noise of her breath were the only sounds in the world.

She was completely alone in a silent, desert upland, where there was no light or sound or any form of life. She was exhausted and hungry and filthy and penniless.

She felt quite content and confident. She astonished herself by how positive she felt. There was something at the end of this drive. If not, not. Really she was past caring.

She stepped out with greater confidence, feeling less need to explore every step before she took it. The drive was evidently a drive, and its edges edges. And she saw a glow of light ahead. If she stared at the light, it disappeared. If she looked away, she could almost convince herself it was there. Intent on deciding if there was really a light ahead, more confident of her footing, she tripped over a stone and fell heavily on the broken gravelly surface of the drive.

She hurt her knees and breast and elbows and hands. She lay shocked for a moment, stretched out on the ground. It was entirely her own fault.

She said, '*Merde*,' very loudly into the darkness, at the stones of the drive, at her own clumsiness. It was the word she had been finding most useful in the whole vocabulary of French.

She picked herself up slowly, painfully. She was stiff and sore. She thought her knees were bleeding, her elbows and hands also, perhaps. Her trousers were torn, those parts of them not already torn.

None of that mattered the slightest bit.

She limped on through the thick darkness, towards a glow of light which was now undoubtedly light, a glow somehow below the level of the ground, a subterranean campfire.

It began to drizzle. The rain was invisible, but she could feel it on her face and neck and on her shoulder where her shirt was torn.

The drive sloped downwards. She had a sense of going between an enormous pair of stone gateposts. The light ahead defined itself as she turned a corner above it. It divided itself into oblongs, many windows of various sizes on many levels, over a wide area.

It was an awfully big house. They had an awful lot of lights on inside it.

Ailie was aware of going downhill through the drizzle, amongst gardens, terraces, running water. This was suddenly a lush and pampered place. It smelled of care, husbandry, expense. Ailie's way was lit now not from the sky but by the dozens of golden oblongs ahead.

Would there be guard-dogs, electric fences, searchlights, guns?

Ailie thought she was not important enough to be savaged by a Rottweiler, but the dog might not know that.

There was no dog, but the drizzle turned into steady, saturating rain just in those last three hundred yards. It blurred the oblongs of the windows, and lowered the temperature of the air by several degrees. It sharply lowered the temperature of Ailie's head.

She thought the rain might make her a bit cleaner.

An English wine merchant had just correctly guessed his adverb. The others, at his command, had been pouring drinks or tying shoelaces in the manner of the word, which was *istrionicalmente*. An elderly female French harpsichordist had histrionically straightened a picture, and so forth. It was rather an easy word.

Elinor was sent out. Somebody had a witty idea. From the landing outside the salon she heard the laughter. She heard the rain becoming heavy against the windows of the landing; she imagined it hissing into the big black river far below.

They called her in. They said her adverb was English. The game started.

To Sandro di Ganzarello, Elinor said, 'Tie your shoelace in the manner of the word.'

Sandro smiled and did nothing. After a moment Mireille de Valangoujard put her tiny foot on a stool and went through the motions of tying a shoelace.

'Ah, fancy stuff,' said Elinor. 'Something like "impersonally" or "indirectly" or "representationally".'

The others smiled. She was already getting warm. She was a clever girl.

To George Napier-Gough, a critic and historian, Elinor said, 'Pour yourself a drink in the manner of the word.'

George smiled and did nothing, except to wave his hands to show he was doing nothing.

Bruno after a moment said, 'Oh, very well, if nobody else wants one.'

Bruno stood up, crossed the room to the table where the drinks were, and poured himself a thin whisky.

'Oh God,' said Elinor. '"Substitutionally". "Otherly". "Alternatively". I know the word I want and I can't grab it. Curse you all.'

She asked other people to perform other more or less ridiculous tasks in the manner of the word. In each case, after a moment, somebody else performed the task.

'Yes, well,' said Elinor, cross with herself. 'Doing it in the manner of the word means having somebody else do it. You are playing by the rules? Yes. You're actually doing what I'm telling you to do, as the rules require. But you're not doing it. Very good. Of course. I completely understand. The word is . . .'

She was laughing. She gestured furiously, still laughing. She knew that it was a perfectly familiar, ordinary word, a word well known to her, which was simply eluding her, as words will.

They all laughed, expecting her to say the word.

Into the midst of the laughter entered Berthe, who grinned largely, involuntarily, owing to coming into a room full of laughter.

Berthe said, '*Madame Elly, une p'tite anglaise, p'tite jeune fille, est arrivée, tout mouillée, fatiguée, gran' faim—*'

'*Jeune fille anglaise?*' repeated Elinor, completely puzzled.

Into the salon behind Berthe came, indeed, a dripping waiflike figure, with a sodden T-shirt glued by the rain to a skinny little body, ribs and small sharp breasts delineated as though sculptured in dirty white stone, pale hair darkened by the rain and plastered to her skull, a small frightened face streaked with dirt.

All the laughter and chattering died. All the glossy people stared in astonished pity at the newcomer.

'I'm so sorry to come bursting in like this,' she said into the silence, 'especially as I imagine I look a tiny bit scruffy.'

Her voice was ludicrously incongruous. It would have been difficult to imagine any voice to fit that miserable, dripping little scarecrow, but nobody would have imagined the voice she had, which was educated, correct, an unmistakable upper-class voice.

She looked round them all, shyly. She said, 'Is Miss Leigh here? Elinor Leigh?'

'I'm Elinor Leigh.'

'No.'

The child looked at Elinor blankly. She was obviously unconvinced. She did not believe that this was Elinor Leigh.

Elinor remembered that she had changed, gigantically, dramatically. She was apt to forget this, because she had become used to looking as she looked: and because she never saw anybody who had known her before she changed.

Who could this be, this frail orphan of the storm who said she wasn't who she was?

A memory stirred. Surely...?

'I am Ailie Huxtable,' said the child. 'I've come about the mural.'

Ailie was aghast.

Everything up until now had been nothing, easy, a piece of cake – crossing France, learning French as she went, hitching lifts, fighting off rapists, stealing food, sleeping on roadsides – that was kid's stuff. This was the frightening bit, dropping unannounced, unexpected, uninvited into a gorgeous castle full of millionaire dukes and haughty duchesses...

Oh my God, said Ailie to herself, what have I got myself into?

The housekeeper or whatever had seemed quite smiley and kind, saying how wet Ailie was (not a difficult comment to make) and trotting along the passage to tell the boss.

The place was evidently full of people. A lot of cars were parked behind, and a lot of lights were on.

There was distant laughter from along the passage. Ailie felt acutely shy. She wanted to stay in the protection of the motherly housekeeper, who would comfort and feed and warm her. She was terrified of the glittering dragons who were breathing satirical and merciless fire at the end of the passage.

Bugger this, said Ailie to herself, I've come all this way, I've been through all those hardships, I can't go any further, this is where I've been headed, this is where I stop, so I'd better tell them that now, and get it over –

They can't turn me out, into this rain. Surely they won't do that?

So she squelched in her ruined boots along the stone-flagged passage, to the brilliant lights and laughter, the silks and goblets of rare wine, the twinkle of jewels, and she tried to put a brave face on it, a little bit brave, not too brave, not impertinent.

That wouldn't do with Elinor Leigh.

Who?

A fabulously beautiful woman, thirtyish, hardly that, breathtaking, marvellously dressed, not dressed much, jewelled, sensational, tall, dark-haired and grey-eyed, with long legs and lovely shoulders and nose and jawline – this magic figure said she was Elinor Leigh.

Oh no. She just wasn't.

We have a calamitous mistake here, two people with the same . . .

But those eyes were familiar, those broad shoulders, long legs.

'I'm sorry, I didn't recognise you,' said Ailie.

'I didn't immediately recognise you,' said Elinor Leigh. 'You were drier when we last met. The mural. Good God. You got my letter. You'd better get dry, before anything else. And dinner? Have you eaten? Have you anything to wear? We can rustle up some clothes, if all your things are wet, anything you need. Then we can get organised—'

'Ailie Huxtable,' said an intensely elegant, rather beautiful old man of about fifty, with a face both hawklike and gentle. 'Good gracious me, what a long way you are from home.'

'Mr Browning,' said Ailie, suddenly very pleased.

'I shall go down in art history as one of your earliest patrons. I expect you remember my cousin Fred? Fred, you remember my friend the landscape painter?'

Ailie did remember Fred, as an amazing cousin for Bruno Browning to have. He still was, fair and beefy like a builder's mate, sitting in a far corner of the big crowded room.

Fred was on the edge of the party. Ailie found herself slap in the middle of it. She was introduced to a dozen beautiful people, who were as friendly as could be. Ailie was offered any of a dozen drinks; she accepted a glass of red wine.

'I came the last bit in a vegetable cart,' said Ailie, answering questions, 'with a man with half a dead cigarette in his mouth. He looked as though he'd go to bed with it, and get up in the morning with it.'

Everybody laughed. Ailie was greatly astonishing herself, holding forth to these people in this place.

'Weren't you frightened all the time?' said a lovely oriental girl.

'Not usually,' said Ailie. 'There's not enough of me for anybody to bother with.'

They all laughed again, gently, kindly. They liked her.

Ailie heard Elinor Leigh asking the housekeeper if there was anything left for Ailie to eat. The housekeeper said there was a great deal of everything.

'Which first, Ailie?' said Elinor Leigh, 'Drink, hot bath, dry clothes, something to eat, would that be a good sequence? Then bed if you're tired, or join us for another drink if you're not exhausted by vegetable carts. Berthe will find you a bed. I can't at the moment think where.'

'Oh God, I'm being such a bore,' said Ailie. 'I've come at the worst moment—'

'Not at all, my dear. What's the point of a house if you can't find room for your friends? Don't worry about anything. Soon all these layabouts will have disappeared, to go and sponge on somebody else, and then we can make you properly comfortable.'

'Thank you very much,' said Ailie.

The others, seeing that she was leaving, said, 'See you anon, *au revoir*, 'bye for the moment, have a good bath,' and other friendly phrases. Ailie was swept out of the room on a wave of goodwill.

'*Ce sont des gents très sympathiques, très gentils*,' said Ailie to the housekeeper.

The housekeeper's reply was too rapid and complex for Ailie to follow in detail, but it added up to agreement.

Ailie found herself led, almost carried, up some stairs and along a passage to a bathroom out of a dream, where Berthe the housekeeper turned on taps and helped her to undress. Berthe saw the unimportant abrasions on Ailie's knees and elbows and breast, the skinned areas, the small amount of smeared blood. She screamed softly, and ran off; she returned in a cloud of violent-smelling disinfectant, carrying swabs and dressings and bandages on an aluminium tray.

Probably the disinfectant was a good idea. There was no knowing what had been on that drive where Ailie skinned her knees. But the smell was not as nice as that of the bath-essence.

That bath was for Ailie certainly the high point of her life up to that moment.

It was not only that the weeks of her pilgrimage across France had been austere and often squalid: that this scented steam, these deep pale carpets, these Redouté prints on the bathroom walls, were in such contrast. It was by no means only that. It was that her whole life had been austere and squalid. This immediate, overwhelming experience was in unbelievable contrast to all of that, too. The big brass taps, the foot-caressing floor, the towels miraculously soft and the size of tennis-courts – these things were as remote from the converted chicken-coop where Ailie's family lived as from the station platform at le Mans.

Berthe came back with a sky-blue quilted dressing-gown which was somehow spare, which had been left behind by someone. This was fine, except that the owner had evidently been a big, tall lady, and into the capacious folds of her dressing-gown Ailie quite disappeared.

Berthe exclaimed, railed at herself for her folly, and was for rushing away and finding a garment many sizes smaller. But Ailie stopped her, Ailie had a sudden feeling that, for the first time in her life, she had a role to play.

The bigger the dressing-gown the better.

'*Ça va très bien, merci mille fois,*' said Ailie, a phrase she had used scores of times, but never with such conviction.

And there were fluffy slippers, also far too big.

Turbaned while she had the bath, Ailie's long pale hair was pretty well dry by the time she was dry. Berthe combed it, hissing as though grooming a horse. No doubt it needed washing, but it shone like metal after Berthe's brushing.

'*Alors, il faut manger, p'tite.*'

Ailie nodded. She smiled at Berthe, who suddenly and tenderly kissed her.

In the big bright kitchen, Ailie met Pierre, wrinkled like a nut, grinning like a monkey, who bowed and shook her hand, and put a chair for her by the scrubbed pine table, and stood behind the chair like a Georgian footman; and Ailie ate gigantically, and drank nearly half a bottle of red wine. The bath, the food, the wine, the sense of welcome and friendliness, took all Ailie's fatigue away, so that she found she wanted, most surprisingly, to rejoin the party.

There was a mirror in the kitchen. Ailie saw herself, in its pearly distorted depths. She saw herself as others might that evening see her.

She would probably never again in her life find herself in this position, of joining a resplendent party when wrapped in a dressing-gown many sizes too big, when cast as a sweet waif, when able to astonish the dukes and duchesses, who had never seen her before, by talking like a lady . . .

This was a chance of making an unforgettable impact, not on any account to be thrown away.

It was not so very calculating. It was harmless. It would please them all. It was not in the least phoney, really – she *was* a waif, a kind of stray kitten; the dressing-gown *was* far too big for her; she *did* speak the way she spoke, thanks to her ridiculous parents, and always had.

'*Je ne suis pas fatiguée,*' she said to Berthe and Pierre, '*parce que j'ai si bien mangé. J'en suis étonnée, mois aussi, mais c'est ça. Je vais rentrer dans le salon.*'

The servants had a short, bitter argument about whether this folly should be permitted, some of which Ailie understood. Berthe thought it would be a shame for Ailie not to rejoin the party, if she felt up to doing so; Pierre thought she should go at once to bed, and stay there for two days at least.

Ailie drank another glass of wine while they argued.

There was a buzz of wonder, sympathy and amusement after Ailie followed Berthe out of the salon.

Elinor noted with amusement that in that short time, in those shocking clothes, all wet and muddy and tattered, Ailie had made a most pleasing impression.

Could it be believed that she was actually a talented artist too?

'Feed her up, she'll be a knock-out, a rave, a killer. She's a beauty. At least, I think so.'

'Don't feed her up, she's just right now, today's look, perfect.'

'Hey, she's already a killer. That shirt. I rave.'

'A painter, Bruno? Talent with it?'

'You have one? There's a painting?'

'What's this about a mural?'

'Elinor has the painting,' said Bruno. 'Would you like to see it?'

'You can all come to it, or it can come to you,' said Elinor. 'It's probably easier if I simply go and get it.'

'I'm afraid it is,' said Bruno. 'Do you mind, darling?'

'I won't be a minute.'

Elinor fetched the little khaki-green landscape, and propped it on a bookshelf. Spectacles were settled on noses; George Napier-Gough screwed his monocle into his eye.

'I like it very much,' said Elinor, trying to keep any note of defensiveness out of her voice.

The others liked it: some not so very much.

No doubt it was more effective in the comparatively muted environment of Elinor's bedroom than in the bright opulence of the salon.

It was not obvious that the artist who had painted this small semi-abstract landscape would be everybody's choice for a large mural where bravura and brilliance would be required.

People continued to scrutinise the picture, and they said it grew on them. They saw more in it, the more they looked at it. This was not a phoney reaction. Elinor had had the same experience.

Perhaps it would be true of the painter as well. One would see more and more in her, the better one knew her. Elinor thought this was very likely what would happen. She was pleased at the thought. She had not made such a fool of herself, writing to the child.

Fred was looking at the picture, with some others. He was not often to be seen staring at pictures. Perhaps he would not have been looking at this one, if Elinor had not put it near where he was sitting.

Why was Fred still grimly sitting up, when he could quite well have gone to bed? Probably only Elinor and Bruno took a moment to wonder. So quiet was Fred, so self-marginalised, that the others simply forgot that he was there.

This was not rude of them. They were not rude people, except when a notable put-down was called for. Fred was deliberately invisible. That was all right, it was what he liked, only why didn't he go to bed?

Elinor wondered about it, without much worrying. Fred was grown up. He could choose to go to bed or to stay up. He was allowed to go. He had been working. He was allowed to be tired. He knew that. Elinor had other guests to amuse.

Bruno did worry a little. He also took the view that Fred was grown up, that he knew he could excuse himself when he wanted to, that everybody would understand that he had been working and was tired. But Bruno was sufficiently devoted to Fred to want him at all times to be content, and sufficiently acquainted with Fred to be sure that he was not happy in this smarty-pants gaggle of fancy people.

Ah well. On with the dance.

Ailie came back after her supper, to everybody's surprise. She looked like a small kitten in a large basket, or a small chick in a large nest. She looked like a very small angel in a very large blue cloud.

Several cynical old hearts were softened.

Ailie gave a squeak when she saw her painting, the prize-winner, propped on a bookcase at the end of the room.

She stayed only long enough for one glass of wine.

She had had quite enough wine. She did nothing silly, nothing discreditable. She said almost nothing, but was seen, almost heard, to be purring. Hands twitched with the desire to stroke her, as though she had been a Persian kitten.

She went off to bed, in a corner Berthe had found. The others began to melt away to bed.

Elinor suddenly said, to a room almost empty, 'So, I'd almost forgotten, what the hell was my word?'

'What word? What on earth are you talking about?'

'That you were doing things in the manner of. That of which you were doing things in the manner. Only somebody else kept doing them.'

'Oh. Ah. Your word. What was it?'

'I was on the verge of getting it, but Ailie came in.'

'Easy to say. Ho. Easy excuse. You never did get it.'

'I never did. A word meaning that somebody else does it for you.'

'You give up?'

'Yes.'

'The word is, "Vicariously".'

'Oh my God,' said Elinor, 'I should have got that. It's easy.'

They all went to bed, and Elinor turned off most of the remaining lights.

She went to the little room where Ailie was sleeping on a camp bed. She opened the door softly, and peeped round it. There was a little light. Ailie lay under an enormous duvet, as dwarfed by it as she had been by the quilted dressing-gown. Now she looked like a mouse in a nest made for a much larger animal, for a bear. She was sleepy but awake. She smiled at Elinor.

'All right?' said Elinor.

'I'm happier than I've ever been before in my whole life,' said Ailie.

'Do you know,' said Elinor, wonderingly, 'I believe I am, too.'

She stretched out a hand, and touched Ailie on the head. She felt an electric tingle in her fingertips, when they brushed the smooth pale hair of Ailie's head.

She closed the door softly, and went away to bed in a mood of puzzled excitement. She did not know why she was puzzled, nor why she was excited.

CHAPTER TEN

RED LEFT in the middle of the morning, having spent a final hour with Bruno and the plans of the new workshops. Bruno was the only person who saw Fred off. Some of the other guests had already left; Elinor was entertaining the others; the servants were being servants; Ailie was invisible, presumed still in bed. Fred did not expect a large and public farewell, and would have been embarrassed at any such incongruous party: but Bruno was sorry that nobody made any fuss of Fred.

He did not *want* a fuss made of him, but still he should not have been so invisible to the others.

Six of the house party remained for lunch.

The six included *il conte* Alessandro di Ganzarello, large, blackish, clever, ugly, popular and very rich, Piemontese, of ancient family but dubious pedigree, forty-five years old, separated from his American actress wife, considered irresistible to women but interested only in women whom everybody else wanted. Sandro often and loudly proclaimed his passionate admiration for Elinor, who indeed had all the glamour and *réclame* that he fancied.

The six included also George Napier-Gough, Anglo-Irish aristo turned critic and historian, in the manner perhaps of an earlier generation, of Harold Acton or the Sitwells. George was comparable in background to Sandro, but in style to Bruno; he changed the ribbon on his monocle to go with his socks; his half-dozen books were accepted as definitive by all except other scholars working in the same fields; his pansy airs and graces camouflaged a healthy, vulgar, old-fashioned taste for barmaids. He also constantly declared his worship of Elinor, although she was much unlike a barmaid.

There were also still in the house a French married couple, and an English and an American woman. The youngest of all of these (the French wife) was ten years older than Elinor. There had been young, but they had left. The effect was relaxing.

The six, and Elinor, and Bruno, foregathered on the terrace at twelve-thirty, where Pierre was opening a bottle of wine and Bruno a bottle of vodka. The river fifty-six feet below was like a steel-green conveyor belt. The far bank was spiked with deep brown shadows, the ground being ruched like a pelmet, and the April sun aslant even at noon. Birds peeped. Berthe far away was singing a Johnny Halliday song. Nobody was in a hurry about anything. The sun was not overpowering or the sky pitiless, nor was there any competitive need to be cleverer or funnier than the rest. It was all as comfortable as could be.

'Where is the child?' asked somebody.

'The muralist. Yes, where?'

'She's been washing her hair,' said Elinor. 'She said it would turn the river black. I should think it's dry by now. She says Berthe can find her some clothes. I can't imagine what clothes.'

'I liked her in that enormous dressing-gown.'

'*Anch'io.*'

'I expect she'll be down in a minute.'

'Ailie,' said Doris the American, who was Features Editor

223

of an important magazine. 'That's a name I never heard.'

'I looked it up in *Chambers*,' said Bruno. 'It's a Scottish diminutive. But a strangely multi-purpose diminutive. It is short for Alice, and Alison, and Helen.'

'It isn't *short* for any of those.'

'It can't be a diminutive of Helen.'

'I am only telling you what *Chambers* says.'

'A mural. She looks hardly strong enough to hold a brush.'

'And she'll need such a big brush.'

'A great, big, heavy, awkward, clumsy brush,' said George Napier-Gough. 'My sentimental old heart is wrung.'

They spoke lightly of Ailie, of her fragility and her adventures, her tattered rags when she arrived, her little painting, her wide eyes and narrow chin: they spoke as though of a small attractive cousin, or a friend's dog: but it was obvious to Elinor that Ailie had made an impression on these people out of all proportion to anything she had said or done.

Elinor was proud of Ailie. Elinor was extremely pleased with herself for having got Ailie here.

Elinor joined the others in speculating about what Ailie would be wearing when she appeared on the terrace – what point her garb would occupy, on the extraordinary spectrum from saturated rags to giant dressing gown.

A little cotton frock? But whose?

There was a sense of expectancy, of drama. The small star was about to walk into the spotlight. It was as though, in a P.G. Wodehouse novel, heavy bets were being laid on what Ailie would be wearing.

Ailie went to sleep in the bosom of a magical cloud.

Since the moment of her arrival at la Moquerie, miracle had piled on miracle. The unquestioning welcome, hot water and huge towels, food and wine, friendliness and featherbeds: Bruno Browning, considerate and understanding and generous: Berthe and Pierre, exuding anxious concern like resinous trees: a little too much wine, which was exactly the right amount: all those lovely people, so unsatirical, so full of goodwill, so readily amused—

And Elinor Leigh. How *could* it be the same person?

'I lost a bit of weight. I got some new clothes. I learned a bit about pictures and stuff.'

That was what she said about herself, when Ailie was trying to apologise for not recognising her. Of course it was true – those things had happened. And other things had happened, which she did not mention. Wands had been waved, by Bruno Browning, and the spirits of this place, and old gods in the stones. Elinor Leigh had become a stunning, a breath-taking beauty, by far the most beautiful person that Ailie had ever seen, beautiful in face and figure and voice and smile, in long limb and tiny detail, thigh and little-fingernail and eyelash, smooth and strong like a big river, like the Loire at Blois where the picture was stolen, internally shining like a secret lantern—

And with a warmth and kindness unguessable in Milchester, when for some reason she was disguised as a guardsman—

And with electricity in her fingertips, a warm vibration, a little shock like the blessing of a small angel—

Ailie's dreams were coloured ivory and cream and pink.

In the morning she found some early sunshine, and some breakfast in the kitchen with Berthe, and a shower where she could wash her hair. She found a sunlit window in a tower where she could dry her hair.

Exploring the tower, she found an unimportant bedroom already vacated by a guest, in which on some previous occasion a child had slept, a young schoolboy. The boy had left some clothes behind. He had arrived in his school-clothes from England, it seemed to Ailie, probably with his parents who were friends of Bruno Browning's, perhaps of Elinor Leigh's: he had shed his school-clothes when he got here, and tucked them away in this cupboard. He had forgotten about them, in the liberation of the sort of clothes he wore in this place. He had gone away without them. Probably he had got into trouble, leaving his school uniform in the South of France.

Ailie, in her giant dressing-gown, had been wondering what on earth to wear by day.

A small unknown schoolboy had unwittingly done her a stunning favour.

Ailie tried on grey flannel shorts, which were held up by a belt striped in green and red. She put on a white cotton shirt. She put on a tie, striped like the belt. She put on a red blazer with a green badge on the breast. She put on a school cap, red and green stripes with a little shield at the front.

She thought that in these clothes she looked like the awning at the front of a shop.

She could see that in the sunlight her ash-blonde hair, new washed, shone with the colour of pewter.

She giggled at her reflection.

Far below she saw people on the terrace, with an air of being about to have drinks.

They might be wondering where she had got to. They might be wondering what she had found to put on. They might not be thinking about her at all – they might have completely forgotten her. But she thought not.

She embarked on the long zigzag descent, and came at

last, blinking, out into the moderate glare of the sun.

Well, what other clothes were there? What else was she to wear, a tea-towel? A couple of pillow-cases? Elinor Leigh's clothes were impossible – she was eight inches taller than Ailie. Berthe was two foot more round the waist. The other three women were all completely different in size and shape from Ailie, and anyway they had not offered to lend her any clothes, and anyway they were all leaving after lunch.

Well, that was all pretty nearly true.

Elinor had hardly seen Ailie all morning, what with some guests leaving and others staying and the housekeeping concerns of the beginning of a week. Ailie could evidently look after herself, appearances notwithstanding. Her journey across France was amazing. She had spirit. Also she had friends. Berthe was already committed to looking after Ailie, in the manner of a hen with one chick; Pierre also, in a sterner and more dramatic manner.

There had been, during the morning, some rapid reference to Berthe finding some clothes for Ailie to wear.

Then, on the terrace, the others were speculating about what Ailie would be wearing when she appeared, if she appeared.

Sandro and George apparently wanted her to go on wearing the dressing-gown, but that would be ridiculous at midday, and the sleeves would get in the soup.

Elinor found herself wondering, with the others. The question was more acutely interesting than it had any business to be.

The answer was one nobody could have predicted.

It was simply astonishing.

The very banality of those little-boy clothes made them

audacious, outrageous, unforgettable.

Ailie's fragile little face under the striped school cap!

Her silvery-blonde hair snaking down the shoulders of the blazer, the red blazer as worn by a young prep-school boy in the cricket pavilion during a house match!

The tie! A school tie! She had tied it very badly. The knot was a mess, and the collar of her shirt was all over the place. A little boy, dressing in the dormitory of his prep school, would have tied his tie like that.

Ailie needed looking after. She needed her tie tying for her, and an awful lot else besides. She needed feeding up. Elinor had been handed the responsibility, it seemed.

Good.

The others laughed, and made much of Ailie. They loved her ridiculous clothes. They cooed. They almost patted and stroked her. They treated her as a young child, as a clever and appealing little dog.

Ailie smiled shyly. She evaded the efforts of the French-woman to tidy up her collar and tie. She kept her cap on, all during lunch on the terrace, raising large innocent eyes to Berthe's shrieks of laughter.

Sandro di Ganzarello went away to Turin, and to Venice and New York. He mentioned, to anyone who asked, that he had been to la Moquerie with Bruno and Elinor; he mentioned even to those who did not ask that his heart was for the first time irrecoverably lost.

He had great difficulty with the name. He could neither remember nor pronounce it.

'Eelah Uctebble. Ileu Octibul. Alla Uthtubel.'

Sandro's listeners were amused because he was amusing. They were interested because he was interesting. People paid attention. Nobody who knew him underrated his taste or intelligence (or income) although he seemed an over-weight *flâneur*. Sandro's friends, in various centres of culture and self-indulgence, heard about a new icon, a small pale sorceress in a striped cap.

It was hard for the French and Americans who heard Sandro's rhapsodies to tell what the hell he was talking about: but it seemed that a new comet had snuggled down at la Moquerie.

Much curiosity was aroused.

George Napier-Gough went back to London, and to Cambridge and York, where he had friends to stay with and articles to write and meetings to attend (he was a member of a thousand boards, quangos and committees). He glimmered at great ladies through his monocle, and fluted about belts and badges and blazers, ivory knees much smaller than a man's hand, pewter-coloured hair and shy sauciness, to a point that made some people think he was becoming senile, others that he was coming out a closet that he had only ever pretended to be in.

People remembered the name, not easily forgotten, and the image George so often painted of a little figure in boy's school uniform coming shyly out into the sunshine.

She was funny with it, George said. She was droll and sparky and talented.

Various people in various cities were pleased at the thought that they might be meeting George's new pin-up.

There was something coltish about Ailie, something jerky and childlike. She had an unco-ordinated quality. This was in extreme contrast to Elinor's graceful certainty of movement, her air of sailing or swimming through life in graceful tranquillity. She was swanlike. She moved with the certainty of not falling over. Ailie seemed all the time perilously close to falling over, so that people were forever darting forward to stop her from hurting herself.

This stuttering and tentative quality became, to Bruno's mind, more marked by the hour. From the moment that Ailie settled into la Moquerie, the contrast between herself and Elinor grew greater.

Little bells of suspicion tinkled at the back of Bruno's mind, and question-marks flickered just out of sight below the horizon.

'Adorable as you look, baby,' said Elinor, 'I think we'd better go shopping, as a matter of urgency.'

'Will you lend me some money? Will you pay me an advance against my fee?'

'Your fee? You haven't even see your space yet. You haven't even been to the building.'

'I'm still recovering from getting here. I'm still getting used to being here. I'm still trying to find my feet.'

'They're not very far away.'

'No. I'm a dwarfish little squit.'

'Summer's almost on us. You won't need many clothes. Do you like clothes?'

'I don't know. I've never had any. I've never had anything new.'

'We must put that right.'

'New clothes. God.'

'Do you want to ring your family?'

'You mean telephone? They haven't got a telephone.'

'Are you serious?'

'They can't afford one. They don't want one. They don't want to talk to anybody. They don't know anybody.'

'Oh my pet, what a funny life you've had.'

'Not half as funny,' said Ailie, 'as the one I'm having now.'

Elinor took Ailie shopping. She took her to le Rozier, in order to get clothes in which she could be seen in Albi.

It was a revelation for them both.

Ailie discovered that she did like clothes. She had guessed she would. She learned also, with a tingle of certainty, something else about herself in the matter of clothes. Bruno had rightly said of her landscape painting that nobody else would have done it quite as she had done it, and that was its value: so she discovered that she should dress not quite as anybody else would dress. She understood that she was to be a kook, what used to be known as a kook. She was the right size for that, and the right age. She had the excuse of being skinny, and the good excuse of being an artist.

The first surprise to Elinor was the fluent confidence with which Ailie spoke French. She had not needed it before – just a few words to Berthe and Pierre. Now in the shops she was voluble. It was pretty odd French, demotic and sometimes unprintable, but it greatly amused and impressed the women in the shops. Ailie would shock François Delalain. It would do him good to be shocked.

The second surprise was Ailie as a clothes-horse. She postured in front of the glass: she twirled and paraded. She was a dwarfish little squit with coltish, unpredictable movements, but she made the little shifts she tried on look like a million dollars.

They loved her, in the shops.

How could someone so small and skinny look so dramatic?

It was carriage and personality, and a lovely long neck and bird bones and a tiny waist, and a sort of bashful impertinence, an urchin quality . . .

It became rather expensive, buying Ailie all the clothes she looked best in.

Elinor remembered her own transformation. She smiled, and swallowed, and wrote cheques.

But Ailie did not wear the clothes the way they meant when they made them. She chopped them in half, and turned them inside out, and mixed this with that, so that it was as Bruno had said of her painting – nobody else had done it, nobody else could do it.

It was not grunge, exactly, because it was skimpy and elegant and high-style, in its strange Ailie way.

Yes, it was Ailie. That was the style it was.

Elinor and Ailie between them had invented a new kind of person to be, an Ailie.

What was an Ailie?

An Ailie could already be defined, after two days' existence, by a few characteristics, habits, habitats, by ways of moving and of being still, by ways of looking and dressing. But a definitive profile of an Ailie would have to wait a few weeks, perhaps months. It depended what Ailie thought of next.

Elinor thought this was all more fun than anything she had ever done – more fun than recreating herself, more fun than recreating the Guardhouse.

Ailie bought clothes for young girls (Elinor bought them) and she bought clothes for young boys also. She bought schoolboy clothes, long shorts, short shorts, smocks, sailor suits. She acquired an awful lot of clothes, and combined them in different ways, sometimes devising a new mix in time for lunch and another in time for tea. But all her clothes were cheap clothes, little cotton things off racks on sidewalks. Elinor had few clothes, comparatively, but those few were expensive.

Ailie seemed to have the capacity to turn cheap tatty clothes into high style, just by wearing them: by stumbling and strutting about in them.

Elinor could never be an Ailie, and nor could most other people. You had to be pretty special, even to try to be an Ailie. You had to have an Ailie look, an Ailie size and shape; you had to make Ailie movements and gestures. It had to come naturally. Sometimes Elinor thought that only Ailie herself could ever be a proper Ailie.

But Doris Loeb the New York editor thought otherwise. Doris ran into George Napier-Gough in Paris, and they laughed about Ailie. They discovered themselves to be founder members of a new coterie, the fans of Ailie. Doris had business in Toulouse, and went there via la Moquerie. She renewed acquaintance with Ailie, and saw in her all that she had seen before, that George Napier-Gough had seen and raved about; she saw much more besides. She saw a role being played with a kind of artless mastery. She was the first outsider to be exposed to the concept of the Ailie.

Doris rang Paris for a photographer. Yet again la Moquerie and the *corps-de-garde* were full of lights and reflectors. Doris had come for lunch, and stayed three days. Elinor tried not to cluck, to nanny Ailie and interfere. She suggested things for Ailie to wear for the photographer, but Ailie knew better. Ailie put on some very ridiculous clothes, and began making drawings in charcoal on the wall where her mural was to be. She was photographed on top of a ladder, and squatting like a mouse on the floor.

Doris was incandescent with enthusiasm about her article, because in that whole world of style, design, fashion, there was seldom anything really new, definable, identifiable, with a name, with a symbolic cult figurehead.

Doris Loeb picked up the idea and ran with it.

Ailie was already a noun. Elinor had been using it as a noun. 'In order to be an Ailie you must do so and so, look thus, say these things, move in that fashion.' Doris turned it into an adjective also: 'That dress is quite Ailie, but it would be Ailier if you took away the belt and added a scarf.' She turned it into a verb: 'You could Ailie this room by giving it a red and white striped ceiling. Would you Ailie this hat for me? Today I'm taking it easy, but tomorrow I shall Ailie.'

Back in New York, with many thousand words and a thousand photographs, Doris sold the idea to her editorial board, there being at that moment, by chance, no other dramatic event in their world. The magazine ran a special Ailie issue, somewhat tongue in cheek, with a lovely picture of Ailie on the cover, with pages of pictures of Ailie.

They had a picture of Ailie with the Tiffany lamp, in the Oriel Room of the Guardhouse. Somebody said the Tiffany lamp was pretty Ailie.

Bruno Browning was in Milchester when the magazine appeared, the European edition running the whole of Doris's piece. Bruno was amused but troubled. He thought that a small joke had got out of hand, and a small person had got out of hand also. He thought it was high time that Ailie stopped dressing up in baby-clothes and got to work on the mural.

Bruno did not know what Fred thought.

Elinor probably thought that Fred had been accepting her hospitality, but Fred thought he was accepting Bruno's. That made it all right for Fred to go to la Moquerie, which would otherwise have been dodgy, by Fred's rules. He had a code about who he accepted drinks from.

Elinor was pretty nearly a no-go conversational area between Bruno and Fred. This meant that Ailie was, too, since you could hardly mention Ailie without discussing Elinor. Probably Fred had no views about Ailie, one way or the other. Probably he had never actually exchanged a word with her.

George Napier-Gough was jealous of Doris Loeb, for being the Apostle Paul of Ailie. He, George, had been one of the original apostles, with Sandro di Ganzarello.

Doris had the advantage of running a magazine, useful in any apostolic effort.

But Doris had a job, an office. She had to be there a lot of the time. George had the advantage of being a free agent. He used it to revisit la Moquerie, to reassert his proprietorial claim to Ailie. It was not so very frivolous, because the Tarn was more or less on his way to somewhere he was more or less obliged to go. It all fitted.

George found Ailie dressed as Ailie doing her mural, and Elinor dressed as Elinor doing the flowers. He marvelled at the contrast. They were two such stunning girls, ten years apart, light years apart. They were stunning in diametrically opposite ways. The goddess, the urchin. Titania, Mustardseed. And so forth: no limit to these conjunctions.

George stayed for lunch, a simple little lunch. He could have done with more to drink than they gave him. Bruno was still in Milchester, earning the wherewithal to pay for the omelettes. George was not displeased that Bruno was away. Bruno slightly cramped George's style, as indeed George knew he cramped Bruno's. (Bruno, for all his learning, was an amateur in a world in which George was a professional; but Bruno was richer, younger and better-looking than George.) George could be uninhibited with the girls, Bruno not there to add his paradoxical brand of respectability to the party. George could indulge in innuendo and casual caress.

Elinor did not mind the innuendos. Ailie apparently did not notice them. She had no experience of the oblique, no capacity for the subtle. In her own conversation, she was startlingly downright, more so in French than in English. Probably she did not know exactly what she was saying in the French she had learned from truck-drivers.

They lunched under the awning on the terrace. It happened that there was a large and intricate cobweb between the metal struts of the awning, which cast a ghostlike, barely-visible shadow on the part of the white tablecloth where the sun struck.

'How beautiful,' said George, tracing the outline of the shadow with his fork. 'Sculptural yet evanescent. It puts me in mind of the work of Naum Gabo.'

Elinor looked blank.

George glanced at her, as though in courteous enquiry. He was pretending to be astonished that she was not familiar with this peculiar name.

'Oh yes,' said Ailie. 'Russian, went to Paris, lots of wire. Somebody said he was like the Seagram Building.'

'Like the *what*?'

'He invented his name, didn't he? Really he was called something quite different. I might do that. But I might not bother. The Seagram Building, you know, in New York. Lots of glass, very simple, very cool. Somebody said Naum Gabo is like that.'

'It's a new thought to me,' said George. 'Damn and blast you, Ailie, now I shall have to dig up a lot of photographs and see if that comparison is as idiotic as it sounds. I might have to go to New York. I've just *been* to New York.'

'I think it's to do with trapping space and light inside a structure,' said Ailie.'

'Yes, I think that might be it,' said George. 'How do you know about that?'

'I'm an art student,' said Ailie. 'At least, I was. Just about now I was supposed to be getting my degree show stuck up on the wall.'

'And you learned about Gabo?'

'Yes. As it happens, yes.'

'Have some more salad, George?' said Elinor, who was being left out of the conversation.

George and Elinor were brought up short by the fact, unsuspected by either, that Ailie knew more about twentieth-century art history than Elinor did. Ailie was not brought up short. She had known it all along. It would have surprised her that anyone would be surprised. Elinor was bigger and better than herself in every single way, more beautiful and cleverer and nicer, but Ailie had been studying the subject for three years.

Elinor contemplated Ailie as though she were a fragile bomb: she might break if not wrapped in cotton wool; she might explode if touched on the wrong spot.

Doris Loeb's article, widely publicised, told a number of people something they had known without knowing that they knew it. They were the people in at the birth of Ailie. They were Bruno and Elinor's party, playing that adverb game when the waif in saturated rags made them all laugh.

People studied the magazine who normally despised it.

People laid claim to knowing Ailie who had really no more than seen her across Bruno's salon.

Other journalists followed Doris Loeb, making pilgrimage to la Moquerie as they had when Bruno was restoring the château, as they had when Elinor was restoring the Guardhouse.

There was more interest – there were more photographs, more thousands of words – because the setting of this new story was already celebrated. It was as though a puppy with two heads had been born in Buckingham Palace. Bruno and Elinor, godparents or good fairies of the new sensation, were already minor icons. Style-conscious readers, ambitious women, had a sense of coming home when they saw all the pictures of Ailie at la Moquerie.

It was the silly season. There happened not to be any new wars. The autumn excesses of the catwalks, the pages of bare-breasted super-models, were still months in the future. Fashion writers cried 'Me too', and a bar called Ailie's opened in the Portobello Road.

Opinion at the Milchester College of Art and Design swung like a drunken pendulum. Many of the boys, and some of the staff, raved to think what they had let slip through their fingers. The smaller and skinnier girls worked at being Ailies. The students described their new paintings as Ailie, and said that they would Ailie their sculptures.

Until the whole thing was suddenly perceived as naff, and the queues in the cafeteria dismissed the Ailie movement as an invention of glossy journalism, an unimportant fraud, a con, a gimmick.

The opinions of art students did not, however, penetrate the lounges of the aspirant, or the low glass tables in the hairdressers'. Ailie was there. Her name was noun, adjective and verb.

Elinor took Ailie to François Delalain, who was thrown into

perturbation by Ailie's accent and vocabulary. He said that he was too old to teach Ailie to speak properly. He said it would take years for her to unlearn all that she had learned in the various gutters of her journey, and he did not have enough years.

As an old-fashioned socialist, François Delalain was not equipped to appreciate Ailie's brand of anarchism, her dash of Dada.

Where would her painting come from? Who would be master of her mural? Could anything be truly Ailie that was so big? She rubbed out all the charcoal drawings she had done on the wall, and began to fill a little book with sketches of Berthe and Pierre, and the men who were repairing the Guardhouse drive.

Bruno came back, exhausted from holding the hands of his senior colleagues in Milchester. He shamed both Elinor and Ailie into seriousness. Elinor addressed herself to a part of the garden which she had long declared her territory, and Ailie began to transfer her sketches to the great spaces of the wall. It appeared that she was visualising a sort of expressionist Bruegel, a most unAilie project.

Bruno had to go away again, to an international conservation conference in Stockholm. He thought that Elinor would come with him. She thought that she would not. It was the first time since they had joined their lives that she had not come with him on such an expedition. She did not go with him to Milchester, where it was all business, but all his other journeys, in his other life, included her. She wanted to come. She loved new places. She mopped up new people and pictures. She was a great help to Bruno, too, in matters of his papers and engagements and laundry. Even for a man who had so many friends and contacts, hotel rooms were lonely in the evenings.

She saw that he was hurt that she would not come. She tried to explain, but she could not tell him why she could not come, because she did not know why. She talked about the garden, and the possibility of this or that person availing themselves of a standing invitation, and about the driveway of the Guardhouse. None of it added up to a credible reason.

Bruno went away, a little forlornly. He left behind a conscientious ghost, making the girls feel guilty if they were too Sybaritic. The weather was now becoming really hot. Bruno's reproachful spirit had to work hard to keep them working hard.

Elinor had to justify not going to Stockholm, by the improvements she made to her piece of garden. Ailie had far more to justify; she could do it by the progress she made with the mural. Bruno at a distance shamed them into working, and they shamed one another.

Bruno telephoned from Stockholm, but he spoke only to Berthe, since the girls had gone out. Berthe said there was no message, no particular reason for the call.

Wearing shorts (a small French boy's very short shorts) and the top of a bikini, Ailie covered herself with charcoal drawing Berthe, at various domestic tasks, on the wall of the Oriel Room.

It seemed to her, to her own surprise, that she was doing a kind of Stanley Spencer, full of allegory and satire.

She became by the end of the morning covered in sweat as well as in charcoal. She was working hard, absorbed in what she was doing, and it was a glaring, windless day at the end of May.

She did not know what time it was. Lunch would be when they wanted it. It was a day when Berthe and Pierre did not come, a day when nobody was coming. At some point Elinor would call her down, and she would have a swim before a drink before lunch.

Ailie wiped her forehead with the back of her forearm, mixing sweat with sweat and smearing charcoal over her face. There was charcoal on her bare knees and thighs and midriff. Sweat glistened in her navel, and stung her eyes.

Elinor wore a wide-brimmed straw hat, and a cotton shirt and baggy cotton pants and espadrilles. She was dressed for the intolerable amount of weeding to which she had committed herself. In a way she quite enjoyed it. It was good to contemplate the square yards of earth between the shrubs, dark and weed-free, waiting to be planted up with the ground-covering subjects she was choosing from the catalogues.

Twelve o'clock, twelve-thirty. A very good morning. A satisfactory result. Pierre would be amazed when he saw it next day.

Elinor straightened, luxuriously, sighing. She was aware of her body, as she uncoiled it from the weeding crouch, aware of its length and strength and slimness, long narrow bones, small waist, smooth skin over sinew. She felt the sweat in the small of her back and between her breasts.

She peeled off her gardening gloves, and inspected her fingernails for damage. She kept her nails short. It was no part of her image of herself that she had the long red nails of an old-fashioned vamp. Her life was too active and unpampered for that sort of thing, even if she had wanted it.

Nearly lunchtime, perhaps. What was there for lunch? There were peppers and green beans in a big oily salad, a fresh pâté and cheese and a melon. All very good indeed.

A swim first. Ailie would want a swim. Ailie had never been swimming in her childhood. Elinor was teaching her to swim. Ailie would be just as hot as Elinor, working indoors. It would feel airless up there, even with the windows wide open. Perhaps they should get a fan, a big slow fan like a punkah.

Elinor took off her hat, and felt the slap of the sun on her forehead and the back of her neck. She felt that her shirt had glued itself to her shoulders. Powdery earth had mixed with a sheen of sweat on her forearms. She guessed there were smears of dirt on her face. Nobody could weed the length of a sweaty morning without getting a dirty face.

Elinor went through the house and out on to the terrace, and along the cliff-face path towards the Guardhouse.

Ailie was surprised and rather disgusted by how much she was sweating. She had thought she was too skinny to perspire, too refined. She had thought fat people sweated, men with beer bellies, sausage-eating Belgians and Bavarians.

Of course she had never in her life before been anywhere hot. Family holidays abroad, even English seaside holidays with bucket and spade, had not been part of her childhood.

Was this part of her childhood? How grown-up was she supposed to be? She had experienced absolutely nothing of a grown-up kind, unless you counted the gropings of yobs with spots, or the grabs of drunken old teachers.

Somebody had said something about the earth moving. It was not to do with bulldozers, but with sex. The phrase was in an article written by a gushing woman, in a Sunday paper rescued by Ailie's father out of somebody's dustbin. The earth moved. Called also climax. What were they talking about? Had her parents experienced that sort of thing? Had it done them any good? Did it do anybody any good?

Ailie was more than ever aware of the isolation she had suffered in her childhood and youth. It was as though she had moved through the world in total deafness, missing everything that everybody else was saying to one another. They all knew about those things, but none of them had told her. Now it was almost too late to ask, without seeming absolutely moronic.

Was Elinor somebody she could ask? How embarrassing would that be?

Ailie felt moronic, rubbing the sweaty palms of her hands on the seat of her little-boy shorts. Her thoughts had rather run away with themselves, perhaps because of the heat.

She decided it was time to stop. She started down the spiral staircase, on her way to bathe and drink and lunch.

Elinor was almost completely unsighted, coming out of the brilliant sunlight into the semi-darkness of the ground floor of the Guardhouse. She groped her way across the hall, her rope-soled espadrilles noiseless on the flagstones. Something stopped her from calling out. She did not want to break the breathless silence. She felt for the wrought-iron newel-post which marked the bottom of the spiral staircase. She started up the stairs.

Feet whispered on the iron steps above her, small bare feet. Slender pale legs were dimly to be seen, slowly descending, above them an area of dark, then the pale smudge of midriff and rib-cage.

Elinor stopped. She might have turned and descended, since Ailie was already coming down. She did not know why she did not do so. But she stood still on the stairs, her clothes sticking clammily to her shoulders and flanks, her hand damp on the stair-rail.

Ailie came lazily down, humming under her breath, her

hand sliding along the iron rail. She was well used to these stairs. She was quite safe. She did not have to look where she was going, and she did not do so. It was dark on the stairs, and she could hardly see anything. She ran into Elinor, standing silent in the semi-darkness of the stairs. She squeaked.

Elinor with her bare forearm felt the soft damp bare skin between Ailie's shorts and her bra. Through the cotton of her trousers she felt Ailie's bare knees. Ailie had clutched her instinctively, in that moment of surprise. Elinor put her arm round Ailie as though to protect her from a fall of which she was not in danger.

They held one another. Either might have let go, but neither did so. Elinor felt Ailie's small pointed breasts through the fabric of her bikini and the cotton of her own shirt. She moved her hands over Ailie's shoulders and back. She pressed her cheek stickily to Ailie's forehead. She kissed her. Ailie returned her kisses, with shy intensity. It was a moment of absolute amazement.

'What are we doing? What is happening?' said Ailie into Elinor's neck. She sounded wondering. She was not frightened.

'I think it is called love,' said Elinor.

'But I am too small and silly for you.'

'Darling.'

'Did you say "Darling"?'

'We are too dirty and sweaty for one another.'

'We had better have a bath.'

'Both of us, a bath. A bath, not a bathe?'

'To get clean,' said Ailie.

'Yes. We shall have to take our clothes off. Let's do that now.'

'Now? Here? On the stairs?'

'Yes, here on the stairs.'

Slippery-skinned, slippery-fingered, they pulled one another's clothes off, and pressed together and kissed, and their hands slipped and skidded over one another, and delicately explored one another, and they purred like cats in the semi-darkness, their clothes strewn over the stairs.

All embarrassment, all inhibition had been caressed away by the time they came to the sun-filled bathroom.

'Oh my God, you are beautiful,' said Ailie.

They ran a bath of coolish, warmish water. In the bath they were coolish, warmish, hot, washing one another with gentle thoroughness, discovering the slippery eroticism of soapsuds, discovering all kinds of things.

There was no threat, no tension, no fright, no pain, no ugliness, no embarrassment, no risk, no man.

They did not talk. Their fingers did the talking.

Ailie ridiculously thought: the high moments of my life have been in baths – my first night here, that bath, and now this bath.

The sensation became so joyfully intense that it became a kind of agony. Ailie moaned and wriggled and relaxed in the soapy water, cradled in the long lovely limbs of Elinor.

Elinor thought: this magical amazing clever sexy beautiful child is the first person I have ever loved and the only person I shall ever love, and I love her completely and I would fight and die and kill for her.

By and by they dried one another, smiling, and then walked together, naked, both, except for shoes, back along the cliff-face path to the château. They put on clean clothes, a few, and lunched in the shade on the terrace, each wishing to serve the other, to wait on the other. They went afterwards to Elinor's room for a siesta, and much later for a walk in the golden evening, hand in hand up the drive and down again, and they lay that night in each other's arms, exhausted by happiness and discovery and love.

CHAPTER ELEVEN

'I THINK I KNEW the first night you came here,' said Elinor.

'When you touched my head. My hair,' said Ailie. 'When you tucked me up.'

'You were so funny that night. You were so sweet.'

'Sweet? I'm not sweet. I'm . . .'

'Dry?'

'Nasty, really. But there. I never knew I was one of those.'

'One of what?'

'One of these. What we are.'

'Dykes.'

'Is that what we're called?'

'I never knew either,' said Elinor. 'Probably I wouldn't be one, if I hadn't fallen in love.'

'Fallen . . .?'

'Fallen in love with you.'

'Oh,' said Ailie. 'Those words are too big for somebody as small as me.'

'Can I come and see your painting?'

'What do you think? I'm doing it for you.'

So Elinor contemplated the two-foot and three-foot charcoal drawings of Berthe cooking, peeling and chopping vegetables, washing and ironing, in a setting as yet only hinted at, but those hints suggesting la Moquerie in a magic landscape.

'This is completely outside anything I could ever dream of being able to do,' said Elinor, after a long moment of staring. 'I'm stunned.'

'Well, I've been taught.'

'Will Pierre go in?'

'Gardening and butlering and cleaning the windows.'

'It's miraculous. People will come from all over the world. Will you have natural colours? Greeny-browns, like your painting I've got?'

'Oh no. Oh *no*. That was boggy old England. A little picture. Ages ago. No, I've got a sort of guide for the colours, a sort of scheme.'

'What guide? Where?'

'You said at the start. You said in your letter, I think. Strong colours. I want Chagal kind of colours. Very clear and strong, strong lyrical colours. Everything but the crimson.'

'Why not crimson?'

'The walls are already crimson. I'll have purple and bright red and light red. And green and violet and various yellows and cadmium orange. There's my guide.'

'What is? Where?'

'The lamp. Your Tiffany lamp.'

Bruno telephoned from Stockholm. He was delaying his return. He would not come straight home, but stop off on his way in London. He had an engagement there. Berthe took the call again, the girls being out. She reported that Monsieur Bruno had not said what he was doing in London.

'I suppose there are thirty million different things he might be doing in London,' said Ailie. 'But I don't know what. I've never been there.'

'I wonder what it is,' said Elinor. 'It's nothing I know about. He didn't say anything about it. I wonder what he's doing.'

She did not wonder very much. Her hands were full. Her mind was distracted and her senses aroused and her emotions engaged as never before.

Bruno was seeing a doctor in London. He was having tests.

He had become aware of certain disquieting symptoms, still undramatic, not yet interfering with his life. He was, of course, aware of his own way of life, the one he had given up in disgust and self-disgust. He had not, when he was young, been aware of taking such risks. Indeed, it seemed possible that when he was very young these risks did not exist. Then the risks arrived, and only after that did they hear about them. They were grave risks, blindly and blithely run by himself and the rest of them. Statistically, he was very likely to suffer that premature death, to be unable to withstand infection.

It had come a long way, this thing, from the dripping malarial swamps of equatorial Africa, to his clean breast, his slim firm body, his decent and moderate lifestyle (now), his diligent and useful activities.

He tested positive. He had known he would.

He had learned what his symptoms meant, more or less, from a curious source: instructional tracts, medical warnings, stuck up in the latrines at the Milchester College of Art and Design. The students were supposed to be warned about that kind of thing.

He might have years to live, usefully, even enjoyably, though becoming progressively weaker, thinner, more easily tired—

And all the rest.

He could not decide whether it showed yet. He stared at himself in the mirrors of hotel bedrooms, and larger, colder mirrors in surgeries and clinics, and sometimes he thought he looked under sentence of death – hollow-eyed, a bad colour, his thick hair lustreless, his lips pinched.

He thought a flight of steps already tired him more than it had done a few months before.

His dreams were haunted.

The other thing Bruno did when he was in London was make a will.

It was all wrong that he had not done so long before. He had funked it, for ridiculous, superstitious reasons; he had postponed it, out of laziness, out of a disinclination to contemplate cerements, holes in the ground or furnaces, out of a kind of timid frivolity. He realised that he could put it off no longer.

He decided not to go to the family lawyers in Milchester, inherited from his parents and Fred's, lawyers of the company as well as of the family, Fred's lawyers as well as Bruno's. Out of embarrassment he decided to go to strangers. The Milchester lawyers would show their surprise about Elinor. He went for this reason to a large firm in the City, to a partner whose name had been given him by George Napier-Gough.

He left la Moquerie and its contents to Elinor Leigh, 'as a memorial to our friendship, and in recognition of her kindness to me.' He left her also a sufficient sum to enable her to go on living there. The money was to be used to endow an artistic or charitable institution in the château, if she decided not to live there. This was not a fixed-choice situation. Elinor was not forbidden by the will to sell la Moquerie. The wish of the testator was stated, as no more than a wish.

The lawyer suggested strengthening the language, making it legally binding.

'You might wish to protect the legatee from an adventurer, a fortune-hunter,' said the lawyer.

'If she wants an adventurer, she'd better have one,' said Bruno. 'I'm not sure she hasn't got one already. A small adventuress. And I don't think anybody can be protected against her.'

The lawyer pursed his lips, looking wise, wondering what on earth his client was talking about.

A bequest went to the Milchester College of Art and Design, to be administered by the trustees of the existing Browning Endowment; this was to provide modest prizes and scholarships for as long as the money could be made to last. Milchester Cathedral, the Milchester Museum and Art gallery, other notable and deserving local institutions received bequests, as did the National Arts Collection Fund, the London Library, and the Glyndebourne Arts Trust.

There were bequests to Berthe and Pierre, and to François Delalain, and to various old servants and secretaries in Milchester.

Fred was executor and residual legatee. Fred would inherit a lot of shares in the company (in which he already had a lot of shares) and considerable other monies, and the lease and contents of the house in the Cathedral Close. He would not want the house, but he might want to keep some of his Aunt Rosa's antique furniture.

Bruno rang up from London, with the time of his arrival at Toulouse. He had a small hope that Elinor would meet him; but Pierre met him.

He had a larger hope that Elinor would be waiting to

welcome him, a bottle on ice. But Berthe was waiting for him.

Berthe said that Madame Elly was inconsolable not to be there to welcome Monsieur Bruno, but she had had to go away urgently, in the little car, with *la P'tite*.

Ailie continued to be *la P'tite* with Berthe and Pierre, because there would have been permanent, inextricable confusion between Madame Elly and Mademoiselle Ailie.

La P'tite as a title, as a form of address, was in no way impertinent, not at all patronising or lacking in respect. It was like Infanta. The servants did respect Ailie, very much: they had seen all the magazines which Elinor left on the coffee tables in the salon. They understood that *Ailie* had become a word. It almost meant 'winged'. (It had nothing to do with garlic.) *La P'tite* was almost winged, a sprite, a mischievous assistant angel, as seen in holy pictures.

Elinor appeared, contrite, overflowing with greeting and apology. She came not up the drive in her car, but along the path from the Guardhouse. She had driven there, to drop Ailie off. The car was there. This arrangement seemed silly but was actually sensible. They would need the car at the Guardhouse in the morning. Ailie was exhausted. She had been overworking. Bruno had made her feel guilty, and she was making up for those days of idleness. She was really very small and frail. The mural was almost too much for her, especially in this hot weather.

'And you?' said Elinor. 'Well? You look well. Was it fun?'

Bruno did not think he looked well.

Elinor looked supremely, superbly well. She was touched by the sun and by something else.

Elinor embarked, some time later, on an elaborate explanation of why she must go to the Guardhouse, why she must sleep there even on Bruno's first night home. She did not after all sleep with Bruno, and had never done so. Ailie had moved herself to the Guardhouse to be near her work, to live with the mural, and in the circumstances Elinor ... Elinor felt that she ... Elinor's responsibilities, Ailie being so young, were ...

Bruno had already known that Elinor would rejoin Ailie in the Guardhouse.

It was all something that ought to have been foreseen. He had not foreseen it, not once considered the possibility. He of all men should have predicted it, but it had never occurred to him. He had been fatuously complacent, thinking that their sweet uncomplicated friendship would continue for ever to be the way of life that they both preferred.

He had seen that Ailie had her hooks in Elinor, but he had not seen what kind of hooks they were.

He felt a great weariness, a sense of irrelevance. He was only a little over fifty, but he felt too old and tired to feel anything other than age and fatigue.

Elinor did not really think he looked well. She spoke casually, politely. She did not think he looked well or ill, she did not closely inspect him, her mind was elsewhere.

Bruno said to himself: I have no business to be hurt. We were never lovers, for God's sake, that was the point of us. We were loving friends, as it might have been two men, or people of widely different ages, as it might have been cousins or comrades. I have no grounds for despair, for jealousy. All that we had, we have, because there were narrow limits to the most that we ever had. It was a little, not a lot. We had that little, no more than that little. Surely we have it still?

Thus Bruno spoke to himself, and he knew it was all a lie.

Ailie said, 'You ought to be with Bruno, his first night home.'

'Darling, there's no need. There never was anything passionate between Bruno and me.'

'I'm not talking about passion. I'm just talking about manners, really.'

'Oh, for Christ's sake.'

'For Bruno's sake. Surely you see? That's why I asked you to drop me here.'

'Why?'

'So I wouldn't be in the way. So you and Bruno could have a private evening together, without the bore of an outsider.'

'You're not an outsider.'

'To Bruno I am.'

'No. You're part of the family.'

'In that case I'll go and be welcoming, even if you won't. He can't be left all alone on his first night back.'

'All right,' said Elinor. 'All right, all right, I'll come.'

Ailie thought Bruno was really pleased that Elinor was, after all, spending the evening with him. She was not sure if he was pleased that she, Ailie, was there. In both cases the feeling could only be guessed at. He was emotionally secretive, his heart worn not on his sleeve but in an inner pocket, a hidden money-belt.

Elinor said that Ailie had forbidden Bruno to be tired after his journey, to want the peace and ease of an early, solitary night. Elinor said Ailie required Bruno to want a party, a beano, a celebration.

Bruno smiled a cool smile, and inclined his head to acknowledge Ailie's interest.

They were awfully civilised, awfully polite to one another.

'He's doesn't look well to me,' said Ailie.

'He never looks well. He never has done. You can't imagine Bruno looking healthy. He always has a sort of haunted look. It's an eastern thing, Slav, something out of Central Asia. You can't imagine Bruno with pink cheeks.'

'He ought to see somebody. He ought to see a doctor.'

'If I suggest that, he'll tell me to mind my own business. Politely, of course.'

'It's not a crime to be concerned about people.'

'Bruno thinks it's an intrusion. He's like a house that's open to the public, but only a bit of it's open. There are red velvet ropes, and signs saying "Private". Locked doors. Bruno's full of locked doors. If there's something wrong with him, he'll keep it behind a locked door.'

Ailie nodded. She knew that this was true. It was probably impossible for Elinor to pry into the state of Bruno's health; it was certainly impossible for Ailie to do so.

That being so, there was not much point in talking about it, worrying about it.

Elinor put it out of Ailie's mind, and Ailie put it out of Elinor's. They had already become very good at putting everything out of one another's minds, in the intensity of physical sensation.

Bruno wondered what, if anything, was worth the trouble.

He had had large plans for the garden. The garden was an investment in the future. His plans for more terracing, tree planting, irrigation, would bear fruit in ten years' time. Then his new terraces would be nice places to sit under his new trees.

Who would be there to enjoy those things?

Did he give a damn?

It was all such an effort. Even if he did not contemplate wielding pick and shovel, or taking the controls of a bulldozer, still there were all those conversations to have, decisions to make, cheques to write: and all for other people, far in the future.

And there was that book he might write. It had been on the agenda for years. It was to have been about attitudes to art, the different kinds of experience to be had from looking at works of art: in part anthology, quoting art lovers such as Goethe rather than professional critics or academics; in part a personal pilgrimage through the world of art, a record of personal revelations and loves and hates. Publishers had thought it a pretty good idea, since his taste and knowledge were in a quiet way sufficiently celebrated. It was a book that would get a lot of serious reviews, if it ever happened.

But the effort. Could it be worth it? Could anything be worth so much sweat?

Once he had had the most abundant energy, fuelling him to be successful in his two completely different worlds. Now he could hardly be bothered to go out on to the terrace with a book. The distance was too great, the book too heavy. In any case he could hardly be bothered to read anything.

He caught Ailie looking at him anxiously. He was not sure he wanted to be looked at anxiously. He did not want to be patronised, with help on the stairs, or cushions plumped up for him.

Elinor was companionable enough, when she had time. She was preoccupied. She talked about all sorts of demands on her time and attention, but really there was only one.

The one was looking extraordinarily well. Objectively, it

had to be admitted that she was an ornament to the place. She often looked extraordinary, and it often worked. It worked for the stream of visitors for whom it was now the season for la Moquerie, and it worked for Elinor.

Of course the Ailie look was a fraud. It pretended to be extempore, improvised, thrown together absent-mindedly, and it was none of those things, far from it. It worked, though. It worked far better than if it really had been last-minute improvisation.

Ailie was not more beautiful than Elinor, but she was odder, more unconventional, more original, perhaps for these reasons more interesting.

A lot of people thought so, anyway. Journalists and photographers thought so.

Elinor herself thought so. Elinor was passionately committed to the cause of Ailie. Bruno was startled at the vehemence with which Elinor leapt to Ailie's defence, after somebody made a mild, unmeant joke about Ailie.

Bruno saw that Ailie was on a pedestal, and that she was not quite happy there.

Ailie preferred being nearer to Elinor, much nearer.

Bruno became to a small extent voyeur, sickening himself by his desire to see what he should not see, sickened by what he saw, sick at how little he was able to see. He had never spied on anybody before, and he would not have believed that he was capable of it.

He was an ill man, and he made himself iller.

After some days, Bruno embarked on the journey to the Guardhouse. The girls had been waiting for him to do so, although they had not nagged him about it.

Elinor wanted to show off this new evidence of Ailie's brilliance. Ailie wanted to show that she had not been idle, that she had been earning her keep.

Bruno took it slowly along the cliff-face path, troubled by the implacable glare of the sunlight reflected by the river, troubled as he had never been before by the vertiginous cliff. He came thankfully into the kindly gloom of the Guardhouse. He climbed the spiral staircase, glad that he had all morning to do so.

In the Oriel Room, he paused for a moment before looking at anything. He did not want his head to be swimming or his breath rasping, when he looked at the painting.

When he was ready, he went straight to the end of the room facing the oriel window. He did not stop to look out of the windows, lovely as the views were. He did not want to be distracted, beguiled. He wanted to be fair and objective. That was what they said they wanted him to be. They all kidded themselves that he would say exactly what he thought.

The picture was completely surprising, although he had been to an extent forewarned. He had known that it included Berthe and Pierre, and the men who had been working on the drive. He was not prepared for the busyness, the activity, the beehive industrial quality of Ailie's design, in which every imaginable domestic and garden task, every item of maintenance and repair, was illustrated as though to teach a beginner how the jobs were to be done.

Ailie had begun with unstartling colours: muted greens and bronzes in the background: then there were slashes and splashes of powerful, almost chemical colours, purples, crimsons, oranges, distributed across the great space, keyed and organised in a discipline that was almost too visibly artful. The effect was oddly medieval.

'It is,' said Bruno at last to Ailie, 'astonishingly unlike anything of yours that I have seen.'

'Or that I've seen,' said Ailie.

'That was something you said to me,' said Elinor.

'What was? What did I say?'

'That I must find an artist who'd never done anything like this before, so that they'd do something completely surprising.'

'Did I say that? What canny advice. I congratulate myself. Are you enjoying it, Ailie?'

'Yes, very much, only it's bloody hard work.'

'In the heat,' said Elinor.

'The colours,' said Bruno. 'They ring a bell or two, don't they? A dated bell, a transatlantic bell. You haven't matched the colours exactly, as Elinor mysteriously did with this crimson, but . . .'

He turned to look at the Tiffany lamp in the oriel window.

It was not there.

There was a lamp there, a lamp being certainly needed at that end of the room: a decent, nondescript lamp on a black wrought-iron stand, with a shade of honey-coloured parchment.

Elinor saw the flicker that crossed Bruno's face, when he looked in vain for the Tiffany lamp.

'You see,' said Elinor, 'the colours in the lampshade are so assertive, so sort of bossy and bullying, that Ailie couldn't achieve her own balance and harmony . . . I mean, as long as the lamp was in the same room, it sort of took charge . . . Isn't that right?'

'It was a bit distracting,' said Ailie.

Elinor was going over the top, describing the tyranny exercised by the Tiffany lamp over Ailie's palette. She was

259

distinctly fanciful. Ailie was playing it down. Those strong colours were a bit distracting: that was the most that Ailie would say about it.

Elinor was protesting too much, to explain why the lamp had been moved. Why was she?

Bruno understood, with a shock, that Elinor had given the lamp to Ailie.

The baton had been passed again.

Elinor was embarrassed that she had given away Bruno's precious gift to her. She had the grace to be evasive about that.

'You gave it to me,' said Elinor. 'So it was mine to give. I'm miserable to think I've hurt your feelings. That's the last thing I'd do. It was disturbing her, those powerful colours. The point is that the colours were nearly but not quite what she wanted. It was impossible for her to do herself justice, with that flaring great icon looking over her shoulder, shouting that she must copy all its colours. She's never owned anything in her life, that child, anything beautiful or amusing, anything of her own. I couldn't not give it to her. It was asking me to give it to her. She'll cherish it and appreciate it and look after it and wash its face very carefully with soap and warm water, and value it even more than I did.'

'No more,' said Bruno. 'No more.'

Bruno's mind went back, that breathless night, to Wenty Pollock.

It went back over his own life.

Bruno had left the world of passion, a thankful exile. His emigration was permanent. He could in no way get a visa to return.

They would not let him in, now. He would be forbidden entry, on medical grounds.

Elinor had come with him into tranquil exile, into an Eden in no need of apples. But she had returned. She was exploring that wild territory, those hidden valleys, the gold mines, the natural springs of wine. She was revelling now in foreign rites and mysteries by which she was hypnotised and dazzled. She was enslaved. She was singing hymns in a different language. She was the slave of a new drug.

Bruno had gone back to Cambridge, leaving Wenty behind.

Elinor had gone away, leaving Bruno behind.

Bruno thought drably about his own future, clinically predictable to the last degree.

Who wanted to climb stairs? Who wanted to write books?

At two o'clock in the morning, the house empty and silent, the moon already down, Bruno dressed himself for a warm-weather journey of moderate length and no hardship.

He wanted to be neat and decent, when they found him.

He did not write a note, though the temptation to do so was strong. There might be people who could think it was an accident. Nobody would be quite sure it was not. That was best. They would think they wanted to know the truth beyond doubt, but it was better if they did not – better for Elinor, for Fred, for Berthe and Pierre and François Delalain, for all the loyal old things in Milchester, and for the smart-assed international arty lot—

For Rosa his mother, if she was looking, if she'd kindly look away just for a minute—

But not Wenty Pollock. Having been there himself, he would not be deceived. A different man in Wenty's position (a different ghost) might enjoy the irony of Bruno's position; but not Wenty. He was too compassionate ever to enjoy another's unhappiness. Wenty would simply see the greyness of a man for whom the game was no longer worth the candle.

I strove with none, for none was worth my strife;

thought Bruno, pretty much honestly, pretty much accurately:

Nature I loved; and next to Nature Art.

Nature? That bit was a bit wrong. Art was easy winner of that.

I warmed both hands before the fire of life;

Yes, Warmed rather than heated, cooked, fried, frizzled.

It stinks, and I am ready to depart.

Very neat, oh, very neat indeed. It can't be a new joke. Somebody must have thought of that one. But it's awfully ingenious, awfully apposite.

More than ever Bruno wanted to leave a note, in which to put the gratifying misquotation.

It was still better not to.

He went out on to the terrace. It was very lonely, with the enormous spaces above and below. He had already started on a journey away from everybody. He had heard of the loneliness of the dying, and now he felt it. He had heard of the dark night of the soul, and he felt that, too. He tried to summon, for comfort, the ghosts of Rosa his mother and Wenty his lover, but he did not think they joined him on the terrace.

He squatted indecisive, for a moment, on the parapet at the edge of the terrace. He was trying not to be frightened.

Wenty spoke from a great way off, his voice chilled by infinity. Wenty said, 'There is nothing for you there. Everything there is done with.'

Bruno let himself fall off the parapet. He was then much surprised by how long it was before he hit the water.

Fred Browning was in his office when they brought him the news.

The body had been found soon after first light by a fisherman, five kilometres downstream from la Moquerie. The cause of death was drowning. There was no reason to suppose that the deceased had entered the water anywhere except la Moquerie. The temperature of the water made it impossible to be precise about the time of death, but it was reckoned to have been between one and four in the morning. The body was fully though casually dressed, in cotton trousers and a lightweight jacket. In the inside pocket of the jacket was a notecase containing credit-cards, driving licence and suchlike, with a little French paper money. Some coins and a cotton handkerchief were the only other things in the pockets. The wristwatch was of a shockproof and waterproof type, and was still functioning accurately when the body was found.

The deceased had last been seen by his companions in the salon of la Moquerie at a quarter to midnight, at which time they had left the château for the Guardhouse.

The body was formally identified by Miss Elinor Leigh, as required by law, although the identity was not in doubt.

The body was little damaged and the features were unmarked.

'Poor old bastard,' said Fred numbly. 'Poor old bastard.'

Fred booked a flight to Toulouse, and set himself to clear his in-tray before he left.

The family and company lawyers knew nothing about any will. They had taken the liberty many times of urging on Mr Brian Browning the desirability of making a will, but as far as they knew he had done nothing about it.

Fred was contacted by a London firm, who had themselves been contacted by Miss Elinor Leigh, who had found their names amongst the late Mr Browning's papers in France. The London firm had a will, of very recent date, which they assumed was the last one, if indeed there were others. Mr Frederick Browning was named as executor, which was presumably no surprise to him. Matters should have been simple, but it appeared that they were not. Other dispositions had been made, subsequent to the making of the will, apparently expressive of the wishes of the testator though not formally registered as codicils to the will. These dispositions having been made in France, French law applied, which as regarded questions of inheritance was substantially different from English law.

How much time had Mr Frederick Browning at his disposal, to deal with what might be a tangle?

The answer was that Fred had no time, but he had as much time as it was going to take.

The terms of the will were exactly as he had expected. God knew what these other documents were, what they said, who would benefit. 'Undue influence' was a phrase that had nibbled at the edge of Fred's mind, from time to time, when he thought about the set-up at la Moquerie. It was a beastly way to be thinking, and he fought against it, but it would not quite lie down. There was nothing Fred could have done about it. There was probably nothing he could do about it now.

He wished he knew more than a scratching of schoolboy French. He left all that stuff to Brian, and got busy with his spanner. There was room in anybody's life for a bit of both, perhaps.

He needed an interpreter and a French lawyer and an English lawyer and about two months of time. The English lawyer was the only one of these things he had.

Fred sighed, and resigned himself to delegating the affairs of Browning Machinery to men who, having run the firm, would not want to stop doing so when he came back.

Brian's trouble, Fred saw, was that he was lonely. He was atypical. He wasn't one of the boys, never could have been.

Why?

Jewishness, a sense of difference. An exotic, unmistakable, Levantine look, which made it impossible for him to be absorbed, to pass unnoticed.

Brains, so that he was never going to be your average man, in the street or on the Clapham omnibus. Taste, discrimination – isolating kind of things, those.

Hormone balance, so that he was always going to be subject to stress, to membership of a minority, to otherness: he was always going to be an object of macho scorn, suspicion, outrage.

And then the mother, that wonderful cannibalistic Rosa, who loved him too much, who asked too much of him, who got from him everything that she asked, at too great a cost.

These things partly caused one another. They certainly exacerbated one another. They produced a man who was never at home, anywhere, with anybody.

Fred thought: Brian never knew what he was, what he

wanted to be. He wanted to be Bruno, but Bruno didn't exist. Bruno pretended to have become what he never really was, without really remaining what he had been.

He came closest to resolution, as far as Fred's knowledge went, in those last two or three years at la Moquerie. But that was a cool business. That was a careful relationship. It was what the old boy wanted, or thought he wanted, but it was bloody bloodless.

It was not the way Fred wanted to live.

But it was exactly the way Fred did live.

Look at him, remarking on another bloke's loneliness – Fred Browning, loneliest man in the South of England. A man in an envelope of plastic, a bubble of oil, with colleagues and acquaintances and a few relations (his mother's boring, decent relations) and no loves in his life, no intimates, no one in front of whom he could cry.

That was a terrible thing, to be a man with no one to cry at.

Not at the end of a weepy old film on the telly, not at the news of Brian's suicide.

Why not?

Fred was not Jewish. He was a beef-fed West Saxon. He was exactly what he looked like.

Fred was not queer, gay, fancy, bent. Not a trace of that, never at any stage of his life.

Fred was not clever the way Bruno had been, the way that separates a man from his fellows, that makes him a member of Mensa, an oddity, a crossword champion. Fred was extremely able in his own areas, but it was not the sort of cleverness that tucked you up on a special cloud.

Fred was a bloke with a spanner in his pocket and a computer on his desk.

He was an island. He had no bridges. He was not plugged

in to any network. There was no one to whom he whispered. He looked warm, but he was cold. He looked human, but he examined himself and found only plastic and ticking machinery, responses as predictable as those of a pendulum.

He could ever so cleverly explain Brian's isolation, but how in God's name could he explain his own?

He emptied his in-tray, tidied his desk, had a long and unsatisfactory meeting with the lawyers in London, a short and satisfactory meeting with Brian's housekeeper in the Close, packed a suitcase (he had nobody to pack a suitcase for him), having noted that it was very hot in south-western France, and had himself taken in a company car to Heathrow.

On the aircraft he studied the specifications of some new American earth-moving machines, and filled in the crossword in the *Daily Telegraph*.

'Who are you? Are you staying here?'

'We have met, Mr Browning,' said the small, lovely girl.

'We can't have. I'd certainly remember.'

'I may have looked a bit different. Both times. All three times.'

'I'm sorry, you'll have to remind me. But I'm not going to believe this, that I could have forgotten you.'

The girl laughed. Her face was small and pointed and sweet. Fred used the word 'elfin' to himself, but he would not have said it out loud to anybody at all.

She said, 'You saw me at the college in Milchester, at the exhibition. With your cousin, with Bruno. With Elinor as well, Elinor Leigh. She'll be back this evening. She'll be very relieved to see you.'

'Milchester. It's coming back. My God. Then it was you who came in out of the rain? It was you in the dressing-gown?'

'That was me.'

'Of course I recognise you now, I really do apologise. I don't understand myself. I'd have said you were once seen, never forgotten.'

'Thank you very much. Except that I was three times seen and completely forgotten.'

'You'll just have to forgive me.'

'Okay. Tea? Coffee? Wine?'

'What are you having? Are you having anything? Am I interrupting something?'

'Wine is the least bad for you.'

Fred laughed.

They drank cold golden wine on the terrace, in the golden light of the late afternoon.

Fred Browning had the feeling that he had been kidnapped, that he was no longer in charge of anything.

CHAPTER TWELVE

'YOU ARE NOT AT ALL as I imagined you,' said Ailie Huxtable. 'You are not a bit what I thought you were, when I met you before.'

Indeed this was not the stolid house-builder or wholesale grocer who had loitered morosely at the end-of-term exhibition, or sat unhappily in the corner of the salon.

Perhaps he was better not in a crowd. He was better when you could see all round him. He was better in a quiet place, and sitting down.

'I feel unfamiliar to myself,' said Fred Browning. 'Fancy me drinking wine on a terrace like this, with a beautiful girl, chatting away as though this was something I do all the time.'

'If you like it, why not do it all the time?'

'I can't.'

'Why?'

'There are other things I do.'

'Stop doing them.'

'I wish life was that simple.'

'Simplify it.'

Fred laughed. It was not an indulgent, a patronising laugh, but one of enjoyment and admiration. The child meant what she said.

Now she said, 'If you can leave your job for a week, you

can leave it for two weeks. If you leave it for two weeks, you can leave it for three. If—'

'And so on, for fifty-two weeks, and if one year then two years, and so on. Yes. Nobody's indispensable, but I'd hate to think they could all get on perfectly well without me.'

'You'll have to get along without Bruno.'

'Yes. It won't be easy.'

'Nor for us.'

'Nor for you.'

They fell silent, a friendly silence, thoughtful, sad because of mention of Bruno.

Fred looked at the girl with simple amazement, trying to relate what he saw to what he had seen – to the farouche and scruffy art student in bovver boots, the tattered and saturated waif, the pet kitten in the oversized dressing-gown. God Almighty, thought Fred, what a transformation. So self-possessed now, poised, chatty, bright, confident, civilised, French-speaking –

French-speaking.

He said, 'How much spare time does the mural leave you?'

'None. As much as it has to. If I have to do something else, the mural waits.'

'I need an interpreter.'

'I don't know if my French is good enough for that.'

'Berthe seems to think it is. She was going at you like a machine gun.'

'Well, I'm used to her.'

'This is something the estate will pay for. It is absolutely necessary. If you can't do it, I'll have to hire a professional.'

'I shan't know what the words mean, the special language, the legal words.'

'Nor would any interpreter, except a specialist legal one,

270

if there is such a thing, and if there is he'd cost a million a minute. We'll get a legal dictionary. The lawyers in Toulouse will tell us what to get.'

'They'll have an interpreter. They'll know of one.'

'I don't want their interpreter. That'd be like buying a horse with a certificate from the vendor's vet.'

'I don't think I can take any money from this, not from Bruno's estate.'

'I'll find out the going rate. I imagine it's paid by the hour. There's an awful lot of pieces of paper in Brian's desk, and I'll have to know what every single one's about.'

'Oh God. Most of them are probably something quite different. Things about the garden, the Milchester college, painting, that book he was going to write.'

'Yes, but I won't know they're about those things until you tell me. I can't throw anything away, until you tell me. I can't assume anything's irrelevant to my job as executor, unless I know what it's about. You see, I really do need you, and if not you, then somebody from outside, which would be a great bore and a horrible expense.'

'I'll have to see what Elinor says.'

'Is Elinor in a tearing hurry for the mural?'

'No, not really, I don't think so, but she obviously wants me to get on with it. It's what I came here to do.'

'We ought to be able to work out a compromise.'

'Yes.'

Poised, charming, chatty, bright, French-speaking, and now on the Browning payroll.

'Welcome aboard,' said Fred to his new employee.

They had never had an employee that looked like this one, a skinny little super-model, in a leather miniskirt and a skimpy waistcoat in a check like a mad tartan, bare feet with toenails painted all different colours, pink and green and mauve and orange, one very big red plastic ear-ring: and she carried off this childish, wildly unstylish combination with a sort of good-humoured panache which made it seem exactly right – for her, if no other, on this afternoon, if no other.

What a girl.

They were right, the magazines in the dentist's waiting-room. He had thought that they were wrong, but they were right.

'I don't want to use his desk,' said Fred at dinner.

'Why not?' said Elinor, magnificent but chilly, stately, too perfect a goddess, an unreachable ice queen.

'I just don't. I don't want to sit in his chair or wear his shoes.'

'There are plenty of desks you can use, spaces, tables, whatever you want. But you'll need to be undisturbed, I imagine. It won't be easy to be undisturbed in this house.'

This was obviously true. Life at la Moquerie was apt to be continuously festive. This summer would be no exception. It would have been ridiculous, incongruous, to respect Bruno's memory by pulling down the blinds and keeping silence. Every party at la Moquerie was a celebration of thanksgiving for Bruno's life. Even Berthe and Pierre understood that they were not to wear funeral faces. Fred understood very well, and he agreed with Elinor. It was true, then, that he would find it hard to work undisturbed in the château.

And Elinor wanted him out of the way: out from under her feet: out of her sight, for as much of the time as possible. She did not want him boring her guests, sitting silent and uncouth among the singing birds of paradise with which her house would be filled.

Fred rolled with the punch. He said, 'Is there anywhere I can camp in the Guardhouse?'

'That would suit me better,' said Ailie, 'if you really want me to help you. When you don't need me to translate something, I can slosh some more paint on my wall.'

'Can you really do that, darling?' said Elinor. 'Just pick up a brush and add a bit?'

'Yes, that's the beauty of oils,' said Ailie. 'I put in a squiggle today and wipe it off tomorrow and put it back different the next day.'

Elinor looked proudly at Ailie, as though Ailie had just brought home a prize from her nursery school.

It was proverbial that doctors never looked after their health, that lawyers and accountants left their affairs in a mess: but who would have thought it of Brian?

In Milchester, his papers were squared up on top of his desk, each pile neat in a clip or under a weight. Fallen petals under flower vases were swept up; ashtrays were emptied and washed immediately after meetings, minutes circulated, questions answered, decisions made. At home he never ran out of sherry or shoe-polish, or lost the corkscrew, or forgot to lock the downstairs windows.

Brian didn't miss trains or forget appointments. He never let the milk boil over. He was a man who did not need a nanny.

But the proverb was proved right again. The big desk at la Moquerie was stuffed to bursting with letters, papers, documents, items legal and cultural, important and meaningless, in French and English and some in other languages: it was a jungle of stuff, a haystack of rubbish amongst which there might be nothing of significance at all.

But there might. Fred knew that and Elinor knew it, and

Berthe and Pierre and François Delalain and several score of friends knew that Brian might have left something to somebody and made a note of the fact. The whole boiling had to be gone through.

It was as though a demon of irresponsibility had taken possession of Brian as soon as he reached the banks of the Tarn. He really did seem to manage his affairs in a completely different way, cavalier, slapdash, his mind elsewhere. That being so, there were almost certainly unpaid bills lost amongst these drifts of paper, forms needing to be filled in for the local authorities, documents relating to electricity supply or sewage or tax . . .

Ailie would need a shelf of dictionaries.

He would need a lot of her time.

It really was as he had said – either she helped him, or he brought in an expensive bilingual secretary.

They loaded everything into the back of a car, and took it the long way round by road from the château to the Guardhouse. It was a lot of trouble, but less trouble than carrying it along the cliff-face path, journey after exhausting journey.

They carried it into the Guardhouse, boxful by boxful (wine boxes, vegetable boxes from the supermarket) and then wondered where Fred should instal himself.

It had to be the Oriel Room.

There was nowhere else where a man could spread papers over a big table, well lit by day and by night, airy, comfortable and practical. A desk in any other room would have been at best a scrubby improvisation, inimical to efficiency, bad for Fred's eyesight.

Fred thought he would not disturb Ailie when she was painting. He thought she would not disturb him. There were many yards of floor between them. Both activities were fairly quiet. When Fred suddenly needed the English-ing of a passage of French, Ailie could put down her brush, and be with him in a moment. Much time would be saved.

So it seemed to them. So it turned out to be.

With the house often full, with Elinor preoccupied, Fred and Ailie and their tasks were rather marginalised. Some days they were seen only for meals. They did not take part in the expeditions to Albi or the organised bouts of pretended labour in the garden.

The girls were parted, though not completely. Their comings together were brief and secret. This was not, as it happened, so great a deprivation as it might have been. They had deliberately, inevitably cooled themselves, after Bruno's death, simply because the extremes of con-quest and surrender, of passion and sensation and self-forgetfulness, seemed inapposite, ungracious, at such a time. A civilised dinner party clashed with no memory of Bruno; but those cries and shudderings did. They were not his cup of tea at all.

This self-denial was without prejudice to the most delirious second honeymoon, when decency permitted.

There was certainly this also, that Elinor was not so liberated, so defiant, so sure of her status in her world, that her relationship with Ailie was to be run up a flagpole while the orchestra played.

They had been marvellously uninhibited when they had the place to themselves, when they could run naked along corridors and drink wine naked on the terrace. They were spoiled. Careful creepings down midnight corridors were part of their future, perhaps, but they had become used to a beautiful blatantness.

Love could go on a back burner, just while the house was

full, just when they were all so busy.

'Who do we think we're kidding?' whispered Elinor to Ailie.

'All the others,' said Ailie.

'We thought it would be easy, giving it up for a bit. Like somebody in Lent, like somebody giving up joints. Oh God. My guts are melting, I'm on fire.'

'It's tricky just now.'

'I wish Fred was in Tierra del Fuego. I wish he'd bugger off to a hotel. Why doesn't he go and stay in a hotel?'

'He's really got more right here than anybody, at the moment. He's got a job to do.'

'Oh, don't be so po-faced. I know all that. I just wish he was the other side of the moon. Then we'd have our house.'

'It won't be long.'

'It will seem long.'

'Yes, it will seem long.'

'The bore about love is that one can't think about anything else. You can't put it into a compartment. I didn't expect that. I didn't expect any of this.'

'Is it your first time, then? This sort, or any sort?'

'You know it is. First and last.'

Ailie smiled, a little quick pussy-cat smile, and trotted off by the cliff-face path to the Guardhouse. Elinor could not follow, to any purpose, because Fred was there with his pieces of paper, and because the others on the terrace would see her go.

Some of the others might follow Elinor along the path, if she went that way, with the excuse of seeing how the mural was getting on, with the excuse of helping Elinor with whatever she was doing. They were a very busy and helpful lot, staying in the house just then. They were great snoopers and tattle-tales.

Ailie got back to find Fred not sitting at his table in the window, but standing in front of her mural.

He glanced at her, when she climbed into the room by the spiral staircase. His face was serious.

Ailie realised, with surprise, that he had a gentle face. She had not looked at him properly before; or her vision had been clouded by preconception; or his face changed. He had a gentler face than the beaky, knowing faces of the people who came to la Moquerie, gentler that Elinor's. Elinor was a Valkyrie, a warrior queen. What was Fred? In face he was not a builder or a butcher. He was not quite a doctor or a priest or a poet. Perhaps he was a man who ran a hospital, or led a team of relief workers into a besieged city.

He had in those first few days of their arrangement asked her to translate two dozen pieces, letters, bills, oddments. There had been nothing obscurely legal. She had needed a dictionary, Elinor's, chosen for her by François Delalain. In asking for Ailie's help, Fred had been considerate and patient.

He was a powerful man. He was only of medium height and build, but he was muscled like a wrestler. This had become obvious when he wore a thin, short-sleeved shirt at his desk. His shoulders and pectorals were indicated, his biceps visible. Ailie had not seen him in the pool. He had got into the way of swimming before breakfast, before anybody else was up, having already done an hour's work at the table. He said he could work more quickly in the cool of the early morning, but he missed Ailie's help.

Now he said, 'It keeps changing. It keeps growing. Every time I turn my back, something new appears.'

'Not much, in the last few days,' said Ailie. 'I've been idle.'

'This bit here, this chap's shirt, that colour.'

'It's over the top, that colour, awful. I didn't mean that kind of mauve.'

'That's what's good about it. A bit of a shock. Unexpected. Sort of electric.'

A week before, Ailie would not have given a damn what Fred Browning said about the colour of a man's shirt in her painting. Now she reconsidered the view she had herself taken. After all, wasn't that vulgar, dynamic colour rather effective here? Working with those other colours, working violently with the hot reds behind . . .

'A few days ago, I wouldn't have noticed it,' said Fred. 'I wouldn't have had the slightest idea about the effect that colour has on the other colours, why you might have chosen it, why you might be doubtful about it.'

'Perhaps I'm not so doubtful about it. You're seeing more than I saw.'

'Only because you've opened my eyes.'

'What? Have I? How?'

'A few things you've said. And then I've been able to watch what you're doing, what keeps happening here.'

'I didn't know you'd been watching.'

'I've been trying not to. It's extremely distracting.'

'I'm sorry.'

'Don't be. I'm not sorry. It's a marvellous way to learn, a piece of amazing luck for me. I remember years ago Brian telling me about a film somebody made of Picasso doing a painting, maybe several. I think they filmed it through ground glass, and he was using some kind of ink, something like a magic marker that showed through the glass. Brian said you learned more about the mechanics of making a painting from that film, than you would from a hundred books or a million lectures. Well, it's been like that for me.'

'I'm not Picasso,' said Ailie after a moment.

'You don't look much like him, it's true. It's funny. This whole situation is really ironic. My mother wanted me to be like Brian, a clone of Brian, academic and arty and a collector and a connoisseur, and she went about indoctrinating me with a sort of . . . I suppose in a very naïve way. My poor old mum. She did mean so well. She pushed Michelangelo and Mozart down my throat, and I just gagged and wouldn't have it. I wouldn't have any of it. Obviously I overreacted. I developed an allergy. I rejected the whole thing. Art brought me out in spots.'

'Literally?'

'No.' Fred laughed. 'But bloody near.'

'That's a pity. It's all a pity.'

'Yes. Oh yes. And I've just now come to realise it.'

'Well, you've still got plenty of time.'

'Yes, thank God. I've got time. It's funny how things go. I had two school friends whose fathers were mad about chess. One was a teacher, one was a barber, believe it or not. They both taught their sons to play chess. The boys both knew how the knight moves even before they could read. One of my friends took to it, thrived on it, began to beat his father, did very well in the national schoolboy championships. Now he writes about chess in the Sunday papers. His dad's plan had worked, absolutely spot on. That was how it was with Brian, right? Rosa his mother gave him the fine arts with her milk. You know what he turned into. It was all absolutely genuine, his thing about the arts, and it all derived from his mother's commitment. My mother did exactly the same thing, with exactly the opposite result.'

'If she'd left you alone . . .?'

'If she'd just been a bit more gentle about it, a bit more sly, spreading the goods on the counter instead of forcing them down my throat . . . Because you see, the thing is, that I'm only now realising what a fabulous countryside there is there, that I've never tried to look at, that I've deliberately turned my back on . . .'

'I'm very pleased if I've helped.'

'By God you have. You've opened my eyes. I want you to open them a whole lot more. Tell me things. Would that bore you out of your mind?'

'No, I don't think so,' said Ailie. 'I don't think it would.'

It was rather awful how little, in a day-to-day sense, Bruno was missed at la Moquerie. Of course it was because he had been impresario rather than star, master of ceremonies, guide, steerer of photographers rather than their target. With Berthe and Pierre, latterly with Elinor also, he had set going a quiet and efficient machine, user-friendly and reliable, not at all cheap, almost invisible; one could imagine the house impeccably comfortable, warm and welcoming, though it had been empty for months. All of this continued to function. It was part of Bruno's legacy. It was in a sense a tribute to him, that his absence made so little difference.

There were those who wondered that the house was full, the laughter unbridled, so soon after so painful and unexplained a tragedy.

One of those who wondered, at first, was Fred Browning the unassimilated outsider, the odd man out. Fred was shocked, at first, when a party assembled almost immediately after his own arrival, itself so soon after Brian's death.

Ailie said, 'It's not like that, not like you say. You're not being fair to Elinor. Think what Bruno would have preferred. Anyway, how long are you supposed to weep and wear black? Six months? A year? The rest of your life, like the poor old bags in a Greek village? Aren't you just talking about convention, Victorian rules? What's any of that got to do with Bruno? With Elinor? With any of us here? You, perhaps. Nobody else.'

'Respect . . .' said Fred uncertainly.

Ailie gave a small, derisive hoot.

'Elinor is showing respect for Bruno by every single thing in the entire way she lives her life,' said Ailie. 'The way she looks, what she eats, everything. Don't you remember what she was like before?'

'I do remember.'

'Well, then. She *lives* respect for Bruno. She doesn't have to give up drink or wear a hair shirt or go to bed after tea.'

'She's not exactly insulting his memory,' Fred admitted.

'No, and if she suddenly died, I wouldn't be insulting her memory, by going on as I am.'

'Elinor didn't invent you,' said Fred.

'Yes, she did,' said Ailie. 'Of course she did.'

Fred laughed. But he saw things at la Moquerie, thereafter, in a different light. He began to see Elinor in a different light.

Fred had known, of course he had known, that he was sharing the Guardhouse with Ailie. The two of them were here together, all night, much of the day. Nobody else, other bedrooms not being needed by the house party. If you had asked Fred, 'Are you sharing a house with Ailie?' he would have thought a moment, and then in a tone of surprise said, 'Yes, if you put it like that, I suppose I am.'

The house they were in was quite on its own, most of the time. Nobody in the château would go there, without a reason for going there. Sometimes there was a reason for going there – to look at the progress of Ailie's mural, to cheer up Fred in his interminable task – but for most of most days, and all of every night, the Guardhouse was illimitably distant. Going there was an expedition, something you talked about before you went, reported on when you got back.

Ailie and Fred were thrown a good deal together. They were both working. They were both serious about the work they were doing.

They talked.

They became accustomed to one another so that, often, they did not talk.

They went along the cliff-face path for most of their meals, because it was easier, because it was more friendly. Everybody wanted Ailie around (though nobody much cared whether Fred was around or not).

Ailie had become, to an extent that surprised herself, immersed in the mural, as she never had been in any of her work before. She was intoxicated by the scale. It was wonderfully huge. A development in one corner seemed to scream for more work in a distant corner, each added or modified splash of colour to demand adjustments to a spectrum of surrounding colours. The corners were indeed distant. Ailie was wearing out the rungs of her ladder. She thought she must be developing enormous calf muscles, but Fred said not. It was a terrific taskmaster, but she was truly falling in love with what she was doing.

She was not now anxious for people to look at it unfinished and experimental as so much of it was. Except Fred. Fred was there anyway. She could bounce ideas of Fred. Fred kept her straight. He was extraordinarily useful given that he knew nothing about any of it, except what she had told him.

It was encouraging to Ailie, that Fred was so positiv

about her work. He really did seem to like it a lot. He would have said so anyway, because he was a very nice man, but Ailie was sure he meant it.

Ailie got into the way of using Fred as a tuning fork, a litmus paper. 'Will this do? Is this too gross? Am I missing a trick here?'

Fred's approval reassured her, and his doubts filled her with doubts.

His taste was more adventurous than hers – more primitive, perhaps, more savage. This was good. A spirit of barbarism entered the mural, compensating for the banality of the things the people were doing.

After dinner, Fred slipped away from the party, incon-spicuous, trying successfully not to put anybody out.

Ailie after a moment noticed that he had gone. Nobody else noticed. Ailie got up to leave. That was noticed, all right. There were cries of reproach, efforts to keep her, to make her perform, to be funny and kooky and Ailie. She said she was really tired, that if she stayed she would only be a bore.

Elinor sat silent through this. Nobody except Ailie saw the way she looked at Ailie. Ailie was embarrassed, in case anybody else did see. Elinor's face was shamingly revealing. It gave away secrets, and there was too much emotion in it.

Ailie went out on to the terrace. She paused by the balustrade, to let her eyes get used to the darkness. She had a flashlight, but she had no need of it.

She was aware of another figure beside her on the terrace.

'Hullo, Fred.'

'Hullo, Ailie.'

'Why are you still here?'

'Waiting for you.'

'Why?'

'Gallantry.'

Fred heard Ailie smile.

This was impossible, but so it was. He could not see her face, and a smile is soundless, but he heard her smile.

He said, 'Time to go home.'

'Yes.'

'Will you lead the way?'

'If you like.'

He followed her close, not too close. He did not tread on her heels.

They entered the thick blackness of the Guardhouse's entrance hall. Fred clicked a switch. There was a split of gold, an audible pop, and blackness.

'Pop,' echoed Fred. 'Got a torch?'

'No,' lied Ailie.

'I have, too, but I don't want to use it. I like the dark. It makes me feel brave. Do you want to hold my hand?'

'Yes.'

So it happened, calm, peaceful, slow and gentle, inevitable.

They were naked and on her bed when Ailie said, 'But I'm a lesbian.'

'No, you're not.'

'Perhaps I'm not.'

'I'm frightened of hurting you. You're so tiny.'

'Too skinny?'

'Adorable.'

'I'm frightened of exploding.'

'Explode. Let's explode.'

'I am exploding. Fred. Darling. Oh my God.'

★

It was even better in the dawn. They could see one another's smiles.

Ailie said, 'I'm crying. Look. I'm crying with happiness. I love you. I'm normal.'

'Let's have a swim.'

'You're supposed to be working.'

'And then some fresh orange-juice and five pints of coffee.'

'And then . . .'

'Are you insatiable?'

'Yes,' said Ailie.

'Hal and Victoria are going to Albi,' whispered Elinor urgently to Ailie. 'Tim and Melanie are going down the Gorges in a boat, Mollie's heard about a woman who's making pottery in Millau, and the others are all leaving before lunch.'

'Yes. People are coming.'

'They rang up. Tomorrow. Not today. Berthe is going off at lunchtime. Darling, the house will be absolute guaranteed empty for four hours.'

'I'm sorry.'

'Come.'

'I can't.'

'You must. Of course you can.'

'I've got the curse.'

'Oh God. Oh well, it won't be perfect, then—'

'It won't be at all. I can't. I'm feeling lousy. I can't face it. I'm sorry.'

'I don't believe you.'

'All right. Don't.'

'Oh darling, I'm sorry,' said Elinor, aghast at the anger in Ailie's face. 'Of course I believe you. I'm just so sick with disappointment. I'd hoped so hard – but we've got the whole of the rest of our lives – just now, all these people, but things will get quieter – I don't think I can stand it. Couldn't we go away for a day or two?'

'You know we couldn't.'

'You don't care. Oh God, I'm sorry, I don't know what I'm saying.'

'No,' said Ailie. 'I must go back.'

'*Why?*'

'I've got work to do. The others will notice. The others already are noticing.'

'I don't care.'

'I do.'

Again, Ailie went back to the Guardhouse. Again, Elinor could not follow.

Ailie felt Elinor's eyes in the small of her back, all the way along the cliff-top path.

'I woke up in the wrong room,' said Ailie to Fred.

'What, my sweet? What room?'

'Elinor's. She woke me up. It was the wrong place to wake up. This is the place for me.'

'It's a good thing you found out when you did.'

'It's a good thing I found you when I did.'

Ailie filled Fred up with what she had been taught at college, and what she had learned from Bruno and from Elinor, and what she had absorbed by the experience of trying to paint and to understand the paintings of others.

Fred took Ailie to Toulouse and Albi in the car he had hired, saying that they had necessary business in regard to Brian's affairs, that he needed Ailie as interpreter. In those great shrines of the arts, Ailie filled Fred up with knowledge and enthusiasm as a vintner fills a bottle from a barrel.

Half asleep at night, half awake in the dawn, Fred babbled of Romanesque and post-impressionist. Ailie smiled proudly and adoringly.

She liked being a woman, not a plaything, a kewpie-doll, a mascot, a trophy.

She very much liked being normal.

She liked Fred.

She liked Fred's enthusiasm, his happy, even-tempered personality, his passionate eagerness to learn, after all the years in which he had deliberately, perversely blinded himself. She liked his simplicity, which was not at all to be confused with stupidity. She liked his ribs and his muscles and his gentle fingers. She liked the trace of West Country burr in his voice. She liked being filled up by masculinity. She liked his joy and her own.

Elinor knew. Of course she knew. Not all at once, but she got to know. She found out. She neither saw nor heard anything, at first, but sensed it.

Love does that, it gives you an extra sense. Love has an alarm system, hypersensitive. Bells rang in Elinor's skull, with a jealous jangle.

Elinor spied on the fornicators, with disgusted fascination. Elinor felt ill with love and with hatred.

Of the men who had come to la Moquerie since Elinor had come there, very few raised their eyes to her.

She was Bruno's. She was said not to be interested in men. She was a general's daughter, more like a general than like a daughter. She frightened the life out of most of the visiting men. She frightened the life out of Fred, who only raised his eyes as high as Ailie.

Ailie was proud of Fred. She was bursting with pride at what Fred had so marvellously become. She looked at him at dinner in the château, discussing painting with the arty-smarty lot who were there. He held his own! He had become a feasible member of this group, not advancing audacious views, or putting anybody right, but not silent in a corner, either.

He looked nicer than any of the others. He was fitter, more of a man, not smarmily handsome in a male-model, shop-window-dummy way, but a solid authentic genuine red-blooded intelligent sensitive gentle understanding manly way.

Ailie was proud of him, and he ought to be proud of himself.

What made Ailie mad was Fred's humility.

He said, 'Modesty, I think, not really humility. In some ways I suppose I am quite modest. I've got a lot to be modest about, as the fellow said about the other fellow.'

'I want to hit you on the head with a brick when you talk like that.'

'Like what?'

'Crawling and whining.'

'Oh come.'

'Whimpering and hiding your face. You ought to be strutting and bragging, Fred!'

'What ever about?'

'Yourself!'

'Well, I doubt if—'

'You never look at yourself! You never listen to yourself! You're worth twenty of any of those wimpish creeps! You can do everything they can do, and a million things they can't do! You can talk about Toulouse-Lautrec, and you ca also fix an engine! You're really attractive. You're exciting, because you're strong. You're formidable, Fred. That's the exact word for you. You give a feeling of power under control, like a very expensive car, like a jet engine.'

'Who is this we're talking about?'

'I want you to swagger!'

'Me?'

'Swank and swagger and spit in their eye!'

'Must I do that?'

'How can I make you understand that you're a gorgeous frightening impressive exciting adorable man?'

She stopped his mouth with hers before he could reply. She thought she might have got something through to him.

It was impossible, for the most modest of men, to hear stuff like that, from a beautiful young girl who was also a fashion icon, without being affected a bit.

Fred contemplated his reflection dubiously. He supposed he passed muster. He tried to assess the impact he had on the various women (more or less weird) who stayed at la Moquerie.

He allowed himself to conclude that they quite liked him.

Ailie said they all adored him. She said they were bound to compare him to the other men, and the moment they did that they were bound to find him six million times more desirable.

Six million? Sixty million.

Fred compared himself, as objectively as he could, to some of the other men. These had been Brian's friends; they were denizens of Brian's world. He would back himself against them in a boxing ring, or in bed with a girl. With any of these women, if you wanted any of them.

Did he?

Elinor swam out on to the terrace, while Fred was amusing himself by speculating about some of the others. She made the others look like milkmaids or housemaids, or drabs, or terrible blue-stocking schoolmarms. Her body was undeniably magnificent. She was one hell of a specimen.

What was it Brian had said? Why she had never married? She was under the thumb of terrible parents, until it was too late, or she thought it was. The general, yes, Fred remembered about the general, a tyrannical selfish dinosaur. Everything inside Elinor was locked up, then; she turned into a bullyragged frustrated spinster.

The situation was unchanged by Brian, of course. She lost a couple of stone, and learned about clothes and painting, but her *essential* situation was unchanged.

Ailie?

The situation was *still* unchanged. Ailie was evidence of that.

What a waste.

She was not the flamboyant, bossy show-off Fred had once supposed. She was flamboyant, because that was how she was. She simply could not be grey and meek.

She could be funny.

She could be kind. She had been very kind to Ailie. Ailie had told Fred about that, and certainly Elinor had been very kind.

She was not a phoney. Her knowledge was wide and genuine, and her enthusiasm was genuine. Ailie said so, and Ailie was in a position to judge.

She was unawakened. She thought she was awakened, but she was wrong.

What a waste.

What had Ailie said about himself? What were all those nice words she used?

How many lives do we have? How soon are we old and helpless? Isn't it better to fail than not to try?

Elinor was that evening aware of Fred watching her. Her hand as she drank trembled with anger and disgust, with sickening jealousy and hatred.

CHAPTER THIRTEEN

I N THOSE HOT LAZY WEEKS of midsummer, Elinor was miserably confused.

She mourned Bruno.

The mourning was not very bitter, the grief not sharp-fanged, because he had departed with dignity. He took his leave like a gentleman. He died as he chose to. His death was in extreme and happy contrast to that of Elinor's father, who died without dignity, falling downstairs having lost his temper. Bruno had had the option of lingering, and had rejected it. He did not fancy that smouldering fag-end to his life. This was obvious to everybody who knew him. The knowledge dried tears.

Elinor mourned him, but not as keenly as she would have done a few months earlier. In the days when he brought champagne or *kir royale* to her bedroom, after her bath, then she would have mourned him, and ached at his absence. But that was long past. It was already past when he died. She had moved on from there. He had been displaced from the centre of her life.

He had never really been in the centre of her life, but she had not realised that until her life acquired a real centre. Ailie filled not a place which Bruno had occupied, but a place which no one had occupied. Bruno shifted to a remoter orbit.

Elinor had loved him deeply and sincerely, but well before he died he had stopped being of high daily importance to her. She had grown up, out of his shadow.

She mourned him deeply and sincerely, but meanwhile there were guests to amuse, meals to plan, flowers to arrange, and Ailie to make love to: and this was all, except Ailie, what Bruno would have wished.

Yes, but—

This was all very sensible and adult. Yes, but: it made Elinor feel guilty. She should have felt keener pangs of misery and loss, deprivation, a longing for time to be turned back. She tried to needle herself into keener grief, with poignant selected memories, but it only worked for a moment or two, and only in the small hours of the morning.

Into this guilt and confusion shuffled the egregious Fred, the peasant, the Milchester redneck. All she needed. Luckily (as it seemed) he took himself off to the Guardhouse, to feel important among bits of paper.

Luckily, as it seemed.

And people came, and kept coming, and she and magical Ailie were forced into haste and furtiveness: effectively they were forced into chastity, which was deeply unpleasant. Elinor went almost mad, looking from her window along the cliff-face, a hundred yards to the golden window of the Oriel Room (no longer blooming with the mad orchid of the Tiffany lamp), looking across the chasm which divided her from Ailie, from Ailie's little breasts and ivory slender thighs and ash-blonde silken fleece . . .

Then when they could have, Ailie wouldn't. Almost petulantly, Ailie refused.

Why? What was going on?

Elinor refused to face the reality of what was going on, for days, almost weeks, while life at la Moquerie was a non-stop party, with Elinor queen of the revels, and Ailie an intermittent Tinkerbell.

In the end Elinor had to face it, that she was rejected and betrayed. She was ditched and jilted.

In favour of a Titan or a Titania, a goddess or demi-god?

In favour of Fred.

Boring common witless Philistine Fred.

Fred, the plumber's mate, the fertiliser delivery-man, the salesman of lavatory cleanser, the junior local government clerk.

A man, at the very best, who told dirty jokes at Rotary dinners.

Bile rose in Elinor's throat, as she thought about treachery, ingratitude. But bile was eclipsed, overwhelmed, forgotten – anger was forgotten – in the screaming pain of desire and loss.

Elinor wanted Ailie back.

Ailie was going through a calamitous phase. She would wake up. She would need help to do so, and help after she had done so.

Fred was not going to go away. Fred was a fixture. It might be phoney, the laborious work he said he was doing – it might be simply an excuse to have an extended holiday in this lovely place, Elinor's place, her castle, night and day screwing an ignorant, romantic child . . .

Elinor gagged at the thought, at the sight, of hard crude male possession of her darling. It made her scream inwardly with the ripping and plunging pain of vicarious rape, with disgust and moral outrage . . .

Fred was Bruno's executor. He could stay where he was exactly as long as he wanted. He could say it was his duty to stay until he had finished. Nobody could call his bluff.

Elinor went to bed, after all the others had gone to bed, went lonely and yearning, miserable and chilly to bed, her guts melting with desire. She looked out of her bedroom window, across a hundred yards of darkness, at the oriel window of the Guardhouse.

She gave a hiccup of surprise.

The Tiffany lamp was in the window.

Fred was using the Tiffany lamp, on his table in that window.

Ailie had given it to him. *Ailie had given Fred the Tiffany lamp*.

That was it. That put the lid on it. It was suddenly another ballgame. The rules were different. There were no rules.

Ailie was dazzled. She was sick and delirious, locked into hallucination. She had to be saved from herself. She had to be saved from Fred.

Fred had to go.

It was instantly obvious, the route Fred had to take. This was la Moquerie, with its history and its Guardhouse. Insolent servants, fornicators, intruders, were expeditiously got rid of, by the simple means of a push.

The river did the rest.

Elinor's blessed big powerful river, the world's most beautiful exterminator.

Ailie felt sincerely sorry for Elinor. She knew Elinor wanted her and missed her. She was sorry to be the cause of somebody's unhappiness. But it was all rather shocking. It had seemed all right at the time – gentle, unthreatening – but in retrospect it was a bit distasteful. It was unnatural. It was not morally wrong, exactly, but it was perverse. It was not what those bits were meant for.

Fred taught her to put all of herself to the right use. She had taught him a lot, but he had taught her something, too. It was absolutely glorious. He was as gentle as Elinor had been, and he was not so demanding, so superior. He did not take the kind of living up to that Elinor did. Ailie did not have to keep worrying about what impression she was making, about saying something silly, about showing her ignorance. She could say anything to Fred. She could relax.

Elinor devised a plan which gave her keen aesthetic pleasure, as might the arrangement of flowers in a vase, or colours in a room. It was a pity she could not tell anybody about it.

In her mind she arranged her agenda, the order in which things were to be done, the gathering of materials, the planting of the need for this or that which the plan required. The searchlight, for instance; the long flex. These things needed groundwork.

The timing was crucial. She had to plan backwards from the house being empty, and the railing of the cliff-face path having been taken away and not yet replaced.

These two things had to coincide. Then also, at the time, the enemy had to want to walk into the trap. She had to have him actually wanting to come along the cliff-face path in the middle of the night, when the rail was not there, when there was nobody about. He must very badly want to do that, at that time chosen for him not by himself but by Elinor. It was no good him coming along before the house was empty, or after it filled up again. It was no good him coming along before the rail was removed, or after it was replaced.

On a night when the servants were not there, Elinor

slipped out of the house and took the bronze putto from the middle of the formal parterres. She wrapped the putto in an old coat, and put him in the back of her car. She scratched at the cement under another of Bruno's acquisitions, the neo-classical marble nymph. In the morning she reported mysterious lights and noises in the garden behind the château; these things were immediately explained by the absence of the putto.

Clearly their security had to be improved. Elinor discussed the matter with the police and with the insurance company. She told the insurance people that the police had suggested a floodlight activated by a photoelectric cell, which would be switched on by the presence of an intruder near the house. She told the police that the insurance company suggested it. She told her friends that everybody suggested it. She would have the floodlight working, she said, whenever the house was empty. She bought the light from a big electrical supplier in Toulouse. Under the circumstances, it was not an astonishing purchase. Many people had such searchlights nowadays, if they lived in remote places, since there was so much crime about.

Elinor announced that she was worried about the rail of the cliff-face path. She said she was getting an expert from the ministry to inspect the concrete uprights and the cast-iron railing. She reported later that the man had come, that he had spent a day tapping and prodding, that he had given her a verbal report: five of the concrete uprights were unsafe.

Elinor set in motion the large machineries of removing the condemned uprights and replacing them with some-thing safer. The removal was speedy, the replacement not. Meanwhile a steel cable was stretched along the path, to fill the gap where the railing had been taken away. Everybody was shown it, and told to be careful.

Pierre was surprised about the concrete uprights, which he had kept an eye on over the years. He thought they were pretty safe. He thought the official who condemned them was a typical interfering bureaucratic busybody. However he accepted that, if the uprights had been found unsafe, they must be replaced, because if there was an accident Elinor would be held responsible.

Elinor measured the length of the flex of the searchlight, against the distance the searchlight would be from the nearest power-point. She needed a long extension lead. She contemplated the narrow grass paths which divided the beds in Bruno's fancy little knot-garden. She decided that an electric trimmer would be the best way to keep the paths tidy. She was clear – she said so, to several people – that the edges of the grass paths must be very, very neat. A scruffy knot-garden, said Elinor, was an abomination. Everyone agreed with her about that. She tried several makes of electric edger, finding the best to be one with a nylon whip like a strimmer. It needed a very long lead, with a plug at each end, because the knot-garden was some way from the house.

Pierre thought it was a ridiculous tool, more trouble than it was worth. He used it when Elinor was looking, but he edged the paths with old-fashioned clippers when her back was turned.

The long extension lead lived on a drum, in the flower-room, when the trimmer was not in use.

Elinor bought a length of clothes-line. She said it was for clothes-line. Berthe said there already was a clothes-line, but Elinor said it was good to have a spare one. That too was kept in the flower-room.

Elinor experimented with clamping her new floodlight to

various pieces of piping in the château. She learned how to do this in the dark. She did not explain why she was doing this, as nobody saw her doing it. She bought a chammy-leather at a filling station, which stopped the clamps leaving tell-tale scratches on anything. She bought a spool of nylon monofilament fishing-line from a sporting-goods store, so that she could switch the floodlight on and off at a distance.

She sold the putto. This was perfectly legal; it was hers to sell. She did not claim on the insurance. She said it was not worth it – the putto was not valuable.

That completed all the mechanical preparations. Now she had to get Fred to raise his eyes to her. She had to be a temptress, a tart.

She had never attempted anything like that, never come within a mile of trying to do anything remotely like that. She supposed she could. She had attracted admiration, devotion, although she had never set out to ensnare. There were women who did. You heard about it. But they were women of a different sort, kittenish, greedy, bimbos with nothing going for them except sex appeal. Could she pretend to be one of those? Was that what Fred would go for?

She had to get Fred to raise his eyes to her: and as soon as he started she realised that he already had raised his eyes to her.

She had long before been vaguely, uncomfortably aware of Fred looking at her, staring at her. He was doing it again, covertly, he was sneaking glances at her. She thought there was hunger in his face.

It was bloody impertinent, but it was certainly convenient.

There would come a night when she was alone in the château, and he was alone in the Guardhouse, and he would come along the cliff-face path to join her.

What did she have to do to bring that about? Smile? Flirt? Melt? Whisper? She was wryly amused that her authority, her famous sophistication, hid absolute ignorance of what every precocious twelve-year-old schoolgirl knew.

There had been some satisfaction to be got from the mechanical precision of her plan, its elegance and ruthlessness. Could any satisfaction be got from playing the vamp?

Satisfaction could be got, triumph could be got, from anything which ended this disgusting situation, this obscene exploitation of her darling's innocence and kindness.

Elinor was fuelled by hatred.

The most squalid and undignified behaviour would be justified. There were no means which this end did not justify. Any act of Elinor's would be justified, which ended those acts which were being done daily and nightly and disgustingly in the Guardhouse.

Elinor that evening smiled at Fred. He looked startled. He looked frightened.

Ailie said, 'While you are here, you must be nice to Elinor.'

'I do try. She is alarming.'

'You don't try really, because you refuse to understand her. It's like what you told me about you and art. You turned your back on all that, because your mother was trying too hard. Look what you missed, all those years. Now you're turning your back on Elinor, and it's silly of you as well as rude.'

'I see the point of her more than I did.'

'I hope so. It's high time.'

To Elinor herself, Fred said, 'I understand better than I did what your life is about.'

'That it's not entirely bogus, not entirely self-indulgent?'

'I'm beginning to understand the merit of your values, your scheme of things, your priorities. Ailie has made me see . . .'

Elinor made herself smile. She touched his hand. He was sitting on the terrace. She was standing beside his chair. He looked up at her, serious, shy.

He said, 'I'm seeing a lot of things in a new light.'

At three in the morning, wakeful and alone, Elinor thought: what a screaming, shattering irony. Ailie has opened the pig's piggish eyes. She's taught him to appreciate me. He'll come along that path.

Ailie has contrived her own salvation, because now I can destroy him.

Ailie will be free. Ailie will come home.

The château had to be empty: the Guardhouse also. Ailie had to be elsewhere. Where, and how? Ailie had not been away for even one night, since the evening of her arrival in the rain, in the spring, in the midst of that party. She had not wanted to go anywhere. There had been nowhere for her to go.

That party. The effect of that party, the people at it. The effect of Ailie on those people, and of those people on Ailie. The cult of Ailie, and the apostles of the cult.

Elinor's mind was sharpened by indignation: it moved with rapid confidence from this point.

Of the people involved with Ailie from the beginning – the new Ailie, born that evening at la Moquerie – three stood out for the noise of their apostleship, for their competitive devotion to the cause of Ailie as Statement. They were George Napier-Gough, the art historian who was enough of a dilettante to be other things sometimes;

Sandro di Ganzarello, who was rich enough to be serious about frivolities, heavy about thistledown; and the journalist Doris Loeb, who certainly thought the whole Ailie concept was her invention.

The point of these people at this moment, Elinor thought, was not their celebrity or their influence, but simply their vanity. They had seen Ailie before Ailie existed. They had spread the word before the word was defined. It was all an unimportant, journalistic in-joke, a piece of hype without even a commercial object: but in that *Vogue–Harpers–Tatler* suburb of real art, or real life, it did them all credit. They would be pleased for everybody to be reminded.

Elinor's plan, then, was for the three of them to give a party for Ailie – a party about Ailie. It would be somewhere not so far away that Ailie would not go, nor so close that she might come back too soon; it would be a party given for a feasible reason, that Elinor would not seem to have invented. It should be fun for Ailie, if possible, because she was going to get a little bit of a shock when she came back.

Not surprisingly, it was all too complex, too ambitious.

Doris Loeb had to be in Easter Island, or if not there somewhere awfully like it. She said she was heartbroken to miss partying Ailie, but she was just obliged to be amongst prehistoric mysteries.

That was a shame. Ailie liked Doris. Ailie would have gone without question, invited by Doris.

She would not go quite without question, invited by Sandro di Ganzarello. Any girl questioned an invitation from him, owing to a reputation fed for years by the gossip columns. But he had a claim on Ailie's notice, as he hardly needed to remind her.

Sandro would make a detour, on his way from Lisbon to Copenhagen.

The reason was pretty neat. Sandro would be there to chaperone Ailie. He would be gooseberry, to protect Ailie and her reputation from the other person who would be there, which was George Napier-Gough.

And George? Oh, George would be there. He had rather lost control of the Ailie phenomenon, to Doris Loeb and her sisters on the glossies. He thought they had gone wrong. He thought they were talking about a style of dressing and moving and behaving, and not what he meant, which was a style of talking, and looking and listening, a style of living.

George was pleased to come to Albi, on the date suggested by Elinor, although he had not planned to do so. He was pleased to celebrate something – anything – with Ailie. It happened that a group of young singers from England were due to perform renaissance music in the cathedral, the sort of thing which often happened there. That was fine with George. It fitted nicely.

George was also agreeable to acting as chaperone, or gooseberry as he himself put it, to protect Ailie from the predatory and irresistible Sandro di Ganzarello, who was to be among those present.

The point of it all, said Elinor, was a party for Ailie, with the people she most admired.

That brought the old show-offs.

Ailie's feelings for Elinor had swung from simple gratitude and admiration, to these things mixed with passion; and then to gratitude with ebbing passion, and then no passion: but with a wish that her lover would appreciate her benefactor, in the simple cause of justice; into this phase came a bit of impatience and resentment, a bit of potential jealousy, as of someone aware of having been patronised, of having been made into a toy.

It was in this mood that Ailie received an invitation jointly from George Napier-Gough and Sandro di Ganzarello, to go with them to the concert in Albi cathedral, with dinner afterwards.

'Make her feel important,' Elinor had said to the men. 'She deserves to be made to feel grown-up.'

This was the tone of the invitation, therefore, which Ailie received – it was from adults to an adult.

Ailie was able to feel important and superior and independent, in accepting such an invitation.

Fred was beginning to think – he was given reasons to think – he thought he was beginning to be entitled to think – that he could aspire to Elinor.

Did he want to? Of course he wanted to. Everybody wanted to.

For a man of his modesty, Elinor was a fabulous prize. The situation was incredible.

Fred became aware that Elinor had arranged for Ailie to be away, at a time when everybody else was going to be away.

Elinor talked about it, in a sort of way, when the house was still full of people.

'By midnight,' Elinor said, one evening, to a crowd, 'the telephone's always gone silent, thank God. Nobody we know is so base as to ring up later than that. I suppose the young in cities do. In American films they do. Our friends don't. We have quiet nights.'

'People used to call by,' said Elinor chattily, another time, 'at all hours of the early morning. They'd be driving through the night to miss the traffic, and suddenly decide to stop here for coffee. We'd switch on lights and bring out bottles. But no longer. The world has sobered up. We all go to bed earlier. I suppose we're getting old. Anyway, we think we're safe from droppers-in after midnight.'

'When everybody else is asleep,' said Elinor another time, 'I'm often terribly wide awake. I rather like it. I remember when I was a child there was an advertisement saying, "Awake in a sleeping world", with a picture of a woman looking haggard and miserable, because she couldn't get to sleep. She should have had a nice hot drink at bedtime, that was the idea. Ovaltine, perhaps. But I like being awake in a sleeping world. I really sometimes like it.'

These remarks were really not terribly interesting, to most of Elinor's listeners. They conveyed no significant message.

The remarks were not directed to most of Elinor's listeners.

They were directed to Fred.

To him they conveyed a very significant message.

'Anyone can tell,' said Elinor, lightly, casually, at dinner, 'when I go up to bed, because my bedroom light shines out over the river, telling burglars for miles around that there's nobody downstairs. I simply can't see any way round that. The problem is insoluble.'

Fred had seen that light, from a distance, from the upstairs window of the Guardhouse. The lamp in Elinor's bedroom had a shade of greeny-gold. That lamp would be switched on at midnight, when there was no fear of late-revelling visitors, of intrusive callers on the telephone.

Fred was publicly yet privately shown, by an ever-so-casual movement, the valley between Elinor's magnificent breasts. He was shown the slope of her thigh. He felt the galvanic touch of her fingertips on his knee.

Fred was not made of brass.

Fred's mouth was dry, and he missed the whole of his

other neighbour's account of her divorce.

Fred had a feeling that Ailie was becoming a little bit possessive. He did not care to be possessed. His marriage, brief and far off, had broken up in part because his wife had wanted to remake him in the image she preferred, that of an indoor man of business rather than an outdoor man of machinery. This was not because it was a better sort of man, but because it was a sort of man she could better control. Ailie was trying the same sort of thing. It was one thing to have opened Fred's eyes; it was another to have acquired a controlling interest in him.

Fred's gesture of independence would, in the event, be a very large one. But a very secret one. Ailie was not to know about it. Ailie was not to be hurt.

Elinor had to repel boarders. A number of people asked themselves to la Moquerie, as so many scores had over the previous few years, at a moment when it was to be empty. An English couple were longing to repeat their visit of two years previously, and had found a little table they thought would be perfect in the Oriel Room; a French widow had had a standing invitation for a year; there were some Americans who had produced rarities for the garden, and promised to do so again. It was difficult to put them all off, and impossible to do so on the telephone when anybody was listening. Elinor could not say that the house had been rendered uninhabitable by rewiring, when no electrician or dust-sheet was to be seen. Elinor had to think quickly and speak tactfully. She managed to change the dates of the English and the French, but the Americans could only come when they said they would come; they were not at all pleased to be told the dates they suggested were impossible having believed, with justice, that they had a claim to priority right.

Elinor was sorry.

Berthe had also to be told that she could on no account spend that night at the château. There was actually no reason that she should be there, but she sometimes stayed the night for no reason. It was difficult to find a good excuse for saying that there was a night when she must not be there. Elinor failed to find an excuse. She just told Berthe she was not to be in the château that night.

Berthe accepted this without visible emotion or surprise. It was impossible to guess what she was thinking. Perhaps she was not thinking anything.

George Napier-Gough came for Ailie in a car in the morning. He and Sandro would bring her back in time for lunch the following day.

Ailie went off in holiday spirits, and in brilliant Ailie holiday clothes.

Fred waved, as the car snaked away up the Guardhouse drive. He was very fond of Ailie, but he felt a sense of liberation.

Berthe and Pierre were not coming in that day, or the next. This was a break in a routine which was often broken. The house being empty, there was not much for Berthe to do. The month being August, there was not much for Pierre to do.

Fred understood that he was not to walk along the path to the château during the day or in the evening. People might call by. It was really pretty likely somebody would drop in. Absolute discretion was required, for very many reasons,

Ailie's feelings not least. Fred understood that. He cared about Ailie's feelings. He kept his eyes on his desk, and gave himself bread and cheese for lunch.

Elinor did the flowers, had a swim, had lunch.

She was wound up as tight as a banjo-string. She was exultant, a fury, a Valkyrie, a girl melting with love and about to recover her lost love.

She was so clever to have played the wanton, while hiding her hatred. She had not supposed herself so good an actress. She had never had to act before. She hugged herself for her cleverness, even as she was aghast at what she was about to do.

Ailie changed, in the hotel room they had booked for her. She did not dress up so very Ailie, for a musical evening in a cathedral with two old gentlemen. By her standards, she was demure.

She wondered a little why she was here, why this was happening. She did not wonder much, because she had become used to being spoiled and pampered and given treats.

She went down to join the others, in the bar of the hotel. They were elegant, in lightweight suits. Sandro had a rose on his buttonhole. They had bread and pâté and fruit and wine, before crossing the *place* to the cathedral.

The cathedral looked extraordinary, barbaric, in the evening light. Ailie felt important and grown up, bowed through the door by her impressive escorts.

If Elinor had been a nail-biter, she would have bitten her nails to the quick. If she had been a smoker, she would have got through a dozen packs.

She prowled in and out of the house, up and down the stairs, consumed by tension and terror and joy.

It was no small thing to kill somebody, to take a life with sudden and irreversible violence.

She had to play God, because God would not do it.

She could not get Ailie back in any other way.

She could not ease her own agony, of loss and betrayal, in any other way.

Fred had become as restless as a flea. The papers on his desk were meaningless to him, dry marks on the paper.

Fred trembled. He felt shy. He felt self-conscious, and frightened of failure. He imagined being too excited, sick with excitement, unmanned by it.

He wanted a drink. He did not want one. He needed one. He was better without. He needed fresh air; he needed to be indoors. He was too hot, too cold, hungry, sated.

He was like a little boy before an important school football match, like a young actress facing a first night in a first part.

He was a pilgrim, a suitor, a beggar.

Once or twice, during the interminable evening, he stopped to examine himself, his treatment of Ailie. He felt uneasy and embarrassed.

The image of Elinor, of Elinor's taut silky envelope of skin over breasts and belly, Elinor's lips and fingers, exploded like rockets in Fred's poor battered brain, and he thought about those things, instead of about little pale Ailie, or his own unimportant conscience.

It was a long evening.

It was a long concert. The seats were hard. But the music was wonderful. Ailie sat between George and Sandro. From time to time both glanced at her. She seemed engrossed.

'*In domum tuam eliminor,*' sang the sweet voices of the choir, 'I am carried over the threshold of thy house.'

The singers repeated the phrase polyphonically, embroidering and enlacing it.

Ailie heard 'Elinor'. She heard it again and again, Elinor's name passed from voice to voice of the choir, sung high and low, loud and soft.

The beauty of the music and of the cathedral filled Ailie with emotion, which Elinor's name defined. The feeling that filled her was guilt and pity and love. Ailie knew that she could not do to Elinor what she had been doing. Suddenly, by the name and by the music which seemed to carry the name, Ailie's love was reawakened, the reality of her heart made evident to herself.

The music ended, and they rose and stretched and began to shuffle towards the south door.

Ailie said, 'I must go home.'

'What?'

'I'm terribly sorry. George, Sandro, I'm really sorry. I must go home.'

Ailie upset them both by suddenly bursting into tears.

'Please one of you take me home.'

'You did the drive this morning,' said Sandro to George. 'I perhaps now.'

'All right,' said George, who was distressed and disappointed, but also hungry. He did not want another drive of an hour and a half each way.

'Do you mind if we go now at once?' said Ailie, sniffing. 'I am truly sorry to do this to you.'

'We can be there by midnight, I guess,' said Sandro. 'Do you want to arrive there at midnight, *carina*?'

'Yes. Yes, I must go there now.'

'*Va bene. Andiam'.*'

Ailie kissed George, and got into Sandro's Lamborghini. They went to the hotel for her case, and started eastwards.

Elinor had bolted the floodlight to the rail, and carried its flex to the plug in the hall, and then taken the nylon line from the switch of the light to the edge of the terrace. She had loosed the wire hawser which served as a rail where there was no rail, and led it across to the inner gutter of the cliff-face path. She had knotted the clothes-line to the hawser, and taken that to the edge of the terrace.

That was it: everything: no more to do except wait. She waited.

Fred looked at his watch, and made himself wait ten minutes, and looked at it again, and saw that it was only one minute.

Sandro did not pester Ailie with questions as he drove. He was not angry. He had experience of love, his own and that of other people, that of many girls. He did not despise anyone for tears or for sudden changes of plan, if the cause was love.

He was sorry about this love that he now saw, because it was a waste, but he respected that it was there.

Ailie sat huddled in her seat, silent, no longer weeping, wakeful, her eyes wide, looking ahead at the beams of the headlights. She sniffed from time to time, but made no other sound.

They came at last to the turning for the Guardhouse, some way before the other turning.

'Here?' said Sandro, slowing. 'Or the other, to la Moquerie?'

'The other,' said Ailie. 'No. Wait. Let me think. The other. No. This one.'

She said that she wanted a clean handkerchief, from her bedroom in the Guardhouse, because the one she had was wet with her tears.

She thought also that she should do something about her face, her eyes probably being red and her nose shining.

Sandro swung the car to the right, and went southwards over the high ground towards the river.

Elinor glimpsed herself, for the thousandth time that day, in the big mirror in the hall of la Moquerie.

'My God, I look wonderful. I have never looked so good. Nobody has ever looked so wonderful as I look tonight.'

Elinor was beautiful as never before because she was excited, because she was filled with happiness at getting her love back again.

Elinor laughed a little hysterically. She said to herself, 'I am dressed to kill.'

Fred heard the car. He was filled with rage and astonishment. He was completely surprised.

A car at la Moquerie at midnight was not unheard of, but an unexpected car at this hour here . . .

'I can't ask you in,' said Ailie.

'I would not come. It is too late for any party, and this is the wrong house. Good night, little one.'

'Oh Sandro, forgive me. I am an ungrateful little pig. I loved the concert. I would love to have stayed – and you haven't had any dinner – I am a selfish toad—'

Ailie burst into tears again. Sandro kissed her, and got back into his car, and drove away.

'My God, it's you,' said Fred, his face almost comically agape with astonishment.

'I must see Elinor.'

'You can't.'

'I must.'

'I tell you, you can't, no, not tonight.'

'Oh Fred, be an angel, get me a glass of water?'

'Sure.'

Fred went into the downstairs cloakroom, as Ailie had known he would, the little dark Gents' loo off the hall, which had by way of window only a three-inch slit in the ancient stone.

The door of the loo had a key on the inside and a bolt on the outside.

Ailie shut the door on Fred, and bolted it.

So heavy was the wood of the door that she could scarcely hear his shouts, or the pounding of his fists on the door.

Elinor saw that it was almost midnight. She switched on the light in the window of her bedroom.

Across the black gulf between the houses, she saw in the oriel window the lurid colours of the Tiffany lamp. Its message reassured her and encouraged her, and told her she was right, and she would be happy.

She returned to the terrace. She took up the clothes-line which led to the steel hawser, and the nylon which led to the floodlight.

She waited in the thick darkness.

She heard a sound which was hardly a sound, and saw a dim rectangle of light appear and disappear, with the opening and closing of the door of the Guardhouse.

She saw the wavering pinpoint of light, the flashlight in

the hand of the person approaching.

At the right moment, Elinor switched on the floodlight, and at that moment pulled the hawser off the ground, so that it threw the person off the path and over the edge; and in that moment she saw the face of the person she was killing.

Taryn Belle is the pen name of Cea Person, a bestselling Canadian author who wrote about her unconventional childhood in two memoirs, *North of Normal* and *Nearly Normal*, both published by HarperCollins. She is a former international model and a businesswoman, who runs a swimwear company with merchandise popularised by celebrities such as Jessica Alba and Kate Hudson. She loves playing board games with her husband and three children, hosting dinner parties in her Vancouver home and crafting out.

Kelli Ireland spent a decade as a name on a door in corporate America. Unexpectedly liberated by fate's sense of humour, she chose to *carpe* the *diem* and pursue her passion for writing. A fan of happily-ever-afters, she found she loved being puppetmaster for the most unlikely couples. Seeing them through the best and worst of each other while helping them survive the joys and disasters of falling in love… Best. Thing. Ever. Visit Kelli's website at kelliireland.com.

GW00480838

If you liked *In Too Deep* and *Matched*
why not try

The Risk by Caitlin Crews
Friends with Benefits by Margot Radcliffe

Discover more at millsandboon.co.uk

IN TOO DEEP

TARYN BELLE

MATCHED

KELLI IRELAND

All rights reserved including the right of reproduction in whole or in part in any form. This edition is published by arrangement with Harlequin Books S.A.

This is a work of fiction. Names, characters, places, locations and incidents are purely fictional and bear no relationship to any real life individuals, living or dead, or to any actual places, business establishments, locations, events or incidents. Any resemblance is entirely coincidental.

This book is sold subject to the condition that it shall not, by way of trade or otherwise, be lent, resold, hired out or otherwise circulated without the prior consent of the publisher in any form of binding or cover other than that in which it is published and without a similar condition including this condition being imposed on the subsequent purchaser.

® and ™ are trademarks owned and used by the trademark owner and/or its licensee. Trademarks marked with ® are registered with the United Kingdom Patent Office and/or the Office for Harmonisation in the Internal Market and in other countries.

First Published in Great Britain 2018
By Mills & Boon, an imprint of HarperCollins*Publishers*
1 London Bridge Street, London, SE1 9GF*

In Too Deep © 2018 by Taryn Belle
Matched © 2018 by Denise Tompkins

ISBN: 978-0-263-93009-6

MIX
Paper from
responsible sources
FSC   FSC C007461

This book is produced from independently certified FSC™ paper
to ensure responsible forest management.

For more information visit: www.harpercollins.co.uk/green

Printed and bound in Spain

MILLS & BOON

First Published in Great Britain 2019
by Mills & Boon, an imprint of HarperCollins*Publishers*
1 London Bridge Street, London, SE1 9GF

In Too Deep © 2019 Cea Sunrise Person

Matched © 2019 Denise Tomkins

ISBN: 978-0-263-27390-8

MIX
Paper from
responsible sources
FSC® C007454

This book is produced from independently certified FSC™ paper
to ensure responsible forest management.
For more information visit www.harpercollins.co.uk/green.

Printed and bound in Spain
by CPI, Barcelona

IN TOO DEEP

TARYN BELLE

MILLS & BOON

For Heather, whose laughter I still hear every day.

CHAPTER ONE

CRASHING WAVES. Sunlight streaming onto his face. A light breeze blowing through the open floor-to-ceiling windows. And a pounding headache.

Alex Stone reached his hand out to the bedside table and groped for his phone, then brought it to life to read the time. 8:37. *Shit.*

He sat up in bed and swung his legs to the floor, cursing his brother as he grabbed a pair of swimming trunks from his suitcase. Ditching his boxer shorts, he slid the trunks over his bare hips and bent forward to dig around for a T-shirt. His head protested.

Alex may not have minded his headache so much if it was the price for an evening of fun, but the case was anything but. After arriving in Moretta from LA last night, tired and jet-lagged—naturally, Alex had refused his brother's offer of a private jet to neighboring Barbados in favor of three leg-cramping commercial flights—his considerate rock-star brother had driven him straight to his place, where a raucous party was in full swing. No amount of sleeping pills or pillows over his head could block out the

noise and music pounding through the walls of his
brother's home, which lasted until, by Alex's estima-
tion, about four hours ago.

He glanced at his phone again: 8:40. His scuba-
diving lesson was due to start in twenty minutes.
He'd taken all the preliminary lessons back in LA,
and today was to be his first open-water dive. But
right now he was exhausted and feeling anything
but mentally prepared for it. It was probably dangerous to dive with so little sleep. He was staying on
the island for a week; there was no rush. He should
cancel...

Screw that. This was something he needed to do.
He'd promised himself he would, and Alex Stone
was a man who always kept his promises.

Alex opened his bedroom door. It had been dark
when he arrived last night, so between the lack of
light and the throngs of bodies crowding the space,
he hadn't gotten a good feel for its layout. Now Alex
could see how breathtaking both the house and
its setting were. Each of the eight bedroom doors
opened onto an expansive piazza with the beach just
beyond it. Between a stand of palms on his right
and a rocky outcrop to his left, the turquoise ocean
lapped gently. As he watched, a tortoise slowly made
its way along the sand in his direction.

Alex turned and walked toward the main house,
noting that there wasn't an empty glass or a cushion
out of place to be seen, thanks to his brother's twenty-
four-hour housekeeping staff. Passing through the
enormous living room, he admired a trio of white

sofas the size of queen beds and the tasteful, original artwork on the whitewashed walls. By the time he got to the stainless-steel-and-polished-concrete kitchen with coffee on his mind, his walk from one end of the house to the other felt more like a quest.

"Hey, little brother," Dev said with a grin as Alex entered the room. Lounging against the counter with a cup of tea in his tanned hand, Dev was the picture of health. For the life of him, Alex would never understand how his brother could party as hard as he did and never look the worse for wear. "Sleep well?"

Alex glared at him as he hit the button on the Starbucks-size espresso machine. "Glad to hear you haven't lost your sense of humor."

"What happened to you, anyway? You missed your own party."

Alex stared at him in disbelief. "*My* party?"

Dev shrugged. "Yeah, man. I haven't seen you in what, four years? My brother comes to visit me—I pull out all the stops."

"And I always thought the guest of honor was supposed to get a little attention at his own party. My mistake."

Dev appeared oblivious to Alex's barb. "Plenty of people there would have loved to give you a little attention," he said with a wink, turning his head toward the window. Through the glass, Alex could see Dev's entourage—including several silicone-breasted groupies—lounging by the infinity pool. Alex gave his head a hopeless shake. There was no denying that he and his brother looked alike—same tall build, dark hair and unusual aqua eyes. The eyes were courtesy of their mother, and, Alex thought, looked devastating on Dev's somewhat prettier face but didn't quite work with Alex's more masculine features. But the similarities ended with their appearance; in every other way the brothers were about as different as guitars and boardrooms, much like their respective careers. "I have to get going," Alex said, downing the last of his coffee.

"Going?"

"Scuba diving. I told you last night."

"Oh. Right," Dev replied, but Alex knew better than to think his brother had been paying attention. It had always been like this between the two of them, even when they were kids—Dev busy entertaining his adoring audiences while Alex hurried along behind in his shadow, just hoping for a shred of his attention. "So, scuba diving, huh? That's kind of unlike you, considering…" Dev trailed off, leaving *the thing they'd never talked about* hanging in the air.

Alex placed his coffee cup down with a thud. He wouldn't give his brother the satisfaction of seeing that he wasn't quite over his fear yet. "Scuba's been on my radar for a while. And what better time to tackle a water sport than when you're surrounded by water?" He started to walk away, and then turned back and gave his brother a cool smile. "You should come with me."

Dev busied himself with fishing his tea bag out of his mug. "Can't risk the old ears, brother. Be the death of my career."

"Of course." Alex left the kitchen, his mood unimproved.

"Take a golf cart," Dev shouted after him.

Nicola Metcalfe was going to be late for work—again. Turning the key in the ignition a second time, she made a frustrated noise in her throat when it gave a dry click…and then nothing. Running an agitated hand through her hair, she jumped off the golf cart and made a beeline back to the tiny staff bungalow she shared with her roommate.

"Kiki!" she shouted furiously as she flung the front door open and strode toward her roommate's bedroom. "You forgot to fill up the cart again! How am I supposed to get to work?"

On her bed Kiki rolled onto her side, her strawberry blond hair spilling over her pillow, and opened one eye. "Oh, God, I'm sorry. I finished work so late last night, and the station was already closed…"

"It's called planning, Kiki."

"Planning. Right," she agreed but was already rolling away again and pulling her pillow over her head.

Nicola sighed, knowing it was hopeless. She loved Kiki—they'd been friends since Nicola had first moved to LA to finish her teaching degree nearly a decade ago, and Kiki was the whole reason she'd moved to Moretta four months earlier, acting as a soft landing for Nicola when she needed it most. After the messy end of Kiki's marriage two years ago, she'd traded in her crazed career as an executive assistant for a bartending job on Moretta. It still amazed Nicola that her friend had had the organizational skills to orchestrate such a dramatic move—unlike Nicola, Kiki was hopelessly scattered.

Nicola left the house again, then she snatched her satchel off the seat of the golf cart and started a slow jog toward the beach along the island's main road. In truth it was Moretta's *only* road, a meandering loop around the entire island with a crisscross running through the center to allow access to its hillside homes, which traded beachfront property for breathtaking panoramic views of the Caribbean Sea. But on a three-square-mile chunk of land sprinkled with only one boutique hotel, one restaurant, ninety-two estates and a few staff cottages, the beach was only minutes away for each and every resident. Seventy years ago it had been a handful of Barbadian and American judges who first recognized the beauty of the tiny island, flocking in to build majestic homes on inexpensive land that soon skyrocketed in value. The influx had earned the island the temporary nickname of "Judgment Isle," ironic considering that it had now grown into a destination known for its privacy and lack of judgment.

By the time Nicola was halfway to the scuba shack, she was breathing heavily and the thin white tank covering her bikini top was soaked through between her breasts. In mid-August it was already ninety degrees before 9 a.m., but having grown up in Hawaii she was used to heat like this. She stopped to catch her breath, placing her hands on her knees as she leaned forward. All was quiet aside from her ragged breathing and the sound of a light breeze riffling through the palm leaves. Gathering her hair off her neck as she straightened again, she found herself wishing for one of the elastics she kept in a drawer at the scuba shack.

In the distance she could hear the whine of an engine approaching. She recognized the sound as another golf cart, the chief mode of transportation around the island. Every home boasted at least two of them—except, of course, *her* home.

Nicola started walking in the direction of the beach again as she heard the cart draw nearer to her. She cast a glance over her shoulder, hoping the driver might be someone she knew—Juan from the restaurant maybe, or Stella from the hotel—but one look told her this was not someone she was going to be bumming a ride from.

The driver was a lone female. Her signature dark wavy hair was wrapped in a pink scarf, and large sunglasses covered half her face. Nicola recognized the woman immediately: Lauren Hayes, just one of the many celebrities who owned a home on the island.

No, Nicola would not be asking Lauren Hayes for a lift to her lowly scuba instructor job.

Nicola lifted a hand briefly in greeting, but the star cruised by with perfectly averted eyes. Nicola shook her head with a small grin. She had no right to complain—this was exactly why she had moved here. On an island overflowing with celebrities, Nicola was an unrecognizable nobody—and that was exactly who she wanted to be.

It was only after Alex had started driving that he realized he wasn't entirely sure if he was going in the right direction. There were no signs, as Moretta wasn't exactly welcoming to tourists—apparently, you either belonged here or you didn't. Even the scuba shack's website was obtuse—*We're located at the beach, of course!*

As Alex drove on, half hoping he was traveling in the wrong direction so he would miss the boat after all, he tried to calm his nerves by bringing his mind back to the whole reason he was here in the first place: John Brissoli. The self-made entrepreneur and ex-lawyer was known to be a recluse, especially since his most successful website had reached stratospheric heights two years ago. The site had spawned a spate of copycats, but Alex was only interested in acquiring the real deal. Never mind that a quick internet search revealed the true scope of Brissoli's work—he had his fingers in many pies, including the porn industry. But Alex didn't see that as his concern. He'd learned a long time ago to separate his own ethics from those he did business with, as there probably wasn't a deal to be made under the sun that didn't have a little dirt on it.

The idea to acquire the website had come from Alex's father, the cofounder of the family media empire along with Alex's mother. Devin Sr. had made it clear to Alex that he was to pay whatever was necessary in order to add Brissoli's site to their company's roster. But of course, it was rarely that simple. Mr. Brissoli had ignored Alex's many emails and calls until a week ago, when he'd sent Alex a one-line response: on moretta if you want to talk.

Moretta. It figured. The same island his rock-star only sibling spent a third of his time on; the same island Alex had been avoiding for that very reason ever since his brother had bought a home here several years ago. Knowing the size of Moretta, Alex had had no choice but to tell his brother he was coming, which maddened him all the more because he didn't actually have a clue what he was going to do once he reached the island. Alex's follow-up messages to Brissoli had once more gone unanswered, so now here he was—four thousand miles away from home with no cell phone number for his contact, no meeting time or place, staying with a brother he'd stopped trying to forge a relationship with years ago. Even the stunning views of the island as he drove weren't enough to cheer him up.

Alex sighed deeply as he rounded a corner in the road, swerving slightly to avoid a crossing tortoise. Beautiful island or not, he couldn't wait to track Brissoli down, get the meeting over with and hightail it out of here.

That was what Alex was thinking when he saw her.

Behind her, Nicola heard another golf cart approaching. She broke her jog, slowing to a walk as the cart pulled up beside her.

"Excuse me," said a deep male voice. When she turned to face him, her breath, which was coming out fast from her run, literally caught in her throat. The man who had spoken the words to her was drop-dead gorgeous. Square jaw, dark mussed hair, and his eyes—they were the exact same color as her own. *No one* had the same shade of eyes as her. When she was little, her mother used to tell her they were proof that she was born with the ocean in her.

"Yes?" Nicola managed to get out.

"Am I going in the right direction? I'm looking for the beach."

The *beach*? Hot or not, it was an obvious pickup line, and a bad one at that. Nicola had heard plenty of those since she'd moved here. This guy was obviously some C-list celebrity staying with an A-list friend and thinking that moved him up two letters in the alphabet. What was it about celebrities that made them think you were supposed to fall at their feet if they deigned to talk to you?

Nicola started walking again, looking straight ahead. In her peripheral vision, she saw the cart crawling along beside her. "Keep driving in any direction. You can't really miss it."

"Of course. The, uh—the main beach, I guess I meant. In the town center."

"Not much of a town, but keep going straight and you'll be there in about a minute."

"Thanks." He paused, and then, "You looked like you were in a bit of a hurry. Can I offer you a lift?"

Nicola turned to look at him again, setting her face in a firm expression of disinterest that belied the flutter she felt in her belly.

God, he was beautiful.

He was wearing swimming trunks and an old gray T-shirt with a rip in the neckline, a flaw in his clothing that only served to highlight the perfection of the body beneath it. She couldn't help herself—she followed the line of his smooth biceps down to his large hands to check for a ring. Now more than ever, married men were a definite deal breaker for Nicola. But his fingers were bare, allowing her to imagine them sliding up her thighs, tugging on the ties of her bikini bottom and…

Stop it.

But she couldn't. Judging from the length of his bent muscular legs, he was at least six foot three— perfect for her, as at five foot nine, she felt too tall around many men. One last look between his legs revealed an impressive bulge that she could imagine undressing, stroking, until he was rock-hard, and then…

Enough!

She was thinking like a sex-crazed teenager, probably because she hadn't actually *had* sex since long before she moved here. Everything that had gone down in LA hadn't exactly worked wonders for her libido.

"I'm happy walking," she lied, and then started

doing just that to prove it. She could feel his eyes burning into the side of her face.

"Suit yourself," he said, shrugged and then drove away.

Really, it was a good thing she hadn't accepted the ride, because Alex was pretty sure there was no way she wouldn't have noticed the swelling under his swimming trunks. Jesus, she was fucking beautiful. Trim, toned figure, long blond hair and those eyes… the same shade as his. Though if she'd noticed that, she certainly hadn't let on. He wasn't sure why she'd been so standoffish with him when he was just asking innocent questions, but he figured it might have something to do with the fact that she looked familiar. Like almost everyone else on this island, she was a *someone*, and she wanted to be sure to send the message that she was way out of his civilian league. Not to mention that a woman as hot as her was most likely off the market.

Alex shook his head, trying to clear it of the image of the glistening sweat between her breasts, the tanned slice of tummy he'd spied between her tank top and shorts, the heavy breathing that had made him think of only one thing. He wanted to hear her breathe like that again, but this time because of his cock driving into her again and again, her nipples thrusting upward to meet his hungry mouth…

Get yourself together. You're about to be sixty feet beneath the surface with nothing between you and a lungful of killer water but a couple of rubber tubes.

Right. He needed to focus. He had come here for two reasons—to close a deal and to once and for all conquer his childhood fear of the ocean, and he wasn't about to be distracted from either of those goals by any woman.

No matter how fucking hot she was.

CHAPTER TWO

TWO INSTRUCTORS, EIGHT STUDENTS. At the dock Nicola did a quick final head count before zipping her dive skin up to her neck. Much to her annoyance, her mind was still on the chiseled god she'd encountered on the road—and the furtive, hopeful glances she kept throwing at arriving students irked her even more. She really did need to get out more.

"Tanks are ready to go," said Zach, her fellow instructor, reaching past Nicola to set the last two metal cylinders on the boat. Nicola smiled her thanks to him. As far as she knew, Zach was one of only a handful of island staff members who had actually been born on Moretta. Raised the son of one of the estate's chefs, Zach had grown up in the tiny staff quarters behind the house and been homeschooled by his mother—just the inspiration Nicola had needed to start tutoring some of the island kids once per week. She didn't think she'd ever become accustomed to the huge class chasm that separated the island natives from the residents who'd taken it over.

"Hi, Miss Nicola," said a quiet voice. Nicola

turned to see one of her students, Raia, peeking out at her shyly from around the corner of the shack.

Nicola smiled at her. "Back to school this week," she reminded Raia with a mix of anticipation and longing. It wasn't lost on Nicola that if she were back in LA right now—back in her old, normal life before it all went crazy—she would be welcoming her first-grade class to their first day of school today. The memory of the children she'd been forced to leave behind two months before the end of the school year still stung.

After Zach and her students had piled onto the boat, Nicola stepped onto the boat herself and started to mentally prepare for the upcoming dive. The fact that she'd been scuba diving since she was thirteen and instructing since she was nineteen, when she'd used it as a part-time job to put herself through college, did nothing to make her take the sport less seriously. It only served to heighten her awareness of its dangers, because with the rising popularity of scuba diving, people tended to lose sight that it was an extreme sport. If done properly it was almost always safe, but there were many things that could potentially go catastrophically wrong.

She ran the upcoming dive through her head, planning the traverse around the reef she would lead her students on. Then she ran through her four students' abilities, assessing each one for potential weaknesses or panic triggers. By the time the boat geared down, pulled up alongside another dive boat and dropped anchor at Sinkhole Reef, Nicola was feeling ready.

"Okay, everyone," she said, pulling her mask and snorkel over her head and letting it rest around her neck. "This will be an easy one. We should have excellent visibility, and we're going for a max depth of seventy feet. You'll see lobsters, stingrays, moray eels, possibly a few nurse or reef sharks. Lobsters hang out in pods, so don't be freaked out if you come across a den of fifty or so. Just keep your fingers to yourselves! Remember to practice neutral buoyancy and keep your fins off the reef. Stay with your buddy at all times, and ascend—slowly, remember—before you have no less than 200 PSI left in your tank."

She walked around to her students to be sure their tanks had been turned to the open position, getting each of them to test their regulators in turn. Then she put on her fins, weight belt and buoyancy control device. Shuffling backward on her fins toward the edge of the boat, she put her regulator in her mouth. Then she held her mask on her face and fell backward to demonstrate a back fall-in. "Now your turn. One at a time," she called to her students once she'd resurfaced.

Focused solely on the safety of the four people under her charge, Nicola was barely aware of the sound of bodies splashing into the water as divers from the neighboring boat began to drop in at the same time.

Alex had thought he was doing okay. On the boat ride he'd run through his entire lesson book in his head, followed by everything he'd learned on the eight pool dives he'd completed back in LA.

He could do this. People did it every day. Hell, there were *teenagers* on his boat who didn't look the least bit concerned that they may very well be taking their last-ever breaths.

Quit it. Not every kid who goes into the ocean has a near-death experience.

After he'd talked himself somewhat off the ledge, he took a deep, calming breath and followed his instructor's orders—tank open, regulator in, mask on. He was standing up, ready to walk backward to the edge of the boat when his instructor pointed at his waist. "Forgot your weight belt," Rusty said. "You won't get far down without that."

Alex groaned. His weight belt—of course. Shit, he was a mess, and his persisting thoughts of that Sienna Miller look-alike on the road this morning weren't helping matters.

Focus.

As he sat down again and unfastened his BCD, Rusty walked over to inspect Alex's belt. The man was huge, which gave Alex a small measure of reassurance—even though his brain told him he'd be practically weightless underwater, if anything went wrong it was comforting to know this guy could probably carry him to the surface on one finger.

Rusty picked his belt up and gave it a heft. "Twenty-two pounds? You're a big guy. I think you'll want another fiver on there."

"You sure?" Alex asked as a vision of himself

sinking to the ocean floor like a rock flashed through his head.

"Yep." The instructor grabbed a weight from the crate near his feet and handed it to Alex. "Just thread it through your belt and you're good to go."

Alex did so, then hefted the belt around his waist and fastened the airline-seatbelt-like closing. It slipped down a little when he stood up, so he tightened it. It slipped down again. Was it supposed to feel this loose? Probably—what the hell did he know? All he was certain of was that he was used to being in control, being the one to show others how things were done, and he was tired of looking like a rookie fool. It was this departure from his comfort zone as much as the ocean he was about to jump into that was causing his anxiety.

In any case, it was go-time. There was no backing out now. Alex got himself ready and fell backward into the open water.

The surface was crowded, as it looked like another group of divers had just dropped in at the same time. It took Alex a minute to locate his buddy, because everyone was unrecognizable to him with their masks and snorkels on. After they inserted their regulators into their mouths, his buddy counted down with his fingers. Holding their inflator controls above their heads, they slowly released air from their BCDs to start the descent to the reef. Alex felt the water close over his head, and then he saw bubbles rise in front of his mask as he exhaled.

He was doing it! He was under the surface of the

ocean, and he was okay! Ridiculously, he felt an urge to let out a *whoop*, then quickly reminded himself of how stupid that would be.

When Alex's feet hit the ocean floor, he spun around in a slow semicircle toward the reef. Then it was right in front of him, and all he could do was blink in amazement. The reef was so much more incredible than any photograph could capture. It was covered in every imaginable shape and color of plant and animal life—waving pink sea fans, purple and yellow tubes of coral—all forming a backdrop for the many animals that called it home. Sea stars of purple, orange and yellow shared space with spiky sea urchins on the coral. A spotted moray eel poked its head from its den, a turtle nipped at a plant, a grouper the size of a coffee table cruised by and a school of tiny blue fish flashed in synchronicity. Beyond it an underwater meadow of seagrass spread into the distance.

Alex turned to look to his left. There, much too close for Alex's comfort, the ocean floor fell sharply away to create a cavernous, eerie-looking dark blue space: the sinkhole the reef was named after. Alex shivered, imagining himself stepping off the edge and falling down, down, gathering speed as the air in his BCD compressed, struggling to swim upward... slipping beneath the surface and sinking while his brother laughed onshore—

Stop it.

He was doing so well; the last thing he needed to do right now was send himself into a panic over something that had happened nearly two decades ago. He tore his eyes away from the sinkhole.

Alex's group was starting to move along, so, remembering his pool dives, he put a little air into his BCD until his fins lifted from the ocean floor. Then he did his best to get himself horizontal—he could only imagine what a newbie he must look like, but at this point he was almost beyond caring—and started swimming after his buddy.

Of all the incredible things to see underwater, Nicola's favorite was probably the very common trunkfish. With their clown-like faces, boxy spotted bodies and you-don't-scare-me attitudes, they practically made her laugh into her regulator every time. She was pointing one out to a student when she noticed another diver swimming past her.

Many divers had trouble identifying people when they were suited up underwater, especially if they were in matching equipment, but Nicola had a knack for it. She could tell this diver wasn't from her group, or even from her boat, and that he was very inexperienced. That was fine—everyone had to start somewhere—but what wasn't fine was that he was on his own with no buddy or instructor in sight, and worse, headed directly for the sinkhole.

What the hell? What was he doing, and why was he on his own?

Checking quickly to make sure her students were all fine, she started going after him. This diver may not have been experienced, but he was very tall, making for a fast swimmer. When he reached the sinkhole, he didn't slow down but cruised right over it, staring down into it as if mesmerized. Then he suddenly stopped, suspended above it.

Nicola was still about fifty feet away from him. She swam harder, not letting him out of her sight. Judging from this diver's behavior, she had a suspicion of what was going on. It was unusual for it to happen at this depth, but certainly not unheard of: nitrogen narcosis. She'd seen it several times in her diving career—a state of euphoria and invincibility, much like that caused by narcotics, induced by breathing air at a higher pressure than the atmosphere. It was imperative that she get to him before he got any bad ideas—like letting all the air out of his BCD so he could swim to the bottom of the sinkhole, for example.

Forty feet away…thirty-five—

Nicola saw something from around the diver's waist drop into the abyss. Her heart stopped.

The diver's weight belt had slipped off, she realized, and now one of two things could happen. Either he would rocket straight for the surface and get a life-threatening case of the bends, or he could panic and very likely spit out his regulator. She hoped upon hope it would be option number two, because then at least she'd have a chance to get her spare air supply into his mouth before he drowned. Muscles burning and heart galloping, she put on a burst of speed, knowing that she still had to keep her breathing under control. If she sucked in too much air, she wouldn't have enough left in her tank to get both of them safely to the surface.

Twenty feet—

Nicola watched the diver's body language as he registered surprise, confusion—he was starting to rise upward—but then the best thing possible happened. She saw his arm shoot out to grab his inflator control, which meant he was doing what he was supposed to—removing the air from his BCD to keep himself from rocketing up to the surface.

Ten feet—

But oh, God, no—he'd hit the wrong button. This, too, was something she'd seen happen before—the buttons were different shapes but close together, so sometimes in a panic a diver would hit the fill button instead of the expel button.

Fifteen feet now as he floated up and away from her—

Adrenaline kicked in, but Nicola's muscles still screamed. Her breath tore out of her lungs—not much chance of giving him air now, but she had to do *something*—and finally she was close enough to take a lunge at him. Reaching her hands up, she used her fins to propel herself upward and managed to close one hand around the tip of his fin. Her other hand closed around the edge of his second fin, then she clawed her way up until she could grab his ankles. She had a hold of him now, but it could still mean both of their deaths if she didn't get to his inflator control to let his air out. She used the same arm she had locked around his legs to let the air out of her

own vest by its built-in button, then used her other
hand to take a slow-motion whack at the diver's forearm. He dropped the inflator control and it floated
slowly down toward her. Nicola snatched it up and
pressed the expel button, doing a strong reverse frog
kick with her legs to try to pull them downward.

And then she prayed.

Long, slow, deep breaths to conserve what little air
she had left. Pretty much impossible at this point,
but Nicola focused on it all the same to try to quell
the adrenaline pumping through her veins. She still
had her arm wrapped around the man's waist with
her head near his hip. She reached for her dive computer to read her oxygen level, though she already
knew from her increasingly labored breaths that it
was dangerously low. The number flashed at her in
urgent red digits—80 PSI. Just enough to get her to
the surface if she started her ascent in about one minute, but that didn't help him any. At least they weren't
rising anymore—they seemed to have leveled out at
around forty feet. Nicola employed a few more reverse frog kicks to pull them down a little farther,
calculating that they'd now have to stay at this depth
for about three more minutes to compensate for their
initial rapid ascent. Going up any sooner put them
both at serious risk for decompression sickness, a
potentially lethal condition where gaseous bubbles
formed in the bloodstream.

Sliding her hand up the diver's chest, Nicola
reached behind his left shoulder and pulled her arm

forward to catch the tube attached to his dive computer. She caught the device in her hand and looked down at his oxygen: 50 PSI.

It was decision time—release him to his possible death but save herself, take both of them up now come what may, or try to share what little oxygen she had left with him.

There was no question. She swept her arm backward to catch her spare air supply, then pulled his regulator out of his mouth, replaced it with hers and hit the purge button.

CHAPTER THREE

WHEN ALEX'S HEAD broke the surface of the water, cold fear was still pumping through his veins. Just moments ago he had been quite certain he was about to draw his last breath. Ripping his mask off with shaking hands, the only thought in his mind was: he'd been a fucking fool to ever think he could do this. Quick on its heels, fueled by his extremely damaged ego, was the thought that he never wanted to face the person who'd been stuck with saving him. Given the choice between terror and humiliation, he chose a third option—outrage.

"What the hell happened down there?" he sputtered to Rusty after he'd yanked his regulator from his mouth. No, not *his* regulator, not even his rescuer's—the device he'd just pulled from his mouth was the spare air supply that his own instructor had had to save him with. After Rusty finally got the memo that things had gone south with one of his students, he'd taken over the job and relieved Alex's *real* rescuer so he or she could surface and save their own life. "You let me lose the group on my first dive? My fucking *belt* falls off?"

Beside him, Rusty yanked his mask down around his neck. "The important thing is that you're all right," he said soothingly, waving to his driver to pick them up. "Let's get on the boat and I will explain." The driver spun the boat in a semicircle and then backed up toward them, expertly placing the ladder within Alex's reach. He grabbed on to it and heaved himself out of the ocean, feeling water gush down his legs as his wet suit drained. Four pairs of eyes—those of his fellow divers, comfortably seated on the benches—turned to look at him as he stumbled on deck. Great. Now he had an audience, as if he didn't feel stupid enough. And he knew very well how he'd just sounded—like one of those pompous assholes that Alex himself hated, the ones who tried to blame everyone else for their failings. Still breathing heavily with exertion and adrenaline, Alex sat down on the bench and leaned his head forward with his elbows on his knees, trying to get himself together.

Rusty dropped down beside him. "Another diver got caught in fishing line, so I had to stop and cut him out. It happens sometimes." When Alex didn't respond, Rusty calmly went on. "You swam away from your buddy. Your belt slipping off was a piece of bad luck. I came for you as soon as I realized you were missing, but thankfully someone else got to you first."

Alex shook his head with his eyes focused between his feet. He still didn't understand what the hell he'd been thinking. He remembered gazing out at the sinkhole from the reef, and then an over-whelmingly optimistic feeling bubbling up in his chest. He would do more than get over his fear, he remembered thinking—he'd fucking *obliterate* it. And then he'd started swimming toward the sinkhole like he was under some goddamn spell or something. To say he was furious with himself was an under-statement. He'd thought he could handle this, could conquer his lifelong fear, and instead he'd only suc-ceeded in making it worse than ever.

"Nitrogen narcosis," called out a female voice from behind him. "At least I'm pretty sure that's what it was. Did you feel giddy and invincible?"

That voice—it was vaguely familiar. Alex lifted his head and slowly turned it to see a woman stand-ing on the other dive boat, bobbing up and down with the waves in an opposing motion to his craft.

No.

It was her. Looking completely different from this morning—wet hair askance, a red rim around her eyes where her mask had imprinted on her now-pale skin, but those aqua irises—he could see them all the way from where he sat. There was no mistaking it: the goddess he had encountered on the road this morning, the hottest woman he'd laid eyes on since forever, was his rescuer.

Alex's pulse kicked into high gear, making his ears ring. Now he truly wanted to die of humilia-tion. Everyone on both boats was staring at him now, including another large, protective-looking instructor at the woman's side. As Alex looked at them, his memory of the recent events fell away, leaving only an intense visceral feeling in his body that was all too familiar. He felt the warm gush of water rushing out of his mouth, saw the crowd of kids staring at him, and his father's furious face as he strode toward him. And then later—the sharp sting of his father's slap across his five-year-old cheek. His father, the person who was supposed to care about him, had only enforced to Alex how badly he'd messed up.

Alex's hands curled into fists on his thighs. He'd learned about nitrogen narcosis in his scuba lessons, but his understanding was that it only happened at depths below a hundred feet. Was she trying to help him save face? Or making fun of him? He knew he owed her his thanks for saving his life, but with his emotions running riot, he feared doing so might reduce him to tears. So instead, he jumped up and strode to the end of his boat, getting as far away from his rescuer as possible.

"Whoa," Kiki said to Nicola as she watched her friend down her second tequila shot in five minutes. "That bad, huh?"

"That bad," Nicola confirmed, sliding her glass across the bar for a refill.

"Care to talk about it?"

Nicola shrugged. "What can I say? I saved some Z-list celebrity today—risking my own life while I was at it, I might add—and he doesn't even have the decency to thank me. I mean, sure, it's part of my job description, but really? The way he was looking at me, it was like the whole thing was all *my* fault or something."

Hands on her hips, Kiki shook her head in disbelief. It was one of the many things Nicola loved about her roommate—that she could always count on Kiki for a big validating reaction to her stories. "Jesus. Where does someone even get *off*?"

"I know, right?" Nicola said, lifting her third shot to her lips. "Maybe it's a Moretta thing." She threw the tequila back with a quick toss of her head, and then clunked her glass down on the counter. "Like as in, maybe I'm just not cut out for this place."

"Oh, no, you don't," Kiki said, slinging her dish towel over her shoulder and leaning her elbows onto the bar to get in her friend's face. Her pretty green eyes narrowed at Nicola. "You've only been here for four months. It's been good for you. You are *not* bailing on this like…" She stopped.

"Like I usually do? It's okay, Kiki, I know."

"Okay. Good," Kiki said, plucking a wineglass from the rack above her to fill an order.

Nicola watched her friend, thinking how grateful she was to have her in her life. When Nicola first came to Moretta, it hadn't been with the intention of staying here. After she'd been fired, she'd known exactly who to call in a fit of tears. Kiki had convinced her that a break from it all would do her good, so Nicola had packed a suitcase and flown to Moretta the following week. It wasn't hard to fall in love with the place, and when she'd gone for a dive and mentioned to Rusty that she was an instructor herself, everything had started falling into place. Kiki needed a roommate, Nicola needed a place away from the spotlight where she could regain her sanity and still earn a living, and they both needed a friend. A few phone calls back to LA was all it took to wrap up her life there. She'd been sharing an apartment with a colleague back at home, and as luck would have it, her colleague had recently started making noise about wanting her boyfriend to move in. Whether her roommate was sincere or just using it as an excuse to kick Nicola out after the scandal, she wasn't sure, but it didn't matter—Nicola asked her to put the remainder of her clothing and few personal items into storage, which she'd happily done. Nicola tried not to think too hard about the fact that it had taken less than a day to put an end to a ten-year chapter of her life, because something about it was downright depressing.

Nicola watched Kiki's eyes following someone behind her. "Dev Stone just walked in," Kiki said under her breath. "Just another day at the office."

Nicola could have cared less, but she caught a glimpse of him in the reflection of the bar's mirror all the same. Hair raked back, careless swagger, a gaggle of groupies in tow. Vomit-inducing. She was just about to say so when she caught sight of another face among the entourage: the diver she'd rescued.

Nicola groaned. This island was much too small, and the scene was so fucking typical that it made her stomach turn. "Don't look now, but it's Mr. Z-lister himself," Nicola told Kiki. "I guess we've unearthed whose star he's hitched his ride to. I have to get out of here." She slid a twenty across the counter and stood up.

"Total asshole," Kiki agreed, crossing her arms over her chest. "Never mind that he's a *hot* asshole."

Nicola rolled her eyes, but she couldn't deny the twinge she felt in her nether regions at the memory of their brief encounter this morning. After everything that had happened, how was that even possible?

"Love you," Nicola said to her friend, and then she was gone.

"You should try the lobster," the woman beside Alex urged him, not even attempting to be subtle about pressing her breast against his arm as she leaned toward the dish. "It's unreal."

"Thanks, I'm good," Alex responded dully, leaning away from her just as unsubtly.

Lobster. He'd seen a whole pod of them today on the dive. It had been amazing to see them all piled together with their antennae waving at him in slow motion—before it all went to shit and he decided he was Poseidon, king of the goddamn sea.

"Hey," Dev said from across the table, the first word he'd spoken to Alex since they'd been seated. As he watched, the woman on Dev's left reached for a platter of plantains and started refilling her master's plate. Alex refrained from rolling his eyes. "How was the dive?"

"Fantastic!" Alex forced a smile, then glanced over his brother's shoulder toward the adjacent bar to check for any new arrivals. He'd been doing this since they sat down in the restaurant an hour ago, just hoping she might walk in. Just hoping he'd have the chance to apologize and thank her the way he should have in the first place. But there was no one new—just the same lineup of bodies seated at the strawberry blonde's bar that had been there since they arrived.

A sharp knife of regret twisted in Alex's gut. He'd acted like a fool. Sure, he'd been furious and terrified, but how could he have let his pride get the best of him like that? He rubbed a hand over his stubbly face. "Hey, you know what?" he said to Dev, pushing his chair away from the table. "It's been a long day, and I need to get some sleep. I'll see you back at the house, okay?"

Dev looked taken aback. "Sure, man, whatever you want."

Alex excused himself and looked around for their waiter. He knew his gazillionaire brother was accustomed to paying—even expected to pay—for everything all the time. Dev wouldn't even check the bill when it arrived. But it was the principle of it that mattered to Alex. Just as he'd refused Dev's offer of the private jet, he would pay for his own meals and any other expenses that arose when they were together. Letting his brother give him a free ride only enforced the shadow Alex had lived in his whole life—especially after Dev's first album took over the charts when he was just twenty years old.

The waiter was nowhere to be seen. Sighing deeply, Alex made his way over to the bar and leaned forward on his elbows. The strawberry blonde bartender was inches away from him, but instead of offering him a drink, she picked up a bar mop and started slowly wiping down the already clean countertop.

Alex cleared his throat. "Excuse me."

"Oh." She rocked back coolly on her heels. "Did you need something?"

"Just hoping to pay my bill. I can't find my waiter."

She tapped a button on the iPad that was sitting on the bar. "Table twelve? Mr. Stone has a credit card on file."

Alex reached into the back pocket of his shorts and pulled out his wallet, then took out a hundred and laid it on the counter. "Then please just put this toward it," he said. He was about to walk away when he caught himself and spun back toward her. "Hey," he said, giving his fists two quick raps on the bar. "There's a dive instructor that works at the scuba shack…blond hair, greenish eyes—"

"Male or female?" the bartender interrupted with a lift of her eyebrow.

"Female." *And hot as hell*, he wanted to add.

"Sorry, doesn't ring a bell," she replied with an exaggerated upturn of her palms, then returned to her cleaning.

Alex stared at her. It was so obvious she was lying

that it was almost funny—she wasn't even trying to hide it. Which could only mean one thing: that she and his rescuer were friends, that his rescuer had already spilled the story and that somehow the bartender had figured out that *he* was the guy who'd made it all go down. God only knew what an asshole this woman must think he was.

"Listen," he said. "I did something really stupid today, and I owe that woman a serious apology. I get it if you're protecting her. But as her friend, think about this—would you rather she went to bed tonight feeling shitty, or feeling like a hero? Because she was my hero today, and I really need to tell her that."

Her eyes widened. "Wow. You're good." She reached under the bar and slid a piece of paper across to him. "I'll give her a note."

CHAPTER FOUR

WEDNESDAY MORNING. Nicola awoke around five thirty to the sound of tropical birds chirping loudly outside her window. Above her bed, her skylight was a dark orange square of light streaked with purple. She tossed and turned for a while, considered getting up—someone still had to walk to the gas station for a jug of gas, and she guessed it wasn't going to be Kiki—but then she fell back into a light sleep filled with strange, twisted dreams. An hour later she woke up feeling foggy and out of sorts.

Today would have been Nicola's second day back at school. She imagined another teacher in her old classroom, organized exactly how Nicola had liked it with her hand-lettered alphabet cards circling the dry board. She thought about twenty faceless children sitting before her, those little sponges who, for eight years, she'd taken so much joy in helping discover their worlds. Then she pictured the faces of her students from last year, stopping to hug her as they bravely made their way to their second-grade classroom.

And Oliver. Sweet Oliver who talked a mile a minute, whose imagination was more intense and whose curiosity was more boundless than any child she'd ever known, the kid who'd stolen her heart from day one with his earnest questions and spontaneous hugs. And the same kid who'd start digging his pencil into his skin when he became bored, who'd physically lash out at his schoolmates and at Nicola herself when he felt overwhelmed.

A severe case of ADHD. Nicola knew the symptoms, had grown up seeing them in her own mother every single day. Her mother hadn't known it because times were different then. But now that Nicola had encouraged her to get treatment, she couldn't help but wonder at how different things might be if her mother's condition had been managed earlier. Not just the instability and poverty that marked her childhood because her mom had had trouble holding down a job, but the calling Nicola felt as an adult to help others in similar circumstances. Would she have still stepped outside her professional boundaries to help Oliver? If not, everything that happened stemming from that one decision—the first photo with Matthew released by *Celebrity Life*, the paparazzi camped on her doorstep, the one piece of dirt the press was able to dig up on her, and the hurtful accusations from parents and coworkers— might never have happened. But it had, and as a result Nicola had had to leave behind everything she knew and loved.

A month ago Nicola had turned thirty. Teaching

scuba diving on an island of celebrities, no matter how idyllic it might appear, was not the life she'd planned for herself at this point.

You have to stop this line of thinking, Nicola scolded herself. Such thoughts could only lead to one thing, and she never wanted to go back to the place they brought her to again. She simply couldn't afford to exist in a world that dark.

Determined to get her day off to a better start, Nicola rolled over in bed—and came face-to-face with her open laptop on her nightstand. Three tequila shots in quick succession were never a good idea, but when combined with Google they could be downright regrettable. A little drunk and still reeling from the dive mishap—and *him*—she'd broken down and searched Matthew's name last night for the first time since she'd moved here. What she'd found hadn't helped her mood. Her screen had filled with the latest news—that his wife had filed for divorce because "their marriage hadn't been able to take the strain of Matthew's alleged affair with elite private-school teacher Nicola Metcalfe." That his wife was asking for spousal support and full custody of their only child, Oliver.

Nicola had felt like she'd been punched in the stomach. She understood why celebrities flocked to this island. There were no tabloids or newspapers for sale at the gift shop, and here you could choose, if you wished, to exist without the internet and TV. The very famous were trapped in a hell of their own making that elicited zero sympathy from the public.

Only by association, Nicola had lived that hell for six endless months, and it had nearly destroyed her. She couldn't imagine what it must be to have the world judging her every word, move and decision—to fuel the voracious appetites of the masses for failure and hope and mistakes—simply by existing.

Heavy thoughts for a beautiful day. Trying to shake off her mood, Nicola tied her emerald robe around her and went into the bathroom to shower and brush her teeth. Her phone was sitting on the vanity. Since moving to Moretta, Nicola had become decreasingly reliant on it, sometimes leaving it at home for an entire day without even noticing it missing— something inconceivable back in her old life. But really, who was going to call her? She'd been shocked at how many of her friends had jumped ship when the scandal went down. Which was another reason she loved Kiki, loyal to the end.

Nicola brought her screen to life to see a text from Kiki. It had come in at around ten thirty last night, long after Nicola was fast asleep.

Z-lister just left you a note. Want me to take a picture of it?

Great—just what she didn't need to improve her mood.

So what was up with that little flutter in her belly?

After showering and getting dressed in her usual work uniform—today it was a white bikini, pink terry shorts and a gray tank top—Nicola went into the kitchen with coffee on her mind. There was a piece of folded paper on the counter next to the coffee maker.

The note.

What could he possibly have to say for himself?

Nicola unfolded it and read: *You saved my life. I acted like a complete moron. Would you accept an apology drink? Alex 555 873 9921*

It was tempting. Nicola could still see his aqua eyes, the lines of his muscular shoulders, how he'd looked at *her* on the road yesterday morning…but no. Anything beyond a drink would prompt her conscience to reveal the truth about why she was here— or rather what she'd run away from to land here—and that was a complication Nicola didn't need.

She crumpled up the note and tossed it into the recycle bin.

From the back pocket of Alex's swimming trunks, his phone signaled an incoming text message. He made a grab for it, but it was just another work message from back home—still nothing from one of the two people he really wanted to hear from right now.

Fuck. It was only day two of his trip, and the whole thing was already off the rails. He'd managed to get John Brissoli's cell phone number last night from a contact of his brother's, who'd made Alex swear on his life he wouldn't reveal his source. The contact said he'd heard Brissoli was staying at the Palms Inn, the island's one hotel, and Dev said he'd never even heard of him. The guy was like some mafia hitman instead of a dude who'd started a website. In any case, Alex's voice mail and text messages to him had both so far gone unacknowledged.

Shoving his phone back into his pocket, Alex strode from the scuba shack toward the tiny gravel lot where several golf carts were parked. He didn't want to wait for her by the shack because this was a conversation that needed to happen in private, but there was nowhere else to wait without looking like a goddamn loitering creep. He was silently weighing his options when he saw her coming toward him.

She was in a golf cart this time, her hair blowing in the wind as she navigated the bumpy road. Beneath her gray tank top her breasts bounced gently. Seeing her like this, still unaware of his presence, relaxed and completely unconcerned about her looks, Alex thought she was more beautiful than ever. She looked strong and capable, and yet there was something about her that made him want to protect her from harm. Which was of course completely ridiculous, given that she'd had to rescue *his* ass yesterday.

The moment was too good to last. The second she laid eyes on him, her expression turned to one of flat indifference. She parked the cart, grabbed her satchel off the seat and strode toward the beach to avoid him.

"I acted like an asshole. You have every right to hate me."

She stopped in her tracks, then turned to look at him over her shoulder. "Why would I hate you?

I don't even know you. I'm sure that underneath it all, you're no worse than any other hotshot with a bruised ego." She resumed walking, so Alex had no choice but to hurry after her. He got in front of her but she wouldn't stop, so he started walking backward. He still had the lingering sense that she was familiar, but that wasn't possible. Though she was as beautiful as any actress, she was quite obviously a scuba instructor and not a celebrity.

"I'm sorry. It was unforgivable of me to not at least thank you. You got a really bad cross section of the worst part of my personality. Under other circumstances, you might even like me. My name is Alex, by the way. Like I said in my note, I was hoping I could take you for a drink. Unless you're, uh… otherwise attached." He tried a smile, but she wasn't biting.

"You're about to hit a tree," she said, brushing past him.

He turned and came face-to-face with the bark of a palm tree. They were almost at the shack now, and he sighed as he watched her disappear into it.

Okay—she gave him no choice.

Alex walked over to the pile of gear he'd assembled earlier and stepped into his wet suit, leaving the top hanging down around his waist. Then he picked up his gear and started carrying it over to her boat.

He was on her boat. She saw him when she started walking toward it with a tank in each hand. To her annoyance, she felt a happy little lift in her chest. She squashed it down and scowled at him.

"I think you're on the wrong boat," she said, swinging the tanks onboard.

"I'm afraid I requested you. You're the best instructor here, and if there's anyone who needs help, it's pretty obvious it's me. I promise you can let me drown this time if I misbehave."

She couldn't help the tiny grin that came to her lips. He was self-deprecating and funny; she had to give him that. And courageous for going back in the water after an experience that would scare many off diving for life. Not to mention that the way his wet suit clung to his impressive build—and the bulge between his legs—wasn't lost on her.

So was that all it took for her? A few cute throwaway lines and all was forgiven?

"Fine. But stay above fifty feet to keep from narcing again. And you're with Zach." She nodded toward her colleague, who was busy casting dark looks at Alex from the stern of the boat.

"You're the boss."

On the ride out to their destination of Camel Rock, Nicola occupied herself with checking the oxygen levels on the dive tanks and checking their O-rings, a job that she knew would have already been done by whoever filled them this morning. It wasn't just that it was awkward having him on the boat—being around him made her feel like a nervous teenager. She couldn't stop the flutter in her belly and the heat she felt in her cheeks when she caught him watching her from his seat on the bench. Those eyes—he was looking at her like she was a freaking ice-cream cone, and the truth was she'd like nothing more than for him to put his tongue in all her sweetest places. It was a weird reaction to have to someone who'd made her life hell twenty-four hours ago.

But then again, nothing had really felt normal since he'd shown up.

"Have a drink with me tonight," Alex said to Nicola as they got off the boat. This was his last try. If she refused him now, he'd have to accept defeat gracefully if he didn't want to risk coming across as a groveling stalker.

She looked at him dubiously, but she didn't shut him down—at least not immediately. She knelt down and started disconnecting her first stage from her tank.

Having just completed his first successful open-water dive, Alex realized that he owed this woman for more than just saving his life the day before. After what happened, he was quite certain he never would have gotten in the water again if he hadn't been driven to go after her—and he'd done it. He'd fought against his fear and won. The reef they'd explored today was possibly even more beautiful than the one he'd seen yesterday, but Alex had been more intrigued by his view of her than of the fish. He couldn't help it—the way that dive suit stretched over her figure made her look like the hottest Bond girl ever. Alex didn't get it. He'd always kept a cool head around women, but somehow one whose name he didn't even know had gotten under his skin.

"Listen. I don't even know your name, and that's going to make for a very bad story when I tell it back home. I'm Alex. Did I mention that already?"

"I believe you did. Nicola," she said, swinging two more tanks onto the dock.

Alex was impressed—the things weighed a ton, and even though she was slender and feminine she lifted them with ease. He reached out for one of them, his fingers brushing against hers. "Can I give you a hand with those?"

"I'm good." She paused, finally turning to face him. Her eyes pierced through him, sending a charge through his body. "It's okay. You're forgiven, all right? I get that you were under a lot of stress. But I really don't—"

"I almost drowned when I was five," Alex blurted out. Her eyes widened, and he shook his head. He'd never told this story to anyone, and here he was about to lay it on a practical stranger. "In the ocean. My mother told my brother to watch me, but he got distracted."

"That sounds awful," she said carefully. "How old was your brother?"

"Ten. And already a rock star—in his own mind, anyway."

Her brow furrowed and then cleared. "Rock star." She grinned. "Dev Stone is your brother."

He shrugged. "I guess someone had to get stuck with the job."

She nodded slowly. "I'm tutoring tonight. Eight o'clock at Pablo's."

"Great! I'll see you…"

But she was already walking away, her long, tanned legs making him ache with every move.

CHAPTER FIVE

"AND IF YOU take the seven away, you get nine. See that?" Nicola flicked her hair behind her ear as she scribbled on her notepad.

Raia smiled slowly in the way she always did when she was starting to comprehend something big, and Nicola grinned with her. Then she stole a glance at her watch. She loved tutoring her students more than anything, but tonight she felt jittery. It was just a drink, she kept reminding herself—not even a date. For all she knew, he could be leaving the island tomorrow. She didn't have to tell him a single thing about herself—least of all the thing that had brought her to Moretta. They'd have their drink, maybe share a few laughs, and then go their separate ways feeling better about what had gone down yesterday.

Except she knew that she was lying to herself. She wanted him, and she could tell he wanted her. Just standing close to him on the dock this morning had made her insides turn to gelatin. When his fingers had brushed against hers, she'd felt a jolt that fired directly to the spot she desired him most.

Nicola closed her workbook and gathered up her pencils. "You did great tonight, Raia. Keep working on your subtraction, and next week we'll do some reading." As she stood and reached for her handbag, she noticed Raia staring at her.

"Are you getting married?"

Nicola couldn't help it—her eyes widened. "Am I *what*?"

The girl shrugged. "Getting married. In Winx, the girls always look fancy when they're getting married. And you look so pretty."

Nicola placed her hand on the girl's head. "Thank you, Raia. That's very kind of you."

Pretty.

Nicola was about as into false modesty as she was into inflated celebrity egos; she knew she had the ability to turn some heads. But as she walked toward her golf cart, she realized how little she'd actually thought about her looks since arriving on Moretta. In LA she'd had a closetful of cute clothes that she wore to work, and had fun experimenting with different hair and makeup styles. But here it was a bikini every day, her hair seemed almost constantly wet and she'd had to actually search for her makeup bag this evening. Out of the four stylish dresses she'd brought to Moretta, she'd chosen a soft gray bamboo one that clung to her figure without being too obvious, paired with strappy silver sandals.

As she fired up her cart and started driving toward Pablo's, she wasn't sure if she was afraid she'd dressed too sexy or not sexy enough.

* * *

Alex drummed his fingers against the table and checked his watch. 8:06. He'd give it another four minutes before he started worrying she was going to be a no-show.

He glanced around the restaurant, taking in the open-air bar—free of the strawberry blonde bartender tonight, he was relieved to see—the casual island decor and the perfectly clear water surrounding the pier his table sat upon. Behind him the indigo sky was streaked with shades of orange and pink. Everything about the atmosphere screamed, *relax, you're in paradise!* But Alex felt anything but relaxed.

He turned back to his table to check his phone, and his breath stopped.

She was standing right in front of him, waiting for him to acknowledge her. He was quite certain he'd never seen anything so beautiful in his life. Her dress, though anything but showy, revealed the perfection of her curves. Her blond hair lay in soft waves against her shoulders, and the small amount of makeup she wore intensified the color of her eyes. Her heart-shaped lips, free of lipstick, shone with a slick of gloss that made him want to bite and kiss them for hours.

"You look incredible," he finally breathed, getting to his feet. He had meant to pull her chair out, but she beat him to it and sat herself down.

"Thanks," she said with what seemed to be a touch of self-consciousness. She gave him a small smile that made the blood rush straight to his groin, and then she lowered her eyes again.

"Thank you for coming," he started, feeling suddenly tongue-tied. When it came to women, they came to him. He wasn't used to pursuing them, and even though he'd had a couple of longer relationships, they'd always been underlain by a feeling of temporariness. A mere distraction from a career that took nearly all of his time and energy to maintain. The woman sitting across from him was giving him the closest thing to a case of full-blown nerves that he'd ever experienced. "Like I said today, I never meant—"

"Forget it. Seriously. The lengths you've gone to to apologize have shown me you're sincere. I'm ready to move on." Nicola met his eyes again briefly, then she plucked the cocktail menu from between the salt and pepper shakers and started studying it. She replaced it and used her hands to sweep her hair off her neck and to one side. As he watched her, he imagined kissing the skin at her throat, trailing his mouth downward— "What is it?"

"Hmm? Oh, just…"

Fuck. He needed to pull himself together.

Thankfully, their waiter appeared just then, so they placed their order. After he left Nicola sat back in her seat, making no move to converse. Alex cleared his throat. "Can I ask you a rather obvious question?"

"Sure."

"Why Moretta?"

Her expression changed immediately into one of… what? Retreat? "What do you mean?"

"I just mean that you're obviously not from here. So what made you choose this island in particular?"

"A few reasons," she replied, ripping the edge of her cocktail napkin into vertical, evenly spaced lines. "I moved here from LA, but I'm from Hawaii. I guess it reminded me of home."

"Hawaii. What was it like growing up there?"

She seemed pleased by his question. "Do you know you might be the first person ever who didn't react to that with, 'Hawaii? Wow, *nice!*'"

"I try to stay unpredictable." He raised an eyebrow. "But since you brought it up…was it?"

She laughed. "Yes and no. Mostly no."

He waited. There was a story there, and if there was anything she wanted to share, then he very much wanted to hear it. But she smoothly changed the focus to him. "How about you?"

He shrugged. "LA born and raised. Westwood. I've tried to fight my way out a few times, but it seems to have its claws in me pretty deep. My brother escaped to London a decade ago, and he takes a lot of joy in reporting how much better it is."

"A rock-star brother. What's *that* like?"

Alex shrugged. "Weird. Normal. Mostly all I've ever known—I was fifteen when he first hit it big."

"I can't imagine what it must be like to go through life in someone's shadow like that."

Alex looked at her in surprise. Nicola had just voiced what everyone else seemed afraid to, as if his ego couldn't take such a frank observation. And it was true, of course—he *had* grown up in Dev's shadow, and however successful he may have become in his own right, it could never compare to the brightness of his brother's rare and phenomenal star. His parents had never tried to pretend otherwise. "Rarely fun," Alex admitted. "I guess the only blessing is that I didn't try to follow in his footsteps. I mean, have you ever heard of the younger brother of a rock star hitting it big?"

Nicola grinned. "Can't say as I have. So what career path did you take instead?"

"I headed an import business until four years ago, when I took over the family company. It wasn't really on my radar, but...my mother died unexpectedly and my father needed help." Of course, this was only the abbreviated version of his father's path to ruthless ambition. Alex's parents started Echelon Media thirty-five years ago, and with a few failed businesses already under their belt, they worked their asses off to make it successful. Eventually, they expanded and gained momentum, even adding print media to their holdings. Then, right after his mother died, the company almost fell victim to a hostile takeover. Losing his wife and then nearly his company had lit a fire in Devin Sr. to buy up everything they could to ensure Echelon's legacy...regardless of the constant strain on Alex to keep up. "My father wasn't dealing well with his grief, so he basically put me at the helm and watched to see if I'd sink or swim."

"Kind of the way you learned to swim?" Nicola's voice was gentle.

"Yeah. Kind of like that."

The waiter arrived with their drinks, so they both stopped talking. Nicola picked up her margarita and took a sip, then she laid her hand down on the table inches from Alex's. He stared at it. Her nails were unpolished, but still long enough to taper to five perfect points. He watched as she bit her lower lip and released it again. Beneath her dress, he could see her nipples straining against the fabric. Had they been that hard before? No—he definitely would have noticed. He felt the blood in his extremities rushing toward the center of his body, creating an unmistakable heat there that only one thing could possibly quell.

Her.

God, he wanted her, and he wanted her *right fucking now.*

Nicola's eyes met his and didn't waver.

An electric jolt shot through Alex's body. Then she lifted her fingers and lightly trailed them along the top of his hand. He shivered.

"I was just wondering," she said, lowering her voice as she leaned in toward him. "If you felt like getting out of here."

He was on his feet and signaling the waiter for the bill before the last word was out of her mouth.

CHAPTER SIX

OUTSIDE THE RESTAURANT there were a few people lingering at the entrance as they chatted or smoked a cigarette. Nicola still couldn't believe she'd been as forward as she had been two minutes ago, but any possible regrets she might have paled in comparison to the urgency she felt to be alone with this man. To put her mouth on that spot right under his jaw she'd been watching all night, to take those fingers she'd finally gotten the nerve to touch and put them on the part of her that was already aching for him.

And he hadn't even touched *her* yet.

"Over here," Nicola said, taking Alex's hand and pulling him around the side of the building toward the beach. He happily obeyed, falling in step beside her as they hurried along the wooden walkway until their feet hit sand. Once on the beach she tugged him up the shore a ways until they were concealed from view of the restaurant by a stand of palm trees. By that time they were both breathing hard, and it was only partly because of their brisk walk.

Alex turned to face her. It was almost dark out,

but still light enough for Nicola to see her own eyes mirrored back to her. He reached out and brushed his hand against her cheek. Just a simple touch, but to Nicola it felt electric.

"I've been wanting to do that since the moment I saw you on the road," Alex said softly. "And so much more."

His hand slid to the back of her head, tangling into her hair. Nicola's pulse raced with the anticipation of the unknown. Would his kiss alight her as much as his touch had?

Alex tipped her face upward and brought his mouth down on hers.

Oh, yes.

A helpless little moan escaped Nicola's throat as she felt his tongue find hers. Slowly, their kiss deepened until it wasn't enough anymore. Nicola wrapped her arms around Alex's hips and pressed into them, feeling his cock stiffen. The rush of wetness she felt made her own feelings obvious. She wanted nothing more than to back up into a tree, have Alex lift her up and fuck her against it right then and there, but was she *really* doing this?

Quickly, before her brain got so addled by lust that she reached the point of no return, she ticked through all the reasons this was a bad idea.

He was a visitor to the island, which ruled out any possibility of a relationship.

But she didn't necessarily want one. In fact, given her current situation, that was probably a bonus.

She'd never been a one-nighter kind of girl, and

she'd certainly never slept with a guy within an hour of their first date.

But she'd never been overcome by such an intense craving for a man before.

She didn't have a condom.

Okay, so that one was ironclad. But maybe he did.

Her hands were inside his shorts—on top of his boxers, grabbing his beautiful ass. Meanwhile, one of his hands had found its way inside the top of her dress. She arched her back as he held her tightly by the waist with one arm and scooped her breast from its bra cup with his other hand.

"Fucking beautiful," he whispered hoarsely before taking her nipple into his mouth. Nicola moaned, desire pumping through every cell of her body.

But then Alex released her breast and kissed her again, still passionately but with more control. When he pulled away, Nicola could just make out his face in the moonlight.

"You're in charge," Alex said to her. "I won't make you cross any lines you're not comfortable with. No guilt, no regrets, okay? Just me. If you want me."

Nicola tightened her grip on him. "I do—oh, God, I do. Not…not everything right now, but soon. Right now I just want to feel your tongue on me. *All* over me."

"Your wish is my command." Alex smiled, making Nicola's insides melt.

Quite simply, this was a fantasy come true. The sound of the waves lapping gently on the shore reminded her that she was on one of the most beautiful beaches in the world. And this gorgeous man was looking at her like he wanted to devour her, like nothing else in the world existed except the two of them. And it didn't, even though Nicola knew they could be discovered at any second. She hardly cared—all she cared about was the intoxicating smell of Alex's skin, his hands in her hair, his body pressed to hers...

Alex ran his hands down her sides, and when he got to the bottom of her dress he ran them back up again, this time sliding them against her skin.

"Back," he whispered, and she obeyed, bending her knees until she was sitting on the sand. He pushed her gently until she was lying down, then he slowly moved the straps of her dress down her shoulders and pulled her bra down. His mouth was on her, teasing and flicking her nipples until she wanted to scream.

"That feels...*so good*," she said between breaths. "But I need more."

"All in time, I promise. First, I want to discover every inch of you."

"What about you?"

"What about me?" He took her hand and pressed it to his still-clothed cock, which felt about twice as big—if that was possible—as it had the last time she'd felt it. "I'm doing just great. Right now I want to feel you come."

Hearing those words from his mouth caused a new wave of heat to sweep through her body. "Please," she moaned, moving his hand to her pussy. "Lick me here."

His hand slid inside her panties, maddeningly close but not quite touching her clit. "I wish I could see them. What color are they?" he whispered.

"Blue."

"Blue like your eyes?" he asked, cupping his hand around her pussy. She moaned and pushed her hips into his hand.

"My eyes are green," she gasped.

"Aqua, actually. Exactly like mine, in case you hadn't noticed."

"I guess I was too busy noticing your incredible body. Now shut up and make me come."

She didn't have to ask twice. Before she could take another breath, his fingers had hooked around the sides of her panties and yanked them down. She moaned as his finger lightly traced her clit and then slid inside her.

He groaned. "You are so. Fucking. Wet."

"All your fault. Now, *please* make me come, or I'll make you fuck me right here."

He nuzzled his face into her neck. "Much too tempting," he said softly into her ear.

And then he was working his way down her body again, trailing kisses down her chest and tummy, then finally—*finally*—pressing his mouth to her most secret spot. She moaned as his tongue took its first sweep across her, and then he was latched on to her, licking and sucking while the heat in her groin built and built…she was already so close…

But then he stopped, transferring his mouth to the inside of her thigh while he pushed it up toward her chest. Nicola made a frustrated sound in her throat. Alex gave a low chuckle, and then slid two fingers inside her. "You're so warm and sweet. My cock is aching for you. But don't worry—plenty of time for that later."

Keeping his fingers inside her, he slid his other hand under her to cup her ass. Nicola felt like she was going to combust. She wrapped her hands around the back of Alex's head and pulled it down toward her again, and that was it—a few more sweeps of his tongue across her clit was all it took. Her entire body tensed as she finally fell over the edge with a frantic moan. Her orgasm exploded out of her so fast and hard it took her breath away, leaving her writhing helplessly on her back while he held her in his mouth.

At last, the final delicious pulse escaped her body and she collapsed onto the sand.

Nicola could only say this: "Oh, my God. Did that really just happen?"

Alex's cock was so hard it hurt. Having Nicola come under his tongue, with his fingers inside her to feel every sweet contraction, had been almost too much for him to take. He moved up and buried his face in her neck.

"We need a bed," Nicola said, reaching out to stroke him through his shorts. "I really, *really* want to take care of this for you."

"Thank fuck. There's just one problem." He felt her tense beside him, so he pulled away from her so

she could see his face in the dark. "I'm staying with
my brother. Not exactly the place I feel like bringing you right now."

"Ohhh…" She relaxed again. "Then we really do
have a problem, because tonight is my roommate's
night off. Nine out of ten says she's at home on the
sofa, and my place isn't exactly super private."

Alex groaned, then got to his feet and extended
a hand down to her. Nicola took it and stood up beside him. "The hotel," he said, snapping his fingers.

"Sure, if they have a room available. They only
have twenty-four of them, though, so the place is
usually full."

"I'll take my chances." Grabbing her hand, Alex
started pulling her back toward the entrance of the
restaurant, but Nicola stayed rooted to the spot. "Are
you—?"

Her mouth cut him off, closing over his, and then
she gave his lower lip a quick nip. "I'm sorry, but
I just can't have you walking around like this," she
said, slipping her hand into the back of his shorts
and then working it forward. She cupped his tight
balls through his boxers, and then ran her fingers
up the length of his aching cock. *Oh, God, yes…*
"There are other women on this island, in case you
hadn't noticed—"

"I hadn't—"

"And what would they think if they saw this?
They'd think it was for them, and I haven't even
had a proper look at it yet." She pushed him firmly
backward until his ass hit the trunk of a palm tree.

"Then please be my guest," he managed to get out, and then she was unzipping his shorts and dropping them to his ankles. His boxers came next, her hands sliding into them at his hips and slowly pulling them down. He felt his cock spring free. He was dying for her to wrap her hand around it, but he was also so turned on that he was afraid a few strokes would be all it took—

Be cool.

No chance. Nicola was dropping to her knees now, palming his head in a smooth, agonizing circle. A groan escaped his chest as he leaned his head back against the tree, focusing on control.

"Very, very nice," she said softly. He could feel her breath on him now, and then her tongue flicked out and gave the underside of his shaft a quick lick.

"Oh, God…" Alex wanted to drive himself between her lips, feel her sweet mouth suck him until he exploded, but he stopped himself. No. He was under her control, and he had no doubt she would take him to a place he may have never been before.

But then she moved away from him and gave his boxer shorts an upward tug. "And now that I've seen it…"

"No!" He gave a tortured groan as he pushed his hands into her hair.

"Just kidding," she said, and then his boxers were yanked down again and he was inside her mouth as she sucked him down. He gasped, keeping his head thrown back. He didn't dare look down at her— even though it was dark, he knew the dim sight of her beautiful lips wrapped around him would be the end of him. Instead, he tightened his grip on her hair, but then she released him from her mouth and flicked her tongue up and down the underside of his shaft.

It felt so good, he could hardly take it anymore. His balls pulled in even tighter, ready to explode—

She had him in her mouth again. He felt his head sliding along her tongue, then his shaft, and then her hand was on his balls as he hit the back of her throat. But then her throat opened and he was sliding in even farther...*sweet Jesus*—

Sensing the exact moment he was ready, as if they'd done this a hundred times instead of just one, Nicola released him into her hand and gripped him firmly. Alex came with a groan, his entire body trembling as wave after wave of heat pulsed from his center to the ends of his toes and his fingertips. He couldn't think, except to know in some deep place that he was experiencing the most intense orgasm he'd ever had in his life. Nicola held him in her hand until he was finished and his legs sagged beneath him, and then she gave his cock one final kiss.

"Now let's go find a room," she said.

The Palms Inn had no doubt seen more than its share of lust-filled encounters during its sixty-four years in business, but Nicola was quite certain that no two people had come close to matching the urgent desire she and Alex were feeling right now. Their time on the beach had only served to fuel their consuming need for each other, made evident by the generous hard-on she felt growing in Alex's pants just minutes after she'd finished him off.

Taking a steadying breath, Nicola passed through the front doors with Alex behind her. The lobby featured dark wood walls and large overstuffed canvas sofas, and she found herself praying they'd have a room available as they stepped toward the reception desk.

"Good evening," the man at the counter greeted them, and Nicola was faintly embarrassed to realize she recognized him. Not that it was surprising—on an island this small, the few staff members who worked in the town center saw each other often.

"Hi, Everly," she said with a smile. Alex's arm snaked around her back and dropped down to her ass, where he gave it a gentle squeeze out of eyeshot. She managed to keep a straight face. "My friend was hoping for a room for the night. Any chance you have any openings?"

Everly gave her a nod that oozed of discreet professionalism. "Would that be a king bed or two queens?"

"Preferably a king," Alex chimed in. "But I'll take whatever you have."

"Let me see if we can accommodate you."

As Everly tapped away on his computer, Alex looked down at Nicola and gave her a wink. Her belly fluttered. God, what was happening to her? Within one hour she'd suddenly become a wanton woman.

But she couldn't help it—that chiseled face, those eyes…she just wanted to lose herself in them. In *him*.

"It appears that we have only one room left. It is the honeymoon suite, so perhaps too spacious for your needs?" He was good—there wasn't a trace of irony on his face.

"That will do just fine," Alex replied, plucking his wallet from his back pocket and producing a credit card.

"As you wish." Everly hit a button on the computer, and a sheet of paper spit out of the printer. He slid it across the counter toward Alex along with a pen. "Just sign here, please."

Nicola blinked at the price tag printed at the bottom of the page. For one night, the room cost about as much as she made in a month. But Alex barely seemed to notice. "Thank you," he said, scooping up the folder that contained their key card.

"Enjoy your stay," Everly called after them.

"I most certainly will," Alex replied, and then he had Nicola around the corner and heading up the stairs with his arm wrapped tightly around her waist. They located their room on the top floor— the only one there—and Alex tapped the key on the lock.

Though they were undeniably here with one purpose in mind, Nicola couldn't help but take a moment to stare when Alex opened the door. It was the most gorgeous space she'd ever set foot in. The floor was polished mahogany, which matched the single beam running along the vaulted ceiling—the only dark contrast to the whitewashed walls and ceiling. Soft faux-fur rugs flanked either side of the bed, and a zebra-print one lay at the foot of the floor-to-ceiling rock fireplace. With a fireplace being wholly impractical in this climate, a giant vase of pink-and-white tropical flowers had been placed where the logs would go. Through a door on Nicola's right, she could see a sitting room arranged with soft pink-and-white armchairs, and to her left a black-and-white-tiled bathroom that was bigger than her kitchen featured a claw-foot tub at center stage.

And directly in front of her was the bed. Four iron posts that were taller than her tapered to points, where they supported a gauzy white canopy that swept down into two graceful curtains. The bed was made up with white linens, on which rested a wooden tray holding a champagne bottle, two glasses and a vase of pink roses. And behind it all, like a picture postcard blown up to life-size, was a flawless, expansive view of the beach and ocean.

"I feel like I'm dreaming," Nicola said, bringing her hand to her chest. "Is this for real?"

"I'll tell you in a minute," Alex replied, leaving her side to cross the room. Walking to the bedside table, he opened its drawer and pulled something out. Pressing it to his chest with an exaggerated sigh of relief, he slowly held it out to her. "It's actually a dream come true," he said with a sinful smile, holding out a box of condoms.

Nicola smiled back at him, but the physical distance between them had given her just enough time to escape the fantasy for a moment. Because that was what this was—pure fantasy, something that didn't happen to ex-schoolteachers who'd lost their job because the world had accused her of wrecking the home of the world's third-highest-paid actor. It didn't happen to women whose best childhood memories were of a fourth-grade teacher who saw an underfed, grungy little girl and decided to take her under her wing for one precious, life-changing year.

Who it *might* happen to was someone who'd grown up being told by her father that all she was good for was attracting a man, who had believed him and then gone out and done something to prove just that—something that the press had dug up to haunt her.

What if Alex found out? What if he already recognized her but was just keeping it mum so he could have a little fun with her?

Alex was in front of her again, pushing a strand of hair off her face as he stroked her cheek. "You okay?"

Nicola gave herself a shake. "Yeah, just... I don't know." She shook her head. "This is crazy. I don't do this sort of thing."

Alex placed a finger under her chin. "Neither do I," he replied.

"Really?"

"Really." Nicola was relieved when, as if sensing exactly what she needed, Alex ran a hand lightly down her back instead of kissing her. "Talk to me," he said softly.

Nicola took a deep breath and locked her hands around his waist. "I'm having an amazing time. But…do you *know* me?"

He blinked at her. "Not nearly well enough. But I sure like what I know of you so far."

"So you don't…" *recognize me?*

But she couldn't say the words—too dramatic, too vain-sounding. And if his answer was no she'd have a lot of explaining to do, which was the last thing she wanted to do right now.

He tilted his head at her. "Don't what?"

She shook her head. "Nothing."

"Hey." Alex ran his hands down her shoulders to grip her upper arms lightly. "If this is feeling weird to you, I totally get it. We don't have to do anything. But even if that's the case, I still want to spend time with you. I think you're amazing—in so many ways."

His eyes were pulling her in, making all her fears melt away. He was perfect…too perfect.

He swept his arm out toward the room. "There are more ways than one to enjoy a beautiful hotel room. I see a bottle of champagne over there with our name on it. Can I tempt you?"

Nicola relaxed a bit. "Sure." After following him over to the bed, she sat down on the edge while he connected his phone to the speaker system on the nightstand. The smooth sound of R&B filled the space.

"This okay?" he asked.

She smiled. "My favorite."

Alex popped the cork on the bottle and poured them two glasses. "To underwater rescues," he said with a self-deprecating grin, holding his glass up. "May I never put you through that hell again."

Nicola laughed and took a small sip. "It wasn't that bad."

"So you've seen worse?"

"I didn't say *that*. But you're not the first person I've had to…lend a hand to."

"So kindly put. Well, I'm glad I went through with it. There were some incredible creatures down there, and the fish weren't bad, either."

Nicola smiled, drawing a leg up on the bed so she could face him. Even though the sexual tension between them had eased a bit since their time together on the beach, she could still feel an electric jolt shoot through her body every time their eyes met.

"Have you always taught diving?" Alex asked her.

She shook her head. "No. I was a real teacher in my previous life. First and second grade."

"Previous life? That sounds—"

"Just an expression," she said quickly. "I became a scuba instructor when I was nineteen and used it to put myself through college. I first went snorkeling when I was ten, after a teacher got me enrolled in a summer camp. I loved it right away. We lived fairly close to the beach, so I used to go off and escape to my underwater world every chance I got." She smiled at the memory. "It's still my go-to stress release. And then a few years later I discovered diving—a whole new world. My family couldn't afford the equipment, but I found a program that allowed teenagers to borrow it free of charge."

"Sounds like you were very self-motivated."

"I had to be." She took a quick sip of her drink as Ariana Grande started singing. The tone of Nicola's response, sharper than she'd meant for it to come out, echoed regrettably in her head. She'd never been a big fan of talking about herself, but since the scandal it had become almost unbearable. "Will your brother be wondering where you are?" she asked to change the subject.

"I doubt it," Alex replied. "He keeps himself pretty well occupied."

Nicola nodded. "I gather you're not that close."

Alex placed his glass on the bedside table and leaned back against the mountain of pillows behind him. "You could say that. We were when we were younger, I guess, but…it got harder later. When his first album went platinum, it was kind of like I lost both him and my parents. He was away touring all the time, and suddenly my parents were completely wrapped up in his success. Nothing I did seemed to matter to them anymore. And now…" He shrugged. "I stopped trying to have a real relationship with him a long time ago. It's like he just stopped trying. Like his fame made him into something so great that it validates every part of who he is, and that's all he needs to define himself. He talks about wanting to live a normal life sometimes, but I don't think he could actually handle it. Being adored by the world puts you in a position that's terrifying to step away from. I get that."

Nicola squirmed a little under Alex's intense gaze. His words made her slightly uncomfortable, because though she'd never have admitted it, there was a tiny, ugly part of herself that *hadn't* hated being in the spotlight for those six months. Having the power to attract such attention from the press and public, to have the world looking at her and wondering what it was that was so special about *her*, Nicola Metcalfe, to snag such a shining star—part of that had been intoxicating, even if she hated what it was doing to all of the lives involved and ultimately made the decision to escape it. "The ego is a powerful thing," she said. "Can you imagine how different the world would be without it? No war, no corrupt politicians. No Kanye West."

Alex laughed.

Hesitantly, Nicola reached out and placed a hand on Alex's shin. "You're here, though, right? That must mean something to him—that you made the trip to see him."

Alex looked slightly sheepish. "I actually came here for business reasons. My brother living here— well, I couldn't put off seeing him forever." Placing his hand over Nicola's, he slowly entangled his fingers with hers. "But I never imagined what else was lying in wait for me."

Nicola's breath caught in her throat. She wasn't new to the language and subtle games of court-ship—she knew better than to place any weight in

casually uttered words this early on. But she'd never
met a man she wanted to get to know so completely
after such a short time. She thought about the many
things she didn't know about Alex—what he liked
for breakfast, what he did for fun, even what he did
for a living—and the history he carried with him
that she knew nothing about. She wanted to immerse
herself in him, to learn every nuance of what made
him who he was. Maybe this would be something,
or maybe it would just be tonight—but she wanted
it, whatever it was. Very badly.

The song changed to Ellie Goulding's latest hit.

"Are you hungry?" Alex asked her.

"Extremely," Nicola said softly. She moved toward
him slowly until she was between his legs, and then
lying on his chest. She looked down at him, and he
stared up at her with an expression that could only
be described as amazement.

"You are so beautiful," he said softly.

She brought her lips to his and kissed him passionately. He kissed her back, but she felt restraint
behind it.

"It's okay," she whispered when they broke apart.
His eyes fixed on her face as she licked her lower lip,
watching her every move like he wanted to pounce
on her. "I want you. I'm ready."

"Are you—"

She cut him off with her lips, and this time he
kissed her back with everything he had, a small
groan escaping the back of his throat. Then he
gripped her arms and rolled her onto her back,

pressing the full length of his body against hers. She could already feel the heat building inside her, her heartbeat quickening—oh, God, she wanted him so badly. "Yes, I'm sure." She reached for his phone and tapped the stop button on the music. "I want to see you, taste you, hear you. Undress me," she commanded breathlessly. "And then you. I want to see all of you."

Lying on top of Nicola, Alex felt intoxicated. It was the only way to describe it—as if someone had opened him up and filled him to the brim with pure desire. And someone had—*she* had. The vanilla scent of her, the softness of her lips and skin—he wanted to lose himself completely in her.

She sat forward and he pulled her dress over her head. Then he reached around her back and removed her bra, exposing her perfect, tan-lined breasts. "Gorgeous," he whispered, spiraling around each nipple with a fingertip. She raised a breast toward his mouth, and he obliged her with a long, slow suck. She moaned. "Alex…"

Slowly. There's no rush.

It was true. This moment only came once in a relationship, no matter how long or short. The first time, that wild collision of anticipation and reality—and he wanted to enjoy it to its fullest. But his cock, already rock-hard, was dictating something quite different.

Her panties were next. He hooked his fingers over the sides and slowly slid them down, revealing a perfect, trim triangle. "I finally get to really see you," he breathed. "As beautiful as every other part of you."

Lowering his tongue, he teased her clit with a few quick licks. Like he was the conductor and she the symphony, her hips curved upward to meet him. Slowly, he parted her lips and slid two fingers inside. "You're ready for me."

"So ready," she gasped.

"And I'm more than ready for you."

"Prove it," she said, reaching for the button on his shorts, but he caught her wrists and gently pushed them over her head.

"Now, now, no touching."

Straddling her waist, he pulled his T-shirt over his head and dropped it on the floor. Then he unbuttoned and unzipped his shorts and pulled them down so they rested across her tummy. His large cock, rock-hard and aching for her, sprang out above her breasts. "You see? I told you," he said.

"You're fucking perfect," she breathed, reaching for him, but he pushed her arms up again.

"You'll have me in a minute," he whispered, bringing his mouth down to her ear and giving her earlobe a quick nip. "Once I'm inside you, you can touch me all you want. Oh, and by the way?"

"Yes?" she managed.

"Get ready, because I'm going to make you come harder than you've ever come in your life."

Her eyes opened wide—pupils dilated, face flushed, she was the picture of lust personified. Alex rose up again, tossed his shorts and boxers aside and got the condom on. Then he lowered himself onto his hands and poised his hips over hers. She opened for him, drawing her knees up. "I need you now…"

"I'll be there soon, I promise. Guess how wet you are?" he teased, dipping his cock down just enough to bury his head inside her.

"The wettest I've ever been."

"I certainly hope so," he said hoarsely. "Because I don't think I've ever been this hard." And with that he slowly pushed himself inside her, a small moan escaping both their lips. He buried himself to the hilt, feeling her warm wetness close around him. It was heaven—the feeling of her, her head thrown back in ecstasy with her eyes locked on his.

He started to move, thrusting slowly at first but quickly gaining speed.

"You feel so good. *So good*," she gasped.

He wanted it to last forever, but it felt so fucking amazing, he just wanted to drive it into her over and over again, faster and faster until—

He forced himself to slow down, and Nicola took the opportunity to wrap her arms around his back and push him sideways. A half roll and she was on top of him, her long hair brushing her nipples as she rocked back and forth. Seeing her eyes closed, completely consumed with her arousal, was maybe the biggest turn-on of all. He caught her arms and slid one hand down to hers to catch it, then he brought it to her pussy. "Touch yourself. Let me see how you do it," he said.

She obliged, using her middle finger to tease herself as she continued to ride on top of him. "Ohhh…" She threw her head back, lost in the moment, and then she pitched forward and braced her hands on either side of his shoulders. Hooking her feet around the inside of his knees to open herself wider, she rocked herself against his pubic bone with his cock buried inside her. That she knew her body well enough to take charge of her own pleasure—a fresh wave of heat flooded Alex's groin.

"Oh, God," she said, inhaling sharply. "Oh, God, here I come…"

"Yes—"

He felt her contractions squeeze his cock at the same time her mouth opened to let out a delicious moan. Alex grabbed her around the hips, anchoring her onto him as she rode wave after wave of her orgasm. It was all he could do to control himself as he watched her beautiful face contort with ecstasy, but he was aching to thrust into her one last time. When she finally let out a long exhale, he held on to her ass tightly and started moving again, building speed as he fucked her upward. The sound of their breathing and flesh slapping against flesh filled the room. Nicola's mouth fell open and her eyelids lowered as she gasped, taking every stroke with a tiny moan of rapture.

That did it. Alex fell over the edge, letting out a massive breath as he drove himself up one last time to empty himself deep inside her. His orgasm ripped from his body almost violently—long, intense pulses of the hottest kind of pleasure that he never wanted to end.

At last his hips dropped down, leaving only the sound of their ragged breathing in the room. Nicola collapsed on top of him, and he rolled her sideways so he was still inside her with his arms and legs wrapped around her. "Was I right?" he asked as he caught his breath.

"What, you couldn't tell?" she replied coyly.

"I don't know. I don't have much to compare it to."

She caught his hand in hers as it trailed up her hip. "Then I guess we'll need to change that."

"I hope so," Alex said softly. "So...no regrets?"

When Nicola didn't immediately answer, Alex began to wish he hadn't asked. He certainly didn't have any. In fact, their union had only made him want every part of this woman—her body, her mind, even her heart—even more. But then she spoke again. "No regrets. And the weird thing is that I knew I wouldn't have any, even though I've never done anything like this before. I just feel...I don't know—comfortable with you, I guess."

Alex smiled. "Me, too."

Nicola gave a short giggle. "Really? I think you feel more than comfortable right now."

"What are you talking about?"

"Meaning you just fucked me. Aren't you supposed to be getting soft?"

"I guess my cock missed the memo," Alex said, wrapping a strand of her hair around his hand and giving it a gentle tug.

"I'm not complaining."

"Oh, no?" He rolled her under him. It was unbelievable but true—just minutes after coming, he was ready to go again. What was *with* this woman?

"You're going to be sore tomorrow," he warned her.

"Then you better make it worth my while."

"Oh, I plan to," Alex replied, taking her nipple in his mouth as he positioned himself between her thighs.

CHAPTER SEVEN

NICOLA AWOKE TO the sound of running water in the bathroom. She rolled over to see that Alex's side of the bed was empty, but a tray of food sat on the desk—coffee and orange juice, a basket of pastries and a plate of cut fruit covered with plastic wrap.

"Hello, beautiful," Alex said. Nicola turned to see him coming out of the bathroom with a towel wrapped around his hips.

"Hello yourself. How long have you been up?"

"Long enough to order breakfast. I thought you might have worked up an appetite." He gave her a devilish grin.

"As a matter of fact, I did," she said, smiling back and sitting up in bed. How many times had they awoken in the night to satisfy their insatiable appetite for each other? Two or three—she'd lost count at some point as the need for sleep finally overcame her body.

Alex came over to her and leaned down to kiss her.

"You've already brushed your teeth. No fair," she said self-consciously, but by the way he was devouring her lips, it was pretty obvious he didn't care. She put her arms around his neck, and he settled down beside her in bed.

"How are you feeling?" he asked, tracing her cheek with a fingertip.

"A little sore. More than a little, actually."

He grinned. "Me, too. But I meant…"

"Oh! Good. *Great!*" she added brightly, but this wasn't the whole truth. A part of her did feel great— *better* than great. She'd just spent the night with the hottest man alive and had had—she may as well admit it—the best sex of her life. And she had to admit to herself that what she felt when she was with Alex reached beyond the physical; how could it be that after less than twenty-four hours together, she already wanted to spend every moment possible with him? But Nicola also felt a creeping anxiety that had stolen her sleep last night despite her exhaustion. Alex didn't live here. He would be leaving. And if they spent any more time together before he left, not telling him the truth about herself would start to be weird. And after she told him, the fantasy would be over—and she really, *really* liked the fantasy.

"I have some work to do today," Alex said, tapping the tip of her nose. "But I'd love to see you later. In fact…" He pressed a palm to his forehead. "I just remembered. It's my brother's birthday today, so he has a party planned tonight. Would you like to come with me?"

She blinked in surprise. "Oh, I… Are you sure I won't be crashing it?"

"Are you kidding? The whole island will probably be there. You'll be the only person I know besides him and his outrageously amazing chef, Rosie, so you'd be doing me a huge favor."

The whole island. If someone recognized her and said something…but then again, there was safety in numbers.

"Well, then, sure. I'd love to." Nicola smiled over the butterflies of unease in her belly.

"Perfect." He pulled her close. "Just make sure my brother knows you're with me. If he lays eyes on you…"

"Oh, *please*." She rolled her eyes, and then glanced out the window at the white sky. "I wonder if he knows there's supposed to be a storm tonight. They can get pretty fierce around here."

Alex grinned. "I'm sure he has his people on it. He's got people for everything."

"Hmm. Sounds weird," Nicola commented with a furrowed brow. Then she pushed her hands into Alex's hair. "You know, there's a very basic question I haven't asked you yet."

He ran his fingers up her arm and clasped her hand in his. "Am I gay? I don't mind you asking, but I thought I answered that pretty well last night."

She laughed. Alex was funny and charming, that was for sure, and he seemed intent on easing all of her concerns. The problem was that only *she* had the power to put her real worry to rest, and the only way to do that was to have a conversation she really didn't want to have. "No. How long are you staying on Moretta?"

He trailed his hand down her side. "How long do you *want* me to stay?"

"That's a dangerous question."

"Is it?"

"Yes. You might not like my answer."

"Try me."

She caught his trailing fingers in her own. "Maybe later. Give me your answer first."

He sighed. "Sadly, I'm due to return to the rat race on Tuesday. Five days from now. But I'll need to extend my ticket if I can't nail down a meeting with the contact I'm here for."

"Wait. You mean you came here on business, but you don't even have a meeting lined up?"

"Yeah, I know. Long story. I won't leave without talking to him, though, whatever it takes."

"Sounds important."

"It is. I've been trying to track him down for months. We want to add his company to our roster, but he's pretty elusive. I won't bore you with the details of mergers and acquisitions—I've yet to see your eyes glaze over, but that would be a surefire way to make it happen."

She nodded slowly. "Okay, so...five days."

"At the least. When I ordered breakfast, I also took the liberty of asking the hotel to extend my stay here." He pushed her hair back from her face and lowered his voice. "And I want to spend every minute of it that I can with you. Staring into the mirror of these beautiful eyes—not that I'm vain or anything."

Nicola laughed again. "Do you ever stop?"

"I try not to." He slid his hand under the sheet to caress her breast. "God, you're beautiful," he said, his voice thick. "Too good to be true. So what's wrong with you? What am I going to find out if I Google you?"

Nicola's heart stopped.

Shit.

She wasn't ready for this.

"You know what I love about Moretta?" she answered smoothly. "It's so close to paradise that you can almost imagine a world without the internet. I kind of love that idea—getting to know someone without the influence of Google. Can you believe the world was actually like that once upon a time?"

Alex grinned. "Can you believe I *remember* what that world was like?"

She smiled back at him, waiting. *It will be better if it's his idea.*

"Okay, so no Google," he said. "Let's shake on it."

Relief flooded through Nicola's body. She hadn't solved the problem, but at least she'd dodged the bullet for now. She'd spend today planning out how she was going to tell him. Anxiety subsiding, she snaked her arms around his neck. "Isn't there another way we can seal the deal?"

"There sure is," Alex said.

"Just one problem," she said, glancing at the alarm clock. "I have to be at work in twenty minutes."

"So that gives us...?"

"About five minutes." Luckily, she kept a bikini in her locker at the scuba shack and could change at work.

"More than enough time."

Alex kissed her deeply, and Nicola felt her body respond immediately. God, what was it about this man? In an alarmingly short time, he'd already become like a drug to her. Dangerous.

She reached out and tugged at his towel, exposing his already stiffening cock.

"See how much I want you?" he said softly.

She moved closer to him, closing the gap between them. "Take me any way you want," she whispered into his chin. "Just make sure you fuck me hard. I need this one to last me for the next ten hours."

"You're sure you're up for that?" he asked, but she could tell by how his body was reacting that he liked the idea—a lot. "I don't want to hurt you."

"I'm up for it," she replied. "And I can see that you are, too."

"You better believe it," Alex responded, sliding a hand down to her pussy. "You're already wet for me."

How could that have happened so fast? But it had—her whole body was already on fire. "Because you make me crazy."

Alex made a growling noise in his throat and grabbed her by the waist, effortlessly flipping her over onto all fours. Then his head was beneath her and his hands were on her ass, pulling her down to his mouth. Nicola moaned, pushing herself into his mouth as his tongue swept at her clit. "Oh, God, I need more—your beautiful cock—"

The words were barely out of her mouth before he was behind her and pulling her hips toward him. And then he was sliding into her, filling her deeper and deeper. It hurt but it felt so good, the most exquisite kind of pain.

"Nicola. You are so fucking amazing." Alex punctuated each word with a thrust of his cock, harder and harder, each stroke building the heat within her. Then he reached his hand beneath her and found her clit, massaging it relentlessly until—

Until she was there with him, both of them cresting and falling together, their moans of pleasure intermingled until finally he collapsed forward onto her back.

"Now, that's what I call a deal sealer," Alex said.

"Okay, spill," Kiki said to Nicola the moment she walked in the front door. She closed it gratefully behind her—a brisk wind had picked up, an early sign of the promised storm—and smiled at her roommate. Kiki was sitting on the sofa with one leg bent up, polishing her toes in two contrasting shades of pink.

"What are you talking about?" Nicola said, trying to look innocent. But it was pointless—within two seconds she burst out laughing. "Fine," she said, tossing her satchel onto the tiny entrance table. "I may or may not have been having the time of my life."

"Assuming you were. Would it happen to be with a Z-list celebrity?"

Nicola could only laugh again. Only a day and a half had passed since she'd sat across from Kiki whining about her Hollywood-wannabe rescuee, but so much had changed since then that she'd nearly forgotten she'd once thought of Alex that way.

"Big misunderstanding on my part," Nicola said, taking a seat next to Kiki on the sofa. "He's Dev Stone's little brother. He's not trying to be famous at all. He's just here for some business deal. We went for drinks, and then… Anyway, he explained to me that the reason he got so upset on the dive was because he almost drowned as a kid. Kind of dramatic, but there you go."

Kiki's jaw dropped. "Dev Stone's *brother*?"

"Wait. Out of everything I just told you, that's your takeaway?" Nicola stared at her friend as she flopped onto the sofa beside her. "You don't have a thing for Dev Stone, do you?"

Kiki stretched her foot in front of her to admire her toenails, then she reached for the nail polish bottle on the coffee table. "Doesn't every woman on earth? I mean, God, look at him! Those eyes…" She shook her head. "But we're talking about you, not me. So tell me. Hot and heavy?"

Nicola felt her cheeks redden. "Wrong color. You're about to put the brush in the wrong bottle."

Kiki stared at the bottle and then corrected her mistake. "You're avoiding the question."

"We had a good time. He's…well, *amazing*, if you

want to know the truth. But he doesn't live here. And he's leaving in five days. And…" She looked away. "He doesn't know the truth about me."

Kiki placed her hand on her friend's shoulder and gave it a squeeze. "The *truth* about you? What, that you're smart and kind and brave and beautiful? That you're a kick-ass scuba diver who wouldn't hesitate to put her life at risk for someone else's? That you're an amazing schoolteacher whose kids made you pictures of themselves bawling their eyes out when you had to leave them? That you just happened to get caught up in a big, fat mess that wasn't even close to being your fault?"

Nicola dropped her gaze again. "You know that's not true. Not the whole truth, anyway." Suddenly, her eyes were filling with tears. She shook her head as she tried to stem the flow with the edges of her fingers. As surreally wonderful as the events of the past twenty-four hours had been, they'd also put her on an emotional roller coaster that she hadn't been prepared to ride.

Kiki moved closer to Nicola so she could put an arm around her shoulders. "It's okay. You've been so strong about this for so long, I think it's good for you to have a cry about it. What happened to you was fucking bullshit."

"Sure, it might have been, but—" Nicola took a deep breath, trying to get her emotions under control. She wiped at her tears and looked at her friend squarely. "Even if Matthew and I never acted on our feelings, we still had them. I can't deny that. Sure, the press blew it into so much more—all that stuff about secret meetings and family outings with his son was bullshit—but that day after our meeting about Oliver… Well, that photo didn't lie. Matthew told me how he felt about me, and I didn't brush him off or tell him to go away or remind him that he was a married father. I let him kiss me. I wanted him to! And after that, I started dreaming about him leaving his wife, about a future with him and Oliver. It was an affair of the heart if not the body—"

"But you did the right thing," Kiki reminded her. "You never touched him again after that. And in the end you left your whole *life* behind to do the right thing! You need to give yourself a break, sweetie."

"I'd like to, but the guilt is still there." Nicola sniffed. "I can't help it. When I think of Oliver now, wondering what happened to his family…I just can't take it. I still feel like it's all my fault."

"But it's not. If a marriage is strong, it's like an airtight room—nothing can get in to destroy it. But when there are big problems, the walls start to wear away, leaving an opening for someone else to enter the relationship. If it hadn't been you, it would have been another woman."

Nicola stayed quiet, but her friend's words made sense. Despite Kiki's scatterbrained ways, Nicola had a lot of respect for her. With her light red hair, freckles and tiny-but-perfect figure, she had the look of an innocent china doll, but Nicola knew that her appearance belied a tough inner strength. She'd come from a childhood that had been traumatic in a completely different way from Nicola's, but she'd prevailed and created the life she wanted on her own terms. And it wasn't like Kiki didn't know a thing or two about relationships—though only thirty, she already had a four-year marriage behind her.

"Okay," Nicola said, taking a deep breath. "Okay, so maybe you're right. But that still doesn't solve my problem. What about Alex? How do I tell him my big claim to fame is being the *10 Things to Know About Matthew Beck's Mistress* girl—not to mention point number ten? Remember that one?"

Kiki shook her head. "Just *tell* him, sweetie. He'll understand—everyone makes mistakes. I'm betting he's got a few under his belt."

Nicola nodded slowly. "You're right. I know—I just have to look him in the eye and *do it*." She took another deep breath, already feeling a little better. Screw it if he couldn't accept who she was—her past wasn't going away, and it was better to know now if this was a deal breaker for him or not. She glanced at her watch. "Speaking of which, I'm supposed to be meeting him in an hour. Hey!" she said, snapping her fingers. "Guess where I'm going tonight? To Dev Stone's birthday party."

Kiki's eyes widened. "Are you freaking kidding me?"

"Seriously. Actually…Alex said the whole island would be there." Said aloud, this statement suddenly gave her pause. The party was bound to have more than a few LA residents attending, and what if one of them recognized her? But then again, compared to Dev Stone's friends and acquaintances, she was hardly considered noteworthy. She added, "I'm sure Alex was exaggerating a tiny bit, but I bet he wouldn't mind if you came along. I mean, if you want to?"

Kiki jumped up from the sofa. "*Want to?* Are you joking?" She brought her hands to her head. "Shit— what am I going to wear?" But then her excited expression was erased by a thundercloud. "What am I saying? I have to work tonight! *Fuck!*"

"Maybe you could get off early?" Nicola suggested.

Kiki snorted. "With Juan managing tonight? Not freaking likely. But, hey—stranger things have happened."

"Yes," Nicola agreed with a smile. "They certainly have."

By the time Alex turned into Nicola's driveway on his golf cart, he was good and ready to leave his day behind. With still no word back from Brissoli, this morning Alex had both left a message at the hotel for him and written him a curt email calling his bluff: leaving tomorrow. get in touch if you're interested.

One of the things Alex had learned in business was that matching someone else's communication style could be an excellent way to get results. He'd spent the rest of the day on the phone putting out fires back home, followed by a brief conversation with his father, who had of course wanted to know only one thing: Had Alex done the deal? Well, that wasn't entirely true—Devin Sr. had also wanted to hear all about Dev Jr.'s latest successes and achievements. "He just continues to amaze, doesn't he?" had been his father's concluding observation before Alex hung up the phone, feeling the old sense of inferiority take hold that he'd left behind years ago—or so he'd told himself. Alex was a grown man, and the fact that he was still seeking his father's admiration, or at least his approval, made him furious with himself.

And now, eight hours after Alex had left his message at the hotel and sent his email to Brissoli, the man still hadn't taken the bait.

It was enough to make Alex regret, not for the first time, that he'd allowed his desire for his dad's acknowledgment to sway him into taking over the family business rather than sticking with his import company, which had been really taking off when he'd sold off his half to his partner. But after his mother's untimely death, his father undeniably needed his help. While Devin Sr. was the more creative partner, his mother had been more business-minded and less emotional—the true head of the company. Alex didn't think it was any coincidence that his mother had died of a heart attack. She worked harder than anyone he'd ever known, and he knew she'd have expected the same from him if she were still alive. And one thing Alex Stone did not do was underachieve or disappoint. So when his dad asked for his help, he had to give it. If he'd walked away, more than the family business would fall apart—his relationship with his father would. And Alex didn't have a lot of other family relationships to fall back on.

Alex parked his golf cart in front of Nicola's tiny bungalow and walked to the front door, trying to shake off his bad mood. Even if his day had gone to shit, he couldn't deny the low-grade buzz of excitement that had stuck around in his mind and body as he went about his work. Nicola. He didn't want to analyze it too much, but she was different from any other woman he'd ever met. Sexier and red-fucking-hot in bed, but it was much more than that. She was also kind and courageous and humble. He knew she wasn't perfect—no one was—but he trusted her to reveal her flaws to him in her own time. Alex couldn't imagine her messing with his head, and he had no desire to mess with hers. He just wanted *her*, straight up, even if it was only for five more days. Right now he couldn't allow himself to think beyond that, because the reality of their situation left him with an empty feeling in the pit of his gut that he just didn't want to deal with.

One look at Nicola was all it took to bring Alex out of his funk. She smiled at him when she opened the door, and it was all he could do not to barge into the room, rip her clothes off and fuck her right there on the floor like a wild animal.

She was wearing some sort of romper thing with shorts that showed off her tanned legs to perfection. The outfit was black with subtle sparkles in it that caught the light when she turned. It was held on to her body by a single skinny strap that looped behind her neck, allowing the fabric to drape between her breasts in a way that was unbelievably sexy without being the least bit cheap. Her hair was done in loose waves with a single skinny braid running along one side of her face, all the better to showcase her heart-stopping beauty.

"Even more amazing than the picture I've had in my head all day," Alex breathed, taking her hand and pulling her close to him.

Nicola reached up to kiss him lightly, but it quickly turned into a long, heated embrace. Pressed up against her, Alex willed his cock to behave itself. "I haven't been able to stop thinking about you," he said when they finally broke apart.

"Me, neither," Nicola said, her eyes sparkling. She took both of his hands and gazed at him as if she was about to say something more, but then she broke eye contact to look over his shoulder. "Looks like that storm's on its way. Shall we go?"

"If we must," Alex said with mock sulkiness. He held his elbow out to her and swept his other arm out toward the golf cart. "Your horse and carriage awaits."

Nicola giggled and took his arm, and they stepped out into the windy darkness.

"I hope you don't mind, but I invited Kiki to come," Nicola said. "She has to work, but she might drop by later. She's…a big fan of your brother's."

Alex laughed. "Who isn't?"

Nicola shrugged as she took her place in the cart. "Me."

Alex turned to face her from the driver's seat. "Really? Don't worry, you can tell me. You didn't dance around your bedroom to 'All the Girls'? Write 'Nicola Stone' all over your three-ring math binder?"

"Maybe that part," Nicola said, looking at Alex with over-the-top coyness, and he burst out laughing.

"Well, I guess I walked right into that one!" he said as he started up the golf cart.

CHAPTER EIGHT

IT WAS AN unwritten rule on Moretta that, out of respect for their illustrious owners, the houses were referred to by their names—Sandy Cliff, The Lookout, etc. While not everyone who owned on Moretta was famous, everyone *was* incredibly wealthy, and they fully expected that wealth to buy them privacy. All the same, word of who lived where spread quickly among the island's staff, and Nicola had been informed when she was hired that part of her job description was keeping those details to herself.

But Nicola needn't have been told. She knew all too well what the need to leave the spotlight felt like, and she had no interest in trying to associate with anyone simply because they were well-known. So when Alex pulled up to his brother's house, she was only vaguely curious about what the inside looked like—which was perhaps why the unexpected luxury of it took her breath away.

Unlike many of the island's massive two- or three-story homes, Tortoise Point was built in the style of a sprawling rancher. As a result the outside looked rather simple and understated, but once inside, Nicola could see that the home had been designed to follow the line of the beach, which started about five steps beyond the house. The entrance to the home was at its midpoint, so looking in both directions, the house went on as far as the eye could see. On the right a row of motel-like doors opened to a huge open piazza. Opposite the doors, thick metal rods ran the entire length of the space. Each rod was draped with white curtains that Nicola imagined usually blew gently in the breeze, but which were being secured against the increasingly blustery winds by a housekeeper even as Nicola watched. To the left was a sitting room featuring massive white sofas and a series of crystal chandeliers, beyond which Nicola could see an impossibly large dining room with a dark wood table at center stage. She counted ten chairs placed around the part of the table she could actually see. Outside, an infinity pool lay at the feet of a crop of palm trees whose trunks were encircled with sparkly white lights. A full bar and buffet table had been set up on the sand, each canopied with white canvas and manned by a staff of three. Were it not for the occasional leaf being ripped off a palm tree and tossed through the air by the wind, the picture would have been perfect.

"Wow," Nicola couldn't help breathing to Alex.

"I know, right?" Alex responded, holding tightly to her waist. "It's quite the place. Dev even had his own studio built in the back."

Nicola thought she heard a note of pride in Alex's

voice. She liked that—that he was secure enough in himself to be happy for his brother's success. She gave his hand a squeeze as she gazed around the room.

The party was in full swing. Raised voices competed with laid-back rap music over the speaker system. Throngs of beautiful people sat in conversation groups or floated by with cocktails. Many of them were dressed in understated but expensive designer clothing, but Nicola noticed that some of the women wore nothing more formal than skirts or shorts with bikini tops. She realized then that it was because of the expected rain tonight—a Moretta party tradition she'd never taken part in. She did a quick mental check of her own outfit—bought at Forever 21, she couldn't help thinking with a private chuckle—and was glad she'd chosen it over the bolder little black dress she'd almost worn, which would have felt much too dressy among this crowd.

"Let's get a drink," Alex said, steering her toward the bar. Nicola happily obliged, glad to have Alex by her side. She wasn't too proud to admit that this crowd intimidated her a bit, and she still held a lingering fear that someone might recognize her and call her out—though she knew it was unlikely. All the same, she kicked herself for not having come clean to Alex before nerves had taken over, burying her courage in doubt.

"I hope you're not the type of guy to leave a girl stranded at a party," Nicola joked as Alex handed her a glass of white wine. The wind blew some sand into her eyes, so she turned her face quickly to the side. Alex moved to shield her from the worst of it. "Because I don't think I have too much in common with my fellow guests."

"You and me both," Alex said, sipping his martini.

"Then you clearly haven't noticed all the women here who are drooling over you," Nicola said, lifting her chin toward a group of females gathered close by. Two of the women were staring straight at Alex as if they wanted to eat him alive, not even trying to be subtle about it. When Alex glanced over at them, they both gave him a suggestive smile as if Nicola wasn't standing beside him with her arm hooked around his waist.

Alex gave them a polite nod, and then he turned toward Nicola and pulled her close to him. Then his lips came down on hers in a deep kiss while his hands went to her ass and squeezed. Nicola kissed him back passionately. If *that* didn't send a message to the circling vultures, Nicola wasn't sure what would.

"You're the *only* woman I want," Alex said, touching his forehead to hers. "Got that?"

Nicola's belly flipped over. *Only woman I want.* It felt incredible to hear him say it, even if she knew better than to read anything into it.

"Besides, I'm just sloppy seconds to my brother. Speaking of which…" Alex said. Nicola looked over her shoulder to see Dev strolling toward them with a beer in hand…and about eight drop-dead gorgeous women in tow.

"Little brother," Dev said, holding his hand up in the air for a bro-shake.

"Happy birthday, Devy. Great party, if you can get past the hurricane that's about to wipe it out."

"Riiight…" Dev replied distractedly, his eyes having already settled on Nicola. "And this would be…?"

"Nicola," Alex said, pulling her close again. "The best thing that's ever happened to me on a business trip."

"I'll say," Dev said appreciatively, and then he tilted his head to the side. "Don't I know you?" he asked Nicola.

Her heart dropped. "I work at the scuba shack," she said quickly as her pulse hammered. *No. Anyone but his own brother. Please, God, no.* "I'm an instructor," she added brightly.

"Oh, yeah…" Dev said slowly, but his face didn't clear entirely.

Nicola turned toward Alex. "Hey, you know what? I'm starving. Could we get something to eat?" She gave Dev a quick smile. "Happy birthday, Dev. It was nice to meet you." She was already pulling Alex away.

"Wow," Alex said when he caught up to her. "Forget to eat today, or just sick of being undressed by my brother's eyes?"

Nicola laughed nervously. "Just hungry, that's all." She grabbed two plates, passed one to Alex and started loading hers up, trying to calm the rapid pounding of her heart. This was officially getting weird, and very stressful—she *had* to tell him the truth.

"Nicola!"

At the sound of her name, Nicola turned and saw Kiki hurrying through the crowd toward her. Nicola smiled broadly—a friendly, familiar face was just what she needed right now. "You made it!"

"Juan let me leave. Can you believe it? Maybe it had something to do with me threatening to tell the world about his knitting habit if he didn't."

Nicola stared at her. "Knitting habit?"

"Forget it. Actually, the bar was dead because of the coming storm. Can you believe this place?" Kiki threw her arms out as Nicola felt a drop of rain hit her head, and then another. She glanced up at the sky, which had turned a threatening charcoal color, but Kiki didn't even seem to notice. Maybe that was what two years of living on a Caribbean island did to you, Nicola thought—major tropical storms just became the norm. "Where's Dev?" Kiki asked excitedly. "Have you met him yet? Can you swing me an intro?"

Kiki's eyes were sparkling, and Nicola hated to tell her she needed to talk to Alex before she was willing to get near Dev again. She turned to look for Alex, but he was at the end of the buffet table chatting with a pale-skinned gentleman. "Just a minute. Let me get Alex—he can introduce you."

"Sure thing. I'll go get a drink." Kiki walked over to the bar, seemingly unconcerned that not only was the rain ruining her blowout, but that she was also completely on her own at a *"Lifestyles of the Rich and Famous"* party. Sometimes Nicola envied her friend's confidence.

Nicola walked up behind Alex, grateful for the canopy's shelter from the rain. Then she touched his arm to let him know she was there, not wanting to interrupt his conversation. He smiled at her and closed his hand over hers. "Nicola, this is John. And his associate, Larry," Alex added, gesturing toward a second man standing behind John.

"Nice to meet you," she said, extending her hand to John. Unsmilingly, he gave her a limp shake. He was extremely thin and had greasy hair. His fly was open. But worse than that was his ice-cold vibe, making Nicola wonder how Alex knew him. She turned to the second man to offer him a handshake, too, but he'd already looked away from her in favor of his cell phone.

"We were just getting down to a little business talk," Alex added, and then Nicola put two and two together. This had to be the man Alex had come here to meet, and now that he had his ear he didn't want to lose it. Nicola was happy to leave them to it, as the man's pale blue eyes boring into her face were making her uncomfortable. "That's fine. Kiki just got here, so I'll go—"

"Nicola Metcalfe?" John said to her suddenly, and her stomach did a sick flop. *How the hell could this creepy guy possibly know my name?*

"Yes," she said, her voice catching in her throat. He nodded. "Thought so. I guess you had to wind up somewhere. You picked a nice place, no? Lots of stars to choose from here."

His voice came out flat, like he could care less that he'd just ripped Nicola's world apart. She swallowed hard. She could feel Alex's eyes on the side of her face, burning with questions.

"Nicola?" Alex asked. His voice sounded far away, like he was in a tunnel. "Do you know John?"

"No," Nicola managed to get out. "But clearly he knows me. Excuse me."

She turned quickly before Alex could protest and hurried away. Her eyes filled with tears as she looked around wildly, wondering where to go. The rain was coming down harder now, but she wasn't about to go running through a houseful of strangers in this state when she didn't even know where the bathrooms were. She hadn't brought her own golf cart here, so she couldn't go home. She needed a place that was dark and deserted so she could collapse in peace. Straight ahead beyond the pool house, she could see an unoccupied area at the base of a rocky outcrop, so she headed in that direction.

"Nicola! *Nicola!*"

She could hear Alex calling behind her, but she didn't stop. If only she'd told him when she had the chance. Now he'd think she was trying to hide it, and even brand-new romances were built on trust.

Nicola was almost at the base of the cliff. The party noise was fading behind her as the rain drenched her hair and clothing—

"Nicola, *stop!* Please!" Alex's hand was on her

arm, spinning her toward him. She yanked it out of his grip and backed away from him a few steps. As the rain poured down between them, she heard a thunderclap in the distance.

"I'm sorry," she said above the din. "I was going to tell you. I should have done it today, but…" She took a swipe at her leaking eyes. "I chickened out."

Alex stepped toward her. "It's all right. You can tell me anything, okay? Let's just get out of the rain."

She shook her head. "I'm not going back in there."

"You don't have to. Over here." Alex walked over to a dry area at the base of the cliff, sheltered by the rocky outcrop, and ducked under it. With the rain now coming down in buckets, Nicola had little choice but to follow. She joined him, wrapping her arms around her legs as she huddled as far away from Alex as the small space would allow. She couldn't imagine how she must look—mascara streaked down her face, hair stuck to her scalp—but that was the least of her concerns. She stared out their little cave for a moment, watching the rain come down in an almost solid sheet as she tried to plan her opening words.

"I'm here for you," Alex said, turning his body toward hers. He had to raise his voice to be heard over the noise of the downpour. "Just tell me what you need to say."

"I can't," she said, shaking her head wildly. "You'll think I'm not the person you believed I was."

Alex held his palms up. "My mind is open. I promise not to judge you. Just tell me."

Nicola took a couple of deep breaths, but a fresh

wave of tears flooded her eyes. Just then the rain started to let up a little, making conversation easier— as if cuing her that it was now or never.

Nicola closed her eyes and began to speak. "Remember how I told you I was a teacher in my previous life? The reason I left it all behind to come here was because I was fired."

"Okay," Alex said levelly.

Nicola squeezed her eyes closed tighter. "The reason I got fired was because my school—it was a private school—decided I was unfit to teach young children. It was the most painful thing I've ever been through. I loved those kids…" She sniffed and took another futile wipe at her eyes. "I guess you don't pay a lot of attention to celebrity news?"

Alex was silent for a beat before he said, "Not in general."

"Didn't think so. Well, Matthew Beck had his son enrolled at my school. Oliver—I taught him first grade. He was a wonderful kid, but he had severe ADHD, so he was often disruptive in class and needed a lot of extra attention. Matthew's wife— Elsa—was off shooting a film in Argentina, so Matthew was the one I was communicating with. He had to come into the school for several meetings, and we sort of bonded because my mother had severe ADHD, too. She didn't know it then, but it's what made it so hard for her to hold down a job. She loved us kids, but she had a very tough time. That's why we moved around so much and never had any money. My father was a lazy son of a bitch who rarely even tried to find work. And he..." She trailed off. One story at a time—if she could bring herself to tell that part of it.

Outside their cave, a flash of lightning lit up the night, followed by a rumble of thunder in the distance. Alex reached for her hand. "It's okay," he said soothingly.

Nicola took a breath and continued. "Matthew is one of the biggest stars in Hollywood, so the paparazzi was on his every move. He'd gotten a court order to keep them away from the school, but they still surrounded it just outside the boundary. I used to see them camped out on my way to school every day. It was—" she shook her head "—pathetic. That so much time was spent trying to get a stupid picture of some guy just trying to get his kid to school." She took a gulp of air. "Anyway, it's not surprising that photographers got wind of a young female teacher he was spending a lot of time with. One day we were out on the playground after school. It had been a particularly bad day for Oliver, and Matthew was at his wits' end. I offered him some comfort, and he put his hand on my arm to say thank you. The next week a friend called to tell me she'd seen a picture of Matthew and me on an entertainment news show. '*Celebrity Life*, America's number one source for entertainment news,'" Nicola quoted sarcastically. "They reported that Elsa was away and that the couple was having marital problems. Then I made the mistake of walking Oliver to Matthew's car one day. Matthew got out of his car, and I had my hand on

Oliver's back because he was feeling agitated. A few days later the same show ran a story with a photo of us looking—" Nicola used her fingers to put quotes in the air "'—very cozy on a family outing with Elsa nowhere in sight.'

"That was it. A bunch of 'sources' popped up claiming Matthew and Elsa had been having problems for years, and that Elsa was saying this might be the last straw. Others claimed that Matthew had confided his feelings for me in them, and that he was plotting to leave Elsa and get custody of Oliver. It was a mess, but then it got messier."

Nicola felt Alex pat her hand reassuringly, but she gave it a quick squeeze and then released it. The worst was still to come, and she didn't want to feel him pull away from her when she finally said the words.

"I won't lie to you. After getting to know Matthew, I developed some feelings for him that were less than professional. I kept it to myself, though, determined not to play to the media or be responsible for the breakup of a marriage. But one day in my classroom, Matthew admitted he had feelings for me. And then he kissed me—it was just a chaste kiss. We were on school property after all, but I still let him do it. And I guess the paparazzi didn't care about the court order anymore, because they managed to get a blurry photo of us through the window. That's when Matthew's fans started sending me hate email, and when the other parents started avoiding my eyes at school. I thought it couldn't get any worse, but then the press decided to see what they could dig up on me."

And here it was, the very worst thing she had to tell Alex. Nicola wondered what was going through his head right now. She knew he was gazing down at her, but she didn't dare look at his face. Placing her fingertips under her eyes, she took a deep breath and started to speak again.

"I've made a lot of mistakes in my life, but I made the biggest one when I was seventeen. My teens were bad. I had my diving, but it wasn't enough for me to escape what was happening at home. My father...he used to sit around drinking beer and watching pornography all day. I was an only girl with two brothers. He wasn't bad with them, but I was a different story. I think he hated women. He used to tell me that the only thing I'd ever be good for was attracting a man, but he used much less kind words than that." She paused, and when she spoke again her voice was filled with painful disgust. "'Your meal ticket is right between your legs.' Really horrible things like that. Anyway, I guess after hearing it all my life I started to believe him. And..." She stopped, her eyes flooding again.

"It's all right," Alex said quietly, replacing his hand on her thigh this time. "Tell me."

"Are you sure none of this is ringing a bell?"

"You might have looked vaguely familiar, but..." He trailed off. Nicola thought his voice sounded tense, no doubt because he was trying to process all that she'd just told him—and decide if she was worth the trouble.

She forced herself to open her mouth. "My boy-friend in high school. He told me we could make a pile of money by doing a sex tape and selling it to some guy he knew. He said the guy had signed some-thing saying he'd blur our faces out, but of course it was all a big lie. I did the tape with my boyfriend, but there was never any money. And when the shit with Matthew happened…the tape was all over the internet, and then *Celebrity Life* picked it up and aired it. *That's* why I got fired."

Alex inhaled sharply. "Oh, God, Nicola. Oh, God. I am so sorry." Nicola finally met his eyes, and he reached for her hands. This time she left them in his. "I can't imagine how horrible that was for you. And your father…" He shook his head. "For him to treat you that way—any female that way—just makes me so furious. He didn't deserve to be your father."

Nicola didn't respond. What Alex said was true, of course, but Nicola knew she was responsible for her own choices. She hated people who tried to blame their actions on their childhood, their parents, their spouses. She had done something stupid, plain and simple.

Alex leaned in toward her, then pushed her hair back from her face. "Nicola, listen to me. We've all done things we aren't proud of. I don't care, okay? I don't care."

Don't care? It was too good to be true. "You don't?" she asked hesitantly.

"I don't. You are an amazing woman, and I'll take it all—the bad with the good, the hard with the easy. Thank you for telling me."

"Thank...?" She couldn't believe it. Could it really be that simple? That a man—not just any man, but *Alex*—could actually know the worst about her and still want her?

She remembered a date she went on after the scandal...her one date before leaving LA. The guy had spent the whole night fishing around for details about Matthew Beck's personal life, and then wondered aloud if Nicola would ever do a repeat performance of the sex tape. Alex was nothing like that. He was...*a fantasy.*

Relief swept through Nicola's body as Alex's hand slipped around her neck and up into her drenched hair. Holding her tight, he leaned in and kissed her hard. To Nicola it felt like a kiss that communicated all that was unsaid between them, the things that were too early to say and the things that were too hard to put into words. From the soil of all the painful experiences that had brought her to this time and place, she felt the first tender shoots of possibility for the life she'd been afraid she could never have. Emotionally raw, she felt laid open with vulnerability—and within that was something strangely but powerfully erotic.

When they finally pulled apart, Nicola was a little breathless. The rain had stopped by now aside from a soft patter. She stood up and ducked out of the cave. "I should check on Kiki," she said, stretching her cramped legs.

"I'm sure Kiki is just fine," Alex replied, joining her outside. Face-to-face, he kept his eyes fastened on Nicola's in the dim light. She felt strangely transfixed, as if his eyes held a spell that worked only on her.

Nicola reached out and grabbed Alex's now-soaked linen shirt in her fists and slowly pulled him closer to her. The flame that had started as a flicker a moment ago was quickly growing into an inferno inside her body. She hadn't felt anything like this before—a magnetism that she was powerless to fight. And it was all because of this one man. *Alex*.

"I want you," she whispered helplessly.

"I want you more," Alex whispered back. In one smooth motion, he lifted her up onto his hips. She wrapped her legs around his damp shorts, feeling the connection between their bodies at their most intimate places. Still looking into Alex's eyes, she slowly moved her pelvis against his. She was gratified to feel an instant response. "Do you have—"

"In my back pocket," Alex replied with a sinful grin. "My room?"

"Too far." One more word came from Nicola's lips, uttered softly but with an unmistakable urgency: *"Now."* She watched Alex swivel his head left and right, weighing his options, and then he carried her the fifty feet it took to reach the pool house. Nicola watched Alex slam the door shut behind them with his foot, and then she found herself in darkness.

Alex was smart. Instead of taking her to the main entrance—the lovely space with the chaise longues and minibar fridge where she could hear guests living it up right now—he'd taken her to the tiny room behind it where the inner workings of the pool were. Though it was private in here, she could hear people through the thin wall as if they were right beside her. But this only served to heighten her pulsing excitement. Still wrapped around his hips, she placed her hands on his face. "I can barely see you. We better be quiet," she whispered.

In answer, Alex's lips found hers and kissed her fiercely. Then he placed her down on something hard, and she realized she was sitting on the pool pump. She could feel it vibrating beneath her, but she could still see almost nothing. Nicola wrapped her arms around Alex's neck as his tongue explored the inside of her mouth. With nothing but the sense of touch between them, every nerve in her body felt alive with electricity.

She heard Alex's shorts unzipping, and then his breath was on her neck. She reached out and her hand ran directly into his rock-hard cock. She slid off the pump until her knees hit the floor, then wrapped her lips around his sweet, thick length and started to suck.

"Nicola, oh, God…"

Holding him firmly at his base, she licked his tip until she felt his legs start to tremble, then she pressed the entire length of him between her rain-slicked breasts. Squeezing her arms together, she moved up and down, letting him slide back and forth in her cleavage. Alex let out a muffled groan, and then his hands were under her armpits, pulling her up and spinning her around. She felt the pool pump hit the tops of her thighs. Alex's hand was at the back of her neck now, tugging at her halter tie. Her top fell forward, exposing her naked breasts. Alex reached around for them while he trailed his tongue down her back. "You taste so fucking good," he said in a low growl.

"Shh...no talking, remember?"

Nicola's outfit was down around her ankles now, and she was about to slide her thong down when she heard a shuffling noise followed by low voices. Just outside their door.

Shit—now they had people all around them. She and Alex stayed perfectly quiet until they heard footsteps walking away.

"Thank fuck," Alex said into her ear with a sigh of relief.

Weirdly, Nicola felt more turned on than ever. The brief moment she'd had when she thought they'd have to abort the mission had made her all the more hungry for what was about to happen. Alex's tongue was on her lower back now, trailing downward as he slid her thong down her legs. She was about to step out of it when he stopped her.

"Just enough space for me," he whispered. He bent her forward, holding her down by the back of the neck until her pussy was resting directly on the vibration. Then he pushed two fingers into her from behind. It felt so unbearably good that she was unable to control the moan that escaped her lips.

Was it her imagination, or did the conversation on the other side of the wall quiet for a moment? She was almost beyond caring—almost. Then she heard the rip of the condom foil, and Alex bent over her and whispered into her ear. "I'm going to fuck you now. And it's going to feel incredible."

That was when she stopped caring altogether.

Nicola tried to back up into him to make it happen faster, but he just pressed her more firmly into the pump. The vibration against her clit was driving her wild, and when he finally slid into her…sheer ecstasy. She felt him hunch over her as he drove into her harder and faster, his breath coming in ragged gasps. The sweat between their bodies created a slick heat on their skin. Alex pushed her legs together until her knees were touching. "Jesus, you are so tight and wet…"

The vibration combined with Alex's thrusting cock—it was the most incredible thing Nicola had ever felt. Her orgasm was close, so close now, and she knew that when it came it was going to spin the earth on its axis. She moaned again involuntarily, and then she was certain of it—the noise on the other side of the wall stopped. They had heard her.

The decent thing to do now would be to stop and stay perfectly silent until they resumed their chatter, but at the moment Nicola cared nothing for decency. She cared only about the incredible electric connection she was experiencing with the man behind her—and about meeting the insane orgasm that was now just seconds out of her reach. By this time their flesh was slapping together loudly anyway, so it probably made no difference, but she found Alex's hand and brought it to her mouth. His fingers crept into her mouth, and she sucked at them greedily as he slammed into her.

And then she was there. Her entire body went rigid at the same time as Alex's did, and she knew he was hitting at the same time she was. As the first wave washed over her, she squeezed her pelvic muscles to intensify the feeling and then rode crest after crest of mind-blowing heat. Her breath came out of her in a long moan that she was certain everyone at the party could hear, but Alex pressed his hand into her mouth as she heard him empty into her with a barely audible growl.

Finally, Alex collapsed onto her back. "My God, woman. What are you doing to me?" he gasped out.

Nicola was wondering the same thing about him.

CHAPTER NINE

For ALEX, sleep would not come. Beside him in their honeymoon suite bed, Nicola slept peacefully with her back curled into him. He disengaged his arm from under her neck and flipped onto his back, staring up at the ceiling in the dark.

What the hell was he going to do?

Alex had figured out who Nicola was the first night they slept together. As he lay staring at her face, her vague familiarity had finally clicked into place. So why hadn't he said anything to her?

Because it was awkward. Since she hadn't mentioned it, he got that it wasn't something she wanted to lay out on their first date—or whatever you wanted to call that first crazy night together. He'd opened the door by throwing the Google question out to her, just in case she felt like talking about it. It had been clear from her reaction that she wasn't ready, and that was okay. He trusted she would tell him in her own time.

Last night Alex's reaction to her admission had been truthful—he really *didn't* care. Alex was a man who believed in forming his own opinions about people rather than letting their reputations cloud his vision. He considered himself a good judge of character, an assertion that had nearly always proven correct in both his business and personal lives. And now once again he'd been right, but not only about Nicola.

John Brissoli. Alex had known he was a slippery snake just from their brief communications, but it was only when he was standing between Brissoli and Nicola at the party that he made a horrible connection in his head.

Nicola had been a victim of the paparazzi. And Brissoli's website, Star*ucker, specialized in taking celebrities—and any civilians that happened to be along for the ride—down for the count. And to make matters even worse, if memory served Alex correctly, it was Star*ucker who had first released the sex tape featuring Nicola's blurred face.

Standing there, Alex had realized there was no way he could admit to Nicola that he'd known who she was. She'd figure out that he was on the island to buy Brissoli's company, and then she'd show him the door before he could say *"huge fucking regret."* Worse, she might even think he was only showing interest in her so he could squeeze some new info out of her.

So he'd let her tell him the whole story as if he didn't have a clue. It had damn near broken his heart, especially the bit about her family, but by the time she got to that part Alex had been too distracted by something else she'd mentioned to be fully present.

Celebrity Life. It was produced by one of the many companies his family's conglomerate, Echelon Media Holdings, owned.

Nicola would fucking hate him.

He should have told her right then and there, come clean exactly like she just had, but he couldn't bring himself to do it. Every excuse in the book had rolled through his head—that she was already upset, that he needed time to plan his words, that maybe he didn't even *need* to tell her because after all, they didn't necessarily have a future together.

But he knew it was all bullshit. Like it or not, he'd already come to care about Nicola a whole lot more than made sense considering their short time together. She wasn't just a lay—she was amazing, and he knew he was falling for her fast and hard. So he'd settled on the best solution he could come up with at the time: he'd deepened both of their feelings by fucking her brains out.

Way to go, Stone.

He would tell her everything tomorrow morning, Alex decided. First thing.

No, you won't. You'll think of an excuse not to, and then you'll feel even shittier.

It was true. It couldn't wait. He had to tell her— now.

Alex took a deep breath, planning his opening words. Then he reached out and gave Nicola's arm a little shake. "Nicola," he whispered loudly.

She made a little noise of surprise in her throat, then she turned over to face him. "Hmm?"

"I need to talk to you," he said, pushing her hair off her face. Her eyes fluttered open. The lamp in the corner, set to its sexy late-night mode, shed just enough light for Alex to see her face. It didn't seem possible, but every time he saw her he found her more beautiful. Even like this—no, *especially* like this, with her eyes hazy and her lips slightly swollen, in his bed for him and him alone.

Until he told her the truth and she gave him his walking papers. After that would he always look back on their white-hot encounter from the night before, remembering that it was the last time he'd ever had sex with her?

His resolve wavered.

"Mmm. I need to talk to you, too," Nicola said lazily, running her hand up his arm under the duvet.

Alex gave a small start. "You do?"

"Yes." She ran her nails down Alex's back, making him shiver.

Steady. Don't get distracted.

Nicola hooked her knee around his leg and rolled on top of him, pressing her bare breasts into his chest. "But I forgot what I was going to say, so I'll just let my body do the talking."

Oh, God...he could feel his cock hardening under her taut belly. He gave one last weak protest. "Nicola, I really—"

"Shh…really what? Really want me on top, or really want to tie me up? Because I just happen to know that a pair of men's socks will do the trick."

Just happen to know.

Alex's head filled with the agonizing vision of Nicola in another man's bed, her arms tied up around her head, moaning with pleasure as he fucked her senseless. It wasn't that she'd done it before that bothered Alex. It was that after he lost her, one day she'd do it again with another man.

That did it. Sliding his hands down to her ass, Alex kissed her with everything he had.

Claiming her.

Needing her.

Consumed by her.

"I'll get the socks," Nicola said breathlessly.

Scrambled eggs, toast and hash browns: Nicola's favorite breakfast. She looked down at her plate of food, wishing she felt hungry. It worried her that she didn't, because she knew exactly why. Nicola had been in love twice in her life, both relationships now a distant memory, but suddenly all the symptoms were coming back to her. Nerves on edge, distracted thoughts of him all day long and loss of appetite. That was how Nicola knew she was falling, and right now she was falling extremely hard for someone who lived three time zones away.

The noise of the Palms Inn breakfast room brought Nicola back to the moment. She picked up her fork and speared a single hash brown, gazing out the window at the storm's aftermath. The sun was back, shining brightly as if last night had never happened. But the palm leaves and debris scattered around the grounds were proof that it had—as was the power outage that had hit the island save for the Palms Inn and Pablo's, which, along with a few of the private homes, had their own generators.

"So," she said to Alex, who was sitting across from her eating a cheese omelet. "I assume you didn't get the chance to talk business last night?" Nicola tried her best to keep the edge out of her voice. It wasn't Alex's fault that he happened to be doing a deal with a man who'd given her the heebie-jeebies and then called her out right in front of Alex. Nicola didn't know a lot about how business deals were done, but she knew it had little to do with personal compatibility and a lot to do with money.

Alex brought his napkin to his mouth and reached for his coffee. He'd been unusually quiet since they got up this morning, but Nicola put it down to work stress. Whatever was going on between the two of them, he had still come here for a purpose that hadn't been met yet. And she realized now she may have made things worse for him by pulling him away from his contact last night.

"Not really," Alex said, after sipping his coffee. "I didn't know he was going to be at the party. I'd sent him an email earlier in the day, and I guess he figured he'd just show up." He glanced out the window. "It's a beautiful day. What do you have planned?"

"Just one dive this morning, then I have the rest of the day off." She hesitated for a beat, and then, "Would you like to do something together? We could hike up the mountain. We'd just have to rent a Jeep from the gas station for the day."

Alex nodded. "That would be great," he replied, but Nicola thought his response lacked enthusiasm.

"Listen," she started. "I hope I didn't cause any problems for you last night? By taking off that way, I mean. You finally got in front of the guy, and I kind of distracted you by leaving so abruptly."

He put his hand over hers. "I wanted to go after you. That was way more important to me than any business conversation."

Nicola gave his hand a squeeze. Alex had given her the perfect response, so why didn't she feel reassured?

Nicola spent the morning trying to convince herself she was imagining Alex's distance, but she found herself distracted both on her dive and as she dressed for her hike with him.

In her tiny bathroom, Nicola tied her hair back into a ponytail and took a look at herself in the mirror. She had skipped the makeup, but she would be lying if she told herself she hadn't chosen her attire with some thought. She wore black short shorts and a khaki tank top, an outfit that was reminiscent of their first meeting on the road—utilitarian but also understatedly sexy in its own way. She'd done this hike a few times before and remembered it as being breathtakingly beautiful, but she couldn't help where her imagination took her when she thought about being all alone with Alex out in nature.

When Alex greeted Nicola with his usual good humor and charm, she started to relax. Everything was fine—it had all been in her head after all. They chatted about her morning dive as they made their way up the road in the open Jeep, the wind whipping Nicola's ponytail around her face. She loved this drive, the way the vegetation thickened into a tropical forest as they climbed. Far below she could see the white crescent of beach contrasted against the turquoise water.

"Did you manage to get some work done?" she asked, placing her hand on Alex's thigh as he drove.

"A little," he replied, but his voice sounded grim. She stayed quiet, focusing her eyes on the dirt road ahead. There was definitely something going on with Alex that he didn't want to talk about. Was it what she'd told him last night? It may have been easy enough for him to tell her it was all fine when she was acting emotional, but now he'd had time to reflect. Was he having second thoughts about her? If so, what about those two mind-blowing sessions last night—had she been a fool to think they were anything more than just a couple more lays to add to his belt?

Nicola took her hand off Alex's leg and held on to the Jeep's roll bar instead. The ongoing silence between them sounded louder than anything Nicola had ever heard before. She couldn't stand it. She wanted to tell Alex to pull over, and then get out of the car and walk home. She was on the verge of saying so when Alex opened his mouth and spoke again.

"I'm looking forward to this hike," he said. "I've heard the view is incredible."

Small talk. *Tourist* talk.

Nicola folded her arms, furious with herself for being such a girl right now. Was she really so insecure that she needed to feel completely connected to a man emotionally and sexually 24/7? What was so wrong with the obvious topic of the mountain they were at this very moment on their way to see?

It was awkward and off—that was what was wrong with it. But at least he was trying.

"It won't disappoint," Nicola responded, and then pointed to a road branching off to the right. "You can park just off there."

Alex pulled off the road and killed the engine. In the distance, Nicola could see a team of men at work on the island's only cell tower. Alex followed her eyes and then glanced down at his phone on the console. "Guess I won't be needing that today," he commented.

"Probably not. The tower goes down almost every time there's a storm. The internet's usually spotty on the island, but now it'll be nonexistent."

Alex pocketed his phone anyway, then patted his pockets for his wallet. Nicola willed herself to get out of the Jeep and start moving, but the sick flip of misery in her belly held her in her seat.

"Listen," she said, turning to face Alex. "I'm getting the feeling… We don't have to do this. You don't owe me anything. I know last night was a lot for you to process. If this isn't working out for you, I totally get it. You're leaving in three days anyway."

She tried to read his face, but whatever it revealed

just bewildered her more. She saw surprise, confusion and something else—guilt?—but it was all overlaid by a carefully curated expression of calm.

"I'm sorry," Alex said, pulling his eyes away from hers to look at the trees. He hung a hand over the steering wheel, and Nicola thought he looked tired. "It's not that. I'm just…dealing with some stressful stuff at work right now."

"Then maybe you should be in your hotel room working instead of climbing a mountain. If it'll get your head straight," Nicola said levelly.

Alex sat silently for a moment, tapping his fingers on the steering wheel and staring off into space. Then he reached for the key and started the ignition. "You're right," he said, turning the Jeep around to head back down the hill.

Nicola was going to cry for the third time in two days, and she hated crying. She'd managed to hold herself together all the way down the hill on the drive home despite the looming, endless silence between her and Alex, and she'd managed to hold it together when he gave her a chaste kiss goodbye and promised to be in touch in a few hours. She'd even managed to hold it together as she walked away and let herself into her house, but now that the door was closed behind her, all bets were off.

Nicola's head pitched forward as a sob tore from her throat. She lifted her hands to cover her face as tears trickled through her fingers.

It was over. It had to be. Something had caused

Alex's feelings for her to change, and the only reasonable explanation was that he wasn't telling her the truth to spare her feelings.

It isn't all about you, you know. He said it was about work.

But her instinct told her otherwise.

"What the—"

Nicola pulled her hands away from her face to see Kiki standing in front of her, still wearing her nightshirt. Her eye makeup was smudged under her eyes, like she'd fallen asleep in a hurry. When Nicola saw her she shook her head rapidly, still crying, but Kiki came over and put her arm around her shoulder.

"Oh, honey…" She led Nicola over to the sofa and sat her down, then dropped down beside her. "What happened? Did you tell him?"

Nicola nodded vigorously, still unable to speak. Kiki plucked a tissue from the box at her elbow and passed it to her friend. "It…went…fine," Nicola said between hitching sobs, dabbing forcefully at her eyes. "He said he…didn't care."

"It's okay," Kiki said soothingly. "Just take your time. What happened then?"

"I don't *know*!" Nicola burst out in frustration. "I have no fucking idea! Everything was fine—like *really* fine—and then today…" She shook her head. "He's been totally distant. We were supposed to go hiking, but we drove all the way up to the mountain and then turned around again. He says it's just work stress, but I don't believe a word of it. He's acting totally off with me."

Kiki held Nicola's hands in hers. "Maybe he's telling the truth. Guys can get really weird when their work isn't going well. It's, like, their entire identity or something." She paused. "What does Google have to say about him?"

Nicola blew her nose loudly. "We promised we wouldn't."

"Are you kidding me?"

"No. I may have sort of suggested it. I didn't want him finding out about me until I was ready to tell him myself."

"Oh. Right." Kiki drummed her fingers on the back of the sofa. "But things are different now. He knows about you—is it really fair for you not to know about him?"

Nicola shrugged listlessly. "I guess it doesn't matter anymore."

"Who knows? It might put your mind at ease," Kiki said, already reaching for her iPad on the coffee table. "Maybe we'll find out he's a serial killer who targets beautiful scuba instructors—in that case you'll be *grateful* he's gone off you."

Nicola watched as Kiki swiped her screen to life and then scowled at it. "Internet's still down," she said, dropping the cover over it again. "He's here on business, right?"

"Yeah. He's trying to buy some guy's company."

"So maybe it's not going well?"

"It's not. Alex told me so himself. And I met the guy he's here for at the party last night—he seemed like a total slimeball."

"Slimeball, huh? So what exactly is Alex's job title?"

"I haven't asked for details. You know what I'm like. I don't like to get into that kind of thing with guys until we've been dating awhile. Especially if they're wealthy—it feels like I'm digging around for income intel or something."

"Most guys would never think that."

"You'd be surprised."

"You've had some bad experiences."

"You fucking *think*?" Nicola jumped up and threw her arms out, but then she sank down again. "I'm sorry. I know you're trying to help. I'm just…super stressed out. And sad." She took a deep breath as a fresh wave of emotion thickened her throat.

Kiki tried switching tactics. "Well. We know he works in media, so maybe—"

"Wait." Nicola blinked at her. "That's more than I know. How do you know that?"

Kiki gave her a furtive glance. "Um, just from chatting with Dev last—"

"Dev?"

Kiki gave her an innocent shrug. "He likes to be called by his first name. Anyway, he seemed very proud of Alex. Kept going on about how he'd had to take over Echelon after their mother died, and—"

Echelon.

Nicola knew that name. She racked her brain, and then she jumped up again. "Oh, my God. Are you telling me that Alex works at *Echelon Media*?"

"He more than works there, honey. His family owns it."

Nicola stared at her friend. "You can't be fucking serious."

"Why? What is it?" Kiki asked in surprise.

"Hand me the phone," Nicola said furiously, reaching out for their landline.

CHAPTER TEN

THE OCEAN'S WATERS were choppy with whitecaps, its normal clear blue dulled under the cloud cover that had moved in again. Swimming on his back, Alex gazed up at the sky and saw thunderheads rolling in from the south. He turned himself toward shore and started swimming in. His pulse was regular. His belly wasn't filled with the cold anxiety that had always gripped him whenever he'd tried swimming in the ocean over the past two decades. Thanks to his last dive with Nicola, it seemed he was finally leaving his fear of the ocean behind him.

Nicola. He'd hated seeing her upset today and knowing he was the cause of it, but he was also confident he'd be able to more than make it up to her once they finally talked. He hauled himself onto the beach and reached for the towel he'd left on the sand. He dried off his torso, grateful that his swim had helped clear his head. Getting a little space from Nicola had been the right thing to do. Alex was an optimist by nature, and he knew what made him tick and what made him stumble. He'd known that if he could just start thinking straight again, he could figure this mess out. Alex had realized this morning that if he was going to tell Nicola the truth about who he worked for, then he needed to have a plan of attack ready to present to her for what action he was going to take to right his wrong. And now it had finally begun to take form.

Until last night Alex really hadn't given any thought to the logistics of Echelon's many media outlets. Of course he knew they produced news, sports, lifestyle, food, gardening, home renovation—and yes, a celebrity news show. But Alex's actual job was so far removed from the workings of these programs that he'd never felt like any of it involved him directly. He spent his days crunching advertising numbers, analyzing sales reports and researching potential acquisitions, not sitting on TV sets reviewing performances. It had never occurred to him that one of their programs might be destroying lives until Nicola had done him the favor of putting a real-life face to the problem. He was willing to admit that it had been irresponsible of him not to put more thought into the ethics surrounding his family's business, and he would agree with her that it needed to stop. And then he would do more than that—he would tell her that when he returned home, he was going to meet with his father about selling off *Celebrity Life*. Of course, Alex was certain he'd have a fight on his hands, but it would be worth it. His actions would prove to Nicola that he was sincere. She had taught him a valuable lesson, and he wanted to be sure she understood that.

And Star*ucker? It seemed that that problem had taken care of itself. Alex hadn't heard anything from Brissoli since the party. Though Alex knew his father would be less than impressed with him when he came home empty-handed. What else was new? Alex was used to his father's disappointment in him. By the time Alex had driven back to the Palms, let himself into his room and changed into some fresh clothes, he was feeling much better.

He was just getting his laptop out when the landline beside his bed started ringing. "A Miss Nicola is on the phone for you," the front desk operator informed him when he picked up.

"Please put her through." Alex grinned. He couldn't wait to talk to her now, to make things right and get this whole thing off his chest. "Nicola," he said happily.

There was a sharp intake of breath on the other end of the line, like she was crying. *What the—*

"Your company is Echelon Media? Is it true?" she asked tearfully.

Oh, God. No.

Alex's mind raced. "Nic—"

"Just answer me. Is it true?"

"Yes, but—"

"Then it was your TV show that destroyed my life. Please stay away from me," she said.

The phone went dead in his hand.

* * *

The knock came at Nicola's door within five minutes of her phone call.

"Nicola!" *Bam, bam, bam.* "I need to talk to you. *Please!*"

Nicola sat perfectly still, staring at the door with wide eyes. She still couldn't believe the nerve of him. After baring her heart and soul to him last night, he'd sat there and played the fucking innocent like his family's company *didn't* own the TV program that had ruined her.

"Nicola! I know you're in there. I'm not going away until you open up!"

And then today. Okay, maybe she could forgive him for not telling her within five minutes of her meltdown last night, but he'd had all day long to cop to the truth. She'd even offered him the perfect opportunity when they'd parked for the hike.

"Come on, Nicola. We need to talk about this. I will out-wait you. You can't stay in there forever!"

So when would he have told her? *Ever?* Or was he just planning to take off in three days and be done with her? A bit of vacation fun and then *sayonara*—

Nicola jumped as Kiki strode out of her bedroom, this time dressed in a hot-pink terry-cloth romper and baseball cap, and yanked the front door open.

"Kiki!" Nicola protested, jumping up off the sofa.

"*What?* I can't listen to this shit anymore. You two do need to talk. *Ciao* for now," she said with a salute, and then she was gone.

Alex stared at Nicola from the open door. His face

looked as pained as she felt, but she wasn't going to be sucked in. Each and every time Nicola had been played a fool in her life, it had been at the hands of a man. Never again.

"May I come in?" Alex asked.

Ignoring his question, Nicola rose from her seat and slowly walked toward him. She stopped when she was still several feet away, crossing her arms over her chest. "Do you know what I used to dream about being when I grew up?" she asked him in a low voice.

Alex held her gaze. "What?"

"A teacher. Not a doctor, not an astronaut, not a Hollywood fucking movie star. *A teacher.* Some might say I dreamed small, but it never felt that way to me. The happiest day of my life was the day I walked into my first classroom. I was a teacher-on-call, so broke I had three roommates and ate toast for dinner every night, but I didn't care. I'd worked my ass off to put myself through college and I'd gotten out of my home state. My life was going to be the one *I* created, not the one that had been handed to me. And for eight years, it was. Then the bloodsuckers showed up and took it all away." She shook her head. "Do you know what my goal was after the scandal? And I'll give you a hint—it wasn't to be a scuba instructor on a Caribbean island for the rest of my life. Hmm?"

"What is it?" Alex repeated miserably.

"To stay hidden. To stay hidden away from the world on this goddamn island so no one can ask me if I really had sex with '*the* Matthew Beck.' And so no one can ask me what it's like to have the world know what my crotch looks like."

Alex swallowed hard. "Nicola, I am so sorry. I should have told you. But I—I didn't *know*. I mean, I knew we owned *Celebrity Life*, but it's not like I really have anything to do with it. My job is at an office downtown, far removed from the studios. It's not my job to know what they're reporting on."

Nicola's eyes narrowed and her upper lip twitched as she advanced on him again. "So basically what you're saying is that it's not your job to oversee the programs your company produces. That whatever connection there is between Echelon and *Celebrity Life* is—let's say, tenuous at best. Your company owns them, but it's not responsible for them."

"Um. Right," Alex responded uncertainly. "I mean, those who seek fame do know that it comes with a price. It's kind of part of the deal."

Nicola was in his face by now, her hands fisted at her sides as she glowered up at him. "Then you're even worse than I thought. It's people like you— people who pass the buck to the paparazzi, the reporters, the public's insatiable demand for celebrity fodder—who are destroying privacy and breaking up families. Oliver no longer has an intact family, and that's partly on you. You should be fucking ashamed of yourself."

Nicola slammed the door in his face.

"Hey, little brother," Dev said to Alex as he grabbed a third beer from the poolside minibar and dropped back into his lounge chair. "I'd say I'm happy to see you cutting loose for a change, but somehow I don't think that's what's happening here." He reached for his own beer on the table between them and took a swig. "Everything okay?"

"Everything's great," Alex said flatly, twisting the cap off his beer and pitching it into the trash bin. "How could it not be? We're in paradise." He took a long drink.

"Funny thing about paradise. Your problems have an annoying way of finding their way into your suitcase."

Alex looked at his brother in surprise. It was the first time he'd heard Dev come close to admitting that his life was anything but a hundred percent charmed a hundred percent of the time. Though common sense had always told Alex that this simply couldn't be the case, Dev never seemed to let his perfect veneer crack. "Maybe for most people," Alex snapped, unable to stop himself, "but apparently not for you."

Dev turned on him. "What the fuck is that supposed to mean?"

"Exactly what I said. You've got people to manage your life, people to deal with your shit, people to crawl up your ass and tell you it smells like roses. Don't talk to me about problems." Alex took a long swig of his beer. He knew he was being petulant and unfair, but he couldn't stop himself. The booze, combined with the fact that he'd just lost the best woman he'd probably ever know in his entire life, had him in a foul mood to end all foul moods. Suiting his temper perfectly, he heard a rumble of thunder in the distance, and then the rain started to come down. But he made no move to leave his chair.

"You're being an asshole right now," Dev said squarely. "You don't know what you're talking about."

"Oh, no?" Alex turned on him. "And how would you know? When was the last time you asked me anything about my life? When was the last time you actually made an effort? Came to visit me—or visit Dad, for that matter? Oh, yeah—I remember. It was when you were in LA to do a show five years ago. You spent the weekend being paraded around town by Dad so he could show you off to all his friends. Probably a big drag for you, but you know what? I'd do anything to hear Dad talk about me the way he talks about you. But I'm not a fucking superstar, so no can do, *Twitch*," he finished, using the nickname Dev's fans had given him.

"Me?" Dev jumped out of his seat and stood facing Alex. "I'm sorry, but did I miss an engraved fucking invitation to your house? Because guess what—I've never gotten one! 'Come and see me,' I always say, and when do you finally accept? When you have a goddamn *business* meeting here—"

Alex jumped up beside him. "What did you want me to do—come here and hang out with your groupies? We've barely spent ten minutes alone since I got here!"

"That's because you've been spending every waking moment with some chick you just met! Anything to avoid—"

"She is *not* some chick—"

"Whatever—"

"Fuck you!"

"Fuck you harder!"

It was something they used to say to each other when they fought as teenagers. Alex glared at his brother, and then he pitched his beer into the recycle bin and stormed away.

He had to walk, blow off some steam. The rain was really coming down now, but he barely noticed. Headed toward the cliff, he passed by the pool house. He threw it a death stare as he walked by, his body still viscerally tuned to the memory of what had gone on in there less than twenty-four hours ago. Even thinking about it made him start to stiffen—*fuck*—

But it wasn't just the sex. Far from it. Nicola was the real deal, the whole package, and he'd fucked it up royally by saying exactly the wrong things to her an hour ago. What the hell was wrong with him? He'd had it all planned out in his head, so how had he messed it up so badly?

It was the sight of her tear-streaked face, the pain he knew he'd caused her…it had thrown him off. Made him think maybe he was the monster in the closet after all. That the business his family had spent thirty-five years building was all constructed around shitty ethics and other people's suffering.

Fuck it. She was done with him—she couldn't have made that more clear.

He turned away from the pool house resolutely and started marching toward the beach. What was done was done. He'd already lost her. There were other women in the world. Someday he'd get over Nicola and move on. He might even find someone he could be happy with. Because that was the way the real world worked—a relationship was a relationship, not some fucking fantasy.

He needed to get out of this place.

CHAPTER ELEVEN

"EARTH TO NICOLA," Kiki said, waving her hand in front of her friend's face. "Open your menu. You need to eat something."

Nicola tore her eyes away from the fuzzy spot in space she'd been staring into and focused on her friend's face behind the bar. "Just some french fries," she said, handing the menu back to Kiki.

"Since when do you eat french fries for dinner? God, you must be in a bad way."

Nicola tugged her fingers through her hair in frustration. "I just—was I too hard on him? I mean, it wasn't really his fault. Not directly, anyway. But…" She shook her head. "No. I have to stop this. There was a reason I broke things off with him, and just because he happens to be slamming in the sack is no reason to cut him slack."

"Sounds like you've got it all worked out, then," Kiki said, filling a wineglass.

"I do."

"Good. Then it won't bother you that Alex just walked into the bar."

Nicola's heart slammed in her chest. "Seriously?"

"Nope. But you should have seen your face. What went through your head when I said that?"

Nicola sagged down in her chair. "I don't know. I mean, what's the difference? He's leaving in a few days. I haven't heard from him since earlier today—"

"Nicola, you slammed the door in the man's face. That's a pretty final statement. In case you haven't heard, guys have this really fragile thing called an ego. Otherwise known as pride. What's he going to do, call you so you can shut him down again?"

Nicola sighed deeply. Her friend was right, of course, just as she always was. And she was sick of talking in endless circles. She glanced around the bar. "It's packed in here tonight."

"It's the weather," Kiki said, gesturing outside to the rain pounding down on the darkened beach. "It keeps them trapped in here."

"Guess this means the power's not going to be back on anytime soon," Nicola commented. "It's taking forever for them to fix the cell tower."

Kiki shrugged. "I don't think it's so bad. We're too attached to our screens as a society."

Nicola blinked at her. "Can you please send my friend back? What the hell was *that* about?"

"Well…" Kiki gave her a sly smile and leaned in close to her. "This whole power outage thing is kind of working to my advantage. You see, I happen to know that a Mr. Dev Stone has his own tech setup. Someone like him can't afford to be out of touch with the world for a day."

Nicola's brow furrowed. "*Happen to know?* How did you come across that tidbit?"

"He may have given me a private tour of his home at the party. Including his studio—which, I might add, is *completely* soundproof." Kiki's eyes were dancing.

Nicola groaned. "Oh, no. Tell me you didn't. That's Alex's *brother.*"

"Or Alex is Dev's brother—depends how you look at it. The point is, he said he'd be happy to let me use his connection whenever I need to, uh… check my email."

"Is that what the kids are calling it these days?" Nicola couldn't help but grin. "Okay. So I take it you had a good time?"

"Only the time of my life," Kiki said dreamily. "Details upon request."

"I'll pass, thanks. But I'm happy for you. Just… protect your heart. Among other things. I don't think Dev's exactly a saint."

"I'm well aware. Don't worry—I'm in it for a good time, not a long time. Speaking of which, I think I'll drop by his house after work. *'Oh, please, Mr. Stone,'*" Kiki said, clutching her bar mop to her chest as she reverted to the long-ago-ditched Southern drawl of her childhood. "*'Won't you help a distressed damsel in search of a little long-lost internet?'*" She batted her eyelashes as Nicola shook her head.

"You're hopeless."

"No, I'm horny." Kiki laughed, sliding Nicola's plate of fries across the bar to her. Nicola looked down at them like they were an unpleasant chore to be gotten through. Despite doing three rigorous dives this morning, she still had no appetite—which irked her no end.

"Don't turn around," Kiki said under her breath as Nicola squirted ketchup onto her plate.

"What?" Nicola said, automatically looking over her shoulder toward the tables near the water.

"I *said*—" Kiki covered her face and shook her head. "Too late."

Scanning through the crowd of people standing behind her, Nicola picked out the back of a lone dark-haired man sitting at a table near the pier.

Alex. Oh, my God.

She quickly turned around again. "Has he been sitting there the whole time?"

"I think so. He just turned his head to the side and I saw that it was him."

"Do you think he noticed us?"

"I doubt it. Your backs are to each other." Kiki punched her iPad and brought his order up. "Table two. Looks like he's on round number three. Drowning his sorrows, no doubt."

Nicola set the ketchup bottle down and lifted her napkin onto the table. "You know what? I'm really not hungry. And I'm not up for this. I think I'm just going to—"

"Run away?" Kiki finished for her with a raised eyebrow.

Nicola glared at her. "Leaving a bar does *not* qualify as running away."

"Actually, it does. You're avoiding instead of facing. I get it—it's your go-to response. We all have them. Me, I try to make light of things and get a laugh or two out of people, even when it's not appropriate to the situation. You have challenges with impulse control."

"Thanks for the therapy session," Nicola snapped, snatching her handbag from the back of her chair. She stood up—and ran directly into Alex.

She blinked at him in surprise, trying to gather her wits about her. He looked amazing, of course. His skin appeared more tanned than it had just hours ago—which was unlikely, considering they'd only had a few spots of sun today—and his aqua eyes stood out in sharp focus. A white cotton shirt showed off his masculine arms and hands, the same hands that had caressed her entire body and then—

No.

"Alex." She nodded curtly.

"Hi, Nicola. I took a trip to the bathroom to see if it was really you."

His honesty was disarming, but he should have tried earlier. "Yep, it's me. Just on my way out." She brushed past him and headed for the door, wondering if he would follow her. Did she hope he would or wouldn't? Both. Neither.

She was at the entrance when he caught up to her. "Nicola. Can we talk? Please?"

She headed out into the rain, walking toward the parking lot. "About what?"

"Everything. I was in such a state today—I didn't

know how to react. I wasn't able to do the most important thing of all, which is to just be honest and speak from the heart."

Nicola finally stopped walking. She crossed her arms and stared straight ahead, her body angled away from his. "Then say your piece."

"Thank you." Alex gestured at the people passing by them on either side. "We're in the middle of a walkway and it's pouring rain. Any chance we could go somewhere a tad more dry and private?"

Nicola shot him a sharp look. "*Not* a good idea."

All the same, she walked back toward the bar to seek shelter in the entrance. Alex followed, stopping directly in front of her. He stood a respectable distance away. He didn't try to touch her. But his eyes rested on her as if they were caressing her very soul. "I am so sorry for what happened to you. And I stand by what I said earlier—that I won't accept direct responsibility for it. *But*—" He raised a hand as her face began to darken. "What I've realized is that that doesn't matter. As head of the company—*any* company—it should be my responsibility to make sure we are acting ethically in every possible way. I can't be the owner of a chain of clothing stores in Kentucky and say I didn't know the clothes were being sewn by children in Bangladesh. It doesn't fly. When I get home, I'm going to talk to my father about selling off *Celebrity Life.*"

Nicola held his gaze.

"Before I took over Echelon, I ran an import business. I loved it, and you know why? The best part of it was flying around the world visiting the factories that the goods I bought were made in. It was extremely important to both my partner and me that the conditions be good and the local laws followed. But somehow when I took over Echelon, that passion didn't transfer over. I guess—I guess I just didn't care as much. It was my family's business, not mine, and even though I tried to get excited about it, that just never happened."

Nicola shrugged. "So why don't you quit?"

Alex shook his head. "It's not that simple."

"Sure it is. Life is short. You don't like something, you change it."

"That's a very simplistic way of looking at things."

Nicola threw her hands up. "It's the *only* way of looking at things!"

"Oh?" Alex said. "Then why are you hiding out on some island longing for your old career?"

"That's different!" she responded testily. "You *know* my situation!"

Alex sighed and shoved his hands in his pockets. "Look, I don't want to argue anymore, okay? Bottom line is that my father needs me, and I'm willing to admit that may have clouded my ethics a bit. I just… I want to make him proud, that's all."

Nicola allowed him a brief nod. He was right— she had no idea what it was like to be in his shoes, what it was to have family expectations to live up to, and she had no right to judge.

"Anyway…" Alex went on, fixing his eyes on hers. "I passed the buck. Just like you said I did. Of course I knew celebrity news could be harmful to the people it hounded, but I guess I assumed that if you decide to pursue fame, you just take the lumps that come with it."

Nicola lifted her chin. "And does your brother feel the same way?"

Alex looked slightly taken aback, but he said, "I doubt my brother even knows which programs we own. He doesn't pay much attention to anyone in our family but himself."

"Maybe you should double-check that with him. It sounds like you make an awful lot of assumptions about how bad your relationship is."

"It *is* bad, trust me. But that's neither here nor there." Alex took a deep breath, puffing his cheeks out. Then he took Nicola gently by the arm and steered her outside. The rain had slowed to a soft patter.

"What are you—"

"I need to say something to you, and I'm not going to do it around a bunch of people who suddenly seem very interested in what we're talking about."

Nicola glanced over her shoulder. It was true—a small, loose crowd had formed at the entrance, clearly only pretending not to eavesdrop. She couldn't stifle a small giggle. Who would have thought *their* conversation would be interesting among such a population?

Alex pulled Nicola around the side of the building until they were out of earshot of the loiterers. Then she backed up against the wood siding and waited.

It was dark back here, but the light from the bar was bright enough to show Alex's features.

"Here's what I want to say," Alex said, gazing into her eyes. "That whatever happened to bring you here, I am sorry for. But whatever happened to bring me here, I'm not. Because I got to meet you. I got to spend three of the best days of my entire life with the most incredible woman I've ever met."

Nicola squirmed. "Alex—"

"I'm not finished. I want you to forgive me—of course I do—and I want to spend more time with you. I want you to give me another chance. But I also want to thank you for helping me learn a valuable lesson."

"Um." She cleared her throat. "You're welcome."

Nicola felt her insides melting. Her resolve to hate him was flattened, and now it was all she could do not to grab him and kiss him. But for what? So they could have a few more nights together, and then she could go back to her little life here while Alex returned to a job that helped exploit people's weaknesses? So he'd sell off *Celebrity Life*—it was probably only one of several questionable assets that Echelon held.

But none of that changed what was in her heart. Yes, her heart—not just her underwear. She wanted him. Badly. And giving in to her desire was a terrible idea.

Nicola crossed her arms over her chest as a last line of defense. "You're forgiven, all right? But I still think it's best if we go our separate ways." Despite her best efforts, her voice came out weak.

"Okay," Alex said simply, making no move to leave.

"All right, then," Nicola confirmed with a nod.

Alex stood looking at her for a moment longer, and then he stepped a little closer. The dim light still caught the shine of his hair, the perfect angle of his lips. "I'll go as soon as you tell me one thing."

"Okay," Nicola replied uncertainly. The suntan lotion and aftershave scent of his skin was making her crazy.

"Do you remember what happened last time we left Pablo's?" he asked.

Nicola looked away. "How could I forget?"

Alex dropped his voice. "Best fucking orgasm of my life. Until the next one."

His words were like a direct line to her pussy. She felt it fire to life with a hot twinge. "Well," she said as her cheeks warmed, "I guess mine wasn't bad, either."

"Not bad? Was that what you called that earth-shattering scream?"

"I don't remember screaming."

"Then maybe I should refresh your memory."

Alex was right in front of her now, their bodies one inch apart. She could literally feel electricity buzzing in the space between them. She licked her lips. "What did you want me to tell you?" she reminded him in a barely controlled voice.

Alex looked down at his shorts, and her eyes followed. His cock was straining impressively against the fabric. "I want you to tell me you don't want to feel me inside you again. My cock thrusting into your pussy as hard as you can take it. I want you to tell me that wasn't the best thing you've ever felt in your life."

It was no use—the last of Nicola's resolve evaporated. Her knees literally felt weak. She tried to control her breathing, but it was already coming out fast. "I don't know. Maybe if you show me what you mean," she said, sliding her hand up her sundress and then down into her thong. No big surprise, she found herself wet and ready. She glided a finger across her clit and pulled on Alex's waistband with her other hand. "Show me."

She'd completely forgotten they were in public, and Alex seemed to care about that as much as she did. His eyes never leaving hers, she heard the delicious sound of his zipper unzipping. She looked down to see him holding himself in his fist. "Oh, that *is* nice. I remember now," she said, still pleasuring herself. "Now pretend you're fucking me."

"Nothing could ever feel that good," he gasped as he started to move his fist up and down. The sight of him turning himself on was making her crazy.

"Just imagine it. How do I feel?"

His eyes were soft, the lids at half-mast as he brought himself closer to the edge. "So wet. So warm and tight. I want to fuck you all night."

"Promise?"

"Promise."

Nicola stopped, bent to her handbag and pulled a

condom from the stash she'd put in there two days ago. "Then let's start right now."

Alex had the condom on in one second flat. Then, reaching under her dress, he yanked her underwear off and lifted her up against the wall. Through her haze of lust, she could feel the wooden siding against her back. She was fully suspended from the ground, but Alex was strong enough that he could keep her there while he guided his cock inside her.

"So good," Alex whispered raggedly into her ear. "So fucking sweet."

Nicola fought the urge to scream out in ecstasy as he started to thrust into her. She felt the zipper of Alex's shorts hit the insides of her thighs with each of his movements, and somehow the fact that they were both still fully clothed with only the most secret parts of themselves connected gave her an extremely erotic charge.

"Come for me, baby," Alex was urging. "Come on my cock. I need to feel you."

Nicola knew just how to get the job done. Grabbing Alex's ass to stop his heavenly thrusting, she stayed there for a moment, enjoying the feeling of being impaled on his rock-hardness. Alex gripped her thighs tightly, keeping her pinned to the wall. Using a circular motion, Nicola slowly started rubbing her clit against his groin.

"Oh, Jesus," Alex growled. "You're going to make *me* come."

"Be my guest," Nicola shuddered with one final gyration, and with that her clit exploded into a thousand fragments. She heard Alex's breath whoosh out of him at the same time and opened her eyes in time to see him mid-orgasm, his eyes closed and mouth open as he rode wave after wave with her. Her body shuddered as she felt herself contract around his cock, drawing out every last delicious pulse. Then, finally, she lowered her legs and slid down the wall. Tilting her pelvis forward, Alex stayed inside her while he kissed her face and neck.

"Stay with me tonight," he whispered.

Watching Nicola straighten her dress and run a hand through her sex-tousled hair, Alex could almost see the cogs turning in her head. Her shiny eyes returned to normal, and the guardedness he'd seen on her face earlier returned. Still leaning against the wall, she reached her hands out and took both of his.

"I do want to stay with you tonight," she started. "Every cell of my body wants that. But I think I should go home. Not because of anything that happened before—I know you're sorry, it's done. It's just…"

"What?" Alex asked softly, stroking her chin.

"I think I need to protect myself. I—"

"From me? You don't need to protect yourself from me. I won't…" But he broke off, shaking his head. What was he going to say to her—that her heart was safe with him? That he already couldn't imagine his life without her by his side? Such statements this early on would run the risk of driving her away if she didn't feel the same.

Nicola didn't wait for him to continue. "I just—I need some time to process. You're leaving and I'm staying. And plus, I was a bitch to Kiki—I need to go back in and apologize to her."

"You're a good friend," Alex said, and he meant it. Alex had a few sports-watching buddies back at home, but no one he trusted enough to really confide in. He'd always managed his hills and valleys and occasional emotional meltdowns on his own. It was something he'd never given much thought to, but suddenly the thought of returning to that life felt empty. Nicola wasn't just beautiful and kind and interesting, she was someone he could talk to about anything— and now that he'd experienced that, it was going to be hard to let it go. No, not hard. Impossible.

"She's the best friend I've ever had," Nicola said. "She caught me when I was falling down a deep, dark hole."

"I wish that could have been me." The words were out of Alex's mouth before he'd known he was going to speak them. Nicola looked at him with wide eyes, and then she dropped his hands. "I'm not trying to freak you out," Alex added quickly. "I guess that honesty pill I took a couple of hours ago hasn't worn off yet."

Nicola gave him a small grin. "You didn't freak me out. And I'm not playing games here. I just need a little time on my own right now, that's all."

"I get it," Alex said, even though he didn't.

Time on my own.

A little space.

It was the language he himself used when things weren't working out with a woman.

"I'll call you tomorrow morning. Okay?"

Alex tried to hide his disappointment. "Sure thing. And if you change your mind in the meantime…"

"You'll be the first to know," Nicola said with a nod, pushing herself away from the wall. She slid her arms around Alex's neck and gave him a long, though slightly restrained kiss. "What just happened was wonderful," she whispered, sending a twinge of lust to his groin. And then she was gone, walking up the pathway without looking back.

CHAPTER TWELVE

NICOLA PLUCKED HER phone from the bathroom vanity and swiped it to life. Still no internet—or electricity, for that matter. Knowing there wouldn't be enough hot water in the tank for her morning shower, she grabbed a washcloth and gave herself a brisk rubdown with soap and water from the sink. Then she walked into the living room and picked up the landline.

"Hey," she said when she got Alex on his hotel room phone. "How'd you sleep?"

"Not as well as I would have if you'd been in my arms," Alex replied, his morning voice still slightly rough.

Nicola's insides went gooey. "You and me both," she replied softly.

"Really?"

"Yeah." She grinned. "We're expecting more lightning, so I'm guessing my dives will be canceled this morning. Meet you for breakfast at the hotel restaurant?"

"Just give me fifteen," Alex replied.

Nicola hung up and pressed the phone to her forehead, still smiling to herself. It had taken all her strength not to call Alex last night, but now that morning was here she was glad she hadn't. She felt clearer-headed, even if her problem wasn't entirely solved. She was ready to move beyond the betrayal she'd felt at Alex's blunder, but the issues of their differing values and respective homes were still glaring. Alex was leaving in two days, the thought of which made Nicola feel downright ill. She was falling for him harder and faster than she'd ever thought imaginable, but it was too soon to talk about a future together without potentially scaring him off. And even if they did *talk* about it, Alex wouldn't exactly be able to move here. The last thing Nicola was going to do was move back to LA—she'd left there for a reason, and Nicola was a firm believer in moving forward, not backward. She'd never returned to Honolulu after she'd left it, and she would not return to LA, either—not for a man and not for anything.

Nicola arrived at the restaurant first and chose a seat by the window. She'd chosen a simple white sundress, not too sexy, for the occasion. She wore small silver hoops in her ears and a matching bracelet. When she saw Alex weaving through the tables toward her in a plain black T-shirt and khaki shorts, her breath caught in her throat.

"Even more beautiful than I remember," he said, bending to kiss her.

"Exactly what I was just thinking."

Alex beamed at her as he took his seat. "I was glad you called this morning."

Nicola adjusted her bracelet around her wrist. "I thought it would be good for us to meet somewhere in public. Otherwise, let's face it. All we'll do is—" she lowered her voice *"—fuck."*

Alex looked at her hungrily. "Since when has being in public stopped us?"

"You have a point." She gave him a small grin. "But seriously. You're leaving soon, and…"

Alex placed his hand over hers. "And what? There's this really handy thing called a phone. I'll teach you how to use it and everything."

"A phone." Nicola nodded. "I've got a better idea. Can we just pretend Tuesday doesn't exist for right now?"

"I think we need to talk about it eventually."

Nicola's stomach rolled over. The thought of waking up tomorrow morning and knowing he was leaving the next day, and then, even if they decided to try to continue things, the emails and phone calls that would probably grow fewer and further between as they both got pulled back into their old lives…it was unbearable.

"Later," she said with a soldiering smile. She took a quick sip of her coffee. The waiter approached their table, and they both placed their orders. "How are things going with your brother?" Nicola asked after the server had departed.

"They're not. We kind of had it out yesterday and haven't spoken since."

"You don't think it would be good to try to sort things out before you leave?"

"I don't think that's in the cards for us. In order for that to happen, I'd have to do all the bending. I honestly don't think he's ever given a thought to what it's like to grow up in the shadow of someone as famous as him."

"Have you ever tried telling him?"

"I wouldn't know where to start. And it would sound like I was playing the victim." He gave a dry chuckle.

"What is it?"

"I was just thinking about when I started up my import business. I was twenty-two years old, and I had no money. I needed a bank loan. When I sat down with the bank manager, do you know what he said to me after he flat-out declined me? 'Why don't you just ask your brother for a loan?' It was humiliating." Alex tapped his menu against the table. "I've never told anyone that story before."

"Then I'll tell you one, too," Nicola said. "Do you know why I became a teacher?"

"Tell me."

"It was because of my fourth-grade teacher, Mrs. MacDonald. She had a perfect yellow bob and wore penny loafers every single day. One day I asked her if I could have the pennies from her shoes. She asked me why, and I told her it was because I was sick of being teased by the other kids that I didn't have two pennies to rub together."

Alex placed his hand on hers.

"I was new—I was *always* the new kid. We moved all the time, whenever Mom lost a job or Dad got complaints from the next-door neighbors because he kept his porn cranked all day. So I spent a lot of time feeling either invisible or teased for my clothes or my bad lunches. But Mrs. MacDonald noticed me. She started leaving food on my chair at lunchtime, and she brought in a backpack of clothing that used to belong to her daughter. There was an Izod T-shirt in there—I'd never been so thrilled. Having someone care like that…it made me feel like I had some value. They say one special teacher can change a child's life forever, and it's true. She was my inspiration."

"Those kids were damn lucky to have you," Alex said passionately. "It's clearly your calling. You need to go back."

"It's not that simple."

"Familiar words."

Nicola gave him a regretful smile. Someday she would teach again—she knew that. It was in her blood and in her soul as much as diving was. But the idea of actually planning and executing her return to the real world—right now it was still enough to make her feel sick with stress.

"Anyway," Nicola continued. "You could say that it was Mrs. MacDonald who was responsible for my diving career. After she got me into that camp for underprivileged kids and I discovered snorkeling, it changed my life. I loved the ocean so much my mother used to say I had it inside me. That that's why my eyes are this color. But I guess you've disproven her theory," she finished with a laugh.

"Maybe mine are this color for a different reason," Alex said softly.

"Oh, yeah?"

"They say the eyes are the windows to the soul. So maybe our souls are a match."

Nicola felt her face growing warm. Could he really feel that way about her? Because she was feeling that way about him—it was completely crazy, but undeniable.

Suddenly, she was filled with a burst of optimism. Maybe, just maybe, she and Alex had a chance. So she wouldn't return to LA—Alex had never said he was attached to it, and there were lots of other places in the world to live. Plenty of couples met halfway around the globe from their homes and found a way to make it work. *Nicola and Alex, Alex and Nicola*— theirs could be one of those stories, too.

She reached for Alex's hand. He was looking over her shoulder, momentarily distracted, but then he brought his attention back to her and gave her fingers a squeeze.

"I wish we were alone right now," she said quietly.

"God, me, too." Alex's voice caught in his throat.

Just then the server interrupted them by placing their plates in front of them. Reluctantly, Nicola pulled her hand away from Alex's and started eating her waffle. After a few minutes Alex put his fork and knife down and leaned toward her. He stroked her cheek. "I want to spend every moment I have left here with you. We still have the room. I just want to be alone with you today. We don't have to...*do* anything. Just be together."

Nicola placed her palm over his hand. "But I do want to do something. More than anything." She looked down at her half-finished meal. "I can eat anytime. But I can't have you anytime."

Alex laid some bills down on the table, rose and extended his hand to help her from her seat. Then he dug the room key from his pocket and gave it to her. "I just have to take care of something quickly. You go ahead—I'll be right up."

Nicola smiled. "I can't wait."

"Mr. Brissoli," Alex called, walking quickly to catch up with him as the man exited the hotel. Brissoli turned on his heel and stared at him as if they'd never met before.

"Alex Stone," Alex reminded him pleasantly through gritted teeth. "We talked at the party."

Brissoli shoved his hands in his pockets. "Uh. Some party."

"It was," Alex agreed.

"So. You got the paperwork?"

"Paperwork?" Alex asked, puzzled.

"For the offer. That's why you're here, right?"

Alex found himself at a rare loss for words. "We haven't even talked about it. You never returned my messages."

Brissoli fixed him with his watery blue eyes. "And

yet here we are, so I assume you're prepared to seize the moment. The stage is yours—talk me into it."

Who the hell did business this way? The guy was a communications nightmare—all the more reason for Alex to be finally doing what he should have done ages ago. "I actually just wanted to let you know that we're no longer interested in acquiring your company. We've decided it doesn't fit with our other holdings right now."

Brissoli gave him a nonchalant shrug. "Suit yourself. Though I think you might change your mind."

Alex shook his head. Man—the dude was just *off*. "I'm afraid our decision is final."

Alex saw the skin under Brissoli's eye twitch. "Hmm. We'll see," he said, turning away.

Alex stood for a moment, trying to shake off the guy's bad vibe. He found it hard to believe that he'd ever entertained buying *anything*, let alone a company, from such a person. A lot had happened in a few days. Actually, if truth be told, Nicola had happened—and Alex realized that meeting her was helping him put many things into perspective.

Alex strode back into the hotel, thinking about the odd exchange as he made his way to his room. It was pretty clear that Brissoli meant to go to his father, and that the battle of wills between father and son would then begin. Alex knew it would be ugly, but he could handle it. In fact, he felt far more certain that he could handle his father than ever before. Was his increased confidence another effect of Nicola? He shook his head, smiling at the thought, and picked up his pace. Right now he had much more important—and pleasant—things to do.

"It's me," Alex said softly as he knocked on the door. Nicola opened up and stood before him with wet hair, her body wrapped in a towel.

"I took a shower," she said. "No hot water at my place."

Alex let the door close behind him and took her in his arms, inhaling the clean scent of her hair. They kissed, and then he held her at arm's length and slowly pulled her towel off. It dropped to the floor, exposing every perfect inch of her. Unsurprisingly, his cock stirred to immediate attention, but he could no longer deny it—his feelings for her reached far beyond his body's reaction. He wanted to absorb every detail of her. He wanted to enter her and stay one with her for as long as she would have him, an act that no longer seemed right to call *fucking*.

"No fair," Nicola said, tugging him over to the bed. "I want to see you, too." Once there she reached out for his T-shirt and pulled it up over his head, then removed his shorts and boxers. Together they lay back on the mountain of cushions and turned to face each other. Nicola gave him a sad smile, and he put a finger under her chin. "I know you think we don't stand a chance," he said. "But I can't imagine a time will come when I won't dream about this face all day long."

Nicola caught his hand and kissed his fingers. "I've loved every minute with you."

"Not true. But please stop talking like it's over."

"This is a fantasy. *You* are a fantasy—"

"Again, not true. I'm all too flawed, as you already know."

"Maybe," Nicola allowed. "But this—" she ran her hand up his side "—is perfection. And this…" She swept her fingers down the trail on his belly that led to the part of him that gave her so much pleasure. "Don't even get me started."

Alex watched her every move, then he pulled her toward him until she was fully enveloped in his arms. His hands slid over her body, memorizing every inch. Then he was on top of her, moving slowly, feeling her breath more like soft satin than an electric current over his skin. Pure sensuality.

"I love fucking you," he said in a voice that melted her. "But right now that's not what I want to do."

She gazed deeply into his eyes, so like her own. "Then what do you want to do?"

Instead of answering he kissed her softly on the lips, and then he worked his way down to her breasts and tummy with his mouth. She pushed her hands into his hair and arched into him as if she wanted to meld her body to his. Then he gently pushed her knees open, exposing her beautiful pussy. His tongue danced on it lightly as her hips moved upward, matching his rhythm and his mood. "Oh, Alex… God, yes."

After a while he rose to his knees, reached for the condom and rolled it on. Then he pulled her up, sat back and lowered her onto his lap, facing him. She gasped as he slid inside her. "God, it just feels better every time. How is that possible?" Nicola whispered.

"Because it's you and me," Alex replied, looking into her eyes. She held his gaze for a moment, and then she wrapped her arms around him so their torsos were pressed together. Her skin felt heavenly and her hair danced over his shoulders as they moved together, their breath quickening as one. Then Nicola leaned her hands back onto the bed, looking down at the place they were connected. "I'm going to miss this so much. Having you inside me."

Alex lifted a hand to her breast, encircling the nipple with a fingertip. "Is that all you're going to miss?"

"Not even close."

"What else?"

"Your incredible body. This face…" She reached out to cup the side of his jaw in her hand. Then she brought herself forward again and kissed him. "Everything about you. *Everything.*" She pushed his shoulders down gently until he was on his back and she was over him. "I never want this to end."

Alex pulled his hands through her hair. Staring into her eyes was magical, like an ocean he wanted to get lost in forever. "You mean *this*? Or us?" He watched her face, daring to hope.

Nicola stilled her hips while she held him inside her. Then she leaned down and put her face inches from his. "Both," she whispered.

Alex's heart skipped a beat. "It doesn't have to," he whispered back. They held each other's gaze for one intense moment, communicating all that was still unsaid between them, and then Alex flipped her onto her back. Through his entire body, he felt an erotic charge unlike any he'd ever felt before—one that didn't stem from pure lust, but rather something much more intimate and deeply personal—something only between them.

Still holding Nicola's eyes, he started quickening his pace. She moaned and threw her head back, losing herself in the moment, and Alex drove into her ever harder and faster, feeling this new desire grow with each stroke. And when she finally came, calling his name again and again, he understood the driving force behind his fervor.

He was making her his, and making himself hers.

CHAPTER THIRTEEN

As ALEX DESCENDED the stairs of the hotel to the reception area, he couldn't help the happy spring that lightened his step. Finally, things were on track. He and Nicola were in a great place—no, a *perfect* place; it had been all he could do to tear himself away from her to complete his task of buying a few groceries at the island store.

After spending several hours feeding their appetite for each other in the room, a hunger for food had gotten to both of them. Nicola had suggested lunch at her place. Kiki was out for the day, and in spite of the power outage, Nicola really wanted to prepare a meal for Alex before he left. Once he gathered what he needed at the store, Alex planned to spend the rest of the day with her. And tomorrow, if she was able to, and then…

But he didn't want to think about that. *Somehow* they would find a way to make things work—he felt sure of it. He would simply not give Nicola up. Now that he'd won her back, there was no way he was going to mess it up again—ever.

"Mr. Stone?" The voice broke Alex out of his thoughts. He turned to face the receptionist, who was holding a slip of paper out to him. Everly—Alex recognized him from the first night. "An urgent message for you. You asked not to be disturbed, so I've been holding it here for you."

Alex almost kept walking. Fuck—Brissoli certainly hadn't wasted any time in getting in touch with his father, though how he'd done it with all communications on the island still down was a mystery to him. His father was the last person Alex felt like dealing with right now, but he supposed he didn't have much choice. "Thank you," he said, taking the note from Everly's hand.

Alex stepped away from the counter and unfolded the note. *Come to the studio immediately. Extremely Urgent. Dev*

Alex frowned. The studio? Extremely urgent? What was going on?

He crumpled the note in his hand thoughtfully. His brother may have been a lot of things, but he was not an alarmist. Whatever the issue was, Alex would look after it and then continue on his day.

"Please let Miss Metcalfe know I'll be slightly delayed," he said to Everly, and then he walked toward his golf cart with a sigh.

Dev was waiting for Alex in the studio. He was standing near the entrance by the seating area, and when Alex got close enough to see him, the look on his brother's face halted him in his tracks.

It was an expression Alex had never seen before—
cold fury mixed with fear. The next thing Alex noticed was that they weren't alone. His mind raced
to place the vaguely familiar woman sitting on the
white leather sofa across from him, but seeing as her
hair was covered by a baseball cap, her eyes were
behind sunglasses and her face was streaked with
tears, it was no easy feat.

"What—what's going on?" Alex asked, bewildered.

"I was hoping you could tell me," Dev replied
sharply. He grabbed the laptop that was sitting on the
glass coffee table and spun it toward Alex.

Alex wasn't sure what he was looking at, other
than to see that it was a Twitter feed. He glanced at
the left side of the screen to see whose feed it was,
and then he froze.

Star*ucker.

To the right of their handle was a Tweet accompanied by a photo.

See how the stars really party! Hang tight for revealing pics of this celeb and more #crunk #nosecandy

Alex's head swam as he inspected the photo. It
was a picture of an actress he recognized. The photo
was taken from up high as if the photographer was
looking down at her, allowing for a perfect shot of
her plunging cleavage. She was holding a cocktail
in her hand, which, judging by the dark stain on her
skirt, appeared to have spilled onto her lap. Beneath
her was a white canvas sofa.

Dev's sofa.

It finally clicked. The photo had been taken at Dev's party. Which meant—which meant that anyone who had been there had been fair game, including Dev himself.

Letting out a long exhale, Alex sank into a chair and scrolled down to the next Tweet. It was an unflattering photo of Dev standing beside the bar, holding a beer with his body partially concealed by the back of a woman with strawberry blond hair. *Coming soon! See Dev Stone's new banana hammock in the flesh. PS she's red-hot...and ready! #letsgetiton*

"Jesus Christ," Alex said, finally looking up at Dev. "How the hell—"

"You tell me," Dev said, pacing back and forth across the polished concrete floor. "And you can fill Kiki in while you're at it," he added, nodding toward the woman. "She's got as much to lose as I do."

Alex swung his head around to her. Kiki. Of course. Shit—she was almost unrecognizable.

Nicola's roommate and best friend.

Fucking *hell*.

"I still don't—"

"These are teasers, you prick!" Dev bellowed. "What the hell else could they be? If photos were all they had, they'd be all over the internet by now! Whoever took this shit has video! *That's* the big reveal—and I can tell you right now it will *not* be fucking pretty! You left the party early, but things got pretty wild at around 3 a.m.—including be-

tween Kiki and me!" His hand slapped down on
the screen, slamming the laptop shut. "I know you
came to Moretta to meet Brissoli and now I also
know that he owns Starfucker. Now, would you care
to tell me what a photographer from the world's
most fucked-up website was doing at my birthday
party?"

"I— Holy shit, Dev. I cannot believe this." Alex
fisted his hands and pounded them onto his thighs.
"Dad's hell-bent on acquiring his company, and Brissoli suggested Moretta of all places to meet, but I
didn't invite him to the party, Dev. I never would
have done that. I ran into him at the hotel this morning and I told him I didn't want to do the deal after
all—the guy's a fucking cesspool, and so is his
company." He shook his head. "I remember now,
though—his associate. Larry Something. He seemed
really busy with his cell phone while I was talking
to Brissoli. I thought he was just antisocial, but it's
pretty obvious now what he was up to."

Dev grabbed a magazine off the coffee table and
hurled it across the room with a roar.

Kiki, who was cradling her face in her hands,
suddenly snapped her head up and fixed her eyes
on Alex. "How long?" she asked in an unexpectedly
strong voice. "How long until the videos hit the site?
How long will he draw this out?"

Alex heaved a deep sigh and leaned forward
onto his thighs, trying to process it all. Suddenly, a
thought occurred to him. "The cell tower is down.
How did you get on Twitter?"

"I have my own VSAT connection," Dev replied.

Alex nodded slowly. "I don't think Brissoli's actually teasing it like this because he wants to. I think it's because he *has* to."

"What do you mean?" Dev asked.

"I mean the storm. After they got the footage, they would have gone back to the hotel to upload everything. The smaller image files might have been sent through to LA from the party, but for the larger files—the videos—they would have had to wait until they had WiFi again. Essentially, the videos are stuck on the island."

"Until the tower gets fixed," Kiki said flatly.

"Or until Brissoli or his photographer can get off the island." Alex paused, calculating. "The internet's already been down for a day and a half. Is that normal?"

"It varies," Kiki answered. "Usually it's just a few hours, but I've seen it take as long as three days. In those cases, they have to bring workers over from Barbados or fly parts in, so things get delayed."

"I saw the damage to the microwave tower yesterday. They're going to need parts."

"How the hell do you know so much about this stuff?" Dev snapped at him.

Alex gave him an incredulous look. Of course— why would Dev remember what degree his own brother had graduated with? Not that this was the time to bring *that* up. "I have a degree in software engineering. Never really used it other than to get my membership in the geek club."

Dev's face remained sullen. "Listen. If this gets out?" He looked over at Kiki, and for one awestricken moment, Alex thought Dev might actually cry. Then he shook his head. "I don't need to tell you how fucking devastating it would be for everyone involved. I can take it for myself, but Kiki? She never asked for this."

Kiki stood up and walked toward Alex, placing herself in front of Dev. She lifted her chin, and Alex found himself impressed by her calm demeanor. "You came here to meet with this guy, Alex. I assume you had a contract ready to offer him? I'd like to see it."

"It's on my laptop." Alex nodded, turning to retrieve the device from his room. Heaving open the heavy door, his stomach gave a painful clench as the implications of the disaster hit him full-force. Throughout this whole ordeal, he hadn't had time to wonder if there were any possible implications for him and Nicola…but now he realized the gravity of just what might be at stake.

A predatory photographer at large on the island.

His and Nicola's public dalliances—on the beach, behind Pablo's and especially in the pool house.

The low voices and footsteps they'd heard outside.

He and Nicola in the heat of the moment, deafened and blinded by lust.

No lock on the door.

Alex felt a punch to his gut. *Jesus Christ.*

He would have to tell Nicola—after everything

she'd already been through. And after he'd just won her back again.

As the door began to shut behind Alex, Dev's hand was suddenly on his shoulder. Then his brother's face was in his, more furious than he'd ever seen it. "Unfuck this, Alex," Dev said to him in a low voice. "Or I will never forgive you."

CHAPTER FOURTEEN

ALEX WAS TAKING FOREVER. Nicola glanced out her window again as she sliced cherry tomatoes on her cutting board, wondering what could be delaying him so long. This being out of touch thing was getting old. Drying her hand on a dish towel first, she then reached out and tapped her phone to check for reception. Still down. She glanced at the clock: nearly two hours since she and Alex had parted.

At the memory of their time in the hotel room, Nicola's tummy gave a warm flutter. His touch was still imprinted on her entire body, but it was so much more than that. Alex was like a dream she never wanted to wake up from. He was doing his best to convince her she didn't have to—and she was beginning to believe it.

Nicola debated; maybe it was time to call Tortoise Point. She was moving toward the landline when she heard a golf cart pull up. Confirming it was Alex with a glance out the window, a small smile came to her lips as she switched her focus to her next problem: whether or not Alex had been able to find avocados at the grocery store. She enjoyed cooking and was excited to make her first meal for Alex, but her menu had been dictated both by the power outage and by what she had on hand. Like everyone else on the island, Nicola traveled to Barbados once or twice a month to shop at a supermarket; here on Moretta, the tiny grocery stocked only basics with a sporadic selection of produce and meat that cost a small fortune. Once she'd gotten home she'd had a small panic attack when she realized she didn't know if Alex had any dietary restrictions, but with little choice in the matter, she'd made a simple dish of wahoo fish from her still-cold freezer, grilled on the barbecue and presented on a bed of salad. But it wouldn't be nearly as good without the avocado.

"Come in," she called, going back to her cherry tomatoes as the knock came at her door. As Alex stepped into the kitchen, she turned to smile at him, but it faded the second she saw his face.

Alex looked like he'd been through a war since she last saw him. His tanned skin seemed paler, his hair was disheveled and his T-shirt was half-untucked.

"What's wrong?" Nicola breathed.

Alex just shook his head as he closed the door behind him. Nicola's stomach rolled over. Everything had been so perfect today—what the hell could have happened in two hours? Numbly, she took a seat at her table for two. Alex lowered himself down across from her as if he was in pain.

"What is it?" she asked again in alarm.

"I have to tell you something," Alex started. "And you are going to absolutely hate it."

Nicola's throat clicked closed as she swallowed. "Okay."

Alex took a deep breath, brought his hands together in front of his face as if he was praying, and then he exhaled. "I've just come from my brother's house. Kiki was there, too."

Kiki?

"O…kay," Nicola repeated cautiously.

"There was a photographer at the party the other night. You met him briefly—the guy with John Brissoli. Only I didn't know he was a photographer at the time."

Nicola's stomach turned over. *Photographer.* Wherever this was going, it was going to be bad.

Alex went on to tell her about the teaser photos that had turned up on Twitter, to Nicola's shock.

"Sooo…?" She looked at him questioningly.

"So the teaser has already named my brother, among others. Dev said things got pretty wild between him and Kiki, and possibly with some of the other guests. And us…"

Nicola inhaled sharply. "Oh, my God. Oh, my… *God.*" She brought her hand to her mouth.

"I know," Alex said miserably. "We don't know exactly what they have, but I think right now we have to assume the worst. They—"

"Who tweeted it? Was it a big outlet? If not, then maybe…"

Dev squeezed his eyes shut as he choked the word out. "Starfucker."

No. *No.*

"You mean Starfucker, the *website*?"

Alex nodded with a pained expression.

This can't be happening.

Nicola gaped at him as the pieces clicked into place, and then she pushed herself away from the table to put more space between them. Just like that, everything she'd believed about Alex seemed like it had been built on a bed of sand.

"That's the website that released the sex tape of me," Nicola said icily.

Alex put his head in his hands.

"And, hold on, you're telling me—you're telling me that you're here to *buy* it? *That's* who your company is making an offer to?" Nicola was incredulous.

Alex was shaking his head. "No, not anymore. Before I came up to the room today—I talked to Brissoli. I told him I was no longer interested, and… I don't know if that's why he released the photos. I think he would have done it anyway, but this—"

"But you *did* want to buy it," Nicola cut in furiously. "You knew perfectly well who you were dealing with when you came here to make him an offer. Because that's what people like you do, right? Study up on the company you want to acquire? Or maybe you're only interested in their numbers and not their content. Have you even *looked* at their headlines? They're enough to turn anyone's stomach!"

Alex threw his hands up. "It wasn't personal, Nicola, it was a business deal! If we only did business with companies who were squeaky-clean, then nothing would get done!"

"There's a big difference between squeaky-clean and St—*that website*." She couldn't bring herself to say the name again. "I mean, come on—you really never thought about how owning that would reflect on *your* company?"

Alex threw his hands up in frustration. "It's my father—he's dead set on acquiring it." He shook his head. "Look. When my parents started Echelon thirty-five years ago, it was a local cable channel with two shows—a fly-fishing program and a courtroom program where you could tune into people arguing their way out of speeding tickets. Dry as shit. Eventually, they started producing a couple of shows themselves and they bought other media like magazines and small newspapers, but it still had a reputation as a bit of an old-school media empire. When my mom died, the board figured with the business management gone—my dad handled the creative side of things—it might be better to just break it up. For my father, I think the double whammy of losing his wife and then nearly losing his company—and the memory of his earlier failures—that's what drives him more than anything. He's terrified of Echelon being irrelevant. For the past few years he's been buying up whatever he thinks the public will eat up, and like it or not, Starfucker is the hottest thing out there right now in celebrity news. You know all too well how popular that makes it."

"I see," Nicola responded flatly. "So this is all your father's fault."

"That's not what I'm saying! I'm just trying to give you some context. Look…" He stood up and walked over to her, trying to reach for her hands, but she pushed them firmly under her thighs. "I know this is a mess," he said. "I wish I could take the time to explain it all to you, to try to make you understand—hell, to try and make *myself* understand—but time is of the essence right now. We don't know how long we have until the tower is repaired. I left a message for Brissoli at the hotel, and I'm going to go over there right now and try to fix this." He stood up. "I'm so sorry," he said, shaking his head sadly.

And then he was out the door, leaving Nicola staring at the empty space where he'd been.

Room 217.

Alex took a deep breath before he raised his hand to knock on the door, trying to rein in his temper. He wanted nothing more than to burst into Brissoli's room and throttle him to death, but while that might solve one problem, it would create many more. He lifted his hand and knocked, settling his face into a neutral expression.

Brissoli opened the door, zipping his fly as if he'd just come from the bathroom…or from somewhere else. Alex suppressed a shudder.

"Right on cue," Brissoli said, giving his watch a cocky glance.

"May I come in?" Alex asked with forced politeness.

"Be my guest."

Brissoli opened the door and Alex stepped inside. The room was a mess—clothing dropped everywhere, an abandoned food tray on the floor, two laptops tossed carelessly onto the unmade bed.

Alex met Brissoli's icy eyes. "I think you know why I'm here, but before we get into it I have to ask—do you really want that kind of litigation nightmare on your hands?"

Brissoli snorted. "Have you *seen* Caribbean privacy laws? And maybe you've forgotten that I happen to be a lawyer myself."

"*Ex*-lawyer, actually," Alex couldn't help but point out. "At least I'm pretty sure that's what they call it when one gets disbarred?"

Brissoli seemed unperturbed by the slight. "Whatever. The point is I know the system. And anyway..." he added, running a hand through his greasy hair. Alex watched with disgust as flakes of dandruff rained on his shoulders. "Starfucker is the hottest thing since Facebook. You've seen my numbers—advertisers are battling to the death for front page. No amount of lawyering up could make more than a dent in that kind of revenue. And this video footage I'm sitting on? Pure gold. Like nothing the world has ever seen. That kind of traffic could shut a site down, but we're prepared for it."

Alex controlled his desire to spit in the guy's face. "So then I don't imagine your moral compass would sway you."

Brissoli looked bored. "Please. All I'm doing is giving the masses what they want. I don't make their tastes—I just feed them. You go out there and make yourself famous, you get what you signed up for. Pretty small price to pay if you ask me."

Alex couldn't help but feel a sense of shame sweep over him. Only a few days ago he'd have said nearly the same thing.

"And anyway," Brissoli continued, stepping close enough to Alex that he could smell his unwashed body over the scent of his Axe body spray. "If I recall, forty-eight hours ago you were pretty hot to do a deal with me." He tipped his head sideways in mock sympathy. "But I guess we had a change of heart once we dipped our dick in 2018's starfucker of the year?"

Alex's hands curled into fists as he forced himself to stay calm. The urge to flatten the smarmy asshole was almost irresistible, but he knew he had to keep his head if he was going to get them out of this. Alex looked at him levelly. "I don't think there's any need to make this personal."

"Oh, but it is personal. That's what makes Starfucker so popular—it's *very* personal. But don't worry—you'll see that soon enough for yourself. All of you will—your brother, that hot little redhead, the homewrecker. And you." He gave Alex a defiant stare.

So Brissoli had it. Not just Dev and Kiki, but Nicola and himself on tape.

Fuck.

Alex reached behind his back, took the folded contract from the waistband of his shorts and handed it to Brissoli.

"Here's what we're prepared to offer. We get rights to all media uploaded as of today's date, meaning you call off your leeches back home—no release of any videos from the party."

Brissoli scanned the papers, and then he went over to the small desk in the corner and scribbled something down on a piece of paper. He walked back to Alex and held it up in his face. "*This* is my new price. You have until noon tomorrow to meet it, or I'm on a plane back home and those videos go live."

"That's extortion." The words were out of Alex's mouth before he could think. Regaining his composure a bit, he added, "That's double what we were prepared to offer. I need more time to get sign-off from our board, and with no phone or internet that's impossible."

Brissoli shrugged. "Maybe my flight will be delayed. Otherwise—not my problem."

Alex looked at him coolly. "This is sounding less like a business deal and more like blackmail."

"I don't like labels."

"Except that you're a lawyer. If anyone knows how these things operate, it's you."

Brissoli stepped toward Alex and tucked the piece of paper into his shirt pocket. "True, but I also know the lengths some people will go to to protect themselves—and occasionally others. Now, if you'll excuse me, I have to pack."

Alex stepped back into the hallway, the number on the piece of paper still swimming before his eyes. It was a price even his father wouldn't agree upon, and Alex didn't relish the idea of explaining to him why it was so astronomically high. No, Alex would sort this out on his own. Going to his father with a mess like this on his hands would only give the man more reason to doubt him.

He walked back down to the lobby, pulling his phone out to check reception. Still nothing. He stopped at the concierge desk and asked to borrow their landline.

Dev picked up on the first ring. "Did you take care of it?" he barked.

"I'm doing my best. But I need your help."

Dev snorted. "Of course you do."

Alex slapped his hand down on the desk in frustration. "Look. We're better working together than apart on this, okay?"

"That would be a first."

"You don't have to tell me. But why don't we just pretend for right now that we're stronger as a team."

Dev heaved a deep sigh. "Fine. What do you need?"

"A couple of things." Alex glanced around and lowered his voice. "Moretta started off as a haven for judges. Are there still any around?"

* * *

For the twentieth time in the past hour, Nicola picked up her phone and checked her reception. Still down—but for how long? How long until she was plunged back into the nightmare she'd fought so hard to escape once already?

She dropped her phone back on the table and paced back and forth a few times, trying not to look at the spoils of her cooking on the counter. The lunch with Alex that had never happened. And just when things were so good between them again—

No. Nicola needed to mentally prepare for the horror that was about to come down on her, and those plans could not include Alex, no matter what her personal feelings for him might be. In fact, it was those feelings that had gotten her into this mess in the first place.

The scene from the pool house flashed through her head. She felt like an unprecedented fool. The encounter had felt so perfect and magical at the time... and now it felt shameful and dirty.

So was this to be her destiny? To keep making choices that led her down a road of sexual shame? The high school sex tape. The kiss with Matthew. And now her act with Alex. All three of them triggered an unraveling of her life—all the more proof that she needed to be thinking with her head right now, because the times she'd let herself think with her body had only spelled complete and utter disaster.

She heard a knock at the door.

Alex.

Nicola crossed the room and opened the door, then she turned away from him again before she could meet his eyes. In her peripheral vision, she saw him slowly enter the room. He stood in the middle of her kitchen. "I'm dealing with it," he told her.

"So I can stop worrying now? My life *isn't* about to turn into a living hell at any moment?"

Alex sighed. "I'm doing my best. I still have more to do, and we have to hope the internet stays down for the rest of the island."

Nicola nodded as Alex exhaled and dropped his head into his chest. "You know all of this might have been avoided if you'd just refused to buy the company in the first place," she couldn't help pointing out.

"It's not that simple."

"I keep hearing you say that, but I didn't say it was simple. It probably would have been one of the hardest things you'd ever done. But isn't standing up for what you believe in more important than—what?—having your father be angry with you for a few days?"

"You don't know my father," Alex said with an edge to his voice. "I'd have spent the next six months hearing about how badly I failed him. He would have dumped Starfucker's traffic and ad sales figures on my desk every day, and when someone else eventually acquired it, he'd probably frame the announcement to remind me of what we missed out on."

"So you have different values—even more reason not to cave to his. Can you imagine what my life would be like right now if I'd let my father dictate my values—?"

"That is *not* what I'm doing!"

"Oh, no? Then what are you doing?"

"I'm trying to do the right thing! Goddamn it, Nicola, can you not see what a tough place I'm in with this?"

"No. I'm sorry, but I can't. If you'd just let your conscience be your guide—"

"My con— Jesus, Nicola. I know you live in some—some *fantasy* here on your Caribbean island, but I have the real world to contend with!"

Nicola looked like she'd been slapped.

"I'm sorry. I didn't… Oh, fuck." Alex shook his head dejectedly, and then he threw his hands up in frustration. "I just feel like I can't win with you. I hold something back, you get upset. I'm up-front with you, you get upset. I don't know what you want!"

Nicola was silent for a moment, and then she spoke in a quiet voice. "You know what we seem to do a whole lot of? Besides fucking, I mean. Arguing. We started off that way, and it looks like we're going to end that way, too."

Alex dropped his hands. "What do you—"

"I mean you're right, we do live in different realities. We live in different time zones. We live with different priorities and expectations. I mean this isn't going to work." Nicola stepped close to him and put a hand on his stricken face. "Look," she said. "I think you're wonderful, I really do. Our time together was magical, and I'll never forget it. But…it can't continue. I can't keep going through life making stupid mistakes that bite me in the ass." She crossed her arms over her chest. "The fantasy is over. It has to be."

Alex shook his head helplessly. "Nicola. Nicola, *please*…"

The look in his eyes tore her heart in two. But she couldn't afford this.

"I think you should go," she said softly.

Alex stood staring at her with his hands clenched at his sides as if hoping she would change her mind. When he realized she wouldn't, he silently opened the door and walked into the cricket-filled evening.

Nicola waited until she heard his golf cart start up, and then she dropped down in a chair and bawled her eyes out.

So this was it. Her life was very possibly about to become a nightmare once again. She'd just spent five days with the most incredible man she'd ever met, a man she'd had to battle thoughts of a possible future with because it just wasn't practical or realistic or cool to fall that fast…and now it was over. Reality hit her like a gale-force wind, wiping out everything she'd allowed herself to believe could be possible. She knew she'd never meet someone like Alex again. Someone, yes—but not *him*. He was too special, too wonderful.

And all wrong for her.

CHAPTER FIFTEEN

THE RIDE TO the airport felt endless to Alex. He'd barely slept last night, tortured by thoughts of Nicola and strange, twisted dreams about his brother, Kiki, the party guests…

He rubbed a hand over his unshaven face as he sat in the passenger seat of the golf cart beside Dev. Contrary to his deadly mood, the sun was out again without a cloud to be seen. Alex thought about how surreal it was that just twenty-four hours ago he'd been feeling on top of the world—and now Nicola was done with him. There was an emptiness inside him that he'd never felt before, but right now he couldn't even afford to grieve her. He had to be fully present for the next hour, or else Nicola's—and Kiki's and Dev's, not to mention his own—future was at stake.

Wordlessly, Dev steered the golf cart into the roundabout that marked the entrance to the tiny open-air airport. Alex scanned it and immediately laid eyes on Brissoli, who was lounging on an outdoor bench alongside his slimy photographer. Both of them were smoking cigarettes as if their greatest concern was getting their last nicotine hit before going airborne—and it probably was.

Until he caught sight of them.

Brissoli's cocky expression morphed into one of outrage as Dev pulled the cart up to the curb. "What the fuck do you think you're doing?" he sputtered, jabbing his cigarette toward the police officers who'd just pulled up behind them in a second cart. Alex and Dev jumped out of their cart and stood in front of Brissoli.

"Bringing the cops to arrest you," Alex said simply.

"For fucking *what*? Taking a few pictures on Caribbean soil? Because that's all you've got on me, and believe me, they could care less."

"Actually, we have you on trespassing," Dev said through clenched teeth, "and invasion of privacy. We take that pretty seriously on Moretta."

"Not to mention blackmail," Alex said, holding up his phone. "Our little conversation is all right here."

Brissoli's nostrils flared. "*Blackmail?* You can't just arrest me for that! You need to build a case—"

"Don't worry, we will. Invasion of privacy and trespassing isn't enough to keep you in jail for long, but it'll buy us enough time to get the blackmail charge to stick—especially after we get ahold of what's in your suitcases." Alex leaned in a little closer to Brissoli and lowered his voice. "I've heard the prisons around here aren't quite as fun as the islands themselves."

The two officers stepped toward the men with handcuffs, placed their hands behind their backs and began reading them their rights. Then one of the officers picked up their suitcases.

"This is bullshit," Brissoli said, but Alex could tell by his shifty eyes that he was running scared in his head. Beside him, his goon photographer looked like he was about to pass out. "You can't just take our luggage! You need a search warrant!" Brissoli bellowed.

Alex shrugged. "Maybe you should have done your research. This island was originally built up as a retreat by judges and senior politicians, and several of the families still own homes here. So it's a lot easier to obtain a search warrant than you might think—especially when one of their sons is on the videos you took."

"How do you know that?" Brissoli asked suspiciously.

"I don't. But he was in the background in one of your teasers, and this particular judge isn't big on taking chances."

Brissoli gaped at Alex for a moment, and then he fixed him with a death stare. "This won't work. I'll be out of here by the end of the day. Be sure and check out the website tomorrow morning."

Alex ignored him. One of the officers held up a single page with a stamp and signature on the bottom. "Shall we take them in, Mr. Stone?"

"Please," Dev said with a wave of his hand. As Brissoli sputtered in protest, the officers led the two men around the side of the airport building with Dev and Alex following. Dev had already explained to Alex that with no police station on the island, the luggage would be taken to the customs room to be inspected—a detail Dev had confirmed with the judge earlier that morning.

Once inside the room, one officer opened the luggage, dug through the suitcases and lifted out three laptops and a hard drive. After removing three smartphones from the men, the other officer added the devices to the pile on the table.

Alex opened the first laptop. "I need your password," he said to Brissoli with his hands poised over the keys.

Brissoli snorted. "I'm not giving you a goddamn thing until I have my lawyer present."

"Of course that is your right, but I'd think someone like you would prefer to make things easier on himself," said a man with a soft Barbadian accent as he stepped into the room. Judge Fenty was tall and impressively built, with only a few grays marring his short black hair. "We can take care of this now or we can detain you at the prison on Barbados until your counsel arrives. Either way the result will be the same—your devices will be searched."

Brissoli glared at the judge, and then his shoulders slumped. He mumbled the password, and after tapping it in Alex quickly located a file named *ns party*. The screen filled with a series of video clips. Scanning over them, Alex saw the image of Dev's face over Kiki's naked shoulder, and then farther down…

a dark, grainy image of his own back hunched over Nicola.

He felt like vomiting.

Judge Fenty stood behind him and pointed to one of the videos. Alex clicked on it, and the unmistakable sound of two people heavily engaged in sex filled the room. He clicked it off and watched the judge remove his glasses. "My son doesn't always make the wisest choices, but for this incident he can't be blamed. What will it take for you to get everything off the hard drives?" he asked Alex.

"Hours of work. I'll need all of these devices and access to a landline."

Fenty nodded. "Keep them as long as you need to." He turned back toward the door.

"Wait!" Brissoli said in a panicked voice, but the judge was already gone. He looked at Alex. "You've got what you need. I've cooperated. Do you really want to go to the trouble—"

"Not everything I need," Alex interrupted, pulling the contract from his back pocket. "I still need your company. Same price as I offered before. More than generous, I think you'd agree, after all that's gone on here."

Brissoli looked suspicious again. "If you're so sure you could send me to prison, why would you still want my website?"

"I don't. My old man does. And making this official will prevent you from finding a way to sue me." It was a bluff—not only had he not clued his father in to these recent developments, Alex had his own intentions for the website—but Brissoli didn't need to know that.

"That's—"

"What—*fair?* I know that's not really your style, Brissoli. So please—don't let me talk you into anything you're not comfortable with." He tucked the contract back into his shorts and nodded at Dev, who pushed open the door to leave.

A minute later the contract was signed.

Nicola's iPad sat on the coffee table, its blank screen masking the horrors on the web lurking behind it. She'd just received a string of text alerts on her phone, signaling Moretta's reconnection to the rest of the world. And now she had to face the worst of her fears—again.

Gathering all of her strength, she swiped the iPad's screen on and opened Safari. Then she typed in the URL to a website she swore she'd never visit.

She didn't dare breathe as she watched the site open on her screen and started scrolling down. The headlines sickened her. *Leona Bragg Flashes Her Cootch on Beach Vacation; Jack Harrison Is Off the Wagon! Passes Out on Barstool—See His Epic Bail; Why Is Chris Lennon Touching His Daughter's Butt?*

She made it to the bottom of the page. Nothing so far, but she knew she couldn't afford to relax yet. The videos could come up at any moment—in fact, they were probably being uploaded right now. There was simply no way to stop the churning worry in her belly.

Nicola shut her screen off, wondering for a moment if Alex would get in touch with her when he had some news to share. Would he call her, text her? Or avoid her? Like Kiki had said, a man could only take so much rejection before he shut down. And she had rejected him rather forcefully.

Nicola rose from her seat and walked outside, taking a few gulps of air to try to clear her head. The sun was shining again, out to fool everyone into thinking it was just another day in paradise. But it wasn't, and Nicola was certain that for her, it never would be again. She thought about the motions of her daily life here—driving her golf cart around, working at the scuba shack and on the boats, going for a drink at Pablo's, eating dinner at the Palms Inn, going for a hike up the mountain. Each and every one of those places now held memories of Alex. She pictured her life in the coming weeks—her conversations with Kiki and seeing Alex's brother around the island, a constant reminder of what she'd lost. Even her tutoring sessions with her kids; it was almost impossible to believe that less than a week ago, she had been ending her session with Raia to go on her first date with Alex. So much had happened since then, some of it beautiful and some of it horrible, but all of it made one thing certain: her life here would never be the same again. She could think of no reason to stay—in fact, to do so would be unbearable.

A few years ago Nicola's oldest brother had moved to Chicago. The two of them had been close growing up, and he'd often told her she was welcome to come and stay with him as long as she wanted.

Yes. It made perfect sense. It was what she needed to do. She couldn't stay here—she was sure of that. Not with memories of Alex, the man she desperately wanted but was certain she could never give herself to, lurking around every corner.

Nicola went back into her house and picked up her phone. Then she hit the button for her brother's number.

CHAPTER SIXTEEN

THEIR MISSION WAS ACCOMPLISHED. As the brothers rode the golf cart home in silence, Alex felt the adrenaline buzz of the past hour leaving his body to be replaced by exhaustion and the long, agonizing slide back into his reality.

"What now?" Dev asked, his voice still grim despite their recent triumph.

"A whole lot of work. I still have to get everything off the drives. Call Dad and talk him through shutting down Starfucker's servers. Not to mention try to explain to him why we just bought a company we're about to shut down. That ought to be fun."

Alex crossed his arms over his chest as he looked out at the passing view of the beach, trying to settle his nerves. If he could have one wish right now, it would be that he'd never come here at all. He'd just created a huge mess that he was still cleaning up, his father was going to lose his shit on him, and Dev still seemed furious with him, meaning their relationship was even worse off than it had been when Alex had arrived.

But worst of all, Alex had spent a week with someone he would now compare to every other woman that came into his life, and he knew they were absolutely sure to fall short.

Nicola. He still felt ill at the thought that he'd lost her. He knew she wouldn't want to hear from him again, so he would send a message through Kiki, letting her know the danger had passed. And then he'd get on a plane tomorrow morning and leave her behind forever.

They were back at Dev's place. Alex grabbed the electronics from the floor of the cart and wordlessly went into the house, then he dropped everything on the coffee table and went to his bedroom. His rage and grief were threatening to spew out of him, and he needed a moment alone. He shut the door behind him and let out a roar.

"Fuck!" he shouted, slamming the heel of his hand against his wall. He picked up the nearest item, a flip-flop sitting atop his suitcase, and flung it across the room. It hit the door and dropped to the floor, where it rested without judgment. But Alex felt no better.

He walked across the room, pulled his door open again and propelled himself into the warm afternoon air. He could feel the fury bubbling up from his belly to his chest, ready to explode out of his body. He needed to walk…or swim…or think of a way to take a hit out on John Brissoli. *Something.*

But none of it would change a thing.

He swerved into the living room and snatched

the electronics off the coffee table. It was time to get to work.

Once inside the studio, Alex dropped everything onto Dev's desk and sank down into his chair. Then he picked up his phone, took a deep breath and punched his father's number.

"Dad."

"Alex. I've been trying to call. Did he sign?"

Alex sighed. "Yeah, Dad, he signed."

"That's good news. At the price we agreed on?"

"Yes."

"Then it's excellent news," Devin Sr. said happily. "I hope you'll have a glass with Dev for me to celebrate."

Alex rubbed a hand over his face and glanced over at the door as his brother walked in. He used his chair to swivel away from him. "We need to shut the site down, Dad. Immediately."

A beat of silence. "Pardon me?"

"Shut it down. We have to. It's a liability, not an asset. We need to clean it up before we can add it to the Echelon brand."

There was a long pause, and then his father spoke again in a low, bristly voice. "Would you care to explain to me why we would shut down a website that we just spent a fortune on?"

Alex raised his eyes skyward. He could tell his father the truth—that the servers contained video images of both of his sons that had almost ruined them. His father may not like it, but Alex knew that the fact that Dev, his father's beloved favorite who could do no wrong, was at risk as much as Alex was would probably work to sway him easily. But that wasn't the real reason the website needed to be killed—far from it.

"Because it's the right thing to do," Alex said. "It's what Mom would have done. She never would have agreed to buy an asset like Starfucker—she would sooner have folded Echelon. But since we have bought it, we need to turn it into something we can live with. And I, for one, can't sell my soul to leech off people just trying to live their lives."

There was another longer pause. "I won't argue with that," Devin Sr. said tightly. "But I will ask you this—why the fuck did we just buy a cash cow website only to re-create it into something that's sure to see a drastic drop in revenues? You could have just left it if you felt that strongly about it. We could have had that conversation."

Alex snorted. "*Conversation?* I don't think so, Dad. Ever since I joined the company it's been, 'You say, I obey.' Maybe it *is* my fault for not pushing back hard enough, but it's always about the numbers for you."

"This is not the time—"

"No? Then I don't know *when* the time is, but you're right—right now I've got my work cut out for me. I need you to get Gene in tech on the line so I can talk him through what I have in mind."

"But why the hell—"

"Because someone else would have bought it!" Alex shouted. "If not now then soon, but either way

it would have continued! And it's a fucking travesty, that's why!"

Dev was in front of Alex now, reaching for the phone. Alex shook his head, but Dev grabbed it from him anyway.

"Dad—it's Dev. Look, Alex did the right thing. If you want to piss at someone, aim it at me, okay? He's had enough for one day."

Alex rubbed at his temples. His brother taking the heat for him—this was a first. If Alex wasn't so down about Nicola and distracted by the job still ahead of him, it might actually make him happy.

He reached for the first laptop and got to work.

Alex sighed and stood up to stretch, his legs cramped from sitting. He glanced at his watch: 8:07 p.m. He'd been so absorbed in his tasks that he'd barely noticed the past five hours slip by, but the files were finally securely in the hands of people he trusted.

The door opened, and Dev came into the studio with Kiki trailing behind him. In his hand Dev held a six-pack of beers. He pulled one out of its plastic ring and passed it to Alex. "I believe you've earned this."

Alex took it and popped the tab. "Thanks."

Dev handed a beer to Kiki, but she shook her head. "I just dropped by to see if there was any news."

Alex nodded. "It's all done. Will you let Nicola know?"

"Why don't you tell her yourself?" Kiki replied.

Alex shook his head dejectedly. "I'd love to, but I'm afraid she made it pretty clear she doesn't want to see me."

"So what, dude? You have to go after what you want in life," Dev said, looking directly at Kiki. Kiki lowered her gaze and turned away from him.

Alex's eyes darted between the two of them and then he cleared his throat. "Anyway," he continued, trying to clear the tension in the room. "I doubt she'd take my call. And last time I went to her place it didn't go so well."

"She's not at home," Kiki said.

"No?"

"No. She needed to get her head on straight. And I bet you can guess where she goes to do that."

Alex tilted his head at her, and then his face cleared. Of course.

"I have to get going," Kiki said, turning toward the door after giving Dev one last glance. "Thanks for everything, Alex." The door closed behind her, and Alex stared at Dev.

"What's that all about?"

Dev shrugged. "I don't know. I really dig her, but I guess we got off on the wrong foot, so now she's shutting me down."

"Which makes her all the more appealing, right?" Alex asked with a grin.

"Whatever." Dev took a swig of his beer, and then he gestured toward the door. "What are you waiting for? Go after her. And when you get her back—don't fuck it up again."

"Thanks for the brotherly advice. I'll give it some thought," Alex said, and then he stood up with a smile on his face.

Screw it. What did he have to lose? He had to at least *try*.

He left the studio. He was going after her.

CHAPTER SEVENTEEN

A SNORKEL, a pair of secondhand fins, a mask that leaked and an underwater flashlight.

How many times had Nicola taken those very same items down to the beach as a teenager? Her equipment may have changed, but her need to escape into another world had not.

On the dock, Nicola fitted her mask over her face and slipped into the water. It was chilly at this time of the evening, and though she'd already had a swimsuit under her clothes, she hadn't wanted to take the time to don a wet suit at the scuba shack. She needed her escape, and she needed it now.

There was a small reef a hundred feet or so off the dock, so Nicola headed in that direction. When she arrived, she shined her flashlight down to the underwater world beneath her. There were many fish that were more active at night, and her beam picked out a small octopus curling itself back into its den. A moray eel slithered by. And all around her was the magical bioluminescence created by the tiny organisms called dinoflagellates. She passed an arm through the water to activate it near her eyes, watching as it came to life in a dancing blue cloud.

This was another world.

But the world above water was one where she could only keep running from place to place for so long before starting over again. It had caused her to lose everything—her career, her friends, her self-esteem and any chance at finding love.

She knew that, but it wasn't enough to hold her here. Right now, more than anything, she needed to leave the memory of him behind.

Alex.

She pictured how his face had looked as she'd turned away from him, all the regret and guilt and caring he had for her. It was so clear. They couldn't be together—not after everything that had happened, and all they had working against them. It was just too hard.

Through the bioluminescence, Nicola's flashlight picked out a dark shape swimming beneath her. She gave a start and then pulled her face out of the water.

The shape was human.

There was a splashing noise beside her, and then a head popped out of the water. The mask was pulled off, and there was Alex. Nicola's eyes widened as she treaded water. "What are you doing? You shouldn't be out here at night by yourself."

"I'm not by myself. I'm with you. What could be safer than that?"

"But you're afraid of the ocean."

"Not anymore." He paused. "Okay, maybe a little,

but it was worth it to see you. I knew you'd be out here. What kind of impression would I have made if I'd just waited for you on the dock?"

Nicola started to turn away.

"It's taken care of," Alex said quickly. "I just wanted you to know. We've got all the footage secured."

Nicola felt relief wash over her body. *Taken care of.* Thank God. But it didn't change things between her and Alex.

"Thank you for telling me. I'm going back in," she said, and started swimming toward the dock. She climbed the ladder when she got there and scrambled onto the wood. Alex had left two fluffy folded towels for them—a step ahead of her. She looked away from them and hugged her arms around herself.

"Don't worry, I won't take it as a sign of forgiveness if you take one," Alex said, hauling himself out of the water. He reached for a towel and handed it to her. "Warm yourself up."

The night air was cold on Nicola's skin. She took the towel and wrapped it around herself gratefully. "Thanks."

Alex held his own towel around his shoulders. The light was dim, but she could still see the aqua shine of his eyes. "I wanted to tell you something else before I left," he said.

Nicola's heart gave a little lift. Goddamn it— sometimes she wished her body could lie to her as well as her mind. "What is it?"

"I bought the rights to your tape. The deal in-

cluded all rights going back five years. Brissoli
doesn't know it yet, but let's just say he was a little
distracted when he signed the contract and maybe he
didn't read the fine print. That footage, along with
anything else pornographic and slanderous, is in the
process of being pulled off the website's servers as
we speak. And the first thing I'm going to do when I
get back to LA is get you a lawyer. You were under-
age when that tape was made, which means Brissoli
was distributing child pornography."

"Wow," Nicola said, pulling her towel more tightly
around her. "Thank you."

"I know it might be too little too late, but..."

"No, really—I'm very grateful." She smiled. "It's
one of the nicest things anyone has done for me."

Alex hesitated, and then he took a step toward
her. "Nicola—"

"No," she said with a quick backward jump. It was
imperative that they had no physical contact as her
heart ached so much she feared that a single touch
might reduce her to tears—or worse, forgiveness, the
one thing she could not afford. "I—I can't do this. I
talked to my brother in Chicago today. There are two
planes out of here each day. You're on the first one,
and I'm going to be on the one tomorrow evening."

"Tomorrow?"

"I came here with one suitcase, Alex. Kiki can
get another roommate. Rusty will understand. He
has other instructors."

"But why? Brissoli? He won't be back—"

"It's not that. This place is tainted for me now.

It seems to be my thing—I have a life, it goes all wrong, and suddenly I need to get out of Dodge." She gave a humorless laugh. "I'm getting well practiced at starting over."

"You mean running away."

Nicola's eyes flashed at him furiously. "Why would I stay? What's left here for me?"

"A lot. Your friends, your students, your diving—your *life*. Have you ever stopped to ask yourself if running really solves anything? What if you just chose to stand your ground, come what may?" Alex caught her eye, and when he spoke again his voice was thick with emotion. "And what if you let me stand beside you while you did it?"

No. She would not weaken, no matter what her heart was screaming. Nicola held his gaze for a moment, and then she shook her head. "That would mean you staying here—and the last time we talked, you made it clear you were going back to the real world. Unlike me."

Alex heaved a sigh, and for one dreadful moment, Nicola thought he was going to walk away.

And who could blame him?

But he didn't. Instead, he moved a little closer to her. "Do you remember when we got off the boat after our second dive together? When you wouldn't let me carry those tanks for you?"

"Yeah." Nicola couldn't help a tiny smile.

"That's when I first knew I was falling for you." Nicola's heart stopped. She stood perfectly still. "And I can't imagine that I'll ever stop falling. I know you don't want to hear this right now, but…" Alex grasped her shoulders. "I love you, Nicola."

Nicola felt her face growing warm in the cool air. *I love you.* Three words she'd never wanted to hear more badly than from this man.

But she couldn't accept them.

She stepped closer to him, then she opened her towel up and used it to encircle his body. "Then make love to me," she said softly. "And we can part ways with an amazing memory."

"But I don't want—"

She pressed her finger to his lips. "Shh…don't talk. Please don't talk. It won't work between us. Just make love to me."

"So I give you my love, and you give me…?"

"Whatever I can in the moment. I'm not trying to hurt you, Alex. I just think that whatever happened over the past week—the good and the bad—we owe each other a beautiful goodbye."

"But can't we—?"

Nicola's lips stopped his words, and after a moment's hesitation he opened his mouth to accept her tongue. He tasted like the salt of the ocean. She gently bit his lower lip while he pulled her body close to his. Then she took his hand and pulled him down the dock to the scuba shack.

It was crowded inside the tiny room—a desk and chair, tanks lined up against the wall, wet suits hanging on hooks. It smelled like wet rubber. Closing the door behind her, Nicola threw her towel down on the hard wooden floor. The bright moonlight shone through the window, illuminating the room.

"Nicola—" Alex tried one last time, but she covered his mouth in hers again, pressed her body to his and grabbed his ass firmly. She kissed him and then went for his neck, pressing her tongue into the sweet spot under his jaw where she could feel his pulse jumping.

It was like something snapped inside Alex. He gave a low growl, and then he had her bikini top off with a single tug of the back string. Then his mouth was on her breasts, licking and sucking like he wanted to consume her completely. She moved her hips against his, feeling an animal heat pump through her veins. She'd never been gripped by such urgency before. She wanted Alex to ravage her, leave her skin marked so she could remember the feel of him for days to come. She wanted to give her entire body over to him, inhale his scent so she'd never forget it, taste his lips so she could dream of them as she fell asleep each night.

"More," she whispered urgently. *"More."*

She worked her fingers into his hair and pushed his head downward, thrilling at the feel of his rough stubble trailing against her skin. Once he was on his knees, he slid her bikini bottoms down and wrapped his arms around her thighs. Then he started licking her exactly where she needed it most, sending a chill up her spine.

"God, you taste sweet," Alex groaned, pushing her firmly back onto the towel, where she lay spread-

eagle and open to him. Nicola barely registered the
hard wood pressing into her back. Alex's tongue
came down on her pussy again, making her moan
as he flicked it across her clit and then pushed it inside her. Her breath was fast, loud, *desperate* for him.
Her orgasm was starting to build, but she wanted
more, much more, before she came.

She grabbed Alex by the shoulder and coaxed him
onto his back. Then she straddled his thighs and ran
her hands over his perfect chest and arms, memorizing every muscle, and then trailed her fingers up
and down his beautiful thick cock. She reached for
a condom from her handbag and rolled it onto him
while she looked into his eyes, which were wild with
heated passion in the moonlight. Then she moved
herself forward until her pussy was resting on his
rock-hardness. Judging from the sound of his labored
breathing, he was riding the same wave of desperate
urgency she was.

"Nicola, oh, God..."

She was wetter than she'd ever been. In one
smooth movement, she scooped her pelvis back and
eased his head inside her. She slid his first three
inches in and out a few times, teasing him, and then
finally she dropped down until she'd completely
enveloped him. Alex bucked upward, grabbed her
hips and started to move. He thrust into her again
and again as she moaned, overcome with exquisite
pleasure. The hardness of the floor made his cock
reach even deeper into her, bringing her orgasm ever

closer. But she wasn't nearly ready for it to be over, and neither was Alex.

Clasping Nicola to his chest, he rolled her over until he was on top. She wrapped her legs around his hips as he moved inside her, taking their rhythm down to a slow and leisurely one, as if they had forever. Alex pulled away so he could look down at Nicola's face, and then he brought a hand to her cheek. "Never forget how we feel together right now," he whispered.

"I won't. I promise," she whispered back. Tears pricked at her eyes, threatening to spill, but she fought them away. And as her sadness faded, it was replaced by a fresh rush of desire.

As if perfectly attuned to her, Alex's lips crushed to hers in a long kiss, and then he rose up on his hands and started driving into her harder and deeper. Nicola could feel his urgent need for her with each sweet thrust. Her entire body broke out in goose bumps that had nothing to do with the temperature in the shack. "Alex. Oh, Alex..."

Her climax was so near now. She let her eyes pass from his muscular arms to his torso, shiny with sweat as he pushed into her, down to the erotic place they were connected, and then back up to his eyes, which were still fastened to hers.

"Don't stop. Please don't stop," she begged him.

"Not until you come on my cock," he promised her between gasps.

Nicola moved her legs together so her thighs were touching, and Alex groaned as her pussy tightened around him even more. And then Nicola arrived with a cry, riding the crest of the most intense orgasm she'd ever felt, shattering her world into a million beautiful pieces. A second later Alex gave a gasp and then went rigid as he emptied into her, his body exploding into heavenly bands of heat that shook him to his very soul.

After they'd recovered slightly, Alex dropped onto his side, taking Nicola with him so he could hold her close to him. She buried her face into his chest, and both of them were silent as their breathing returned to normal. Alex's skin smelled like the sea mixed with his sweat. She could hear his heartbeat through his chest. Nicola kept her eyes closed, willing the moment to never end.

Finally, Alex spoke. "How can I ever give this up?"

You don't have to, Nicola almost said, but she caught herself.

No. It simply wasn't going to work, no matter how much they both might want it to. Their chemistry might be combustive, but there were still too many odds stacked against them.

Different cities. Different lives. And though she knew deep down Alex was a good man, despite everything he'd done to prove himself, was he really going to change his business dealings for good?

Nicola pulled herself away and looked at Alex's face in the moonlight. She ran a hand through his hair. "That was the perfect goodbye," she said sadly. "But it *was* goodbye."

She got to her feet and found her swimsuit, pulled it back on, and grabbed her handbag. Alex didn't move, just stayed lying on the towel as he watched her prepare to leave him for the last time. Nicola dropped down on her knees and lowered her face to his, gazing into his eyes for a moment, and then she gave him a gentle kiss.

She stood up and left the shack.

CHAPTER EIGHTEEN

ALEX SAT LISTLESSLY in the passenger seat of the golf cart, listening with half an ear as Dev, who was driving, recited his upcoming tour schedule to him. "...European dates end in late October, then I'm on to Australia, and then I kick off the North American leg in Los Angeles. January eighth, I think. I should have a day in LA before the first show, so that could work," Alex caught. He only realized Dev had stopped talking when his brother gave him an energetic punch on the arm.

"What was that for?" Alex asked irritably, rubbing his biceps.

"Have you heard a word I just said?"

"You were giving me your tour dates."

"And suggesting we spend a day together before my show in LA. But if you'd rather not..."

"No!" Alex said quickly, cutting off Dev's go-to passive-aggressiveness. He and his brother may have made some positive strides in the past few days, but some things would probably never change. And Alex was learning that that was okay—their relationship didn't need to be perfect to be good. "I'd love to," Alex said. "I'm sure you'll be booked in at some palace, but how about staying with me instead?"

Dev gave him a satisfied nod.

Alex suppressed a sigh as they passed the island's one and only sign for the airport. Dev glanced at him sideways. "That bad, huh?"

"Worse. Not only have I lost the love of my life, I'm also going back to a job I hate." He stopped short. It was a strong word to use, but in that moment Alex realized it was true.

Dev was silent for a moment and then, "You know, I'll admit I've never given much thought to how hard it must be working in the family business. Taking the reins from Mom—that's a lot of pressure."

"You don't have to tell me."

Dev shook his head. "I couldn't imagine having a career I didn't enjoy."

"I know you couldn't—and I mean that in a good way. I've always admired you for pursuing what makes you happy, no matter what anyone else might think." They rode in silence for a few moments, and then Alex began to smile.

"What is it?" Dev asked, giving him another sideways glance.

"I'm going to quit."

"Are you crazy? Dad will fucking freak!"

Alex laughed. "You sound like the *old* me. Who cares—he'll get over it. What choice does he have?"

Dev shook his head. "Good on you, man." They both fell silent again as they bumped over the dirt road, and then Dev cleared his throat. "Hey, I meant to tell you. I get that the whole Starfucker thing wasn't really your fault, okay? I'm glad we worked together to fix it."

"Is that your way of apologizing?"

"You know me—I never apologize. I just open the door for others to tell me I'm forgiven."

Alex laughed dryly. "Same old Dev. You know, I guess I have to admire that. You've always known who you are—and screw the world if they don't like you."

"Plenty don't."

"You think so? I don't," Alex lifted his hand to the roll bar. "Can I ask you something?"

"Ask away."

Alex took a breath. They'd never talked about what he was about to bring up, and he was pretty sure Dev wouldn't like it. But if he'd learned anything over the past week, it was that subjects left unspoken did much more harm than good. "The day I almost drowned. I remember it clear as day. I was working on a sandcastle while you danced around it, and I kept yelling at you that you were going to break it. Mom left to go do something and asked you to watch me until Dad got there." Alex stole a glance at Dev's face, but he was staring straight ahead with an unreadable expression. "No one told me not to go in the water. So why did you lie to Dad? You told him that Mom forbid me to go in the water, but I disobeyed. I mean, I get that you didn't want to get in trouble, but I nearly died. Wasn't that enough of a punishment for me?"

Dev sighed. "Hey. You and me, we're pretty different, right? You've always been so self-assured. I guess I envied that. Still do, if you want to know the truth. Me—I've always needed an audience. I guess I measure my value...externally. And you measure yours internally. That day...my friends were there. I wanted to impress them. I had this air-guitar thing I'd been working on, and they started chanting— 'Twitch, Twitch'—and it sounds pathetic, but it was kind of like a drug. I always knew I wanted to be a performer. It's my strength, but it can also be my weakness. That day it was. I was more concerned about what they thought of me than I was about my own little brother. When Dad came at me...I guess I was embarrassed. Ashamed. You always did everything right, and I was always the one who needed to be 'corrected.' So I threw you under the bus."

Alex couldn't help but chuckle. "I'm not as self-assured as you might think. And in case you hadn't noticed, it's you who could do no wrong in Mom and Dad's eyes after you hit it big. Now I'm the one trying to do whatever I can to get Dad to throw me a bone."

"Not everything's a competition." Dev shrugged.

"That's easy to say when you're always the winner."

Dev finally turned to look at Alex, and his face looked genuinely surprised. "Then I think we live in two different realities. Whenever I talk to Dad, he's always going on about what a great job you're doing running Echelon. I always hang up feeling like the shitty 'artistic' son." He made quotes in the air.

Alex looked at him and burst out laughing. "Well. That's fucking awesome," he said.

Dev steered the golf cart around the roundabout and parked it at the curb of the airport. The brothers got out of the cart and exchanged an embrace. "Great having you, little brother. I mean that."

"It was great seeing you. I mean that, too." Alex managed a smile. "Until January, then."

"Until January." Dev started to walk back to the driver's seat, and then he turned around. "And, hey— about Nicola? I've been there. It'll pass, I promise." He lifted his arms in an expansive gesture. "The world awaits you," he said with a wink, and then he was off again.

Alex allowed himself a small grin. *He's been there?* That was news to him—as far as Alex knew, Dev had never taken a relationship beyond a two-week stand. But Alex was beginning to see that there was a lot more to his brother than he'd once thought—even if he was certain Dev's situation had never been like Alex and Nicola's. Alex was crazy fucking in love with her, and she was all but done with him.

Cursing under his breath, he yanked his suitcase handle up and rolled it into the tiny combined departures and arrivals lounge. The lounge contained two rows of benches, three check-in kiosks, a coffee shop and a small gift shop. He glanced around hopefully, wondering if Nicola might have changed her mind and shown up to see him off, but no such luck.

As his eyes tracked back to the gift shop, a spinning rack of magazines caught his eye. He stepped closer to it, shaking his head disdainfully as he examined the tabloid covers. A week ago he would have rolled by them without a glance or a second thought, but now the headlines screamed at him.

Booze, Brawls and Bimbos—Mary Bonneville and Jed Ricker on the Brink of Divorce.

Winona Powers, Are Those Really Your Thighs? See the Stars' Worst Beach Shots.

Caught Red-Handed! Mark Giller Getting Cozy With His Hot Young Co-Star.

"Pretty pathetic, huh?"

Alex snapped his head up at the sound of the voice. Could it possibly be—

It was.

Nicola.

Alex's breath dried in his lungs. She had stepped out from behind the rack, and now she stood in front of him. She looked tired, but to him her beauty could not be dulled—there were those blond waves cascading over her shoulders, those perfect heart-shaped lips and those aqua eyes shining at him in the morning light. It was all Alex could do to stop himself from snatching her up and swinging her around like the hero in some cheesy movie.

He glanced down at her side. "Where's your suitcase?"

"I left it at home." She stepped a little closer to

him as his heart skipped a beat. Then she reached for his hands. He released the handle of his suitcase and gave them to her. "I was up most of the night," she said. "So I'm a little tired. But I came here to tell you something. I've decided I'm not going anywhere—not now, anyway. I won't live on Moretta forever, but I'm not going to run anymore."

"That's wonderful," Alex said, not daring to hope this changed anything between them. "I'm proud of you. I know that couldn't have been an easy decision."

Nicola shook her head. "It wasn't. But it wasn't the only decision I had to make."

"Oh, no?"

She squeezed his hands. "I had to decide if I could live without you. And the answer is no."

"No?" Alex repeated dumbly.

"That's right. I can't do it. Someone like you comes along once in a lifetime."

Alex swallowed hard, finally allowing a smile to come to his face. "I—"

"Shh…" Nicola put her finger to his lips, and then she put her arms around his neck. "I love you, Alex. I love you more than you can imagine. And we can make it work. It may not be a fantasy all the time, but that's okay. I want real life with you—the good *and* the bad."

"Oh, Nicola…" Alex took her face in his hands, and then he kissed her deeply. "You have no idea how happy that makes me. This is amazing. I love you so much…" He kissed her again.

"But you have a plane to catch," Nicola said, sliding her eyes to the clock. "Don't worry. I'll still be here when you land. Call me when you get in, and we'll figure out when I can visit you."

Alex took her in his arms again and closed his eyes. She loved him. They were going to make it work. It was the best thing he'd ever heard. No, more than that—it was all that mattered right now. "You know what? How about I don't."

Nicola tilted her head at him questioningly.

"I mean, what am I going home to? A furious father. He can rail at me over the phone just as well as he can in person. I think it might be time to make some big changes in my life—and the first one I want to make is today's schedule. I'm staying."

"Oh, my God. Really?" Nicola's eyes shone excitedly.

"Really. I'll have to go back eventually, but...you think you could handle a couple more weeks with me?"

Nicola tilted her head and lowered her voice. "If they're going to be anything like the past week, then...yes. I can't wait to enjoy every minute."

"Then let's get started," Alex said devilishly, wrapping his arms around her.

And then he couldn't resist: he picked her up and spun her off the floor.

* * * * *

MATCHED

KELLI IRELAND

MILLS & BOON

This book was an absolute blast to write, and it is my strongest wish to dedicate it to every reader out there who has been brave enough to pursue their dreams with undiluted, unapologetic passion. You inspire me to do the same. For that? You have my eternal gratitude.

CHAPTER ONE

ISAAC MILLER WORKED to control his breathing, his heart rate, his every response as he stared out over the New York skyline. Behind him, his brother paced. Jonathan had never been able to settle when nervous anticipation got the best of him, even when they'd been children. But Isaac was less concerned with his brother's anxiety than the predicament his younger sibling had finagled Isaac into this time.

He turned, every step controlled, his hands locked behind him. Less chance to strangle the little genius who stood in front of him if he kept his hands occupied. "I agreed to fund your new app, Jonathan, but I did *not* agree to be a test subject. You're well aware I only answered the questionnaire to help with your testing. I neither intended nor authorized you to use my profile as part of your initial trial."

"I know, Isaac. I know." Jonathan paced back and forth, his steps precise, his pattern across the room as tight as any military formation.

His brother would be counting every step to ensure he spent the same amount of energy crossing the room as he did coming back. Same number of steps to and fro. Same view from every window. Same length of stride, as if he'd measured it. The guy was obsessed with patterns and, as part of that, the accuracy of those patterns. He wouldn't have made a mistake like this. He wouldn't have accidentally put Isaac Miller, CEO of the capital investment group Quantum Ventures, in a speed-dating pool that would test Jon's newest app—a *dating* app—tentatively named Power Match.

But, somehow, Jonathan had done just that.

Isaac crossed his arms over his chest. "Just remove me from the pool of desperate singles willing to allow their love lives to be determined by digital algorithms."

His brother looked at him, regret and tension etching stress lines across his brow. "I can't."

"Yes, you can. Just delete my profile and remove me from the group. If it creates an odd number, replace me with someone else. In fact, use someone from the office." He pulled out his desk chair and sank into it. "I'll send out a request for participants. I assure you, someone *will* volunteer."

"You can't send out a request," Jonathan said in a tone Isaac rarely heard from him. It was a tone that was firm, even demanding. A tone that brooked no argument.

"I beg to differ," Isaac said softly. Brother or not, Jonathan was here as a client—the head of a start-up venture that Isaac had financed. He believed in his brother's vision. Even more, he believed in his brother's history of success in creating apps that went viral. But no one—*no one*—told Isaac what he could and couldn't do. He hadn't become head of one of the world's premier capital-venture firms by allowing others to dictate what he did, or did not, do. Even family.

"I'm serious, Isaac." Jonathan dropped bonelessly into one of the guest chairs across from Isaac's desk. "I input all the data and the app has already pre-paired test subjects for tonight's meet and greet. To take you out, I'd have to find someone with your identical personal parameters."

"So do it."

"I. Can't." Jonathan slid lower in the chair. "You've already been matched with three volunteer subjects the app determined would suit you. Well, two, anyway."

Isaac arched an eyebrow.

"According to Lucky, you're, uh, apparently a bit…" Jonathan waved his hand in a dismissive manner. "Anyway, I can't just—"

Isaac leaned back in his chair and steepled his fingers. "I'm a bit what?"

Jonathan dipped his chin, the younger brother overshadowing the tech genius as he mumbled an indiscernible answer.

"Speak up."

Jonathan's head snapped up, his eyes ablaze. "You sound like Dad."

"I've been insulted more gravely than that," Isaac said. Though not by much, or by anyone Isaac cared about. The coarse observation stung, but he buried the emotion behind the facade he wore like a custom-fit suit. "Go on, then. I'm a bit *what*?"

Jonathan crossed his arms over his chest. "Lucky says you're difficult to get along with."

"And who, pray tell, is Lucky, and why should I give a good goddamn about what he thinks?"

Jonathan snorted. "Lucky is the app's nickname. You know, like 'get lucky.' It's a play on the common vernacular for getting laid."

"I get it," Isaac growled.

"When's the last time you got lucky? Because, brother to brother, you sound like you could use a little somethin'. Why don't you shed your corporate persona for a single night, stop suspecting that everyone wants something from you and simply work on getting laid. We'd *all* be grateful." The last was muttered with more than a little snark.

Jaw set, Isaac stared at his younger brother. "My private life is off the table."

"In other words, it's been a while." Jonathan shook his head. "When are you going to relax?"

"When it's reasonably justified."

"Which will be when…never?" Jon ran both hands through his mop of hair, pushing it off his forehead as he closed his eyes. "I know what this is. I'm not stupid. It's about Mike. Like everything is always about Mike."

The name hung like a silent condemnation, and Isaac fought to keep his face neutral as his brother continued, blissfully ignorant of the pain just the name could elicit.

"When are you going to let go of his death, Isaac?" The question was delivered softly, but there was an unmistakable need to understand within the words. "He's been gone more than twenty years now. And what happened wasn't your fault. No one blamed you for it. Not even Dad. We all knew it was an accident. There was no way you could've stopped it."

An accident. No way to have stopped it.

Isaac refused to let his brother lure him into discussing the past. They were here to discuss the future. More specifically, the risk he'd taken on Jonathan's new project. This app was an unknown. That made it dangerous in its own right. It was one thing to invest in it, given Jon's history of success. It was another to be subject to the initial testing of an unproven product. "Take me out of the test pool, Jonathan. That's an order."

A finely shaped eyebrow rose in sardonic, wordless response. "An order? You really do sound like dear old Dad. Look, Isaac, you clearly haven't been listening to me. What do I need to do to make you understand that what you're ordering me to do can't be done? Do I need finger puppets? Flash cards? I'm telling you, Isaac, I can't take you out of tonight's test run without scrapping the whole event. My team and I collected information on roughly six hundred volunteers and entered all their data into the software. Your profile was accidentally included and, God only knows how or why, you made the cut.

Lucky selected the top ninety-eight that were most likely to find a suitable match. If we pull one participant, we have to find an identical replacement. That's not possible. So we'd have to cancel tonight's event, collect a new sample group, reenter their data, rerun the program and reschedule the test event. We can't do that. Not even for you. The app is set to launch in thirty days, Isaac. I don't have time to start over with a new test pool."

"You're sure there's not someone who could pose as me?" A last-ditch hope, yes, but Isaac didn't want to do this, didn't want to sit across from strange women and see what did, or *didn't*, spark between them. He opened his mouth to tell Isaac to simply remove the women he was supposed to meet with when his brother played the one card Isaac had never been able to say no to.

"I need your help. Bad. I don't want this to go south, Isaac. Not for me and definitely not for my team. They're depending on this to pay out. I don't have the same financial demands thanks to my trust fund, but…" He sat up and leaned forward, forearms propped on his knees, and looked at Isaac with undeniable, wholly authentic sincerity. "They have families counting on them. Most of them have kids. You're my only family. Forget the capital-investment side of things. Just—" Jonathan tunneled his fingers through his hair "—use an alias for all I care. These people don't run in your social circle. The chance that anyone will recognize you is slim. I need *you*, Isaac. As my brother. Please."

It was the *please* that broke him. That and the reminder that, with their father gone and their mother suffering severe dementia, the two of them were truly all that remained of their family. They had each other. Brothers.

"Don't expect me to 'hook up' with one of the test pool or whatever you're calling them."

"TPCs. Test-pool candidates."

"Whatever. I'll show up tonight, and then I'm out. Nothing more, Jonathan. Promise me you'll remove me from the unalterable 'TPC list' when the night's over. No finagling me into a second event. Are we clear?"

Jonathan beamed. "Absolutely. I'll make sure you're declared unsuitable for the project at the end of the night. That way you won't be selected for future events. I promise."

Isaac sat back in his chair and looked out at the New York skyline. He'd do this for his brother before he slipped back into the predictable solitude of life as he'd crafted it. A life he lived alone.

And alone suited him just fine.

CHAPTER TWO

RACHEL STEPHENS GLANCED at the clock on her bathroom wall for the fourth time in ten minutes. If she called a cab now, she'd be early. The last thing she wanted was to be the first person there. But she didn't want to be late, either. If only she hadn't agreed to participate in this ridiculous dating-app test. Her best friend, Casey, had pushed her to apply a couple of months ago during a stay-in movie night—a night that had involved too much wine followed by too many hormone-igniting Chris Hemsworth flicks. Devastating consequences always occurred when she indulged in too much of a good thing. And the wine *had* been good. But Chris…oh, Chris. He made her thoughts go in directions that were decidedly unsafe.

Rachel's phone buzzed on the bathroom counter. Her stomach clenched. Around the office, rumors were flying that a big case was coming in, a case that could make or break a junior attorney's career. Her boss had intimated that, if the filing came through, he would be selecting her to work with him. If he called now, she wouldn't have to go to this dating-app trial.

A glance at the display dashed her hopes. She swiped to answer, then tapped the speaker icon. "I still blame you for getting me into this."

Best friend, coworker and fellow junior attorney Casey Bass snickered. "You know you're glad you were drunk enough to accept the challenge. I'm just pissed that I didn't make the final cut. I could've used the compensation they were offering to help pay for our trip to the Dominican Republic in March. Who was it that told us becoming attorneys would make us rich?"

"A private student-loan officer who spun wild tales of riches beyond our wildest dreams."

Casey sighed with enough drama for the both of them. "I'm still waiting for my ship to come in."

"So that's why you're always hanging out by the docks. And here I thought you were just trolling for sailors."

Her friend's laughter soothed her nerves some. "Whatever works."

"Look, I'm just happy I was able to afford real chicken and fresh vegetables on my grocery list this month. And the trip to the Dominican will help ease the pain I experience every time I write out the current month's student-loan check."

"True enough." Casey sighed as she shifted her bedding around, and Rachel could imagine Casey curled up in a nest of blankets and pillows with her laptop, working, as some random Netflix show looped in the background. "So. What are you wearing?" Casey asked.

"If you'd asked me that in a deeper voice, I'd tell you." Rachel leaned forward and applied her mascara with care. "As it is, you'll have to wonder."

"Just promise me you're not wearing your black power suit, black heels and carrying your black Burberry bag. You think it's stylish, but you look like a monochromatic ad for a high-end funeral home. A gorgeous one, mind you, but still. Wear something with color. Oh! Wear that dark green dress—the one with the V-neck and the slit up the thigh."

"Casey, that dress was the result of a sip-and-shop event. Seeing as tonight is a result of another night spent with wine as my intimate companion, I've decided the fermented grape and I are absolutely *not* friends."

"I disagree. Wine is generally the catalyst behind your best decisions."

"You're an enabler." Rachel capped the mascara and stepped back, taking in her black power suit, black heels and black Burberry bag, which sat on her bed. When had she become so—so…predictable? She used to be spontaneous, fun, outgoing. A bit of a rebel, if truth be told. The way her life had played out over the last several years had made her overly cautious, had taught her to be conservative when making decisions. She'd become content blending into a crowd instead of standing out. Truth? If someone accused her of being a total bore, she had no defense.

"Safe," she whispered. She would argue she was safe.

"What's safe?" Casey asked.

The question hung between them, and Rachel had no doubt that Casey knew exactly what was going through her head.

"Stop playing it safe, Rach. Jeff left, but you survived. It's time to thrive. Take the fact that you made the cut for tonight's little experimental soiree as a sign that it's time to start living again. Maybe even time to get laid."

"Casey!"

"Oh, c'mon, Rachel. It's not like I don't know you and your vibrator are ridiculously intimate."

"No more than you and yours," Rachel countered.

"Not denying it. But at least I'm out there, playing the field, looking for someone. Even if he's a Mr. Right Now versus Mr. Right. You need to do a little of the same. No one is ever going to be one hundred percent safe, Rachel. No one is ever going to be able to chase away your demons. You're the only one with that power." She paused, took a deep breath and let it out before continuing, her next words so much softer. "Honey, you have to stop holding on to Jeff's memory. He was an asshole. You can't see it now, but trust me. I'm begging you. His walking out? It was a good thing and, deep down, you know it. He changed you, nearly suffocated you with his dos and don'ts. He tried to make you into the breadwinner, the Stepford wife *and* his personal fetch-it girl. For God's sake, he was unemployed more than half your married life."

"He managed to snag an heiress." The admission was thick. Heavy.

"An heiress whose family made their money by revolutionizing the laxative industry. A shit for a shit. It's so apropos."

The sound Rachel made was half laugh, half sob.

"Like I said, what you need is Mr. Right Now, Rachel. Stop disqualifying every man who comes on to you. Instead, look for the opportunity to have fun. It's the only way you're going to break that last tie, Rach. And it's time. Let. Him. Go."

She knew Casey was right. Even if it was just for a single night, Rachel needed to try to relish every moment. She needed to be adventurous instead of cautious, a sexual creature who took chances despite the odds and dared Fate to strike back.

It was time she proved to herself that, though Jeff might have left her damaged, he hadn't been able to break her.

No one was that strong.

Casey's voice was softer when she spoke, as if she knew where Rachel's thoughts had taken her. "Pull your hair down out of the predictable chignon, put on that damn green dress and go have a good time. Don't do it for me, though. Do it for you—for the woman you were and will be again. Starting now."

Familiar doubt crept in. She'd once been brave, adventurous, more than a little bit wild. She'd liked herself then. Jeff had liked her, too. It had changed after they'd married, his concept of wifely behavior so different than the woman he'd married. It wasn't lost on her that the woman Jeff had left her for was exactly the type of woman Rachel had been. The woman who was on everyone's invite list. The woman who was full of enthusiasm and possessed an easy way about her. Someone with a quick wit and an adventurous spirit.

"Don't go down that dark path, Rachel. Please."

It was the *please* that did her in. Casey didn't beg. Ever. And here she was, reduced to pleading with Rachel to live her life?

"You make a hell of a compelling closing argument, Case."

"You always said cases are easy to win when you know you're right."

With shaking hands, Rachel undid the buttons on the black suit jacket, then shed the heels and the pants. She pulled out the dark green sheath dress, cut off the tags and slipped it on. Next, she grabbed the pair of black patent-leather stilettos from the back of the closet—shoes she'd sworn to only wear when she finally worked up the moxie to wear the dress.

Tonight was the night.

Pulling the pins from her hair, she let the mass of mahogany waves tumble down her back. She bent at the waist and flipped over her hair, fluffing it with her fingers until it was free and loose and a bit wild. She flipped it back and turned to face herself in the mirror.

She couldn't help but smile. The woman looking

back at her was someone she hadn't seen in far too long, but she would have recognized her anywhere. A quietly confident laugh escaped her, the sound also something she hadn't heard in a while, and she had missed it.

"You did it," Casey whispered. "You put on the damn dress."

"I did."

The other woman let out what could only be described as a whoop. "Go get him, tigress! Own tonight!"

"No apologies."

"No regrets," her best friend in the world said. "You better come by my office the minute you get in tomorrow morning because I'm telling you now, I want deets. Dirty, *dirty* deets."

"We'll see if there's anything to tell. I have to make a connection first. And it has to be real."

"Let's agree on this now because I know that if you tell me you'll do something, you'll do it. Always. You don't break vows."

Rachel swallowed hard. "Agree on what, exactly?"

"The three qualifications Mr. Right Now has to have to pass the Rachel Stephens test."

"Three?" Rachel squeaked.

"Three."

"A guy has to have more than three qualifications for me to consider getting down and dirty."

"No, he doesn't. If we were discussing Mr. Right? Sure. But we aren't. This is *Mr. Right Now*. So three it is."

Rachel scowled.

"You're almost six feet yourself, so he has to be tall," Casey said, starting the list.

"Kind," Rachel countered.

"Kind is for counselors and protein bars."

"Casey," Rachel warned.

"He needs to be seriously hot."

"Intelligent," Rachel countered. While a guy being hot was nice, his looks did nothing to help a conversation along if he wasn't bright.

"Intelligent can be a bonus qualifier. This is a one-night stand, Rach, not someone who's boyfriend material."

"Fine. But, Casey?" She stared at herself in the mirror, trying to imagine what strangers might see when they looked at her. "There has to be chemistry. *Real* chemistry. That's not negotiable."

"Then there's your list."

"What?" Panic nearly choked her. "That's not enough!"

"Yes, it is. For a one-night stand, it's plenty." That tone—it was one Rachel recognized.

That tone meant Casey had reached the point she was about to let down the facade she sported, the one of the fun-loving, slightly ditzy blonde femme fatale. One could push Casey only so far and then boom! She dropped the facade and the hard-ass took over. Rachel had her own version, she supposed. Or she had once. Regardless, she didn't want to fight with Casey. She needed her too much right now.

"Now promise me—*swear to me*—that if you

meet a guy with these three qualities, you'll make a play."

Rachel swallowed once, then twice, through a throat clenched tight in history's unyielding fist. She took a deep breath, admiring the way the dress made her full B-cup breasts look just a little larger, the push-up bra making her cleavage just a little more substantial than it really was. "Remind me to send a thank-you note to Victoria's Secret for their water bra."

Casey laughed. "Deets, girlfriend. I want the down and dirty tomorrow because I'm telling you now, there *will* be a connection tonight."

Rachel closed her eyes and smiled. Maybe Casey was right. Maybe tonight was the night she'd back take her life.

No. No *maybes* about it. Tonight *was* the night. She would own it, and whatever happened? Happened. "I promise," she whispered. "Casey?"

"Yeah?"

"I'm back."

The other woman sniffled, the sound small but undeniable, and her voice wavered a bit when she spoke. "I've missed you, Rach."

"Me, too, honey. Me, too." She stood up straight and took one last look at herself in the mirror. "Now, if you'll excuse me, I have men to meet and connections to make." She paused for a split second, trying to find the right words. Then she said, "Thank you, Casey. Thank you for standing by me and for reminding me who I really am."

"Thank you for finally listening. Now go slay the last of your dragons, and do it without remorse." The grin on her friend's face translated seamlessly to her tone.

"No regrets," she affirmed.

Casey disconnected the call without another word.

Rachel grabbed her satin clutch and dropped her bold red lipstick inside before snapping the little bag closed. One last glance in the small mirror beside her front door confirmed that the woman who looked back was ready.

Her eyes shone with a vitality she had missed for a very long time. She took a deep breath and pressed a fist against her abdomen in an attempt to settle sudden nerves fluttering behind her belly button. It didn't matter if the man she connected with was Casey's brother, the bartender or one of the software engineers for the Power Match app. If there was chemistry, she was going to see this through. A liberation, of sorts. But more, a definitive reclaiming of her life.

A small, involuntary smile pulled at the corners of her mouth.

No regrets, indeed.

CHAPTER THREE

ISAAC STOOD AT the bar, the crowd at his back, and sipped a dirty martini. Two olives. Shaken, not stirred. Alcohol—something he rarely indulged in—was the evening's only saving grace.

Seeing as he had no intention of actually trying to find a partner tonight, it seemed pointless to pay any attention to the singles milling around the room. That included the three women who had, one at a time, attempted to engage him in conversation. He'd politely excused himself to speak to an acquaintance here or there, or to go back to the coat check to retrieve the phone he'd claimed he'd forgotten. Each woman had been irritated but had accepted his unsubtle dismissal. Not an ounce of real moxie in any of them. It surprised him that he was mildly disappointed.

Behind him, the crowd mingled and made small talk as they tried to figure out whom in the group they might end up paired with. There was a great deal of forced laughter from women and posturing from men. Both groups were trying too hard. So Isaac continued to sip his drink and ignore them all.

The moderator entered his peripheral view, and he watched as she took over the small platform where the DJ likely held court on any given night. The woman, whom Isaac recognized from one of the meetings between his investment firm and Jonathan's lead team, fiddled with the mic. What was her name…? Jamie? Janie? Something like that. She'd been impressive; he remembered that much. She was the team's lead psychologist, stolen from a competitor, and the person singularly responsible for creating the personality-profiling system that Jonathan had turned into code.

Jaline.

Her name was Jaline.

The mic screeched, and the crowd winced before someone started clapping and everyone followed suit.

Jaline took a mock bow, then lifted the mic. "Good evening. My name is Jaline. You're all here because—"

Half listening to Jaline's presentation and half developing the following morning's agenda, Isaac pulled his phone from the inner pocket of his suit jacket. There was no reason the interim couldn't be turned into productive time. Opening the phone's note-taking app, he began to tap out a rough outline for the first of three meetings scheduled before noon.

A round of applause had him lifting his head and looking around. People had begun to move en masse, approaching the makeshift stage from where Jaline had been speaking.

Isaac signaled the bartender. "What did I miss?"

"Instructions on how to find the love of your life, apparently." The guy grinned. "If it were that easy, I'd be out of a job."

Shaking his head, Isaac handed the guy a twenty. "Another drink, my friend, and the CliffsNotes version of the speech I just ignored."

"Make your way to the table, pick up the paperwork with your first name, last initial and unique participant ID. Men go the numbered table to which they've been assigned." The bartender shook the drink with expertise and poured it with little more than a glance at the glass. "The app's magic algorithms ensure that at least one woman who has a compatible personality and similar interests will make her way to your table. If you're lucky, Cupid will follow before the clock strikes twelve—" he slid the drink to Isaac "—or the bar closes at two. Whichever comes first."

"Funny guy," Isaac murmured into the glass before taking a sip.

The alcohol burned his throat, and the pungent fumes left him craving clean, unfiltered air. Maybe this weekend he'd head up to the Poconos. For all that he loved the city—its vibrancy, international community and resulting diverse culture—there was nothing like New York's mountains in the fall.

"Isaac?"

He turned toward the familiar voice. "Hello, Jaline."

She handed him his packet and visibly cringed. "Sorry. Jonathan said to make sure you didn't skip out."

Irritation prickled along his hairline and he rubbed at the sensation, trying to get it to go away. "I told him I wouldn't bail on him, and I won't."

"Fair enough. My job is to get you your paperwork and see you seated at table twelve. Then? I'm out, and you're on your own with the women Lucky paired you with."

"Fantastic." In reality, this whole thing was anything but.

Taking the paperwork, he made his way to table twelve, well aware the woman watched his every move. He had to wonder what she'd do if he feinted toward the door, but he didn't. He was many things—unnecessarily cruel wasn't one of them. That he'd even considered it was evidence as to how much the evening had worn on him. Only brotherly affection kept him from walking out. Jonathan had made it clear he needed Isaac to see this through. And at the end of the night, Isaac would be disqualified for any future test runs of the Power Match app.

Whatever. It amused him that he would end up being declared insufficient. That hadn't ever happened to him before.

Sinking into a chair, he set his drink and paperwork on the table and then shrugged out of his suit jacket. Less than two minutes passed before he found himself putting the jacket on again.

"This is ridiculous," he muttered, yanking the jacket so it hung straight and then rearranging his tie. "It's a couple hours of one night of my life. Nothing more. I've been civil for far longer and under worse conditions." He picked up his martini glass and gave Jaline, who still watched him, a somber salute. "I'll survive."

With the lyrics from that same iconic 70s song ringing through his head, he smiled benignly as the first woman approached his table.

Rachel leaned over the ladies'-room counter and reapplied her lipstick. The sound system had been piped into the spacious room, so she heard the moderator calling participants together to attend what was deemed their final "power match." The woman's enthusiasm grated on Rachel's nerves, particularly since her first two meet and greets had been unmitigated catastrophes.

"Calling all lab rats together for the final observation session of mating behaviors as they occur in an urban environment," someone said from behind a closed stall door.

"In a *controlled* urban environment," someone else qualified from another stall.

The two commentators laughed.

Rachel didn't.

Were they right? Was that all this was—a structured environment where psychologists would watch with an educated eye and report their findings back to the mysterious people who designed apps like this? What would they do with the personal information when the app went live? She racked her brain, trying to remember the contract language regarding using an applicant's personal information for advertising and promotional purposes.

Damn it. Wine haze had her questioning what she thought she remembered.

She *knew* better than to sign anything, even her bar tab, when she'd had that third glass of red.

Could she back out? Yes, but she needed the cash offered to participants to pay off the remaining balance on her March trip with Casey to the Dominican Republic. If she didn't collect the two grand, she'd be seriously hard-pressed to make that vacation happen. And she *needed* that vacation. Two weeks in paradise. No incessantly ringing phones. No senior attorneys treating her like she was a secretary instead of an active member of the New York State Bar. No ten- and twelve-hour days ending with cold Chinese takeout. No Saturday mornings or Sunday afternoons in the office trying to catch up. No insane commute that involved crowded subway stations, jostling crowds at every crosswalk or attempts to avoid the unpredictable weather.

Two weeks of complimentary drinks, fine dining, spa services and beach chairs situated just out of reach of the surf.

"For that, I can tolerate a hell of a lot more than being called a lab rat," she said to her reflection.

An attractive woman left one of the stalls, stepped up to the mirror and began fussing with her hair. "You here for the dating thing?"

"Yeah." Rachel glanced over. "You?"

"No. I'm Jaline's assistant."

Rachel searched her brain for the name but came up empty. "Jaline?"

"Jaline Harkins. The moderator." Making an O with her mouth, the woman used a piece of tissue to clean up the places she seemed to think her lipstick had feathered. "She's the doctor—well, she's a psychologist but has her PhD—for the app developer. She worked for the number one dating app in the United States, developing the software that helped them get to where they were. But the guy who came up with the app that paired powerful men and women? He came in and stole her right out from under the competition."

A warning bell sounded in Rachel's head. "If she had a noncompete, and I can't imagine she didn't, she's violating the terms of her employment." And any reasonably intelligent employer would have had a noncompete in place if this woman, Jaline, had exclusive access to proprietary information like the competitor's software.

Jaline's assistant elegantly lifted one shoulder with obvious indifference. "No idea. All I know is that Jaline took me with her." The stranger casually glanced at Rachel from the corner of her eye. "Jaline even got me a raise out of the whole thing. She told me that the guy who scooped us has some pretty serious capital backing. And with Jaline handling the psychology between good and bad matches? This new app is going to be a huge success."

Rachel had no idea what she was expected to say to that, so she just nodded.

"What do you do?" the other woman asked.

"I'm a lawyer."

"Cool. Your first two matches—what did you think?" The woman didn't give Rachel time to answer before continuing. "If you'll excuse me, she'll need me on the floor as the men try to navigate the paperwork for this final power match. Even men deemed professionally powerful need an assistant if forms are involved. Best of luck finding Mr. Right," she called over her shoulder as she left the bathroom and returned to the bar.

"I just need to find Mr. Right Now," Rachel said to the empty air. Neither man she'd been paired with so far had even come close.

The first man had her looking around to see if the whole event was actually a practical joke…one made wholly at her expense. Unfortunately, it hadn't been. "King John" owned a line of portable toilets used at construction sites and such. "John ain't my name. It's Bruce," he'd said. "But I'm talkin' 'John' as in shitter, sweet cheeks. Get it?"

The "King" had tried to pump her for legal advice for the first thirty minutes of their forty-five-minute introduction. When she'd said that she didn't give legal advice outside the office, he'd shrugged. Then his face lit with enthusiasm. He offered to take her on a tour of his "personal facilities" as he slid his filthy booted foot up the inside of her bare leg while waggling his eyebrows and asking, again, if she "got it."

She stood, told him she definitely "got it" and said that if he didn't get *out* before the next session, she'd have him *thrown* out. Then she went straight to the bar and ordered a mojito.

The second man she'd been matched with had been so initially forgettable that he seemed harmless—he reminded her of an actor who played a scientist on a popular sitcom. As irony would have it, the guy was actually a scientist. He held a doctorate in astronomy from MIT. But he also lived in his mother's basement and was a certified conspiracy theorist. He had spent the entire time telling her that the evening's events were part of a breeding study being carried out by the government.

When the bell announcing the conclusion of the second match sounded, Rachel had nearly tipped over her chair as she stood and headed for the bar. That hadn't stopped the guy from calling out an invitation to go back to his mom's place "to copulate in the name of science."

Her second drink had been a shot of tequila.

So had her third, and she hadn't even met the third man she'd been paired with.

She also hadn't been the only woman at the bar. The bartender had been pouring as fast as he could for the mass of women crowding the counter, all of them sporting some level of shock.

If she was honest with herself, it seemed most prudent at this point to simply cut and run. She wasn't even opposed to leaving her coat. It could be replaced. Her sanity? No such guarantees. Yes, she needed the money for her vacation. But she was more than willing to eat a ramen-only diet to pay off the trip's outstanding balance. And if that wasn't enough, she'd borrow from her 401(k). Anything had to be better than this.

Decision made, she left the women's room and headed for the exit.

Someone lightly touched her arm, and Rachel spun to find the moderator, Jaline, looking at her. "Is something wrong?"

"You could say that. First, I was felt up by the steel-toed work boot of the man I wouldn't have selected as a partner if humanity's very existence hung in the balance. I told him to leave without consulting you, but I also likely saved you sexual-harassment charges. You're welcome, but make sure he's taken off the roster for future events. I mean it." She knew she sounded as crazed as she felt, but there was no reining it in. "My second match is a conspiracy theorist who probably believes *Star Trek*—*any* generation—was a documentary. He offered to procreate, in his bedroom in his mother's basement, in the name of science. I don't know where you found these guys, but they aren't even *remotely* the type of partners we were promised. They aren't like-minded. They aren't civilized. And they *certainly* aren't gentlemen. Given the looks on most of the women's faces at the bar, you're going to need to provide post 'power match' therapy to help them get over the horrors of agreeing to this farce."

Chest heaving, she turned to go, but Jaline stopped her, this time grabbing her arm with enough force to startle Rachel. The woman's eyes were wide, her expression harried.

"Please, Ms. . . ."

"Stephens. Rachel Stephens."

"Please, Ms. Stephens. Rachel. I'll personally en-sure the first man is removed from our test pool and flag his application as an automatic rejection if he tries to reapply. I'll also have the second man's ap-plication reviewed to see how he got through to the test phase. Neither of these men represents Power Match's ultimate bachelor. Please, stay through the last round of introductions? As a test applicant, your participation helps us sort out any glitches in the app before it goes live." The diminutive woman shud-dered. "Can you imagine what would happen if we didn't figure this stuff out first?"

Rachel hesitated. "I appreciate the position you're in, but it's been a colossally bad night, Jaline. I just want to go home."

The woman held out her hand for Rachel's crum-pled paperwork. "I'll make you a deal. Let me per-sonally vet the final candidate you've been paired with. If I don't think he's a good match, I'll see you out myself and sign your paperwork so you can still collect the compensation."

Rachel clutched her paperwork. "Let me get this straight. If he's not legit, if he's another 'glitch,' I get to leave and I still get paid as if I'd sat through all three rounds."

"You have my word." Jaline eased the paperwork from Rachel's fist and flipped through several pages. "By choosing to stay, you're helping to ensure this doesn't happen…" Her gaze snapped to Rachel's. "You're going to want to stay."

"Why?" Skepticism weighted the one-word question. "Who is he?"

"Your next power match is…" Her cheeks flushed, and she fanned herself.

Rachel's eyebrows shot up. "You're actually blushing. Who is this guy?"

"I'll allow him to introduce himself. But I'll promise you ahead of time that he's incredibly easy to look at, he's the very definition of corporate success and he's a gentleman through and through. You aren't going to want to miss this introduction."

Curiosity always got the best of her in the worst situations, and this evening certainly qualified as a personal "worst."

Jaline seemed to sense her hesitation and leaned in close, speaking low enough that only Rachel could hear her. "I'll stay within sight. If he says or does anything you don't like, just…" She looked around and ended up pulling a rubber band out of her little bag. "Put your hair up in a topknot and I'll come running." When Rachel still didn't agree, the woman took her by the arm and steered her across the room, every step taken with undeniable purpose. They neared a table at the far corner of the dance floor. A man sat alone, his back to the room, balancing his chair on the two rear legs. The lazy way he rocked forward and back announced to anyone and everyone that he was thoroughly bored.

His short, black hair was neatly trimmed. His suit

was cut so it framed his broad shoulders and, even slouched as he was, he was tall.

"That's him?" she asked, squashing an unexpected wave of anticipation.

"Yes." Jaline threw her a little side-eye. "He'll be worth your time. Trust me."

Rachel scowled at her. "I never trust people who say 'trust me,'" she murmured.

"Wise," the man said.

She shot Jaline a wide-eyed look. "Supersonic hearing?"

Jaline slapped a hand over her mouth to stifle her laughter.

He turned just enough to offer her a glance at his profile. "Nothing so extraordinary. I'm just used to people talking about me behind my back."

Tall.

Check.

From what she could see? Smoking hot.

Check-check.

If chemistry sparked between them?

A shiver ran up her spine.

Rachel pulled out her chair and slowly sat, facing the man she hadn't expected to find.

Mr. Right Now.

CHAPTER FOUR

ISAAC LOOKED UP as the chair opposite him was pulled away from the table. A woman in a dark green dress sank onto the seat with incredible grace, setting her clutch in her lap before crossing her legs in a controlled move that drew his attention. His gaze rested on the dress's short hem before he realized that her legs were bare. In October.

Isaac shifted slightly in his seat. He had always appreciated the way women's bodies appeared deceptively softer, their more subtly sculpted lines and lithe forms imbued with inherent grace. And when a woman worked to enhance those fine lines and fluid form? He appreciated it all the more. Without a doubt, the woman who had taken a seat across from him put in more than sufficient time to hone her form. She'd done such a magnificent job that, embarrassingly, Isaac found himself staring.

Appreciating.

Craving.

The woman began tapping a well-manicured fingernail against the small bag in her lap. "Let me know when you're done with the physical assessment. The timer on our little meeting starts in—" she twisted in her chair, then twisted back "—about three minutes."

"Plenty of time, then."

"Time for…"

"Surely you've heard how important first impressions are."

Her finger—the one tap-tap-tapping her handbag—went still. "And what, exactly, are you doing to secure that all-important first impression?"

"I'm sitting here trying not to intimidate you."

She laughed then, the sound as promising as room-temperature bourbon poured over chilled whiskey stones.

"Do that again," he said quietly, his gaze hovering at the highest point of the slit in the dress, the one that exposed a thin strip of smooth skin on the outside of her upper thigh.

"Do what again?" she asked in that sin-and-redemption voice.

"Laugh."

"Make me."

Isaac leaned back in his chair and crossed his arms over his chest. Who was she, this stranger, that she thought she stood a chance in hell of ordering him to do anything at all?

Had the dress she was wearing been displayed in a museum, it would have been called "Temptation in Textiles." And with just cause. It was cut so that it showcased her best physical assets—long legs, trim waist, pert breasts, pale skin and that elegant neck, half-hidden by the mass of loosely curled mahogany hair. That strong jaw.

He liked defined characteristics in a woman— knew men who much preferred their women softer, both in form and personality. Not him. As far as Isaac was concerned, strength was strength. And strength trumped softness each and every time.

Whoever this woman was, she understood the value of strength.

But she didn't realize whom she was facing off with.

He tried to decide what color he'd call her skin. From that glimpse of thigh to the line of her jaw, the tone was that of diluted honey—warm but not quite tan. The sun would give her more warmth if she spent much time outdoors. But he knew she didn't. The finger that had tapped her bag was too smooth, unblemished, to belong to someone who did anything outside besides, perhaps, run.

Another look at her legs and, yes, she was a runner.

She smiled, and his attention shifted to her lips.

Lush but not bee-stung. Not thin. Lips that framed a decidedly smart mouth.

For now, that was amusing. And now was all they'd have. He glanced at the meeting timer. Forty-three minutes.

"If you're bored, you could try conversation. It's a universally accepted means of passing the time."

One corner of his mouth twitched. "Are you always so…"

"Quick-witted?" she offered.

"Snarky."

She shrugged. "Semantics."

He quieted, waiting to see what she would add in the hanging silence.

She stared at him, also waiting on…something. What? Conversation? Yet the longer they sat there, the more clear it became that she might just be able to wait him out.

Seconds passed, crossing the one-minute mark and dragging on before she couldn't stand the building tension and broke the silence.

"Okay," she said, leaning forward and resting her forearms on the table, her breasts pressed together by her biceps so that her cleavage nearly doubled. "I'll get the ball rolling. What's your name?"

He rose.

She followed suit.

He held out a hand.

She stared at it for a moment and then offered her own hand in return.

A jolt of awareness passed through him not unlike a mild electrical shock. "I'm Isaac Miller."

"Rachel Stephens."

"And what do you do for a living, Ms. Stephens?"

"Please, call me Rachel."

He didn't blink, didn't look away. "Isaac."

"I'm a lawyer…Isaac."

He sank back into his seat and folded his hands across his abdomen. "You're a rare woman, Rachel."

"And how did you come to that determination in

under five minutes?" There was a smile hidden in the question as she sat down.

"You're an attorney."

"Yes."

"Are you successful?"

"Each person measures success against different markers."

"By your own, then."

She lifted one shoulder, her head tilting to the side as she considered him. "By my measure? Yes. But there are still mountains to climb and glass ceilings to shatter."

He nodded in agreement. "You'll get there. You clearly have a mind that complements your appearance."

"I look smart?" Surprise played through her wide gaze.

He fought the urge to smile. Letting go of his iron control now wouldn't do. But she deserved clarification. "You look absolutely stunning, to be frank. What I meant was that your mind seems as attractive as your—"

"My body," she said, surprising him.

He had wanted to say "body," but that wasn't acceptable. Not by his or society's standards.

"Admit it," she teased. "That's what you were going to say, but you backed yourself into a conversational corner."

"Certainly...not." One corner of his mouth turned up against his will when Rachel laughed again. The sound shot through him, landing at the base of his spine, making his balls draw up tight.

She leaned forward and, in a stage whisper, said, "That was a pathetic cover."

"It was," he admitted. Curiosity rarely provoked him to action, but tonight it won over his typically analytical approach. "May I ask you something, Rachel?"

"That's what we're here for."

"Is it?"

"Isn't it?" she countered. When he paused, she pressed. "I'm looking for honesty, Isaac. Not word-play."

He sat back in his seat. A woman who openly asked for honesty...and, he believed, meant it. Isaac's curiosity was more piqued than ever.

"Fine. Long story short, I wasn't supposed to be a candidate, but I came tonight to appease the app developer."

"Who is he to you?"

"A...client." Isaac rolled his shoulders. She didn't need to know who Jonathan was. It wasn't relevant.

"A client." She tilted her head to one side, considering him. "And what is it you do, Isaac?"

"I work with a capital-investment firm."

"So your company bankrolls ideas and software or software applications other people come up with and then you...what? How do you get back your initial investment?"

"We essentially buy into whatever the idea or product is and, in exchange for start-up funding, we become part owners in the new venture. If that venture is successful, my firm is paid something equivalent to dividends on that success."

"So you help people get started and then ride their coattails indefinitely." She gave him an innocent look that forewarned him that whatever came next would be sharp. Or clever. Perhaps both. "Sounds a bit like a high-end pyramid scheme."

Both.

And it fascinated him. Here sat a woman who didn't stroke his ego. A woman comfortable in her skin. A woman who knew her worth. He hadn't experienced anyone like her before. Similar, but no one had ever possessed the entire package—the one that made up his perfect woman. But here she sat, wearing confidence like a cloak, sexuality like stilettos, and wielded her curiosity like a sword.

He would have to mind himself. Because by doing nothing more than being true to herself, Rachel Stephens threatened Isaac's vow to get in and out of tonight's social experiment without making a connection.

The alarm sounded, signaling they had just fifteen minutes before their time together reached its scheduled end.

Realization that this meeting was nearly over moved Isaac to act, something he never did without weighing the consequences, measuring pros and cons. Not now, though. Now? He had to admit he wasn't ready to walk away from this woman, and he'd do whatever he had to do to ensure their time together wasn't finished.

Not yet.

Whatever he did, he had to figure out what the hell was happening between them.

Anticipation hummed along every nerve in Rachel's body, but the feeling was, without a doubt, most concentrated in the most inconvenient places. The back of her neck. Her breasts. The lowest part of her pelvis. Her entire sex. There was no denying that Isaac Miller scored one hundred percent when graded against the Mr. Right Now trifecta scorecard.

She could've added a few extra attributes—maybe humility or even… Oh, who cared. Nothing so mundane would really matter when it came down to brass tacks. Or silk sheets.

So, with fifteen minutes left in the evening, she had to admit that she had found a man who qualified as Mr. Right Now. And she owed herself a win.

That meant figuring out if Isaac was interested in her before the final bell rang and, if he was, how to get things to go down the path that ended with rumpled sheets and a little pillow talk prior to saying their farewells.

But before she could test the waters, he parked his elbows on the table and pressed his hands together, almost as if he was praying. Dark blue eyes that had been casually guarded all night were suddenly serious. "How confident are you in your poker face?"

"Very," she replied without even a moment's hesitation. "I'd be a pretty shitty lawyer if my face gave away everything I was thinking."

"Do you consider yourself a good lawyer?"

"I do." She offered no apology for her surety. Why should she? Then an idea struck. Scooting forward until she sat on the edge of her seat, she crossed her arms and placed them on the table. "What about you, Isaac? Are you any good at your job?"

"The best."

She'd anticipated as much.

Putting her weight on her elbows, she decided to test the waters. "And how's *your* poker face?" She spoke softly so that he'd have to either lean forward to hear her or ask her to speak up. Her gut said that if he was into her, he'd lean in. If he wasn't, he'd ask her to repeat what she'd said.

He leaned in on the first word.

Score one for intuition.

"Also the best."

"Are you willing to make a little wager, maybe see which one of us possesses the superior poker face?"

"Perhaps." He blinked slowly, the heat in his gaze making her clench her thighs. And when he next spoke, she found herself leaning forward to hear *him*. "And how do you propose we do that?"

"A game." God, was that breathy voice actually hers? "Seven-card stud. One round. Winner takes all."

"What's the prize?"

The urge to put herself out there overruled her common sense and any reservations she'd held on to up until that point. "One night." She looked down, gauged her timing, then slowly looked up. Met his blazing gaze, licked her lips and lowered her voice even further. "Together. No strings. No regrets."

His gaze locked on the bare skin of her thigh and lingered longer than could be deemed polite. She tapped the table and his attention snapped back to her.

"Deal."

A sharp thrill coursed through her and she rose from her seat. Isaac reclined and hooked an arm over the chair back, looking up at her. "I don't suppose you have a deck of cards handy, do you?"

"What, you don't keep a set on hand for situations just like this?"

"My spare is in my other suit jacket."

"Of course." She swept low and retrieved her clutch and then, with all the casualness she could muster, she inclined her head toward the front door. "Shall we?"

"Shall we what?"

Her stomach somersaulted, rolling over and over before coming to a shaky halt. Thank God it was right side up.

This was the moment when she had to decide. Be bold and brazen, or reserved and, likely, peppered with regret come dawn.

"Bold," she said so softly that Isaac's attention focused on her mouth and he seemed to be trying to read her lips.

"I'm sorry," he said. "I couldn't hear you."

Rachel closed her eyes, searched and found her

emotional center and whispered a small promise to never again forget who she was, no matter what happened in the next thirty seconds.

She opened her eyes, held out her hand and said, "What do you say we get out of here and find a deck of cards?"

CHAPTER FIVE

ISAAC IMPATIENTLY WAVED off his driver and opened the town car's rear passenger door for Rachel. He jogged around to the other side and stopped for a moment, his hand resting on the door handle, to regain his composure. Getting his heart rate down into the normal range—a range it hadn't visited during the last hour—wasn't optional.

The woman flustered him, and he wasn't sure whether he hungered for it or abhorred it.

She threatened his self-control like no one had before. Ever.

And she was as sexy as she was impulsive. Impulsiveness was, at best, difficult to predict. At worst? It was dangerous. And without being able to predict her actions and reactions, he was flying blind.

If the conversation with her had proven anything, it was that he didn't have a solid grip on his reactions to her. For God's sake, he'd smiled! Impulsively. He'd let himself relax in her company. She was a veritable stranger despite the forty-five minutes they'd spent together. And when he'd tried to withdraw, she'd followed him, leaning across the table and using that seductive voice of hers like a siren. Her offer of one night of unmitigated, irresponsible, unparalleled pleasure had scrambled his brain.

"Poker," he said softly and shook his head, the urge to grin striking him again without warning.

This time, Isaac managed to quell it, his iron-clad emotional control slipping back into place. He could do this. He could play a game of poker with her, enjoy their time together no matter how they spent it and then issue a kind but definitive farewell come morning. That was absolutely within his emotional wheelhouse.

Impulsive or not, Isaac wanted—needed—to see where this might go. Rachel's spontaneity was a challenge. She kept him on his toes, forced him to engage in the conversation and be wholly present.

It was an odd thing to be that present in a personal conversation. He honestly couldn't remember the last time he had.

The door opened and his driver stood, twisting to face Isaac. "Sir? The woman in the back seat…" He hesitated, fidgeting with his tie.

"Yes?"

"She asked me to relay a message."

"Then relay it."

"I don't want to lose my job."

Isaac's mouth twitched, though whether he hovered on the border of irritation or humor he couldn't say. "Just tell me what she said. Verbatim," he added.

"She said to tell you to either get your ass in the car or take her home where she could play solitaire."

Laughter nearly choked him, and he couldn't stop it from breaking free, a sharp sound that was entirely unfamiliar. Realizing his driver's eyes were nearly bugging out at the fact Isaac was laughing, he tamped down the outburst, cleared his throat and said, "I'm getting in. Run the divider up, pull into traffic and drive."

"Destination, sir?"

"I'll let you know." The man moved to reenter the driver's seat, but Isaac stopped him. "Oh, and David?"

"Sir?"

"As far as anyone—*anyone* else is concerned, I left the bar alone. I don't care if it's family, friend, coworker or corporate rival, you didn't see me with anyone tonight."

"Yes, sir."

Letting himself into the car, he settled into the plush leather seats and breathed a short sigh. There was familiarity, even comfort, in the known, and this car was known. It was his. Something he had arranged so that each and every component suited his preferences.

As directed, the driver raised the partition between the front and back of the car before pulling away from the curb.

Rachel glanced out the window. "I assume we're going to get cards."

"If you prefer."

She looked at him, expression open, not an ounce of pretension or any sign of an agenda visible. "Where would you normally go to get cards?"

"Wherever you prefer." Light from a smartphone screen lit up the interior, and Rachel started rapidly tapping on the screen. "No need to Google directions. Tell me where you want to go and David will get us there."

"I'm not Googling directions. I'm texting my emergency contact to let her know where I am, where I'll be and when I'll be back."

"Seeing as I'm with you and don't know that information, maybe I should give you my cell and you could text me, too."

She glanced at him then back to her screen, smiling. "Smart-ass."

"Seriously, Rachel. Where to? David can drive the city for hours, but a destination would be nice."

Fingers pausing over the screen, she worried her lower lip with her teeth.

Isaac leaned forward and hit the intercom button. "The boat, please, David."

"Boat?"

"It's as good a place as any for me to school you in seven-card stud."

She laughed, that true laugh of hers that was low and sultry and a type of foreplay all its own. "Where's the boat?"

"On the harbor."

"That's a given, Isaac. I need the name."

"The Marina."

Her tapping resumed, but she paused to read a response and then shot him a sharp look. "*The* Marina?"

"The one and only."

"Are we going to the clubhouse or do you have a boat?"

"Boat."

"Slip number?"

He relayed the number and added, from memory, the manager's name and number as well as his driver's name and number, watching as she sent all the information to this mysterious emergency contact.

Rachel continued to clutch her phone even when she'd finished typing. She was clearly a good deal more nervous than he'd believed.

Sighing, he reached over and touched her forearm lightly before withdrawing. "Would you prefer I take you home?"

"No." But she didn't look at him.

Doubt began to weasel in, its insidious voice filling his mind with all the things that could go wrong, until he finally asked, "What are we doing here, Rachel?"

She swiveled around to face him, then. "My friend made me aware of who you are, Mr. Miller."

"Isaac, please. And just what did she tell you?"

"That you're the CEO of Quantum Ventures. That you're—you're…" She looked away, worrying her bottom lip.

His breath faltered, an unwilling captive trapped in his chest. He waited. Then he waited some more. When she didn't continue, wouldn't look at him, he forced himself to control his breathing. Every inhale and exhale felt forced. Possible attributes this stranger had saddled him with raced through his mind, each one hitting him with surprising, almost crippling force. Admittedly, his own imagination was likely far crueler than the simple truth. Without making a conscious decision, Isaac suddenly found himself filling in the possible blanks out loud, though in a low voice.

"I assume, based on your reaction, that your friend decried me as evil. Or am I perhaps corrupt? Has she found my name on some government watch list? Did she tell you I'm cold? Callous?" All truths—things he'd been called or labels that had been attributed to him at one time or another—that he didn't want her to have heard. Surprised at his outburst, the shock of it caught him just below the diaphragm and made him suck in a short, sharp breath. Forcing himself to slow down, to regain control of himself and his runaway mouth, he offered a more lighthearted response. "I can confirm for you I'm neither evil *nor* corrupt, but the watch-list thing? Odds are pretty good she's right."

"Cold and callous?" she asked, her voice oddly soft.

"Depends on where you sit on any given issue, but yes. I've been called both. I even earned it once. Maybe twice. Okay, fine. Three times. But that's all I'm copping to."

"Fair enough." She sighed and made a show of tucking her phone back into her clutch. "In the interest of full disclosure, you should know I've been called psychotic, a ball-busting bitch, heinous, criminally motivated, a ladder-climbing whore and a few other things that make me a potentially unsavory individual to be seen with."

He slid his glance sideways and found her mouth twitching slightly as if she was fighting the urge to grin. The breath he'd been holding escaped in a surprising rush. "I would expect you to be wise enough to bury those bodies in places they'll never be found."

She grinned and waggled her eyebrows. "Those who sleep with the fishes—"

"Have no tales to tell."

Rachel chuckled, her smile authentic. Then it faded. "She told me you're rich." A pause and she shook her head. "No. That's not accurate. Casey said you're 'filthy' rich."

"And if I told you all my money has been thoroughly laundered?"

"I'd ask if it was truly clean."

"Lily-white," he said without hesitation. "Smells like Gain detergent."

"Good to know."

Shifting to face her, Isaac looked at the first woman to have ever made him forget himself during simple conversation. "Is it a problem, Rachel? That I'm essentially criminally wealthy?" When she hesitated, he felt himself mentally stumble and raced to fill the void. "Ah, I get it. You're regretting that you didn't bet more on this poker game now that you know I'm good for it."

Her peals of laughter rang through the car. "You might be good for it, but I'm not raising the stakes, thanks."

"We don't have to do this, Rachel."

It took a moment for him to realize he was clutching the door handle in anticipation of her answer. One more facet of his control she'd fractured, and the fact irritated him. Forcing himself to breathe slowly and deeply, he released the handle and laid his arm across the back of the seat, fingers resting just inches from her tousled hair "You said it yourself earlier. Honesty. No word games."

Her chin lifted so rapidly he feared she might suffer whiplash. But when she spoke…

"I don't want you thinking I made that offer based on your net worth." She shook her head at the same time she laughed, the sound still rich but somehow a bit smaller in the vast backseat of his town car. "I had no idea who you were."

"Should you have? Known, that is."

The look she gave him, one so deep and clearly considering, stalled his next breath. He waited on her answer. Would his money matter? Would it influence her unjustly? He had never given a right damn about what anyone thought about him or his projected "worth." A man was more than the number of commas on his bank statement. And Rachel's thoughts where his true worth was concerned? For whatever reason, he felt as if her opinion of him mattered. Like *she* could matter if he paid this whole evening any attention at all.

Her opinion *matters. Nothing more*, he mentally clarified. He wouldn't allow her to get under his skin any more than she already had. He would retain control of himself, would not cede it to a woman he hardly knew, no matter how intelligent, witty or attractive she was. "I'll ask again. Should you have known, Rachel?"

Her scowl spoke volumes. "Probably."

"Why?"

"Because…" She bit her bottom lip, her eyebrows winging down as she considered her words. "Just… because."

"That's not much justification."

"I don't think I owe you justification."

"You don't owe me anything." His voice was even lower now than it had been moments before. Soft, even. Not the voice of the infamous hard-ass the business world knew as Isaac Miller. His boardroom opponents would laugh if they could see him now.

"That look on your face." She smiled, her features softening in the ambient lighting. She shifted onto her hip to better face him. "May I ask you something?"

"Of course."

"That was an easy yes."

"I don't have anything to hide."

"Fair enough. How in the world did the software program pair us, Isaac? I have to be blunt here. We're as different as day and night."

He lifted his hand from the back of the seat and

raised a single soft curl from her temple. Pausing, he gave her the chance to object.

She didn't.

"I have no idea how we were paired. You must've answered the questionnaire with great care to land such a catch."

Her eyes sparkled despite the dim lighting. "Or you did."

The laugh caught him off guard as it rushed up from somewhere deep and all but inaccessible. He reveled in the endorphin rush. When was the last time he'd laughed like this? The sobering thought tamped down the laughter, though not before he caught the surprise on her face. "You're right," he murmured, twisting the curl with care around his forefinger. "Perhaps it was I who answered with more than a little luck."

But he hadn't.

He had rushed through the questionnaire, giving it less than even half-assed answers. He'd had no intention of finding a potential partner. Not even a partner for a single evening. He'd been helping his little brother. Nothing more. But to admit as much to Rachel would be to insult her, to say that his thoughtless answers paired him with such an interesting woman while hers paired her with a man who didn't give a shit. So he shrugged. "The program was created to dig deeper, to find the common ground that superficial assessments miss. Perhaps there's more to this thing between us than simple chemistry."

"In my experience, chemistry—true chemistry—is rarely simple."

"Then maybe the program's doing exactly what it was designed to do." He tugged gently on her curl, his pulse thundering through his head louder and louder as she voluntarily moved into his space. His hand. His touch.

"It's important to me that you know I didn't come with you tonight based on your net worth. I couldn't care less, Isaac."

"Trust me. If I thought otherwise, you wouldn't be here right now."

"You're the second person to tell me to trust them tonight."

"So I am." He let go of her curl, watching it gently bounce back. Then he asked, "What do you want, Rachel? What do you truly want out of this evening?"

"A promise."

His hackles rose, and she laughed out loud. "Nothing like that. All I want is the guarantee that, whatever happens, it's all consensual, no strings attached, and we part ways on good terms with no expectations for anything more."

"Thank God." He laughed then, entirely self-deprecating.

Rachel smiled, the look a soft one she hadn't shared until that moment.

"What?"

"You don't laugh much, do you?" More observation than question.

"I don't typically find much to laugh about." The

admission made him sound cold, even callous, to his own ears, but before he could expound on the statement, she responded.

"Then you're not looking."

That stung, and he snapped back without thinking. "A bit presumptuous, don't you think?"

She seemed entirely unfazed, blowing off his little spew of temper without comment. "Do you have an executive assistant?"

"Now you're answering questions with questions?"

"Irritating...isn't it?" She gave him a wide and genuine smile.

He snorted and shook his head. "Two." At her confused look, he clarified. "I have two assistants."

"Surely one of them could schedule some downtime for you to laugh a little."

"Is laughter so important to you, then?"

The look in her eyes softened and appeared to be far, far too close to pity for his comfort. But the question that followed her look—*that* made him wince. "Is laughter not important to you at all?"

"I don't make money by scheduling 'downtime' or laughing."

She smiled softly, a bit sadly, and reached out, the move slow enough to give him time to reject her by withdrawing, but he left his hand resting on the seat between them. "You don't know what you're missing."

When she laid her hand over his, he experienced that same jolt of awareness that had hit him when they'd initially shaken hands. The sensation was stronger this time and held a level of intimacy he didn't believe had been earned. His instinct was to pull away. But he let her hand stay, resting atop his. What she said next proved to be his undoing. And once again he hadn't been prepared.

"There's so much more to life than making money, Isaac."

"Prove it."

She tugged on his hand at the same time she leaned toward him. Isaac went where she directed, not ceding control, but, rather, allowing his curiosity to be sated.

His rational mind shut down the moment their mouths met over the center seat.

Heat roared through him, a deafening rush of sound and sensation that consumed his senses and rendered him deaf to all but the small sigh loosed by the woman in his arms. She was a study of contradictions—pliant but firm, leading him even as she followed his lead, curious yet certain, innocent but tempting, angelic yet sinful.

Isaac fumbled around in the dark until he found the button that hailed the driver. David's voice came through the sound system. "Sir?"

"Take the long route to the Marina."

"Yes, sir."

Then Isaac turned his full attention on the woman at his side, his mouth finding hers as if they'd done this a hundred times before.

Rachel made a small, hungry sound, and Isaac

swallowed it down like a starving man given his first real food in weeks, months, *years*. He fed from her mouth, sipping until he couldn't contain himself. Then, for the first time he could remember, he loosened the hold he had on his control.

And desire took over.

Their hands were still joined, but he ran his free palm up the outside of her bare leg, under the edge of her dress until he reached her hip. An inch, maybe two, higher, and he found a scrap of lace that constituted her underwear.

The lace was no match for the strength of his hunger, and the fabric was gone, torn away between heartbeats.

She whimpered, a pleading, needy sound made as she suckled his lower lip. He must not have responded fast enough because she gave it a quick and demanding nip.

His cock swelled harder and faster, tenting his trousers and giving *her* free hand a destination.

She gripped his length through the linen and wool, and moaned without reserve.

"God, Rachel," he said into her mouth. "More. Tell me you want more." And she would have to tell him clearly. He wouldn't lose all control, wouldn't let a sexual haze take over and confuse what she wanted with what she consented to.

"More," she whispered, tracing her tongue down the line of his jaw.

He ran his hands through her hair and forced himself to pull away, to focus on her and wait until she focused on him. "How much more? Spell it out. I won't have misunderstandings here. Where is the line we don't cross?"

"If I say stop—"

"We stop," he interrupted before she could finish. "That's the only line."

Isaac closed the distance between their mouths without another comment or thought, and let his carnal cravings take over. The back of his brain roared with victory even as his conscious mind warned him to proceed with caution. But caution took time, calculated thinking, reserve.

None of these were available to him just now.

He pushed up her dress to her waist as she parked her knees on each side of his hips and straddled his lap.

Still gripping his cock through his pants, she pulled his member toward her and rode the ridge with abandon, rubbing the broad head where she most needed stimulation.

He reached between them to unbutton his pants and pull down his zipper. The move set free his raging erection in one efficient move.

"Sweet, bleeding hell," he said on a groan as the heat of her sex skated over the most sensitive parts of him.

Nibbling her way down his jaw as she rubbed along his length, she got to his ear and nipped the lobe, then whispered, "Condom."

Fumbling like a teenager on prom night, Isaac dug out his wallet and prayed to God he still had something in there. When he found the gold tin, he could have wept with relief. He scrabbled to find the tab, then ripped the thing open, pulled the condom free and slid it down his length. Before he could move his hand, Rachel gripped his cock by the root and sank down on him one merciless inch at a time.

Her sheath was so tight she felt almost virginal. Only his control kept him from giving in to the instinct to lunge forward and bury himself in her welcoming heat.

With his hands resting on her waist so she could set the pace of their lovemaking, he let his head fall back against the headrest. His hips slid a little lower, stopping at the seat's edge to give Rachel more room to move freely. She took advantage of the change in position and began to ride his length.

Eyes wide open, Isaac gave himself over to a wild passion, one that hovered so close to unfettered freedom that he'd never imagined it could exist.

Not for him.

CHAPTER SIX

RACHEL COULDN'T BELIEVE this was happening. She'd seized the moment and initiated that first kiss with Isaac Miller. Things between them had gone from a simmering boil to an uncontrollable inferno in roughly 0.02 seconds.

She rode his thick length with abandon, reveling in his size. Women who claimed size didn't matter had obviously never had the choice between an average penis and an above-average penis. Isaac was well above average, stretching her to the point that pleasure and discomfort converged, and separating the two became impossible.

And she loved every damn second.

Her inner walls quickly stretched, accommodating his length and girth, and she took him as deep as she could with every downward stroke. Grinding her mons against his pubic bone, she stimulated her clitoris, rocking and rubbing with more primal hunger than finesse. That would come next time. And there *would* be a next time. She wanted nothing more than to lose herself in him tonight.

She reached between them and begin to strum her clitoris, pushing herself higher as she rode him harder, crying out with frustration when he moved her hand, only to hum with appreciation when he replaced it with his own.

He worked her like a maestro, plucking and pulling and pressing at just the right moments, pushing her so far that she could no longer think, could only grab his shoulders and give her body over to his control, inherently trusting him to give her what she needed. That was when she felt it—the orgasm bearing down on her, rushing through her with a force that threatened to shatter her.

Isaac wrapped his free arm around her hips and pulled down at the same time he drove his hips up and pressed the broad pad of one thumb on her clitoris with calculated strength.

Rachel's release nearly tore her apart, ripping a shout from her throat that left her exposed, completely at his mercy as he pushed her through the first orgasm she'd had with a partner in more than five years. With his cock buried in her and her walls contracting around his solid length, it was only seconds later that she felt the repeated pulse of his orgasm work through him.

Head thrown back, the tendons in his neck strained as he rode out his own pleasure in relative silence, a single, sharp gasp the only sound he made.

Rachel couldn't have looked away even if she'd wanted to.

Small waves of sensuality rippled through her as

Isaac's hips jerked one last time, his orgasm finding its end. She wanted more, wanted to repeat that over and over tonight, so that she was physically sore tomorrow and thrilled with every aching muscle she earned between now and then.

She collapsed against him, breathing in the scent of warm wool, hot skin and the spicy yet earthy remainder of cologne on his collar. Saltiness spread across her tongue as she traced the tip of her tongue over his neck and, again, nipped his earlobe.

The car struck a bump in the road and jolted Rachel so much that Isaac had to help her retain her balance, though he withdrew from her even as he held on to her shoulders. She moved then, returning to her side of the car, and pulled her dress down around her hips as she searched for the scrap of her underwear, though she couldn't find it in the dimly lit interior.

Beside her, Isaac worked to set himself to rights. Between rustling clothes and rapid breathing slowly returning to normal, he glanced her way.

"Rachel?"

She looked up, pleased at the high color riding his cheeks. "Yes?"

"We're here."

"What do you mean 'here'?" She set her clutch beside her as she tried to wrangle her breasts back into the revealing but nonsupportive V of her dress.

"My boat."

It was then that she realized the car had stopped moving.

The windows were tinted too dark to see out of, so she moved to open her door.

Isaac reached out and stayed her hand, resting his across her forearm. "Let David get the door for you."

"David knows what we've been up to. I doubt he's inclined to open my door."

"No man will treat you as anything but a lady in my presence, Rachel."

She turned toward him, laughter catching on her huff of breath. "You know, I can't seem to decide if you're old-fashioned or contemporary, noble or a certifiable megalomaniac. Which is it, Isaac? Who are you?"

A strange look passed over his face. "Label me however you see fit. Just promise me you'll stay to-night."

He left her feeling off-balance and more than a little unsure of where they stood with each other. Conversation with him swung between easy and something that resembled a contest of wills she was never sure she won. Yet she wasn't convinced she'd lost, either.

But there was one thing she knew without a doubt, one truth that couldn't be disregarded. They were highly, *highly* compatible as lovers.

If she intended to follow through on her promise to herself and find pleasure for one evening with Mr. Right Now, she had to stop trying to understand Isaac and, instead, give herself permission to simply enjoy him. He fit her list of immediate needs, and he fit it well. Trying to force him into the mental and emotional mold she'd created for Mr. Right wasn't fair to either of them because she doubted he would, or could, qualify.

Isaac gently reached out and curled his forefinger beneath her chin, regaining her attention. Eyes on hers, he gently stroked her bottom lip with the pad of his thumb. "Stay." If he had couched a question somewhere within the command, she didn't hear it. But Mr. Right Now didn't need to defer to her, didn't need to act the gentleman all the time. He had to respect her rights and know how to get the most out of her body.

Isaac had proven that he fit both requirements.

She gave a short nod. "For tonight."

Then she stepped out of the car and gasped at the yacht the driver had pulled up to.

"This is what you call a boat?" she asked.

"By definition, it qualifies."

If this was what he called a "boat," she'd be interested in seeing what he called a "house." She was certain they had very, very different definitions. But, for tonight?

She could live with that.

CHAPTER SEVEN

WITH RACHEL'S HAND in his, Isaac led her to the moored yacht. He normally didn't give the size of the boat a second thought, but he'd been oddly concerned that Rachel would balk at his suggestion they come here if he'd made it clear that the boat was, in fact, a yacht.

His personal assistant, Collin, stepped out and inclined his head in greeting. "Mr. Miller."

Isaac let go of Rachel long enough to step onto the rear deck's planking, then turned and took her hand again, helping her step across the wooden gangway and onto the deck.

"Welcome aboard the *Patent Pending*."

Her laughter rang out across the still night air, and warmth spread through Isaac's body with an effect similar to that of a generous shot of whiskey. The sound was so uncomplicated. Pure. Authentic.

Isaac found himself smiling in return.

Rachel turned toward him, and what had been a look of amused curiosity on her face softened, evolving with every beat of his heart until her expression settled on something far more intimate. She seemed to realize she had revealed something quite personal and abruptly turned away. Approaching Collin, she held out her hand. "I'm Rachel. Rachel Stephens."

Instead of shaking her hand, Collin kissed her knuckles. "The pleasure is entirely mine, madam. My name is Collin. I'm Mr. Miller's personal assistant."

She shot Isaac a funny look, one that silently asked, "You have a personal assistant?"

Isaac shoved his hands in his pockets, rocking heel-to-toe and back as he answered. "He prefers that particular title over 'butler.' I indulge him because it keeps him in my employ."

"Why do you need a personal assistant?"

"It's my job to keep him in line and, at times, focused, Ms. Stephens," Collin interjected.

"Collin tends to grossly overestimate his value and underestimate my self-sufficiency," Isaac grumbled good-naturedly. "I don't have the heart to correct him for fear he'll lose his obviously tenuous grip on reality."

"Had I known I was agreeing to spend the evening with a yacht-owning philanthropist, I might have been a bit nervous." She leaned toward Collin, laid a hand on his arm and, in a stage whisper, said, "It's a good thing he pretended to be a rather self-involved, disinterested, somewhat self-deprecating individual. That managed to keep my expectations for the evening in check when I found out he was, actually, filthy rich."

Collin glanced at Isaac, unable to mask his surprise. True, Isaac normally would have taken someone to task for calling him self-involved, be it true or not. He would even agree that he did, indeed, have a penchant for keeping his world ordered. That might make him come across as self-involved in some situations. But to agree that he was self-deprecating? At all? No one would believe that description. Ever. He was completely confident, both in himself and in the world he'd created with money and sheer force of will.

Still, this was Rachel. He was clearly inclined toward leniency where she was concerned. And his current easygoing nature was, without a doubt, a direct result of the mind-blowing orgasm he'd just experienced.

Collin clapped his hands together and rubbed them briskly. "What are the evening's plans, Mr. Miller?"

He looked out over the inlet. "How's the water tonight?"

"Calm. Wind is out of the northwest at roughly five knots. Skies are clear. If I may, sir, I'd suggest a short sail out into open waters. Ms. Stephens might enjoy the night sky absent the city's light pollution." Collin gave her a small smile. "The stars are magnificent when viewed from the upper deck."

"Please, call me Rachel. And while it sounds lovely," she murmured, "I wouldn't want to create any unnecessary work."

"Work is, by definition, necessary to one's continued employment." Collin gave Isaac a sharp nod. "I'll have the captain point us to sea while I put together some finger foods and drinks." He strode off with purpose, leaving Isaac and Rachel alone.

"Are you up for a short sail?"

She moved to the nearest railing and watched as the crew worked to release the moorings and push off from the dock. "It's fine with me, though I'm not sure how my friend would reach me if I needed to call her."

"The boat has Wi-Fi. The password is *penniesand-pounds*."

She snorted rather indelicately. "Of course it is."

Isaac stepped up behind Rachel, pressing his chest to her back and resting his hands on either side of hers on the railing. "Do you need to call her, Rachel?"

She shook her head. "Do you do this with every date?"

"I don't date."

Leaning her head back, she rested against his shoulder and stared out across the dark water. "What about lovers? Surely you take a lover now and then."

"I haven't had a lover in… Let's just say it's been a very long time."

She huffed out a small sound of disbelief.

"It's the truth. I haven't had the time or the inclination to get involved with anyone."

"That's a lonely way to live."

"I'm surrounded by people all day every day. Each one of them is constantly making demands of me. By the end of the day, all I want is to sit down, alone, and have a beer in silence. No one asking me for anything. No one giving me news, bad or good, that requires my action. No one expecting me to fix whatever is currently broken. No one pitching me an idea from their mother's bunco partner's son's grandson in the hopes they can bypass the process and have a direct 'in' to the decision makers.

"I'm alone, Rachel, but that doesn't translate to lonely. Not by any stretch of the imagination."

"That's fair."

"So what about you? Boyfriend? Lover? Husband?"

She stiffened and then pointedly moved one of his hands aside to push past him. "If I was in any type of committed relationship, even if it wasn't going well, I wouldn't be here right now. I don't condone cheating and won't tolerate being cheated on. I'm worth more than that."

"A simple 'no' would have sufficed."

"Under most circumstances, I'd agree with you. But that won't cut it with me, Isaac. Not when we're discussing faithfulness." She crossed her arms tightly under her breasts and turned to watch the receding city lights. "You should know that up front."

"This is obviously a sore spot."

She continued to stare out over the pitch-black water.

"What happened?" When she still didn't answer, he pushed. "Who cheated on you?"

"I'd prefer to leave my history where it belongs." Her gaze met his then, full of heat and fury and such a clear, raw pain. "Behind me."

She'd been hurt. Badly hurt. That much was obvious. And whoever it was that had hurt her had done so by breaking promises. The extent of those promises, Isaac could only guess. The very idea insulted even his somewhat stunted sense of chivalry. There were things one just did not *do* when involved in any type of committed relationship, or any relationship for that matter. Cheating was at the top of the list, right after physical abuse. Tied with lying.

The idea of Rachel's pristine skin suffering any untoward handling had him clenching his fists as he asked through gritted teeth, "Did he hit you?"

"What? No!" She shook her head, her hair making a susurrous sound as it slid over her shoulders and along her arms. "No," she repeated, more in control of her response. "I'd have cut off his testicles while he was sleeping."

He liked this side of her as much as her softer side, liked that she was, again, the perfect vision of strength and self-sufficiency. "Good."

She shook her head and turned back to the sea, the wind carrying her words to him. "I would have thought that you, as a man, would be offended at the idea of any man's preciouses being mistreated."

Settling one hand on her waist, Isaac stepped close enough to lean in and press his lips to the hair that covered her nearest ear. "It's inexplicably sexy, this image of you strutting into prison to a standing ovation."

She shook with silent laughter beneath his hand before settling her back against his chest, her ass against his groin. It wasn't lost on him how well they fit, and he would have thought he'd be fighting the urge to step away and reclaim his space.

He wasn't.

But he did.

She didn't follow but, rather, held her place at the railing.

Part of him had wanted her to pursue him. That was a known element. This—her ease with herself and her self-assurance where he was concerned—was new. So new it was an anomaly. When he asked himself why it mattered what she did, there was just…nothing. No immediate answer. No forthcoming answer. Hell, nothing at all. The only thing he received was internal silence paired with slight unease.

God help him, this woman had turned him into a damn mess.

So Isaac moved in close, rested his hands on her waist and urged her back against him.

She came to him without hesitation, snuggling back so that his cock nestled in the crease of her ass. That? That worked just fine. Particularly when he began to harden again as they shifted to keep their balance, the result being a gentle stroking motion against the sensitive head of his cock.

Rachel hummed her approval and wiggled against him to bring him closer.

Lowering his face to her neck, he dropped a slow, openmouthed kiss against skin that smelled faintly of expensive perfume. He'd smelled it before but couldn't name it. Whatever it was, it was green and woody with a hint of musk—a perfume suited to a confident woman.

Perfect for *this* woman.

"Like that, is it?" Arms crossed over her abdomen, she laced their fingers together. "And here I thought we had come to the 'boat' in order to play cards."

"The 'boat' is good for many things. Playing cards is just one of them."

"You'll spot me a cigar and a beer, right? If I had known I'd need a stogie tonight, I would have carried a larger handbag."

For the second time tonight, he busted out laughing without thinking it through and staying the reaction. And just like before, the action—reaction?—irritated him as much as it surprised him, though this time wasn't quite as jarring as the first had been.

She let him spin her in a dancer's twirl and pull her back into his embrace, where he began swaying to and fro. "You muddy what is normally a clear mind. For me, anyway."

The smile she gifted him was breathtaking in the starlight. "You're welcome."

"And why is that?"

"You don't seem to laugh much. That's a shame."

"And why, again, is that?" he asked, curiosity piqued.

"Your laugh is sexy as hell." Rachel went up on her tiptoes and nipped his chin, encouraging him to lower his face to hers. He did as she wordlessly bade, and she rose again, this time stealing a kiss.

They stood there on the dark deck.

She tasted him.

He tasted her.

They explored each other, and their hands followed their mouths' joint precedent. Her small sounds of pleasure pushed him higher, encouraging him to go farther, to find bare skin.

Breaking the kiss, Rachel dropped to her heels. "I'm guessing that Collin, your butler-who's-more-personal-assistant-and-finger-food-chef, could walk out at any moment."

"He better not," Isaac all but growled. "I pay him better than that."

She chuckled even as she took his hand and backed toward the nearest pair of sliding glass doors. "Surely this rickety dinghy has a horizontal surface *somewhere*."

"Dinghy, huh? I don't think she's ever been so insulted."

"She'll survive."

"I'll have her brass polished and make Collin sweet-talk her while he does it."

"Rich men are such snobs."

Taking her hand, he rested it over the length of his throbbing cock.

"Hmm." She palmed him before changing to long, slow strokes. "You need to see a doctor about this, sir?"

"I'd rather see a particular lawyer in this case."

"Lucky for you, I'm on a one-night exclusive retainer."

She closed the paper-thin distance, opening herself to him. His hands. His kiss.

Isaac plundered her mouth, his tongue tracing her

lips, her teeth, before seeking hers. It was an intimate duel, one of thrusts and parries, with an outcome that would have two winners.

She returned his attention with equal fervor. Every move she made affirmed for him that they weren't yet done with each other. Every sound solidified her intent. Her every touch declared that she intended to slay the demons he'd roused.

And his body was her weapon of choice.

Anyone could see them, standing as they were on the open deck. Rachel pulled away from him and, grabbing his hand, backed up, trusting him to guide her. Or at least keep her from falling overboard.

His lips were swollen from the passionate kiss they'd just shared. A small smudge of lipstick—her lipstick—marked his collar. She couldn't help but think the deep brownish red, labeled Jungle Vixen, was a good color on him.

"Which way to the bedroom?"

He smirked. "She has six. Take your pick."

"'She' again. Why is that?"

"Every good boat is a 'she.'"

"I'll make sure to let the United States Navy know they need to rechristen a few of their boats."

He stumbled. "Boats? Good God, Rachel. Don't let the navy hear you call their warships 'boats.'"

"Boats. Ships. Warships. Why are the 'warships' not classified as 'she'? Seems a little inequality might be at play here." She paused. "You don't think women are warriors?"

He moved closer with panther-like grace. "If I'd ever been so foolish as to entertain that idea, you would have changed my mind tonight." Leaning in, he nipped her lower lip.

"Good save." She couldn't help but wonder if he always knew what to say to when backed into a corner.

He slid an arm around her waist and then bent and hooked the other behind her knees, lifting her with ease.

She squeaked, a sound she found embarrassingly feminine. "Don't carry me, Isaac."

"Why?"

"I'm too heavy."

"Bullshit." But he stopped and looked at her. "Let me carry you to bed, Rachel. Please."

"Just…" Heat burned up her neck and across her cheeks. "You swear I'm not too heavy?"

"Don't impugn my manhood here, woman. I shouldn't have to tell you that my carrying you is a wildly romantic gesture."

Burying her face in his neck, she murmured, "Don't do something ridiculous like throw your back out."

"I won't. I'm curious, though. Where's the concern coming from?"

She kissed his neck and couldn't help but feel empowered when he shivered. "I'm not done with you tonight. An emergency-room visit for a slipped disc isn't part of my plans."

"If I slip a disc, it'll be because I'm rushing. You

have no idea how sexy you are or how much I want you to carry out your plans for the evening."

"And if those plans are simply a card game?"

"I'll spot you the cigar, as promised. But, Rachel?" He paused and leaned down, bringing his lips to within a hairbreadth of hers. "If you told me all you wanted was a poker game, I'd honor that."

"I know."

"That's all that matters." He toed open the sliding glass door and strode down the narrow hall, carefully twisting and turning, as if to ensure he didn't bang Rachel's head or feet on a wall.

She gasped when he stepped through a doorway and kicked the door shut before settling her on a massive bed. Looking around, she feigned indifference. "An actual king-size bed. I'm impressed."

He arched an eyebrow. "What did you expect?"

She grinned at him. "Bunks? A U-shaped dinette? Maybe a fish-gutting table."

Isaac peeled off his jacket and tossed it toward a chair in the corner of the not insubstantial room… and missed. "Not on this dinghy." Then he started working on his tie.

Rachel rose to her knees, then crawled across the bed, stopping only when she placed her hands over his at his collar. He stilled, looking down at her. For a moment, her mind went blank.

His blue eyes, framed by black lashes, had darkened several shades and developed an immeasurable depth. But they held something new.

Excitement.

His facial features were as defined as before, but they were decidedly less harsh.

Softened.

And the flush of his skin might be attributed to the brisk wind that had buffeted them on deck, but she saw something else there, as well.

Anticipation.

She hadn't taken the time to pay attention before, and the car's dark backseat hadn't been conducive to noticing the small things. Admittedly, she hadn't been interested in the small things, either. All she had wanted was him. His body. An orgasm.

The memory made her thighs clench and her sex ache.

Isaac lifted a hand and gently cupped her jaw, tracing his thumb along her cheek. The tip of his thumb brushed her lower lashes. He smiled when she blinked. "The way your pupils expand when you're turned on…"

"Surely they're not any larger than a dime."

"Try a pair of Lincolns," he countered.

"No way."

"Two nickels, on my honor."

"Do you always have to be right?"

"No. It's just that I *am* always right."

"Mmm-hmm. Keep believing that. It's bound to keep your bed warm."

"Tonight, I have you."

"Tonight." The affirmation was unexpected. Worse? It stung.

She knew she had no reason to expect more. Hell,

she'd been the one to initiate this one-night stand. Not once had she thought beyond the moment, she'd been so intent on reclaiming her life with Mr. Right *Now*. Isaac fit that bill.

There was no denying he was well outside the type of man she had traditionally looked for, dated and, yes, even married. They were from such different worlds. His "dinghy" bedroom was larger than the one in her apartment. His annual club membership was likely more than her annual salary. She had only just scored approval to hire a paralegal, whereas Isaac had two executive assistants…and a private *personal* assistant. But they did have raw, undisputable chemistry.

That was all a one-night stand required.

Leaning down, he brushed his lips over hers. "Where did you go, Rachel?"

"Mental walkabout."

"Come back to me."

Her chest tightened, and she couldn't help but wonder what it would feel like to hear him say those words with meaning. Purpose. Desire. Not that he didn't want her, but if he truly *wanted* her.

Sinking back to rest her butt on her heels, she let one hand wander down the buttons on his shirt. "I assume you have a tailor?"

His brow furrowed. "I do."

Gripping the front tails of his shirt, one in each hand, she pulled. The first button popped off, pinging across the built-in dresser's marble top.

"Objections?" she asked, her voice low. Sultry.

"None."

That was what she'd wanted to hear. With a single swift yank, his shirt buttons pinged around the room. The shirt hung open and left his chest exposed, his skin still bearing the last vestiges of a summer tan. Mission accomplished. The temptation to take him in in visual gulps almost overwhelmed her. Forcing herself to slow down was almost more than she could stand. But this moment and this man were meant to be savored.

So she did.

His pecs were much more defined than she had expected and so firm she could have bounced a quarter off the top of each muscle. The planes of his abdomen were sculpted but not egregiously so. He clearly worked out, took care of himself, but he wasn't muscle-bound.

With his belt loose and his pants hanging low on his hips, his obliques created funnels to the ultimate final destination. But Rachel still wanted to look and luxuriate in his sheer maleness. To appreciate him for the way he'd not only taken care of but had also sculpted his body. If it was a shrine, she planned on worshipping there with fervor all night.

Tracing her hands lower, reveling in every peak and valley, she reached his waistband and paused before curling her fingers over the edge. Her fingertips brushed the tip of his erection and came away damp with arousal.

He sucked in a breath. "Enough play."

"Never." She worked his zipper free and let go, watching his pants pool around his ankles. His cock strained at the boxer briefs he wore, the head breaching the elastic waistband.

Impulse drove her to lean in and quickly trace her tongue over the exposed crown.

Isaac's hips jerked forward as his hands flexed open and closed, seeking something to hold on to.

She kneeled before him on the bed. "Honest question."

He gripped his shirt front and pulled down until the fabric strained over his shoulders. "You want to *talk*? *Now*?"

"Yeah. I do."

"I'll trade you conversation for losing the dress."

She reached for the zipper at her back and paused. "Answer my first question and I'll drop the zipper."

"The whole dress."

"And you want to negotiate now?" Folding her hands in her lap, she smiled demurely. "Not happening."

"Damn it, Rachel. You're killing me. I want to see your body. All of it. In the light. Not try to make out details by the diluted light of oncoming traffic. Just…" He tunneled his hands through his hair…and immediately finger-combed it into a semblance of submission. Then he set about picking up the buttons that had scattered when she'd removed his shirt, gathering them all before opening a drawer on the built-in dresser and depositing them inside. When he retrieved his shirt, folded it and set it on top of the dresser, her suspicions were confirmed.

Isaac Miller was a man who needed order and control.

Part of Rachel wanted to panic. Jeff, her ex, had tried to control her. No, not control exactly. More that he'd tried to dominate her in every aspect of their relationship. Isaac had kept his need for control to himself. Literally. He'd not once tried to control *her* but, rather, had tried to negotiate what he wanted while keeping his own person and his surroundings controlled. When it came to his treatment of her? There had been nothing but respect. That made Isaac different than Jeff. And different was what she needed tonight.

She shifted her body to give him a good look at her cleavage, teasing him and, in an unexpected turn, being teased by him when she saw the way his eyes flared as they took her in. Running a hand up the front of her dress, she hooked her pointer finger over the fabric and tugged just enough to expose more flesh. "Answer my questions, Isaac, and the dress comes off."

He cursed, short and swift and colorful, then gave a curt nod. "At this point? Ask me anything and I'll answer just to see you lying across my bed with nothing but the shoes on."

"When was the last time a woman went down on you?"

His eyes tightened, small crow's feet appearing at the corners. "Does it matter?"

"If you want this to come off—" she let one shoulder of the dress slip "—you'll answer me, and not with another question. What happens next is up to you."

"It's been a while."

"Which translates to how long?"

"I don't know for sure."

Her eyebrows winged up. "Are you serious?"

He dragged a hand down his face. "This is a bit uncomfortable for me."

Without a word, she dropped the dress from her shoulders to her waist and revealed the long-line bra she wore. All of it—the deep V in the front; the low corset back; the demi cups that supported her breasts; the lace edge of each cup that barely revealed each dusky nipple's crest.

Isaac let out a soft groan. Jaw clenched, he reached for her and then stopped himself, letting his hand fall back to his side.

He didn't look away, though, and Rachel swore the weight of his gaze was so heavy it could have been measured.

His cock kicked, pushing away from his belly before the elastic pulled it back against his abdomen.

"Rachel," he said, not pleading, exactly, but not far from it. "I'm going to assume you asked about my history for a reason."

"I did." Lifting her left breast from the lace cup, she gently rolled the nipple between her thumb and forefinger.

He watched without blinking.

A growl rumbled up from deep in his chest. "I can't think with you touching yourself like that."

"Good."

He shot her the briefest glance. "Good?" he choked out.

She lowered her voice. "That means we're even."

Isaac let his head fall back and he groaned loud this time. "Please, Rachel."

With decided casualness, she removed the bra and tossed it onto the floor, where it landed across one of his feet.

Rising up, she shimmied the rest of the way out of her dress. He'd done away with her underwear in the car, so all she had on were the shoes.

As requested, she left them.

Slipping off the bed, she stood before him in nothing but the shoes, her hair tumbling around her.

He touched her then, tracing a finger down her neck, across her décolletage, between her breasts and then under so he could palm one breast. When he dragged his thumb across her already swollen nipple, he did so with the softest touch.

Her sex clenched tight when, without warning, he dipped his head and suckled that same nipple with just enough force that her knees nearly buckled. She ran her fingers through his hair and held on to him, encouraging him to show the other breast the same attention.

"Greedy, are you?"

"Hungry," she said on a gasp. "Hungry for you, Isaac."

"You've got me."

And that was what she wanted right then. Him. Only him.

Seduction had been her sole intent. *Her* seduction of *him*. But he had flipped the tables so fast that she was forced to take a step back before she begged him to take her against the wall.

All from a little breast play.

Like she'd realized early on, chemistry wasn't a problem for them.

But she still wanted to taste him, to have him at her mercy, to hear him call her name and beg for more. And she knew the fastest way to get exactly what she wanted.

Stepping back, she ignored his protest and went to her knees. With intentionally slow movements, she gripped the bottom edge of his boxer briefs and pulled, watching as the elastic waist slipped down and his cock sprang free. She chanced a quick look up, thrilling at the wild look on his face, the way he instinctively spread his legs and reached down to cup his balls.

He wanted this as much as, possibly even more than, she did.

Running her hands up the insides of his thighs, she encircled the base of his cock, pulled the head away from his abdomen and took him all the way to the root. Took him so deep that her nose bumped his pelvis. She rose at a leisurely pace, letting his cock slide along her lips until the crown popped free.

Isaac gasped, his hips lurching forward with such lack of control she knew he had stopped thinking and, instead, started experiencing. And that? That was what she had wanted all along—someone to go on this wild, one-night ride with her, a lover invested in their *mutual* satisfaction versus someone who had a one-sided agenda.

Rachel nibbled the flushed head of his cock, using her teeth to tease and add another layer of sensation.

He leaned back and, using one arm, braced himself against the dresser. "Oh. My. G—"

She swallowed him to the root again, this time working her way up and down the length of him in rapid up-and-down movements that simulated the sex act and left him pumping his hips in time with the pace she set.

Continuing to slide up and down his length, tasting the building evidence of his pleasure, she was surprised when he rested his hand on the crown of her head and encouraged her to slow down. She was about to balk when he ran his fingers through her hair and whispered, "Your mouth is magic, Rachel. Sheer magic."

He shifted, changing the angle at which he thrust between her lips.

She accommodated the change, which required her to go even slower.

"Your tongue…" He sucked in a sharp breath as she traced the underside of the crown. "God, right there."

And she focused on the spot that drove him wild.

He started to move then, and she followed his lead, gently nudging aside his hand so that she could palm his sac and encourage him to find his release.

Isaac bent his knees and lost himself to the culmination of the pleasure she'd brought him.

He swept down and, for the second time that night,

scooped her up in his arms. This time, he settled her in bed with a kiss on the forehead and climbed in beside her. "My turn," he said, lips pressed to her forehead.

He left a trail of kisses as he worked his way down her body, his lips and mouth and teeth doing things to her that made her mind blank and her nerves fire in rapid bursts of sensation. When he got to the apex of her thighs, he didn't slow down. Instead, he parted her legs wider and worked her clitoris between his upper lip and tongue until she was writhing with pleasure, crying out as the first orgasm hit. Isaac didn't give her a chance to recover before he drove her to her second orgasm, an experience just as intense as the first.

Lying limp beneath him proved the best she could do as small aftershocks played across her nervous system. A slight tap-tap-tap of a finger against her hip tried to get her attention.

"Rachel is busy having an out-of-body experience. Please leave a message at the beep," she murmured. "Beep."

"No message necessary," he responded, and the bed shifted with his weight as he prowled back up her body.

The familiar sound of foil being torn had her turning her head to one side and watching with anticipation as he slipped a condom over the length of his hardened cock.

"You do things to me," he said softly, not looking at her.

"What kind of things?" she asked, trying not to smile at the sound of her voice—so satiated—and failing.

He lifted one shoulder. "Things I can't really articulate."

Then he moved between her thighs, nudging them wide and then wider, before taking her left leg and draping it over his shoulder. She must've looked a bit surprised because he smiled as he propped himself up and slipped his free hand under her ass.

"Better—" he rapidly thrust forward and down "—penetration."

Rachel lost her mind as he filled her, stretching her sensitive flesh and driving into her without slowing. She thrashed beneath him, trying to move in time with him, but the way he held her, the way his cock thrust so rapidly and his pelvis ground against her clitoris, all she could do was experience.

One moment she was caught in the throes of passion, and the next her fourth orgasm of the evening was wracking her body. There was no warning. No sense of impending release. It simply happened, threatening to tear her limb from limb as she thrashed beneath Isaac's weight, crying out and demanding more, demanding cessation.

Both.

All.

None.

Until she couldn't take it anymore and simply gave herself to the pleasure, to the man who owned her body and played it like a maestro.

She was coming down, every muscle lax, when

Isaac made a small sound that drew her gaze to his. He watched her; never looked away. Muscles in his neck were corded with the strength of his own release, and his movements became less and less controlled until he pumped his hips in a frantic way and then she felt it. The pulse of his orgasm. The way it worked down the length of his shaft.

Lazily lifting her hand to his shoulder, she felt the desperation leave his muscles and he collapsed atop her, his lungs working like an industrial bellows as he fought to regain control of his breathing.

She'd brought him to this point, this place where he'd nearly given up control.

And she liked that she'd been the one to make it happen.

Almost, anyway.

Without a word, he rolled to the side, pulled her against him and spooned her, his hand cradling her hip.

Her eyes grew heavy and she let sleep come. She was almost across that dark threshold when she thought Isaac said something—something that sounded suspiciously like "We're far from done."

She hoped that was exactly what he'd said.

But first, she needed sleep.

CHAPTER EIGHT

SUNLIGHT BREACHED THE windowsill and crept across the pillow until it struck the strand of hair Isaac had been rolling between his fingers. Rachel was lying in front of him, her lips, still slightly swollen from the night before, parted just a bit as she breathed deeply and slowly.

Asleep.

He knew the agreement they'd had—they would enjoy each other for a night. They'd done just that. Man, had they ever.

He wondered which direction she'd take things this morning. Would she bolt? Would she linger? Maybe insist they share a leisurely breakfast? Would she try to get him to confess to having some un-named feeling for her?

Chances were good she wouldn't try to make their night anything more than it had been. More realistically, she'd discover they were docked and call for a ride—either the friend she'd referred to last night or a cab.

Would she ask to see him again?

He wouldn't bet on it.

He scowled. What was it about *that* that pissed him off? Women routinely wanted to see him again, wanted to create something where nothing existed. Those women were easy enough to gently send away. No need to hurt feelings. But Rachel was…different. Could he let her leave, let things go under the pretense that nothing really existed between them?

Not going there.

Would she leave him her number?

He knew the answer to this one without a doubt: she would…if he asked.

And he wouldn't.

Isaac had seen and done a great many things in his life, but pursuing one woman exclusively didn't make the list.

And it never would.

There was too much at risk; too much that couldn't be predicted and, therefore, protected.

Rachel made a small sound in her sleep and snuggled deeper into her pillow.

God, she was beautiful in the early-morning light.

"Beautiful in any light," he whispered.

The way his life was structured suited him, and he didn't see the value in changing something that worked so well.

But doesn't she work well for you? The question, one he hadn't even been aware he'd been bandying about, was a legitimate one.

She did, in fact, suit him in many ways. Sure, she was his opposite. And the way she tested his control made him mentally itchy. But she drove him insane in an entirely different manner when their clothes came off. And *insane* was the right word considering that he was even entertaining the thought of seeing her again.

There was something so undeniably different about her. She was the first woman he could remember who made him want one more moment with her, another round between the sheets. One more of anything that would keep her within his reach.

His phone buzzed, and he realized with a start that it was Friday.

A workday.

And he was late.

Isaac was *never* late. Particularly for work.

Gently rolling away, he dug his phone out of his jacket pocket and saw his brother's number flashing on his display.

"What time is it?" Rachel asked, her voice raspy with sleep.

Isaac sent his brother straight to voice mail before he turned to the woman in his bed. "It's seven forty-five."

The covers flew back and she nearly fell out of bed. "Shit! Shit, shit, shit! I have to go!"

Every component of the conversation he'd had with himself—every argument for not seeing her again, every rationale for letting the morning be the end of things—evaporated. Only one single word came to mind. "Stay."

She paused, pushing her mane of hair out of her

face and revealing eyes gone wide with surprise. "What?"

"Stay." He cleared his throat. What the hell was he thinking? But he carried on despite the idiocy of the request. "Stay. Today. With me." *What the hell. In for a penny, in for a pound.* "We'll go somewhere for the weekend."

"And what?" she croaked.

"Spend time together."

"Doing what, exactly?"

"Plotting world peace? Just spending time together, Rachel. I enjoyed your company and was under the impression you might have enjoyed mine." He shifted to better see her. "We can take the weekend and figure out what this is, figure out what's going on between us."

Rachel sank down on the edge of the bed, twisting the dark material of her dress until it was a crumpled mess, her bare toes curling into the plush carpet. "Where?"

He shrugged. "Anywhere you want."

A small laugh escaped her, and she slapped a hand over her mouth. "Sorry," she said, looking down with obvious dismay to find she'd turned her dress into an impossibly worse mess. She smoothed the wrinkled fabric, stretching it this way and that in a futile effort to straighten it even moderately before she gave up and slipped it on. "I can't. I have to go to work." She turned and presented her bare back. "Zip me up, would you?"

"I'm not throwing this out there without some

thought, Rachel. I would very much like you to spend the weekend with me."

She glanced back at him, her face a riot of emotions. "I'd like that, Isaac. Truly. But I have to go to work. You might be the one the Lord goes to for a personal loan, but I, unfortunately, don't have that type of financial freedom."

"You're an attorney," he stated, as if she might have forgotten.

"Right. With all the student-loan debt that accompanies the job title. I don't have a choice." She shook her head, then darted across the room to grab her shoes. "Then, when you add the outrageous rent I pay for a one-bedroom studio in the city? I have to work. I did try, once, to get my landlord to accept *Monopoly* money for my rent." She grinned over her shoulder, the look bright and unfettered. "He wasn't amused."

"Call in sick." He knew he sounded irascible, but he didn't care. He wasn't ready for this to end.

Shoes in hand, she turned to face him. "Excuse me?"

"Call in sick." He shrugged. "People do it all the time."

"'People' might, but I don't. Ever. It's not ethical."

"Be that as it may, it tells me you have the time on the books. You must get at least five days a year. If you don't 'ever' use them, then the days are available. So use one."

"And where would we go?"

"Like I said, anywhere you want."

"Dublin."

"Ireland?"

"No, Isaac. Dublin, Ohio."

"I'm not sure what's there, but if that's where you really want to go? Sure."

She moved so fast he didn't have time to avoid the pillow she chucked at him. Before the first one hit the floor, she'd armed herself with another and was poised to pitch it, as well. "Yes, Ireland. Dublin, Ireland. If you meant it when you said anywhere, it's the place I want to go more than anywhere else in the world. For the chance to go, even for a weekend? I'd call in."

Satisfaction moved through him like a warm wind. If visiting Ireland was her greatest wish? He could make that happen a hundred, even a thousand times.

Moving with deceptive casualness, he retrieved his phone and tossed it to her. It landed on the bed, inches in front of her. "Call in."

"You're serious."

"I would think you'd realize by now that I don't make offers I can't, or won't, follow through on, Rachel. I don't play games."

"You're insane." Grabbing her clutch, she seemed as if she was about to leave. Instead, she pulled out her phone. A few taps to the screen and she held the phone to her ear, her pointer finger hovering over her lips in a shushing gesture. The sound of ringing, a recorded greeting and, finally, the beep cueing her to leave a message. She looked at him with wide eyes, her hesitation as clear as the crisp blue sky outside.

He nodded once toward the phone.

"Jim, I won't be in today. I have to take care of something that came up unexpectedly. I'll use a personal day to cover the absence. Feel free to call if there's an emergency and I'll do my best to get back to you before the day is out. Otherwise, I'll talk to you Monday." She disconnected and let her hand fall to her side, the phone slipping free and hitting the floor with a muted plunk.

He stepped across the room and bent low, sweeping her phone off the floor and deftly turning off the ringer. "I thought you were going to call in sick."

She lowered herself onto the edge of the bed. "I didn't want to lie."

The woman was an anomaly, without a doubt. But he appreciated that about her. "I admire your honesty."

"I wish I felt better about it being actual honesty." She slumped forward and sighed, then abruptly stood. "I can't go to Dublin wearing a dress that needs to see the cleaner before it sees the light of day, so I need to go back to my place and pick up some more appropriate clothes. And I'll need my passport."

"We'll get something at the airport that will tide you over. There are always sweats available. And, if you'll allow it, I'll have Collin go by your place while we're getting ready. He can grab your passport and bring it to the airport."

"It won't be easier to just have me get it and some clothes?"

"By the time you decide what to wear, what you want to take versus leave, what makeup you want and so on?" His mouth curled at the gentle truth. "To be blunt? No. It won't be more sensible let alone easier."

"Fine." She dug out her key and handed it over. "And then what?"

He smiled. "Before anything? A promise."

Her brow furrowed. "What kind of promise?"

"An easy one." He retrieved his own phone and made a point of showing her he was turning off the ringer. "No work this weekend. No taking calls, sneaking to read texts in the bathroom, et cetera. If we're going, we're going all out."

"I won't if you won't. Deal?"

He saluted her with his phone before depositing it in his pants pocket. "Deal. Let's get to the airport. We're on the front side of rush hour, but it'll still be a solid hour to get there. We can be in the air by nine thirty and in Dublin in time for a late dinner. We'll shop for weather-appropriate clothes first thing tomorrow morning."

She laughed out loud, the look of joy on her face absolutely priceless. "I can't believe I'm doing this."

"Neither can I."

"Then why *are* you doing it?"

Gathering his pants and buttonless shirt, he dressed so much as he was able and left the room without answering her, because the truth was something he couldn't quite put into words, and to lie to

her would mean setting a precedent that had histori-
cally proven all too easy to fall into where women
were concerned. So he said nothing. That didn't stop
the truth from ringing through his head, though.
Why was he doing this?

Because I want to.

CHAPTER NINE

RACHEL LOVED THE smell of Irish wool. Silly, she knew, but there was something different about it, like it held the warmth inherent to the few Irish natives she had met in the single hour she'd been in Dublin.

Isaac had been efficient, arranging for their flight and a car and driver to meet them at the private strip at Dublin's international airport. They'd been whisked away to a shop where Isaac was now outfitting her against the damp chill of the Irish fall. Outside, rain fell in a singular sheet that created a steady percussion, the sound creating white noise that threatened to lull her to sleep where she stood. The shop was warm and she'd been plied with tea and biscuits as she settled in to try on the growing mountain of clothes her lover seemed to think she needed, but all she wanted to do was sleep. And see the city. And go back to bed with the man who'd brought her to this amazing place.

This whole trip seemed surreal—an out-of-body experience her logical mind couldn't make fit. Couldn't rationalize. The experience was one she didn't want to make sense of, though. It was simply too incredible to let reality seep in, because reality would ruin everything.

The first thing it would dismantle would be the man at her side. She was enamored with him, more so than she had ever deemed possible and certainly more than she cared to admit. This—this... *thing* between them was supposed to have been her one-night, take-her-life-back stand, and it was fast developing into something more. Something she was afraid to put a name to, afraid to speak out loud, as if acknowledging it would somehow make it all disappear like a curl of smoke in the wind. Likewise, she was terrified that if she tried to hold on to it, this new and fragile and wild thing would slip through her fingers. So what was she to do?

"Did you find an emergency exit and bolt?" Isaac asked, his tone infused with a sense of humor she had only caught a glimpse of since they'd met.

The last time had been on the flight, right after the pilot advised them to buckle their seat belts as they prepared to land. She'd lost all sense of cool and scrambled to the window with childlike enthusiasm. It was, after all, Ireland—her first glimpse of the Emerald Isle up close. She'd waited a lifetime for that particular moment. Isaac had impulsively tugged her hair and told her to sit down so they could land. She had huffed in impatience and flopped into her seat, and that was when she'd seen it—that glimpse of a genuine smile that lit his face from within. As desirable as anything, or anyone, she had ever seen in her life.

That was also when she had experienced that first real awareness, when like called to like, and she saw him not as a momentary lover but as someone who could be more if he cared to be. The realization had scared her silent, the awareness acting as an anchor that weighed her sharp retort so it fell off her tongue, down her throat and into the rising abyss of remorse left by her ex-husband.

She had been grateful Isaac hadn't pushed her as they landed, hadn't tried to get her to own what was bothering her. Instead, he'd left her alone. Almost too much so. That he was warming to her again made her relax. Breathe easier.

"Rachel?" he called again. "Come out and show me your outfit or I'm coming in there."

"You wouldn't dare," she replied, more in control of herself than she'd been even seconds before. "That would cause a scandal in such a conservative country, and the last thing you want is your name in the paper."

"I couldn't care less," he answered, closer this time. "You have ten seconds to come out, or I swear to you I'm coming in."

"Would serve you right," she mumbled, tugging at the sweater's hem and adjusting the fit so the garment hung evenly just below her natural waist. The jeans he'd picked out for her fit like a glove, but she still needed comfortable walking shoes, a couple pairs of underwear, basic toiletries—all the things to get her through a weekend in Dublin. "Dublin," she mused aloud.

The dressing-room curtain was yanked aside, metal rings clattering against the curtain rod, and there he stood. A smile toyed at the corners of his mouth. "If you don't make a decision, all you're going to see of Dublin will be the inside of this dressing room."

"It's a lovely dressing room," she replied.

He pinched her ass.

She yelped.

He stepped in close and kissed her, silencing any admonishment she might have come up with.

He was thorough, exploring her mouth with leisure, even when a woman nearby cleared her throat in an obvious attempt to get their attention. The second, louder throat-clearing made her gently break away.

"Stop," she whispered, heat burning across her cheeks. "We're causing a scene."

"I can only say I wish my man looked at me with such open admiration," the woman said, eyebrows raised. "I brought the extra jumper you asked for, sir."

"Thank you, Linda."

The saleswoman all but melted at Isaac's gratitude, her appreciation visibly doubling when he slipped her a twenty note. "Enjoy the rest of your shopping. Let me know if there's anything else I might do for either of you," she said before fading away without further comment.

Rachel took the sweater he handed her. "You're incorrigible. And I can't afford this sweater."

"I told you—this weekend, all of it is my treat."

"I don't want you paying for everything, Isaac. If you had just let me go by my place and get some clothes, this wouldn't be necessary."

"It would have taken a couple hours in rush hour to get to your place and then back to the airport. Every hour we spent trying to gather belongings for a spontaneous weekend away made the trip less spontaneous and…" He swallowed and looked up at the ceiling, seemingly searching for inspiration. Or that escape hatch he'd mentioned.

"And what?" she prompted.

"And every second we weren't in the air was a second you could change your mind." He stepped in close and pulled her into his embrace. "I wanted this time with you, Rachel."

She let herself relax in the circle of his arms. "I wouldn't have gone back on my word."

"I know that. Or, at least, now I do."

"Because I'm here?"

"In part. But also because I'm getting to know you better."

"True." Leaning back so she could see his face, she waited until he met her gaze. "Thank you for bringing me."

He kissed the tip of her nose. "Let me see that sweater she just brought you."

Rachel slipped out of the one she'd been wearing and into the one he'd chosen. Sliding past him, she crossed the dressing room and stopped in front of the full-length mirror. The clothes she wore fit her exceptionally well. Curling her toes against the cold seeping through her feet from the tile floor, she worried her bottom lip. This was going to be an expensive shopping trip. The last thing she needed was to spend the money, but she didn't want him to provide her with everything she needed, either. That wasn't the deal. At least, not in her mind. She'd provide for herself so there was no misinterpretation about what was going on or who they were—or weren't—to each other. But this was going to seriously damage her vacation fund.

"You look incredible, you know."

She looked up and found Isaac's reflection in the mirror. He still stood outside her dressing room, one shoulder leaned against the door frame as he watched her through hooded eyes.

Tugging at the sweater, Rachel shifted her attention away from him, instead taking in the fit of the jeans and the sweater's muted colors. "I like it."

"Then it's yours."

"I'll buy it, Isaac."

"I want to get it and whatever else you need."

"No." She faced him then, forcing her hands to stay relaxed while keeping her arms at her sides. "I don't want you buying everything I want. I need to do this for myself." She drew a deep breath. "But thank you for the offer."

He started toward her, steps slow. Steady. Kept coming at her even when she was less than an arm's length away. He moved her back and into the vacant dressing room beside the floor-to-ceiling mirror. And pulled the curtain shut behind them.

Rachel's nipples pearled at the sheer dominance Isaac exuded. To maneuver her like he had, to pull the curtain shut without even looking— He wasn't intimidating her. Not even close. What he was doing was turning her on. She shook her head and looked away, trying to keep her cards close to her chest. Never had she been the woman who found overbearing men attractive, but this man? The whole thing simply *worked*. She wanted to tear off his clothes at the same time he shredded hers, then she wanted to go at it like frenzied animals. In a semipublic venue. Which was so, so not her style. But he brought out that part of her, made her feel alive and sexual and emboldened to take chances the old Rachel wouldn't have thought of, let alone suggest. He empowered her as well as celebrated her empowerment, and the realization was enough to have her gaze whipping up to meet his.

He stared at her as he worked both hands under her sweater's hem and found bare skin. He ran his hands around her waist, then splayed them across her lower back, his fingers dipping below the waistline of the jeans until they caressed the upper globes of her ass. Thumbs followed.

"Unzip your jeans."

"Here?" she whispered.

"Yes." His voice had dropped an octave. Or three. He cupped her backside the best he could without the jeans being unbuttoned and unzipped, then slipped his knee between her legs at the same time he pulled her against him. He raised her leg until her sex was pressed against his thigh, setting a rhythm— up fast, down slow, up fast, down slow—that had the knot of denim sewn in the crotch rubbing all the right places. Dipping his face to her neck, he nipped her jawline as he squeezed her ass.

It took a moment for the small part of her mind that was still functioning to realize he'd stopped directing her speed and means of riding his rigid thigh and left her to keep going with the pace he'd established. She faltered a bit at the reality, but he pulled her back into the moment when his mouth found hers, all lips and teeth and demand.

She opened to him willingly, meeting his sexual hunger with her own. She tasted him, reveled in him and demanded more. He gave her what she wanted on a soft groan.

Outside, someone coughed rather delicately. "You're finding everything you need for your visit, ma'am?"

The saleswoman who helped us. What was her name?

Rachel broke the kiss and tried to put distance between her and Isaac, but he refused to let go of her ass. His eyes shone with twin sparks—one lust, one humor. It was the latter that stopped her, kept her silent.

"We're fine, Linda. We'll be out in a moment with her selections."

Not another word, only the sound of the woman's footsteps as she hustled away.

"You really are incorrigible," Rachel chastised. She wiggled and pulled at his arms in her attempt to get away.

He leaned in and nuzzled the sensitive spot just below her ear. "Hearing that in such a school-matron tone is turning me on in ways I'm almost ashamed to admit."

"Did you go to Catholic school?"

Pulling away just far enough to meet her stare, his eyebrows winged down as he gave a small shake of the head. "No. Why?"

"Because while I'm all for a little role-playing in the bedroom, I am *not* putting on a nun's habit and fulfilling some odd schoolboy fantasy you've been harboring all these years."

The laugh that rumbled out of his chest was rusty but pure, and the look on his face said he was as startled as she was. He coughed and then cleared his throat. "I'll remember that about the role-playing."

"But you're clearly not denying the nun-in-the-habit fantasy."

"Just keeping the mystery alive."

She snorted rather indelicately. "We're so new to each other that it seems there's more mystery than established fact between us."

Isaac sobered but didn't say anything. Instead, he removed his hands from her pants and stepped back, looking her up and down before his attention rested on her eyes. "True," he said softly. "But mystery's death most often comes at the hands of truth." He pulled back the curtain and motioned for her to go first. When she reached the dressing room doorway, though, he shot his arm across her path and stopped her in her tracks. "I'd rather let the mystery live a bit longer than escort it to its death by laying my sins on the table for your perusal."

She didn't know what sins he referred to, but just then the specifics weren't as significant as the weight of his words. That kind of weight made the listener weary. Whatever truth Isaac carried could be nothing less than life-altering.

Reaching up, she cupped his cheek. The urge to comfort him overwhelmed her, and she didn't think, didn't *over*think. She simply went with the moment, offering him the first words that came to her. "There's little anyone can do that cannot be forgiven."

"Some actions might be forgiven, but they're never forgotten." He closed his eyes and drew a deep breath, leaned into her hand and then opened eyes that were bleak in a way she'd never seen them. "Not ever."

Stepping back into the dressing room, he gathered several items she'd tried on and then walked out, arms loaded with clothes she hadn't intended to buy. He paused and looked back, clearly fighting to lighten the mood. "Don't pay attention to my morose side, Rachel. I would've left it in New York under lock and key but its keeper was busy. Let's get you some shoes and blow this Popsicle stand, shall we?"

Rachel didn't know what to do with the knowledge that wasn't really knowledge, so she simply nodded. "Sure," she said softly, following him toward the shoe department because, if nothing else, one thing held true.

Even an unanticipated emotional minefield would be traversed more easily in a good pair of shoes.

CHAPTER TEN

ISAAC HAD BEEN to Dublin often since his company's European headquarters was in the city, so he had mentally mapped out the places he'd take Rachel. That way she would get the most out of their short visit. To his surprise, however, she had her own ideas. He suggested they take the hired car to see the city.

She insisted they walk.

He suggested they hire a local historian as a tour guide.

She wanted to talk to the people she encountered in the marketplace.

He suggested they dine at a well-known, Michelin-rated restaurant.

She insisted they find a pub and order local fare—catch of the day and a Guinness.

At that, he balked.

"Rachel," he said as calmly as possible, "I'm not going to take you to a public tavern for your one dinner here."

She arched an eyebrow. "Too good to rub elbows with the common man, Isaac?"

"No, but there are so many better choices we could make," he answered, trying not to acknowledge the pleading in his voice. He didn't want fish and chips. He wanted a six-course meal that involved both beef and lamb, maybe a main course of fish, a fine tart for dessert. Good coffee. Better beer. But none of what he had in mind would be served in a basket on a bed of fries, and, if they went to the tavern Rachel was currently navigating toward, that's exactly what was in store.

Her hand settled on his forearm. "Isaac?"

He had begun to crave the intimacy of her voice. So much so, in fact, that he found himself circling the reality of his feelings like a wounded animal. "I don't care for crowds." That was all he could manage.

"Why not?" She rubbed his arm with slow, gentle strokes. "It's not much different than addressing employees in the workplace."

He couldn't help but shake his head. "Not in that number or that proximity."

Her hand stalled, resting lightly near his wrist. "You don't talk to your employees in company meetings?"

"Never en masse, no."

"Huh. Who does, then?"

"Whoever is most appropriate for the topic at hand. It's usually not me." He took her hand and tried to pull her in the direction of a restaurant he favored. "Let's go—"

"There," she said, pointing to someplace over his

shoulder…and in the opposite direction than he'd intended to go.

He glanced back and had to fight to keep from groaning. "O'Sullivan's Public House? No, Rachel. Please, no. Let me take you somewhere there aren't grease stains on the menu."

She tilted her face up to his and beamed. "C'mon, Isaac. Please? Pretty please? We can go somewhere nice for brunch tomorrow. You can pick anywhere you want and I'll go, no questions asked. But this may be my only chance to experience an Irish pub on a Saturday night. I don't want to miss it. I am absolutely *craving* something fresh off the local fisherman's boat and an expertly built Guinness. Maybe three." She batted her eyes playfully, trying to win him over.

What she didn't know?

She already had.

All she had to do was make her wishes known, throw in a little flirting and he would move mountains just to lay the world at her feet. If all she wanted was dinner in a pub? He'd buy the damn pub if need be.

"Damn it," he grumbled for the sheer sake of appearing to balk. "This is ridiculous."

"Please?" she asked again, her enthusiasm as contagious as the viral flu.

Grabbing her hand, he ducked his head against the increasingly heavy downpour and pulled her along toward the pub's entrance.

They were thoroughly soaked by the time they

crossed the threshold. Both laughing and cursing under his breath at not having thought to buy an umbrella, he shook like a dog exiting a lake before pushing his hair off his forehead, taking a fortifying breath and entering the melee, Rachel in tow.

People were crammed into O'Sullivan's tighter than sardines in a can. He scanned the pub and quickly found what he was after.

The bar.

Working his way through the crowd proved more difficult than he'd anticipated. It had been so long since he'd been in such tight quarters, surrounded and unable to move freely. His chest tightened as if a vise had been twisted around it, forcing him to breathe through his mouth just to get air. He shouldered past a man and received a shove back. Isaac didn't care. He just needed to get to Rachel and the bar, sit down and order a drink. Then this feeling would subside.

It had to.

The bar seemed to get farther away instead of closer as he worked his way through the crowd. He was stronger than this, could get her there safely. It wasn't like she was in imminent danger.

They made it with one last push forward, and his luck seemed to have changed—two barstools were vacated at the same time. Isaac guided her onto the nearest one and then slid onto the stool beside her, scooting his seat closer to her at the same time.

"This is the experience you wanted?" he asked, forced to nearly shout over the din.

She beamed at him and nodded.

The man next to her draped an arm over her shoulder and drunkenly slurred, "Well, hello, lass. This bloke you're with?" He gestured toward Isaac with his pint glass. "Guarantee I'll do you better."

Before Isaac could react, Rachel turned to the man, said something quietly and gave a little finger wave when the man took off as if he'd been told the devil was here and refused to leave without him.

Isaac shook his head slowly, staring at Rachel as she turned back to the bar. "What did you say to him?"

"I told him we should run away together, and the faster the better seeing as I'd just discovered you were a serial killer."

"You didn't."

She shrugged. "Maybe. Maybe not. Either way, he won't be hanging around trying to befriend at least one of us tonight."

Again, Isaac found himself shaking his head. "I don't know whether to take you seriously or not."

She shrugged and then waved at the bartender, made a random hand signal he acknowledged before pointing to a table currently being wiped down. Then she took Isaac's hand. "C'mon. There's a table opening up."

"I feel like there's a whole different language being spoken, and I'm not at all fluent."

She tossed back a grin. "I took a chance and mimicked the signal I saw that resulted in a Guinness being delivered. I made it two. Or I ordered a double shot of whiskey. Either way? It ought to be good."

They slipped into chairs, but not before Isaac helped Rachel with her coat. Sitting in the chair nearest her, he asked, "I don't suppose you saw a hand signal that would get us something to snack on?"

"I did." She flagged down a server. "Could we get two menus?"

"Right. Two seconds while I drop off these drinks and I'll be with you." Then the girl sped off.

"You're making me feel like I have zero experience in a city I've been to more times than I can count."

Again, she shrugged. "Seems bar language is universal." Then her brow furrowed. "But I'd be willing to bet you don't often 'end up' in this part of town on any given Saturday night with a woman you hardly know on a trip that wasn't planned. Cut yourself some slack."

"Thanks for that." His dry tone said more than the few words.

The waitress returned and slipped laminated, single-sheet menus in front of them.

Rachel glanced at it briefly before turning to the waitress. "I ordered something to drink from the bar, so I'm ready for a meal." She rubbed her hands together. "What's the special tonight?"

The young woman appeared harried as she flipped through her order pad and rambled off the day's catch as well as a soup of the day and the night's signature drink.

Rachel leaned in, listening closely, and repeated back everything she'd said. The young woman looked up, eyes wide, and then burst out laughing. Rachel smiled, and Isaac had the feeling the two had just had one of the mystifying female-bonding moments that automatically excluded all men in the vicinity. He waited and was proven right.

"No one listens that closely. You're not from around here, to be sure."

"The United States."

The girl's eye lit. "Where?"

"New York City," Rachel answered.

"Oh, man. I've always dreamed of going to New York." A dreamy smile slowed the girl's whirlwind demeanor.

Rachel smiled in return. "Ironically, I've always dreamed of coming here."

Isaac was mesmerized, watching as Rachel connected with a total stranger in a strange land. The woman had a gift for making others feel at ease, as if they'd known her far longer than they had and far more intimately than was warranted by the few words they'd exchanged. She was incredible with people.

Including him. Even though he had been intent on keeping her at arm's length, she'd managed to get past his first-line defenses and become a comfortable piece of his private life. But what had changed between the Power Match meet and greet and now? Truly, the answer was "nothing." The last thing Isaac needed was the complication of any type of relationship. He wasn't built for commitment, didn't have the emotional capital he would need to invest to ensure any relationship he entered into would thrive. And if he couldn't ensure any investment would perform above and beyond the mean, he didn't invest.

Period.

Yet having spent only two nights with Rachel, having taken a spontaneous trip with her, he had to wonder where his head was. It certainly wasn't screwed on straight. Had it been, he wouldn't be sitting in Ireland with a woman he hardly knew, marveling at her ability to charm complete strangers. Things hadn't been terribly difficult between them, and he knew she was the reason. Had he been solely responsible for making things between them work? He'd have ended up going home alone, again, that night. And every night thereafter. He wouldn't have had Thursday and Friday night to revel in her companionship, wouldn't have tonight…perhaps even more…to look forward to.

Yet recognizing that he was the problem in this equation didn't sit well.

At all.

But what was he supposed to do—change who he was to suit another person? How could she come in and make him consider upending his whole life?

Because that's what he'd done. He looked around. No. That's what he was *doing*. Actively.

As he saw it, he had two choices. He could either let the weekend play out and then do his level best to walk away without a backward glance, having enjoyed the woman's company and their shared sexual experiences before parting ways with a friendly but final farewell. Or, more realistically, he could see the weekend through and find a way to see Rachel again.

Isaac's temple began to throb, the headache striking him without warning.

Having a woman in his life would complicate things, add to the list of people he was responsible for keeping safe. Did he want that? Did he want the additional responsibility that came with opening one's life?

More troubling, did he want to give up the control over himself he'd fought so hard to master? Because there was no doubt that Rachel threatened his control. An epiphany hit, and he realized that she hadn't just threatened it. She'd *taken* some of it away from him without trying. That the act was an unconscious one didn't matter at all. She did what she did, was who she was, and that was good and well for her. But for him?

No.

Glancing around, he realized this wasn't who he was. Not this pub, not this place, not this spontaneous decision-making, not yesterday's shopping excursion. None of it.

"None of it."

"Pardon?"

He looked up and realized the waitress waited on his order. "I apologize. I'll have what she's having, drink and meal alike."

The waitress jotted down a couple of notes before

promising to have their drinks back quickly. Then she turned and was swallowed by the crowd.

Isaac knew the feeling of being consumed, swallowed whole and lost in a familiar place. That's exactly what he was experiencing right now.

Truth? He didn't want to change his life. He didn't want to see things uprooted, didn't want the threat of loss added to his emotional baggage. To bring in Rachel would be to ask her to change who she was seeing as Isaac was pretty damn sure he, himself, wouldn't change.

So he would do what he did best. He would build a plan around logic and then execute the plan to the satisfactory end—an end where he and his lover would bid each other goodbye. Then he would go back to the life he'd created for himself, the life that he knew, the life that had structure. That was predictable. That was safe.

But for the first time in as long as he could remember, the safe thing didn't feel safe at all.

Rachel had watched a bevy of emotions play out across Isaac's face, from fear when they'd arrived to what she could only label resoluteness as they waited on their dinner. Isaac had been dismissive when she asked if he was okay, so she'd left him be. Instead, she focused on the people funneling into the small pub, watching as several arrived with instruments and grouped themselves by type. Brass sat near the fireplace. Fiddles were closest to the bar. Handheld drums she believed were called bodhrans were near the front entrance. And two guitars were close to her and Isaac's table. Groups of men began to move tables out of the center of the pub at the same time the waitress returned with their order.

"What's going on?" Rachel asked, tipping her head toward the men's activity.

The waitress didn't spare a glance. "There's a *craic* tonight."

"A…"

"Craic," the waitress said slowly. "It's like…" She tapped a finger against her chin before her eyes lit with the answer. "It basically means a good time. Fun. Entertainment. See the folks scattered around with the different instruments? The players will play familiar songs, joining in on the ones they know, getting up and wandering about as the vocalists sing and patrons dance. That's why the menfolk are moving the tables. You and your man will have to get up and give it a go around the dance floor after a bit." With a wink and a nudge, she was off, quickly swallowed by the ever-growing crowd.

Your man.

Rachel's insides fluttered at the waitress's reference to her and Isaac. He wasn't hers. At least, not in the traditional sense. For the weekend, though… That was a matter of opinion. She didn't want to be tied to one man again, wouldn't allow her life to be dictated by his wants and needs. She was reveling in her freedom, rejoicing in having just managed to reclaim her sense of self. Yes, her choices regarding Isaac were, without a doubt, one aspect of her new-found freedom—sort of an exclamation point at the end of her declarative sentence. But he was somehow more, no matter that she didn't want him to be.

Even though he was from society's upper echelon, a group she had never felt entirely comfortable with, she found she actually *liked* him. It was the oddest thing. He was her opposite—cautious to her jump-first mentality, logical to her natural free-spiritedness and, despite his spur-of-the-moment offer to take her to Ireland for the weekend, highly structured in the face of her spontaneity.

Rachel nearly choked on her Guinness. As if that wasn't a *massive* spontaneous act—taking a weekend jaunt to Europe. She'd have to strike that off her list of differences, or at least weight it accordingly. Regardless, there was something about Isaac that called to Rachel. It was a call she didn't want to hear and one she did *not* want to answer. Not when she'd just found her feet again. She'd been nothing but a pile of raw, exposed emotions after her ex-husband left. And they'd been compatible from the start. But she and Isaac? Not even close. She didn't need to get seriously involved with a man who was, in so many ways, her opposite. That was like begging the Fates to weave trouble right into her lifeline. No, no, no. No relationships for the next year. At least. Maybe two.

Relaxing a little on the heels of her inner pep talk, she tried to think of a neutral topic for conversation. Glancing up, she found Isaac watching her in an almost predatory way. It was a look she'd only seen in the bedroom. He seemed to be measuring her for the right size of bedsheets.

"King," she said without thinking, reaching for a handful of pretzels and popping a couple in her mouth. They would, after all, need room to move.

"King?"

She choked on her drink.

Isaac lunged for her so fast he tipped over his chair. It had barely hit the floor when he had her in the universally approved position for assisting someone with an obstructed airway.

"Rachel?" he said, full of authority. "Raise your hand if you can breathe."

She wheezed and raised her right hand.

"Take a deeper breath."

Struggling past the embarrassment of the pub patrons' watching her publicly choke to death, she managed a deeper breath that dislodged the offending pretzel, thus clearing her airway.

"Thank God," Isaac muttered, clutching her so close and so tight she had to struggle to breathe all over again.

"I'm good," she croaked. "It's okay, Isaac. I just choked."

"Things can go wrong so, so fast, and you can't undo what happens in that blink of time," he said against the back of her neck.

Air rushed across her skin as he drew his own fortifying breath. "We're good," he said to those around them. "International incident averted."

Several people chuckled, and Rachel could

only be grateful when the waitress shoved her way through the crowd with a glass of water. "Here you go, ma'am. Scared the evil right out of me, you did, choking like that. Good thing your man was here to intervene!" And she was off, calling back that their food should be ready "soon enough."

Isaac took his seat, then leaned down and swept his napkin off the floor before asking as quietly as possible over the din of the crowd, "You're sure you're okay?"

"Sure. Just one more time I wished a sinkhole would have opened beneath me so my actions would have gone down as heroic versus 'died by choking on pretzel salt' or 'inhaled piece of lint and perished.'"

He smiled, but the tightness around his eyes prevented her from buying the gesture as genuine.

Anxious to discuss anything but what had just happened, she plucked the first conversational topic that passed through her mind and took off with it. "How do you think Power Match ended up putting us together? I mean, I know we sort of joked about it before, but what do you think we did differently than most of the other participants to end up with a decent match?"

"Decent, huh?" This time, his grin reached his eyes. "I don't know if I should be amused or insulted."

She closed her eyes and shook her head. "That came out wrong."

"Moving along," he said with obvious mercy. "I'm

curious. Why do you think the meet and greet didn't go well?"

She gaped at him. Literally. Gaped. "Why…? Did you not look around? Did you not talk to another woman? Did you not ask the other two women you were paired with how their introductions had gone?"

"Um, no?"

There was an opening for a tirade regarding men and paying attention, but that would wait. This wouldn't. "Isaac, I went to the ladies' room before meeting you. I didn't hear a single woman in there discuss anything positive. Some were making pacts to leave if the next match was as poorly done. Others were hiding out in the restroom until it was all over. And others still were talking about the fact that Power Match couldn't hold a candle to Date Me and how they'd be going back to that app exclusively."

Leaning back in his chair, he crossed his arms over his chest. "I had no idea."

"Maybe it was a glitch?" she suggested.

"No way. My brother is the app developer. It wouldn't be in my hands if there was a glitch."

"What if you missed it, though?"

"If I had, someone else on Jonathan's team would've caught it. There are checks and balances."

With a look of relief, he tipped his chin at something over Rachel's shoulder. "I'm going to guess this pile of bar food is ours?"

"Every last crumb," the waitress said, balancing the serving tray on one hand and pulling dishes with the other.

Rachel rubbed her hands together with glee. This was the Irish experience she wanted. Fish and chips paired with a well-built Guinness on a Dublin Saturday night. "There's enough here to feed half a dozen people!"

Isaac grinned, that rare grin that came from somewhere he didn't realize he guarded so heavily. "You look like you're prepping to eat every last bite."

"I'm going to put a hurting on this basket. Don't doubt me." She took a bite of her fried fish fillet and nearly groaned with pleasure. "Oh, man, this is good."

Isaac leaned forward and dragged his thumb across her bottom lip. "You had a little something right there."

Rachel almost choked. Again. She hadn't been the only one to change direction without warning. Isaac's touch had been purely sensual. Almost carnal. As if he had been flirting with undisguised intent, and Isaac didn't strike her as one to flirt. At all. Confused, she down set her fork and picked up her beer, focused on taking a drink to buy herself time to respond.

Isaac chose that moment to pick up his fork and stab a bite of fish. He saluted her with it before taking the bite, his eyes closing in bliss. "This really is excellent."

"As good as the restaurant you wanted to go to tonight?"

He opened his eyes and looked at her, the solemnity of his gaze a weight she didn't fully understand. "Better."

That one word, his acknowledgment, freed a part of her she hadn't known was still chained by insecurity, a part of her that would stand her ground but still wanted his approval. Unsure what to say that wouldn't make her sound like a blathering idiot, Rachel elected to fork up another bite of fish and chew slowly. She wouldn't talk with her mouth full, but she did smile. And he smiled back.

Who knew she'd find safety in good manners.

CHAPTER ELEVEN

Isaac was off center. Proof?

He.

Had.

Danced.

And he'd enjoyed himself. Immensely.

That hadn't been part of the plan. Not that there'd been much of a plan to start with, inviting an essential stranger to Europe for the weekend. This was a prime example of why he lived a structured, pre-planned, well-thought-out life. Surprises didn't suit him one bit. This whole thing—the woman, the trip, dining in a pub, dancing with locals—had been one hell of a surprise.

Not to say he wasn't rolling with it. He was. Mostly due to the joy that seemed to bleed from Rachel's pores and saturate anyone within a three-block radius. The woman was *alive*. Truly living. In the relatively short time they'd spent in the pub, Isaac had wondered for a brief moment what it might be like to be that free, what his life might have been had Mike not died under his watch. He had a snapshot of who he might have been, and it was sobering. Enough so that he'd handed off Rachel to a local man and walked off the dance floor.

She hadn't followed.

Part of him had wanted her solace and was irritated she didn't seek him out.

Part of him had been proud of her for holding on to the person she'd clearly been working so hard to become. Or, more aptly, reclaim.

From his corner booth, he'd watched Rachel twirl around the floor, watched her attempt a step dance similar to *Riverdance* and laugh wildly when she got tripped up. Had envied her the freedom she displayed as she kicked off her shoes and tried again. Publicly. And failed. Again. All while laughing aloud at her best effort that just hadn't quite been good enough.

She'd moved in time with the music as she made her way to his table. More than once she'd kindly passed on an offer to dance or to have another round courtesy of a local. By the time she'd made it to Isaac, she'd spoken to half the bar, and she'd known the names of half the people she'd talked to.

"You want to take another trip around?" she asked.

He considered her, with her hair pinned up in a messy bun, tendrils curling slightly in the pub's humid warmth, the flush of exertion on her cheeks and the bright light of joy radiating from her eyes.

"I'll be sore tomorrow, but it will have been worth it." She grinned even wider. "Did you see me try to step? It was a complete train wreck, but it was fun."

She reached across the table, she took the pint he'd
been spinning slowly between his palms and downed
half of it. "I'm going to need several bottles of water,
too. Badly. The hotel will have it, don't you think?"

"Mmm-hmm." He imagined her as she'd been last
night, flushed and sweating for a different reason altogether, and his cock roused in his jeans.

As if she could read minds, she slid closer and
rested her chin on his shoulder, speaking directly
into his ear. "You've given me the most amazing
weekend."

"It's not over."

"No. It's not." She discreetly nipped his earlobe,
holding it for a second between her teeth before letting go. At the same time, she slid her hand up the
inside of his thigh, reached his groin and cupped
him gently, massaging his balls with her fingers as
she traced his length with her thumb. "The evidence
would suggest you enjoyed watching me dance, Mr.
Miller."

Isaac shifted in his seat. Shivers ran through him
when she laughed, her hot breath washing over his
ear and neck and down the edge of his collar. His
cock swelled even more, and Isaac began to wish
away all the pub patrons.

He twisted in his seat just enough that he could
put his cheek next to hers and speak into her ear.
"Rachel." Gently taking her wrist, he stilled her
hand. "You're going to make it impossible to leave
without causing a scene."

Her breath caught as his chest rubbed against her nipples. "So, it seems, are you."

"What do you suggest?"

She traced the tip of her tongue along the outer shell of his ear. "A brazen, unapologetic...rapid exit."

"I'm good with that."

"To the hotel?"

"Unless you truly want to cause a scene, yes."

"Where's your driver?"

"Gone for the night. We're just a couple blocks from the hotel."

"Hurry."

The need in her voice made him want to stand on the tabletop and beat his chest like a maniac. She wanted him as much as he wanted her. Heady stuff, that.

He slid out of the booth and was amused when she cleverly angled herself in front of him so that the bulk of her coat hid the majority of his groin. She reached back and draped his arm over her shoulder to keep him close as they worked their way to the exit, she shouting goodbyes to her new acquaintances and receiving hearty farewells in return. They spilled out onto the sidewalk, the voices and music from the pub growing muffled as the heavy door shut with a *whump* behind them.

"Which way?" she asked as she looked first left and then right.

"Right." He turned her and pointed. "See the bright light? That's where we're headed." He took a step toward the hotel and stopped, looked back and held out his hand.

Rachel looked from his face to his hand and back, clearly confused.

He waggled his ungloved hand. "C'mon."

She took his hand in her own, laced her fingers through his without comment, and they started toward Isaac's favorite Dublin hotel.

The rain fell softer now, but it was still their steady companion as they made their way down Dublin's busy sidewalks, past more well-lit pubs brimming with Saturday-night revelers and darkened storefronts locked up tight.

Isaac held her hand without comment, but his insides warred. He knew he was treading a line that threatened to trip him up. And if he fell? He was screwed.

He wasn't stupid. Rachel would want more. She would deserve more. And he simply didn't have it to give.

So he would enjoy this weekend and, as planned, say farewell when they returned to the States early Monday morning. He'd return to his life, she'd return to hers and they'd have this weekend to look back on. Fond memories, but nothing more.

But what if…?

The forming thought made Isaac miss a step, and he actually stumbled.

Rachel tightened her grip and grabbed his elbow with her free hand. "Little too much to drink, Isaac?" she asked with a broad grin.

"Must've." It was all he could come up with.

Because no. No, no, no. No what-ifs.

But…

He couldn't stop himself from wondering what it would be like to change "goodbye" into "see you later." As in, later in the week. Or later in the day. Something. Anything other than a shake of hands and quick buss on the cheek and a permanent parting of ways.

"Isaac?" Rachel tugged on his hand. "Isn't this our stop?"

He stopped and looked back at her, at the doorman, a man he recognized from previous trips, who was holding the lobby door open for them.

"Yeah. It is."

"Serious wool-gathering going on in that big brain of yours." She tugged his hand again. "Unless you've changed your mind, let's go upstairs."

That voice of hers should come with a warning. Hell, she should be required to have it licensed.

She smiled at him, the look slow and sultry and entirely suggestive. "I'm tired of walking."

"What would you rather do?" He had to know, had to hear her say she wanted him. And she came through as if she knew what he needed just then.

Stepping into his personal space, she tilted her chin up until their gazes locked. Then she went up on tiptoe and kissed him softly, barely breaking away so that, when she spoke, her lips moved against his. "I'd rather be in our room, wearing nothing but the little silk number I picked up when you were so determined to go to the shoe department, watching you grow hard as I touch myself while thinking of all the things I want you to do to my body before sunrise."

"God help you." He closed the fractional distance between them, hungry for her, devouring her mouth even as she devoured his in return.

A discreet cough had him swimming to the surface of consciousness and looking about. An older couple shot them a disapproving look even as the doorman coughed again, still holding the door open.

Isaac dug out a random Euro from his pocket and passed it to the man, not sure if he was giving him a five or a century note and not caring either way. He all but dragged a laughing Rachel in his wake, through the lobby and into the elevator, where he swiped his key card to the upper floor of the hotel.

"The penthouse," she said softly. "I'm sure this is common for you, but I'm not sure I could ever get used to living like this."

He didn't look at her.

Couldn't.

Not if he had a hope in hell of making it to the room versus hitting Stop and taking her right then.

Never in his life had he wanted a woman the way he wanted Rachel.

"Have the rules changed at all?" he asked, his voice low and almost ragged.

"No."

He turned and pulled her into his embrace, kissing her with almost manic fervor, touching her where he knew she liked to be touched, and trying to take her higher even as he drove back the voice in his head that warned him he was treading far too close to the line he'd vowed to never cross.

The line that would make her his.

Forever.

Rachel's body hummed with anticipation, every nerve charged. Electrified. What awaited her in their suite—*suite!*—was sheer, unapologetic pleasure. Hers for the taking. She would never be able to repay Isaac for what he had given her in this trip, but she could definitely do her best to create memories with him that would last them both after they said farewell.

His mouth on hers was demanding, making it hard to think about anything but the moment at hand. Hard, but not impossible. Images fluttered through her mind, each one a snapshot of something different that she wanted to do with him. To him. For him. She wanted to give herself over to his keeping, knowing he'd take her so high she'd struggle to breathe, fight for oxygen and free-fall back to earth, where he would catch her...and do it all over again. The relief of having that in a lover was beyond definition. She knew she'd be taken care of, left satisfied, and would sleep in his comforting presence tonight and wake up in the morning to the security he offered.

He broke the kiss and gave her a hard look. "You're thinking too much."

"Sorry."

"Don't apologize. I'll just have to redouble my efforts to fog your brain."

"If you double down, I'm going to die."

"Can't have that, now, can we?" He moved his lips to her neck, obliterating any thought but where he might go next. They were in the elevator alone, and it was unlikely they'd be interrupted. The threat was still there, though, and it was a complete turn-on.

Rachel let out a short, breathy laugh. Who knew she had a little exhibitionism lurking in her closet?

"What in God's name have I done to make you laugh?" he asked, his voice saturated with mock annoyance.

"I was just imagining what I want to do in this elevator, and it struck me as a little funny that I would be so daring in what amounts to a public place."

"You had your hand on my cock in the pub," he reminded her.

Heat burned across her cheeks. "So I did."

"That was about as public as you can get."

"Maybe, but I still contend that that little exhibition wouldn't hold a candle to me having your cock in my mouth if the elevator were to stop and the doors open to an old couple who hadn't expected a pornographic peep show until the doors closed."

"Or they passed out."

"Or she gave me pointers."

"You don't need pointers. Trust me." The smile in his voice was clear, and unexpected laughter rumbled through his chest.

She had been responsible for that. *She* made him

smile. *She* made him laugh. *She* made him relax. Only *she* had managed to bring out this side of him. She was sure of it. The few times he'd let himself smile or laugh, the action had seemed to catch him off guard.

"I have no idea what else you're imagining doing in this death trap, but I'd be interested in a play-by-play."

To her dismay, the elevator chimed as it stopped. "Seems we'll have to save the verbal rundown for another time. We're here."

"Or the old couple's on the other side of the door."

She glanced at the floor number displayed. "I doubt it."

He leaned back to see her face. "Promise you'll tell me later."

"Why don't I just show you now?"

His eyes darkened, pupils growing wide with his elevated arousal. "More than a fair compromise."

With a fistful of his shirt, she backed away and pulled him with her, letting him guide her—a little pressure to the left. A little to the right. Before she knew it, he was squeezing her hips and backing her into the door.

He let go of one hip and slipped the key card into the door. The electronic latch buzzed then clicked, and the door swung open. With a deft move, he spun her around, held her close until the door latched, then backed her into it again.

She arched an eyebrow even as she hooked a leg

around his upper thigh, pressing her sex against his rock-hard erection.

Isaac stared at her, so serious, his eyes dark with passion.

She let him look until she couldn't stand the tension anymore. Running her hands through his hair, she pulled his head down to her as she rose to meet him, claiming his mouth in an open declaration of intent. She would have him here. Now. The way she wanted. He need only agree.

And he did.

Lips fused, they explored each other, teeth nipping, tongues dancing, until his breath was hers and her breath was his. This wasn't a seduction but a culmination, the place they'd been headed all day through flirtatious words and teasing touches. There was nowhere else they could've ended up but here, in each other's arms.

Rachel fumbled with the hem of his shirt, pulling it free before waging war with the buttons. Frustration peaked fast, and she tugged, sending buttons flying.

"I'm going to have to send you my tailor's bill," he said against her mouth.

"I'll give you my address."

"Later."

Isaac rolled his shoulders and shed the shirt, leaving his chest bare for her to explore.

Eyes closed, Rachel feasted on the tactile experience, letting her fingers run across the ridges and planes of his chest and abdomen, the sculpted perfection of his six-pack and up again across his pectoral muscles. He was perfection. Everything she wanted. Everything she craved.

Isaac responded in kind, pulling her sweater and then her shirt over her head, leaving her clad in only her bra, jeans and boots.

"Lose the boots, Rachel."

She had to step back to toe them off, but he took her hips and pulled her close when only one was off. Going to his knees, he laid kisses along the bare skin of her belly and whispered, "Too slow. Taking too long."

With efficient care, he removed the other boot, then stripped her out of her jeans in seconds. Then he sat back on his heels and took her in, letting his gaze rove over her in a leisurely manner.

Rachel reached for him, but he gently pushed her back against the cold door and held her there. "Let me look."

"Isaac." She didn't care if she sounded needy. Hell, she *was*. He could look later. Right now, she wanted him, needed to feel his skin against hers. She pulled at him again, and this time he came to her in a rush, surging to his feet and pressing his full length against her.

Hooking his arms behind her knees, he lifted her so she could wrap her legs around his waist and he could pin her to the door with his hips.

Rachel wrapped her arms around his neck, as well, letting her head fall back against the door as he nipped her jaw, her ear, her neck, her collarbone.

The heat of his mouth seared her skin, and she reveled in the burn. Hungered for more. Wanted him to possess her body and use it as he would.

She ground against his cock, riding the length of him, his jeans abrading her tender flesh through the satin of her underwear. Friction brought her close, and she whimpered, trying to ride harder, faster, to hit the right spot that would send her over the edge, but he shifted and denied her.

An animalistic snarl left her, a noise she didn't recognize, as her body demanded more from him.

"Patience," he rasped.

"Screw that," she bit out, pushing her hips down against his. "Don't make me wait, Isaac."

"Rachel." Her name from his lips issued against the skin on her neck.

She gripped his hair and pulled his head back until their eyes met. "Love me, Isaac."

"Rachel," he said again, a strange note of concern creeping in.

She realized what she'd said and tried not to panic at the request. Instead, she clarified. "Love my body, Isaac." Lowering her face to his, she watched him fight to control his breathing as his nostrils flared and his chest heaved. "Take me here. Now. Command my body and make it your instrument of pleasure. Please."

Those words proved to be his undoing. He surged against the door, his hips grinding into hers with delicious force as he let go of one of her hips to fumble with his jeans. She shoved away his hand and undid his belt for him, letting him work the button free, and then pushed at his jeans and boxers with her hands until she could get them hooked on a heel and shove them down to his knees. His cock sprang free, and she groaned at the feel of his scalding heat against her sex.

"Condom," Isaac muttered.

"Let me."

She took the condom he'd pulled from his pocket, ripped it open and slipped it down his length as she shook under her ministrations.

Sheathed, he pulled her back into his embrace, ripped off her underwear with a sharp jerk and, burying his face in her neck, thrust his hips up and forward, filling her in one stroke.

She cried out and he froze until she tightened her arms around his shoulders and began to move. "Not hurt," she gasped. "Fuck me, Isaac. Please. Please. Please," she begged as she fought to move, pinned as she was between him and the door.

He must've heard her through the haze of lust. Shifting, he rapidly established a deep plunge-and-retreat rhythm that dragged the root of his cock over her clitoris with every stroke. This—he—was wild, and she gave as well as she took. Rachel scored his back with her nails as she fought to hold on, to hold out, until there were no options left but to come apart in his arms.

He reached between them, found her clitoris and pressed her with his thumb at the same time he drove deep into her.

The effect was cataclysmic.

Rachel shattered, crying out as she rode Isaac as hard and fast as she could, aware of nothing but the raging sensations that ripped through her body. She was left shaking and limp as they receded and only the aftershocks rocking her internal muscles remained.

He pressed her back against the door and shook as he rode out his own orgasm in silence, his thrusts growing erratic until he stilled and only the sound of their heavy breathing filled the air.

Rachel laid her head on Isaac's shoulder. She was limp as a rag doll but sure in the knowledge that he wouldn't allow her to fall.

And he didn't.

But there was more than one way to fall, and Rachel had a sinking feeling she'd taken the first major step toward falling for Isaac in a way he wouldn't be able to save her from. And probably wouldn't want to. But that was the thing about falling.

Once someone truly began to fall, stopping that forward momentum was nearly impossible.

CHAPTER TWELVE

THE CLOCK'S GREEN digital display read seven minutes after three. Just past the witching hour. And Isaac had no doubt Rachel Sullivan had worked some type of magic on him. There was no other explanation for what he was experiencing. Thinking. Feeling. And it was the latter that most terrified him. He had worked to become immune to feelings, capable of shutting down his inner self with brutal efficiency. Yet in only a couple of days, one woman had unraveled what had taken him twenty years to build and then master.

She had him thinking about how they might make things between them work.

In the dark beside him, his bewitching woman shifted but didn't wake. Easing onto his side, he studied her profile. Even now, seen by nothing more than the alarm clock's faint glow, she was beautiful. Not a traditional beauty, exactly, but more the girl next door who suddenly, one day, stepped out of her house a grown woman. A woman who had come into her own, who commanded the space around her and drew people—men—like bees to pollen. Her nose was narrow and straight. Her mouth was a little wider than convention deemed attractive, but it made her smile all the more radiant. Her jawline was strong but perfect. Her eyes were expressive, although, if she tried, she could shut down their communication.

Then there was her body. It was lithe, pert and perfect for him. Small, firm, high breasts. Trim waist and narrow hips. An ass that would stop New York traffic. Toned legs that turned a pair of high heels into weapons of destruction.

And then there was her mind. She was sharp. Brilliant, really. Accomplished and successful in a male-dominated field, and that was no small feat.

He'd never wanted any woman like he wanted Rachel…despite the fact she often infuriated him.

She turned her face toward him, eyes open just a bit, a small smile playing around the corners of her mouth. "Hey, you. What are you doing up at this ungodly hour?"

"Watching you."

Her laugh was thick with sleep, little more than a heavy exhale. "That's weird, Isaac. Stop watching me sleep."

"Make me."

"Jerk."

"Not denying it."

"Look, then. I'm too tired to care."

"Rachel?"

"Hmm."

Her eyes drifted closed and her breathing settled into a slow and rhythmic pattern. Moments passed and she said nothing more, so he whispered her name again. "Rachel."

No response.

Her silence empowered him to ask the question that had been dogging him, the question that would have explained to her why sleep had eluded him—would continue to elude him—tonight. "Where do we go from here?"

As he had expected, she didn't answer.

That was actually preferable to the alternative. He didn't want to hear her say they went back to New York—to their own lives—and never looked back. He didn't want to hear that he was allowing emotion to confuse the signals between them.

Damn his brother for forcing his hand where this app was concerned.

"I don't know, Isaac."

He jolted as if he'd been shocked. "What?"

She yawned and rolled toward him, eyes still closed. "I said I don't know where we go from here."

Oh, God. She'd heard him. He'd been sure she was asleep. What did he do now? He couldn't have this conversation. He couldn't—

"Calm down," she muttered into the arm covering part of her face.

"I'm calm," he said, ignoring the way his voice lacked conviction and hoping she'd do the same.

"Really?"

"Yes."

"Then why is the bed shaking?"

"It's not."

She moved her arm, sighed and propped herself up on her elbow so she was looking down at him, eyes wide open. "Liar." Then she smiled, and the look melted him.

Something inside him loosened, and he could breathe. "Am I so easy to read?"

Rachel dropped bonelessly onto her pillow before rolling onto her back. "I can honestly say I've never met anyone more difficult to read than you."

Compulsion drove him to touch her, so he laid his hand on the bare skin just below her exposed breast. "You never did show me that satin number you picked up."

She groaned. "My body rejects your suggestion that it rise and retrieve the aforementioned unmentionable just to satisfy your curiosity."

"Spoken like a lawyer."

"Layman's terms? You can see it later."

"Isn't it a bit early to cry off with a headache."

She snorted. "I didn't say I had a headache. I said I wasn't getting up."

"How quickly the romance fades."

She laughed. "Your early-morning attempts at humor require me to be caffeinated."

"Do you know that I've smiled more since I met you than I have in…well, in a long, long time?"

"I wondered."

Reaching out, he finger-combed the flyaway bits of her hair that sleep had mussed. "Why?"

"It didn't seem like a normal response for you at first."

"And now?"

"You tell me."

"It feels good."

She leaned into his hand, and he instinctively cupped her cheek. "You should smile more. It suits you."

But did it? Really?

She was the catalyst for his smiles and laughter. When she was out of reach? Nothing else seemed to move him the same way she did. And she did it with such grace. So effortlessly.

He sat up and scrubbed his hands through his hair.

"Isaac?"

"I..." He swallowed hard enough he was sure she heard him. What could he say that wouldn't be an utter lie? That life had stolen his joy, his humor, when it robbed him of his brother? That he didn't feel he had a right to laugh because he'd stolen that gift from his parents, as well? That he'd become entombed in a gilded cage of his own design where love and laughter weren't part of the decor? All of those things sounded like pathetic excuses, yet each and every one was anchored in truth.

"Isaac?" she asked, softer this time. She pushed back the covers, sat up and kneeled before him, naked save for the riotous tumble of hair cloaking her shoulders. "Talk to me. Please."

The pang in his heart wrought by her plea hurt more than it should have given how little time they had known each other. And yet, for all that, he found words welling up in his chest, tumbling over each other in a rush to be the first spoken, the first heard.

"I don't typically smile or laugh, Rachel. I haven't in years."

Leaning forward, she rested her hand on his bicep. "But why, Isaac? Why punish yourself by omitting joy from your life?"

"Laughter and smiling are emotions."

"And?"

"I don't *do* emotions."

She started to retrieve her hand, but he placed his own down on hers and held it against his skin, craving the connection, knowing he would have to have that connection, her strength, to have this conversation.

"But…why? Why in the world would you do that to yourself?" She was honestly confused, didn't understand what would warrant exiling one's self from joy.

"I killed my middle brother. He died right in front of me." The confession spilled out of him without his consent, as if he'd been bound to tell her and suffer the consequences. And maybe he was.

"H-how did you kill him, exactly?" She took a deep breath, visibly slowing herself down as she controlled the exhale. "What happened?"

Isaac cursed his subconscious choice of words, no matter their accuracy. He'd scared her, and he was an ass for doing so. Even if what he'd spoken was the truth.

"I was home from college for spring break. New York had seen a lot of rain, so the creeks and rivers were swollen. I loved the outdoors, loved hiking, camping, rock climbing." He swallowed again, fear making the action painful. "Kayaking. I wanted to run the rapids on a local river, and Mike asked if he could go with me." He paused, and she waited in silence, seeming to understand he could only tell the story in fits and starts.

"Mike wasn't as strong a kayaker, didn't have the experience I had, and he was a little nervous, but I told him he could come along. I said we'd use the tandem kayak—one made for two people—and I'd let him lead or sit in front. I'd be there to—to..." Looking up at the ceiling, Isaac took a moment to slow down, counting backward from twenty to zero, inhaling and holding his breath for a count of eight and releasing it on a count of ten.

"Short version of the story is that the kayak flipped. I got out and he got trapped in the rapids, upside down, the kayak stuck against a boulder. I couldn't get to him to flip the kayak and he didn't have the skill to do it. I watched him drown. I stood there as he died because I wanted to conquer the rapids. I was arrogant, Rachel. I knew he wasn't experienced enough, but I was certain—so damn *certain*—that I was better, stronger, more capable of overcoming anything that came up. It never occurred to me that he could die. But he did. Mike died because I didn't keep my promise. I didn't keep him safe. I lost control of the situation, and he died."

Rachel sat perfectly still, unspeaking, for several moments as Isaac fought the rising panic that he had kept at bay for so many years. No more. It all came rushing in. Right here. Right now. He would suffer,

would lose any hope he had with this woman, and
he would accept that. It was just one more penance
he would pay for taking his brother's life.

She started to speak, then stopped, and Isaac saw
it for what it was.

The end.

Rachel had to choose her words carefully or risk
alienating Isaac forever. He hadn't killed his brother,
but that wasn't what he'd spent a lifetime telling himself. He believed he was responsible, and that had
shaped the man he had become and the burdens he
had carried since the tragic loss. Giving in to her
urge to pull him close and cuddle him would only
drive a wedge between them. After all, he had flat-
out told her he didn't "do" emotions.

Caution. She had to proceed with caution.

She must have taken too long because Isaac
started to move away from her.

Reaching out, she grabbed his hand and yanked.
Hard. Hard enough to spin him around and force him
to face her. "Don't walk out on this, Isaac."

"Don't pretend to understand."

"I'm not pretending anything." She refused to let
go of his hand, knowing there was no way he'd physically shake her off. Even angry or hurt, he wasn't
that man.

"Please sit down and talk to me, Isaac. I want to
be clear about a couple of things."

He sank down on the very edge of the mattress,
as far away as he could be and still hold her hand.

The choice wasn't lost on her, even though she was relatively sure he didn't realize what he'd done.

Rachel closed the distance between them, tightening her grip on his hand when he tried to retrieve it. "I haven't asked for much, Isaac, but I'm asking you for this. I need you to listen to me. Please."

Isaac eyed her with something far too close to distrust for her liking, but it wasn't enough to deter her.

"I know you think you killed your brother."

"I did."

"No. Your brother drowned."

"Under my care."

"Yes."

Her agreement stunned him into silence. If that's what it would take, fine. She'd run with it.

"But you did not 'kill' him, Isaac." He started to argue and she squeezed her hand around his. She couldn't lose him at this point. "Let me finish."

"You're going to piss me off."

"Anger is an emotion. You don't do emotion, so subdue it until I've had my say," she bit out. When he did nothing but glare, she went on. "To kill someone is to act with intent, be it malicious or self-defense. By definition, you didn't kill him. You didn't even take his life because his life wasn't yours to take. I know you feel guilty. It's understandable. You were unable to save him in dangerous conditions. But, Isaac? Hear me on this. You did *not* kill him."

"He's dead," he replied, his words flat. His tone vacant.

"Question. Had the roles been reversed, had you

been the one in the front of the kayak and trapped against the boulder, would you have been able to extricate yourself from the kayak and get out of whitewater rapids and safely to shore?" When he began mulling it over, she shifted closer and pressed her free hand against his chest. "Yes-or-no answer, please. Would you have been able to get out given your skill level on that particular day and under those conditions?"

"No. But—"

"Then what are you guilty of?"

She was entirely unprepared for the emotional eruption that followed. Isaac shot off the bed, distancing himself from her. Slapping his palms flat against the wall beside the bed, he leaned forward. His breathing was labored, a sheen of sweat running along the column of his spine.

"Isaac?" she asked with uncertainty.

"I should have told him no, Rachel. Don't you get it? I should have known there was a strong likelihood we'd get into some sort of trouble and he wouldn't be able to get out of it."

"Why should you have known?"

"Because the moment I agreed to take him, he became my responsibility. The last thing my mother said to me was 'Make sure to take care of your little brother.' He was thirteen, Rachel. *Thirteen.*" His shoulders sagged, dragging her heart down, as well. "If I'd had better instincts, I would've told him to stay home. I wouldn't have let him tag along. He would be alive if I'd been smarter. More careful. More aware. Less arrogant."

"In other words, if you'd been able to predict the future and, by knowing, control the outcome," she said softly, and it all fell into place. His need to control everything in any given situation. His unwillingness to let go and laugh or smile spontaneously. His inability to let go entirely during lovemaking and give his pleasure, his well-being, over to someone else's keeping. All of it and so much more. He had achieved success in the capital-investments game because he was unable to live with himself if he failed.

Isaac wasn't the prodigy the investment world thought him to be. He simply went with the outcomes he could be certain about. Concrete guarantees. Outcomes he could influence. Outcomes he could, in a very real sense, control.

Isaac hadn't entered into a long-term relationship because he couldn't predict the outcome of any given emotional "investment" he made. People, and relationships, just weren't predictable. And his need to control himself, his need to keep things predictable and to keep those he cared for safe, made it impossible for him to love unconditionally. Love came with all kinds of ups and downs, bumps and bruises…and no promises of forever. Rachel had learned that firsthand.

Going slowly so as not to startle him, she slipped from the bed and moved in close to him.

"Don't," he rasped.

She ignored him, her own instinct telling her he wasn't pushing her away but rather he was trying to hide from the exposed truth. His major character flaw as he saw it. But that wasn't what Rachel saw. In front of her wasn't a failure but a fractured soul. With extreme care, she rested her hand on his shoulder.

His skin twitched like a horse aggravated by a fly. She didn't move.

Isaac's head dropped lower.

"You aren't to blame, Isaac."

"You say that like you were there."

Ignoring the bite in his words, she moved in closer, resting her other hand on his hip and her forehead on the outside of his arm. "I've never lost a sibling, so I can't say that I understand. But I've lost loved ones, some to death, one to abandonment. I may not have been there, but from what you've told me, you aren't to blame. Your mother…did she, or does she, blame you?"

"No." The word was as sharp as a rifle report. "It would be easier if she did."

"Your father?"

"He's bitter, angry at the world." He sighed. "But he's always been that way."

"What about your other brother, Jonathan?"

"He's the baby of the family. And no, he doesn't blame me." His voice softened with affection. "In fact, he was in my office Thursday morning and told me I had to let Mike's death go."

"Sounds like a smart guy."

"Brilliant in many ways. In fact, I owe him. Huge." Isaac gently turned and pulled her into his arms. "He's the one who browbeat me into going to the Power Match meet and greet after my information was inadvertently used. He's the reason we met."

Rachel settled into the circle of his arms, nuzzling his chest. "No offense, but I have to question his 'brilliance.' The app wasn't exactly a success in matching us, you know."

Again, laughter rumbled through his chest. "No, it wasn't. Truth?"

"Truth."

"Apparently I'm such a pain in the ass that the program had trouble finding matches for me within the test pool."

"And here I thought I was special."

She stilled as Isaac rested his lips against the crown of her head, gave her a soft kiss and said, "You are."

Whatever happened between them tomorrow, she'd deal with it then. Now, in the quiet of their hotel suite, Rachel had seen beyond the outer shell Isaac had created and had met the part of him that he'd kept hidden from the world. She had stood beside him, hand in hand, and looked into his personal abyss, one brimming with more than a decade of remorse and immeasurable guilt. An abyss that had been so dark, but now, she thought, held a glimmer of something akin to hope. Something that might lead him toward self-forgiveness. If she could be part of that for him, part of the healing he so desperately needed, she would be content.

No. Not just content.

She would be happy.

CHAPTER THIRTEEN

THE BATHROOM DOOR opened and steam billowed out like a drumroll in advance of the woman who followed. She smiled, her face softening at the sight of him. "Hey, handsome."

He cleared his throat. "Hey."

Moving with languid grace, Rachel crossed the room, wet hair wrapped in a towel, another towel around her body. Barely.

Isaac couldn't help but think that the Europeans had the right of it, using smaller towels. Particularly given the way the edges separated to reveal an expanse of thigh right up to her bare hip.

"You need breakfast."

He looked up rather stupidly. "Huh?"

"You're eyeing me like I'm on the menu."

"If you're not, I'm filing a complaint with hotel management and going back to bed."

"Hotels like this—I'm sure they'd hate to have such an influential customer leave dissatisfied." She leaned forward, the movement pulling the towel edges farther apart. "Particularly when the solution is such an easy one."

Isaac leaned up and claimed her mouth. She tasted like hope overlaid faintly with toothpaste. She smelled like mint and rosemary. Beneath his hands, she felt like a combination of absolution and carnal sin.

He was good with that.

He wanted—*needed*—both. From her. Only from her.

He pulled her to the bed and laid her down with care, worshipping every inch of skin he could reach. There would be time to slow down later, to worship her body as it deserved to be worshipped. Right now? Isaac needed her. Needed to be inside her. Needed to be lost in her. And from the sounds she made and the way she moved her hips, the way she pulled him to her, it was clear she felt the same.

Sliding up her body, he entered her with a tenderness that was new between them.

Rachel moved beneath him, meeting his thrusts by lifting her hips, taking him deeper than he'd thought possible, holding his face in her hands and watching him for every cue, every tell, every nuance. He saw the reactions in her face as he watched her for the same.

Without warning, he rolled over, taking her with him. This put her on top, empowered her to set the pace, to control the culmination. He still worked her body with care, finding her clitoris and exposing it so he could gently thrum it and push her experience higher.

Hands on her hips, he encouraged her to slide up and down the length of his cock.

She took advantage of the moment. Letting her head fall back, the tips of her hair brushed over his thighs in an erotic sweep.

Isaac groaned, gripping her hips with more strength, bending his knees a bit and encouraging her to ride him with more fervor.

Again, she complied.

Leaning forward, she parked her hands on his chest and pistoned herself up and down his full length, her eyes glazing as the orgasm moved in. She curled her fingertips into his skin. Short, blunt nails would leave crescents.

He hoped they did. That he could wear them as a badge of their lovemaking for as long as possible.

Rachel began to ride him harder, grinding her pelvis against his. "Isaac!" she shouted, and that's when he felt it. Her walls tightened and her sex worked him—squeeze, release, squeeze, release—over and over until he thrust into her one final time and his own orgasm claimed him. He worshipped her body, was a slave to sensation and a willing servant of pleasure's demands.

Rachel collapsed on top of him.

Their breaths came hard and fast, their hearts pounding out competing rhythms with every thundering beat.

Isaac was relatively sure he could lie there for-

ever and be content. And he was, shockingly, okay
with that.

She was lying on her side, eyes declaring her sa-
tiation, her pale skin flushed from exertion and release. With nothing more than a soft, swift kiss, she
left the bed and went into the bathroom, shutting the
door behind her. Water ran, and he heard her moving
about. She hummed a popular song. The tune was
drowned out by the sudden squall of the hair dryer.

He took the opportunity to order room service and
donned a robe to receive the meal when it arrived.

Rachel finished drying her hair before she
emerged from the bathroom, naked. Crawling into
bed, she pulled the sheet up and tucked it under her
arms.

"Feel free to pamper me as you will. I like my coffee with two sugars and a lot of cream. Toast? Thoroughly buttered. I'm not skimping on calories this
weekend." Her dimples emerged. "Not when there's
fresh Irish butter to be had."

"You're the last one who needs to worry about calories." He fixed her coffee and created a plate loaded
with both sweet and savory goodies—including well-
buttered toast—with that very statement in mind. He
set it on the nightstand beside her, then leaned in for
a swift kiss that would have undoubtedly led to more
had her stomach not growled.

Dipping beneath the arm he had propped on the
headboard, she snagged a strawberry and bit into
the fruit with a groan. "I could get used to this," she
said after downing the entire berry. "I'm curious

about what you do, though. Particularly how you got involved with Power Match. I mean, I know your brother is responsible for the new program, but how, exactly, did *you* end up as a test subject?"

"Purely by accident."

She rubbed her hands together and waggled her eyebrows. "Sounds salacious. Do tell."

He snorted and shook his head. "Far from salacious, I'm afraid. It was a mistake. Jonathan had to have an individual's information to show how the software would pair that person to test-pool subjects. Having a known candidate allowed the board to see how the analysis worked, how it would pull from personality traits, preferences and more to successfully pair potential couples. He asked if he could use me since those sitting on the investment board knew me. I balked. He pleaded. I caved. That's the short version."

"And the long version?" she prompted before taking a sip of coffee.

"It involves structural planning, infrastructure of Jonathan's company, staffing decisions, a few bloody fistfights, name-calling and some hair-pulling, the last of which wouldn't be believable on the retelling."

She choked, sputtering and wiping the coffee off her chin. "Did you just make a joke? As in, a *joke*-joke?"

He gave a short bow. "My bag of tricks is endless, madam."

"I'll say," she murmured, glancing at the part in his bathrobe.

He tied the waist tight again. "Lusty wench."

She shrugged. "Your fault."

"In that case, declare me guilty and get on with my punishment."

She chuckled. "I'm an attorney, not a judge."

"Do you want to be? A judge, that is."

"No." Her answer was swift, even a bit vehement. He waited.

"I…" Rachel pulled the sheet up until it was tucked tightly under her arms. "It sounds so, well, I guess it sounds hypocritical to discuss glass ceilings and gender discrimination while I'm sitting here with you, naked, in a bed you paid for."

"This—" he waved a hand between them "—has nothing to do with gender beyond the fact that you're a deliciously sexy woman I wanted to treat to a weekend away. Okay?" When she looked down at the plate she had moved to her lap, he sat on the edge of the bed, curled his finger under her chin and gently lifted her face to his. "Okay, Rachel?"

"Okay."

Isaac stood, dropped his robe and then retrieved his own plate and coffee before crawling into bed beside her. "Now, out with it. Tell me what you want from your job."

"A career" was her immediate answer.

"Lay it out for me."

She crossed her legs tailor-style and twisted just enough to face him. "I've been a junior attorney for years. Longer, in fact, than every man that was hired by the firm the same year I was. If they survived the grueling hours, they were promoted by year five. Not me. There was always some reason I was passed over." She paused, took a sip of coffee and hummed in appreciation. "That's good stuff."

"Agreed. Now, go on."

"Are you always this bossy so early in the day?"

"I'm an early riser by nature. I'd have been in the office at least—" he glanced at the clock "—three hours by now."

"I'd have been there two."

He tipped his head in acknowledgment. "Two workaholics sitting here lounging in Dublin. Who'd have thought?"

She huffed. "Not me."

"Me, either, but I'm glad we're here."

"Me, too."

"What do you want, Rachel? From your career, I mean." He clarified quickly, maybe too quickly, afraid that her answer might be more than he wanted to hear just then.

She continued as if his abrupt clarification meant nothing. "I want to make junior partner this year. There's an opening…" She swirled her coffee in her cup, eyes glued to the muddy-looking drink. Then she looked at him, her gaze fierce. "I want it, Isaac. I've *earned* it, probably ten times over. There's another attorney who has thrown his name in the hat for consideration, but I've been there two years longer than he has. I have more experience, more hours in court with twice the recorded wins that he has. I've *earned* that position."

"What would it mean for you to get that job?"

She looked over his shoulder, her eyes softening. "No more worrying about having to give up my one-bedroom apartment to get a roommate. No more eating ramen for dinner to be able to pay my student-loan payments. No more scrabbling to make ends meet when I need to cover business expenses or manage to pay for an actual vacation."

She looked so fierce sitting there, hair hanging in waves around her bare shoulders, eyes bright with ambition, mouth thin with determination. Isaac knew she'd get what she was after, come hell or high water. She wasn't the type to settle for less than what she deserved. He recognized the same trait in himself and knew just how far he would go to achieve the next pinnacle of success, particularly when it was so clearly within reach.

"You'll get there," he said softly, offering her a bite of bagel covered in cream cheese.

"I have to, Isaac. If I don't?" She took the proffered bite and chewed slowly. Swallowed. "I can't let this position go to someone who hasn't put in the time. I'll do whatever I have to do to get the partners to see me."

A sudden thought crossed his mind, made his stomach perform an unwelcome flip-flop. "Did this trip affect your chances?"

"No," she answered quickly. "I wanted to do this, Isaac. Wanted to do this with you. It's been the reminder I needed that, sometimes, you have to let your hair down and live a little. All work and no play makes Jack a dull boy and Jill a dull girl, after all."

"Truth." He raised his coffee cup and clinked it to hers.

"Truth," she repeated. "What do you see happening with Power Match after Jonathan's test run?"

"I'm not entirely sure." He rolled his head from side to side and popped his neck.

"I can tell you what *I* think needs to happen," she said as she forked up a breakfast sausage.

Test-subject insight would be invaluable, so he waved her on.

"You need to find the glitch in the software that seems to pair opposites versus like-minded individuals."

"Don't tell me you think we're a bad match," he said, voice laden with ironic disbelief.

"Not a bad match," she affirmed. "Just not a match I'd have ever sought out on my own."

"Because…"

"We're opposites." She reached out and traced a finger along his jaw. "For all the ways we seem to be perfect for each other? We're really, truly opposites. You can't tell me you'd have sought me out in a crowded room if we'd been left to our own devices."

"I'd like to think I would have." An unfamiliar pang in his chest told him he wasn't being honest with himself.

Or her.

When he was alone in bed in the middle of the

night, he'd look at the truth more closely. Until then? It was something he'd tuck away and let lie.

"What are your aspirations for Power Match?" Rachel asked, shifting to reach for a sausage on his plate.

He picked it up and fed it to her from his fingertips, trying to keep his mind on the conversation. "I'd like to see the app replace Date Me as the number one app that singles, particularly corporate singles, use to find their perfect partner."

"You'll need to work out the glitch. Oh, come on. You know we're a glitch." She scooted closer and snuggled into his side, easing the sting of her words. "The best glitch ever."

But still, by her admission, a glitch.

Unwilling to go down that path, he set aside his plate, flipped the covers back, stood and stretched. "Well, my sexy glitch, what do you say we abandon this fine establishment and go see as much of this city as we can before we're required to return to real life?"

Rachel scrambled out of bed and reached for her little suitcase filled with new clothes, retrieving what were unquestionably his favorite pair of jeans on her and a heavy wool sweater. "Let's blow this Popsicle stand."

"What do you want to see first?"

"Everything," she answered as she pulled her sweater over her head.

"I'll do my best," he declared.

And he meant it.

They spent the day exploring as much of Dublin as they could on foot before, with more regret than he could ever have anticipated, it was time for them to gather their things and head to the airport, where his corporate jet waited.

They talked the entire way home, arguing at times over differences of opinion. He loved that she had no problem holding her position, even if he battered her beliefs with irrefutable facts. She didn't cave, held firm and gave as well as she got.

The woman was one in a million.

She slept the last leg of the trip, rousing only when he woke her for their descent into LaGuardia.

"How are we here? I just went to sleep," she mumbled into her pillow.

"That was three hours ago."

"Whatever." She buried her face in her pillow.

"C'mon, Rachel. You know the drill." He hooked an arm around her shoulders and sat her up, using his free hand to lean her seat forward. "Seat in the upright and locked position."

"Blah, blah, blah." She scrubbed her hands over her face. "What good is being rich if you have to follow all the rules?" she grumbled.

"You're cute when you're irritated."

"Then I ought to be damn precious right about now."

He grinned. "You are."

"Don't patronize a sleepy woman. I need coffee first."

He laughed, warming when she turned away to hide her answering smile.

The lights of New York City were brilliant, reflecting off the overcast sky so that the city itself appeared to glow.

"Seems we brought the gloomy weather home with us."

She harrumphed, sliding down in her seat and resting her forehead against the window. "I don't want to go back to real life," she whispered.

"Neither do I."

She didn't respond, and Isaac wanted to prod her, provoke her into saying something, anything, that would open the conversation for him to demand she see him again. Not ask. *Demand.* After all, she claimed he was always irritating her or pissing her off. Might as well keep to his record.

But she said nothing, and he wasn't sure how to play his cards.

"What has you looking like you need a package of prunes and a magazine?"

"Nothing."

"Liar."

"Perhaps," he answered, just to annoy her.

But she surprised him and, instead, laughed. "You're far too predictable at times, Mr. Miller."

The pilot's voice came over the intercom, interrupting the exchange with the announcement that they'd been cleared to land.

Rachel gathered her few belongings and started rummaging for her cell phone.

Isaac laid a hand over hers. "Have to wait until he clears us to use electronic devices. Cell phones can interfere with his communication from the tower."

She sighed rather dramatically. "Like I said, what good is being rich?"

Isaac waved his hand like a game-show hostess presenting the interior of the jet as a prize. "Oh, it has its perks."

She chuffed out a short laugh. "Smart-ass."

"I've been called worse."

"No doubt."

"Rachel?"

She looked up at him, eyes wide and entirely receptive.

"I don't know how to do this."

Her face closed up tight. "I have a pretty good idea where this conversation is going, Isaac."

The skin on the back of his neck prickled. "Do you, then? By all means, enlighten me as to what's going through my head."

"Despite the wonderful weekend, you've made it clear numerous times that you don't do long-term relationships. Ever. So this is the point where you issue the gentle 'it's been fun' parting line and offer to have your car service take me home."

His stomach had tied itself in multiple knots as she spoke, crowding his lungs so he couldn't get a deep breath. "You're wrong," he finally responded.

"Oh?" She looked out the window. "Then pardon me for borrowing your language, but 'enlighten me.'"

"Look at me, Rachel." She didn't turn, so he

waited. "I'm not having this conversation with the back of your head."

She rounded on him, eyes dangerously narrowed. "Say what you need to say."

"It would serve you right if I let you ride home thinking whatever it is you're thinking. But you're so damn stubborn you probably wouldn't take my call tomorrow."

She blinked owlishly. "Call? Tomorrow?"

He closed the distance between them and kissed her, putting everything he had into the kiss—frustration, lust, fear, passion, longing and, most terrifying of all, hope.

She responded without reservation, and he couldn't help but release her seat belt and pull her into his lap.

"We're landing," she murmured against his lips.

"What the hell good is it being rich?" he replied.

She laughed before returning to the kiss with such passion he couldn't think of anything but the woman in his arms.

The plane lurched to a stop at the gate, nearly unseating her.

Isaac helped her to her feet and then rose to stand beside her. "Let me see you home."

"I'll let you see me to a cab."

He sucked in a breath. "Rachel."

"Isaac." She reached up and traced the line of his jaw. "If you see me home, I won't be able to help myself. I'll ask you to come up. You will. We'll be up in a couple of hours doing what we do, and you'll be there tomorrow morning when my alarm goes off far too early. You'll ask me to call in again. I'll be tempted. I can't make senior attorney if I keep calling in just to get laid."

He laughed. "Fair enough."

"So see me to a cab and kiss me farewell with a promise to call me tomorrow?"

"Promise."

They gathered their bags, and he didn't balk at her insistence she carry her own belongings. The airport was far busier than he would have expected for a midnight arrival, but they managed to remain side by side and talk all the way to the cab lineup.

She went to the front of the line, opened the cab's rear door and turned to him.

He kissed her with all the promise he had in him, let her get in the cab against his better judgment and watched her disappear in traffic.

The alarm went off way too early—confirmation that real life was back. Shuffling to her tiny kitchen, her eyes still working on getting with the concept of "being awake," she put the coffee pod in the machine and pressed what she hoped was the brew button. Thank God for single-serve coffeemakers. No measuring. No adding water. No thinking. Very little waiting. Cup in hand only a few seconds later, she made her way back to the bedroom and sat on the edge of the bed, trying to wake up. Jet lag was a very real thing and a bitch to boot.

Reaching for her cell phone by rote, she was confused when it wasn't on her bedside table, where it belonged.

"What did I do with it?"

Forcing herself to get up, she went to where she'd literally dropped her bags last night, just inside the doorway. She hadn't had the energy to put things away just then, so she'd left her bags where they fell with the promise to sort things out after work today. Then she'd gone to bed.

Her cell had to be in the clutch she'd carried the night she met Isaac. She'd taken it to Ireland and then shoved the whole thing into the messenger bag she had purchased. Digging through the sparse but jumbled contents, she found the little evening bag wrapped inside the dress she'd worn Thursday night. She opened it and, sure enough, there was her phone.

And it was as lifeless as Jimmy Hoffa.

"Crap." She should've plugged it in, but she hadn't had messages when she checked it Friday night when they'd arrived in Ireland. And, if she was honest, she'd forgotten about it entirely after that.

Taking the phone, messenger bag and her one small suitcase back to the bedroom, she plugged in the phone. It was so dead that it wouldn't power up with the cord in place. The best it could do was show the blinking red battery icon. Served her right. She'd just let it charge while she showered and put herself together. That would let her check her messages on her way to work. She'd plug it in at her desk and let it fully charge there.

Admit it. You want to know if Isaac has called.

"Nope. Not going to worry about that."

Liar.

"Perhaps," she said, smiling. She'd never be able to hear that phrase without thinking of him.

Rachel went through her morning routine, loaded her new messenger bag with her work items and then grabbed her phone. If she didn't step it up, she was going to miss the bus to the subway and end up late.

She had to run for the bus, but she made it. Taking the first seat she came to, she sank into it and retrieved her phone. Which she almost dropped when she powered up the screen.

"What the hell?"

Nineteen text messages.

Nine missed calls.

Four voice mails.

That wasn't Isaac's style. She was sure of it. And that meant something had happened.

Hands shaking, she had to try twice to enter her passcode. All she could think was that something had happened to her mom while she'd been off playing pretty princess with New York's most sought-after bachelor. Or maybe it was her dad. Or it could be Casey. The phone couldn't connect to service fast enough for her.

She went to the texts first.

There were eight from Casey. Her boss, Jim Franks, had sent six. Three had come from her mom. Then there were two from Isaac. Saving his for last, she tapped her boss's name, scrolled to the first text sent Friday morning and started reading her way up.

Friday, 11:05 a.m.

Rachel, I know you called in asking to take a personal day, but I need you to come in. One of our high-profile clients is bringing a time-sensitive suit against a competitor. I need you to draft and file a cease and desist order and have the defendant served before the end of the day. I want you to take the lead on this case. It could be the one that gets you the senior attorney's position you've been after.

Friday, 11:59 a.m.

Rachel, I need you to get back to me ASAP.

Friday, 12:21 p.m.

Rachel, I've had Tom start drafting the cease and desist order until you get here. I need you to come in and take point. I can't have you out today.

Friday, 2:05 p.m.

Rachel, Tom has drafted the order. I'm going to go over what he has. The process server is already here and waiting. Get in here as soon as possible.

Friday, 3:01 p.m.

This is going to require you and your team to come in and work this weekend to have the full complaint filed first thing Monday morning. Just come in as soon as you can.

Monday, 7:47 a.m.

My office as soon as you're here.

With every message, the nausea roiling in her belly grew worse until, by his last text, she felt like her insides were being tossed about on brutal seas. Closing her eyes, she rested her head on the bus's cold window and tried to slow her breathing.

How the hell had she not seen these? Why hadn't they come through?

Hands shaking worse than ever, she went back to the phone and tapped on Casey's messages.

Friday, 11:12 a.m.
Call me as soon as possible.

Friday, 11:24 a.m.
I'm not joking. Call me. Now. Don't leave without talking to me.

Friday, 11:49 a.m.
For the love of God, do NOT get on that plane, Rachel. DO. NOT.

Friday, 1:00 p.m.
Why the hell aren't you answering your phone????

Friday, 4:44 p.m.
Call me. NOW.

Friday, 7:58 p.m.
Just got home. Rach, not naming names here for good reason, but I'm telling you, extricate yourself

from last night. Please. Trust me. Just do it. Catch commercial and come home no matter the cost.

Saturday, 9:04 a.m.

You didn't turn on international calling, did you? Damn it. Your career's in deep shit, my friend. Get your ass home.

Sunday, 10:10 p.m.

Worked all weekend trying to cover for you. Why? Because I love you and I'm worried sick. If you have any sense of self-preservation, call me before you go into the office. Jim is LIVID. Your ass is on the chopping block and you need to be prepared.

She glanced at her mom's messages. Just chatter. So she went to Isaac's messages, her heart hammering so hard in her throat she wanted to puke.

Monday, 3:42 a.m.

At the risk of appearing pathetic and just a bit stalkerish, I miss you.

Monday, 7:57 a.m.

There are a great many things I could say, but I'll only bother with this: I never would have taken you for such a power-hungry woman that you'd use your body as a weapon and another's emotions as leverage to reach the next rung on the corporate ladder. Consider our affiliation terminated.

Bone-numbing cold swept through Rachel's body as she blindly grabbed for the stop cord. The driver pulled to the curb, and Rachel staggered off the bus, bent down and retched, but nothing came up. Stomach cramps kept her bent forward. She blamed the tears on the urge to vomit.

Liar.

Forcing herself to rise to her full height, her damnable mind running through a thousand different scenarios, she keyed her phone open, selected her list of recent calls and tapped on Casey's name. The call went through, rang just once and her coworker and best friend in the world came on. "You on your way to the office?" Her somber tone said everything, cementing the weight of the situation and confirming Rachel's fears.

"Yeah." Someone shouldered past Rachel with a sharp "watch it," and she stepped out of the path of commuter foot traffic to lean against a storefront window. "How bad is it?"

"Hold on."

Rachel heard Casey's heels click across the floor. She stopped and told her paralegal to give her ten uninterrupted minutes. More heels on hardwood, this time approaching the phone, and then she was back.

"It's bad, Rach. Really bad. How far away are you?"

"I'm going to spring for a cab in the hopes of getting there faster. So give me the short version."

"You're familiar with the dating app Date Me."

"Sure. We've both used it."

"For years, it's been the world's number one dating app. Friday morning, the investment section of the paper reported on Thursday night's test run for Power Match and publicly predicted that it would become the new go-to for professionals who wanted to essentially skip dating and go straight to wedding bells. The capital-investment firm run by one Isaac Miller released a statement that touted advancements over Date Me's psychological matchmaking methods, claiming to have built a better, more accurate system that will make Date Me's app obsolete the moment Power Match goes live."

"Sounds like a standard marketing ploy to generate interest."

"It would have been…if the client hadn't scooped Date Me's lead psychologist—the same psychologist who developed Date Me's proprietary questionnaires that determine the most effective means of matching couples. Rach, she had a watertight noncompete in place when she left. No working for any company that could be considered competition for two years. And no using, developing or in any way modifying software deemed proprietary for five years from the date of separation."

"Oh, shit." She couldn't tell Casey what she knew. Not without making her culpable should the firm's management or, worse, founding partners question her. So she swallowed the urge to tell what she knew and, instead, listened.

"It gets better." Casey lowered her voice. "She only left nine months ago and Date Me is claiming she didn't give them notice as per her contract. She just packed up and left. They found out, through the news report, about her alleged improvements to the selection software she originally created for Date Me, and they're claiming that their primary global competitor is not only using their proprietary software, but also trying to damage Date Me's market share, investment security, client retention—the list goes on. Their legal department outsourced this case to us Friday morning. They asked us to file an immediate injunction to stop all work on Power Match's development and release, enforce the noncompete for the psychologist and seek damages from both the developer and the capital-investment firm funding this project. You know who Caffeinated Brainiacs obtained capital funding from, Rachel."

Casey didn't say his name. She didn't have to.

The company was Quantum Ventures.

The CEO was Isaac Miller.

Rachel maneuvered through foot traffic to the curb and hailed a cab. "Does Jim know where I was?" she asked as a cab pulled up. She slipped inside and slammed the door at the same time she gave the driver her destination.

"I don't think so. You didn't tell anyone but me where you went, did you?" Casey paused; Rachel waited. "And you didn't tell anyone else who you were with?"

"No."

"Then I don't know *how* he'd know. But, Rachel, even though Tom drafted the order, Jim assumed you would call back or at least come in this weekend, so he listed you as the attorney of record on Friday's filing. If Quantum Ventures' legal department knows, or if *he* told them…"

"They would have filed a countermotion to have me removed from the case."

There were four things that Rachel was certain of just then.

First: her boss knew where she'd been.

Second: he knew whom she'd been with.

Third: what had been the best weekend of her life was almost certainly going to cost her the career she'd fought so hard for.

Fourth: Isaac Miller, the man she'd begun to fall for, believed she had betrayed him.

CHAPTER FOURTEEN

"WHAT THE HELL were you *thinking*, Jonathan?" Isaac rarely raised his voice, but the breach in his emotional dam—that *Rachel* had created—had grown. Continued to grow, in fact, and he found himself unable to rein in his temper. "What you did? It's beyond irresponsible. It easily qualifies as flat *stupid*!"

Jonathan sat slouched in the same chair he always chose when he came to Isaac's office, a hangdog look on his face. "I'm telling you, Isaac. I asked her if she was clear to work for us and she said yes. What else was I supposed to do?"

"What…else…" For a second, Isaac thought he might rupture a vessel, perhaps develop an aneurysm and collapse where he stood. When that didn't happen, he began to pace. Back and forth in front of his floor-to-ceiling windows, repeatedly shoving his hands through his hair. Grabbing fistfuls at the crown. Pulling until he thought he might yank himself bald. Spinning to face his brother, he forced his hands to his sides. "What else should you have *done*? Tell me you aren't serious."

"We did the in-depth preemployment background check we do on all employees. Shit like noncompetes don't show up on those reports, Isaac. The most I can do is ask. If someone lies, I have no way of knowing."

Scrubbing his hands over his face, Isaac tried to slow his breathing. "Your human resources department should have called her former employer and asked for references. That person should have asked if there were any legally binding agreements in force that would prevent her from working for the competition."

"Part of her condition of employment was that we didn't contact her current employer for a reference. She said she didn't want them to know she was looking for another job. Happens all the time, so HR didn't think anything of it."

He closed his eyes and counted. First to ten and, when that didn't work, to twenty. Then he looked at his brother and forced himself to remember that the kid was, in fact, brilliant. And more often than not, brilliant minds did not come equipped with add-on faculties like common sense. Case in point.

Sighing, he dropped into his chair. "We're in a hell of a mess, Jonathan. Our investors are furious and they, and their lawyers, have been bombarding us with questions we can't yet answer. Our legal department is scrambling to figure out how to salvage something, anything, in relation to this project so that we don't lose millions. *Millions.* And our best efforts may be irrelevant as the entire project appears to be going tits-up thanks to social media. Quantum Ventures' reputation for ethical business practices is, as we speak, dissolving like sugar cubes left on the sidewalk during a monsoon."

Jonathan sat forward and rested his forearms on his knees, hands dangling, chin tucked to his chest. "I'm sorry, Isaac. I'm good at ideas. I'm great at execution. It's the other stuff that trips me up."

"Yeah, it does." No point softening the truth.

Or so he thought until Jonathan looked up, eyes wide, face pale as fresh milk. "I'll pull the project."

"It's not that simple, Jonathan. We have to answer the legal complaint, prove we've stopped work as ordered by the judge and figure out how we recoup the money we've invested so that those financial backers I mentioned don't jump ship and take their money elsewhere."

"How do I make this right?"

He thought about what to say, thought about telling Jonathan that they were so far up shit creek that a paddle was pointless and even an eight-cylinder outboard motor would likely do them no good. But the kid was a mess, and all Isaac had done was add to his stress.

It wasn't his fault that, on the inside, Isaac was a bigger mess than the developing corporate calamity. He hadn't been able to sleep last night, his mind awash in weekend memories, his body craving one woman's touch, his heart feeling odd in her absence. Texting her at 3:42 a.m. had been foolish. But as he sat in the dark, empty highball glass dangling from his fingers, mind softened by alcohol, he had realized he was falling in love with Rachel. More the fool was he. He just thanked God he hadn't said as much in his text.

Then there was the other truth of the matter, particularly as it related to Jonathan. Isaac couldn't deny that he, himself, was more to blame for this debacle than Jonathan. As Quantum Ventures' CEO, he should have been more careful in the application stage. He should have thoroughly vetted the senior members of Caffeinated Brainiacs' development team. He should have had his legal team confirm there weren't any noncompetes in play, particularly with those senior team members. And he should have ensured that every *i* was dotted and every *t* crossed instead of assuming someone from Caffeinated Brainiacs would handle the finer details. Bottom line? Isaac had handled Jonathan more like an indulgent older brother than the renowned capital-venture expert he was.

But what was done, was done.

Now? He could shout, stomp, point fingers, terminate contracts and even terminate people, but it wouldn't change the truth. Isaac could blame no one but himself.

He was searching for the right words to convey that singular truth when his phone chirped, the sound soft and unobtrusive. The caller ID flashed an internal extension belonging to the head of Quantum Ventures' legal department, Ben King.

Mustering every ounce of control he possessed,

Isaac picked up the phone and greeted the other man with a facade of calm confidence. "Hey, Ben. I'd tell you to give me the good news, but I know better if you're phoning rather than delivering it in person."

Ben chuckled. "No worries. I'm a lawyer. It's part and parcel of my job description. 'Deliver bad news succinctly and from a distance.' I'm just sorry to say it's definitely bad news."

Isaac turned away from Jonathan, not sure he could keep his worried expression out of his brother's line of sight. "Might as well lay it out there, then."

Ben didn't mince words. "Taylor, Lord and Mitchum, the firm representing Date Me, intends to file suit for patent infringement and intellectual-property theft, and they're not only naming Caffeinated Brainiacs, but they're also going after Quantum Ventures."

Isaac pinched the bridge of his nose. "I'm not surprised."

"They're filing in federal court."

His stomach dropped. "I'd like to revise my answer."

"I thought you might."

"What does that mean for us, Ben?"

"It means a hell of a lot of media coverage. They're seeking an injunction that would halt any and all work related to the development of Power Match as well as financial remedies for damages done and claims made by the psychologist, Jaline Harkins, alleging the inferiority of the Date Me app when compared to Power Match."

"They're built on similar software platforms," Isaac said through gritted teeth. "If she said Date Me sucks, she's implying Power Match sucks, as well."

"Not necessarily. Date Me's parent corporation, Clockwork Machinations, could be entitled to damages for defamation, loss of investor faith and damage done to public opinion. Jaline was a highly disgruntled employee, and she's been running her mouth and giving interviews without the knowledge or consent of Brainiacs' senior management. She acknowledged as much when I questioned her this morning. But it doesn't matter. Legally, we're on the hook."

"What are we talking about in dollar figures, Ben?"

"Easily seven figures if we settle. Likely eight if we go to court."

Swiveling his chair, Isaac moved the mouthpiece away and focused on Jonathan. "Has Jaline Harkins been terminated?"

"No."

"Do it. Now. Tell her Legal will be contacting her with a termination agreement."

"I'll get it done and have the draft to you this afternoon," Ben promised.

"The Power Match project is shut down, effective immediately." He knew Quantum Ventures would take a huge loss, but there was no other choice. The liability Quantum Ventures was exposed to was enormous, significant enough to negatively affect their stock values as well as business expansion and profitability over the next five to ten years. "This has to be done if you have any hope of salvaging Caffeinated Brainiacs' future, Jonathan."

"I get it." His little brother stood, dug his cell out of his jeans pocket and held up the phone. "I'll just go out in the hall."

"Use the conference room. Better to do it as privately as possible. Even my people talk."

Jonathan gave a single nod and left the room.

Isaac returned his attention to the attorney. "Ben, make sure that the termination agreement does *not* offer her a damn dime in severance. She's lucky we aren't pressing charges. If she balks at all, tell her I'll put everything I have into making sure she can't even get a job dumping slop buckets on a pig farm."

"Remind me to never piss you off."

"I shouldn't have to."

"I can always count on you to tell it like it is. And, Isaac?" He waited until Isaac hummed with irritation. "I think we need to be proactive—go to plaintiff's counsel, tell them everything we're doing to resolve the issue and offer a private settlement. Include an airtight nondisclosure so the numbers are private, but we should make a good-faith effort to intercede before filing our response."

"Do you think they're willing to negotiate?"

"It can't hurt to at least propose settlement, include some public statements from Quantum Ventures that make it clear we didn't intend to cause Date Me any harm. Point out that they're a good service—good enough we thought they were worth competing with."

"Run the numbers and let me know what we're talking about, but go ahead and see if they're willing to meet. I don't have to tell you to do what you can to make this go away, Ben."

"No, sir, you don't."

"Get me a solid settlement figure as well as talking points at least two hours before we meet. I'll want to go over them with you and discuss strategy so we're on the same page in there. You and me. No one else from legal."

"You think that's wise?"

"Unless you tell me it's a dumb-ass move, that's my plan. Appear as confident and in control as possible. Don't give them even a crumb of proof this shit is shaking the foundation of Quantum Ventures."

"Yes, sir."

"How soon can you make this happen?"

"If they agree? I can try to get a meeting today."

"Whatever it takes, do it." And he hung up.

Leaning back in his chair, he locked his hands behind his head and propped his feet on the corner of his desk. Anyone who saw him would think he had everything under control. Superficially, he might. But he still had one huge problem to deal with. He was going to have to sit across the table from the attorney listed on the injunction, the attorney who had warmed his bed right before she sold him out for an office with a better view.

Rachel Sullivan.

* * *

The cabbie pulled up to the front of her office. "Twenty-seven even."

She handed him thirty and got out, standing on the sidewalk and staring up at the glass-and-chrome high-rise. Her future, or what was left of it, waited beyond those doors.

She crossed to the revolving door and was in the process of entering the lobby when a single idea settled at the forefront of her mind.

What if this was all a bunch of smoke and mirrors?

Isaac had all the information on Caffeinated Brainiacs. He must have had an employee roster. Wouldn't he have questioned the psychologist's credentials and work history *prior* to agreeing to fund the app's development? Theoretically he would have had access to all the candidates' applications…including hers. What if he had selected her knowing her firm had represented Date Me in previous filings, from the initial patent to the lawsuits corporations of its size were always involved with? He could've easily used his access to Power Match's information to single her out and ensure that any suit brought forward was compromised.

But how could he have known you *would be the one tapped to represent Date Me?* her subconscious whispered.

She ignored logic and embraced fury. Anger, so long as she managed it, would carry her much further than fear and its inherent weaknesses.

Whatever happened, she wasn't going to let someone, boss or lover, browbeat her over something she had possessed no knowledge of. Period.

No man had the right to play her like a pawn on a chessboard. She had lived that life, suffered for it and she was done with it. Never again would she be any man's pawn. If she was anything, she was a queen.

And it was about damn time the other players on the board realized it.

She headed straight to Jim's office, where she tried to explain her actions. Jim wasn't as sympathetic as she might've hoped. Once she'd finished speaking, he made a call, stood and directed her to the elevators. They rode up in silence, exiting on the top floor.

Rachel followed Jim to a large conference room she'd never seen before. A long mahogany table gleamed under unobtrusive lighting. There were only two unoccupied chairs on their side of the table. Across the massive expanse, perfectly centered and sitting shoulder to shoulder, were three older men, all of whom Rachel recognized: Andrew Taylor, Christopher Lord and Bradley Mitchum. They were the founders of what had become one of the most prestigious corporate law firms on the East Coast.

Jim sat down without looking at her, pulled out his pen and shuffled through his papers over and over, reorganizing them to the point his every action seemed absurd.

Rachel had a moment of stark clarity that struck so suddenly she almost laughed out loud.

Jim had always espoused teamwork and team values, claiming he would fight for any member of his team under any circumstance if they were in the right. Rachel had been honest with him. She'd done her best to prove beyond a reasonable doubt that she hadn't been in the wrong for what had occurred outside the office, in her private life, without knowledge of the brewing conflict. She knew now that every word she had uttered had been irrelevant—nothing more than wasted breath. Jim wasn't the man she had come to respect over the last seven years because he wasn't the man she had believed him to be. Looking at him now, she knew with absolute certainty that he wasn't here to defend her. He was here for the opportunity to distance himself from whatever she was deemed guilty of. And, on the off chance she salvaged what was left of her career, he would be there to stand up and act like he had believed in her all along. In the end, he would do whatever was required to save his ass.

Rachel was on her own.

Andrew Taylor gestured toward the plush chair clearly reserved for her. "Have a seat, Miss Sullivan."

"Sir." She sat and crossed her legs, folding her hands in her lap. She'd brought nothing with her. No cell phone, pad of paper, pen. Nothing. So she would sit and answer their questions respectfully unless— and until—they gave her reason to do otherwise.

Christopher Lord leaned forward, rested his forearms on the table and laced his fingers together. "I'm sure you know why we've asked to speak to you, Miss Sullivan."

"I believe it has to do with how I spent my weekend, sir."

Christopher Lord's brow furrowed, his heavy jowls wobbling as he sharply enunciated every syllable. "Not only how, Miss Sullivan, but with whom."

She inclined her head in acknowledgment. No way was she going to roll over and give them her belly. Absolutely not. The only information they would get from her would be answers to questions she deemed relevant to her position within the firm. The rest of it was none of their damn business, no matter how furious she was with Isaac.

"It has been brought to our attention that you took a trip with the CEO of Quantum Ventures, a company against whom a prominent client of our firm has asked us to file suit."

Again, she inclined her head.

"Please respond verbally, Miss Sullivan."

The nape of her neck prickled with unease. "May I ask why, Mr. Lord?"

"For clarity's sake."

"Was my nod of acknowledgment not understandable?"

"For God's sake, Rachel, just answer out loud," Jim snarled under his breath.

"Certainly," she said, her voice so arctic she was surprised it didn't condense on the air. "When I understand why."

Christopher Lord's face flushed. "Because I've asked you to, young lady."

Like that, was it?

She met his gaze head-on. She didn't blink. Didn't flinch. "Am I being recorded, sir?"

Bradley Mitchum jotted down a short note on his legal pad before unbuttoning the single button on his suit coat and crossing his arms. "This needn't be a hostile interview if you don't wish it to be, Miss Sullivan."

In other words, if she played nice and answered the men's questions, they'd pat her on the head and maybe allow her to keep her job.

Nope. All kinds of nope happening here.

She waited, and Mitchum gave her a patronizing smile. "Did you or did you not spend the weekend with Isaac Miller, CEO of Quantum Ventures, the primary defendant in an injunction your immediate supervisor directed you to file last Friday, October seventeenth?"

"I did," she answered.

He stared at her for a moment before continuing. "And did you or did you not allow Isaac Miller to cover your travel expenses via his corporation, Quantum Ventures, again identified as the codefendant in the injunction you were directed to file?"

"I didn't allow it. The use of the corporate jet was exclusively his decision."

"But you didn't request that he travel commercial or, at the very least, allow you to meet him at your final destination, which, I believe, was Dublin, Ireland?"

"Mr. Mitchum, you and your two fellow partners are obviously aware that I spent the weekend in Ireland with Isaac Miller and that I traveled to and from the country via Mr. Miller's corporate jet." The corners of her mouth turned up, but the gesture, the look, was far from anything one might constitute as a smile. "In the name of expediency, let's allow that to stand as established fact. This way you can skip the inane questions and move on to those that you most want answered."

Christopher Lord turned positively puce. "Don't be irreverent, girl."

"With all due respect, don't call me 'girl'...*sir*."

Andrew Taylor held up a hand, staying Christopher Lord's response. "Miss Sullivan, answer me this. Did you or did you not engage in inappropriate activities with Isaac Miller between the hours of 7:00 p.m. Thursday, October sixteenth, and midnight Sunday, October nineteenth?"

Her mind filled with memories of her time spent with Isaac, from their initial meeting to what proved to be their final goodbye. No matter what he thought of her now, no matter what these men *ever* thought of her, she would not under any circumstances label anything she'd done with Isaac as "inappropriate." Sitting up impossibly straighter, she looked each man in the eyes before answering. "No, sir, I did not."

Christopher Lord looked at her with undisguised smugness. "You're lying."

"No, sir, I'm not."

He leered at her, looking her up and down. "Do you deny you engaged in sexual intercourse with Mr. Miller?"

"Among other things? Yes, I did."

"Do you contend that sleeping with the defendant in a complaint you were ordered to file is not a serious conflict of interest?" He looked so pleased with himself, the bastard, that he might sully what she'd had with Isaac.

At the time, what they'd had had been authentic, untainted by the lives they led during business hours. She had to believe this was true, couldn't entertain the ideas that had flooded her mind earlier—that he might have known, might have used her. The man she believed him to be wouldn't have done something so—so...cruel.

"It would have certainly been a conflict of interest had I known he was going to be named as a defendant in a case one of our clients hired us to file and pursue. But, for the record, I did not know that this firm had been retained by Date Me. Nor was I at any time during the weekend aware that I had been assigned to represent our client in any action involving either Quantum Ventures or Isaac Miller."

Andrew Taylor again held up a hand to stop the others from questioning her and, when he spoke, his words held more gravity because of his soft delivery. "You expect us to believe that you didn't receive any of the texts, emails or phone calls made to you by employees of this firm despite the fact you carry a smartphone for which you receive a monthly stipend and, per your employment agreement, you are to keep on your person at all times?"

He had her there. She was going to have to admit to her own stupidity and, perhaps, Isaac's request that they leave their phones off for the weekend. Sitting up straighter, she looked from man to man and then answered. "I did have my phone on me. I checked my texts and calls prior to departing. There were none. Then Mr. Miller and I left the country, and I turned my phone off preflight." In a split second, she chose to keep Isaac's request to herself. What good would it do either of them if these men decided she'd been used? Her shoulders sagged a fraction before she forced them back in place.

"The true problem arose later when I failed to turn on the international-calling feature on my phone. I've never traveled abroad before, so the thought didn't cross my mind. I did power my phone up when we arrived in Dublin, but, without international calling enabled, I didn't show any missed texts or calls all weekend. When we returned to the United States, I was exhausted. I went home, dumped my bags by the front door and went to bed. Alone," she said with emphasis as she looked over at Mr. Lord. "I woke this morning and immediately retrieved my cell. The battery was completely dead, so I plugged it in and got ready for work. I checked my phone on the ride to the subway and discovered all of the messages that I'd failed to receive while out of the country. I immediately got off the bus, caught a cab and came into the office as directed."

Andrew Taylor nodded, but she had no idea what he was nodding *about*. "Did you have any messages from Mr. Miller, Miss Sullivan?"

She swallowed past the dense regret that threatened to choke her. "Yes, I did."

"How many messages did you have?"

"Two."

"And what were they?"

She recognized the look on his face, and knew it for what it was. He was setting her up for the kill. Like hell would she give him the satisfaction. She knew her job here was over. The hostility and disdain she'd been subjected to had made that clear. She wasn't going to give them the satisfaction of carrying out what amounted to a public execution.

"The messages from Mr. Miller have no bearing on this interview."

Bradley Mitchum had been slowly twisting his pen between thumb and forefinger. "I'm sure you can understand that we might see things a bit differently."

"As is your collective right, Mr. Mitchum. But I will not disclose the content of those messages. I've had no further contact with Mr. Miller and would assume there will be no personal contact moving forward. I've also been advised by my immediate supervisor that I've been removed from the case, so, again, there's no merit in disclosing the content of personal messages."

Mr. Mitchum leaned back in his seat and stared at her.

It was a good stare…if one hadn't been stared down by Isaac Miller, and recently.

"Miss Sullivan, I will allow you to keep the content of those messages to yourself. However, it is imperative that you disclose any and all conversations, written or oral, that you had regarding the development, strategies and/or marketing plans for Quantum Ventures' client, Caffeinated Brainiacs."

So there it was. The ultimatum. To keep her job—but no doubt give up any hope of promotion—she would have to turn on Isaac and tell this panel of misogynistic assholes everything she knew about Power Match, about Quantum Ventures and, without question, about Isaac Miller. Sure, she'd remain employed. But for how long? And was her job worth it? Was it worth tearing down a man whom—as furious as she was with him—she had come to respect… and possibly, very possibly, care for?

No matter what the weekend had been to him, it had meant something very, very real to her. It had been the best weekend of her life, and he'd given it to her. Whether under pretense or not was debatable. But the truth of her feelings was hers to interpret, and she wouldn't sell out that part of herself for any amount of money, let alone superficial job security.

Folding her hands in her lap, she let herself grow still. She needed to let her heart catch up with current events before she answered. "I'm sorry, gentlemen, but this weekend was a private affair. I won't share information that was shared with me in good faith that could now destroy not only Mr. Miller, but also his corporation."

"You're treading a very fine line here, Miss Sullivan."

"And I'm of the opinion that I have conducted myself in a professional manner and have answered each and every question that is relevant to this matter, sir."

Christopher Lord slapped a hand on the table, and everyone jumped. "You've behaved like a woman whose morals are loose and whose ethics are, at best, questionable. You will address this panel with respect and answer any question we ask. Do you understand?"

Rachel stared, as shocked at the outburst as she was at essentially being called an unethical whore.

Jim reached over and grabbed her arm with more force than was either necessary or professional. "Answer him, Rachel."

And that—Jim grabbing her—was her breaking point.

In the small, rational corner of her mind, where she found herself watching the fallout with interest, she realized she had wondered where that point would be, if it would come, and what she would do if it did.

Now she knew.

She stood with enough force that her chair careened across the room, one caster catching on the carpet and nearly tipping the seat over. She yanked her arm free from Jim's bruising grasp, straightened her jacket and then faced Jim. "Do not ever, *ever* grab me again, Jim Franks. You have no authority to touch me without my consent and never, *ever* in anger. Do you understand me? Please respond verbally as I've been required to do."

"Get out," Jim growled at the same time Christopher Lord bellowed, "You're fired, Miss Sullivan."

She rounded on the rotund man with slow control, channeling Isaac Miller, mimicking movements she'd seen him make with ease and grace. Lifting her chin, she met the gazes of the three men who had created the firm that had been her professional home for the last seven years. No more. She'd sworn she would never, ever give another man power over her, and this was where she took her stand. Not only for Isaac Miller and what they might have had, but also for herself. "You can't fire me, you arrogant, judgmental, pompous sons of bitches. I quit."

And she walked out of that conference room with her head held high knowing she'd taken the final step in asserting her freedom from her past.

Rachel Sullivan had opened the door to her future.

CHAPTER FIFTEEN

BEN KING HAD done exactly as Isaac had asked, but the plaintiff's counsel claimed extenuating circumstances and had put off the requested meeting until Wednesday afternoon. When Isaac and Ben arrived, they were as prepared as could be for the media, saying nothing more than "no comment," over and over as they pushed their way into the high-rise, crossed the lobby as fast as possible and stepped into the first available elevator car to open its doors.

The digital display silently counted the floors as the car climbed, and, with each level they passed, Isaac found his chest growing tighter and tighter. He slowed his breathing, counted backward from twenty, focused on his heartbeat, pictured a sunny beach and the sound of the waves—all things he'd taught himself to do to beat back panic attacks.

Yet this time, nothing helped.

Rubbing the heel of his hand up and down his sternum, he knew he had to look fierce. He *felt* fierce. In five minutes or less, he would be facing off with Rachel for the first time since they'd said goodbye.

The first time since he'd learned she had lied to him.

She had played him, and it wasn't something he was proud of. Worse, she had managed to pull years of suppressed emotions to the surface—emotions he wasn't equipped to handle.

On cue, his chest tightened another degree.

The elevator stopped and the digitalized feminine voice announced they had arrived at the forty-sixth floor.

Ben stepped out, tugging his jacket straight and adjusting the messenger bag he carried. The doors began to close before he realized he was alone. He looked around and, seeing Isaac still standing in the elevator, slapped a hand on one door as it began to close. "You coming?"

"Yeah." *No.*

"That would require you to actually get out of the elevator, Isaac."

"Yeah." *No.*

But he did, his steps leaden, his movements far from smooth.

Ben cleared his throat. "Ah, Isaac?"

"Yeah."

"You're going to have to pull it together and say something other than 'yeah' when we're in there. If you aren't up for this—" the slightly older man whipped his head to the side and popped his neck "—now would be the time to tell me."

"I'm good."

Ben studied him with open concern. "You sure?" He held up a hand. "Wait, wait. I know the answer. 'Yeah.'"

Shaking his head, Isaac turned and approached the double doors that led into the firm's reception area.

At the desk, a young man worked the phone lines with practiced ease, holding up a finger to indicate he'd be right with them. After transferring the call he'd been on, he smiled at Isaac. "How may I help you?"

"We're here to see Rachel Sullivan and Jim Franks."

"Certainly. Your names, please?"

"Isaac Miller and Ben King."

The receptionist issued two visitor's badges before instructing Isaac and Ben to take a seat.

They did and were left waiting an inordinate amount of time.

"Stupid power games," Ben muttered. "Piss me off."

"Which is exactly what they're supposed to do," Isaac answered.

"Sure, but they aren't nearly as effective when each party recognizes the other's common strategies."

A feminine voice interjected. "It's the uncommon ones you have to guard against."

Isaac looked up and found a tall woman with short dark hair and cool green eyes standing over them.

She held out a hand. "Gentlemen, I'm Casey Bass."

Isaac let Ben stand first and shake hands before he rose and followed suit. "Pardon my directness, but we're here to see Miss Sullivan."

Her eyes cooled further. "I'm sure you are."

There was an underlying hostility that Isaac didn't understand, but he knew he wasn't imagining it when Ben shot him a mystified look.

"Follow me, please." The dark-haired woman started down a long, nondescript hallway, moving at a sharp clip.

Isaac followed, rolling the woman's name around in his mind. *Casey Bass. Casey Bass.* Why did it sound so familiar?

Rachel called a woman named Casey before we left for Ireland.

"Excuse me," he said, increasing the length of his stride so that he passed Ben and caught up to the woman. "Are you Rachel's friend, Casey?"

"I am," she answered, not bothering to slow down let alone look at him.

Irritated, he refused to be deterred by her attitude. "I was under the impression we'd be negotiating with Rachel—Miss Sullivan," he quickly amended.

The woman stopped so abruptly that Isaac had to scramble to keep from running over her.

She shot him a bitter look, her mouth a hard, inflexible slash across her face. "I'm sure you did, Isaac...Mr. Miller."

The way she amended her address of him was less correction and more verbal sneer.

"Do I know you, Ms. Bass?"

"No, Mr. Miller. You don't."

"Then may I ask why you're treating me with such open disdain?"

"Yes, you may." And she started down the hall-way again.

He caught up to her in four long strides and began walking shoulder-to-shoulder with her. "And?"

She stopped again, and this time Isaac had to turn back to face her.

"You're free to ask. That doesn't entitle you to an answer. I'm of the opinion that the lines between personal and professional relationships have been crossed one too many times of late, and you're clearly not the one to have suffered the consequences." She reached around him and shoved open a door. "We'll meet in here. Mr. Franks will join us momentarily."

She strode in, not offering them refreshment or even choice of seating. She simply went to the other side of the table and sat down, folded her hands and stared at the door.

"Ms. Bass, I'm certainly not trying to provoke you."

"Then stop asking about Rachel," she snapped.

He knew he should let it go, that the very lines between personal and professional that she had ref-erenced were blurring, but she was pissing him off. "We came here under the impression that we'd be dealing with Miss Sullivan."

"Don't you think you've 'dealt with' her enough?" she asked.

The question wasn't lobbed at him with aggres-sion, as he'd anticipated. Instead, it was dropped at his feet, the weight of accusation so heavy he felt smothered by it. "I don't understand."

"That's on you, not me. And it's *certainly* not on her."

"Loyalty is admirable," he bit out, "but not when it's misplaced."

Ben looked between him and Casey. "Clearly there's subtext here, and I'm missing it entirely. Someone want to bring me up to speed?"

"No," Isaac and Casey answered at the same time.

"Isaac." Ben's warning was clear.

"No," he repeated but with less heat.

The side door opened, and a middle-aged man with dark circles under his eyes and a serious paunch entered. "Mr. Miller. Mr. King. I'm Jim Franks." Everyone stood, and the men shook hands.

Casey just glared.

"Ms. Bass," the older man said with a note of warning. "Mind yourself."

"Yes. Sir."

Curiosity was eating Isaac alive.

The negotiations began, but Isaac only half listened. He knew Ben would handle it. The cold glances Casey kept shooting him were of far more interest. Even more was Rachel's absence. They hadn't been notified that she'd recused herself from the case, and there hadn't been any notice of a change of representation. That meant, in theory, she should have been there.

Isaac had been prepared for her to be there.

Hell, despite it all, he'd wanted to see her, ask how she could live with herself after selling herself out like she had—going to Europe and subtly obtaining information about Power Match and Quantum Ventures that she could now use to bring him down. She'd been so smart. So devious. And he was so damn hurt.

For all that, though, something wasn't sitting well with him, namely Casey's undisguised animosity.

Without warning, he shoved back from the table and stood. "Ms. Bass, I'd like to speak to you privately."

"Step out that door, Casey, and you can follow in recent footsteps. Catch me?" Jim Franks asked in a quiet, firm voice.

Casey hesitated for a split second before she stood, grabbed a piece of paper and scribbled something out before sliding it across the table to her superior. The man read it, his eyes going wide, but she paid him no attention whatsoever. "Outside, Miller."

He followed her not just outside the conference room, but down the hall and into an office where she began opening drawers and dumping the contents into a giant reusable grocery bag.

Isaac ran a hand around the back of his neck and pulled, trying to exhaust some of the tension racing through him. "I have to admit I don't have a clue as to what's going on here."

"No shit," Casey muttered. "First intelligent thing I've heard you admit."

"Pardon?"

She rounded on him, and the only thing Isaac could think was that he wouldn't want to meet her in a dark alley.

"She worked for more than two years—*two years*—to recover from what that bastard of an ex-husband did to her. She clawed her way out of the hole he nearly buried her in, and she took a chance on you. Why? Because I pushed her to do it. I should've let her rediscover herself a little more slowly—" her eyes shimmered with unshed tears "—but I *missed* her. I missed the fun-loving, gregarious, always-ready-to-take-a-chance-on-life woman I knew. Or had known." She pounded a fist over her heart. "She was on her emotional deathbed, and seeing her resurrected? I was selfish, and I wanted more for her. Instead, she got *you*."

"Just a damn minute!" Isaac reached out and took the bag from Casey's hands, stopping her from stuffing it with pens and pencils and Post-it notes. "She *lied* to me."

Casey yanked the bag back and resumed stuffing it with anything within reach. "Really? When?"

Isaac opened his mouth, closed it and opened it again. Nothing came out.

Casey laughed, the sound bitter. "That's right, Captain Intelligence. She didn't lie to you. She didn't *know* she was being assigned to this case. That happened after you two were on your way to Ireland. The girl's never been out of the country, so she didn't even think to turn on international calling on her phone. And it wouldn't have mattered anyway, seeing as she made you a promise that it would be a no-work weekend. Rachel keeps her promises, no matter what."

A sinking sensation was building in Isaac's gut, gathering speed with every word Casey spoke.

She looked at him, then, and for the first time he saw compassion on her face. "You really thought she lied to you? That she whored herself out for a promotion." Casey shook her head, and the first tear broke the dam of her lower lashes, streaking down her cheek. She didn't bother to wipe it away. "If you knew her at all, you'd know better than to ever assume that of her. The woman is the most loyal, loving, compassionate person I've ever met. That you thought so little of her? You don't deserve her."

"Where is she?" he asked, voice ragged.

"She got fired for refusing to flip on you."

She gave up her career. For me. The thing she'd worked for since college, the hours she had put in, the shit she had tolerated, the ground she'd forged toward breaking through that glass ceiling. All gone. All for me.

"You didn't know," Casey said softly.

"I swear I had no idea. Where is she now?" He stepped closer and took Casey's free hand. "Please. I need to… I have to…"

Casey paused and considered him. "Why?"

"Because, I—I…"

"If you can't say it to me, I don't trust you to have the balls to say it to her."

"I need to tell her. I—I have to make this right."

One corner of her mouth curled up and caught the next tear. "That's the best you've got?"

Isaac looked at this fierce guardian and knew the

fastest way to Rachel was through her. So be it. He took a breath and leaped. "I love her, Casey."

She dug out a Post-it note and jotted down the address. "Go. Now. And don't screw this up. I don't look good in prison orange, but I *will* eviscerate you if you hurt so much as a single hair on her head."

"I won't," he said, starting for the door. He stopped and looked back, curiosity temporarily winning over his desperation. "What was on that piece of paper you handed that guy in the conference room— Franks, I think his name was?"

She grinned, and her beauty shone through the tears. "It was a rather creative, if brief, resignation. It consisted of two words. I'll let you guess what they were."

He laughed and yanked open the door, and then, with the address in hand, sprinted down the hall.

Isaac waited for the elevator because forty-six flights of stairs might kill him and he caught the first cab he could hail. He had to repeat the address twice after initially shouting it at the driver and getting nowhere. Finally—*finally*—the driver pulled away from the curb at breakneck speed when Isaac offered him a one-hundred-dollar bill if he could get there as fast as possible save for a single stop at the nearest convenience store.

He had an apology to offer, some groveling to do and a declaration of love to make.

Pronto.

Rachel watched *The Ellen DeGeneres Show* with the knowledge that, if she didn't get a job soon, cable was going to have to go. Shame, that. She really liked Ellen.

She had just risen from the sofa to retrieve her last pint of Ben & Jerry's when someone started pounding on her door like the end times were nigh. Of course, she screamed. First, in fear. Then, in anger.

Storming to her door, she let her anger precede her to the peephole. "What the hell is your problem, you psychotic piece of... Isaac?"

"I've been called worse," he said, leaning against the door frame.

"Go to hell," she said, the words soft but firm, as she turned away, trying valiantly to ignore the shaking and nausea. He had to leave. She couldn't do this, couldn't pull herself together, if he was going to come here and berate her, make empty accusations or attempt to destroy the fragile sense of self she'd managed to forge in the fires of her career's decimation.

"I've been living there since we said goodbye at the airport. It sucks. Let me in. We need to talk."

"I think your last text was pretty clear. Hey, I have an idea. If you want to see me, why don't you call my pimp? You clearly think I'm for sale—morals, ethics, the whole package. Might as well add my body to the list." She closed her eyes and waited, hoping to hear the sound of receding footsteps. Instead, a piece of paper slipped under her door.

On it, in clean, crisp penmanship, were two sentences.

You promised me a game. I'm here to collect.

"Don't do this to me," she whispered.
A second piece of paper followed.

Five-card stud. One game.

She waited.

Open the door, Rachel.

"No," she said even more softly.
A fourth piece of paper.

Please.

Isaac Miller rarely said "please."

With trembling hands and, issuing a quick prayer that this wasn't the biggest mistake of her life, she opened the door.

He looked incredible in his power suit, but his hair was a mess. It looked as if someone had taken a leaf blower to it. She wordlessly gestured to his mop.

He rolled his eyes up and patted his head. "I just took the most harrowing cab ride of my life. Offered the guy a hundred bucks if he'd break every traffic law necessary to get me here in record time. I'm pretty sure there are some traumatized pedestrians out there. I should probably offer to cover their therapy costs."

"Probably," she whispered on a wavering smile. "Isaac, what are you doing here?"

"I, uh… I imagine I look like hell."

"Never." She hated herself for the admission, but it was the truth. Never would she offer him less.

"May I come in?"

"Why?"

"Honestly? I'm new to apologies and I would imagine there's going to be some groveling—all mine, I assure you—and I don't want to do it in public."

She stepped back and let him in.

He closed the door quietly behind him and stood there, looking more than a little lost.

Everything in her wanted to go to him, to comfort him, but she held fast. If they were going to find their way through this, it had to start with him. And he had to mean it.

Clearing his throat, he took off his jacket. "Where should we do this?"

"Uh, do what?"

He shot her another sheepish grin. "Play cards."

"Cards? You came here to play cards?" she asked, fully aware her mouth was hanging open.

"You promised me a game."

"I did, but—"

"Casey said you keep your promises."

"You met Casey? When? Why?" If her head spun any faster, it would pop off and drill a hole in the ceiling.

"It's a long story." He looked around, saw the sofa and headed for it. "This'll do."

"Isaac, you can't just walk in and…and…" She threw her hands in the air. "You can't just play cards because someone promised you a game."

"I'd let it go if it was anyone but you. But it's not. And I can't. Please, Rachel."

Arms wrapped around her torso, she sat down across from him and waited.

"You know the rules?" he asked, shuffling the cards.

"I do."

"I want to change the wager."

"I'm unemployed, Isaac. I can't afford to bet."

He fumbled the shuffle and picked the cards up. "One game. Winner takes all. And if you want me to leave after we've played, I'll go. My word on it."

Oh, what the hell. It's not like he can take me to small claims court if I lose.

"Fine. One game. What are we betting?"

"Everything."

Her gaze shot to his face, but he didn't look up from his shuffling. Like a pro, he dealt the first card facedown and the second card faceup. She received a three of spades; he had a jack of hearts.

"What are you willing to wager, Rachel?"

"Truth." She looked at him. "Any question asked is guaranteed an honest answer."

"Done."

He dealt the third card.

She received an eight of clubs; he received a ten of hearts.

"Did you stack the deck?" she demanded.

"Nope. You saw me shuffle, drop half the deck and also deal."

Mumbling random curses on his most prized personal parts, she waved him on.

"What's the bet, Rachel?"

"Another truth. Same as before."

"Done."

He dealt the fourth cards.

She received a six of diamonds; he received a king of hearts.

Rachel closed her eyes. She was going to lose. She knew it. And she'd be stuck answering whatever questions he wanted answered before she could kick him out.

"I'll bet you a single kiss I'm going to win."

"No kissing."

"What would you propose, then?"

"Whoever wins has to…" She couldn't think, not with him staring at her so earnestly. "Has to reimburse the other for the cost of clothes in Ireland."

"Done."

He was going along too easily. Something was up.

He dealt the last card.

She received an ace of spades; he received an ace of hearts.

"What are the odds I would win with a royal flush?" he mused.

She closed her eyes. God, she was dumb, knowing how her luck had been. Letting him in had been a mistake. Still, she picked up her first card and couldn't help but groan. Jack of clubs. She officially had nothing.

"Go on," she said, waving toward his hand. "Prove to me how you never lose."

He folded his cards and put them in the deck.

"What are you doing?" she demanded.

"I'm folding. You win."

"What? That's not how you play this game."

"It doesn't matter where the queen of hearts is, Rachel. I know where the queen of my heart is. She's sitting right across from me. Every other queen? Absolutely, totally, irrevocably irrelevant." A sad smile played at the corners of his mouth, but he was so serious. "Ask your first truth, Rachel."

"Did you lie to me? About Ireland. Did you take me because you wanted to or because you knew Date Me was filing suit?"

"Two questions, but I'll answer both. First, I never lied to you." He met, and held, her gaze. "Not once. I took you to Ireland because I was desperate to spend the weekend with you."

"Why?" she asked, hating that her voice cracked, hating that she was showing such weakness in front of him and yet unable to stop herself. "Why me?"

This time, the smile that spread across his face was warm. "Have you seen yourself? My God, Rachel. You're incredible. Amazing. Wonderful. Funny, warm and caring. Charming. Smart as hell. A vixen between the sheets. A powerhouse mind who can hold her own in any conversation. You're the whole package, Rach. The real deal."

Her face flushed and, despite her fierce admonition that she would not cry, a single tear broke free. She swiped at it, angry he'd reduced her to the weepy woman. She was stronger than that, and he needed to know it. "I hate you for that—that single tear. Just so you know."

He nodded. "You have every reason to hate me. I acted like a complete ass. But I realized something when I was at your firm and it was Casey, not you, who walked through that door. I wanted to rage that I wasn't getting to see you just one more time. And that's when it hit me. One more time would never, ever be enough."

He moved to her slowly and held out a hand, waiting for her to come to him.

"I'm scared," she admitted, voice thick with emotion as she took his hand.

"So am I. It's part of the thrill, I think."

She laughed a nervous laugh, the sound escaping before she could swallow it down.

He just looked at her with undisguised affection, running one hand through her hair and working out the tangles with tender attention. "I need you, Rachel. There's a difference between want and need. I definitely want you. History proved that repeatedly." And he had the grace to blush. "But I need you even more than I want you." He pulled her close then, wrapping her in the warm safety of his arms. "I'm asking you to trust me," he said with his lips against her temple. "Give me a chance to prove that I'm the man who will fight for you, who will go to bat for you, who will always have your back."

"What about the lawsuit? I'm still liable to be called into that mess."

He shook his head. "I pulled the funding on the project and made an offer to settle out of court."

"Isaac!" she said, pulling away. "You can't do that to your brother!"

"I can, and I did. I won't expose you to any additional risk or put your career in jeopardy."

"I don't have a career. I was, well…they tried to fire me. But I quit."

"That's my girl," he said, pride saturating every word.

"Wait. You're proud of me?" She was so confused she didn't know which way to turn.

"No one gets to treat my woman like I hear they treated you."

"Casey," she growled.

"Also an excellent choice in friends. She's by you in this, too, and didn't hesitate at all when she threatened me within an inch of my life if I hurt a single hair on your head."

Mind reeling, Rachel stood and went into the tiny kitchen to make a cup of tea. Not that she wanted it. She just needed something to do, anything that would keep her mind off what was going on between her and Isaac. But the damn Keurig gave her less than ninety seconds to sort her mind out before the tea was done and she had to face him.

Turning, she gasped and would have spilled the

tea had he not been there to intercept her fumble. He stood so close she could smell his cologne, faint but woody.

"I want to give you the world, Rachel."

"It was just a poker game," she whispered.

"It was never just a game. Not to me." He reached out, hesitated and let out a breath she didn't know he'd been holding when she laid her cheek in his palm. "You are my chance at redemption, the opportunity to be happy. I can't lose that. I won't lose you." Tracing a thumb along her cheek, he continued. "I realized something today, something that seems impossible in such a short time. But there's no other explanation."

"What's that?"

"I'm falling in love with you, Rachel Sullivan, and I don't want or need to control it. I just want to experience it. All of it. With you." And he kissed her.

Shock rocked her to the core, making her slow to respond.

He leaned back, and she saw authentic fear in his eyes.

"Isaac," she said, her voice thick with emotion. She kissed him then, reveling in the feel of his lips against hers, the way he felt beneath her roving hands. She'd never thought she'd experience this—him—again, and yet here he was.

"I won't ask you to say—"

"I love you," she said quietly. "I knew it when we said goodbye at the airport. I couldn't wait to see you again, to see if that feeling was even more powerful. Then I received your texts."

He cringed. "I'm so sorry."

"I've kept them both." She slipped her arms around his waist and snuggled in.

"Why in the world would you keep that awful second text?"

"There'll come a day when I need it for leverage, I'm sure."

Laughter rumbled through his chest beneath her ear. "Clever girl."

"Take me to bed, Isaac. Show me a thousand ways that you mean what you say."

"My pleasure, Miss Sullivan. My pleasure."

But he was wrong.

The pleasure would be theirs. Always theirs.

Together.

* * * * *

COMING SOON!

We really hope you enjoyed reading this book. If you're looking for more romance, be sure to head to the shops when new books are available on

Thursday 31st October

LET'S TALK
Romance

For exclusive extracts, competitions
and special offers, find us online:

f facebook.com/millsandboon

🐦 @MillsandBoon

📷 @MillsandBoonUK

Get in touch on 01413 063232

For all the latest titles coming soon, visit
millsandboon.co.uk/nextmonth

MILLS & BOON

THE HEART OF ROMANCE

A ROMANCE FOR EVERY KIND OF READER

MODERN

Prepare to be swept off your feet by sophisticated, sexy and seductive heroes, in some of the world's most glamourous and romantic locations, where power and passion collide.
8 stories per month.

HISTORICAL

Escape with historical heroes from time gone by. Whether you passion is for wicked Regency Rakes, muscled Vikings or rugg Highlanders, awaken the romance of the past.
6 stories per month.

MEDICAL

Set your pulse racing with dedicated, delectable doctors in the high-pressure world of medicine, where emotions run high a passion, comfort and love are the best medicine.
6 stories per month.

True Love

Celebrate true love with tender stories of heartfelt romance, the rush of falling in love to the joy a new baby can bring, ar focus on the emotional heart of a relationship.
8 stories per month.

Desire

Indulge in secrets and scandal, intense drama and plenty of hot action with powerful and passionate heroes who have it a wealth, status, good looks…everything but the right woman.
6 stories per month.

HEROES

Experience all the excitement of a gripping thriller, with an romance at its heart. Resourceful, true-to-life women and str fearless men face danger and desire - a killer combination!
8 stories per month.

DARE

Sensual love stories featuring smart, sassy heroines you'd wa best friend, and compelling intense heroes who are worthy
4 stories per month.

To see which titles are coming soon, please visit

millsandboon.co.uk/nextmonth

JOIN US ON SOCIAL MEDIA!

Stay up to date with our latest releases, author news and gossip, special offers and discounts, and all the behind-the-scenes action from Mills & Boon...

 millsandboon

 millsandboonuk

 millsandboon

It might just be true love...